Sharon —

Enjoy my book, I really
Enjoyed meeting you!

The author

Barbara Jones Harman

Shadow of the Pines

A novel about two families and the revival of an age-old vendetta that involves romance, greed, murder, vengeance and retaliation.

by

Barbara Jones Harman

authorHOUSE™

1663 LIBERTY DRIVE, SUITE 200
BLOOMINGTON, INDIANA 47403
(800) 839-8640
WWW.AUTHORHOUSE.COM

First published by AuthorHouse 10/12/05

ISBN: 1-4208-6375-4 (sc)

Printed in the United States of America
Bloomington, Indiana

This book is printed on acid-free paper.

DEDICATION

I dedicate this book to the memory of:
Sarah Emily Ann Mullins Jones
Who told me the story of the Pound Mountain massacre.

To all her Grandchildren who never had
The pleasure to sit at her knees and hear
From her lips what I have related herein.

TODAY IS PAST AND GONE,

TOMORROW'S YET TO COME.

IT WILL SURPASS THE DAY THAT'S DONE

YESTERDAY'S A MEMORY

WE'LL SHARE THEM ALL, YOU AND ME.

Robert Lee Jones
Emily's Grandson

I wish to express great appreciation and deepest gratitude to my daughter-in-law Janis Jones and a niece Marcia Roberts for their hours of work and unrelenting encouragement in this effort. Without it I would have never made it this far!

B.J.H.

PREFACE

When I was a young woman I married a man from the hills of Kentucky. His mother told me a startling history about her father who was, at the time a deputy marshal and faith healer. It was hard for me to believe the stories she told me, but I was curious and wanted to know more. I knew I had to visit the places where these things had taken place. My husband and I planned a vacation to the beautiful, magnificent hills of the Blue Ridge Mountains between Kentucky and Virginia.

Friends and relations confirmed the incidents and told me more. I knew it was my duty to reveal the stories to our children and grandchildren in a way they would not easily forget.

It may seem impossible that this hatred lasted for over a hundred years, but it did; until vengeance and retaliation almost destroyed three families. I have tried to keep my story as close as possible to the truth. Although the characters, places and incidents have been fictionalized, all events in this book are true.

TABLE OF CONTENTS

INTRODUCTION

Rueben James Tandy and Booker Thomas Phelps were men as different as two men could be. In 1782 their paths crossed in a way that changed their lives and families for years to come.

Tandy was a man of English and Welsh descent with a temperament hard as cast iron. He expected everyone around him to do his bidding. Rueben joined the American patriots in 1775 to fight for freedom and was injured before the war was over. A shell fragment embedded in the left side of his face left it deformed and paralyzed. This along with his strong will earned him the nickname of 'Iron Jaw'.

When Rueben returned home he found his old friends were not eager to accept his disfigurement and shunned him. He longed for a place to hide away from the stares of the world. He heard about vast tracts of land the government was selling for homesteads in the Carolina territories. Perhaps he could find the place he longed for.

Rueben along with his wife of only a few months left their home in Pennsylvania. They began a journey that would end in a beautiful valley deep in the heart of the Blue Ridge Mountains, a place remote and unsettled where 'Iron Jaw' Tandy could hide from the stares and ridicule of the world. He was overjoyed at his discovery and without first filing a claim, happily started a home for himself and Gerda.

Booker T. Phelps of Scottish heritage was frugal and extremely loyal to his family in all endeavors. This included coming to

America and fighting together in the war for freedom. After the war the clan agreed to find a place in this new free country that would resemble as closely as possible, their beloved Scotland. Phelps also heard of the vast tracts of homesteads for sale. Along with his family they searched and found rolling hills as green and plush as their homeland. Wisely he traveled back to Norton, Virginia where he filed and deeded the claim to his property. When he returned he found a stranger clearing and building on his land.

Booker T. and his family with a caravan of four wagons approached the stranger. The group was concerned with the settled-in look of 'Iron Jaw's' camp.

"Booker T. Phelps here, T for Thomas. To whom are we having the pleasure of speaking, sir?" Booker T. introduced himself and offered Rueben his hand in friendship.

"Rueben James Tandy," Rueben mumbled forcing the politeness with difficulty, not eager to make conversation. He deliberately ignored the hand Phelps extended him.

"I believe you are on my land." Phelps dropped the bombshell. His English was blurred, but Rueben understood him well enough.

Rueben's Welsh stubbornness flared with determination. He thrust his chin forward, tightening his facial muscles until the side of his jaw was like iron.

"This is my land. I am building here, an' I am stayin'," 'Iron Jaw' Tandy stated emphatically.

"You have made a mistake building on this land. I have measured and staked out this claim. My deed is registered. Eight hundred acres west and three hundred acres east, all north of the river is legally mine. My uncle is a surveyor and is settling on up the mountain. Nothing has been claimed south of the river. He would be glad to measure out another claim for you," Booker T. offered in a neighborly way. He could see Rueben was not going to admit he was wrong.

Rueben took into account the threatening look of the caravan. Large draft horses, Percheron and Grays, were hitched to the wagons. There were two men on each of the wagon seats, a driver and another man who carried a gun across his lap. Rueben was certain they came prepared to force him off his land.

"There were no buildings on this land. Wasn't that part of the deal? You had to build and improve the land? I intend to file on this land as soon as my buildings are up." Rueben was certain of his rights.

"You should have a claim filed first. How can you know where to build? You can't just pick a piece of land and squat on it! That wouldn't be legal." Booker T. was trying to keep his patience.

"I have made no mistake, but I see you've brought your army to drive me off my land." Rueben's voice was ice, his eyes even colder.

"Mr. Tandy, believe me, I am sorry about this. I will pay you whatever you think would be right for your building." Booker T. offered, wanting a peaceful solution to the problem.

Rueben's shoulders straightened. He would not give them the joy of seeing him leave like a whipped dog. He would not look at Phelps.

"Come, I will show you on the map how the land lies. I filed my claim twenty days ago. I am sorry you have gone so far as to start building on this spot. There is still plenty of land remaining," Phelps offered amiably. "Believe me, Mr. Tandy; we are willing to help you in any way."

"I want nothing from any of you. You can be assured this will never happen to me again." Rueben's face was a dark mask of fury.

'Iron Jaw' knew it would be futile to argue further. There was no way he could win against the burly lads that made up the Phelps-Baldwin clan. Sullen and silent, he hitched his team and helped Gerda onto the wagon seat. He crossed Pound River and followed a small branch of water. Once again he searched for a place away from the stares of the world. He found a secluded spot high on a mountain covered with pines, dogwood trees, shrubs and a vast amount of vine and fern.

This time Rueben returned to Norton and made it legal. He christened his corner of the world 'Tandy's Mountain'. He declared angrily, but with pride to his wife; "This is my land! No one will dare come on my mountain without my consent, least of all any of the Phelps tribe!"

Rueben James was not convinced that he had been wrong about the land in the valley; he still considered it his. He had been pushed off and forced to leave the home he had begun. He had been ridiculed, disgraced and humiliated. This conjured up a burning hate in Rueben's heart and he nourished the hostility toward the Phelps clan. He hoped with a fervent desire for his wife to become pregnant. He wanted a family of strapping lads, an army of his own, to get even with Booker T. Phelps.

One day, Booker T. and his uncle Tap Baldwin dared to make a social visit to Tandy's Mountain. Neighborly like, they offered to help Rueben raise another cabin.

"I thought I told you to stay away from me. You're lucky I didn't kill you before you got here. I want no help from the likes of you! The only thing you bastards can do for me is to stay off my land! Keep your stinkin' noses out of my business an' plague me no more! Now get before I fill your damn backsides with lead. That would pleasure me to no end. You'd better stay on your side of river. Now get off my mountain!"

Rueben moved Gerda so far back on the mountain, she was afraid they would slide down the backside. He so isolated their home, that folks would say, "If 'Iron Jaw' allowed you on his mountain, you had to ride a ways on a mule, walk a ways, then swing in the rest of the way on a grapevine." They swore the place was so remote that the hoot owls made love to the rattlesnakes. Rueben was not happy with the bleakness of the land, but was satisfied with the intense wilderness of his mountain.

Rueben James Tandy again made a vow to get back his land in the valley. He pledged to kill Booker T. Phelps and all his clan. He would see to it's doing, as soon as Gerda supplied him with the family of boys he needed to build his army.

And so it began; the hot and cold feud that lasted over a hundred years, until it came to bloody draw on Pound Mountain.

Chapter One

O n a cold January night in 1815, Rueben James Tandy lay ill from a severe case of pneumonia. There was no medication or effective treatment for the illness. 'Iron Jaw' knew he was dying.

His life had been a failure. He had not completed the vow to get his land back in the valley. There was no family of burly boys he'd longed for. Gerda bore two children, a son, who died in infancy and a daughter, Dorsey.

In his last dying moments Rueben demanded his wife and daughter be at his bedside. In a weak effort to stay alive, he struggled to draw a pledge from them to keep his vendetta.

"Booker Phelps still lives on my land. Promise me you will destroy him and get it back!"

"We promise, yes, we promise."

His struggle to talk caused a hoarse cough. Rueben's throat filled with phlegm and he could not speak. In a last vain attempt to hear their pledge, he attempted to raise and reach for Gerda, but fell back on his pillow. A long rasping breath left his body, and his struggle was over.

After Rueben's death Gerda and daughter Dorsey could do little to carry out the promise they had made. Dorsey was thirty-one and thought marriage had passed her by until she met Frank Mitchell from Kentucky and hastily fell in love. Four childless years later she gave up hope of having an army of boys to destroy the Phelps family.

Unexpectedly she became pregnant. Their only child, a daughter, Hilga, was born June, 1821.

Frank Mitchell was a man of dark complexion and equally dark disposition. Blazing black eyes added to his foreboding good looks. He proved to be shiftless and lazy with only one ambition, making whiskey. He had no intentions of taking up a vendetta that meant absolutely nothing to him. Their daughter, Hilga, also had no desire to pursue the feud.

"You don't think I'm gonna march down there an' get killed over a damn disagreement that should have been buried with Grandpa 'Iron Jaw'," Hilga informed her mother.

Hilga at sixteen looked like her grandmother with golden hair and Dresden skin. It was her blonde beauty that attracted a traveling pan salesman. She had little trouble convincing him to take her with him to Richmond when he left. A year later when she became pregnant he abandoned her. She had no choice but to return to the mountain.

Hilga hated returning and swore when her child was born she would leave again and never come back. Her child's birth in May 1838 was difficult for Hilga. The hard delivery pushed the baby's soft skull into a pointed shape. At the top grew a small amount of blonde fuzz.

Because of the child's strange looking head Grandpa Mitchell said he looked like a Jaybird and that was what he called him. The strange look of his head was temporary and rounded normally. The blonde fuzz turned black and grew thick and curly, but 'Jay Bird' was the name he carried throughout his life.

When Jay was a year old, Hilga kept her promise. She packed her few belongings, left and never looked back, leaving her son with grandparents who hated the responsibility and stigma of raising an illegitimate child.

Dorsey's life with Mitchell was a living hell. Frank was cruel to his wife and had been brutal to her mother Gerda. Baby Jay carried his grandfather's genes in looks and personality. This always reminded Dorsey of how much she hated Frank. As a result she could not stand the child and only let him in her sight when necessary. During these rare moments grandma would tell him of the "theft" of their land by the Phelps's.

Grandmother Dorsey demanded Jay hide under the bed when any of their few visitors came. At night he slept in the corncrib and became friends with the rats and mice that crawled around him. In the winter he was allowed one down quilt. Jay was certain it was his friendship with the dogs as bedfellows that kept him from freezing to death.

Grandfather Mitchell's meanness found a new battleground when Jay came onto the scene. He could always find an excuse to beat the boy. As a child, Jay lived in terror of his grandfather and the heavy leather strap. He found solace and comfort in dreams of getting old enough to take up his great-grandfather's vendetta. He tried to understand why 'Iron Jaw' hadn't taken back the land that really belonged to the Tandy's.

"Why didn't great-grandpa shoot them all? That was his land." Jay, at thirteen, was asking his Grandma Mitchell again why the promise to kill the Phelps clan had never been kept.

"Why do you suppose, you simpering nin-cum-poop! There was too many of them and only one of your great-grandpa, 'Iron Jaw'." His grandma slapped him so hard with the back of her hand that the blow staggered him backward against the wall.

"Now I'm a tellin' ya boy, get yerself a strappin' woman. Have you a passel of burly boys, raise em' mean an' ornery. March down there an' take back what's really ours. It wasn't your great-grand pappy's fault. He didn't have the family of boys he wanted. There was only me, yer grandma. What could we do? They'd a come up here like a swarm of locusts an' done us in. On his deathbed, he made me promise to get revenge. I promised to marry an' have a family of boys and raise them to be strong an' mean; our own army to destroy the Phelps's." Grandma's eyes squinted as she looked at Jay with contempt and disgust.

"But it ain't happened, as you can see. I married your grandpa, Frank Mitchell, which was a big mistake. He ain't good fer-nothin', 'cept makin' whiskey, an' slappin' folks around. The only kid I had from him was yer ma an' she run off with another good fer nothin'. He never even married her. She came back here, her belly full of you. She had no shame in what she'd done, just waited to hatch you and get back off the mountain quick as she could. Abandoned you is what she done!" The memories brought a raging anger into Dorsey's voice.

"But you could change things, boy! You could get growed up and kill all them Phelps's an' get back our land. The years are gone an' things are still the same. We're up here, an' they're down there. It ain't right, it's got to change. They're the thieves. We belong down there, not up here on this rock pile where nothin'll grow 'ceptin apples, trees an' goats." Grandma put her hands on her hips in exasperation, opened her eyes wide and screamed at her grandson. "Ya got to do it. I'm tellin' ya; take that land back fer the Tandy kin! It's yer vendetta now! Quit yer snivelin', get out'a here an' help yer grandpappy. You know the harness strap stings lots worse than the back of my hand!"

Jay knew the sting of the harness strap. He'd felt it often enough. In spite of all the cruelty, he grew tall and broad of stature with hidden emotions. A deep scar on his left cheek, where a harness ring had cut deeply, only added to his rugged handsomeness. The deep marks on his body were slight compared to the ones left on his mind.

Jay's childhood was filled with terror and hate. Repulsion from his grandmother and brutality from his grandfather sculptured a man, callous and mean. He developed a dour saturnine personality. His grandmother drilled him often on the vow she made to his great-grandfather. But Jay had no time for killing the Phelps's. He was too busy cultivating a burning hate for his grandparents, which was demanding revenge. Then something happened to push the hate into the back of his mind.

Jay lost his heart and all his reason when he met a young woman at a Fourth of July celebration in Gladeville. Her long brown tresses and laughing gray eyes beguiled him. He was filled with anxiety when he found out she was the daughter of Abe Baldwin, a member of the clan who were his hated enemies. He felt desperate but would not be turned aside as he went courting.

"Jay Mitchell, you've gotta be out of your head! Marry my daughter? In a pig's butt! You'll see me dead first. Your family has always hated everyone on this side of the river. What makes you think you can change that with a wedding? Never! Your great granddaddy would turn over in his grave. Now get back on your mountain an' stay there!"

"I love Mattie. My great granddad, 'Iron Jaw', has been dead for nigh onto thirty years. I'd be willin' to forget all that. I'd make her happy," Jay pleaded. He was determined and he would not be deterred. If he had Mattie, the old hate would be buried. He'd build them a cabin away from Frank Mitchell and his drunken brutality.

"That's all well an' fine, Jay, but Mattie has already been promised to Ira Phelps. Good day!" Abe Baldwin informed him and slammed the plank door in his face.

"I'll kill Ira Phelps. I'll kill him! I will have you, Mattie. You'll forget Phelps, I promise you! Come with me Mattie, come with me," Jay's voice fell muffled against the heavy door. The desire of his heart was a desperate dream, but he could see clearly it was just that, a dream.

Mattie should have been his by rights. But the Phelps's seemed to have a way of getting everything that belonged to the Tandy's. Just like the land that by all rights should belong to him. The Phelps's would take everything they could get, then take more, and didn't care who they stepped on. Well, he would forgive Mattie, but he would never forgive Ira Phelps for winning her hand.

Strange events began to occur on the mountain. Grandpa Mitchell was trampled to death by a mule he'd owned for twenty years. Soon after they buried him, grandma fell down the springhouse steps, broke her hip and died a few weeks later. It seemed odd to the neighbors that Jay showed no sympathy or grief. Most of them cared little for the Mitchell's, but felt a certain duty to see them buried. All of a sudden there was concern; they turned on Jay with venom.

"Twas Jay's wicked, evil ways, mind you, that's behind all this. Damn sure you could lay odds that it were his neglect that caused his grandparents to be laid in their graves," they declared, certain that Jay knew more than he was telling. "Never will amount to much, his ma's leavin' him an' all. He was blessed having such wonderful grandparents."

Their talk concerned Jay little. The prattle of chattering women did not cause him to forget the whir of the strap. It could not stamp out the sight of blood that oozed from his cuts. The gossip did not erase the memory of the gray-eyed girl he loved. Only one thought filled his mind, he must leave this hateful place.

There was no one to be afraid of any more and he vowed there never would be again. He was eighteen and old enough to care for himself. Nailing up the cabin, he prepared to move to Richmond. The pledge made by his grandmother had become his inheritance now. He buried it and the dreams of Mattie on Tandy's Mountain.

Jay had not bargained for the big city of 1856 or working for a living, and found both very distasteful. Although he had worked hard on the mountain, ambition was never one of his attributes. With no education, trade, or craft, it was impossible to find employment of his liking. Out of total desperation and hunger he took a job cleaning gutters, which he detested. He listened unconcerned to the political discord that filled the streets. A person by the name of John Brown had been hung at Harpers Ferry. This meant nothing to Jay. He cared little for the state of the country. He was only worried about his own state. It seemed to Jay that the years dragged by slowly.

The only thing about the city Jay found to enjoy were the houses of ill repute. The women found him to be strange, quiet, and moody, with an unquenchable thirst for the clear, high proof whiskey of the mountains. He had a passion for cruelty and gave in frequently to his violent rages. The shady ladies hated to see him come. They were glad when his visits stopped.

Tired of paying the high cost for his pleasure, Jay went searching for a wife. At a shop he became acquainted with a young widow, Sarah Wilson. Soft red hair and amber eyes attracted Jay first. Her talent and wages as a dressmaker encouraged his desire further. He soon made her his bride.

Sarah's first marriage had been childless, although, her union with Jay was fruitful and provided them with two sons, Rueben James II, and Blaine. Their marriage was not filled with love and ecstasy as she had hoped.

Jay was twenty-four. In 1861 the state of Virginia had become the central battleground for the dispute over slavery. Not being a slave owner, Jay decided long before he would not be drawn into a political war that meant absolutely nothing to him. Tandy's Mountain would be a good place to hide. Taking Sarah and the boys, they traveled from Richmond back to the place filled with haunting ghosts and terrifying memories. On their journey to the Blue Ridge Mountains, they met a doctor, his wife and their young daughter, Hail.

Dr. Travis D. White was also running, trying to find a place to hide from the war. It didn't take Jay long to persuade the doctor to buy a piece of his mountain. He convinced him that Tandy's Mountain was the secluded spot he was looking for.

Hail White, at the age of twelve was scrawny and small. Her large emerald eyes and pale face were surrounded by a mass of copper colored hair. She watched as her father counted into Jay's hand the amount of money in United States currency that Mitchell required for the purchase. She lowered her eyes as she felt the man's blazing gaze.

Jay Mitchell's dark good looks were impressive, but it was the fire in his eyes that stayed in Hail's mind. It frightened her and the feeling stayed with her as she grew older.

During the remaining war years Jay tried to be satisfied on the mountain but he found the old memories were not dead. They returned often to torture his nights and haunt his days. The scars of childhood had grown deeper and never left his thoughts. Even after his marriage to Sarah dreams of Mattie often filled his quiet times.

The home that 'Iron Jaw' built for Gerda was still standing. On this spot the timber grew thick and dense. There were places that seldom felt a flicker of sunshine. It was a dark place of hiding for Jay. It matched his sullen and moody disposition. He had become a man of miserable unbending will. Life on the mountain was lonely and desolate. Jay became broody and restless. Sarah felt sympathetic with Jay's misery. She was as miserable as he. Time had not been kind to Tandy's Mountain. New trees and vines grew everywhere. Underbrush and Scrub Elm choked the orchard. Stock had to be bought and a place prepared for them. Sarah swore the soil on Tandy's Mountain had more gravel per yard than anywhere on earth. Longing for the low lands, Sarah pleaded with Jay to return to the city.

9

Jay found no love or compassion for life and intended to give none. However he developed a small liking for his two sons, but he cared more for his horses and pigs than he did for his wife. She was only considered as a laborer to work for him, obey him, and always be sexually convenient whenever he demanded.

The war was over and Jay was in dark despair at being on the mountain. He decided to give into Sarah's desire to return with his family to the city. He was preparing to tell her of his decision when she dropped a bit of shocking news upon him. They were going to have another child!

Jay Bird Mitchell's uncontrollable temper flared into a fused rage. Another child did not fit into his plans for returning to the city. He told Sarah, in not too gentle terms, exactly how he felt blaming his wife as if the fault was hers alone.

"For cryin' out loud, Sarie! Why'd you go an' do that fer? We ain't never gonna leave this damnable place. Never! You can have that kid right here, an' Doc White can take care of you. You're gonna stay in these damn trees until you rot an' die!" He shouted angrily at her.

"Reckon I'm doomed to stay on this God forsaken mountain forever!" Jay grumbled fiercely to himself, stomping out of the cabin, letting the heavy door slam behind him.

Staying on the mountain was not a satisfying decision, it only meant more misery for him, but he would stay. It would serve Sarah right. "Just what she deserves!" He kept muttering to himself as his long angry strides were closing the distance to the barn.

He hadn't thought much about Phelps since his return. He heard through the grapevine that Mattie's family still considered him part of the dung heap. The despair he felt brought it all back. He recalled vividly his Grandmother Mitchell's words, "get growed up an' kill all them Phelps's an' get back our land. They are the thieves. We belong down there. I'm a tellin' ya, take that land back for the Tandy kin!" Jay could feel again the sharp slap of her hand.

"You're too wimpy! Get out of my sight, you ratty boy! Out o' here! Out'a my sight!" Grandma had screamed as she pushed him out the door. Her words still haunted him, "You'll never be man enough to kill anyone, least of all the Phelps's!"

As he waited for Sarah's child to be born, he thought often of Grandma Mitchell's words. They became a burning fire in his mind. He would kill the Phelps's. He would be the man his grandmother wanted him to be. He would raise his sons to hate anyone who bore the name, Phelps. He would prove his Grandmother Mitchell was wrong about him. He'd show them all he wouldn't be wimpy. He would be strong and get the land that really belonged to the heir of 'Iron Jaw' Tandy. And Mattie would live long enough to regret that she had chosen a Phelps over a Mitchell.

Jay would conceive a plan to even the score. He would take out his anguish of being on the mountain and develop a scheme to get rid of Booker T. Phelps's great-grandson squatting in the valley below.

"I'll get rid of all you Phelps's! I'll get back 'Iron Jaw's land. I don't know how or when, but I'll do it! So, Ira Phelps, you better be on your guard! If I catch any of your damn family on my mountain, they are good as dead!" He muttered to himself as he saddled his mule.

Jay would ride wildly into the thick trees, cursing his grandfather, and nurturing his hate for Phelps. It might take years for a plan to come around, but it would come. The thought brought a bright light to surface in Jay's black eyes. The flickering spark soon flamed into a raging fire. A blaze that burned there as long as there was a Phelps left on Pound River to torment him.

On a hot lazy day in August 1872, Jay Bird Mitchell lay beside a gushing stream on his mountain. Here in the plush greenery Jay hid from the world, but he could not get away from the ghosts that always haunted him. Phelps's were still in the valley and he was still on Tandy's Mountain.

At the thought of Phelps, Jay stirred and sat up. He pulled on a string tied to a bush and fished out a jug of whiskey cooling in the stream. Removing the cork, he took a long swig. He wiped his mouth with an open hand and smoothed his mustache and the beard he had grown since his return from Richmond. Jay gave a loud belch of enjoyment then leaned back against the tree. Setting the jug on the grass, he prepared to enjoy the remainder of the hot summer evening beside the coolness of his spring. He would not return to the old memories with their bitter thoughts. Instead he would think of the present and how his life had changed to a wonderful realm of happiness.

In the years that followed the war, the state of Virginia struggled to recover from the devastation. Jay took up making whiskey and killing Phelps's. He found two of them trespassing on the mountain while coon hunting. They never left. He buried them there along with their dogs.

Ira Phelps struggled to finish the mill he started during the war, on the property that really belonged to Tandy's. Jay would be kind, he would let him finish before he got rid of him. The property would be even more valuable. Contrary to Jay's personality, he would be patient and wait, so long as Ira stayed out of the whiskey business.

The settlement of Gladeville had only been a small stopover when 'Iron Jaw' and Gerda came into the hills. It was now a prosperous town. After coming into the valleys on the Virginia side of Pound Mountain and lower on the river, there was now another place of business. The hill people called this small village of no consequence, 'Donkey'. It had its share of wild times and gunplay. It boasted a general store, blacksmith and a man named Trace was building a tavern. Jay was quick to seize the opportunity to cement relations with the owner. The village was also a stopover for shipping supplies across Pound Gap into Kentucky. Donkey soon became the central playground for illegal whiskey running.

Sarah died giving birth to their third child. Jay blamed the child for his stay on the mountain. Being left with three boys, one of them a babe put Jay at a loss. Fortunately, his neighbor Bess Stewart, having just lost her own newborn, was able to wet nurse Jay's little son. Her heart went out to the motherless boys. Grieving for her own child, she filled her home with thoughts of Jay's boys and baby Bob.

Jay worried little about the boys, knowing they were in good hands. He filled his mind with thoughts of killing Phelps and planning revenge against Dr. White, who he blamed for letting Sarah die. He turned his idle days into busy ones making whiskey and taking it into Kentucky. Then, two years after Sarah's death a wondrous thing happened. He found a girl living with a band of Irish gypsies on Elkhorn Creek in Kentucky. She became his wife and a stepmother for his children.

Beautiful Mae, was wonderful and wild as a marsh hare. She loved Jay with a love like he had never known and was filled with a tender understanding that amazed him. And beyond all comprehension, he returned the feeling. Jay had never loved anyone since Mattie. Now Mae was going to have his child and this time Jay felt a pang of happiness. Desperately he hoped it would be a girl as beautiful and warm as Mae. Maybe he would call her Taynee. That was almost like Tandy, yes, Taynee would do very nicely.

Jay was even beginning to enjoy being on the mountain. Anywhere with Mae was a beautiful song. His life had never had much music and he loved her deeply. Even his miserable temperament had mellowed.

Along with loving Jay and caring for his boys, Mae filled Jay's days with gypsy songs and dancing. She warned him against black witches and their wicked ways and told him the things they could do to bewitch a person. She told him how they could change themselves into small animals and put spells of bad luck on those they hated. Jay loved her so much, he wondered if she had cast a spell on him. Hating the Phelps clan was second place now that his life centered around Mae.

Jay felt drowsy as he watched the water play around the rocks at his feet. He thought lazily how the small spring flowed through the apple orchard 'Iron Jaw' had planted for Gerda. As it filled Tandy's branch it gained momentum and rushed down the mountain to join the main river above the Phelps place.

Hateful Phelps's! The war had slowed them some and now Ira was having a hard time finishing the mill. It had always been his aggravation that the Phelps family prospered and the Mitchell family had become lazy and uncaring. With Mae on his mind, he had become lax in teaching his sons to hate their enemies in the valley.

Thinking of Phelps again, his eyes opened wide. He fastened a watchful stare on a bright orange and green terrapin making its way to the water's edge. As he thought angrily of Ira, his hand closed tightly around a small rock. He threw it with aggravated assault upon the unsuspecting turtle. With the impact the small amphibian quickly drew in its head and legs protecting itself with natural instinct from the enemy.

"You're just like them damn Phelps's. They always have a way of protecting themselves. But there'll come a day, there'll come a day!" He muttered to himself.

Jay settled back against the tree, prepared to doze. Then he heard a faint noise, unfamiliar to the quietness of his world. He tilted his head, and listened intently. There it was again. Was he hearing the murmur of voices? Perhaps, he thought, leaning back slowly, it was only the bubbling of the spring.

Closing his eyes, he returned to dreaming of Mae, smiling to himself as he thought of the hard smooth rounding of her belly as his child grew inside her. So desirable was the warm, firm fullness of her breast under the touch of his hand.

He moved with a start as his ears again became alert to the slight but definite rumbling of turning wheels. Reaching for his rifle, he raised his tall body with surprising agility into an upright position. With long strides he broke into a swinging run through the thick apple trees.

CHAPTER TWO

On Tandy's Road, as Jay enjoyed the quietness of his domain, Mattie Phelps crossed his mountain. She guided the young mare pulling the buggy with expert hands and watched with discomfort, the rippling trails of heat waves filling the road ahead of her. The hot breeze stirring the leaves in the numerous trees did not ease nor lessen the intensity of the sweltering climate. The steep hills cupped the heat, refusing to let it escape, until her body was encased in a stifling steam bath. To add to Mattie's discomfort, the shrilling of the birds throbbed persistently inside her head. It was as if they were trying to out sing each other in a last, vain attempt to close out the day, reminding her that it would soon be gone.

Tall brush and low creeping undergrowth pressed with strong will against the road's edges, pushing with firm intent toward the middle. Lush blue-green grass grew tall in the center of the otherwise rocky, seldom traveled road. The low bed of the small one-seat surrey pushed the high grass flat, leaving a silver streak with its passing. The green carpet would spring back quickly, erasing the slightest evidence of a passer by. The horse moved the buggy rapidly across the mountain.

Mattie and her oldest son Tom sat with their backs straight on the seat. The buggy was Mattie's prize possession and she kept immaculate care of it. The red corduroy covering and black leather trim of the interior showed only slight signs of wear and heavy use. The wheels moved easily, without a squeak on their well-oiled shafts.

Although Mattie held herself strictly erect, she sat only slightly taller than the young boy beside her. An abundance of dark brown hair was smoothed across her ears and twisted into a roll at the back of her head. A small black straw hat modestly trimmed with black ribbon and net perched on top of the massive bun. The poke-style bonnet was held safely in place with soft silk ribbons tied securely under her round chin.

She drove the young, high-stepping sorrel mare with expert hands, never slacking her attention on the reins, steadying the horse at just the right pace to make the many curves in the winding road. Mattie felt the severe heat of the day. Her condition and the strain of the journey to the mountain had worn a pattern of weariness upon her face. Her usually pleasant mouth was drawn into a tense line. Her shining gray eyes clouded with fatigue as she allowed her mind to review the happenings of the past two days.

The previous morning she awoke from a restless night of troubled dreams about her friend, Hail White. The dreams seemed like a warning and she felt compelled to see for herself if everything was all right. She must try to convince Ira to let her go and settle the turmoil in her mind.

After much discussion over the breakfast table, persuasive looks, and increasing persistence, she had coaxed consent from her husband. He, however, insisted that she was in no condition to be gallivanting around the hills alone. It was his unyielding demand that she allow one of their two sons to accompany her. Ira watched their leaving very closely; making sure Mattie took the turn down Pound Road toward the Stewarts. He let them go with a wave of his hand and a firmly shouted order to stay clear of Tandy's road.

It took most of the first day to reach Hail's, down Pound Road, and up the long slope of the mountain. Mattie was delighted to find Hail well in both body and spirit. They convinced themselves that the dream meant nothing. They laughed at Mattie's fears and put them out of their minds.

The two women giggled and chattered the next morning away. They kept their hands busy stringing beans and finishing a small quilt Hail had on the frame. Until, to their surprise, the sun was beginning its journey down toward the west, and Mattie realized she must leave. No amount of coaxing on Hail's part would change her mind.

"Land's sakes, how the time's flew!" Mattie exclaimed, gathering herself up from the chair and reaching for her hat. "It'll be dark before we'ins can get down the mountain to Stewarts! We must go down Tandy's road. It's the quickest way. Come now, Tom, we must hurry."

"But Maw, Paw said not to go on Tandy's road. He said not to. We'ins hadn't better!" her young son interrupted with concern, shaking his head decisively.

"Hush, Tom! You must learn to keep your place!" his mother answered looking at him with disapproval.

"Don't go that way Mattie! It ain't safe for you, please don't chance it." Hail added her plea in a soft voice, husky with distress. "You stay over again. It'll be no trouble at all. You can get an early start in the mornin' an' go back 'round by Pound Road, the way you came." Hail suggested, becoming nervous as she watched Mattie shaking her head in refusal.

"If you're not a mind to stay with me, you go on down the mountain an' spend the night with Bess an' Jan. They'd welcome your company. Oh, Mattie, Please! I'll worry to no end if you're a mind to go by Jay's!" Hail pleaded with Mattie, her large eyes filled with concern as she watched Mattie tying her bonnet securely with no intention of obeying.

"It's not safe, Mattie. You know that Jay has forbidden any of you to set foot on his part of the mountain. Aren't you afear'd?" Hail's jade eyes clouded with deep emotion. She looked intensely at her friend.

"Don't you fret none Hail; I ain't scared of Jay Mitchell, or the likes of him! And don't you be either," Mattie assured her, the soft burr of the hills becoming more slurred as her voice filled with anger toward Jay.

Sadness clouded Mattie's eyes as she thought of the desperation of Hail's loneliness. But Hail seemed to have recovered and the pale was beginning to leave her face. She shook her head to free it from the ache of remembering.

"I told Ira I'd be home before dark. He's been feelin' poorly lately. I dare not leave him for too long, or he'd work himself to death. We have tarried longer than I had a mind to. We'll head on across Tandy's road an' no one will be the wiser!" Mattie's voice was strong with conviction. She patted Hail's hand reassuringly.

"I ain't afear'd of Jay's bunch Hail. I'm only afear'd of the dark, dear, an' the first bitter sting of death when the reaper comes to take me to the glory land. I'm only hopin' an' a prayin' that the Lord'll be willin' to let me see my youngins' raised," Mattie stated firmly with an encouraging smile.

"It's ever so much closer. Jay's never home anyway an' we'll be down the mountain in a bit. Besides I'll have Tom to take care of me." She flashed another smile at her son. Mattie said her last decisive words on the subject, climbed into the buggy beside Tom, and lifted the reins.

Hail stood on the porch waving them goodbye, watching them leave the gate and pull down into the road, headed for Tandy's orchard. A deep apprehension filled her heart as she thought of her own deep hate for Jay. She had no choice but to let them go. She sent them on their way with a cheery smile on her face and a prayer on her lips for their safety.

As Mattie traveled through the intense wooded area between Hail's and Jay's orchard, her mind erased the thoughts of the day. There was never a more beautiful spot than Tandy's Mountain. The late afternoon sun filtering through the many leaves on the enormous trees spattered rays of flickering light in transcendent fantasies along the road. As she turned the horse onto Tandy's road, she could not contain herself any longer. She had to pause and feast her eyes on the beauty surrounding her. Bringing the horse to a slow walk as they reached Mitchell's orchard, she pulled it to a stop and set the brake.

The misty haze that usually shrouded the valley was absent this day. The high rolling hills were engulfed in a variety of giant trees; oak, dogwood, sourwood, maple, and groups of stately pine. The vibrant beauty spread over the hills like a bolt of soft green velvet.

Occasionally, a high rock jutted out to spoil the emerald softness. Even these extruding surfaces were almost hidden with moss and vine. Taking a deep breath, she was amazed at the wonder of God's hand upon the earth. Engrossed in the sight, she forgot the time, the boy beside her and for a moment her growing weariness.

Mattie could see into the tree-choked valley below. Shining in the fleeting sun rose a wooden skeleton, a tower of rafters that would soon be Ira's mill. A project her husband started with his cousin Valdean Bentley. The two had talked and dreamed together of building a central gristmill to grind their neighbor's corn. Before they had scarcely begun, the high hills felt the impact of the *War Between the States*. At the same time Jay returned to Tandy's Mountain to hide from the war, Valdean left Pound to join forces with the confederate army.

When Val returned home, he found the hills suffering from the devastation of war. The armies of both sides had taken everything eatable, wearable, spendable, and anything with the possibility of being made into war material.

Ira had not been spared, his funds were depleted and work on the mill had stopped completely. Ailing health had kept him from the army. Suffering from an illness that often racked his body with uncontrollable shaking and weakness; he was unable to work for more than a few hours at a time.

Val knew there was only one means of making money quickly in the hills and that was making whiskey. There was no way he would be involved in moonshining. There had to be cash for the huge grinding wheels and gears, or there would be no mill. It was decided he should be the one to find a job elsewhere to supplement their finances. Leaving a sweetheart, he promised to return soon with increased wealth and a wedding ring. However, due to unforeseen circumstances Val made a decision to never return to Virginia.

Ira's health took a turn for the better. He accepted the fact that Val was not coming back. The dream of a gristmill was his alone to complete. At first Val sent what money he could, but in time that dwindled. Out of loyalty and love, and because of the funds he had provided, Ira made his cousin a partner in the mill. Val's letters became fewer until they stopped completely.

Mattie was sad knowing she would never see Val again. She worried over Ira's insistence to finish the mill. He worked relentlessly to complete the building. During the last few weeks, Mattie had seen his energy lag, not totally from the heat. She worried his illness might return. The ailment would cause her husband to spend days in bed. She suspected he kept his true condition from her. Mattie was not one to nag and Ira would not volunteer anything concerning his health. She could only watch with a heavy heart as his strength declined. It was enough of dwelling on the years gone by. They could not be brought back nor decisions turned around. She must move on. The day would soon be over.

Mattie lifted the reins to start the horse. Her eyes caught a flash of sunlight resting on the shining apples in Tandy's orchard at the bend of the road. The fruit tempted her, bidding her to pick one and have a bite. A yearning rose inside her, a desire she felt often these days. She could subdue the desire no longer. She was aware that it was wrong to tarry in this spot, but she had to have one of those gleaming apples. She turned to the boy beside her, "Hurry, Tom. Jump down; I must have some of them apples. I simply will not go one step further till I do!" Mattie's voice was set with decision. She licked her tongue across her lips as if tasting a luscious morsel.

Tom sat quietly as his mother guided the horse through Hail's gate. He watched in silence as they crossed the crest of the mountain, and took the curve joining Tandy's road. Through a density of limbs above their heads, he had watched the sun. It was rapidly heading toward the top of the mountains where it would soon drop from sight.

Tom had always loved the Cumberland Mountains and the strip of Blue Ridge that separated Kentucky and Virginia. He would have been delighted with any place other than this forbidden spot. He kept his head bowed, not wanting to look around. The constant turning of the wheels and the bobbing of the horse's head made a rhythmical pattern in his mind. His eyes closed, his head nodded, and he dozed.

His mother's words brought him back to the day with a start. He had not been eager to accompany her in the first place and the events of the days were boring to him. The short nap made him even more cantankerous and he was quick with a sullen answer.

"Tain't right, Maw, it's stealin'!" Tom offered cautiously.

The giant apple trees had grown together in huddled masses, long branches gnarled and tangled, evidence of total neglect. An abundance of fruit twinkled dimly in the rays of the late afternoon sun, imparting to Mattie a tantalizing invitation to be picked. She could not suppress her desire any longer. Her gray eyes glistened with anticipation. The moment of hesitation turned to one of action. Wrapping the reins around the whip handle, she climbed out of the buggy. Taking a basket from the carrier at the back, she motioned for Tom to climb down.

"Come now, Tom. You must hurry an' fill the basket!" she again commanded, smiling coaxingly. A dimple appeared bewitchingly at the corner of her mouth. "Hurry and be quick, before someone sees us."

Tom, still hesitant climbed down from the wagon seat. He crawled over the fence with the quick agility of his youth and shinnied up the tree to obey her command. He wondered silently why his mother dared stop at this forbidden spot. But he had learned in the last few months not to question anything she set her mind to, not understanding the sudden change in her. Without cause she would become cross and irritable. Contrary to her usual pleasant self, she would shout loudly at her family. Then, realizing she had been short tempered, she was just as quick to tell them she loved them. She would then apologize for her hasty words and burst into a torrent of uncontrollable tears. To the boy, her sudden tears were more unbearable than her quick temper.

"Be for hurrin', Tom. It'll be gettin' dark 'fore long." Mattie's anxiety leant a note of harshness to her usual soft, gentle voice.

"Paw'll skin us for sure when he finds out what we'ins have been up to. Them Mitchell's is a hatin' us awful bad, Maw!"

Mattie shrugged away the boy's reminder and handed him up the container. Resting the basket in the crook of a limb, Tom began his task.

Mattie picked an apple from a low hanging branch and bit into the succulent fruit. How good it was! Lifting her long skirt, she wiped away the juice that ran down the corner of her mouth. With a small hand, she felt the hard swelling of her belly. She had been confident for some time of her pregnancy. For years after her second son, Matt, was born she hoped to have another child, but it had not happened. Now, with happy certainty, her hopes were realized. She knew it was the reason for sudden tears and quick bursts of temper. Then there was this crazy, unrelenting craving for green apples. Apples, just right half ripened after the sun brought forth the sweet tangy juices to tantalize a body's taste buds. She was filled with the satisfaction of her pregnancy and savored the sweet and sour goodness of the half-ripened fruit she was eating. Taking another crunchy bite, her body quivered as she felt the baby move. Smiling happily to herself, she was certain without a doubt that the baby would be a boy. Already she had picked a name, Billy Dean.

"Tain't right, Maw. No ways!" Tom grumbled to himself, but continued filling the basket, sticking an apple for later eating into his pocket.

"Dad-blame it youngin', hush your mouth! What's got into you anyway? I should have left you home an' brought Matt, but I figured you bein' the oldest an' all, you should be the one. Now be for hurryin'!" Looking up at the boy with warming gray eyes, she smiled sweetly, softening the harshness of her words.

"Your paw don't know what it's like to be wantin' somethin' so bad."

Mattie reached the filled basket and placed it in the carriage at the back of the wagon. Climbing back onto the seat, she straightened her skirt and waited for the boy to settle himself beside her. Lifting the reins, she released the brake and turned the horse back into the wagon tracks, starting the mare out slowly.

"Mitchell will kill us for sure! He doesn't cotton to anyone takin' anythin' that's his!" Tom declared, still displeased at his mother's disobedience.

"If we get out a here, he'll never find out. Now hush your mouth, Tom! You are too much of a youngin' to be puttin' your nose into grown-up affairs! Besides, I ain't tendin' to see or talk to that hateful man, ever, after what he did to Hail!" Mattie said, spitefully. Her voice held a touch of bitterness with a twist of hate.

"What'd he do, Maw, huh? What'd he do?" Tom asked, looking up at his mother, his water-blue eyes opened wide and sparked with questions.

"Never you mind, Tom. You are much too young to understand such things. If we-ins don't get home, you'll see how riled your paw can get! We best be gettin'!"

Tom wanted to ask her, if he was too young, how come he had to be part of this little thievery. He held his silence wondering if she would ever consider him to be anything but a youngster. His thoughts were angry at his mother's attitude toward him. If he was such a child, why was he allowed to accompany her in the first place? He took the apple from his pocket and began to polish it on his leg. He pushed the apple with such force that he could feel the warmth from the friction through his homemade breeches. Taking a bite from the apple, he turned his head and watched the side of the road, feeling much older than his nine years.

Leaning forward slightly, Mattie took the whip from the bracket and gave the horse a light flick on the rump. As she clicked her tongue in the roof of her mouth, the young mare broke into a swinging trot. The many branches of the tall trees formed a ceiling over their heads, making a tunnel for them to travel through.

Suddenly, thundering through the thickness of dense trees, a shot rang out sharply behind them, then another! The sound on the still mountain air chilled Tom's blood and filled him with terror. The repercussion echoed across the mountain, back along the valley walls, and settled in heavy around them.

Mattie stiffened and was immovable with fear, thinking it must surely be Mitchell. He would kill them both. She had endangered them by coming this way. She would never live to have the baby she so desired nor see her family grown!

Tom turned to look over his shoulder. Through the back window of the buggy he could see a tall figure of a man, running behind them on the road, a dark moving blotch blending into the flickering shadows of the tall trees. A flash of stray sunlight reflected sharply on the barrel of the gun Jay was firing as he ran. The sudden flash of reflecting light bounced sharply in Tom's eyes, blinding him for an instant. He turned back to his mother.

"Whip her harder, Maw, whip her harder! Make her run fast, let's get out of here!" Tom shouted, tossing the apple and pounding his knees with clenched fists.

Tom's clear-blue eyes, peering from under the brim of his battered old hat, were wide with fright. In boyish desperation, he reached for the reins. Lifting them forcefully from his mother's tense hands, he flipped them up and down on the horse's rump. Frightened by the shooting, the horse snorted loudly. Then, feeling the sharp whack lifted its head and broke into a high run down the treacherous winding road.

"We-ins' have gotta get out-a' here fast! I'm scared Maw! I'm scared good!" Tom yelled at his mother, his voice rasping and trembling with fear. He was trying desperately to guide the horse down the road.

Jay reached the edge of the orchard just as Mattie's mare broke into a swinging trot. Hurdling over the rail fence his great grandpa had built, he turned into the dusty tracks of the road, firing as he ran. As they moved away, Jay recognized Mattie's horse and buggy. The last bright rays of the sinking sun and the movement of his body prevented him from getting a good shot. They had moved far ahead of him and disappeared into the heavy trees. He threw the long Winchester with angry force into the tall grass in the middle of the road.

"Damn Phelps's. Damn you, damn you! Ain't nothin' safe when you'ins are around! I caught you good Mattie, stealin' my apples. Your bunch thinks they own the whole damn valley an' the mountain too! Well, I'll show you this mountain belongs to Jay Bird Mitchell! I'll get you. I'll see to the rapin' of your mealy-mouthed, pasty-faced women too! I promise you. I'll kill you all!" Jay shouted, waving his arms above his head but his voice fell unheard within the thick trees.

The rocking of the wagon and the snorting of the horse brought Mattie back to reality. Shaking herself to clear her head, she took the reins from her son. Pulling the horse under control, she kept it moving rapidly down the hazardous road. Tom clung tightly to the side of the buggy to keep from toppling out. The basket filled with apples bounced high, tipping as it came down, spilling the contents

24

onto the road, leaving behind a shimmering trail of red and green in the dusty wagon tracks.

After the episode at Tandy's orchard Mattie lived in fear, expecting some kind of reprisal from Jay, but there was none. She told Ira nothing and drew a solemn promise from Tom to never mention it. Ira never knew of their disobedience.

Four months after the apple incident, Taynee Mitchell was born. Jay's happiness was complete. Two nights later, Mattie gave birth to a son, Billy Dean. The Phelps's home was filled with joy. On the other side of Tandy's Mountain, in the early morning chill, Hail White endured her labor alone. Her house was filled with hate and despair.

In the five years that followed, times on Pound became lawless and disturbed, outlawing and moonshining became prevalent. Gunfire and murder were a way of life. Many people claimed Jay had his fingers in it all.

Ira Phelps finished his mill and added on an implement store. Much to Jay's consternation, Ira took up moonshining and was fast becoming the kingpin in the whiskey running business.

Another knot was added to Jay's rope of bad luck. His darling Mae died giving birth to her second child, stillborn. Jay was grief stricken. Life handed him another devastating blow. Left a widower again, this time with four young children, he became more frustrated and bitter. To ease his sorrow he would desert his children and leave Tandy's Mountain for months at a time. He left his oldest son Rueben to be responsible for Blaine, Bob and their five-year-old sister, Taynee.

A few days after Mae's death, Mattie Phelps was found dead. The Phelps's dogs discovered her body lying on the path leading to the huckleberry patch behind the mill. Ira, like Jay, was left with a motherless family.

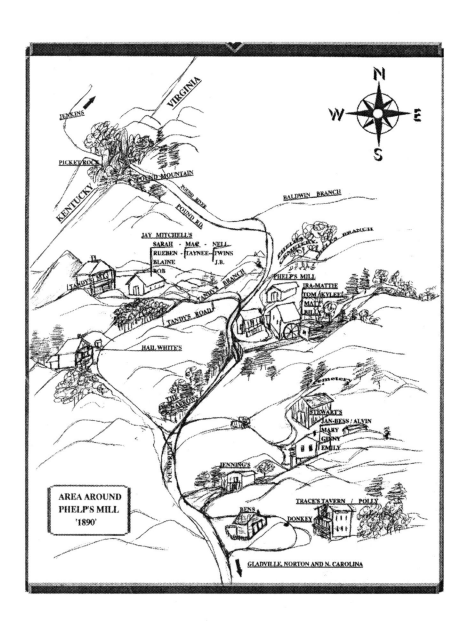

AREA AROUND
PHELP'S MILL
'1890'

CHAPTER THREE

-1890-

"Thank goodness that messy job is done," Kylee Bentley exclaimed as she wiped the back of her hand across her forehead, leaving a dark streak of sticky syrup behind. She gave a heavy sigh of weariness and continued the job she started at dawn with her father.

The day was beginning to be stifling hot and unbearable. The green and yellow leaves hung limp, without a flicker on the huge trees. Even the noisy chatter of the gray squirrels had ceased, waiting for the cool of the evening shade. In August of 1890, Oldfort, Tennessee began as always with sorghum making, a job Kylee always detested. The hateful task, however, did not keep her from singing at her work.

Early morning started with the assembling of the grinding mill and building a fire in the outdoor furnace. Then with team and wagon they headed for the fields to haul in the cane. After stripping the leaves and berries, her father would feed the long stalks into the sorghum mill.

Their old mule, Maudie, diligently pulled the long pole in a circle, slowly turning the grinding wheel. When the thick green syrup came from the mill Kylee strained it through a clean cloth into a large oak bucket and carried it to the furnace.

Kylee watched the fire inside the furnace as she carefully poured the green syrup into the metal container on top, called a boiling box. It was hot, insufferable work, stirring the boiling liquid and skimming off the foam that formed on top with a long handled wooden dipper. The syrup would thicken and turn a soft brown color. Kylee then dipped the finished sorghum into large storage barrels.

After the sorghum was finished, her father cleaned and polished the grinder. Kylee helped him put the mill and long poles into the wagon. It would be ready for a neighbor to borrow, along with the old mule, Maudie. Kylee busied herself washing the boiling box and rubbing it with a piece of pork fat to prevent rusting.

"I'm headin' for the house daughter. Soon as you finish gettin' the lard spread, fetch a fresh bucket of water to the house. I'll spread them grindin's on the field in the mornin'. I have to leave for town now. I'm needin' to talk with you, so be for hurryin'!" His voice was firm and decisive, not the soft slow easy drawl she was used to.

Valdean Bently headed for the house, a heavy burden on his heart. How was he going to tell Kylee of his decision? There was no reason to worry he kept telling himself. Kylee had always been an obedient child.

Another decision he made over eighteen years before had completely changed his life. At the time it had been as hard to decide as this one. But, he had stuck with it and never returned to his home in Virginia.

When Val left to find work and raise the money needed to finish the mill, he never dreamed his life would take such a change. He worked mines in Kentucky, but soon learned the long hours and coal dust only aggravated an old wound he received in the war. A letter from his sweetheart stated plainly she had grown tired of waiting and found another love and begged him to release her from the promise she had made. He was broken hearted and devastated. Desperately needing a friend, and missing Ira and Mattie, he made a decision to find a new life. He decided to travel to Chattanooga, Tennessee and find an old war buddy. The last time he had seen Dolf Trudman was when they were both recovering from war injuries in a military hospital on Lookout Mountain. He remembered Dolf's lovely young sister, Nan who visited often. She was a ray of sunshine to all the lonely patients, encouraging each one, reminding them of a sweetheart or family waiting at home. As Val traveled into Tennessee he began to think often of the beautiful young woman, a vibrant girl with brown hair and sparkling dark eyes. He found Dolf and was informed that Nan was still single. Val was delighted and began seeing her often with marriage in mind.

After they were wed, Val built a cabin on a piece of ground given to them by Nan's father. After the first year of marriage and there had been no child, Nan was crestfallen. Everyone had a child within the first nine months, even sooner, she complained.

Then they were blessed with Kylee. A baby with green eyes, more beautiful than any child they had ever longed for. Nan was ecstatic and entwined her life around the baby. Val felt left out and neglected. When Kylee was three, tragedy struck. Typhoid fever raided the valley. Death moved as the silent reaper, taking many lives including Nan, her father and her mother. Dolf and his family were spared, as were Val and Kylee.

Brokenhearted and grief stricken, Val's first desperate decision was to give the child up for someone else to raise. But a deep love and devotion to the child would not allow him to forsake her. The task was not an easy one. He asked for no one's help and promised himself that with some sacrifices and God's help, he would get the job done.

As Kylee grew up, he constantly reminded her, "you gotta be a lady, hon, no matter what! It's what your mamma would have wanted. No matter what you got or ain't got, folks are gonna notice you, if'n you're a lady. A real lady has values an' ideals. You can respect yourself if'n you stand up to your moral commitments. It's up to me to see to it that you learn good moral ideals an' values!"

"I ain't never had no education Kylee gal. There weren't schools back where I come from. There's one here an' you're goin'!" He emphatically informed his daughter.

Dolf, his wife and four strapping sons had a farm that joined Val's and Kylee soon became close friends with her cousins. They took her to the little school in the village until she could ride a horse and care for herself. As she grew older Val taught her the art of pickling and preserving and how to dry the orange pumpkins and big banana squash. She could bleach apples with just the right amount of sulfur. She learned how to wash and cord fleece, spin yarn, dye the thread, and weave it into cloth. Kylee became a fine cook under Val's supervision. He bragged often of her accomplishment.

"That daughter of mine can make the best darn scrabble in the state of Tennessee, maybe even Virginny!" he would declare with a far away twinkle in his eyes.

They lived hard at times, but managed to stay together. Even with his two failings, booze and gambling, he provided for Kylee and saw to her raising.

He shook his head to clear it of the memories. Looking back was no good. If he let these feelings possess him, he would back out on Kenus Hall. He would be tempted to take Kylee to Virginia and the beauty of the Blue Ridge Mountains. He shook his head again knowing this was an impossible thought.

Now he arrived at a place where he regretted his nugatory habits. They would cause him to lose Kylee. The old condition in his lungs grew worse to aggravate and trouble him. Too much whiskey and long hours of working in the dust on his farm had not helped. It became harder each day for him to breathe. The deep cough and rattle in his lungs were with him constantly.

He had a gut feeling that his time here was limited. Kylee had to be provided for if anything should happen to him. Kenus Hall made him a good offer and he had no other choice but to accept. Kylee would be well taken care of. She would be married to a man of means and position. Although Kenus was three times her age, it must not interfere. She would just have to accept the arrangement. The amount of money Hall offered for her had blinded Val to all reasoning. Now, as he thought about the deal, he had a deeper urge to back out. But the arrangements were made and there was only one way to tell Kylee, quick and to the point.

Val watched his daughter at the well, admitting to himself what a fine young woman she had grown into. Thick auburn-brown hair hung in one heavy braid down her back to below her waist. He could hear her singing '*Roosters crow in the Sourwood Mountains, ho-hum-come a teadle-dum-day. She won't come and I won't fetch her, ho-hum-come a teadle-dum-day*'. It was hard to think about Kylee being gone. The home would be lonesome without her lovely face, happy smile, and joyful song. She had indeed been a joy and had filled his life completely after Nan died. Yes, he would miss her.

At the well, Kylee filled a washbasin. The hot day combined with the heat from the furnace and heavy stench of pig lard almost caused Kylee to lose her insides. The water was cool and refreshing. She washed away the fat that rolled into balls and stuck to her hands from the cold water. Splashing the water over her arms, she rubbed hard on the sticky syrup that trailed down to her elbows. She was fighting off the flies that were aggravating her in swarms.

Curiously she wondered what it was her father had to tell her. Drawing fresh water, she washed her face, giving special attention to the brown streak on her forehead. The water cooled her flushed face. Quickly she dried on a towel hanging on the well post.

A small breeze whirled its way across the yard, picking up the dry dust and rattling the leaves on the maple trees behind the barn. It coaxed a curly wisp of hair from the tight braid to blow across Kylee's face and tickled her sunburn nose. She regretted her decision to not wear a sunbonnet. Thankful for the breeze, she breathed in deeply. Removing her long apron, she doused it in the basin of water to soak out the gooey syrup mess. Filling a wooden bucket that was sitting on the edge of the well with water, she headed for the house, wondering again what it was her father had to tell her.

Her father had silently ignored her through the day, scarcely speaking two words. He was strangely different from the father who was always joking and exchanging jest with her. It puzzled her even more when he hadn't taken a minute's pause to have his usual nip from the flask in his hip pocket. Every effort she made to converse with him had been turned aside.

There were no lighthearted words for the old mule. As the day progressed, he neglected to give the animal a taste of the sweet foam Kylee had been skimming from the sorghum. When sorghum making started, the old mule, Maudie, would suddenly develop a sweet tooth. When Val forgot to feed her a ration of fodder the faithful servant reminded him with a screeching bray.

The evening cool was beginning to settle in. Kylee could hear the squirrels resuming their noisy chatter. The whirlwind danced away to find another yard to play in. Maudie stood nodding contentedly; glad the long day of work was over. As Kylee crossed the yard she reached over the fence and stroked the animal's soft nose. Remembering her father's instructions to hurry, she broke into a run up the stairs, splashing cool water from the bucket over her bare feet with the sudden movement. It felt so good. She had to suppress a driving urge to spill the entire contents of the bucket over her warm body.

"I'm done Paw," she informed her father as she entered the room.

Her father was standing as she had seen him many times. Back to the fireplace, hands fastened behind his back, an unlit pipe between his teeth, staring blankly out the open door. He rocked slowly back and forth as if in deep thought.

"What took you so long, girl?" Val questioned as he unfastened his hands and took the pipe from his lips.

Turning around, he knocked the ashes loose on the inside wall of the fireplace. He set the pipe on the mantel next to a tintype of Nan. He hated to tell Kylee of his decision, but the deed had to be done. Turning back around slowly, he faced the young woman.

Dark eyes that usually sparked with laughter when he talked were now seriously clouded. Kylee could not tell what emotion he was hiding. But she felt again the difference in her father. There was something that spoke to her of disaster. He dropped his news upon her, harsh, blunt, and definite.

"I've promised you to wed Kenus Hall!" he spoke hurriedly, without feeling. Kylee heard the definite decision in his voice.

Stunned by his words, she stopped in the middle of the room. The shock of Val's news stiffened her body. She flexed her fingers and dropped the bucket with a loud crash. The water spread in a puddle and was quickly absorbed into the dry planking of the kitchen floor. When the clanging of the fallen bucket subsided, the room became deathly silent.

After she had absorbed the impact of Val's words, anger crept in. She took a long deep breath. The sudden intake of air broke through the heavy silence in the room. Stretching her small body to its highest, almost reaching five-feet, she let her breath out slowly, releasing some of the hostility.

"No, Paw, no! I won't! You can't make me. I'll run away first."

Never in her life had she spoken in such a way to her father. Kylee's usual calm nature had quickly arrived at the boiling point. Her fair complexion became flushed with the strain of keeping her temper from flaring. Her rosy cheeks soon matched her sun burnt nose. She was struggling to find a way to think rationally. Under no circumstances would she agree to marry Kenus Hall.

Kenus, with his little pig eyes looking her over, and the thought of his sly, sneaky, suggestive grin sickened her. She raised her chin high with renewed defiance. Green eyes sparked with fiery disobedience. Val did not miss the unrelenting decision in her voice or the refusal glowing in her jade eyes.

"Are you plannin' on disobeyin' your paw youngin'?"

"I ain't a youngin' no more, Paw. I'm almost nineteen and I'm old enough to have some say." Her full lips tightened and began to tremble as she spoke. "What's happened? You always said that a lady needed values, an' should marry for love!"

"That was when you were a youngin' girl an' believed in fairy tales. Circumstances change! You forget such nonsense! You'll do as I say as long as you're under my roof," her father told her harshly. "It's time you were wed."

"But why Kenus, Paw?" Kylee couldn't believe this was happening. "He's older than you."

Kylee could tell by the firm set of her father's jaw that there would be no changing his mind. But why had he chosen Kenus? He didn't even like him. He had told her so often.

"Age matters little. I want you married to a man who can care for you in a fittin' manner. Heaven knows I haven't given you much Kylee," Val apologized. "You can be gettin' your things together. There'll be no weddin' at first."

"I'll not stay in his house without bein' wed. It wouldn't be fittin', Paw. Oh, Paw, what's happened to you?"

"You'll be like a housekeeper. He said he'd respect you as such. The Preacher will marry you proper when he's back at the church at Thanksgivin' time," he added seeing the shocked look on Kylee's face. "Kenus promised me that much. He pledged to be a man of his word."

"I'm happy with what we got. It's all I need," Kylee insisted.

"You be ready in the mornin'. Quit your snivlin'!" he shouted at her when he saw the tears well up in her eyes and roll slowly down her cheeks. Then his voice softened as he remembered the love he had for her and how lonely he would be when she was gone.

"You'll be close, darlin', an' I'll be to see you often. I'll make sure he's treatin' you right. He's got money an' can give you all the things a gal hankers for. It's for the best. I had no choice. You'll have to set your mind. The deal has been made an' there's no turnin' back. He'll be to get you tomorrow. You be ready!" His statement was final. He could not allow himself a moment of reconsideration.

"Oh, Paw, how could you promise me to Kenus without even askin' me first? I won't do it! I won't! I won't!" She screamed, trying to enforce her words, struggling hard to control her tears. Her body weakened, her anger was fading. Only cold desperation remained. Clinching her hands into small tight fists, she stomped a bare foot firmly upon the plank floor. The sound was loud in the small room and hung heavy under the low ceiling.

Val's patience grew thin; his nerves close to the breaking point. He hadn't planned on Kylee's reprisal. She had always been an obedient child, but now he could see she was not a child anymore. Because of her smallness, he had failed to notice how much of a young woman she had developed into. Looking at her now the full realization swept over him. It was not hard to understand why Kenus desired to have her. The deal was made. He could not allow her to get the upper hand. With a long stride he closed the distance between them and struck her sharply across the cheek.

The blow surprised and staggered Kylee. She reached for the table to steady herself and leaned heavily against it. In spite of the tears that flooded her eyes, she did not cry out, but raised her head defiantly, ready for battle, rebellion sparking peridot stars deep within her green eyes.

"Disrespectful youngin'! You might as well know you'll do exactly as I say! Get your things together. Be ready to leave when Kenus comes for you. I'll not tolerate any more back talk, you hear? Be ready! I'm goin' to meet Kenus now. I'll be back 'fore dark. Have supper ready!" he demanded as he crossed the floor.

Val reached for a battered hat that hung from a peg beside the door, kicking the bucket aside that was in his way. He slapped the old hat on his head with angry force. He stomped out the door and down the steps heading for the barn. The black hat sat too far down on his head, resting heavily upon his ears and causing his hair to stick out at the sides, giving him the look of a circus clown. Kylee always laughed at the funny old hat but on this hot autumn day, there was no laughter. Not even a smile followed him down the path lined with green and gold buttonwood sycamore.

Kenus Hall was known as a man of means, owning most of the property on the surrounding hills and in the small community. What he hadn't acquired by inheritance, he cheated people out of through gambling. He kept in their good graces by financing a large portion of the schools needs and paying an enormous tithing to the church. The card games he held were well known throughout the territory. This evening he was waiting, without patience, for Val's arrival to begin a game.

"You don't know my cousin Talt Hall across the table there?" Kenus questioned Val, the anger showing clearly on his face at Val's late appearance. "The other man there is sort of a relation, but that's neither here nor there."

The small man, Talt Hall, had no resemblance what so ever to his cousin. Kenus being a tall man of stature and stout in build. Talt wore two guns strapped around his slight hips. Kenus wore his gun in a shoulder holster under his suit coat. Their eyes were their only resemblance, eyes that look past you, not at you. A stare that made you feel like slime on a rock. The 'sort-a-relation' was a tall skinny man with graying hair.

"Val Bentley here, he's the one we've been waiting for. Let's play cards!" It was clear Kenus was tired of the delay, the protocol was over, and the game began.

The night wore on; one game after the other until it was long after midnight. Valdean always the loser until his IOU's mounted into a stack.

"I'm going to Chad's for some booze. Hold things until I get back." Kenus pushed his chair back and rose to leave.

It was time for flexing knuckles and stretching knees. There had been little exchange of conversation. The men were estranged by the difference in the personalities.

"So you're Kenus' cousin," Val addressed Talt, trying to kill the silence.

"That's what he said. I'm gonna take a walk." The answer was as cold as his eyes. He said no more and left.

Val walked slowly around the room eyeing the other man, wondering if he should start another unwelcome conversation. The silence bothered him along with his growing stack of IOU's.

"I guess my luck's no-good tonight. I don't think Kenus mentioned your name, are you from around here?" Val questioned the other man.

"No I'm here from farther south. I'm Hall's brother-in-law," the tall man counted and re-stacked his chips over and over, running them through his fingers allowing them to fall on the table.

"Brother-in-law? You mean you're married to his sister?"

"No, I'm his brother-in-law, like he is married to my sister."

It grew late and the long shadows darkened across the barn and blended into the night and Val had not returned. Kylee patiently put the dishes she had set out back into the cupboard. The meal she prepared of mustard greens, side pork, and corn bread went on the hearth to keep warm. The small home was plain and free from any frills or fancies, but Kylee had been happy here. There was no money for luxuries, and their clothing was as plain as the home. Kylee hadn't minded; no one in the valley had better, except Kenus.

The thought of him sickened Kylee. His money and fine home were of no importance to her. With a woman's instinct, she feared becoming a wife to Kenus. She grew ill at the thought of his puffy hands on her. There would be no joy, only hate and repulsion.

She would not wait for a fate such as her father and Kenus had planned for her. She removed her father's valise from under his bed. He had told her many times how it had traveled through the war, never leaving his side, even when he was captured. It was with him through his stay in the hospital at Lookout Mountain. He carried it on his journey home, then back to the mines in Kentucky and down the road to Tennessee.

"It has memory value, girl. The things inside have no meanin' to anyone 'ceptin' me." Val explained.

Kylee remembered the valise always being there, under his bed. She took the keepsakes that were in the bottom and put them in a small wooden box that was attempting to fall apart. She pushed the box under her father's bed. She filled the valise with her few belongings then tucked it under her cot.

It was too late to leave tonight. Val would come home from a night of drinking and sleep well into the next day. By the time he awoke, she would be far back into the mountains, living in some cave as the early settlers had done. She would stay hidden until they gave her up for dead. Then she would go to a big city and find a job. She had schooling through the eighth grade, more than most females of the time. It would entitle her to a teaching position in many places. Sewing and cooking was a breeze for her also. She was certain she could care for herself. It was about time she did.

The small fire she built to cook supper was all the light needed. Now as the fire burned low, the cabin was bathed in darkness. Kylee took the lamp from the mantel and placed it on the table in the middle of the room. She fired a small stick on the embers of the hot coals. Lifting the chimney, she lit the wick. Then she tossed the flaming stick onto what was left of the fire and secured the chimney back into place.

The soft glow from the lamp filled the room and warmed Kylee's spirits some. She closed the door because of the various small varmints that liked to find a sleeping place in a corner of their home. She longed for the fire to die soon. The room was becoming hot and sticky.

Removing her dress and petticoat, she readied herself for bed. She washed her face, hands, and feet, then brushed her hair. Kylee had never owned such a luxury as a robe and always slept in her underclothing, which included a chemise and bloomers. In the winter she was allowed to wear her stockings for added warmth.

In her rebellious mood she wondered if she dare allow herself to sleep without any clothing, the night was so hot and sultry. Then she reprimanded herself for such a thought recalling the promise of the ladies at the church, "sure fire, hell, an' damnation if a young lady allowed her thoughts in any way to dwell upon the naked body."

There was no way of understanding grown-ups. She liked her cousin Jess's theory better, "the Lord had given you a body, why was it wrong to acknowledge you had one?" Kylee agreed. The only thing certain in the world was hard work and being pushed around by someone.

She seated herself well into the middle of the room, away from the heat of the fire cross-legged upon the floor, clad only in her underclothing. Undoing the heavy braid hanging down her back, she flipped the loose hair over her head letting it rest upon the floor. She began the long process of brushing one hundred strokes, both sides and back. Her long tresses were thick and slightly curled, encouraging tangles and making her task difficult. She counted diligently. Her father said it was part of being a lady. It was what her mother had always done.

The fire had almost died. There was only a slight glow from the embers to catch the reddish highlights of her dark hair. The brush popped bright electrical sparks caused from her vigorous brushing, as her strokes became stronger and more rapid. A cool breeze touched the back of her neck as Val opened the door and entered the dimly lit room. He's even drunker than usual, Kylee thought flipping her hair back. She watched with concern as he leaned heavily against the wall.

Val hung his hat on a peg and staggered across the room. There was paleness in his face, an ashen quality, different from the usual whiskey redness. The startling pallor sent a message to Kylee. She rose to help him as he stumbled into the table. He reached and held to the edge with a shaky hand. Kylee was quick to ease him gently onto a chair.

"Oh, Paw!" She exclaimed in terror as her hand grasped the sticky wetness on his shirtfront.

Frantic, she filled the gourd dipper hanging over the water bucket on the washstand and offered it to her father. He refused feebly and pushed it away weakly.

"Paw, Paw, what's happened? Tell me, what's happened? You're hurt an' bleedin' bad! What can I do to help you? Please let me help you."

"Oh God, Kylee babe, it's too late; it's too late. I'm hurtin' bad," Val began coughing, a rasping wheeze coming from deep inside, draining his strength. Blood ran from his nose and mouth and gushed from a bullet wound in his middle.

"I'm so sorry, Kylee. I didn't realize. That dirty bastard shot me when I found out what he was up to." Val took a deep breath and held a hand to his stomach.

"Hush, Paw. Hush right now. I ain't gonna listen to anymore. You're gonna come an' lie down. I'm goin' for help. I'll get Uncle Dolf. Come on now, that's a good Papa."

Putting her arms around Val, she tried to lift him, urging him gently to the bed in the corner. "Leave me be, it's too late, Kylee. It's too late," Val declared faintly, pushing her arms away.

Tears ran down the deep gullies of his wrinkled, weathered cheeks. The sight of his tears filled Kylee with panic. Taking a towel from the shelf over the water bucket she unbuttoned his shirt and pushed it against the gaping wound.

For the first time in her life, Kylee was seeing what a thirty-eight pistol could do to a man. The sight wasn't pretty. She grew weak looking at the blood oozing from the hole in Val's middle.

"Hold it Paw, hold it in hard!" Kylee ordered. "Maybe it will slow the bleedin'. I'm gonna get Uncle Dolf. He'll know what to do. I don't care what you say!"

Val began coughing again, breathing in short quick gasps. Kylee frantically began wringing her hands. Her father drew in a deep breath and held the towel firmly to catch the rush of blood that came gushing out. He reached for Kylee pulling at her arm.

"No, don't leave me. Please don't leave me. I have to tell you somethin' you need to know. I tried to raise you right, girl. It wasn't easy after your Maw died, it wasn't easy. Heaven knows, but we got it done, didn't we?" He smiled faintly at Kylee through his tears, his eyes asking her forgiveness. "I'm so sorry I struck you Kylee."

"Oh Paw, don't talk of that, it was your right. I'll do anythin' you say, just don't die," Kylee pleaded with her father.

"You're never gonna marry that bastard. Never! You understand Kylee? I told him it would have to be over my dead body. He said he'd see to that, an' have you too! Well, maybe I'll be dead, but he'll never have you. Ain't got any conscience, a man like that, ain't got no conscience." Val's voice was coming in long gasps. "He was crazy mad 'cause I found out he was already married. No one here abouts knew 'bout it. He's kept it hid, but his wife's touched in the head. Some sister of hers is takin' care of her in Chattanooga. He left her there when he came here. He thought he was safe and that no one would find out. Well! I found out! Her brother let it slip. Kenus is only lookin' for a pretty young thing to play around with, an' take care of his big house." Val was struggling to finish his story. "He needn't look at you anymore, ain't none of mine going to marry up with a man that's already got a wife!" His voice sounded firmer and stronger. He started slipping back into the brogue of the hills, which he had almost lost.

"Quick now girl, hurry an' get me the ink, quill, an' stationary in the chest. Hurry now. I have to write a letter. We must make plans to get you away from here. You set over there, Kylee."

Kylee hurried to set the writing material in front of her father. Totally puzzled at the fact that he didn't want her to watch what he was writing.

"He shot me. He left me for dead. Thinks he's gonna have you, but I'll show him. I ain't dead yet!" Val said with conviction.

Val reached and slid the lamp closer, turning up the wick. The flame flickered brightly, vibrating and catching the heavy uneven rhythm of his breathing. His hand shook uncontrollably tipping the lamp and dangerously rocking the chimney. It settled and righted itself upon the table. Splatters of ink fell in splotches upon the white paper as he lifted the quill from the inkwell. He began slowly, writing with extreme difficulty.

"Let me do it for you Papa, please. I can do it for you."

"Sit down, girl, leave me be! I'll do it myself. Gotta hurry 'fore it's too late!"

Val pushed her roughly aside. Kylee sat down in the chair across from him. She was crying quietly to herself, tears flowing down her face. A cold chilling silence fell upon the room as Val proceeded to write. She sat in quiet desperation watching her father struggle to finish the letter that seemed to be of such importance.

"I'm done, Kylee dear," he spoke haltingly, gasping for air.

The bleeding stopped, the blood drying on his lips. The soiled towel slipped from his lap, forgotten.

"The letter is to Ira Phelps. You remember? I told you 'bout my cousin Ira from Virginny. We were more than just cousins. Our paws an' maws were sisters an' brothers. Without being direct family, you can't get any closer than that, Kylee. Our folks all died with a sickness that came to the hills when we were boys, 'fore the war. It took a lot of folks. We were lucky. We were left to raise each other." Val breathed in hard for air.

"Ira will take you. I know he will, if he's still living. He owes me. I did a favor for him once. Heaven knows I ain't ever been sorry for it." He looked at Kylee across the table with a deep love for her shining in his clouded eyes.

"Kenus will never find you there. It's too far back in the mountains. Anyway, it used to be. I suppose it's changed some by now. It's been so long, so long," his voice trailed off, his mind fading into memories of his childhood and the glorious beauty of the Blue Ridge Mountains between Kentucky and Virginia. He came back to the present with a start that shook his body and the shaking didn't stop.

"Get your things ready. Your Uncle Dolf will take care of everythin' for you. He'll get you away." He signed and folded the letter shakily. Slowly he put it inside the envelope rattling the paper loudly with his trembling hands. He sealed it and addressed it carefully.

"Don't cry, Kylee dear. I can't bear to see you cry. Please, no tears. Can you do that for your ole' Pappa? Listen to me Kylee, listen good. Kenus is never to have you! Never! No way, are you to go with him. I'm sorry, babe. It was all because of my stupidity an' greed. It was my fault. I have loved you, girl. Don't ever forget.....I....Lovvv...." his voice trailed, then stopped with a loud gurgle that rose in his throat choking him. He slumped to the tabletop; his arm stiffened, then straightened, knocking the ink and letter crashing to the floor.

A loud sob came from Kylee. She jumped to her feet, "Oh, Paw! Don't be dead! Don't be dead!" She was crying. But, he was dead and it was over for him.

Her father, a small man, slight of weight was no problem for Kylee to lift from the chair and drag to his bed in the corner. Gently she closed his eyelids, washed the dry blood from his lips and face and covered his body with a blanket.

Sitting down at the table, her tears dry, she laid her head on folded arms and waited out the night. She heard the rain start, slowly, and softly at first, as if reluctant to fall upon the low roof. It grew heavier as the night progressed until in the gray dawn it became a steady oppressive downpour.

As if in a dream, Kylee bent and picked up the letter at her feet and laid it on the table. She rose wearily from the chair, stiff and chilled from her long night in one position. Pulling on a heavy tweed cloak and tying a scarf over her long hair, she went out into the pouring rain. In her haste, she didn't take time to saddle her horse, Buttons, but mounted him bareback. Unconcerned with the wind and rain, she ducked her head into the storm and rode three miles to Uncle Dolf's.

CHAPTER FOUR

Kylee depended on her uncle and aunt to take care of everything. They helped her see to her father's burying. She had no intentions of leaving her home. She was staying and the devil could take Kenus Hall!

Uncle Dolf was kind and sensitive to Kylee's feelings and considerate of her needs. Kylee watched silently as her uncle built her father's casket. She said not a word as her Aunt Aggie dressed her father's corpse in his Sunday suit. She had never understood why he called it his Sunday suit. He never wore it on Sunday. He never went to church, but saw to it that Kylee went on Sundays, Christmas, and Easter, too with her aunt and cousins.

Kylee combed her father's hair tenderly and placed the battered old hat on his head. Shocked by her actions, Aunt Aggie was quick to reprimand her.

"Really Kylee dear, you can't do that! It wouldn't be proper."

Kylee's nature was shy and withdrawn to most people, but she also had her share of fortitude and stubbornness. With no disrespect intended toward her aunt, she left the old hat on Val's head.

The Trudman family took turns sitting with Kylee and her father's corpse, receiving family and friends, as they readied for Val's services.

"It is time we have the grave open. It would be fittin' to get the buryin' over with. You get the things you need, an' put them in the wagon next to the shovels an' pick. There'll be no need for you to come back here. The boys an' I can see to the other stuff," her uncle kindly instructed her.

"I feel badly girl. There's nothin' we can do 'bout your paw gettin' killed. The law's on Kenus's side. Said they had a witness that saw your paw try to kill Kenus. It's self-defense where Kenus is concerned. I think Kylee, we'll find that your paw had most everything signed over to Kenus. Your paw told me that. I'm sorry, Kylee," Dolf continued regretfully.

"Your Paw came to the house that night. May heaven forgive me, I should have known right then that somethin' was wrong. He wouldn't come in, stood talkin' at the door. I thought his stagger was from drinkin'. I was angry with him for bein' liquored up. He told me then that he had backed out of the deal with Kenus. I couldn't understand why he kept insistin' that if anythin' happened to him, I'd see to it that you got away from here. I told him to hush up, go home an' sleep if off, that he was gonna live a long time. He know'd then that he was dyin', he know'd. It's the way it'll be, girl. Kenus has it fixed to get everything you own. Things are already in progress."

"He might legally have everything my paw had, but I am the one thing paw owned that he ain't never gonna have!" Kylee said definitely. "I'm not leavin' here either!" Her mind was made up. She was not about to give into Kenus's whims.

Uncle Dolf drove the big wagon with the boys, the casket, and Kylee's belongings. Aunt Aggie and Kylee took the buggy. The full leather top would shield them from the rain that was threatening.

The cemetery was on the hill behind the church. They buried Val beside Nan underneath a tall elm. Kylee felt in her heart that he was happy to be resting beside her mother. The lonesomeness of being without a wife and the struggle to raise a child had ended.

Dolf watched Kylee as they buried his old friend, admiring her courage, as she stood quiet and desperate beside the grave. The rain came suddenly before they were finished, gathering force until it became a steady downpour.

Kylee's head bowed lower to its pounding as it fell unmercifully on her dark grief. It kept on and on, untiring and never ending it seemed. It drummed steadily upon the crude homemade casket in the grave before her. The shovels of mud were falling upon it with dull soggy thumps, as if it were a hollow thing, echoing loudly in her ears. Kylee stood alone, silent and separated from her family and friends, in bleak despair. In her dark mourning attire, she cast a lonely dark figure against the dismal sky.

Uncle Dolf read a few verses from the Bible in the absence of a preacher. Her four cousins sang a medley of sacred songs, which Kylee had sang with them often. The songs were a comfort in her grief. They worked now, struggling to fill the grave, trying to beat the rain. The friends that gathered left as the storm began.

Kylee turned away and started slowly down the slope of the hill. The wagon that carried the casket and Kylee's belongings was parked under a small tree as close to the grave as possible. She decided to wait at the wagon until they were finished. Listening to the shovels of mud falling upon the casket filled her with the stark realization of her father's passing. Her legs felt as if they were going to give away underneath her. She needed to sit down.

The rain slowed and stopped as suddenly as it began. Kylee removed the black scarf from her head and gave her dark auburn hair a shake as she walked. The heavy rain had penetrated the soft silk material, leaving her hair damp and gleaming with wetness. Small corkscrew curls framed her small face. Tight ringlets tickled her ears as her long hair fell in loose waves down her back. Raindrops gathered and hung in clusters to each curl's end. They clung there for a moment then dripped slowly onto her already wet clothing.

At the wagon she sat down beside Val's valise filled with her few articles of clothing and personal items. Dangling her feet she swung them to and fro. Aware of the added weight in the wagon, the horses moved ahead, whinnying nervously.

"Easy Joe, easy Cleo," Kylee spoke softly to quiet them. It will be a sunny day after all, she thought. Through a small clearing in the west, she could see the sun making a vain attempt to shine.

Behind the valise was a box of books belonging to Kylee covered with a canvas to protect them from the rain. She had packed them tearfully, determined not to leave them for Kenus to get his greedy paws on. *Five Little Peppers and How They Grew, Hans Brinker, Heidi, Little Women, Under the Lilac,* and *Tom Sawyer,* were all books she treasured and knew by heart. It was the one luxury her father allowed after she learned to read. He loved for her to read aloud to him and it became a thing of enjoyment to both of them. It became a tradition for him to add a book to her collection as a birthday gift or for a special occasion.

The container consisting of Val's souvenirs was tied carefully inside a shawl to keep it together; it sat beside the box of books. Kylee carefully untied the bundle and opened the box. There were some childhood toys, a child's pair of buttoned shoes wrinkled and dried from age, a small pair of wire framed reading glasses in a black case, and a square tin. She supposed the childish things had belonged to her. There was a faint memory of her mother wearing the wire-framed glasses.

The tin can was painted with lovely ladies around the sides and a lid trimmed and decorated with garlands of roses. She lifted the lid and looked inside. It was filled with old army insignias, a baby's knit cap beginning to fill with holes, army papers, and several letters addressed to her father. The envelopes were so crumpled and stained with what appeared to be teardrops that she declined opening them. There was no time and her tears would only add to the task. Her father had never spoken to her of these treasures. The letters meant absolutely nothing to her. But they were a small part of her father and she would keep them in his memory. She tucked them inside the tin can and back into the box tying them together again with the shawl. That's where they stayed, unlooked at, unread, and soon forgotten.

Kylee looked at her boots and the chunks of wet earth gathered around the soles. Breaking a limb from an overhanging branch, she scraped the edge of her shoe patiently. The boots were badly worn and the soles beginning to break away from the upper shoe. She sighed wearily, thinking of her father's promise to resole them. A faint smile touched her lips at the squishy sound her feet made inside her shoes. The moisture and dirt had seeped in around the split soles leaving a bed of mud for her feet.

Now that the burial was over, the tears that she had been trying to control came easy. Kylee cried quietly, hugging herself closely, glad for the chance to be alone, letting the tears flood her face and feeling better from the sudden surge.

Jesse was coming down the hill running carefully between the headstones and graves. Her uncle, aunt, and other cousins followed walking slowly, carrying the pick and shovels. The tears stopped, she dried her face on the scarf and promised herself there would be no more.

"Hey! We're done, Kylee," Jesse called to her. "We're goin' to town. They are havin' lunch at Elmer's place for us all." He settled himself on the wagon beside her. "Cause of your paw."

Cousin Jesse, the younger of the boys, was not as tall as his older brothers but built with tenacious strength. Everyone who knew him stood a little in awe of Jesse, cautious not to cross him. With Kylee he was always guardian and protector.

"I think not. I'm not up to it, Jesse."

"You'll have to tell my paw. He'll expect you to go."

They watched Dolf and Aggie coming closer. Kylee apologetically made her excuses. The three days it took to get Val buried and sitting up with the corpse for two nights exhausted Kylee. Her nerves were frazzled and her body was weary. There had been no time for rest. Dolf pushed them constantly, insisting they must finish with the burying. There was an urgency to get Kylee safely away from Kenus's clutches. But for Kylee there was no hurry, she had no intentions of leaving.

Uncle Dolf reluctantly agreed for her to go to his house. Understanding her need to be alone, but he suggested that Jesse accompany her.

"No, please Uncle Dolf. I'm just needin' to get some rest an' be alone. I'll be fine. Give my apologies an' appreciation to the ladies."

Dolf, a short stocky man, removed his hat as he talked to Kylee, exposing his almost bald head. He smiled kindly as he helped his niece up into the buggy and watched as she started the horse out slowly.

The ride to her uncle Dolf's small farm was restful and pleasant. The warm rain was gone, leaving behind a sweet clean smell and it filled her with peacefulness. Moisture gathered on the big leaves of the sycamores along the road glistening in the sun, causing small dancing rainbows to appear. These colorful illusions cheered Kylee and her spirits rose.

Guiding Buttons through the wide gate, Kylee drove around to the back of the small white farmhouse and into the barn. She unhitched her horse, took time to brush him down and turned him loose to graze.

As she returned to the house, there grazing in the back yard was a horse she quickly recognized. Reins dragging, saddled and bridled, it was nibbling grass dangerously close to her Aunt Aggie's favorite flowerbed of marigolds.

Kylee knew as she walked up the pathway to the house who the visitor would be. She wanted to run but lifted her chin proudly and climbed the steps. Behind the sheltering cover of morning glory vines Kylee heard the creaking of the porch swing as it moved to and fro. There sat Kenus Hall with his back straight and his arms folded across his chest as if he owned the place.

A sinking feeling told Kylee that the creaking of the porch swing was a chorus to her doom. She walked slowly across the porch, her head held high, filled with decision. The sooner she told this horrible man of her intentions, the better.

"Afternoon Miss Kylee. I come to offer my condolences at your father's death." Kenus offered with perfect manners, slowly getting up from his seat. "I reckon you know it was his promise that we could wed. I been stayin' away waiting for you to bury your paw," he went on to say in a voice soft and smooth as satin.

Kylee felt sick with despair. The desperation only added to the weak feeling in her middle. She watched his thin lips twist into an obnoxious smile. She couldn't stand the sight of him, and hated everything about him. How could he dare have the audacity to offer his sympathy? Where did he get the guts to stand here before her and demand she marry him after killing her father? Well, never! Never would she consent to such a thing.

Kenus was finely attired in a fashionable three-piece suit of dark blue pinstripe serge. A man in his early sixties, he was very suave and young looking for his age. His black hair and mustache was showing no gray. At his age, Kylee thought in disgust, it shouldn't be that black. There was no doubt in her mind that he colored his hair and mustache too.

He was immaculately clean with well-groomed nails and neatly combed hair trimmed high above his ears. A square jaw was set firmly with the determination of a man accustomed to having his own way. A large swooping mustache was waxed and twisted at the ends, in the style of the day. He drew his graying brows down over narrow deadly eyes that penetrated with a cold, chilling stare. Kylee felt as if she had been undressed with his glance.

Kylee often despaired at what her Aunt Aggie called plainness. Her nose was pointedly sharp and her eyes round and green.

"Green-eyed greedy gut, go 'round an' eat the world up," classmates would often tease. Her soft complexion was fair with warm color on her cheeks. "What you a blushin' fer Kylee?" another would taunt. But Kylee had a champion protector in her cousin Jesse. He was always ready to take up a battle for his cousin with the freckled face.

The few light brown dots that sprinkled her nose were her major grief. One consolation was her hair, hanging far below her waist, thick and abundant, dark brown with orange red highlights, hanging far below her waist. Her father told her it was her crowning glory and warned her never to cut it.

She had a childish shyness that troubled her; afraid she would never outgrow it. Small and slight of build, she had been slow to receive her share of roundness. Now a firm full figure thrust hard against the dark homespun dress that she had worn for many years. The strain on the material looked to be more than it could stand and seemed to be in danger of bursting. Kenus was hoping for such a happening to take place while he was in a spot to get the full view. As he leered at her, she began to regret not letting Jesse accompany her.

He grinned at her slowly showing large white teeth. Kylee thought he looked like a jackass and guessed that his thoughts were of the pleasure she would bring to his bed. She had news for him.

Kenus's thoughts were just as Kylee surmised. But he was also thinking that she would be a good worker. He would keep his thoughts and desires to himself for now.

49

"Naturally, I'm a sympathetic man. I aim to give a proper amount of time for grievin'. I'm a fair man, but not a patient one," he informed Kylee, licking his wet tongue across his dry shapeless lips.

Taking hold of Kylee's arm, he gripped it tightly, bending down to look closely into her eyes. Kylee felt his breath and the saliva he sprayed with each word. She tried to pull away. His hold on her arm was firm and unrelenting.

"You listen to me, girl! You're gonna belong to me!" Kenus warned her sensing her withdrawal. A woman as small as Kylee would be easy to subdue. He had no intentions of waiting long.

"Don't take too long with your grievin'! Under the circumstances I figure a month would be plenty. After that I'll be to get you. Be ready! Don't be for gettin' any ideas about leavin'. I'd just have you brought back. Understand?" He gave her arm a twist that shook her body then released her.

"I have no plans that include marryin' you, Mr. Hall," she told him scornfully, raising her chin higher. His appearance at this time totally unnerved Kylee.

"It's not fittin' for a gal your age to be a traipsin' 'round the hills with no paw or maw. First thing you know, a gal as handsome as you could wind up bein' a woman of sin." With that statement, he picked up his hat from the porch swing. Putting it on his head, he gave it a sound thump on top pushing it firmly into place.

"Nonsense!" Kylee retorted, shocked at the insinuation. She was trying hard to keep her body from trembling. "All the same, I have no intentions of marryin', least of all the likes of you! I'd rather be a woman of sin!"

"You can be forgettin' me, the sooner the better. I've other plans that were my paw's true wishes. If there was any justice at all, you'd be in jail, waitin' to hang for killin' my paw!" Fire blazed through the grief and weariness in her eyes.

"He told me about the wife you're keepin' hidden. Now get an' leave me be!" she screamed. Turning quickly into the house, she slammed the door leaving Kenus with an angry red face as he mounted his horse and rode away.

Kylee knew it was not the last of Kenus. Growing weak with desperation, she wanted to scream, to cry. Remembering the promise to herself that there would be no more tears, she bit hard on her bottom lip. Slumping against the doorframe she let her body give way to lonesome despair.

She had to get away from that terrible man. Deciding emphatically and without any further procrastination she would mail the letter to Ira Phelps! Sliding down onto the floor, she slumped into a crumpled heap of exhaustion and weariness.

The days passed and grew into weeks and the month Kenus had given her was closing in. Kylee had mailed the letter to Ira Phelps and there had been no reply. She began to doubt the possibilities of his existence, telling herself over and over that it was just a dream to have a home and haven drop from the sky. There was no reason this person in Virginia should be anxious to accept a complete stranger into his home and under his protection. The more she thought about it, the more certain she became that it would not happen.

Dolf settled her affairs in the only way possible. Kenus started his legal actions to insure his take over of her property. Val had signed his deeds over to him and the rest went to pay IOU's and other debts. When it was finished, all that was left for Kylee was her horse, Buttons and the buggy. After the property was settled, Kenus became persistent in his rights to have Kylee.

At her lingering refusal, his threats turned to Dolf and his family. Kylee began to fear for their safety and knew she could wait no longer for a letter from Phelps. With her out of the way, Kenus would leave them alone. With lagging spirits, they made ready for Kylee's departure to a sister of Aggie's in Ohio.

Aggie, christened Agatha Jean, was a tall stately woman. She was bone thin, leaving the lines of her face chiseled and sharp. The strict reserved look was quite contrary to her cheery, warm personality. She wore her thin hair pulled severely up, rolled and twisted into a skinny tight bun high on her head.

Kylee loved her aunt dearly. She was the closest thing to a mother she had known. Aggie longed for a daughter but was content and happy with her four sons. After Nan died, she grew very fond of Kylee and would have showered her in girlish things, but Val refused to let her spoil Kylee. Now she had her chance to indulge her niece.

They mended and patched Kylee's badly worn underclothing. They put together a new robe and nightgown. When Dolf scolded at her extravagance, she insisted that Kylee could not appear at her sister's without proper bed clothing. It would be a reflection on them.

Then proceeding slyly, laughing behind her husband's back, she sewed a new pink-checkered gingham dress. She tucked and smocked the front, and then fashioned elbow length puffed sleeves, trimmed with a touch of lace. The dress was finished with a wide Dutch boy collar. Triumphantly Aggie added a matching sunbonnet.

The week arrived for Kylee to leave for Ohio and her heart was heavy. How could she leave the place where she had spent all her life and grew up with four cousins who adored her? She assured them she would write often. Tearfully she laughed and joked with her cousins. Kylee coaxed them with a beguiling smile to come visit her when she was settled, reminding them not to forget her.

Uncle Dolf left for Chattanooga to sell Buttons and the buggy to buy her a train ticket. Before he returned, a letter arrived from Ira Phelps in Virginia, a letter that would change the course of Kylee's life completely.

CHAPTER FIVE

Billy Dean Phelps, the youngest of the Phelps clan, whistled loudly to himself as he guided the team of mules carefully along the rugged road. Jack was docile and obeyed the pull of the reins. Old Red resented the restriction of the double tree and neck-yoke. Billy had to concentrate strictly on keeping her in line.

High in the Cumberland Mountains, between Virginia and Kentucky, nestles a strip of mountains called the Blue Ridge. The hills had changed little. They were still as breathtakingly beautiful as when Mattie sat enjoying her apple and looking out over their loveliness nineteen years before. The remoteness and inaccessibility of the terrain discouraged interference from outsiders. People of the hills were becoming firmly enslaved to the restraining bonds of tradition but were growing away from the practice of teaching their young. Rapidly regressing into illiteracy and superstitions they were falling behind in a world growing and progressing.

On this warm fall day, as Kylee was arriving at her destination, Billy was traveling to meet her. His thoughts however were not on the duty of his journey, but on the possibility of taking time for a visit at the Stewart's. He had been so busy with the fall grinding that there had been no time to see his friend Mary Stewart.

Mary was alone on the porch. She waved at him gaily as he crossed through the creek where the bridge had washed away and drove up to the steps. The Stewart's home perched precariously upon the side of a steep tree-covered hillside. The long porch and the two-storied house were supported against the hill by tall posts. The grassy yard was mowed and well tended. A variety of flowers were blooming fluently in wide beds on each side of the stairs.

Mary sat on the rail, enjoying the warm fall sunshine that spilled in a flood on the porch. The buzzing bees made a happy sound in the honeysuckle climbing the rail on the west side. The girl smiled happily at the young man coming up the stairs, excited and surprised at seeing Billy, she was overjoyed at his appearance. They sat on the rail talking and laughing, eyeing each other as if for the first time.

"I swear Billy; I never heard tell of such a thing!" Mary declared, giving a long braid a toss over her shoulder. Ducking her head, she looked up at him from lowered eyelids lined with thick heavy dark lashes.

"It's the gospel truth, Mary." Why was he so nervous explaining, he had never before been ill at ease with Mary. They were like brother and sister; their families close, sharing every facet of their lives. Now, sitting beside her, hat in hand, he felt clumsy and stupid.

He had never noticed how dark brown her eyes were. It had meant nothing before that her long yellow braids sparked with golden highlights in the sun or that those dark eyebrows were a startling contrast against her blonde hair. He felt tongue tied and awkward. He wished he had never mentioned the strange contraption. He should have waited until he knew more about it, but he always shared everything with Mary.

"It's true Mary, there's a machine that carries your voice through the air over a wire, or somethin'." His voice edged with a hungry longing for knowledge.

"They've had them in Louisville since '79. They say most everyone in the big cities have one in their homes. They're going to start puttin' them in the courthouse an' other places in Gladeville. That's gettin' pretty close, Mary, an' I just learned 'bout them. Don't you see Mary; we need a school here 'bouts to learn things that are happenin'. Wouldn't it be great to be able to read?" He looked into the girl's dark eyes, but could see no encouragement there.

Somewhere a dog barked, the sound lost in the vast thickness of trees. Billy in his confusion fastened his gaze intently in the direction of the sound. He tried hard to control the trembling in his stomach that was beginning to affect his knees. He wondered again at his extreme nervousness at being with Mary. She had been his friend since they were children. They had swum naked together in the swimming hole below the mill, slept together when they had stayed over. He had known all his life he loved her but had never thought about her as a man would a sweetheart. Now looking at her, he was seeing her for the first time as a beautiful, desirable young woman with a wonderful maturing body. He wanted to grab her, hold her close, and kiss her red lips.

"You're folks at the Association? Where is everyone?" he stammered, changing the subject, still perturbed over his ignorance and trying not to look directly at the beautiful girl before him.

"Paw took the family into Gladeville. He's lookin' for a buyer for the tobac'. Uncle Alvin's in the barn buildin' hangers. I'm just here talkin' to you. How come they let you get away from the mill? We don't see too much of you'ins any more," Mary questioned, talking fast, wanting to keep Billy close for a moment longer.

"Paw an' Matt have gone into Kentucky. Tom's suppose to be horse tradin' for paw in Gladeville, but you never can tell about Tom, he could show up anywhere. Paw's got his mind set on havin' a new team an' he thinks Tom knows as much about horseflesh as he does."

"We have a cousin comin' from Tennessee. I'm on my way to meet her in Donkey. Her paw died an' we'uns is the only kin she's got. Paw says it's our Christian duty to take care of our own, what's in need."

He smiled at the girl. Mary sure got pretty since he'd seen her last. How could a girl change so much in just a few weeks? He couldn't believe how her newly developing breasts filled out her dress. Swallowing hard, he tried to continue.

"Paw says he don't know what we're gonna do with a female around. We'uns has been livin' without one for so long. He's been tryin' hard enough to talk Matt or Tom into bringin' home a wife. But they ain't about to pleasure him with such a thing. They's too busy squabblin' over Polly." He slapped his hat against his thigh and let out a laugh of merriment at the thought of Matt and Tom's mutual attraction for Polly Trace.

"He ain't gonna have a bit of trouble marryin' me off. I'm ready. I know exactly who I'll choose." His face sobered and he looked seriously at the young woman before him.

Warmth spread across the back of his neck and turned his ears a vibrant pink. Then he realized the girl had not missed the implication of his words, nor his look of admiration. A bright smile filled his face, making the dimples flash in his tanned cheeks.

"I got to be goin'," Billy declared, jumping from the railing all feet and legs. Mixed up and confused with his rediscovery of Mary, he replaced his hat with trembling fingers.

"Gotta go. See ya," his voice was gruff with embarrassment. Lowering his head, he stomped hurriedly down the steps.

"Bye Billy," Mary called after his retreating back, laughing at his awkwardness and wondering why he left in such a hurry. He seemed uneasy; she wondered if it was her fault.

Mary was very aware of his admiring glances. She was also having new feelings sweeping through her body, encasing her in glowing warmth and she liked it. She watched Billy close the distance between the house and wagon with long strides.

"You bring your cousin. You all come an' see us, you hear," Mary shouted after him. But the wagon had already disappeared into the thick trees. She could hear the big wheels splashing thunderously crossing the creek. Billy was driving the big mules hard down the rough road.

The wagon moved rapidly along. In places the hills came together so closely that Billy had only to spread his arms to touch them. In these intense hollows, he had to follow the creek bed, which made it a hard journey on man and beast.

Pines grew high in thick patches, a sea of green engulfing the traveler. Blue-green so dominate that it created an illusion of mist hovering over the valley he was descending into. The beauty of the broad-leafed trees decked in new colors and the fall wild flowers blending brilliant colors together, escaped Billy this day. His thoughts were busy with his new discovery, the wonder and beauty of Mary. He had even forgotten the baffling telephone.

All around him pine branches and the rustling of dying leaves made music to ride upon a passing breeze. The crisp sigh rose in the air and settled around Billy. A gentle whispering to mingle with his dreaming of Mary and it soon became a soft sweet melody. Mary, Mary, the song whispered in his ears.

He was remembering the sparkling lights shimmering in her golden hair and her eyes warm and dark brown, laughing and gleaming with glowing promises. "Her lips Billy, her soft red lips." The symphony became a loud overture to Mary and she was the only thought that filled his mind.

Billy knew that if he were to kiss her sweet red lips, they would burn with a desire that would match his own. He would kiss them tenderly, cautious not to crush their petal softness. Then, oh, wonder of wonders. She would push her firm rounded body against him, demanding in a hushed voice. "Love me Billy, love me!"

Then, as she gave herself to him, he would discover that the promise in her eyes was real. His face became flushed and his breathing heavy as he imagined what joy it would be to hold Mary in his arms. With his dreaming he made a vow to himself and shouted it out to join the music of the trees.

"I'll marry Mary, by darn! I'll marry her after her birthday; she'll be sixteen, if her paw'll be willin'."

He could tell from the pounding of his heart that it had better be soon. The waiting would be unbearable. In his eagerness to have Mary, he whacked the mules to enforce his decision. Startled from the sudden flop of the reins, the unsuspecting team jumped quickly and pulled sharply to the side of the road. The wagon tipped dangerously.

The jolt revived Billy from his dreaming. He pulled the team safely back onto the road, got everything under control and resumed traveling at an even pace. Billy tried hard to keep his concentration on driving the team but found that Mary was now imbedded deep in his thoughts.

The afternoon was becoming hot and humid. The air was sticky without a touch of a breeze. The orange and gold leaves hung inflexible, unstirring on the tall oak and chestnut. A flicker of air could not stir through the barrier of trees.

Billy wrapped the reins around the whip holder and let the mules make their own way down the road. Taking a shiny new Hohner harmonica from his pocket, he blew into it easily, coaxing a tune from the instrument. The clear sharp notes drifted out on the air to mingle with the trilling of the birds. The sound filled him with pleasure and a sudden yearning for the music. For a moment he forgot Mary. The desire for her had been momentarily replaced by another penetrating love, a love for the music he played.

Early the same day as Billy was discovering the sudden blossoming of Mary, Jay Bird Mitchell headed up Tandy's Mountain. He rode fast and hard until he reached the crest of his mountain. Then he pulled his blood bay Morgan sharply to a stop. He sat looking out over the valley below.

Sitting tall and straight in the saddle, he stretched his neck to see. The wooded hills were a deep green speckled with bronze and gold as far as the eye could see, interrupted only by occasional patches of pines shedding long shadows upon the earth. Jay had no feeling for the green and gold splendor before him, but he respected it. If there was anything in his life he respected, it was the deep densely wooded hills. They were vast enough to hide even his meanness.

He had become a man of moods, filled with bitterness and hate. The hills had shown him no mercy. After Sarah's death and he found Mae and the mountains became a little more tolerable. Then after a few years of happiness, the hard life of the mountain claimed Mae too. Jay was broken hearted and withdrew into a dark grief, paying little attention to anything around him, not even his three sons and small daughter. He even pushed his hate for Phelps into the back of his mind. He lived in a world of his own, leaving the mountain for long periods of time, abandoning his children to care for themselves.

Tiring of his lonely life, covering his grief with a shell of meanness, he again searched for a wife, a mother for his children. He bought a fourteen-year-old girl from a large family in Kentucky. The war of slavery had been fought and was over, but this type of slavery still went on in the hills. The girl's name was Nell.

In the first year of their marriage, Nell gave birth to twins. The young woman was different from Jay's first wives. She loved the mountain. Coming from a large family, she was used to hard work and poverty. There had been no other children until now, the twins were eight and Nell was pregnant again.

As Jay sat looking over his mountain, he thought with regret of Nell's condition, hoping it would not be twins again. He allowed himself no joy in showing love toward anyone. When he had loved Mae, she had been taken away. He was not going to be hurt again.

For Nell there was only Jay's demanding. He had a small amount of pride for his sons who had grown up wild and restless, but the feeling could hardly be called love.

Women to him had only become the means to an end. Then he would say they weren't even good at that. As far as Jay was concerned, after Mae died, they weren't good at anything.

"Ain't nary one of them a bit good at playin' cards. They's none of them, I've know'd of that knows the first thing 'bout makin' good clear whiskey. They's a knack to makin' good whiskey, you gotta start with clean spring water. It's gotta be cooked off at the right time an' proofed just right. Then you gotta let it sit a spell in a charred barrel, the longer the better."

He wiped the tobacco juice from his whiskers with the palm of his hand and rubbed it off on his trouser leg. Jay was good at making whiskey. It was the heritage his grandfather Frank Mitchell had left him, along with dark hair, good looks, and a raging temper.

"The only thing most women are good for is hoein' corn an' workin'. Most of them don't know a darn thing 'bout cookin'. Can't even boil water without burnin' it. Ain't nary a one that is much to brag about in bed. I'd lay you odds, ain't more'n one or two that I've come by that know a thing about pleasurin' a man. Now there was Mae, Taynee's maw." A shining gleam would come to his eyes and sadness in his face at the memory. "I reckon, Polly could, perhaps from the looks of her. Taynee maybe could be, as hot-blooded as her maw, she looks enough like her."

Sitting looking over the treetops, his thoughts dwelled on his daughter Taynee. She'd be most nineteen now, beautiful and wild. He could not get the little twist of her body as she walked, out of his mind. He wondered if she knew what it could do to a man. His eyes rested on the top of Phelps's mill, showing above the trees that had grown tall enough to almost cover it. That damn mill! He would be glad when it was completely engulfed. Then, when he looked out over his mountain, it wouldn't block his view.

There was another eyesore on his mountain, Whites' cabin. He wanted Hail off his mountain. He had waited a long time but she was still there. Why didn't she leave? She had no kin, no one to keep her there. Her life must be lonely. It was, he told himself, to torture him. Hail was always there, squatting on his mountain. Her father had been dead for almost twenty years and still that aggravating woman was there to curse his days and haunt his nights.

Jay believed that her miraculous healing powers did not come from above. He was convinced in his own twisted mind that Hail was a witch. Hadn't Mae spent hours explaining to him about such things? She told him about black magic and its evils of spells and curses. Hadn't he watched Hail appear from the mist and take the form of a howling dog? Maybe she would be a mad fox chasing him through the trees until he fell on the ground in a fit of fright. Then twisting and shaking he would beg her not to hurt him.

He had a strong conviction that Hail had laid a hex on him. It was turning his family into a bunch of cowardly weaklings. It caused the death of his wives and stillborn children. Oh, she had her wicked ways that she inherited from her father, he assured himself. Hadn't Doctor White let his first wife die when Bob was born?

The only person Jay was afraid of was Hail. A fear so real that he was certain if he killed her, he would die a horrible death. But he told himself there was a safe way to kill a witch. He would see her burn in the hottest fire hell had to offer. There was a reason he had let her stay this long. Hail was the only granny woman around and if Nell had complications, she would need her. The grim thought straightened his mouth and tightened his jaw. After Nell's baby was born, he would get rid of Hail. The mountain would be all his again, and soon, very soon, the valley and Phelps's mill also!

Jay pulled the reins hard to turn his horse around. Enough of this, there was no time today to brood upon the things that filled him with rage and fury. He had to hurry and get the money at the cabin to complete a horse trade he had made in town. Perhaps he would allow the boys to ride back with him. After he paid for the horse and played a card game, a jug of good corn whiskey would finish the day in good shape.

CHAPTER SIX

The train ride for Kylee was long and tiring. She felt as if she had crossed half the nation. Her back was tired, her legs were numb, and her bottom felt like it had turned to stone from sitting so long. The journey for the most part had been interesting. She met a variety of people and had seen a lot of country. It was enjoyable, but exhausting.

Then the thing that cinched the saddle was the ride from Norton through Gladeville to Donkey. She thought the journey would be made on a stage. How wrong she had been! Her carriage was a supply wagon loaded heavily, its destination, Kentucky by way of Donkey, Virginia. The wagon jarred her unmercifully as they traveled the winding road into the Cumberland Mountains.

The driver spoke more often to the mules than he did his passenger. He was concentrating on driving the big team. She was glad of the silence and rode clinging to the seat, concerned only with her survival and praying for her deliverance.

Donkey was the most ridiculous name she had ever heard of for a town. She wondered if it would be as silly as it sounded. It was almost, the few buildings that made up the small village were built close to the wide street. A blacksmith, tavern, and general store rested along the slant of the hillsides. The porches in front created the only sidewalks, narrow and accessible only by steep stairways and covered with sheltering roofs. An added wing back captain's chair or bench made a welcome retreat on a hot day. The buildings spaced a distance apart made up the extent of the small town.

A tavern, a two-story red framed structure with white shutters and trim, sat slightly apart from the other buildings. Behind it grew a massive grove of colorful elm and dogwood climbing the hill. Hanging underneath the three gables of the second story and above the heavy door, a wrought iron sign proclaimed this to be Trace's Tavern.

Goods and supplies were bought in Norton, Virginia and hauled into Kentucky. The trip across the mountain was thirty-five miles of hardship on both man and beast. Donkey was the last stop before crossing Pound Gap. The drivers would welcome a night of relaxing at Trace's Tavern.

Saturday, September 18, 1890, was what the hill people called Association. The town was decked in red, white, and blue streamers hanging limp in the still air. Occasionally a firecracker exploded adding to the nervousness of the horses on the overcrowded street. People and buggies flooded the town and the air was filled with noise, laughter, and loud talking.

The celebration was like a country fair. It was a time for displaying crops, buying and trading stock, and exchanging breeding techniques. The hill people gathered together, dressed in their Sunday best. They packed lunches and prepared to spend the entire day in the village. Women visited, exchanged gossip and recipes with neighbors; shopped at the general store and watched the children play. The men spent time at the stockyard behind Ben's livery horse trading, drinking, and talking over a possible candidate for the next year's election.

Sparsely populated Donkey had not been considered a threat politically until now. The Deputy Marshal, Tanner Hensely, distributed law from Gladeville. But the people of the hills began to feel it was necessary to have a law officer of their own and petitioned for a Constable. It would come up for consideration along with candidates for the job at the next election. The possibility created much discussion around the area.

The citizens wanted their own peace officer to be where he was needed. Tanner always managed to be somewhere else. If he was around, he had a way of twisting things to his advantage. He made deals with lawbreakers in order to line his pockets. Until now they had kept their eyes shut and turned indifferent backs to his affiliation with outlaws and renegades. But robbery and murder had increased and the people in the community were becoming concerned. Moonshining was considered a necessary sin and Hensely had been casual about the whole thing until Ira Phelps became involved.

The mountain law under Tanner Hensely turned a blind eye on the whiskey trade, for a price, except for Ira Phelps. Ira wouldn't pay the high price for the whiskey made in the hills or the cost for Hensely's 'blind eye'. He went into Carolina and bought his whiskey cheap and bootlegged it in Kentucky for a fair profit. This little act of sly business under Tanner's nose tormented the Deputy Marshal. He vowed to put a stop to Ira's activity.

It was mid afternoon when Kylee arrived, the sun was scorching, the air still and humid. Outside of Trace's two old veterans of war leaned their chairs back against the tavern wall enjoying the porch shade and snoozing, totally unaffected by the commotion around them. Flies buzzed, hovering over their long whiskers with a low sibilant sound. Occasionally a loud snore would escape and the flies would scatter, only to return with persistence. A large hound dog slept placidly under one chair.

The strong stench of animal droppings was heavy in the air. People were coming and going everywhere. What a miserable little town, Kylee thought. The driver helped her down and sat her belongings on the dirt floor of Ben Hardman's blacksmith's shop.

"Here's a traveler for you, Ben. Her ticket said to deliver her to you. Here she is safe an' sound. I'll unhitch an' put the mules in the corral. I'll be in town for a few days; I ain't headin' on up the mountain today. I'll be at Trace's if you need me," the driver called into the man at the forge, tipped his hat to Kylee and went about his business. It was the most she had heard him say.

Ben finished pounding a mule shoe, dipped it into a bucket of oil, laid down his tools and walked over to where Kylee stood in the double doorway. Taking a large kerchief from his back pocket, he wiped the sweat from his face, hands, and bare arms.

"You're the Bentley girl, kin of Ira Phelps?"

"Yes," Kylee stated meekly.

"Ira told me to keep an eye on you, when you arrived. He told me Billy would be here to fetch you. I'm sorry Ma'am, I just carry on. I'm Ben Hardman, blacksmith an' stable master," Ben announced and reached to shake the young women's hand.

Kylee liked the strength in his firm handshake. It put her at ease.

"Can't make out why he didn't just have you go on up the mountain with the mule skinner. But no tellin' what Ira has on his mind." Ben scratched the top of his head, puzzled. "Billy will be along to get you. Phelps's are men of their word. If they say they'll be here, they'll be here, sooner or later," Ben promised her, looking out into the dusty street but seeing no sign of Billy.

Kylee sat on a bench watching the children running and playing among the heat waves and dust. Wagon wheels, horse's hooves and numerous pairs of feet had trampled the dry earth into a fog. It hung suspended around the few buildings muffling the loud talking and animal sounds. Somewhere above the dust a dog barked incessantly.

The nauseous stench of animal sweat and droppings converging with the intense heat was overpowering. Then the smell that caused Kylee to breathe in deeply floated through the fog of dust; it was the unmistakable aroma of fried chicken from someone's picnic basket. She had eaten her last apple and jelly sandwich from her paper bag long before noon. She was weary and hungry and the sharp smell made her stomach churn.

When the letter arrived from Ira Phelps, she was impressed with its warmth and friendliness. Ira had enclosed train tickets and made arrangements for her journey. He enclosed a substantial amount of money in the form of a bank draft for any other costs she may have. Uncle Dolf arranged everything; there was no doubt about what was necessary to complete her travels. He mapped and coursed the journey to her destination. He also telegraphed a reply to Ira telling him of Val's death and when Kylee would arrive.

Much to Dolf's consternation, Aunt Aggie had made a decision. Some of the money from the sale of Buttons and the buggy would be spent on a good traveling suit for Kylee.

"After all," she stated, with firm conviction, "It would not be a tribute to Val's memory to arrive among Mr. Phelps's family, them strangers an' all, lookin' totally poverty stricken." Aunt Aggie's statement was somewhat exaggerated, but it was her final ultimatum. "It wouldn't be fittin'!"

Dolf shook his head, giving his wife a stormy look. It was his opinion that Kylee might need the money for food and other necessities.

"First impressions are mighty important husband; she'll have enough for whatever she'll need. It appears to me, Mr. Phelps is a man of means an' he sent the extra money for just such a purpose. It's my opinion he does not want her to appear to his friends as the poor relation."

"What about the pink dress you made for her?"

"Really, Dolf, she cain't travel in that."

"Wal, it was good enough for her to go to Ohio in."

"That was different, she couldn't afford anything else, an' now she can."

"It appears to me that it'd be a mite more impressive, if she were to arrive with some money in her hand instead of in fancy trappins', like a circus pony," Dolf replied, disgusted. Fancy clothing to him was a total waste.

"I intend to see she's properly attired for the trip anyways." Aunt Aggie would not be shaken.

They traveled to Chattanooga and Aunt Aggie promptly saw to it that Kylee had a fine pearl gray traveling suit. Navy blue would have been better Kylee suggested, but her Aunt simply refused. Blue did not go with her green eyes, was the dear lady's opinion. A white blouse with just a touch of lace, for a feminine air was added, as was a new pair of boots, several pair of gloves, and a box of linen handkerchiefs. The conscientious aunt still persisted that a hat was needed. A sailor type skimmer of silver gray straw was chosen, delicately trimmed with a bouquet of pink silk roses, white tulle and fuchsia ribbon completed the chapeau. After underclothing and hose were bought, Kylee was ready. Aunt Aggie was appeased.

When Kylee boarded the train, she felt as elegant as any of the ladies appearing on the tin box tied inside the shawl. Her long thick auburn brown hair, rolled and piled high was held in place with long toothed combs and wire hairpins, a fitting throne for her fine new hat. The soft material of the suit fit the curve of her full breasts and hugged her small waist with elegance. As she lifted her skirt to step upon the train coach, one could catch a glimpse of new leather boots, buttoned snugly around her shapely ankles.

Aunt Aggie was proud of her niece's appearance. Jesse and the boys gave their cousin admiring glances and low complimentary whistles. Even Uncle Dolf had smiled his approval as they waved her goodbye. He had to admit Kylee certainly looked every bit a lady. Her father would have been proud.

The excitement of new clothing had faded. Only the weariness of the long trip from Tennessee remained. Kylee grew bored with just sitting; she had been doing that for too long. Leaving her belongings under the protective eye of Ben, she walked aimlessly into the street. Her intent was to join the group of people at the stables behind the blacksmith shop. She stopped to look at the two old veterans asleep on the tavern porch, smiling to herself, wondering how they could stay so unconcerned with the bustle and noise around them.

While Kylee was standing, a bee attached itself with persistence to a silk rose on her new hat, making loud buzzing sounds. Terrified of bees, she remembered her father always said to stand still and they wouldn't sting. Fists clenched, eyes closed tightly, she stood very still at the corner of Ben's blacksmith, waiting, hoping to discourage the little beast so it would move away.

Standing with her eyes closed she failed to see the rider coming down the street. He guided the horse skillfully around her unconcerned with the storm of dust raised by flying hooves. Kylee gasped as the dust went up her nose. She opened her eyes in time to see the rider pull to a stop at Trace's hitching rail and dismount. In two strides, he topped the stairs and disappeared inside.

When Kylee recovered her breath, she was furious. What ill manners! She cleared the dust from her eyes with the small wad that was the remainder of her dainty white handkerchief, and began brushing the dust from her skirt. Her efforts only resulted in ugly pink streaks left from the red Virginia dust and the damp hanky.

"Oh, you beast!" she gasped, her nose full of dust and her attitude dismayed. "My beautiful skirt, it's ruined!"

No one heard or cared. Even the bee had been discouraged and gone on about its business to parts unknown. Kylee was wishing she had never seen this miserable town. She was a stranger, so far away from anyone who loved or cared about her. Filled with despair and loneliness, she longed for the sight of a friendly face, or to see Jesse's broad shoulders. He would never have let such a rude person get by with treating her so. Looking at the ugly streaks on her new skirt, she wanted to cry. Then remembering the promise she made at her father's grave of shedding no more tears, she lifted her head trying to muster new courage.

The ill-mannered young man came from the tavern and crossed the street. A young woman who looked to be about her own age was hanging possessively onto his arm. Black hair fell in long ringlets down her back. Numerous curls about her face were held in place by a shimmering band of blue satin ribbon, tied in a layered bow over her left ear. Her white dress flowed in ruffles to just above her ankles, revealing white silk hose and white patent leather pumps.

Packaged like a present, Kylee thought, all wrapped and ready to open. Kylee noticed with a bitter twinge, her clothing, unlike her own, was unblemished, free of any dust streaks. The couple laughed and talked as they crossed the street, passed Kylee, and headed to the stockyard behind the livery. She could hear the man telling the girl, "You are a picture this day, Polly. You're surely the fairest gal in town." He told her in a low voice, husky and soft with a slight Scottish burr that still touched the dialogue of the hill people.

Hill people were not to be confused in anyway with hillbillies. Original people of the hills were a genteel breed. Later the hills were infiltrated with groups of people slovenly in their ways, deserving of the nickname, hillbilly. Hill people would be grossly insulted if they were to be called hillbillies! The attractive young woman laughingly accepted his compliment clinging tighter to his arm and looking up at him adoringly.

Kylee followed them absently as a child would a pied piper, hoping to get a closer look at the lovely girl. The pair was soon engulfed in the gathering of people and animals. She forgot her weariness and was soon enthralled with the beauty of the horses, pushing closer to watch the buying and selling. It brought back memories. Recalling a special occasion when her father had taken her to the sale ring in Chattanooga and bought her horse, Buttons. Oh dear, here it came again, that lonely despairing feeling. She must not let this happen! She lifted her chin higher with firm determination.

At the center of the group, sellers walked their merchandise. The horses pranced or stood proudly, heads held high, displaying long legs and rippling muscles. Kylee spotted the couple she had followed just ahead as they stopped to admire a strikingly beautiful Palomino mare. A superb animal standing with pride, legs straight, two hands higher than any other horse in the ring. The owner was carefully grooming the horse with a currycomb and talking gently to the mare as he brushed.

"If the mare is for sale, what's her price?" the ill-mannered young man asked.

"Sorry mister, I have a buyer. I'm waitin' for him to come back with the money," the man grooming the horse replied.

"I'll top his price!" Tom Phelps offered. His clean-shaven, square jaw set in firm determination.

The smile Tom had for Polly was gone and his face clouded with seriousness. His generous top lip tightened, drawing the skin firmly across his high cheekbones. Eyes clear blue as thin ice on a frozen millpond burned with desire for the horse. It was love at first sight. His mind was made up. He would have the mare.

Tom had not grown as tall as his brothers, Matt and Billy who took after the Phelps clan; he was shorter with a muscular frame. He was broad through the shoulders and blade thin at the hips. As he grew to be a man he developed a very distinct taste for clean stylish clothing. He had long ago given up his battered old hat preferring his head bare to the elements except in the winter or when the rain came.

Tan riding breeches with winged legs were tucked snugly into calf high, highly polished black boots laced at the sides and instep.

A navy blue sack jacket with a matching vest topped a white muslin shirt without a collar. Tom wore a soft silk brocade scarf knotted and tucked into the neck opening. He was comfortable and at ease in his stylish attire. Feet planted firmly apart, he wasn't budging. A slight breeze ruffled a strand of blonde hair across his forehead.

Kylee eyed his immaculate cleanliness. There were no dust streaks showing on his clothing! Disgusted with his just scrubbed appearance, she thought he looked like a dandy. It caused her to think of Kenus. She hated the young man for reminding her.

"Name your price. I have the money," Tom said taking some money from his pocket. He held the bills firmly but casually in his hand, knowing actions spoke louder than words.

"I've been offered a hundred and fifty," the owner stated and stopped his brushing, resting his arm on the mare's rump as he eyed the money Tom held. The other guy might never show up, he had better get the money while there was a chance.

"What's the blood line?" Tom questioned.

The girl in white was still hanging tightly to Tom's arm. She sighed as she listened to the history of the mare. Pulling slightly on Tom's arm she tried to encourage him to leave, her dark eyes clouded with boredom.

Tom gently loosened her hold on his arm. Walking slowly around the horse he lifted its legs examining them closely. He rubbed his hand across its honey colored hide, making sure the color was true. People were known to tint a horse's hair to enable a sale. He was not going to be fooled. The butternut color of the Palomino had not yet become popular in the East as it was in the West. Tom was mesmerized and had to have the mare.

A man pushed in front of Kylee blocking her view. She had to stretch to her tiptoes to see around him and see what was taking place.

"I'll give you two hundred'n fifty and the Tennessee Walker hitched at Trace's," Tom said looking over the top of the horse at the owner, deliberately counting through the money he held.

"Well," the owner scratched his unshaven jaw, making a rasping sound with his fingernails, taking a closer look at Tom and the money. "I guess it weren't really settled anyways. We never shook hands. I sure didn't see any money!"

"I guess the big feller ain't comin' back." He took his watch out and scrutinized it closely. "It's been over six hours. I ain't seen hide nor hair of him. Looks as if he ain't comin' back." He tucked the watch back into the pocket of his vest and looked at Tom.

"Well dad-blame it! We never signed any papers, so I reckon it weren't a bindin' deal no-ways. If you got the money an' you bring the Walker, I reckon the mare's yours."

Tom's smile was back. He handed the little man the counted bills and some silver to make up the balance. He offered his hand and they shook.

"It's a deal! I'll get my horse; you make out the sales slip to Tom Phelps. I'll be back shortly." Tom turned to move through the crowd.

"Just a darn minute, you damn polecat, that horse is mine!" A loud voice boomed across the gathering.

Ice blue eyes froze as Tom watched Jay Mitchell elbow his way to the center of the crowd with insolent forcefulness. A wide brimmed black hat towered above the tallest. A large pistol, 38-caliber, hung strapped around Jay's dark gray wool pants. His shirt was lighter weight but the same gray color with full raglan sleeves. Dark telltale patches of moisture covered his back and showed at his armpits caused from his long hard ride. His two sons with pistols strapped around their hips in the same manner followed close behind.

"Sorry mister, it had been so long I thought you weren't comin' back. This feller made me an offer. He had the cash money. I couldn't wait no longer. The deals made, the horse is his," the horse owner explained watching the ashen pallor lighten Jay's dark face.

"What you talkin' 'bout? We dealt for that horse. I went an' got the money. That's a long ride. I got the hundred'n fifty you said you wanted. Now that horse is mine, I'm takin' it!" Jay tried to push past the smaller man and untie the horse.

The owner took the reins firmly in his hand and stood his ground. Taking a plug of tobacco from a vest pocket, he bit off a chew, watching Jay closely.

"Now just a darn minute!" Tom stepped up, his voice showing anger, bristling and harsh. He fastened his steel blue eyes on Jay.

"I've dealt for that horse, I paid the money. Ain't no one gonna say different, least of all a Mitchell. Get out of my way Mitchell. That's my horse, bought an' paid for!" Tom ordered, taking the reins into his hand.

Jay looked Tom straight in the eye, unconvinced. Cold fire bolted in his black eyes. A big hand came back to rest on the butt of his thirty-eight, resting easy and light, scarcely touching it but the action spoke loudly.

"Men have been killed for less, Tom."

"You ought to know!" Tom implied, still holding the reins as he stroked the white blaze on the horse's nose.

"I've been waitin' for a chance to kill some of you'ins. I guess now's a good a time as any," Jay informed Tom in a cold harsh voice, unconcerned with the people watching.

"If you want to kill a Phelps so bad, what's holdin' you? Now would be the time, sure enough. Cause I'm takin' this mare!" Tom's voice was calm but chilling. The steel glint in his eyes enforced his words.

Handing the reins back to the seller, Tom pulled his coat back at the side with his free hand revealing for all to see he was unarmed. The horse pulled nervously against the tight rein.

The crowd spread out, backing away from the argument, wanting no part of the quarrel. The Mitchell-Phelps feud was well known in the hills. Even the people that settled after the Tandy's and Phelps's became familiar with the conflict and stayed clear from any part of it.

Horses whinnied nervously sensing the excitement. They tromped restlessly in the soft ground stirring the already dusty air into a heavy fog making it more difficult to breathe. Kylee moved back with the crowd, wishing she had stayed at the front of the livery. Someone might have come for her. She had been totally caught up in the excitement that filled the gathering. The girl in white had disappeared completely. A growing suspense hung over the crowd.

"There'll be no killin' in town today!" A medium built man announced pushing his way through the people. "You all hear me good now! If you folks from Pound want to kill each other, do it on the mountain. You keep your squabble up there. There'll be no shootin' here! We have women an' children in town today." The new arrival in the crowd stated, demanding respect with haughty arrogance.

Tanner Hensely, Deputy U.S. Marshal from Gladeville, tucked his coat carefully and slowly with definite purpose behind the butt of his pistol. He waited for the two men to get the message. Hensely was not overly concerned with the safety of the people, but he saw them as possible voters when Marshal Snow retired. He knew Phelps was favored among the crowd. To make himself look good he would settle this little confusion. Deliberately, as everyone watched, Tanner took a long cigar from his suit coat pocket, bit off the tip and spit it out. Placing the cigar in his mouth, he motioned for a bystander to light it.

"There ain't gonna be any trouble if I get what I bargained for. I aim to have that horse. Fair's fair, Hensely." Jay's temper flared. A flame flickered deep in his dark eyes.

"Is that right? Does the horse belong to Mitchell?" the deputy questioned the owner.

"Tell him. Tell him that horse is mine!" Jay ordered, assured that his friendship with Hensely would get him the horse.

The man holding the horse spat a stream of tobacco juice between the mare's legs. He better settle this deal once and for all before someone got killed; it could well be himself. Nodding toward Tom he motioned toward him with a scrawny thumb. "The young feller there paid me for the horse."

He nodded again toward Tom still steadying the horse. "He's the owner, the deals been made. Far as I'm concerned, cash on the barrel head seals the deal!"

"Why you scabby little pip squeak! I'll send you to hell first! Then I'll take care of that bastard from Pound! It'll make the mountain a better place to live!" Jay stated hoarsely moving toward the little man. But the smaller man was quick, more agile, and stepped behind the mare putting its body between them.

"Just a minute, Jay. The man has accepted the money. The deals made, let it go. Let's keep down the trouble here. You an' the boys

SHADOW OF THE PINES

step on over to Trace's with me, easy like. We'll have us a card game an' some refreshments. What do you say? Come on now," Tanner placed his hand firmly on Jay's shoulder trying to ease him in the direction of the tavern.

"Let Tom take the horse, peaceful like. I'm not wantin' to make any arrests today."

"You ain't a meanin' that you'd arrest me or my boys now, do you Tanner, for defendin' our rights?" Jay questioned, pushing the Marshal's hand roughly from his shoulder.

"How 'bout arrestin' them two? They's the ones that messed up this whole deal. By rights that horse is mine! How 'bout it, Marshal? It's their fault, every bit of it." Jay's face turned a shade of purple, his eyes wide with uncontrolled anger. Damn Phelps's! What's the matter with Hensely anyway? Had he forgotten who his friends were?

"Only trying to keep law and order, Jay. If you keep persistin' in this, yes, I reckon I'd arrest you an' your boys. Quicker than scat, far as that goes. Understand?" Tanner tried to communicate a message to Jay with his eyes, hoping to make him understand that he had to make a good impression on all these prospective voters. It would be better if Jay would calm down so he could get him away from the crowd.

Hensely could see Jay cooling off some. There was a slight relaxing of his tight facial muscles. Maybe Jay would like to sever their friendship. It was not the time to worry about that now.

"You ain't never gonna arrest me! An' remember this, you better never lay your hands on any of my boys. You better hear me good, Hensely! I said, you ain't never gonna arrest me, or mine!" Jay's voice was deadly. His hand came away from the butt of his pistol where he had been resting it, waiting nervously. He closed his hand into a large fist and shook it under Hensely's nose.

Tanner never budged, he was afraid of no man, least of all Jay Mitchell. He'd talk to him when he calmed down. As for Phelps, he hated his guts. He'd just as soon let Jay kill him, but not here, there were too many people watching. Best to put it to rest for today.

"Mind what I said, Tanner. You better never lay your hands on one of us Mitchells!" With the warning he turned away, pulled his black hat down over his fiery eyes and made his way through the crowd.

"You mean that's all?" Rueben, his oldest son asked, the disappointment apparent in his voice. Walking with short quick steps he tried to keep up with his fathers long hurried stride.

"Are we gonna let them get away with that? Are we Paw?" Rueben's voice was filled with disappointment. "We ain't gonna let that bastard Tom live are we?"

"Why didn't you kill him Paw?" Blaine, the taller son, questioned. "If you want me to Paw, I'll go back and kill them all! I'd kill every one of them stinkin' bastards for you Paw, Hensely too, if you want me to!" Blaine tried to push his brother out of the way so he could be closer to their father.

"Hush your mouths!" was Jay's loud irritated answer.

Jay burning with rancor at the outcome of things sullenly mounted his big bay and thundered up the street. His two sons straddled their mounts and were hot on his heels.

Kylee walked slowly back to the front of the livery in a tired dejected mood. She hoped someone would be there waiting for her. The crowd moved away gradually. The happy joyous feeling faded after the disturbance. She was glad there had been no shooting, even if she did hate the young man with the bad manners. Remembering the gaping hole in her father she knew she wouldn't want to see that happen to anyone. She dropped the incident in light of her own problems. Weary and hungry, almost to the point of exhaustion, she questioned Ben again about the Phelps's.

"Ira'll have someone here to fetch you. You needn't worry your purty head none 'bout that. Step on over to Trace's an' get a bite of vittles, everythin'll look better then."

As she crossed the street and approached the tavern there was the young man again. This time he was leading his black horse toward the stable lot behind the livery. She surmised he was ready to complete the trade that had caused the afternoon trouble. The pretty girl in the white dress stood on the tavern porch waving him goodbye. Kylee could hear her saying:

"You-all hadn't better forget the picnic I'm fixin' for Sunday. This day has been a total fizzle with all this horse tradin' an' all!"

A haughty look followed her words, then a bright smile. "I'll not tolerate any more of that. If you don't want to make it up, well, maybe Matt'll be 'round. He likes fried chicken as well as you," Polly said the last under her breath. She doubted if Tom heard a word, he was so wrapped up in his horse-trading.

Polly turned and slipped into the tavern. She gave an unconcerned look toward Kylee coming up the stairs. Kylee found the inside of the tavern dark and cool, a complete change from the heat of the dusty street. She hoped her last dollar would buy her a meal.

A large stairway filled the middle of the room leading to the second story. A bar ran the length of the wall underneath. Tables and chairs filled the rest of the room. Through a doorway at the left of the stairway, Kylee could see into a small kitchen at the back.

The heavy red velvet drapes at the windows kept the room dark inside, making it necessary for the gas lanterns to burn at all hours. The place was crowded with men. Polly stood talking and laughing with a group at a table in the corner. Inside, the room was filled with cigarette and cigar smoke. The smell of tobacco juice, Kylee thought, was worse than the stockyard. Swallowing hard she tried to keep her insides down and made her way up to the bar.

The bartender, a husky man with a whiskey red face, friendly eyes, and a heavy swooping mustache above thick lips, smiled kindly at Kylee. She asked shyly if it were possible to get something to eat.

"Sorry lady, I don't have a thing left. These galloots cleaned me out early. Ain't too many in here now that's interested in food. Now you might get something down at Hannah's. Her husband runs the sawmill over on the hill. She's been fixin' lunches for some of the mill workers. Could be she'd have somethin' left. It's the white house, tuther end of town. It's a ways but you cain't miss it. Sides," he said behind his hand bending closer to Kylee, "It's a mite nicer for a lady."

Thanking him in a soft voice, she turned toward the door. Kylee dreaded going back into the heat outside, but she couldn't stay here.

"Why'd ya send her away for, Trace? Wasn't she a purty little thing?" a bystander at the bar remarked. "I ain't never see'd her before. Have you ever seen eyes like that?"

"They's lots you ain't never see'd afore Grady. They'll keep 'em hid from you if they's smart," Trace remarked in a teasing manner.

Laughter and admiring glances followed Kylee to the door. She could see Polly standing behind the bar looking at her with contempt, taunting her for being in such a place! She was very conscious of the many staring eyes following her as she crossed the room, little pig eyes, glaring, reminding her of Kenus and the fate she had so narrowly escaped. Eyes filled with lust and greed, laughing and jeering at her. Served her right for being here! Faster and faster she moved, almost at a run, reaching for the door handle. Leaning the weight of her body into the heavy door, Kylee gave it a hard violent shove. To her astonishment the door opened outward with ease totally upsetting her composure, causing her to stumble. Without grace or dignity she fell headlong out the door.

CHAPTER SEVEN

When Ira received the letter from his cousin, Val Bentley, Billy had been excited. But he thought it strange that his father was so secretive about the letter. He carried it around in his pocket, slept with it under his pillow as if someone were going to steal it, and only shared bits of it with the family.

Billy thought it would be great to have a girl about the place. Thinking perhaps she would be old enough to help with the cooking. His father told them very little about their cousin only that she was coming to live with them, declaring that he really didn't know too much about the girl. It had been so long since he had heard from Val. Ira warned them all to be patient and kind with her or he would have their hides.

The stop at the Stewart's had so confused Billy that he forgot his enthusiasm about the unknown cousin. The involvement with his thoughts of Mary and the enjoyment of the harp were his only major concerns. Besides, the day was too beautiful to be in a hurry, he knew Donkey would be hot and crowded. Even the mules had jogged along patiently giving into Billy's lazy mood. Drawing his slouched body up, he sat straighter on the seat. As he came into town much of the crowd was dispersing.

"It must be later than I thought," Billy muttered to himself. His idling had worn away the day. He waved to a buggy load of friends passing on the road and hurried down the hill past Trace's Tavern and up to Ben's livery.

"Hello, Ben!" Billy shouted into the blacksmith shop as he climbed down from the wagon seat.

"Hello Billy!" Ben greeted him coming from inside the shop to stand in the wide opened door.

"Did you see anythin' of a gal that came in on the supply wagon?"

"Sure 'nough. She was a little upset when you weren't here to meet her. She was afeard you folks had forgotten her. I told her not to worry; you'd be here. Them's her belongin's on the bench there."

Ben spat a stream of tobacco juice at a beetle wandering blindly in a pile of horse droppings and smiled at his perfect shot. He wiped his mouth with his hand, lifted his leather apron and rubbed his hand dry on his breeches. He was looking at Billy waiting for an explanation for his lateness.

"Well you know Ben; it takes a while to get here. Sides, I was sure that the supply wagon wouldn't get here 'til later. I thought there was plenty a time. I appreciate your lookin' out for the gal." He thought he better not let his paw hear about this. It was his paw's firm orders not to get the girl upset or worried. He offered his hand to Ben for a handshake.

"Well it came in a little early today because of the celebration. You should have been here earlier, Billy. There's been all kind's of goin's on. I see'd Tom ride by just a minute ago. He went up the shortcut toward Pound. You didn't see him, did ya? I was gonna stop him and ask him about the gal. But he almost rode me down he was in such a hurry. Looked like he bought a new horse. Doesn't he usually ride a black Walker?"

"No Ben, I didn't see him. But when he's a ridin' he don't see no one. He was suppose to be lookin' for paw a team, but you cain't never tell about Tom." Billy scratched his head under his black hat, puzzled. "Yah, that's the horse he left home with, a black Walker."

"Wal, I better fetch that gal an' get back on the road. Where can I pick her up, Ben?"

"She ain't much of a girl, Billy. More of a woman dressed real purty. Had the looks of a real lady. Little bit of a thing. No bigger'n a minute. I sent her on over to Traces to get some vittles. She was beginnin' to look a little puny. You ain't aimin' on takin' her on home tonight, are you, Billy? That's quite a trip for a little lady what's already been on a long journey."

"Thanks for your concern. We're not making the whole trip today. I think we'll head on up to Carl's an' spend the night. I want to see the young'uns anyway. It'll give the gal a chance to rest before we head on up the mountain. I'll go on over to Trace's an' fetch her. Is it alright if I leave my wagon there a spell?" Billy stretched his long arms behind his head, fastened his hands and flexed his fingers. He hated the thought of getting back on the wagon.

"Sure enough, Billy. I'll throw the little ladies things up in the back here an' cover 'em with that tarp you've got tied behind the seat. You'll be ready to head on out. See ya next time 'round." Ben waved his hand to Billy as he lifted Kylee's belongings into the wagon.

Billy went on a high run across the street, took the stairs at Trace's two at a time, crossed the porch in one stride and reached for the door handle simultaneously with Kylee. The timing was perfect. Kylee was completely thrown off balance by the sudden release of the door and stumbled headlong into Billy.

Surprised, Billy stepped back catching his shoe heel on a raised board in the flooring. Completely losing control he staggered backward sprawled onto the porch floor taking Kylee with him. They were covered in a pile of gray skirt, white petticoats, and Kylee's legs encased in black stockings and knee length bloomers.

Kylee's exhaustion reached the breaking point. In spite of all her promises of 'no more tears', she began to cry. Her body became as a rag, limp and sagging, she had no strength left to raise herself, there was no control over the tears rolling down her cheeks. Hair damp from perspiration crept free from the twisted rolls and now hung in loose curls about her neck and ears. Dismayed, she tried to pull her skirts down to cover her under garments.

A passer-by witnessing the fall, offered in a gallant manner to help Kylee to her feet. Adding to her embarrassment he smiled teasingly, but politely inquired if she was all right. At the nod of her head, he went on into the tavern and closed the door.

"Oh, I am sorry. You just came out'a nowhere," Kylee declared through the flood of tears rolling down her cheeks.

The surge of tears and dusty air had dried her throat until her words came out shrill and rasping. The squeakiness in her voice and the absurd spill tickled her funny bone and turned the tears into a giggle.

The sudden shocking surprise along with the jolting fall knocked the breath from Billy's body. It took him a few minutes to regain his breathing. He raised his long lean body to a standing position with Kylee holding his arm trying to help.

Seeing her tears upset him further and like most men, he was totally dismayed at the sight. Spotting her handkerchief on the porch floor, he picked it up and put it in her hand. The hound dog under the chair of one old veteran raised its head, curious about Kylee's laughter. With drooping eyes, the dog looked over the situation.

"Stars an' garters, ma'am. I am sorry! But you sure surprised the daylights clean out'a me. Please don't cry!" Billy begged, confused further at her silly giggling.

Kylee's tears and laughter were almost to the point of hysteria. She was not hearing much of what he was saying. Smoothing out the wad of hanky, she attempted to dry the tears and blew her nose loudly. Her introduction to Virginian men had not been very promising.

Billy bent to look into her tear-stained face. "Are you all right?"

Her hat had shifted to a precarious perch over her left ear and she looked totally ridiculous. Could this be the cousin that he was supposed to meet? Ben said she was a little one. This one sure wasn't any bigger than a minute. Oh, Lordy! If he'd hurt her in anyway, his paw would skin him good.

"I'm Billy Phelps, Ma'am. I'm lookin' for a Miss Kylee Bentley. Would you by any chance be her?"

Billy was glad her tears had stopped. The moisture was still in her eyes, mixing with the merriment, sparked emerald stars deep in her jade eyes. She nodded her head at him.

Finally, finally, someone had come for her. She blew her nose again and gave a good look at the person who had so rudely upset her. Standing with the hot breeze ruffling his sandy brown hair, he looked innocent enough, but didn't look to be much more than an overgrown boy, tall and thin, to the point of being skinny. He didn't appear to be the type that would deliberately knock her down.

"I'm fine, really. I'm just glad that you have finally come for me."

Billy thought she looked like a pixie. She wasn't hurt, everything was all right, and her laughter was proof of that. Relieved, he found himself laughing with her, the tension easing. He picked up his hat where it had fallen, took Kylee's elbow and guided her down the stairs.

"I guess we did look purty ridiculous," Billy offered.

The confusion had no effect on the two old sleeping veterans. They continued to snore. The old hound laid his head back upon his paws and closed his eyes.

Billy helped Kylee up to the wagon seat. She tried not to be depressed at the prospects of another wagon ride. At least someone had come for her and she was headed to her destination. She tried to regain her composure remembering she was a lady and to be a credit to her father's memory.

Billy climbed onto the seat next to Kylee. She was trying to re-anchor her hat and get it stationed in a more suitable position. Picking up the reins, he slapped the mules on their slick rumps. They pulled out slowly as Billy turned them around in the wide street and headed back out toward Pound Mountain.

Watching the girl closely, Billy hoped she wouldn't start crying again. A small person he noted with enough hair for two people her size. The soft reddish brown color was capturing shining highlights from the late afternoon sun. Her smooth cheeks were flushed pink. Perhaps, Billy thought, she'd had enough of the Virginia sunshine for one day.

The sky began to darken; it couldn't be that late already, Billy pondered. A dark cloud covered the sun, spreading and drifting on into the sky until the entire Northwest was gray. The dull sky deepened the shadows among the trees, casting a depressing air of gloom upon the world.

Kylee felt as if a bucket had been put over her head, adding to her deep homesickness. She slid closer to Billy.

"I know'd it was too powerful hot. A day this hot is bound to stir up somethin'. Sure enough, cousin, we're in fer a real storm."

Billy looked down at the young woman beside him. Her smallness reminded him of his mother. He reached and tucked her hand into the crook of his arm. "Set closer, ma'am. Everything's gonna be fine, you'll see. We'll get to Jennings 'fore that storm hits."

"Will it rain hard?" Kylee asked, huddling closer to Billy. "I don't want it to thunder, the thunder scares me, I don't like the rain neither." Remembering the night her father died a dark grief clouded her green eyes. "Everything bad happens when it rains."

"Nothin' to be afear'd of cousin." Billy smiled assurance at the huddled figure beside him.

His straightforward smile calmed Kylee. Something about the dark blue eyes filled with concern reminded her of Jesse. Feeling she had found a friend, she ducked her head preparing for the onslaught of the storm.

Billy's smile turned the corners of his mouth until the dimples, so like his mother Mattie's danced in his cheeks. He was worried at Kylee's dejected mood hating to see anyone sad. Billy loved nothing more than making others happy.

His mother always taught him that the Holy Scriptures said to love one another; this was Jesus' commandment to his disciples. Billy didn't have any trouble with that commandment at all. He was eager to love everyone, insisting to his brothers, that it was even possible to find something about the Mitchell's to love.

"But there's gotta be somethin' about them you could love. Taynee's always been my friend. She ain't a bit like the rest."

"Don't worry about lovin' any of them, little brother. They's all polecats, you'll start hatin' 'em soon enough. You better not let Jay catch you hangin' 'round with Taynee; he'll kill you both. I thought she had left the hills. I ain't seen her taggin' along with them Mitchell boys for a couple of years. In fact, I ain't see-d her nowheres," his brother Matt related.

Billy displayed his love for living best with his music and watching people laughing and dancing. He was the happiest when playing the fiddle he crafted himself. Tom read him an article in a magazine he brought from Norton. The article told how people built their own violins. Billy set his mind to make a fiddle, and he did!

He copied the pattern in the magazine and went searching for the right wood. He carved and sanded until he thought the pieces were just the right shape, then glued them tediously together. After waiting for the glue to dry, he took much pain putting on the coats of varnish. Then he fashioned a fine bow, balanced with the right weight, then filled it with fine horsetail hairs, washed and dried.

When he was finished, something wasn't right. The tone was screeching and dull, each string sounding the same. He ordered new strings from the mail order house and put new horsehair in the bow. Still it wasn't right. He gave up in bitter disappointment.

Then one day, Toad Jones, a well-known fiddle player from Gladeville came by to make a whiskey deal with Ira. He informed Billy that he had made a few fiddles himself. The young Phelps was delighted to show off his craftsmanship. Admiring Billy's violin, it didn't take Mr. Jones, the fiddler, long to discover what was wrong.

"Boy," he said. "You gotta have a sound post. That's what makes the sound ring true an' sweet! You gotta place it, just 'bout there." Toad pointed at a spot inside the fiddle. "Then you go right up there on the ridge of the mountain. Kill you one of them big rattlers that's up there. Save the rattle buttons an' put 'em right inside that fiddle. Then listen to it ring when you're a playin', *Sally Goodin'*. Sides, it'll keep out the spiders!" he added, giving Billy a playful shove, a quick wink, and a joking grin.

Billy, with his pocketknife fashioned and smoothed the little post and seated it carefully inside the fiddle. To his amazement, the sound rang sweet and true. After much practice and consternation to his father, he could play a few tunes. After long hours of practice he learned to play others. The imperfect melodies were beautiful and satisfying to Billy. With perseverance and hours of struggle, he became very proficient at his music. The happy sound of Billy's fiddle became part of him and it was in demand wherever he went.

For Billy, the sound post in his life was love. Without it, his life would be incomplete. He knew he loved Mary and he felt a love for Kylee the moment he looked into her moisture filled pixie green eyes.

It was his warmth and loving personality Kylee felt sitting beside him now. She watched the blue Virginia sky turn into a dark swirling mass of stormy clouds.

"Nothin' to worry about Kylee, we'll thump these ole' mules harder. We'll be at Carl's in a swish of a lamb's tail!"

He flapped the reins sharply on the animal's rumps and they moved swiftly up the road. It was evident the storm brewing was going to be a bad one. It could fill the creeks and branches to overflowing with turbulent waters, sweeping the timber and brush down the steep hillsides into the ravines and hollows.

"Hang on tight to me, Kylee. I ain't gonna let nothin' happen to you. No sirree. If I did, my paw would skin me alive!"

Dusk gathered the stormy shadows together in dark creeping masses among the thick trees, closing out the remaining daylight. Black clouds and tossing tree branches merged as one gray mass on the murky skyline. A roll of thunder rumbled faintly over Pound Mountain as they drove up Jenning's branch to Carl's place.

The rain started slowly, falling gently in huge splatters. Billy raised his head to let the cooling dampness caress his face. A sweet clean smell emanated from the road as the big drops raised the dirt in white dusty puffs. The musty wetness filled his nostrils causing him to breathe in deeply. He loved the touch of the wet rain as it fell softly upon his cheeks.

Something else touched their senses, sweeter than the rain. The aroma of food drifted out on the heavy air to welcome them. Kylee had forgotten her hunger as they traveled. Now a sudden pain stabbed her in the middle, renewing her desire for food. She felt faint from the goodness of the smell as it hovered temptingly about her nose.

Carl Jennings greeted them warmly and hurried them in out of the rain. Carl was a short, stocky man with wide shoulders and powerful arms. Dark laughing eyes and thick lips smiled through a graying mustache and beard. Offering his hand to Billy he greeted them warmly. Patting Billy affectionately on the shoulder, he eyed Kylee curiously. Billy explained her presence, introducing her casually as the family watched her with reserved feelings.

A low fire burning on the hearth was the only light in the cabin. The fire was necessary for cooking and felt good after the cooling dampness of the fresh rain. Four children sat on the floor before the glowing fire. The bright firelight cast long elfin shadows on the cabin walls. The weird shapes danced around, bowing in and out, playing hide-and-seek with the stationary shadows dwelling among the furnishings. The children, after a long day in town, were waiting patiently for their supper.

"I'm afear'd that storm's not gonna let up 'fore mornin'. You two settle yourselves and plan on stayin' the night. Wouldn't think of you a headin' out with a wagon on a night like this. Might slide right into the creek. We'll have it no other way, will we wife? I'll go on out an' unhitch your team an' put the wagon in the barn so's your things in the back'll stay dry. You never mind, Billy. Stay in here an' dry yourselves. I'll have it done in no time," Carl said going out the door.

"It's good to have you, Billy. Give me your hat young lady an' I'll put it up on the shelf. No one will bother it. My, ain't it a purty one," Nettie Jennings smiled at Kylee, admiring the hat. "You're more-n welcome. Supper's on. You-all sit up an' eat hearty. The fixin's ain't fancy, but they's plenty. You eat all you've a mind to. Carl'll be right along. You help yourselves, I'll see to the youngin's."

The friendly smile Nettie gave Kylee made her feel instantly at home and she was too hungry to be bashful. Their acceptance of Kylee was unusual. Most hill people did not take so readily to strangers, "furiners," they called them. She was with Billy, which made the difference. It was clear to see they loved and adored Billy Phelps.

The children kept their heads down during the meal, watching Kylee curiously from lowered eyes. The meal progressed with friendly talk between Carl and Billy. Nettie served the table, encouraging the little ones to hurry and finish. The oldest, a boy about seven, excused himself and went around the table to stand timidly behind Billy.

"Did you bring your fiddle, Billy? Did you?" he questioned shyly as Billy swooped a piece of corn bread around his plate getting the last bit of molasses.

"Darn it, Seth, I sure didn't," Billy said, licking his fingers, relishing the last bit of goodness. He turned an apologetic smile on the boy.

Billy without his fiddle was unheard of. When he saw the disappointment clearly on Seth's face, he took the harp from his pocket. The unhappy look in those big eyes would never do!

"I brung this instead," Billy explained to the boy. "It's a bit easier to carry."

"You gonna play it fer us?" Seth questioned in childish curiosity.

Billy shook his head. "It's yours! You can learn to play it yourself. Next time I come, you can play me a tune. All you have to do is just blow in right here, like this, until you get it to sound the way you want." Billy wiped his mouth on his shirtsleeve and blew a short tune into the harp as Seth watched with big eyes.

"You think I can do it, Billy? Gollee!" he exclaimed as Billy nodded his head in assurance.

"You gotta promise though, not to plague your maw an' paw. You gotta do it quiet like, or they'll have our hides."

Billy remembered his father's consternation at his first musical attempts. Ira would chase him from the house to the back field. Billy would sit on an old stump and play his fiddle for the raccoons and squirrels.

"I promise Billy!" Seth declared, his excitement running high.

Returning to his place in front of the fire, he blew into the harp softly, careful not to raise a rebuff from his mother. The three younger sisters gathered around him, watching in rapt wonder, coaxing for a turn.

Kylee had been so hungry she was ashamed of how much she had eaten, consuming quantities of cornbread with white butter and molasses. There was a large pot of mustard greens with side pork and a lot of fresh green onions. Afterward there were blackberries with thick cream in little wooden bowls. Kylee ate until she reluctantly had to move away from the table. It was all she could do to keep from groaning; her tummy was so full.

"I would be more than happy to help with the dishes," Kylee offered. "In appreciation for the wonderful meal."

"Oh no, you never mind. I won't have you spoiling your lovely clothes."

"My goodness, my skirt is already ruined; a little dishwater will not matter," Kylee sighed and took a towel and began drying the dishes.

Nettie moved the lamp she had lit for the table and set it on the sideboard. Their task proceeded with little talking, listening mostly to the conversation between Carl and Billy.

The Jenning's place was the first on Pound River, which was no more than a creek filled by various streams, called branches, flowing down the hollows from the back hills. The cabin sat back from the river on the Jenning's branch and was visited often by travelers heading out of town too late to make it across the mountain, or merrymakers in no condition to travel further. There was always tobacco and pipe for a weary traveler. Although Carl was not a drinking man, there was always whiskey or brandy for those who so desired. One could, if in the mood, more often than not, find a card game in progress at the Jenning's cabin. Carl reached the tobacco tin from the mantel, filled his pipe and offered the tin to Billy.

"I ain't ever smoked Carl, but I'll try a chew."

Carl handed him a twist of tobacco and sat down in a large hand carved rocker nodding for Billy to sit on a stool next to him. He prepared to relax and enjoy visiting with the young Phelps'.

Billy hoped the tobacco wouldn't make him sick. He wanted Carl to know he was man enough to handle it, but just the thought of tobacco in any form usually sickened him. His brothers tormented him unmercifully because of his total denial of booze and tobacco. They thought it was a sure sign you were a man if you could hold your liquor without falling down and chew your tobacco without turning sixty shades of green, which was exactly how Billy was feeling, green.

"I guess Ira was really upset about that escapade in Gladeville. I can understand why he didn't want to pay all those taxes. Then when they confiscated his whiskey…well, that hurt. But it was better than getting' jail time. I don't see why they killed your cousin that was driving for Ira. I reckon it was Jay that pulled off that little stunt. Hensely seen to it that he got clean away with that. Jay is always lookin' for any excuse to kill some of your folks. Your paw has got to be more careful, Billy." Carl puffed on his pipe slowly; a deep concern crossed his face.

"It's easy for Hensely. With Jay's help, they have the law around here sewed up pretty tight. Jay proved that when he got smack dab away with killin your paw's cow. Yep, he got out'a that slicker than a greased pig in a poke. Unless you have an in with Hensely you can forget the whiskey business. Things will get even worse when Snow retires, if Hensely gets his job. We gotta get someone to run against him, Billy. You think Tom might consider the job?" Carl suggested watching Billy closely. Carl puffed on his pipe hard, making his short beard bob. Squinted his eyes drew dark brows together in a thoughtful scowl.

Billy thought over the situation, chewing the tobacco slowly, swallowing easy. Trying not to allow too much of the brown juice into his stomach. He spat quickly into the fire. The spit lay sputtering on the hot ashes. Not too experienced at spitting, the juice ran freely down the corners of his mouth. He hurriedly wiped the brown juice away with his shirtsleeve and hoped no one noticed his embarrassment.

Kylee watched him from the corner of her eye, covering a smile with her hand. His prominent Adams apple jogged up and down as he chewed. He had a very nice nose, she thought, straight and finely sculptured. He was much too thin for his prominent bone structure. Some weight to fill out the hollow places around his cheeks and eyes was needed. Large ears protruded like flaps and were probably a constant target for teasing. His thick light brown hair was slightly curled and inclined to be very unruly. A happy, alert face matched his sociable personality. Kylee concluded she was glad he was her cousin and would be happy to have him for a friend.

Carl pretended not to notice Billy's confusion. He reached and stirred the fire in a pretense of doing something.

"I don't know why Snow ever appointed Hensely for a deputy. The way I see it, he must a had somethin' on him. He's a worthless excuse as a lawman. An outlaw with a badge is all he is," Carl said in disgust.

"I sure wouldn't vote for him if I was old enough. Paw was sure enough upset about the whiskey and Gerald's killing. He thought Jay should a paid for that. The cow deal made it worse. Matt was sure enough ready for killin'. It took some doin' for Tom to git him calmed down. It kinda looked as if Jay had a right, but he should have kept that damn bull penned up. You know how it is, Carl, with a cow when she comes in season, she just bellers all the time." Billy's ears began to turn pink, but he continued.

"Well, that big Durham bull Jay just bought wanted to do the neighborly thing. Down the hill he came right to Daisy. Well, she were so tickled with his company, she wouldn't let him go back home without her. So, she just followed him on up Tandy's Road, headed straight for Jay's. It was right there that Jay found them. He up and shot them both, claimed no bull of his was gonna breed a Phelps's cow. He left them both lyin' there, dead in the road."

"Well, Paw thought maybe the law would make Jay pay for our cow, but that was a laugh. Takin' him to court made Jay even meaner. Paw let it drop, but I don't think Matt'll forget it. Ol' Daisy cow was his. He'd had her since she was a little bitty calf. He loved the ol' cow! Maybe Mitchell was entitled, but it sure seems a waste of good stock. Sometimes I think that man is plumb tetched. Don't seem like he has a lick of sense," Billy expressed thoughtfully, wondering about Jay's weird ways.

"But, you know Carl, that ain't all. It's been somethin' or other all along, even 'fore I was born. An' still ain't nothin' settled at all. You suppose there'll ever be an end to it?" Billy asked, shaking his head in bewilderment.

A loud knock interrupted their conversation. As Nettie opened the door, the smell of wet grass and trees invaded the room. A refreshing breeze followed the sweet scent. The scant light fell across three men framed in the doorway; a carving in blackness, black hats, black rain slickers, and black beards, their forms blending into the darkness of the stormy night.

The three moved into the room, not waiting for an invitation, bringing with them the wetness that covered their clothing. A cool dampness hung heavy around them. They made no effort to remove their raincoats. Water ran from the brims of their hats and traveled in rivulets down their long coats and splattered loud upon the wide boards of the plank floor.

"Thought we'd get up a game, Carl. Everyone's drunker than hell in town. Reckoned you'd give me a chance to win back some of what I lost the other night," Jay Mitchell announced, unbuttoning his slicker as if readying to stay. His tall, massive body seemed to fill the small cabin. It was Mitchell's habit to be a visitor in the darkness.

"Well, I would be willin' for a game Jay, but we have visitors. Reckon I'll pass tonight." Carl rose from his chair and moved toward the men, puzzling in his mind the strangeness of circumstances. They were just speaking of this man. The old adage came to his thoughts, 'speak of the devil, an' he's sure to appear'.

Jay peered hard into the dimness of the room and spotted Billy standing close to the fireplace.

"Well now, ain't that Ira's little boy? You reckon the dried up old cripple would like to try another round in court?"

"Damn Phelps's, they's all over the place." Jay peered leeringly into the room trying to see Billy's face. "Tom ruined my day in town. It looks like your gonna spoil my night. I've had a belly-full of Phelps's fer one day. How in the hell did the baby Phelps get away from papa's apron strings, anyways?"

The two young men behind Jay pushed their hats away from their faces, grinning, trying to see into the room. Blaine's interest fastened on Kylee.

"If you've a mind, step outside Mitchell. I'll show you I ain't the baby you're a thinkin'," Billy retorted in quick anger, forgetting he was going to find something about this man that a person could love.

"You better be a worrin' about your baby boy. Ain't he old enough to ride with the big boys yet?" Billy tried to keep his voice from shaking. He knotted his hands into fists, which he opened and closed nervously.

"Ain't no business of yours about Bob. He could take care of a whipper-snapper of a Phelps any day!" Jay sneered, leaning toward the center of the room.

Carl stepped between the two, not about to have the Mitchell-Phelps feud come to a bloody draw in his home. "Let's have no trouble this night," Carl said calmly but meaningfully. "You can take this quarrel up somewheres on the mountain, if you're a mind to, but not in my place."

He looked hard at Jay; cold significance lighting steal sparks in his eyes. Jay backed away; he would respect Carl's wishes, valuing his friendship. Besides, Billy was only the baby Phelps; he wasn't too interested in babies. He addressed Billy in a low hushed voice filled with disdain:

"You tell Tom, I'll get him fer that slick horse trade in town today. I'll get my horse back, one way or tuther. Seems as if the Phelps's cain't keep their hands off anything that belongs to me!"

With that statement he turned, waiting for his sons to move out before him. They had kept silent, too interested in Kylee to worry about one puny Phelps.

"There'll be another time, Phelps!" Jay turned to say before he closed the door.

Kylee could see the rain behind the men through the open door, a heavy veil against the night. A deep chill ran through her bones causing her to shiver. It was raining hard and steady. She could feel Blaine's blazing dark eyes upon her, burning into her flesh. Hugging her arms tightly around her body, she tried to warm herself. The joy of the evening was gone, looking at Billy's sad unhappy face as he stood looking into the fire she knew it would not be recaptured. The only thing left for them was bed and the sweet forgetfulness of slumber.

In a fuming rage, Jay gave the reins tied to the porch post, an angry jerk. But his anger was not aimed at Phelps.

"I'd like to know what the Sam-hill's the matter with that milksop, weak-kneed brother of your-n'. He'd druther stay home and slop the hogs, or plant flowers for Nell," Jay curled his lip back into a sneer. "Ain't got no guts at all!"

He reached for the saddle horn and mounted. Different from most Virginia men, Jay preferred the high Spanish saddle horn. He liked to rest his hands while riding.

"Cain't get him interested in travelin' with us at all. Sometimes I wonder what kind of a man he's turned out to be. He'd druther spend his time tendin' to chores with Taynee than swarpin' an' whorein' with his brothers. Cain't figure him out!"

Jay started out slowly up the mountain following the creek with the water splashing high around him. Each glistening drop mingled exuberantly with the sparkling rain that had slowed to aggravating drizzle.

"I bet he'd want that one if he'd see'd her, Paw. You reckon? Weren't she a beauty? Little-n cute, that's what I like, little-n cute with shinin' hair. I wonder who she be? I ain't ever seen her 'fore," Blaine shouted, following close behind his father trying to be heard above the slowing rain and the pounding of the horse's hooves.

"Might a know'd you'd notice a purty one," Jay yelled, smiling with pride at his second son. He had been too involved with Billy to notice Kylee.

"If I see her again, I aim to get me a piece of her. I bet she'd be a good'n, right Paw?"

Blaine's statements fell on deaf ears. His father had pulled out far ahead, riding hard crashing through the creek. His older son Rueben followed close behind him. Blaine had to stop his dreaming of Kylee and ride hard to keep up with the two men riding far ahead of him in the sullen night.

CHAPTER EIGHT

They were up at the crack of dawn to get an early start. Kylee's eyes were heavy and puffed from her sound sleep. Her night's rest had been complete, except for an occasional small foot placed at different points in her back. The stay at Jennings had been a welcome diversion, one she had enjoyed and needed.

There is nothing like sharing a bed with four small children to close the gap of strangeness. By morning Kylee had become like an old friend. The children begged them to stay longer. Billy laughingly promised them another visit soon. He reminded them of Dee Rueberry's 'one year after' funeral preaching at Stewart's cemetery later in the fall.

The chickens were already scratching and clucking busy finding the day's food. A fat pig rooted lazily in the warm ground hoping to find a bit of rubbish. Billy reminded them again, regretfully, that the day was getting on and they must resume their journey.

Waving goodbye, Billy started the mules out slowly. The road wound increasingly upward ascending into tall pine, maple, dogwood, and a variety of other trees filling the hollows and crevices with heavy shelter for copperheads, black snakes, and all manners of four legged varmints. Streaked in patches across this green lushness were vibrant patches of red and orange announcing that fall would soon be the reigning season, in all its blazing glory.

Kylee tried shyly to make conversation with Billy, but he was strangely quite. Even his happy-go-lucky smile was absent. She was certain the events of the previous night were responsible for his stillness. Not knowing the boy or the circumstances surrounding the event, she felt it was not her place to pry into his mood. So she withdrew her conversation and rode in silence.

The sun rose hot and sure of itself in the blue Virginia sky. Kylee opened the valise Billy had tucked between them on the seat and took out her sunbonnet. Carefully she put the straw hat into the valise. The twist and curls of her piled hair had loosened and she replaced them with a large soft coil at the nape of her neck. Already it was beginning to creep loose from the severe restriction to hang in curly swirls about her face and neck. Covering her head with the sunbonnet, she tied it loosely under her chin. Kylee anticipated the day would be a long hot one, the heat already becoming intense. She removed her jacket and turned it lining side out, folded it neatly and laid it across the valise. The bright sun was trying to dry out the world, but the wet earth was remaining a steaming mass of humidity. It seemed to Kylee that the heat of the Indian-summer days that were upon them penetrated one's sweat glands with intensity.

Billy's thoughts were busy on the events of the past evening and he was only slightly aware of the girl beside him. The hatred between the Phelps and Mitchell families was a raw wound to Billy. The feelings went back long before the cow or court incidents. The old grudge handed down for generations and the accumulations of current incidents keep it always fuming. Hensely wasn't helping matters with his fondness for Jay and his hatred for Ira. Billy felt sure it was bound to wind up in a killing before long, much to his dismay.

Gossip traveled the hills; the bitter confusion had grown into a legend. It had become a fireside topic. If someone were found dead in the Pound region, it was quickly blamed onto the Phelps and Mitchell feud. The dispute boiled at times, then eased off a spell, then flamed hot again. Neighbors began to call it the hot and cold feud. They suspected that before it ended one or both families would be destroyed.

Most folks believed the worst about the Mitchells. A reputation for being mean and ornery followed them everywhere, blaming Jay's renegade ways and hard-nose attitude for keeping the quarrel going.

They were quick to take sides with Ira, feeling a compassion for his disability. Besides, in one way or the other, either Ira or his wife Mattie, were related to almost every family on Pound Mountain.

The Mitchell family kept mostly to themselves, shying away from social gatherings. Occasionally the third son, Bob, would show up at a preaching trying to be friendly with the young people. But he soon found they were not eager to be friendly with any Mitchell. Blaming his father for the way he was treated, he quickly developed an attitude that resulted in bitter feelings toward Jay. He wore the well-known chip high on his shoulder. He withdrew from his father and brother's coarse and wild ways, conscious of the favoritism his father shown for Blaine.

Jay's only daughter Taynee would sneak away to visit with Mary and they both became constant companions with Billy. But as they grew older, the two girls became involved with women's things. Swinging on grapevines, swimming, catching guppies and terrapins, playing hide and seek, were all considered childish. Jay kept Taynee close to home to help Nell. It was now seldom that she saw Mary or Billy. Occasionally they would meet on the bridge below Stewart's and dangle their feet in the water and tell each other their grown-up dreams and secrets.

Mary Stewart, with her warm sweet nature, and because Taynee was her friend, had been kind to Bob. With his loneliness and desire for attention, he was quick to misjudge her kindness for something more. Mary became an active scene in his mind and his feelings for her soon became much more than friendship.

Billy was concerned over Bob's attraction for Mary. Knowing the Mitchell reputation, he was afraid it would end in unhappiness for her. When he talked with her about it, she assured him the young man always treated her with kindness and respect. Billy had been pacified; deciding Bob was only searching for a friend. But he thought it wouldn't hurt to keep an eye on the situation. Now with his new found love for Mary and the encounter with Jay, Bob rested heavy on his mind. He could think of nothing else. The intense hatred between their families was felt severely by Billy.

He stopped about noon to rest the mules and let Kylee stretch. He helped her down from the wagon and she thanked him gratefully for the momentary break.

"I reckoned you were gettin' a mite tired," Billy said removing his black hat that had grown steadily white with dust. He knocked it firmly against his thigh.

The dust lay heavy upon the cover over Kylee's box of books in the back of the wagon. The moisture from the previous rain had only barely settled the top layer of dirt. The road was already dry and dusty.

"Is it much farther?" she questioned Billy.

She brushed the powdery film from her long skirt with short tender strokes. The fact that her long trip had successfully ruined her new suit made her cross. How much further must she go? Billy pulled to the side of the road where heavy brush and wide trees hid the creek from view. Kylee could hear the tinkling music as it danced across its rocky bed. The trilling song did not lighten her growing weariness.

"It ain't far now!" Billy declared. "I'll give you a minute to yourself."

His ears turned a bright pink as he made the weak apology for leaving her alone and headed for the cover of the thick brush. Kylee took advantage of his disappearance to find a high wide rhododendron bush to lift her skirts. She climbed back into the wagon and was ready and waiting when Billy returned.

The road wound steadily into the intense hills. Trees grew so increasingly thick; it was impossible to see any distance on either side of the wagon. On the winding road, the vision ahead was not much better. This country, with its steep, rolling hills, and countless hollows was a place her father had dearly loved. Kylee felt a kinship to these lovely mountains. She was beginning to understand her father's devotion and was finding a permanent place in her heart for the serene beauty of the Blue Ridge. If her father had so revered this place, why had he never returned? Had he done something so bad he couldn't come back? The questions stuck in her mind but she put them aside. There were more important things now.

The road straightened, hugging close to the side of the hill. She could look down and finally see the creek they had been following.

"If we had time we'd stop an' see the Stewarts. They live there, across the creek." Billy nodded his head toward the right where a bubbling branch spewed into the main creek. He was thinking of Mary with her warm brown eyes and sweet smile. Kylee could see nothing but a carpet of green and gold with a trail of smoke curling into the blue sky.

"But we had better be gettin' on." He slapped the team sharply with the reins to move them on faster, anxious to be home.

Bush and vine increased. Long tree branches closed out the sky causing dark shadows to form over the narrowing road. Billy indicated, with a nod of his head, to the left where there was a strip of heavy trees and brush nestled into a deep crevice between two hillsides. A place so close it seemed you could touch both sides at the same time. Dark and ominous, a place the hill folk shied away from.

"That's the 'narrows', Kylee. No one goes there 'ceptin' spooks an' haunts. It's on Jay Mitchell's mountain." Billy told her, then added more to himself, "I wonder how many folks he's killed an' dumped in there."

Bitterly his thoughts returned to Jay and the previous night. Then looking at Kylee he added one of his encouraging smiles, no need to frighten her. He'd said too much, he must get his mind on something else besides Mitchells. So he let his thoughts turn to Kylee.

Kylee bent to peek around the young man beside her, but could only see a strip of darkness spreading into a hollow. A sudden chill cooled her body and she shivered. For an unknown reason the place frightened her. She could understand why no one wanted to go into the 'narrows' and was glad when they had passed the spot.

As their journey continued, she began to feel like a wart on a toad. Kylee had been sitting so long on the hard wooden seat that she was certain if she tried to move, the seat would never release her. They traveled closer to the stream sometimes splashing through the rocky bed. The rain filled the creek to over-flowing; it swirled in eddies along the banks.

Silver rays of sunlight lingered upon the churning water, raising a thousand sparks upon the surface. What a beautiful free spirit the stream was, Kylee thought, rushing without hesitation to its journey's end. Would she ever reach her destination, wondering again about what a 'far piece' she had traveled away from her home? At least she was free from Kenus. There was no need to worry about him. He would never find her in these intense hills. She reflected upon her father, memories brought back the sadness at his loss and an oppressive loneliness filled her. She bowed her head and studied her lap, one hand clinging tightly to the side of the wagon.

They moved out of the thick trees around a bend and into an open spot that spread like a saucer between two hillsides encircled with pine, chestnut, oak, and slippery elm. Lush patches of berry bushes and wild flowers grew along the edges. Intense blue-green coloring of trees and foliage, vibrant blue sky converging with the overwhelming humidity gave an illusion to the eye of a smoky haze shrouding the valley. The vague film added a touch of mystery to the spot. Kylee felt as 'Iron Jaw' and Gerda had when they first discovered the plush meadow, in total awe and complete love.

The Phelps house was situated in a wide yard on the north side of Pound River. At the end of the driveway and against a hill was the barn. Across from the house was the gristmill Ira had worked so hard to build. A small branch of water filled the pond behind the mill. A wall made of rock and mortar held the reservoir of water back. An iron door built into the face of the damn was open, letting a small amount of water flow through, releasing the pressure on the wall. Water was easing its way down a wooden flume to trickle lightly over the big wheel, turning it slowly. After the water spilled over the wheel it formed a stream that flowed under the bridge and joined the main creek on the south side of the road. Behind the millpond stood three majestic oak trees, spreading enormous branches over the water reflecting their fall attire in a magnanimous display of color. The giant oaks reminded her of the tall trees behind the barn at home and Kylee felt still another pang of homesickness.

"That's the mill, Kylee," Billy exclaimed excitedly as they crossed the bridge.

The wide planking thundered noisily under the mules shod hooves and clattered loudly with the added weight of the wagon. Billy guided the team from the main road into a curving drive and up to the front porch of the house.

"We're here Kylee," Billy said glad to be home.

The house was bigger than Kylee had expected. She caught her breath in wondrous surprise. Never in her wildest thoughts about her new home had she imagined such a house. It was even more impressive than Uncle Dolf's farmhouse. The two-story white frame building sat separate from the barn and mill. A sheltering roof covered the wide porch, running two sides of the house. The second story had several dormer windows overlooking the porch roof indicating bedrooms on the second floor. The foundation was rock and mortar that raised the porch and house four feet from the ground, giving it a tall look of elegance. Billy stopped at the front step, jumped out and hurried around to help Kylee down. He handed her the jacket and valise, then lifted her things from the wagon and set them on the bottom step.

"You go on in Kylee, make yourself to home. I'll be right along soon as I put the wagon away an' feed this ole team. Go along now; I'll only be a minute," Billy told her with a smile that flashed his dimples as he climbed back into the wagon.

Standing on the wide bottom step Kylee watched Billy drive the team to the barn behind the mill. He waved back at Kylee as he passed and disappeared into the barn.

Looking back down the drive, Kylee could see across the bridge until the trees swallowed the road. Realizing how far she had journeyed from her home into these green and gold mountains, she felt like the only person in the world. Kylee accepted the fact that she would never see her Uncle Dolf, Aunt Aggie, Jesse, or her other cousins again. Blinking hard, she tried to hold back the tears she had promised not to allow herself. She must not be a boob and be a credit to her father. The feeling of immense stillness folded around her.

She glanced around at the grass growing heavy and unattended in the wide fenced yard. Trailing arbutus with lavender-blue blossoms fading and drying in the fall sun, left to their own initiative climbed aimlessly around the porch. Mountain laurel leaves turning red and gold, wandered down the rail fence. Underbrush and bushes were left to grow wild, thick, and uninhibited. Everything was green and musty smelling from the rain.

"What a place for snakes," Kylee thought, shuddering, wrapping her arms around her body as if to protect herself.

Behind the barn and built over the stream that filled the millpond was a springhouse, a place to shelter hams and cool the milk. Grapevine and wild fern grew over the top, making a soft cool covering.

At the side of the house was a well. Beside it grew a gnarled apple tree, the trunk encircled by a slivered cracked bench. To Kylee, it appeared a place of rest, a haven from the chores of a hot day.

On the northwest side of the house grew a small apple orchard. Everything had the appearance of total neglect, grass had been left unmowed, the rail fence splitting and peeling from want of paint, and the springhouse roof was beginning to sag from a split beam.

Kylee turned and walked slowly up the stairs and across the wide porch haltingly. She was dragging her feet, hoping Billy would not be long. Pushing the front door open she went inside. The center room was large and spacious. An enormous fireplace engulfed the back wall. A trivet had been built inside for cooking and heating water and an oven built in at the side for baking. In the ceiling, beams had been left unpainted and exposed.

Kylee leaned her weary body against the door and surveyed the room. On the wall at her left a door stood open, she could see inside to a room with a tall bed, neatly made. On the same wall was a wide staircase leading to the second story with a coat closet built in underneath. Another door also under the staircase, she would learn, opened into her Uncle Ira's bedroom.

To her right a third door had a window and Kylee could see it was easy access to the back porch and well. Also on this wall was a built in cupboard. Beside it was a buffet with a marble counter top. A washbasin and empty water bucket sat on the marble counter, fastened to the wall was a wooden rod holding a badly soiled towel. Above it was an oval mirror with a carved brass frame. A bamboo calendar and razor-strap hung on the wall. Beside the mirror were three shelves holding an array of shaving mugs, with brushes, straight blade razors, hair pomade, and a variety of shaving cologne. A large oblong table of dark oak and six chairs occupied the center of the room. Two wood rockers and several small benches sat in front of the fireplace. Filling the wall next to where Kylee stood were three tall windows built into a bay, with a wide seat at the bottom. Ruffled curtains of Irish lace, worn and faded, were tied back to give full view of the drive and mill. Kylee noticed that one of the curtains had lost its tieback and had been tied in a large knot to keep it out of the way.

A large spinning wheel and butter churn sat in the corner, dusty and unused. An oval braided rug of many colors covered the floor under the wheel and churn adding warmth and color to the interior. Kylee immediately liked the room, but overnight without a fire and the coolness of the rain left it chilled and damp. Feeling more alone than ever, she backed out onto the porch filled with late afternoon sunshine to wait for Billy.

Billy unhitched the team, gave them a measure of oats, and turned them loose in the fenced meadow behind the barn to graze. The big barn was clean and neat with everything in place. Harnesses and doubletrees hung on the walls. Saddles were soaped, oiled, and stacked on wooden sawhorses made of logs. The side stalls for the big teams and the places for the wagons Ira used for hauling were clean and dry. Billy filled the stalls with fresh straw. Things were ready for his father's return.

Ira Phelps was a businessman of extreme talent and caginess, making two trips a month or more, when the weather permitted, into North Carolina. From the people there he could purchase whiskey at a dirt-cheap price, for less than he could make it himself. While in North Carolina he would purchase an extra team and wagon, fill the wagons with whiskey, hiding it under cover of supplies purchased for his mill and hardware store. After returning home and spending a few nights resting, he would then take the whiskey on into Kentucky, bootleg the whiskey, sell the extra wagon and team, and make a considerable profit. Because of a crippling illness that left him disabled, he was never without a companion. He was always accompanied by one of his older sons, Tom or Matt, leaving the other one with Billy to help tend the store and mill.

Traffic increased over Pound Mountain as more settlers began to move into the hills, steadily increasing the store and mill business. This gladdened Ira's heart since things had been desperately slow. His father taught him that land was the way to invest money and Ira had learned his lesson well. Along with the whiskey trade, his small business, and thrifty 'Scotch' money planning, Ira became a wealthy man.

Ira's prosperity only added to Mitchell's irritation. Jay was regressing even further into his lazy, slovenly ways after Mae's death. He had taken up outlawing to make a buck after Ira beat him at the whiskey business.

Congress slapped strict controls on the whiskey trade. Laws were passed to protect the health of consumers and revenues to insure the government's share of the profits. Each state and county was allowed to decide if it was to be wet or dry. The people of the hills felt the controls and taxes were unfair. Whiskey making had long been their heritage and they were proud of being the best in this profession.

Many counties of Virginia and Kentucky voted to be dry; which meant it was illegal to produce whiskey for pleasure or profit. Moonshiners took advantage of these dry areas. It was places like this that kept the trade flourishing. The government sent agents to keep close watch on the moonshining activities in the hills. The people nicknamed them 'Revenuers' and laughed at their inability to put a stop to the whiskey making. The dense wilderness of the mountains made perfect hiding places to produce the homemade liquor.

The whiskey trade became tougher each year. Ira managed to get his wagons through using his business as a disguise. The bitter-hate between the Phelps's and Mitchell's only aggravated the situations and Hensely's friendship with Jay hadn't helped matters.

The trial at Gladeville, that Carl had mentioned was a result of a charge brought against Ira for moonshining by Tanner Hensely. Jay and Tanner were both disappointed when Ira got off scot-free and continued to moonshine under Hensely's nose. The Deputy Marshal couldn't pin anything on him. It caused an enmity between the two men that would be disastrous for Phelps.

After Ira finished the mill, his health failed steadily. He was stricken with a long feverish illness. When he recovered, he was totally paralyzed from the waist down. Moving his arms was difficult and he had to be fed and dressed. With determination and help from his very dear friend, Hail White, he regained the use of his arms, to the extent that he became partially self-sustaining. His dependency on others to be moved made him cross, irritable, and short-tempered. The only thing that made his life worthwhile was his sons, his friend Hail, and the trips he made into North Carolina.

Ira apologized constantly for being a burden on his sons. They assured him that he was no problem and were happy to be able to help him. However, they added, he could at least allow them sometime for a little pleasure. He made it almost impossible for them to find time to sneak away and spend a few stolen hours with Polly.

Billy hung the harnesses and headed for the house, waving to Kylee standing by the door as he crossed the yard. When he reached the stairs, he picked up the box of books and tucked them under his arm. He lifted the valise in his hand and the small bundle in his other and went up the stairs, smiling pleasantly at Kylee.

"Welcome to the mill, Kylee," he told her, indicating with his head for her to go back into the kitchen ahead of him.

"I'm sorry about the way thing's look," he apologized setting her belongings on the window seat as he passed. "We-uns never get much time for cleanin'. It's supposed to be my duty to keep the house, but I don't get much chance. Paw an' Matt are gone most of the time and Tom's off galavantin' somewhere. I gotta tend the store an' what comes in at the mill. I cain't be two places at once. Then I gotta clean the barn too, so's I don't get much time at the house."

"I try to keep up; paw gives me a share of what he makes. Next year I'll get to take my turn going with him to Caroline. Paw an' Matt are in Kentucky now. Who knows where Tom's at, horse-tradin' somewhere, I suppose. They'll be in tonight sometime, or tomorrow. The rain probably slowed 'em down. Gollee, it's sure gonna be nice havin' a woman around." Billy's voice was filled with happiness as he looked across the table at Kylee.

"Where's your maw?" Kylee questioned curiously in a small, tired voice, standing strictly reserved as if afraid someone would jump out and grab her.

"My maw died when I was a youngin'. Paw says there'll never be another like her. There hasn't been, least ways not for him. I hope you won't get too lonesome without some womenfolk around. I'll take you over to Stewart's; they've got lots'a girls over there. They ain't got no boys at all, ceptin' Jan an' Alvin. I'll fetch some water."

"You can wash the dust off your face. That'll make you feel better. I don't usually talk all the time, Kylee." He picked up the bucket from the marble counter as he talked and was out the side door and across the yard before Kylee could answer.

"I'm sorry about your maw an' all," she called after him, but he was out of hearing range.

As Billy left the bottom step, his stride broke into a run. Before he reached the well, Kylee watched him jump high into the air, swinging the bucket he held and clicking his heels sharply together before landing upright on the ground. Kylee was too far away to hear what Billy said.

"Thank you Lord! Thank you for sendin' Kylee to us!" he exclaimed as he rose into the air and lifted his arms.

Kylee watched Billy at the well drawing water. He set the filled bucket on the edge and disappeared into the springhouse.

He came into the house, carrying the bucket filled with cool water. Cradled in his other arm was a small brown bowl filled with butter and he held a chunk of smoked side pork in his hand. He unloaded the meat and butter on the table and set the filled bucket on the counter.

"Gee whiz Kylee, ain't you gonna take off your bonnet? I was hopin' you were gonna stay for a while," he told her with a teasing smile, thinking how pretty she was.

"Matt an' Tom are sure gonna like havin' someone as pretty as you around." His bright face filled with mischief as he thought of his brother's conflict over Polly. Maybe now they'll stay home more. He understood how you sure could get lonesome for the sight of a female. His eyes filled with merriment and he added, "Me too, I'm gonna like havin' you here. A lot!" Tossing his old worn out hat onto a peg beside the door, he turned to the cupboard.

"Bess Stewart sent over this butter. She's always doin' things like that, 'specially since we lost our cow. She is always tellin' us that we-uns need a woman 'round here. Claims that men need women folk to look after them. She worries no end 'bout us. She'll be mighty pleased that you're here. Yes sir-ree, Kylee, it's sure gonna be nice havin' you!" He exclaimed again, smiling shyly. "I'll get a fire goin'. Reckon you're gettin' hungry, I am."

Kylee removed her bonnet and took an apron from the valise, eager to help, smiling at Billy's apparent confusion. His confession of being glad she was here made her feel wanted and accepted.

"You better not say that yet, Billy. When you see what a terrible cook I am, you might be sorry I'm here. Sides, I'm the one that's glad," she declared, thinking of her long journey and Kenus.

They fried the side pork and stirred up a skillet of corn bread. There was cornmeal, baking powder, soda, salt, and sugar in the large cabinet. A bowl and the things they needed for mixing were on the counter, clean, neat, and covered with a clean towel to keep away the dust and flies.

The meat was good, but the fire was hot and cooked the bread too quickly. As a result it was heavy and soggy inside. Tired and hungry, they were glad for the food, laughing at their first attempt at cooking together. The laughter and the meal had eased the tensions and Kylee felt more relaxed in her new surroundings.

As they were eating, she noticed a hole in Billy's shirtfront that needed a patch. A button was missing from one sleeve cuff and it hung undone. Kylee felt sorry for the boy who had no mama; she knew about having no mother and understood Mrs. Stewart's concern. It was apparent that at least one Phelps was in need of someone to care for him.

After finishing their meal, Kylee washed and dried the dishes and polished the table. Billy swept the floor and brought in a supply of wood and water. Braving the tall grass, Kylee picked a handful of fall flowers growing about the porch railing, put them in a bowl, and placed them in the center of the table. The dark shining top reflected the beauty of the blossoms. Their sweet sent filled the room with a heady aroma. The reflection of the colorful bouquet faded as the evening dusk gathered. The dark shadows began to thicken around the tall pines and Billy said to Kylee:

"Come on Kylee, I'll show you the rest of the house, and your room."

The room under the stairs had been Billy's, but would now be Kylee's. A tall bed stacked with feather ticks and quilts occupied the center of the room. A small rock fireplace with decorative wood skirting filled one wall, an open closet the other. Above the head of the bed were two windows with wide sills and no curtains. Kylee could see across the yard, down to the mill. Along the wall beside the door was a tall dresser with a round mirror. A small black rocker sat before the fireplace and a large braided rug covered the entire room. Kylee could not believe such luxury was meant for her, but Billy was assuring her in a soft voice.

"This will be your room, Kylee. I moved in with Tom. He'll have to put up with me. My maw used to sit in that rocker an' read me stories from them books on the mantel. But she died before she ever got to teach me to read. I see'd you had some books Kylee, do you read? I sure would like to know how. I'll put your books right up there beside those others. I got everythin' out 'ceptin' for that banjo an' fiddle hangin' there." Billy nodded toward the instruments hanging next to the dresser. He rambled on not waiting for Kylee's answer.

"I made that fiddle myself, 'ceptin' for what Tom helped me with. He bought the banjo one time when he was in Caroline. He says them folks are great banjo pickers. I'll be goin' with Paw to Caroline in the spring. I can hardly wait. I'm takin' along my fiddle. I aim on havin' some real down home pickin'!" Billy grinned. Billy's grin marched across his face like a parade band making music in Kylee's heart.

"I'll get your things, Kylee. I sure am sorry I talk so much. But sometimes there ain't anyone to listen to me. So when there is, I cain't shut up. Paw's room is behind yours. He has an iron stove in there. He says the fireplace just don't keep him warm enough. Tom an' Matt's rooms are upstairs. I'll be fine in Tom's room. Don't you fret none, 'bout that. Sometimes I can get a heap mad at him, cause he puts up pictures of pretty women all over the walls. Sometimes they ain't dressed much, and that embarrasses me. But not Tom, nothin' embarrasses Tom. No-sirree, don't nothin' embarrass him!"

Billy's ears turned pink realizing what he had been saying. He became silent, looking to the floor.

"I can't take your room, Billy. I don't want to do that," Kylee said slowly. "I can have a pallet on the floor."

"That would never do!" Billy was shocked into lifting his head and looking directly at Kylee stating emphatically, "Paw would split my back side for sure if I had you sleepin' on the floor! Now, you settle yourself right there in that rocker. I'll bring your things."

"I'll leave that banjo an' fiddle hangin' there if you don't mind. There ain't much room on Tom's walls what with all them pictures an' things."

He became flushed again as he thought about the pictures on Tom's bedroom wall. One was a pretty blonde women dressed only in her drawers, top bared, her large bosom daringly exposed. It confused Billy to think of what a woman might look like without her clothes on. He thought about the loveliness of Mary, his confusion was complete.

"Thank you, Billy. The fiddle an' banjo will be just fine there." Kylee smiled at Billy as she sat down in the rocker. "And yes, I know how to read." Her body sagged into the contour of the rocking chair with weariness. She felt as if she belonged there and had just returned from a long journey. She wished silently that she would never have to leave.

"We'll get busy an' teach you to read."

"Oh-my-gosh, that's great, Kylee. Just great." Billy forgot Mary, the pictures, and his confusion with the thought of learning to read.

"I'll bring you some water; you can heat it over the fire an' have a bath. That'll make you rest better. There's a latch on your door; you can have all the privacy in the world. When you get done, just holler, an' I'll be here to take the water out for you. I'll bring you a lamp too," he told her as the room began to darken.

Billy moved to the door with reluctance, hating to part from Kylee's company and wanting to talk more. But he knew she was tired and he was too. Looking at his new cousin sitting in his mother's rocking chair, his heart filled with a happiness he had not felt for a long time. It was as if the chair had been waiting for her. He hoped she would never leave and stay with them forever.

CHAPTER NINE

It was late when Ira Phelps and his middle son, Matt returned. Billy had emptied Kylee's tub of water and told her goodnight. He sat down in front of what was left of the fire and had promptly fallen asleep. Matt opened the door and came in loud and boisterous, his presence filling the dim-lit room and waking Billy from his sound slumber.

"Hi baby brother, you still up? Thought you'd be in bed by now," Matt greeted Billy playfully ruffling his hair, a habit that followed from the younger brother's childhood.

Matt was tall and good-looking, lean of stature with long limbs and bony knees and elbows. He was never able to buy clothing long enough in the sleeves. He looked like an overgrown schoolboy with a short dark curly beard. Heavy dark brows jutted out over warm dark blue, to the point of being black, round eyes. Owl eyes, Billy called them teasingly. Eyes that filled with love when he looked at his younger brother. A sharp hawk nose added a stern look to his face denying the merriment in his shining eyes. Contrary to the easygoing attitude in his happy face, he was a man of quick temperament. Matt was different in looks and personality than his brothers and was often in discord with them and his father.

"You fetch the cousin, Billy? I was hopin' to get a look at her before Paw starts yellin'. I suppose she's tall an' skinny, or round an' dumpy, or drab lookin'. Maybe she's just a brat of a kid huh, brother?" he laughingly questioned Billy. He didn't expect too much from a stranger, especially when they were relation.

"Yeah, I brung her, but she was tired an' it was gettin' late. Didn't think you'd be in this time of night so I sent her off to bed."

Billy stood, stretched, and smoothed down his unruly hair trying to awaken fully. He would not attempt to describe Kylee to his brother. Matt would have to wait and see for himself. Was he in for a surprise! Billy was thinking she was about the most perfect thing he'd ever seen, except for Mary.

"Wal now, what's this here?" Matt asked, tossing his wide brimmed hat onto a peg by the door. "Ain't that sweet, kinda nice wouldn't you say? For a bunch of varmints like us?" Matt eyed the flowers on the table.

Taking some packages wrapped in plain brown paper from his coat pocket, he scattered them across the table. He hung his coat next to his hat, sorted through the packages and handed one to Billy.

"Here's what you asked me to bring you. I sure hope they'll be a fittin' present for a gal like Mary. Cain't believe my little brother has a sweetheart." Matt flashed a teasing grin at Billy, showing fine white teeth against his black beard and mustache.

Taking a cup from the cupboard he filled it from the coffeepot hanging over the almost dead fire. He drank the steaming liquid down without waiting for it to cool. Taking a twist of tobacco from his vest pocket he bit off a chew and offered it to Billy.

"Thanks Matt, no." Billy refused shaking his head, recalling his earlier experience. "Where's Paw?" he queried as he unwrapped the package Matt handed him.

"He's down at the barn with Tom, they're a comin'. Paw wanted to go to the barn first an' unload the things we brung with us before we came to the house. Guess he didn't trust me to put things away without his tellin' me exactly where to put each thing. Tom came in before I had a chance to bring Paw to the house. They're jackin' their jaws about some horse trade Tom made in town. I was too tired to wait around. Tom said he'd bring Paw in," Matt explained as he sat down stretching out his long legs. He leaned back, raised his arms and folded his hands behind his head.

"Boy I'm dead tired, Paw never lets down. When he gets on a wagon, he don't give you no chance to drag your feet. I can't understand how he keeps goin'. He could stay an' run the mill with you. Me an' Tom could make them long trips. But no, he don't think we can do it right or he's afear'd he'll miss somethin'!" Matt stated as he watched Billy open the box that had been inside the package. A strand of crystal beads sparkled inside. "Can't believe little brother has a sweetheart."

"Aw Matt, you know we've been friends forever. I was aimin' on givin' her a present for her birthday, that's all. She'll be sixteen."

Lowering his head, Billy hoped Matt would not guess how much he longed to be more than a friend to Mary. Thinking of the girl, he knew it was not the heat from the low burning embers that warmed his body.

"Sure do thank you, Matt. They'll do fine." Billy beamed at his brother immensely pleased with the beauty of the beads.

"That's okay kid. It'll come out'a your share of the whiskey we sold in Kentucky. Paw got a good price for the lot," Matt explained watching Billy closely. It wasn't hard to read the telltale look on his face, even in the scarce light of the fire.

"I'd better stir up the fire. I hear the wagon comin'. Tom's bringin' Paw. That rain has chilled the night some. Paw'll be cold. I can hear him now. He's still naggin'. I'm glad it's Tom he's onto this time an' not me!" Matt rose to put a log on the fire and added a couple chunks of coal.

Tom Phelps pushed the heavy oak door open with his foot as he carried his father easily in his strong arms. His father was a stout man, heavy almost obese. His legs had become shriveled and twisted from his crippling illness giving him almost a dwarf look. Tom carried the man without effort, distributing the balance of his load onto strong legs. The muscles in his calves rippled against the tight fit of his riding breeches.

"Push Paw's chair out here, Matt. Thought you'd have it ready, you know'd we was comin'."

Matt disappeared into their father's bedroom and returned with the heavy, cumbersome, high-backed wheel chair. It was the means of Ira's freedom from depending on his sons when he was home. In a moment of inventiveness Tom built a long ramp from the porch to the yard making it possible for his father to move independently back and forth to the mill. Tom set his father in the chair faking a sigh of relief.

"I'm tellin' you Paw, you've got to lay off that corn bread an' sowbelly. Them folks over in Caroline an' Kentucky feed you too good. That fat meat is gonna kill you, an' that whiskey don't help either. You're gettin' too fat for your own good. Soon you'll have to stay home an' sit in this durned old chair," Tom teased his father fondly, carefully tucking a bright colored quilt around his lifeless legs.

"It ain't the cornbread an' sowbelly he needs to give up. It's that buttermilk an' green onions. They make his farts smell so bad you can't stand to ride on the same wagon with him. Then I gotta sleep at his side out there on the road," Matt said his bit as they laughingly continued to tease their father.

"That's right, go 'head an' keep on bellyachin' 'cause you have to carry me an' sleep by me. We could hire a driver. You know what happened when we tried that. You wouldn't have to be bothered with me but you'd not get a share then, either. I told you Tom; I'd come in with Matt. But no, you had to have a talk. So's now you had your talk, hesh up your grumblin'. You're both gettin' too big for your britches. Sides that good clear corn whiskey burns up that sowbelly." Ira retorted a slight twinkle beginning to show in his clear blue eyes, scarcely visible beneath heavy white brows.

"Come on Paw, we weren't complainin'. We was a joshin'. You're gettin' so you cain't take a joke at all. You're gettin' ornerier then a sore-tailed tomcat. I'll take the wagon back to the barn an' unhitch," Tom declared disgusted with his father's lack of humor, failing to see the twinkle in his eyes.

"You do that, Tom. You just do that!"

As Tom drove the wagon back around the drive and up to the barn, he recalled the days before his father's illness. Remembering his ambition and never ending energy, how he worked the fields and drove himself when building the mill between planting and harvest. He had felt his father's great courage and determination during his long illness and the terrible sadness after they found his mother dead on the ground where she had been picking berries.

He knew it was a bitter potion for his father to depend on others. Tom loved his father more than anyone in the world and admired his fortitude and courageousness. Under his shell of orneriness was a kind-hearted man. Tom was glad he was able to help his father. He only teased him to lighten the burden.

It was hard sometimes to stand the moments of irritability and temper, sometimes almost unbearable. Then he would reprimand himself realizing the handicap his father struggled with. He would be ashamed for being cross with him. Tom suspected his father envied their youth and constant energy which caused them to be the target of his ill moods.

He hadn't felt like facing his father this night. He had hoped that Ira hadn't returned yet or had retired for the night, certain he could better explain the purchase of Jole' on a new day. When he saw the lantern light shining from the barn, he knew Ira and Matt had arrived just ahead of him. Now as he unhitched the big team of perfectly matched grays, he realized how old they were getting. He understood why his father was angry with his purchase of a horse that would be no service to them, only pleasure.

"You got a right to be angry Paw, but I had to have her," he explained to his father as Matt left the barn leaving Ira sitting on the wagon seat talking to Tom.

"I could understand son, if she were built to make you some money, but the only thing I can see that she'd be good for is a brood mare. She's too big for a racehorse; she'd never be fast enough. She's bigger than I'd want for ridin'. She's even bigger than Jan's sorrel. She ain't got the hooves or legs for a plow pony. It'd take a lot of trainin' to put her with another horse an' make a team for haulin' a wagon. She'd be too frisky for pullin' a buggy."

"I gotta admit she is a beauty. Purty as any horse I ever saw, an' I've see'd some purty ones. It's like I've been tryin' to tell you galloots, buying a horse is like choosin' a woman. Looks aren't everythin'. There's lots of other things to consider such as durability an' performance. But you never listen to a thing I say. Think you're gettin' too old for advice from your paw! Think you know it all!

Now tell me, how come you spent as much on that worthless mare as you would have on a good team, which we're a needin'. Look there at Bawli an' Dawli, they're gettin' too old for these long trips." That was Ira's hard-nosed appraisal of Tom's purchase. He was admiring the horse and liked the palomino coloring, silver white mane and four white stockings on the young mare.

"I don't know, Paw. I took one look at her an' I guess you could say it was love at first sight. I had to have her! I'll pay you back from my share of the whiskey," Tom promised his father and picked up a currycomb and began stroking the horse's shining blonde mane. "I'm gonna call her Jole' Blonde, Paw."

"Jole', what kind of a name is that?" Ira asked stroking his long white beard thoughtfully.

"Well Paw, it seems if I remember right, someone told me Jole' is a Cajun word meaning beautiful. This horse reminds me of a beautiful blonde, a tall blonde with long legs an' soft arms, a warm-blooded blonde with red lips an' big bosoms. An' willin', Paw, willin' for anything. Her only purpose would be to give you pleasure."

"That's the way I think it'll be with Jole'. When you straddled her, she'd be right there to give you a pleasurable ride. When you started up a mountain, she'd be with you all the way. She'd never balk on you. She'd still be a goin' for you when a lot of others would drop. She wouldn't leave you stranded in the middle of the night without a ride; like that ol' reprobate of a mule Red has done me many a time." Tom hoped his father understood. He kept brushing the horse's mane.

"Well, done is done, Tom. Reckon I never thought about no horse like it were a woman. But I reckon a man has some good in him, when he loves horses as much as you do. You always were good to your animals, Tom. Treatin' 'em almost like they were people."

"Wal, Paw. There was another reason I had to have this particular horse," Tom confessed, looking around the animal's nose at his father setting above him on the wagon seat. "Someone else wanted her almost as bad as me."

"Now who could have wanted that lummox of a horse, sides you?"

116

"Jay Mitchell," Tom answered slowly, his voice so low that Ira had to lean forward to hear him and almost toppled off the wagon seat.

"Who was that you said son? Speak up! You never had a problem speakin' up before."

"You never had a problem hearin' before, Paw. I said, Jay Mitchell."

"Jay Mitchell," Ira's head came up, his back straightened. "You don't say! You mean to say you snickered him out'a that horse an' got it for yourself?"

"Sure is a fact, Paw! Bad as I wanted this horse, I'd got her one-way or 'tuther. But it sure pleasured me no end to plague that man."

"That brightened up my day, Tom. Yes sirree, that brightened up my day!" Ira exclaimed slapping his lifeless legs. His voice held a note of triumph and his eyes glowed like flames on a newly lit candle. His delightful laughter rang through the barn.

"It was a good haul this trip, but that brightened my day!" He stopped laughing long enough to catch his breath.

"You mean he never gave you no fight? Let you walk away with that mare he was a wantin'?" Ira asked, knowing full well that where Jay was concerned there had to be more to it than that.

"Oh, he wasn't gonna let it go without a fight. But I had already paid for her an' he could see I was without a gun. Not like it would matter to Jay. But there were a lot of folks standin' 'round. Just as things were gettin' warm, who should happen by? No one else but Deputy Marshal Tanner Hensely." Tom looked up at his father with a sheepish grin. "Yep, there he was, big as life an' twice as ugly. Stuck his big nose right in the middle of things. He thinks he's somethin' all right. Struttin' 'round like he never done nothin' wrong in his life. Too many of us know better. Don't know how he ever got that position in the first place. Must'a had somethin' on Snow. He trusts him beyond reason. Guess it's like you told us, when it comes to politics, you have to make strange bedfellows, an' money talks." Tom stopped brushing and became serious. "It'll even be worse if he gets Snow's place as Federal Marshal when he retires next year. Too bad ain't someone with enough guts to run against him." Tom was wound up, disturbed by the political situation in the vicinity. Jole' was forgotten for the moment.

"I guess it was a good thing he happened along. I know he ain't got no love for us, but his appearance probably kept someone from gettin' killed. At least Jay backed off. He left madder than a hornet. You know Paw, it sure would stop Jay's cahoots with the law if someone from Pound Mountain would run for Snow's job. Someone needs to stand up against Hensely," Tom said thoughtfully, stopping his brushing to watch his father.

"He's got another year to go, Tom. If you got any intentions, you need to declare yourself."

"I didn't say I'd do it Paw. I wouldn't have a chance. I was thinkin' of someone like Jan."

"Jan already said he wouldn't do it. You could do it son. I'd be behind you an' so would Jan an' Carl. You could be sure of all the Baldwin Branch an' the Mullins bunch too. Think about it Tom, I'd be proud. Proud indeed! If money talks, we got enough to be heard, loud an' clear!"

"You can bet Hensely wouldn't take it lyin' down if I was to run against him. He already hates our guts. He's made up his mind to put us out of the whiskey business. If he cain't do that, he'll kill you Paw. He's gonna get you out of the way, one-way or tuther. I worry 'bout you. If I run against him, it would be just another thorn in his side. Tanner an' Jay together are capable of anythin'." The enjoyment that came to his eyes at the thought of upsetting Hensely clouded as he thought of the danger to his father.

"There is danger in lots of things, Tom. I've lived with danger all around me. Never knowin' when Jay would cut loose on a rampage an' kill us all. If I'd let a little fear keep me from living my life, I'd given up an' died long ago. We'll do it, if you've a mind to." Ira paused, pleased with the thought of his son running for office. "Let's say no more. There is one thing I want you to do, Tom. First thing in the mornin', I want you an' that horse, you think capable of wonders, to make a run over Pound. You remember that piece of ground up next to Jay's, the one that belonged to Tap Baldwin's family?"

"Yeah, Paw."

"Wal you know it were Jay what run him off. Tap said he couldn't take no more of bein' shot at. He sold that land to Will Tackett. Now Tackett ain't never lived there, never could get him to leave Kentucky. Now he wants to head out West. He wants to sell all his properties. I want that piece of land. I've heard from Carl that Jay's wantin' that land bad. I ain't lettin' him get his grubby hands on it. Your Uncle Tap would never want that to happen. It's a prime piece of land son, timber an' coal. Someday it'll be worth a bundle."

"I've given you an' Matt your piece of land. Yours includes the house an' mill. Matt's joins the Stewart place. I want this piece of land to give to Billy on his birthday. I want you to seal the deal for me. Offer him more than he is askin' if you have to, but get it! Tackett's living over in Jenkins. We didn't haul over there this time, but you'll be able to find his place without any trouble." Ira waited for a nod from Tom.

"I'll do it for you, Paw."

"Take me to the house now, Tom. I'm weary to the point of dyin'. Like you said, we ain't heard the last of this horse deal."

"It ain't likely Jay'll forget bein' whipped by one of us. When he wants somethin', he usually don't give up until he gets it!" Tom added as he prepared to drive his father to the house.

After putting the wagon away and unhitching the team Tom walked slowly back to the house. He was thinking over seriously what his father had said about putting his bid in for Marshal Snow's job. It was time someone stood up publicly to Hensely. Marshal Snow trusted Hensely unquestionably with the policing of Donkey and Pound Mountain. The increasing friendship between Jay, Hensely, and the outlaws on the mountain had become a festering sore with the people who lived there.

When he entered the house again, he noticed the bright cheery look of the floral bouquet. Billy must be out of his mind picking flowers for the table. Whatever it was, he was all for it because it really brightened up the place. Then he could hear his father telling Billy:

"Well, I've had my coffee now an' rested a bit. You fetch Val's girl. I want to take a look at her."

That explained the flowers and the neat look about the house. Billy had brought home the new cousin from Tennessee. Well, he might just as well have a look at her too, might prove interesting.

"Aw Paw. She was really tired out. I put her in my room like you said. She'd be asleep by now. Cain't it wait until mornin'?" Billy coaxed, pouring his father another cup of coffee as a means of persuasion.

"It ain't that late. I don't want to wait until tomorrow. I've been waitin' long 'nough. I'm gonna look at her now. Fetch her!"

The fact the girl was coming had occupied most of Ira's thoughts lately. He had tried to be home earlier but the rain had delayed them. He wasn't waiting another night to take a look at Val's girl. He sipped slowly on the hot coffee, letting the warm black liquid soothe the taut strings of his ragged nerves and the weariness of his body.

"Ain't no one in this house tired until I say they are," Ira told them loudly, his voice cracking with increased irritation. "I want to have a look at the gal. I don't mean tomorrow, or the next day. I mean now, right now!" Ira's eyes, so like Tom's, flashed light blue in the firelight. "Fetch her! Be quick boy!"

"Now calm down Paw. We'll have a look at the cousin. You don't want her to see you all red in the face from hollerin', now do you? You've probably already woke her, shoutin' so loud."

Tom spoke softly, to calm his father, who could at times, really get wound up. He refilled his father's coffee cup as a means of pacifying him. Nodding his head for the younger brother to bring the girl and not rile their paw further.

Billy knocked on Kylee's door. She answered immediately from where she stood behind the door listening; hearing Ira's loud demanding voice.

"Is something wrong, Billy?"

"It's nothin' Kylee. Paw's home an' he's wantin' to see you. Hurry fast as you can, he's in no mood for waitin'. He'll be bellerin' loud enough to bring the cows from the next holler, so hurry." He gave her a warm smile of encouragement.

Kylee moved back into her room to find her cover-up. Thanking Aunt Aggie under her breath for the new robe as she slipped it on.

120

Its dark green color brought out the red in her hair. She was quite presentable. She wouldn't have to be ashamed of her attire.

The kitchen was dark except for the low flickering of the remaining fire. The men in front of the red glow cast long shadows into the high rafters of the ceiling. Huge apparitions with distorted shapes waited to gobble her up. She moved in close to Billy for courage and strength.

"Here she be, Paw. This is Kylee. Take it easy, will you. Remember we're new to her. We don't want to scare her away, do we?" Billy cautioned placing a hand on Ira's arm, which his father irritably tossed aside.

"Hesh-up Billy, I don't need no youngin' tellin' me how to act. Hold your tongue, I ain't gonna gobble her up," Ira said looking at Kylee.

"Come closer, girl!" he told her with a softening in his voice. "Light a lamp, Billy." Ira stroked his beard deep in thought looking over every inch of the young woman.

Billy took a lamp from the mantel, lifted the chimney and lit the wick turning it to a high position. A pale gentle light fell softly around Kylee as she moved closer. She felt more frightened than ever as the increasing light spread to the corners of the room.

Ira took the lamp from Billy and lifted it high letting the glow cascade around Kylee, studying her for a long minute. Tom and Matt did not miss the slightest detail. The long thick braid hanging down her back, the shimmering light dancing like fireflies in the tangled curls hugging her chin and neck. They looked her over with sweeping scrutiny.

Kylee hated them all, except Billy. They made her feel like a prize pig being purchased at an auction. She wanted to turn and run but Ira had set the lamp on the table, took her hand, and held it firmly.

"Are you in health? You look a little puny. You ain't got much for size." Ira scrutinized Kylee, peering in close so he could see her eyes better. They were, as he knew they would be green as the ivy that grew around the rocks in the damp places of the forest in early spring. For a fleeting moment he recalled a young girl with eyes just as green.

The possibility of having a young woman in his home delighted Ira. He had been eager to accept Val's request to give Kylee a home. He would have never let Val send her to someone else, she was family, and Kylee's place was with him. They would find a way to make her feel at home. He would have to keep a close eye on Tom and Matt. He had seen the bright light sparkling like flint in their eyes. Noticing her smallness, Ira was quick to misjudge her ability.

She could feel the nervous knot tying in her stomach. Was it going to be impossible for her to stay? Her Uncle Ira thought she was puny. Maybe he wouldn't want her. Would he deny her without giving her a chance to prove her capabilities? Standing taller, she tried to stop the trembling in her chin and was quick to defend herself.

"Not really sir. I've always been shorter than anyone else, but I can do my share," Kylee answered with spirit.

"You a good worker?"

"Yes sir," she answered meekly this time, trying to keep the quivering from her voice and pulling to ease her hand away from Ira's.

Ira was aware of her trembling and felt the slight tug of her hand. Patting her hand in comforting gesture, he released her with a warm smile. The smile spread so wide it moved his white beard down to rest on his chest, filling his face with warmth. He was delighted with the young woman.

"I be a heap sorry for your paw's death. I've been grieved over it. We were like brothers. I remember them times that are gone. But that's enough of that. You're welcome here Kylee, Val's youngin' is surely welcome. I guess you can tell this place needs a woman. I've been tryin' to get them two whippersnappers there to bring home a wife, that ugly one standin' is my eldest Tom. The one there in the chair, the uglier one, is Matt. But they are so darn ugly, no one'll have them."

Ira's statement brought a slight grin to Kylee's face and her chin steadied. It didn't take more than a look to know the words were a jest.

"You met Billy, he ain't so ugly. But he sure is bashful!" Ira gave a laugh and looked with fondness at his younger son who was standing protectively close to Kylee.

"I've been tryin' to tell them two uglies to stay away from Polly, find 'em a worth while girl instead of layin' 'round rubbin' bellies with a no good!'"

The two young men looked to the floor embarrassed at the referral to Polly in front of the new arrival. Matt rose from his chair and stood next to Tom.

"There ain't a woman 'round that would have a worthless half dead thing like me." Ira continued, pounding his lifeless legs without mercy. "Ain't no-one in their right mind gonna waste time on the likes of me. Not with these hot-blooded youngin's 'round. If they treat you in anyway disrespectful, you let me know. I can still take a harness strap to them." Ira took another long look at Kylee. "Well, I'm off to bed. I'll see you in the mornin'. Your duties, girl will start with breakfast. I'm an early riser. Have my breakfast on the table. You can call me uncle, I'd like that." The meeting was over as far as Ira was concerned. He said good night and wheeled the clumsy high-backed chair into his bedroom and closed the door.

"Good night ya-all. I'm goin' to bed; it's been a long day. I'll be up early Kylee to give you a hand. I can soften Paw's early mornin' disposition." Billy smiled at Kylee. He took the stairs two at a time, in a hurry to be off to bed and glad his father had accepted their new cousin.

"I'll be up early too cuz, to give you a little moral support. Paw really ain't too bad in the middle of the day, but early mornin' he's a bearcat! Wouldn't want a tender little thing like you to brave the bear in his den without plenty of help. It's gonna be nice havin' you here. I'm hopin' your stay will be a long one!" Matt touched Kylee's shoulder slightly, stooping to look into her eyes. She sure was little he thought. Just looking at her abundance of hair reminded him of his mother.

"Good night," he said to her and was gone, taking the stairs a little slower than Billy had.

Kylee moved to return to her bedroom. A firm hand closing around her arm detained her.

"Don't hurry away Kylee. I want to show you where things are. You're a shakin' girl! Don't be afear'd, things'll look better in the mornin'. Paws bark is a lot worse than his bite, you'll see. Why that's all he's been talkin' about for weeks is when you would get here. Now you're here. I know he's pleased to no end." Tom turned on his best smile, flashing straight white teeth against a beardless face.

"Billy's been doin' the cookin', an' I gotta tell ya, anythin's gotta be an improvement. You sure don't look like most of the cousins I've seen. You're a heap purtier," Tom continued.

He felt the muscles tense in Kylee's arm. She was trying cautiously to free herself. He took a last look at her lowered eyelids lined with dark thick lashes. Her small nose was sharply defined in the limited light. His eyes lingered on her mouth, lips dark pink and almost too full for her face. She had bitten on the bottom one until the color had drained. Her firmly rounded chin was trembling visibly. Tom thought from the looks of her that she'd had enough of his family for one night and released her.

"Paw likes biscuits an' gravy for breakfast. I'll be up to show you where things are in the mornin'. Good night," he added taking one last look; he turned to the fire dismissing her.

Kylee thankful for her release went to her room. She tried to swallow but her mouth was dry. Tom had held her arm so firmly it ached. Through the open window over her bed, the night was dark with no moon. The fresh air filling the room was sweet and smelled clean. The gentle swishing of the pines swaying in the slight breeze made a soft whispering sound.

Closing the door and dropping the latch she felt her way across the room and laid back into the softness of the bed. Her body was weary, but her mind was so busy reviewing the night's events she couldn't sleep. She was shocked at her uncle's condition. No one had told her he was an invalid. The nearest thing she had ever seen to a cripple was Uncle Dolf when his old war injury flared up, usually during a rainstorm. His knee would become stiff and he would rely on the aid of a cane. But Uncle Ira looked to be totally handicapped. Oh well, she would adjust to that and help him all she could.

She should try and sleep but was afraid if she closed her eyes she would sleep for two days. That would never do. If she didn't get up early to have breakfast ready, her uncle would be angry. She couldn't chance that. She must prove herself worthy of being taken into his home. Finally out of total exhaustion, she fell into a troubled restless sleep. The place where Tom had held her arm still pulsed like a band around her flesh, squeezing and making her arm ache. The clear blue of his eyes reflected the glow of the lamplight and shone through the darkness.

From somewhere she recognized those broad shoulders and slim waist. The clean face with the deep cleft chin was not one a person easily forgot. Blonde, slightly wavy hair lifting in the breeze then lying to rest upon a tanned forehead stirred a memory. Her restless dreaming returned to chilling blue eyes, glowing in the firelight, as they looked her over, eyes burning with determination as they gazed with desire at a golden mare. The dream was a sudden discovery that brought her up to a sitting position in bed.

"You're him! You're the one that ruined my beautiful new suit," she said out loud.

Realizing she might be heard, she covered her mouth with both hands. Laying back into the soft pillows, her eyes filled with realization as she stared into the night.

"You're him! I'd never forget those eyes, those neat clothes, and such bad manners!" Kylee muttered to herself wide-awake. The brother that Billy mentioned and the man at the sale were one and the same. Admitting to herself Tom's identity, she was glad he had in no way been aware of her presence in town. Kylee filed Tom and the incident of the ruined skirt in the back of her mind along with Kenus. She would never forgive him for his unconcern, bad manners and the way he held her arm. Pulling the quilts up snugly under her chin, she let out a long sigh and fell into a sound sleep.

CHAPTER TEN

Billy sang joyously as he went about his early morning chores that included filling the wood box under the eaves that opened from the outside into the kitchen. It was also his duty to keep a supply of wood on Kylee's hearth and a bucket of coal from the bank behind the house for his father's iron stove.

It was one of those beautifully warm fall days when the insects are the stickiest and the birds sing the loudest. A swarm of aggravating pesky flies buzzed around Billy's ears constantly causing him to swear softly under his breath. The only way he could close out the noise of the birds was to sing louder than they did. So he raised his voice in song as he chopped, carried, and stacked the wood. His loud clear baritone voice reached out to Kylee where she sat on the bench under the apple tree churning butter.

> *"There are folks building homes as sweet as can be.*
> *They're plantin' their yards en plantin' their trees.*
> *But my little hut, I'll just let it be,*
> *Cause Jesus is buildin' a mansion for me!*
> *A mansion for me, a mansion for me,*
> *Built by my Lord upon Calvary.*
> *My little hut, I'll just let it be,*
> *Cause Jesus is buildin' a mansion for me.*
> *A mansion for me. A mansion for me......."*

Billy finished the wood and went inside to remove the ashes from the fireplace grates. Things had gone amazingly well since Kylee's arrival. It had been over three weeks since the first day she came and Billy felt as if she belonged to them. Already she had become like a sister sharing the work that seemed to never end.

One of the older brothers would go with Ira into North Carolina and Kentucky. The one who stayed behind would help Billy at the mill and the hardware store. Billy had strict orders from Ira to do Kylee's bidding and never leave her alone.

Kylee would often sit on the wide steps mending or peeling apples in the warm fall sunshine and watch the wagons come and go at the mill. She delighted at the sound of the big freight wagons rumbling across the bridge heading for Pound Gap and into Kentucky.

The Phelps men liked their new addition. Kylee kept a neat house. Their clothes were always ready, washed, starched, and ironed. Clean bedding was always on their beds, fresh and sweet smelling. Amazingly, she was a good cook too. In fact, they thought she was almost too good to be true.

Kylee shed her nervousness and was no longer ill at ease and enjoyed being part of their family, except for Tom. Not allowing herself to be friendly with him, she carefully shut him out wearing a covering of indifference toward him. Tom found her attitude difficult to understand wondering what he had done to deserve such treatment.

After her arrival, she began immediately to organize the house. With Billy's help, they repaired the chicken lot and rounded up a few hens Ira had let run wild and a scabby old rooster. There were fresh eggs for breakfast now.

Kylee was ambitious and no stranger to hard work. Billy was always there to help her. They cut away the unwanted brush in the yard, piled, and burned it and mended and painted the fence. When they were finished everything inside and out was clean, neat, and shining.

Remembering what Aunt Aggie had told her about protecting her skin, she diligently wore her sunbonnet. It would also shelter her hair from the drying effect of the sun and discourage the golden freckles that so readily marched across the bridge of her nose. She would sing and hum at her work, often smiling at the men folk as she called them. Except for Tom, she'd be darned if she would have a smile for such an ill mannered young man.

As Kylee worked with Billy they developed a mutual fondness that tightened as the days went by. They made a deal to exchange their talents. If Billy agreed to teach her how to play the banjo she in return would teach him how to read. So every spare moment away from work and daily chores was spent in the learning process. Once again, Ira was annoyed with the provoking shrill notes of the musical beginner. If it hadn't been for his growing affection for Kylee he would have run them both off. He warned them that their instrumental endeavors had better take place while he was away or out of hearing range.

After completing the dirty job of removing the ashes and cleaning up the dust that settled, Billy removed his shirt and filled the washbowl. He washed his face, hands, and splashed cool water over his head and shoulders. He looked proudly at the developing muscles in his skinny arms. With a sheepish grin he tightened his fists and watched the muscles swell. Matt couldn't kid him about having teeny weeny muscles anymore. Futilely he tried to comb his course light brown hair into some shape of tidiness.

The bamboo calendar hanging beside the mirror reminded him it had been a long time since he worried about what day it was. A circled date demanded his attention. Could it be possible? He looked closer. It was the 16th of October. Mary's birthday and Dee Rueberry's funeralizing was tomorrow!

It was a tradition in the hills to have a second funeral one year after a person was buried. It was a special occasion for the family to bring friends and relation from miles to attend. There would be preaching, gospel singing, and lots to eat. Billy had been so concerned with Kylee's arrival that he had forgotten the funeralizing. Mary's birthday had even slipped his mind along with the crystal beads in the black box tucked into the corner of Tom's trunk.

As he thought of Mary, a hungry longing filled him. How could he have forgotten such a vision of loveliness? He was anxious to share with Mary his new developing ability to read. Then a chilling thought came to his mind. What if Bob Mitchell had been pushing his attention on her all this time? Perhaps he had even won Jan's permission to court his daughter. There was a sick feeling in Billy's stomach as he thought of Bob with his darling, touching her, maybe even kissing her. Perhaps Mary had fallen in love with him. After all, he was considered to be the better looking of the two with his black eyes and hair, dapper mustache and long sideburns. Girls were funny; they set great store in dark, swarthy looks. In a twinge of jealousy, he was prompted into action. He would not let another day pass without seeing Mary. Tossing the towel carelessly into a heap on the counter top, he ran up the stairs two at a time, as was his habit.

He found the box with the beads where he had left it. He wrapped it in a piece of tissue paper he found in his mother's old sewing box and tied it carefully with a string of red yarn. He put on a clean white shirt, tucked the package into a pocket and went back down stairs excited to find Kylee and tell her of his plans.

Billy found Kylee at her job of churning butter. Dots of perspiration were beginning to form on her forehead from the heat of the day. Even under the shade of the old apple tree the heat was intense. She wore the dress Aunt Aggie had made her and had folded the skirt into her lap away from the splashing churn. White bloomers were pulled above her knees. Kylee had indiscreetly rolled her long black stockings to her shoe tops letting the air caress her bare legs. She hesitated a moment now and then to shoo away the flies that were attracted to the lip of the churn.

The job had taken longer than usual today and she was beginning to wonder if the butter would ever come. Ira had purchased a jersey cow from Jan Stewart to replace Matt's loss of Daisy. The young heifer had calved since Kylee's arrival. Even after the calf had drunk his belly full from a bucket, there was plenty of thick yellow cream to become an added chore.

"Hey Kylee, you 'bout done?" Billy called, waving his arm at her. "Come on. I want you to go to Stewart's with me."

"Gosh a Friday, Billy! What you a yellin' 'bout?" Kylee looked up from her concentration on the churn to watch Billy cross the yard. Startled by his sudden appearance, she quickly tried to cover her knees with her skirt and quickly rolled her stockings back into place. It would never do for him to see her bare legs. She flipped her long tresses that were hanging loose, out of her way.

Sitting in the shade of the twisted, gnarled tree she looked as if she had been painted there. As Billy crossed the wide yard he watched her in questioning wonder. He marveled at how so much sweetness could be gathered up in one pink gingham dress. He let the feeling sweep over him, the fantasy that she had always been there. He suddenly realized how empty his life would be if she should decide not to stay.

"Come on Kylee. We're goin' to Dee's funeralizin'. The preachin's tomorrow, but hurry we're goin' today," he laughingly pleaded with her.

"Billy, make sense. I can't just leave. I have things to do!" her reply was definite and she continued with the up and down movement of the churn handle.

"The cow has to be milked an' there's eggs to gather. Supper has to be set on for the men folk."

"Tom'll take care of those things." Billy lifted the lid and looked at the golden chunks of butter floating to the top.

"Look here Kylee. That butter's near done. Paw'll have fresh buttermilk. You can make him a cornbread before we leave, that'll make him satisfied. There's that ham you baked yesterday, an' sweet taters. They'll make out; they ain't starved yet, that I've know'd. It won't hurt 'em a bit to take care of things for a change. They'll do it. Come on now Kylee, hurry. I'll help," he coaxed and promised at the same time. "'Sides Tom's here."

An apple fell bouncing soundly on top of Billy's head then dropped with a bang on the lid of the churn. He grabbed the injured area. "Ouch, you little bugger. Just for that, I'll eat you!" he exclaimed picking up the apple from the churn lid. Billy had always been told that his love for apples stemmed from his mother's superlative urge for the fruit when she was pregnant with him.

Kylee couldn't hold back the laughter that bubbled up at Billy's enthusiasm. She shook her head in refusal, at the same time realizing this skinny, lanky, bashful boy had become very dear to her. How could she deny him anything? She was weakening, giving in, like butter in his hands.

"You'll like the Stewarts, Kylee. You'll get to be 'round some women folk for a change. There's Mary, an' Ginny, an' little Emily. No one can help fallin' in love with little Em." He grinned at her in a most appealing way, the happiness shining in his eyes at the thought of seeing Mary.

"Well, if you think Uncle Ira won't mind. I wouldn't want to anger him."

Billy finished eating the apple and tossed the core over the fence to old Red, the mule. He lifted the churn and headed for the house.

"I'll have to work the butter first. Then set out somethin' for supper." Her words went over Billy's head, ignored. She straightened her skirts and hurried to keep up with Billy's long stride. Knowing he had not listened to a word she said.

Kylee worked the butter and set a pan of cornbread to bake on the hot coals of the fireplace. Then she set about brushing and twisting her hair into a tight bun, securing it at the back of her head. She was setting the cornbread off the fire, getting ready to leave with Billy when Tom came in from the mill. Billy quickly gave him a detailed report of their plans.

"I've been thinkin' on goin' over to Jan's myself. I have his meal ground an' loaded in the small wagon. I was lookin' for a chance to take it over an' stay on for the preachin'. I ain't seen Preacher Andy for a coon's age. Or the Stewarts," Tom said as he poured hot water from the kettle into the basin.

He cooled the water with a dipper full from the bucket and began to wash. He watched Kylee through the mirror wrapping the cornbread in a clean towel.

"Paw an' Matt'll be back from Kentucky before dark. We'll leave a message. Matt'll milk Daisy an' handle things 'till we get back." Tom's mind was spinning as he talked.

He had been trying to plan a way to have some time with Kylee. Since her arrival Billy had occupied her completely. He was allowing himself a pang of anger toward his younger brother for monopolizing all of Kylee's spare time. He watched her closely through the mirror. Why did she always twist her hair up in that snug bun? Thick shining hair like Kylee's should hang loose down her back in a long fall, to be admired.

He could see her tying some cookies and a cake inside a tablecloth. He smiled with satisfaction as an auburn curl crept out of the tight restriction to hang freely on her shoulder. Tom sharpened his razor on the strap getting ready to shave. Kylee tucked the stubborn curl impatiently back into place. Tom shook his head in disbelief.

"If you'd like Billy, you can ride Jole'. I'll drive the wagon. It's loaded an' ready to roll. Kylee can ride with me."

"You mean you'd trust me to have a ride on Jole'?" Billy couldn't believe his good luck. Tom was totally tight-fisted where Jole' was concerned.

"Well then, hurry up you two, let's go!" Billy exclaimed anxious to be on his way.

It was too easy, Tom thought as he climbed onto the wagon seat beside Kylee. He had felt certain Billy would insist on staying beside the pretty cousin.

The low bed of the wagon was loaded level with sacks of meal. A high seat with no back bounced roughly above the wagon bed. The goodies Kylee had tied into the clean white tablecloth were tucked securely between them on the seat. The sweet smell of the blackberry cake she had baked that morning hung suspended over the wagon. It's spicy fragrance; pure torture to Tom, reminding him it had been a long time since breakfast. So engrossed were the trio in getting ready, they had forgotten to take time for lunch.

Kylee smiled to herself as she saw Billy hang Tom's banjo over his shoulder. Carefully he wrapped his fiddle in an old shawl of his mother's and placed it with loving tenderness inside the wagon against the tailgate.

The day was becoming hot and the chirping of the birds filled the air with a pending excitement. They crossed the bridge below the mill and the thick trees closed in around them. Deep ruts in the road left by the big freight wagons had filled with a soft powdery dust creating a perfect cover for the rocks that became a constant threat to the smaller wheels. Tom held the team steady, moving at a rapid pace down the winding road.

Billy rode out ahead, anxious to be on his way. The beautiful day and the thought of seeing Mary put him in high spirits. He guided Jole' in and out among the many trees along the edge of the road staying ahead of Kylee and Tom. Billy loved the hill country; it was the only place he knew. He adored its beauty with a strong passion. He marveled at the elusive haze that hung over the valleys on a hot day. He enjoyed the feel of the mountain rain on his face and the rustle of the wind in his hair.

He delighted in the first frost of winter that disguised the grassy meadows and broad leaf fern with a white peppery covering reminding Billy of hominy grits. On a hot fall day like this, he would long for a soft wet snow. White blankets clinging to the trees and bushes turned his world of green into a fairyland of white. Even the droughts that dried the streams emptied the wells and left the earth baked and dying did not upset him. They never lasted long and the pines even then stayed cool and green. With his increasing love for Mary he wanted to marry her and raise his children in this corner of God's green earth.

His heart was almost bursting with happiness. Wrapping the reins around the saddle horn, he slid the banjo around to his front and picked a tune. The sound of the banjo rang sharply upon the atmosphere joining with the whispering pines. He joined his voice to the melodious song.

> *"One thing that would make me happy,*
> *two little babes to call me pappy.*
> *Ho-hum! Black eyed Susan, Black eyed Susan Brown....."*

Jole' went along with the mood prancing and stepping fancy holding her head high. The flies hummed around the tails of the horses Tom was driving. He guided them expertly down the familiar narrow road. Beside him Kylee was very quiet. Tom wondered why her silence disturbed him. It was what he had wanted, to be alone with his lovely cousin. Now he was nervously at a loss for words, must be because of his mixed up feelings about her. Never before had he been ill at ease with a female. This one however, certainly unnerved him, especially when she sat so unreasonably silent.

Tom watched her from the corner of his eye as he guided the horses. Kylee sat rigidly straight, clutching tensely to the wagon seat trying hard to keep her balance. Was he driving too fast for her comfort? Reining in the team, he held them down to a slow rolling trot.

The ring of the banjo and Billy's song drifted in on their ears. It was a magnificent day and the music eased the tension. Tom found himself joining in Billy's song, his strong clear tenor reaching easily to the top of the highest hill.

"Love my wife, an' I love my babies.
Love my biscuits sopped in gravy.
Ho-hum! Black eyed Susan,
Black eyed Susan Brown..."

Feeling the relaxing effect of the music, Kylee loosened her grip on the wagon seat. Patting one hand on her knee she kept beat with the music, humming softly to herself.

Tom wrapped up in the music, failed to see the large rock that had rolled into the road. A front wheel struck hard, rolled back, then bounced roughly over the barrier tipping the wagon dangerously. Quickly catching his balance, Tom's song stopped in midair. He concentrated on controlling the team and keeping the wagon upright. Reining the horses in firm and steady, he managed to keep them gentle.

Kylee lost her sitting position and squealing in fright fell backward into the wagon bed. Fortunately the sacks of cornmeal received her graciously, cradling her gently. Kicking her legs frantically at the empty air, she attempted to right herself succeeding only in wedging her body firmly between two sacks, legs straight in the air.

Tom, quick to realize her plight, pulled the horses to a stop. He held the reins firmly in one hand and offered the other to help Kylee. A brilliant flush covered her face as she struggled to right herself. The wire pins holding her hair in place loosened and it tumbled free. She looked around for her sunbonnet; it had to be somewhere, underneath her she supposed.

The sight of Kylee's green eyes round with surprise peeking between two black stocking clad legs and white bloomers tickled Tom's funny bone. Laying his head back, the laughter rang through the trees. He was not making light of her dilemma; it was just that she looked so dog gone funny stuck there with her feet waving in the air. Kylee was quick to take offense.

Ahead of them, Billy heard Tom's laughter. Looking back to see what caused the merriment, he decided it was nothing he couldn't hear about later and rode on.

Kylee flushed with anger, blamed Tom for her upset. Disgusted at her own clumsy awkwardness, she struck out furiously at the hand he offered her. She struggled to lift herself to a sitting position. Tom drew back his hand and waited as she climbed back onto the seat. Her face was scarlet from her effort and hair hanging wildly about her shoulders.

Tom still smiling with amusement looked into the trees. He waited as she struggled to straighten her skirts and gain control of her wayward hair succeeding only in a large soft bun at the nape of her neck. Big improvements over that tight wad on the top of her head, Tom thought. He liked the loose curls left unrestrained about her face and ears. Reaching back for her sunbonnet he handed it to her in a polite gesture.

Without gratitude she snatched it from his hand and placed it with wild abandonment on her head. She was exhausted from her struggle, breathing heavy, face still flushed, and her attitude was hostile. She was trying hard to regain her composure but was close to tears. She realized her face was red, that her hair was a mess, and was quick to blame Tom for her misery.

"You're completely hateful!" she told him spitefully, closing her lips in a thin tight line. The cutting chill in her voice froze the warm happiness of the day. Her low opinion and dislike for Tom complete.

"I sure am sorry, Kylee, 'bout the rock. It wasn't really my fault." Tom's laughter was silenced; not even a smile remained. He could see she was very upset and would not be talked out of her self-indulged hostility. It was very apparent that she found no amusement in the situation.

"Come on now, Kylee. If you're riled 'cause I saw your under things, you needn't be so all-fired upset. I've seen stockin's before an' bloomers. Matter a fact, they were on girls when I seen 'em," Tom confessed, looking sideways at the young woman as he started the horses.

She was not softening and he was becoming a trifle perturbed at her coldness. He had apologized, what more did she want? She even refused his gracious offer to help. Well, if that was the way she was going to be and hold to her indifference, he would just even the score with a little teasing fun.

"Maybe I've seen a mite more. Without stockin's, or bloomers!" he told her, a crooked grin twisting his lips.

Perhaps that would bring a smile out of her. He could see his teasing was only receiving a frozen look of distaste. His effort to appease the situation had only made things worse. Turning his eyes to the road he became quiet and sullen. He flicked the reins lightly on the horses' rumps.

"Giddee-up," he instructed them.

Horses, now there was something worthwhile. They had a heap more sense than women, except old Red, but then she wasn't a horse, just a dumb old mule.

"I'll just bet you have!" Kylee sullenly responded to Tom's statement. Thinking of the pictures she'd seen in Tom's room when cleaning.

But Tom was not listening. Kylee didn't care if his teeth were the whitest she'd ever seen. It didn't matter that he was even better looking than her cousin Jesse. It didn't give him the right to leer at her as he had done, then add insult to injury by laughing at her unfortunate tumble into the wagon.

Hating him fiercely, she wished she didn't have to finish the ride with him. She watched the side of the road and added the incident to her mental file under, 'Hate Tom!'

Tom tried to understand why his attempts to be friendly with this new member of his family only offended her. The happiness Billy's music had brought was ended. A tense quietness settled in around them. The afternoon was hot, as only a fall day can be and was becoming uncomfortable. Only the movement of the wagon creating its own slight breeze made it bearable.

They turned from the road and crossed a bridge over Pound River, which was little more than a stream this time of year. Underbrush grew thick and tangled. Dogwood and chestnut spread enormous branches twining together over the water making a heavy cool shade along its banks. They followed a narrow road for a short distance then forded Baldwin's Branch. The bridge Jan was going to rebuild was still in the, 'I'll do it later stage'. The road extended upward a few yards and widened out into a clearing.

The Stewart's house, sat close to the side of a hill surrounded by a grassy yard. A large rock chimney engulfed the center of one side. A wide porch spread the length of the front wall. Long posts under the porch held the house securely into the hill. Billy waited at the bottom of the wide steep stairs leading to the porch.

"Hall-lo the house!" he shouted, removing his hat and waving for Tom and Kylee to hurry.

At Billy's call, the screen door banged open and three girls appeared. The yard came alive, chickens clucked and pigs squealed. The quiet afternoon was vibrant with noise.

"It's Billy an' Tom!" the girls called.

"Mommy, mommy. Come see who's here! We'uns have company already!" the littlest girl called into the house jumping up and down flouncing her long ringlets about her shoulders and clapping her hands gleefully.

Billy dismounted and was up the steps two at a time, lifting the little girl above his head.

"Hi kitten. What a darlin' you're getting to be. Growin' so big, too. Still my sweetheart?" he questioned her, lowering her enough so he could see into her brown eyes shining with love. Holding her close, he touched his nose to hers. Chubby arms encircled his neck in a vise-like grip, hugging him tightly.

"Yes. Yes, Billy, I love you!" Emily confessed and planted a kiss soundly on Billy's mouth. "I ain't never gonna love no one else! Never!" she assured him, nodding her head up and down to enforce her words.

"Come on now, Em. That's enough of that. Billy has come to see us all. Now don't pester," Mary told her little sister, lifting her from Billy's arms and standing her on the porch floor.

"Hello, Billy," Mary looked shyly at Billy, her face beginning to flush.

Emily turned her interest to Tom and Kylee driving into the yard. Ginny, the middle sister smiled a happy welcome at Billy along with a verbal greeting. Her carrot orange hair was kinky curly and her light brown eyes flaked with yellow stars. She still had the chubbiness of childhood into her fourteenth year and was often depressed with the thought of never slimming down.

"Hi, ya'all. We've come for the preachin'. We come a bit early to help get things ready," Billy spoke to all of them, but his eyes were only for Mary.

Beautiful Mary. It was almost frightening to look at such loveliness. Her milk white skin had a high blush on her cheeks from the sight of Billy; her eyes veiled and dark brown, glowing with happiness and pleasure at his presence. Breathing a sigh of wonder, Billy hoped he hadn't waited too long.

Mary returned his searching look with a sultry smile and eyelids lowered just enough to entice him. How handsome he had become with his summer tan. It seemed ages since she had seen him last. Why had he waited so long? He used to visit so regularly. She was certain the time had passed slowly because of the dreams she'd been having about Billy. She tried to understand how come skinny Billy with the knobby knees had suddenly become the most important thing in her life. A blush covered over her face, a warming surge filling her entire body. Ducking her head she hoped Billy wouldn't notice or guess her thoughts or discover the fact that she was very new at the flirting game.

"Look at Mary, she's a blushin'. She's a blushin' 'cause Billy's here," Ginny teased jokingly, flashing a smile at Billy.

"Hush your mouth, Ginny!" Mary gave the younger girl a shove into the house wall. The jolt flipped Ginny's red hair and brought a spark of fire to her amber eyes.

"Well, you are too a blushin'. Just look at you, all red an' dewy eyed." Ginny, with her teasing ways, was not about to give up on such an opportunity. Mary was ignoring her and had turned to welcome Tom and his new cousin.

Tom hesitantly offered Kylee a helping hand down from the wagon expecting a refusal; to his surprise she accepted, but was not about to pleasure him with a look or an expression of gratitude. Fastening her eyes on Mary's back Kylee followed the girls into the kitchen.

The kitchen filled the lower level of the house. It was crowded with furniture and a large round table with chairs. A small fireplace was built into the back wall and a large Monarch iron and chrome range dominated the room. The huge black cook stove had been a wedding present from Bess's father. The young married couple had hauled it into the hills to their new home on Baldwin Branch. At that time it was the only one of its kind in the vicinity of Pound Mountain. A narrow bed built into the wall close to the fireplace served as a bed and a settee. Windows filled the south side of the room, letting in an abundance of sunshine making the room a happy cheery gathering place.

Hill life was hard for women, but Jan Stewart had tried in every way to lighten his wife's burden refusing to have her work in the fields, a place that was common to most hill women. To him she was a beautiful treasure to be pampered and cherished. He loved her and the three daughters she had given him with warm tender passion after the death of their baby son. Jan always longed for another son, "but the Lord had not seen fittin'", he would say. He lavished the longing for a son on his Cousin Mattie's boys. They were like his own. In return for his affection and kindness toward them, they loved and respected him.

Bess Stewart, a tall beautiful pastel blonde, bent and lifted a golden brown apple pie from the stove oven. Laughing at her little daughter as she dragged Tom and Billy into the stifling hot kitchen filled with luscious aromas.

"Billy, Tom, what a nice surprise! Didn't expect to see you all 'til tomorrow," Bess greeted them in her soft husky voice. Her cheeks flushed from the heat of the stove. Her brown eyes filled with joy at the visit from the two young men. Setting the pie on the warming oven to cool, she reached in and removed another and set it beside the first one and closed the oven door.

"I'm glad you've come. Of course you're stayin' the night," she said turning to give Billy a fond embrace. Bess reached for Tom to give him what she thought would be a quick hug, but Tom held her securely. He planted a kiss firmly on her cheek as she turned her head to look at Kylee.

"What a sight you are. You're so beautiful, Bess," Tom whispered in her ear.

"Go-on with you now, Tom," she quickly answered him, trying firmly to push him away.

"Is this Val's girl?" Bess questioned, trying to divert Tom's interest.

"Yes, this is Kylee, Bess. She's come to live with us," Tom stated, holding Bess closer.

Bess pushed forcefully on Tom trying to loosen his hold on her, very aware of the observing eyes in the room. Her face and neck became warm and pink, not from the heat of the oven alone but because she felt a warmth and eagerness in Tom's embrace that shouldn't be there.

"No wonder Jan never leaves home, even for a card game with a beauty like you around," Tom offered, still serious but offered a smile, releasing her reluctantly.

Early forties only increased Bess's golden blonde beauty. Shoulders held firmly erect, a rare beauty was there, soft, warm, and ever a pleasure for those who gazed upon her.

"By the way, where is Jan?" Tom asked, looking out the window trying to keep his eyes away from Bess.

"Him an' Alvin are out at the barn stackin' an' tyin' tobac. They'll not be in 'til that sun starts down behind the hill," Bess told him.

Mary and Ginny sat down on the stairs that led over the fireplace to the second story bedrooms and listened to the playful bantering between Tom and their mother. They eyed the stranger thoroughly. Kylee stood timidly in the door holding her sunbonnet. Emily was still hanging tightly to Billy.

"Come Mary, we must finish with dinner. Fetch the butter an' milk. Quick now, that's a dear. Ginny ready the table," Bess instructed the girls.

Mary took a brown bowl from the cabinet as she admired Kylee's heavy shining hair, still in disarray from the tumble in the wagon, and the cool greenness of her wide eyes. The Phelps's young cousin was almost as pretty as her mother, Mary thought. She had never seen anyone prettier than her mother, except maybe Taynee, or

Polly. Polly was awfully pretty, but not as beautiful as her mother or her friend Taynee.

"You sit here an' be comfortable," Mary said to Kylee pulling a chair out from the table in an offer of friendship and hospitality.

Emily promptly attached herself to Kylee's knee leaning heavily against it. She looked up at her with wide dark brown eyes. The four-year-old was all awe and curiosity. It was not often that they had 'furiners visit.

"Look's as if Kylee's in good hands. Come on Billy, we-uns'll go on out an' give Jan an' Alvin a hand. I brought Jan's meal an' feed. We'll stack it in the corn crib for now." Tom was out the door with Billy following close behind.

The long days had shortened. It seemed too early in the day for the sun to be setting. Tom hated the change from fall to winter, but loved the hot Indian summer days that were upon them. His eyes gloried in the burnished colors of autumn. The temperatures heated the days into the 80's and cooled the nights to almost freezing. Dry leaves covered the ground and if you were quiet you could hear a deer fifty yards away rattling around on the frozen earth.

No matter what time of year it was, Tom had to admit he had a passion for Bess Stewart. As he grew into a man, his warm friendly affection for her had developed into something much more. He was still thinking of her magnificent beauty as he climbed into the wagon beside Billy and headed for the tobacco shed.

"Are you a-likin' your new home?" Mary was venturing to know Kylee better. A shy smile followed her question.

"Yes, Uncle Ira an' the boys have been kind to me."

"We're sorry 'bout your paw. Ira will be glad having you here. He's kind, but he'll work ya too. He was good at drivin' his wife, Mattie. He'll see you're kept busy one way, tuther. Dear Mattie, she had so much to do, mindin' the boys an' the mill when Ira was so ill. After Billy was born, she weren't too well herself. Then he started them trips across the mountain, draggin' her an' the boys along all the time. Never allowed her a minute's rest. Carin' for that big house, too!" Bess was truly indignant of Ira's treatment of her friend.

"Workin' the fields while he was gallivantin' off buyin' whiskey," Bess rambled on. "Listenin' to his bellerin' all the time. Bein' afear'd of the Mitchell's didn't help her nerves any, neither. Never took no store 'bout it bein' her heart that gave up, the way they found her an' all. I know there was more to it than that," Bess sighed, thinking of how Mattie died, speaking in a stilled hushed voice looking out the window, her thoughts ages away. "It was strange. Very strange," her voice trailed.

The late afternoon sun coming through the windows lit a ball of light around her flaxen hair that was wound in a thick double braid about her head. She stirred the gravy and looked at the changing trees outside the window. Lifting the corner of her white apron, she dried away a tear rolling down her warm cheek.

It had been many years since they had found Mattie on the path. Bess still thought it strange, the black and blue mark that encircled her neck. As a young bride and new to the hills she was close to Mattie. They had been like sisters, raising their children together and sharing every facet of their lives.

"Now, Mommy. That ain't true 'bout Uncle Ira not bein' good to Aunt Mattie. He loved her very much. He's been terrible lonely since she died. It was her that wanted that big house, so it was up to her to care for it. She had the nicest clothes of anyone here, at least ways that's what I been told, an' her own buggy, too!" Mary spoke up strongly in Ira's defense.

"We must hush 'bout them things Mary, it's over now. I reckon I did put it a bit harshly, but I still miss Mattie so!" Bess looked apologetically at Kylee. "You must keep your place Mary, dear. You're not a grown woman yet."

"Ira is a good man. He'll be takin' you along with him too. He likes company on them long rides of his. You pay us no-never mind, the way we-uns ramble on. Guess Ira's told you that we are some relation, on Jan's side. Mattie was a cousin to him, so that makes you some relation to my girls there. Everyone on the mountain is related some way or 'tuther, 'ceptin' the Mitchells. Ain't many would claim them as relatives. I know it was Jay Mitchell's doin's what happened to Mattie. Ira just won't admit it!" Bess was back into the past again.

"Now Mommy, let that be. Kylee's not wantin' to hear 'bout them things even if'n she is our cousin." Mary was delighted to have a new cousin to share with Billy. She was a grown woman even if her mother didn't think so, anyways, almost. Didn't her feelings for Billy prove that? Hadn't her mother been married and expecting her first child when she was her age?

"You hold your tongue Mary, an' fetch the butter an' milk," Bess instructed her daughter again returning to the present and the preparation of the evening meal.

Bess looked at Kylee sitting tensely on the edge of the chair. A touch of fear filled her eyes. If Jay found out there was another woman at the mill could it mean danger for her? Would she end up as Mattie had? Bess shook her head to clear it of such thoughts. It was well known that Jay had promised to rape and kill all the Phelps's women.

Emily Ann had grown more curious of Kylee. She pushed her lips tightly into a half smile imbedding the dimples deep in her rosy cheeks. Her brown eyes snapped with mischief.

"You're really our cousin, our very own? You're gonna stay over with us?" The little girl declared looking directly into Kylee's eyes and asked seriously.

"Are you in love with Tommy-kins? Cause I seen you lookin' at him in that funny way when he was a huggin' mommy. Same way as Mary looks at Billy. Oh, she don't think I notice, but I do! I ain't as little as she thinks!"

"Hush, you little goose! Leave Kylee be. You could plague a mule to death," Mary declared lifting Emily onto a chair and setting a plate of green onions in front of her.

"There now, you peel those skins off them onions, darlin'. That'll keep you busy," Mary instructed her little sister, kissing the top of her head fondly.

"I don't want to, Mary. They make my hands stink," she wailed.

"Do it anyways! Would you like to come with me to the spring house, Kylee?" Mary invited, picking up the brown bowl and ignoring Emily.

"Wash your hands with a little salt." Mary told the child.

"Don't mind Em. She's little an' don't know what she's talkin' 'bout," Mary explained, noticing Kylee's confused look when the little girl had mentioned Tom.

Dogwood and persimmon trees lined the path to the springhouse. Interplaying lights of late afternoon traced patterns of shadows upon their moving bodies.

"If'n we hurry Kylee, I got a little tobac an' I secretly borrowed one of Uncle Alvin's pipes. We-uns can have a smoke," Mary confessed.

Mary's long blonde braids hung forward over her shoulders swishing back and forth across her breasts as she walked. Soft highlights sparked a soft sheen from her golden hair reminding Kylee of corn silk drying in the sun.

"Uncle Alvin would a let me have it anyways." Mary smiled mischievously at Kylee.

Mary pushed open the heavy oak door to the springhouse. Rock steps lead down to a room below. A steady stream of spring water flowed through the bottom, keeping the inside far cooler than the temperature outside. A blue enameled pail of milk covered with a white cloth was cooling in the running water. A bowl of butter, pickles and jars of jam sat on wooden shelves around the walls. Cured hams and bacon hung from the rafters safely away from the heat outside. A black snake appeared between the crocks of pickled corn and beans. It slithered back into a secluded hideaway next to the rock wall unconcerned with their presence.

"Shoo," Mary said, swishing her apron. "You're after that milk again." The snake was oblivious to her attempts to frighten it and slid slowly behind the rocks and out of sight.

Inside the springhouse was cool and the musty smell of wet wood and earth was heavy in Kylee's nostrils. It was the smell of rain on dry ground and a vegetable garden as your hoe turned the earth. It also smelled of growing things, and the scent of a rose garden in the early morning dew. It was the smell of burying, as her father's casket was lowered into a muddy grave. Kylee shivered as the damp air touched the back of her neck.

There was Mary heaping the little bowl with butter, setting it on the step and lifting the blue milk pail out of the water. Kylee shook herself, this then was reality, and this was what she must think about.

Mary dried the bottom of the bucket on her apron. She set it on the step beside the butter.

"There now, that's ready. Sit down, Kylee," Mary said, sitting down on the rock step motioning for Kylee to sit beside her.

Pushing the heavy door ajar, Mary made a crack to let in a small amount of sunshine, propping it open with a small rock. She took a clay pipe filled with tobacco and a long stick match from her apron pocket. Wiping the moisture from a flat rock with the apron, she struck the match. It flared slowly in the dim coolness. Holding it over the pipe, she sucked in slowly until the tobacco began to smoke then shook the match out and stuck it between two rocks. Putting her elbows on her knees she prepared to enjoy the pipe. After a minute Mary handed the pipe to Kylee.

"I don't know Mary, I never did this before," Kylee said nervously.

"You mean you never smoked, dipped snuff, or chewed? It's the easiest thing Kylee. Tain't hard at all," Mary promised as Kylee put the pipe in her mouth.

"Just draw in slowly, like you were gonna swallow, only don't. Easy now, you gotta keep puffin' or it'll go out." Mary laughed at Kylee's struggle.

Kylee was getting the hang of it, but the tobacco was fresh and hot and bit her tongue sharply. She handed the pipe back to Mary, covering her mouth with her hand as she choked back a gasp and started coughing.

"How long did it take you to learn?" Kylee asked between coughs. "Did someone teach you?" she questioned watching Mary puff on the clay pipe letting out little puffs of smoke from the side of her mouth like an old pro.

"My friend Polly taught me. She knows lots'a things. She ain't terrible at all like all them ole' tongue waggers say! They's all jealous 'cause their men folk go gallivanting 'round all the time. They're either off playin' cards or drinkin' whiskey, or makin' it, or both. Hangin' 'round Polly an' leavin' their women to hoe the corn en' tobac'," Mary enlightened Kylee, watching the head of the black snake as it appeared again at the bottom of the step.

"My man better not be lookin' at her! Least wise not that way, I aim to give him all he needs to keep him at home. I'll see he don't have no excuse to wander off." She smiled dreamily as she watched the snake slither away along the stream of water.

"We'd better be gettin' back." Mary stood up and offered the pipe to Kylee, but she shook her head in refusal.

"Mommy will be wonderin' what's keepin' us. She'll send Ginny along to see what we're up to. Ginny can get all kinds of notions. She can imagine all sorts a things."

Mary knocked the ashes from the pipe on the rock step and tucked it back into her apron pocket. Taking the rock away from the door she picked up the bowl of butter and handed Kylee the pail of milk. Letting Kylee out first into the startling evening sun, she pulled the heavy door closed behind them.

"Gosh-a-Friday, Mary. You must know lots. Me, I'm such a dumb-bell. I'd never know what to do to keep a man from wanderin'. Ain't they supposed to do that to keep you from gettin' pregnant? My Aunt Aggie an' the ladies at the church back home said if'n you sat on a man's lap you'd get pregnant for sure!" Kylee had never had a girlfriend to confide in before. She was spurred on by Mary's friendly smile.

"Really, Kylee! Polly says it takes lots more'n that. She ought a know. Mommy ain't had a baby since Emmie was born. She sits on Poppy's lap all the time. My cousin Eloise said, her momma told her, that if'n you let a man touch your knee you would die for sure! Lessen you're married of course. I don't aim on takin' any chances. Don't seem like there would be any harm in just kissin' a man. It'd pleasure me no end to kiss Billy. Maybe if'n he'd ask I'd even sit on his lap." Mary giggled ducking her head and blushing at the thought of what fun it would be to kiss Billy.

"Mary!" Kylee said in shocked astonishment, but returned the giggle.

"I know, Kylee, but..." Mary stood still and looked seriously at the other girl. "I'd even be willin' to have his baby. I think I'd like that." She stared out across the grass, watching a blue jay land in a tall tree next to the porch rail.

"You'd want to be married first, wouldn't you? That would be the proper thing." Kylee was definite.

"Oh, of course. I want to marry Billy. I guess I have loved him forever. I just cain't get myself to think of no one else. I suppose I love him better than anything in the world. But he ain't even looked like he was about to ask me to marry him." Mary thought of Billy's bashful ways and the day on the front porch.

"He's so bashful, he'll never do it! Tomorrow's my birthday; I'll be sixteen. Most girls here 'bouts are married before then. You don't think I'll be an old maid, do you?" Mary questioned her new friend, turning to see into Kylee's green eyes.

Kylee took a close look at Mary. Golden hair and dark brown eyes, smooth satin skin, long dark lashes, and eyebrows a dark contrast against her Dresden beauty. She shook her head.

"No Mary. If anyone'll be an old maid it'll be me. I'm almost nineteen an' I ain't even kissed a man," Kylee confessed and the two were happy over their secrets.

"We're best friends now, Kylee. When you're best friends, you're bound to keep things secret. You promise?" Mary said seriously and turned to watch the path again.

"I will, I promise I'll never tell anyone. But you know what Mary? Maybe you should tell Billy how you feel," Kylee suggested, shifting the pail of milk from one hand to the other.

"I could never do that. It wouldn't be proper." Mary flipped a blonde braid back across her shoulder smiling shyly at Kylee. "But I'd like to!" she added with another giggle.

A heavy dark cloud was forming over the forest behind the house and floated leisurely upward darkening the deep shadows around the pines. It rested with stubborn persistence across the bright blue sky.

"Now then, would you look at that?" Mary said with dismay. "It surely is a thunder cloud." She watched the dark cloud cover the tossing boughs of the trees.

"Maybe it will blow away," Kylee offered, looking at the sky. She swallowed hard, feeling sick and wishing she had never seen Uncle Alvin's pipe.

Suddenly Mary shivered feeling the wind blow across her. She froze. Her face became ashen, her breathing stilled. She stood transfixed, motionless on the path.

"Mary, what is it? What's wrong?" Kylee frantically questioned. "Has the tobacc' made you ill too?"

Kylee forgetting her own sick feelings was concerned for her new friend. Taking Mary's arm, she shook her firmly. Mary only looked at her blankly, not seeing. Kylee set the milk pail down on the path and shook her harder with both hands.

"Mary! Mary! Tell me please, what's the matter?"

"Oh, Kylee," Mary said shakily as the color returned to her pale face. "I feel just awful. It ain't the smokin'! I had a feelin' of dread. That cold wind chilled me to the bone." Mary was trembling so hard it was difficult for her to talk.

"It was awful! Like mommy says, it's as if someone had stepped across your buryin' place." Mary's brown eyes were wide with fright.

"I know, I just know it was a warnin'. I have this heavy dread upon me. I know somethin' terrible is gonna happen. I know it!" Mary took a deep breath. "Oh dear, I ain't gonna let it spoil my day. I ain't!"

"Nothin' is gonna happen Mary, at least not nothin' bad. Tomorrow is a special day. All your folks'll be here. 'Sides it's your birthday. When that ol' wind came up it chilled ya 'cause it's been so hot. There now. See, you're not shiverin' anymore." Kylee picked up the pail and put her other arm around the younger girl as if to protect her from a further onslaught of dread.

"You'll spend this evenin' with Billy and you're gonna see, he loves you too. I know it. Everything'll be wonderful. You'll see!" Kylee promised and hugged her arm around Mary tighter.

"I'll pray it don't rain an' spoil everything for tomorrow," Mary said, returning Kylee's hug. Thinking of Billy she had almost forgotten the moment before.

The heavy clouds still persisted overhead. Kylee shivered, she too would pray for a sunny day tomorrow. Once more the sorrow at her father's death closed in around her. She recalled again the pounding downpour on the night he died. Suddenly she felt very lonely. As they walked toward the house, she remembered for the first time in weeks, the hateful face of Kenus Hall and was glad again for the distance between them.

The two girls climbed the stairs and crossed the porch still arm in arm. Mary's dread of something terrible happening and the incident of the pipe were pushed into the back of Kylee's mind filed in a place beside the memory of her father, Kenus Hall, and Tom's intolerable behavior.

CHAPTER ELEVEN

The evening meal was a jolly affair filled with merriment, teasing, and laughter. Kylee felt the strong bond of love and affection between the Phelps men and the Stewarts.

The men had returned from the barn just as the women finished preparing the meal. Kylee liked Janice Stewart the moment he ducked his tall body through the door and came booming into the kitchen. Long arms encircled Tom and Billy's shoulders, towering above the two younger men. The frivolity they had just exchanged left them all flushed and winded from laughter. Kylee surmised the joke was of an indecent nature because Billy's face became even more vibrant pink when he looked at Mary.

Janice's six-foot-seven inches of muscle and brawn were topped with an abundant crop of reddish brown hair. 'Crop' was the only fitting word for Jan's deeply waved unruly, auburn mane. It sprang from his head like a well used feather duster. His orange red beard and thick hair made it impossible for Jan to keep a neat, well-groomed look. His eyes were dark brown as black strap molasses and twinkled with deep merriment. There was a hesitant question in them when he acknowledged Tom's introduction of Kylee. He stood always, with a slight stoop as if apologizing for his outrageous stature.

A small man with gray hair followed on the heels of the others. Kylee was to learn the pale bent man was Bess's brother, Uncle Alvin, owner of the pipe and matches. A long stay in a northern prison during the war and years of hard work in the coal mines left their mark on the man. He had come to Bess and Jan's to spend his aging years. The white of his eyes had yellowed from what Hail diagnosed as a liver disorder. But Ira insisted it was only his infernal habit of constant drinking. A small drop of moisture gathered at the end of his nose to hang there suspended indefinitely, never dropping.

After the meal was finished, Jan set out the pipes and tobacco. While the women washed the dishes and straightened the room, the men enjoyed their tobacco and a glass of brandy before the fire. Billy politely declined the offer.

Bess gathered her mending, which seemed to never end. If she could just keep Emily from climbing every tree and rock around, perhaps there would be a catch-up point. Sitting at the end of the table, she let the breeze from the open windows cool her body. The evening meal always tired her and she was glad it was over. On top of everything else, there had been the food preparation for the next day.

She had enjoyed the surprise visit of Tom and Billy and looked fondly at the two. Her eyes did not linger too long upon Tom for fear he would put something into her glance that wasn't there. Bess was very aware of Tom's increasing attraction for her. She wondered again about Kylee, thankful for her presence at the mill. It would lighten the Phelps's burden of being without a woman greatly. She was glad for Mary to have someone close to her own age to visit with. Taynee never came to see them any more and Polly, well, she didn't exactly approve of that young woman. She could tell from the laughter and giggles that ensued during the dish washing that Mary and Kylee had already become fast friends.

"Now Emily dear, you musn't be a nuisance. Quit pestering Billy. You could plague a body to death," Bess spoke gently to her little daughter who had been coaxing Billy to get his fiddle since the meal had finished.

"Perhaps Billy's too tired to pleasure us with a tune," Bess added, knowing full-well Billy was never too tired for some music.

"Okay, okay, little darlin' you've got me!" I'll play the fiddle if'n you'll coax Tom to get the banjo. Ain't never too tired for a tune,"

Billy assured Bess. "We're gonna have us some rip-snortin', toe tappin' music. You ready to do the dancin' Kitten?"

Emily stepped a little dance to prove her readiness then turned her beguiling ways to persuading Tom. "Please, please, Tommykins! Please do. My feet are just itchin'! Hurry, get your banjo." She was tapping her toes and clapping her hands to enforce her eagerness.

"We'll do it, sweetie! We sure will do it." He laughed at the little girl. Never would anyone have dared call him such a pet name as Tommy-kins, except an elfin little girl, his favorite, Emily Ann.

Billy drew the bow across the strings in a 'rip snortin' hoe down as Emily danced. The others clapped their hands keeping time with Emily's flying feet. She clapped, twirled, and bounced her curls. Tom picked and Billy fiddled. They tapped their toes, keeping time as the old tunes rang out. *Cripple Creek, Ragtime Annie, Turkey in the Straw,* and *Boil Them Cabbage Down:*

> *"Boil them cabbage down,*
> *Turn them hoecakes 'round.*
> *The only song that I kin sing,*
> *Is boil them cabbage down."*

Tom sang loudly, stepping a dance along with Emily as he played and clicking his heels in the air.

"Ya-hoo!" Jan yelled loudly and joined his clog to the dancing.

The tempo increased until Bess feared for the safety of the house. Emily finally gave out and fell exhausted against her mother's knee.

"Oh, what fun, what fun! Do some more, do some more!" Emily laughingly coaxed.

Uncle Alvin sat unnoticed on his cot in the corner, his jug of whiskey close by. He patted his foot quietly in time with the music, nodding his head until the drop of moisture at the end of his nose bounced up and down, but never dropped.

Tom laid aside the banjo and rested his elbow upon the mantel. He had watched Kylee clapping her hands happy with the music, apparently enjoying herself. He could tell she was still angry with him. She hadn't spoken or given him a glance all through the evening. Still puzzled, he wondered what he could do to get her to smile at him the way she did Billy.

Tom turned his glance to Mary sitting on a bench beside Kylee. He watched her closely but her eyes were only for Billy and she flirted with him brazenly. Billy was very aware and enjoying every minute. Tom couldn't help but laugh at Emily, her face rosy from the exertion of dancing, her brown eyes flashing with excitement. His eyes traveled to Bess where she sat under the lamp concentrating on her mending and tapping her toe. A smile crossed Tom's lips as he looked upon her loveliness with longing. A veiled look filled his eyes.

They were all exhausted from the exertion but Emily still coaxed for a story song. She tugged on Tom's sleeve, bringing him back from his dreaming of Bess.

"The one 'bout Pretty Polly," she pleaded.

Tom couldn't refuse the impish smile on her elfin face. Picking up the banjo again, he sang the history of *Pretty Polly*:

> *"Polly, pretty Polly, come take a walk with me*
> *"We'll go get married, some pleasure's to see.*
> *Oh, they went over hills and valleys so deep,*
> *Until pretty Polly she began to weep."*

Emily sat herself on Kylee's lap, hands folded listening intensely. Tom could see a tear glistening in her eyes as he sang of the unfaithfulness of Polly that led to her cruel murder.

> *"Oh, they went a bit further and what did they spy?*
> *A new dug grave with a spade lyin' by.*
> *He shot her in the heart and the blood it did flow.*
> *Down in the grave, pretty Polly did go.*
> *He put the dirt oer' her and turned away to go*
> *Down to the river where the deep water flow."*

At the last sad note of the song, they sighed, thinking of Polly's fate and the suicidal death of her sweetheart.

Jan dropped down in his rocker weary from keeping up with his small daughter's twirling feet. Lighting his pipe, he leaned forward, pondering the words of the song.

Ginny sat beside her mother content to be a part of such a happy group. Tom could hear her humming softly to his song. He could see the signs of the woman she was going to be. It wouldn't be long until she would be just as pretty as her sister Mary.

As he closed the song, his eyes rested again upon Bess. How beautiful she was. The angels in heaven would surely have the same warm glow. There it was again, the feeling he had for her. Why did he always feel this way when he looked at Bess? He didn't think of her as being older, only that each year his desire for her grew. As he thought of her it was as if he were singing for her alone. He wanted to hold her in his arms and lay his head upon the softness of those full breasts.

As he watched Bess he thought of his mother and the night they had found her. There had been a feeling in the air, a hushed feeling, the same as he felt now. The night birds had been singing just as they were outside this night. He shook his head with a start and brought himself back to the group in the room.

Jan fastened the screen door to the outside wall and closed the door from the moths that gathered to the lamp. They were in a small world of their own inside the room; everything and everyone outside, forgotten. A loud knock broke Tom's reverie and brought them all back to reality.

Janice opened the door as a second knock thundered demandingly into the room. The tall dark visitor framed in the open doorway was Jay Mitchell. Tom stiffened noticeably; his body became rigid, motionless. He was like part of the rock in the fireplace wall. Billy's flushed face paled.

"Evenin' Stewart," Mitchell greeted Jan. Wiping his sleeve across his mouth, Jay removed the tobacco juice from his lips. He offered his hand in a quiet gentle manner, not at all like the Mitchell Jan was used to. Removing his wide brimmed hat, he smoothed his uncombed hair waiting patiently for Jan to invite him in.

"Come in Jay," Jan held the door back to make room.

"You reckon we could talk out here, Jan? I wanted to see you private like." He tried a twisted smile for Jan's sake.

"I have no secrets from my family, Jay. However, we could talk outside, I reckon."

Jay backed away from the door and Jan stepped out onto the porch. The night was dark with no moon. Deep shadows hanging from the tall trees increased the blackness. Frogs croaked loudly, their cries sharp on the still night. Occasionally the song of a night bird could be heard. Jan made no move to close the door. The light fell sharply across the darkness of the porch.

"I've come to ask you, Jan, about Mary," Jay's voice was strong and forceful.

"She's a likely lass an' marryin' age. My boy Bob has a hankerin' for her. So I'd feel proud if you'd be willin' for them to marry up. Me an' the boys'll build them a cabin of their own below the orchard, for a start. She'd be well treated. Bob's a pleasurable boy an' does no chasin'. He's takin' with your gal. I can't get him interested in anything else." Jay straightened himself and replaced his hat as he spoke.

"Tarnation, Jay! The gal's only fifteen. I was hopin' to keep her at home for a while longer."

"For hell sake, Stewart! When I married Taynee's maw she was only fifteen. Nell was just fourteen. She had a set of twins before she were Mary's age! I tell you Jan; a girl's the sweetest at an early age! The boy's twenty-three an' grows idle from wantin' a woman. I can't get nothin' out'a the boy, mopin' 'round all the time! I keep tellin' him a visit down the mountain to Donkey might help. A go with Polly or some other no count girl would get his ambition back. But he ain't gonna listen to me; he's only got one gal on his mind, that's your lass. I cain't convince him that the way to forget one gal is to get another." As Jay talked he pushed his hat back and scratched his head puzzled.

"Now you'd think it would be them other lunk heads that would be a thinkin' about gettin' hitched. But they's not interested. They's too busy with other things. I'd like your hand on it, Jan." Mitchell's aggressive attitude filled the night. It was as if he expected even the darkness to do his bidding. He spat a long stream of tobacco juice across the porch rail.

"I never thought he had it in him to get married up," Jay continued, shaking his head. He reached his hand to Jan as if the matter was settled.

Jan ignored his out-stretched hand. He had not thought of Mary as the marrying age, she was still a child to him.

"I'd like your hand on it, Stewart!"

"I reckon I had best see if the lass would be willin', Jay, before I give my hand on it. After all she's the one to say." Jan had made a promise to Bess never to marry the girls off unless they were willing.

"Now Jan, you know you gotta put your foot down with women folk! If you let them have their way your knee deep in cow shit. They'd never let you have a drink of shine, nor a card game, ever!" Jay responded a note of anger filling his voice.

"I aim to let her have her say, anyway," Jan was definite and he stepped back into the room. Jay followed waiting, filling the doorway, the dark night a black frame around him.

The group in the room had remained silent, each with their own thoughts. The conversation on the porch had been hushed and low. Each time Jay raised his voice to a high pitch they could hear Mary and Bob's names filter into the room. Mary was certain, without a doubt what Jay's visit was about. She shivered and again the dread was upon her.

On occasion she met Bob in the woods. He would come to the cornfield at the back of the house when they were tying fodder and would want to talk. Realizing he was a lonely person she was nice to him and let him help her herd the cows into the barn for milking. She would have him help her dig roots for Hail. When his attention became more demanding and he mentioned marrying, she treated his proposal as a joke and had laughed at him.

"I'm not ready for marryin', least ways not with you Bob. We're just friends."

Bob had been angry, almost in a rage. He grabbed her roughly, holding her in his arms, trying to force an unwanted kiss upon her lips. Struggling to free herself, she pushed him away roughly. She remembered Bob's unhappy voice following her as she ran to the house.

"I'm sorry Mary, come back. I never meant to frighten you. I only wanted you to know I love you. I want to ask your paw for you. Please Mary, come back! Mary!" His loud call had followed her down the trail.

She had seen him watching her from a distance. But he had never approached her again. She thought he had forgotten his thoughts of marriage. Now as she listened, she was afraid her father might consent to Jay's proposal. A chill filled her. She began to tremble inside. It was her duty to honor her father's wishes.

"Come here, Mary," her father's voice was kind and gentle. He held out his arm for her to come to the door. Jan could feel her trembling and held her close with a long arm.

"You needn't be afear'd child. Jay has come to ask if you'd be willin' to marry up with Bob. I told him it was for you to say. Marryin' is a serious business. I want for you to be sure. If you're willin', then I'll give my blessin'."

Mary loved her father very much at that moment. Feeling the strength of the big man, she knew she had nothing to fear. With head held high she faced Jay Mitchell.

"Your Paw's tellin' you right. My Bob's wantin' to marry with you. It's not like as if he were a stranger. You've knowed him since you was kids. You couldn't do better, Mary. He's a good boy," Jay announced with some pride at last in his third son.

Very aware of Tom and Billy's presence in the room, Jay hated them for being there. Here they were, damn Phelps's, cluttering up his life again. As far as he was concerned, the incident was over, a wedding to plan.

"I'm sorry Mr. Mitchell. I cain't marry Bob. I feel no love for him," Mary offered, and gave the man a weak smile.

She had always feared Jay's dark looks and demanding ways. It was not his forcefulness that made her draw away now, but the blaze of fire in his black eyes. Bowing her head, she leaned heavily into her father as Jay's anger began to show.

"That's a little thing, girl!" Jay's voice boomed.

Jay had tried hard to keep his temper down and not frighten the girl. He could not control the hostility coming to light in his eyes. Finally the rage engulfed his face. There was no longer a need to pretend to be something he wasn't. He hated these people who thought they were better than he. A determination filled him. He would have the girl for his son. No one dared refuse Jay Bird Mitchell.

"You'll learn to love him after you've a passel of youngin's an' a cabin of your own to care for!" Jay's voice was hard with anger.

"I think not Jay. My daughter says no. We'll respect her wishes an' close the matter!" Jan informed the man and patted Mary's shoulder, reassuring her. But Mary could see Jay was not going to accept the no as definite.

"The hell we will! Love is a little thing. It's a firm hand that counts!" Jay growled.

"No, poppy, NO!" Mary whispered to her father.

Jan turned Mary back into the room and reached for the door.

"The girl has made her decision Jay. She says no. We'll respect that an' say goodnight!" Jan told Mitchell decisively.

Mary gave Jay a faint goodnight smile.

"You are a lovely one!" Jay sneered. "You think yourself too good for a Mitchell?" Jay was not satisfied. He saw Billy's eyes on the girl. It was plain how he felt. It was there for all to see. Taynee was right; Mary loved Billy Phelps. Well, he'd see about that.

"I reckon that's not so," Jan said calmly.

"I'll give her a little time to change her mind." Jay's voice held a sinister warning. "You both change your minds, or someone's gonna be sorry. You put your foot down with women. Right on top of them, if you have to." Jay turned sharply and left in angry haste not waiting for another answer.

"Is that a threat, Mitchell?" Janice leaned out the door and called after Jay.

The only reply he received was the silence of the night. Then the faint echo of horse hooves crossing the creek below the house reached his ears.

"It's settled," Jan informed the family as he turned back into the room. "Ain't gonna be no more of it!"

Jan was visibly upset over the matter. Through the years, even with the disapproval of the families in the hills, he had stayed neutral when the feud flared because of his close friendship with Ira and relationship to Mattie. It had not been easy, but he had managed to stay on speaking terms with both the Mitchell's and the Phelps's. He could not take Jay's threat lightly. He was concerned for Mary, certain they had not heard the last of the incident. But no matter, he would not be intimidated.

"Off to bed now! There's pallets on the floor for Tom an' Billy. The girls will share with Kylee," Jan instructed.

Bess, with Mary's help, spread the corn shuck ticks and feather quilts on the floor. Uncle Alvin was already sound asleep on his cot in the corner, fully clothed. Bess lovingly covered him with a patchwork quilt and tenderly smoothed the graying hair from his closed eyes. She remembered the man he used to be before the war and constant drinking had claimed his health.

"Night, ya'all. Come along wife, tomorrow will be a busy day. We must rise early an' make ready."

While Jay and Jan were talking, Emily had cuddled herself into Kylee's lap and was immediately engulfed in slumber. Her father lifted her sleeping form into his strong arms and carried her up the stairs.

"Say your goodnights girls, an' up to bed." A smile found its way through Jan's massive copper colored beard.

Bess followed him carrying extra quilts and the lamp from the table, leaving only the glow of the fireplace to light the room. Ginny followed close behind them, yawning widely. It hadn't taken any coaxing for her; she was ready for sleep.

Tagging along behind, Kylee waited on the second step expecting Mary to follow. When Mary moved toward the stairs, Billy reached to detain her.

"Wait, Mary. Can we talk?" Billy asked in a low voice. Taking her arm he guided her over to the fireplace where Jan had started a small fire for light.

Feeling Billy's touch, she was confused and shy. She hung her head and looked at the floor unable to look into his eyes. They stood for a long moment looking into what was left of the fire.

"I have somethin' for you, Mary. It's for your birthday, but I want to give it to you before tomorrow."

Tom left the cabin. He could see he was not needed at this particular moment in Billy's life. On the porch he stood waiting for his eyes to adjust to the heavy darkness. Then he headed for the little outhouse tucked against the wooded hill.

SHADOW OF THE PINES

Inside, the cabin was dim, the fire only a bed of glowing coals. Long wispy shadows danced on Mary's and Billy's faces. Billy took the package from his shirt pocket and handed it to Mary with a wide grin.

"Happy birthday, Mary."

Mary ducked her head and studied the knot as she untied the yarn, hoping that Billy would not notice the shaking in her hands caused from his nearness. Dropping the wrappings on the remainder of the fire she slowly lifted the lid on the black box with trembling fingers.

"Oh, Billy!"

The crystal beads lying in a circle on the red lining reflected the flame as the tissue paper blazed up the chimney. Bright red and blue lights flashed about the rafters.

"Oh!" Mary caught her breath. "They are just wonderful, Billy!"

In a moment of extreme pleasure she forgot her nervousness and the chilling dread. She stood on her tiptoes and kissed Billy soundly on the cheek. Then realizing her boldness, she backed away and ducked her head fastening her gaze upon the beauty of the beads.

"They are the most beautiful things I've ever seen." Mary ventured to break the silence that was settling between them.

"Thank you. I hope Poppy will let me keep them. You know how parents feel 'bout gifts from boys. They say boys expect somethin' in return." Mary's cheeks flamed crimson.

"No Mary, no. That isn't the reason at all. I wanted to tell you in some way how I feel. I would have died if your paw had a promised you to Bob. I gotta tell you now before it's too late." Billy had been spurred on by Mary's bold kiss on his cheek.

"I love you Mary. I love you so much I cain't bare it. If you don't feel the same 'bout me, I'll die."

Mary looked up with an ecstatic look directly into his eyes. Her flirting glances through the evening had imparted to Billy a message that she would welcome his embrace. Billy took the box from Mary's hand, closed the lid and set it on the mantel.

In a daring move, Billy put his arms around her waist and held her firmly. Mary tilted her head back and put her lips in a dangerously close position. She took a quick intake of breath as Billy boldly held her tighter. He smiled at her, the light in his eyes almost teasing. Then his usual shyness turned to total seriousness.

"If you love me, Mary an' you'll be my wife, tell me when I can speak to your paw. I cain't wait long," Billy told her, the teasing gleam in his eyes turning into dark pools. His voice was soft, low, and husky with emotion.

It was here. The moment Mary had been dreaming of. The moment she thought would never happen. Billy was asking her to marry him! His arms were around her, her lips a fraction away. Maybe, just maybe, if she leaned a little closer he would kiss her and not wait another minute. She pushed her body into his. It was all the invitation Billy needed. He lowered his head to meet her trembling lips. Reaching her arms around his neck, lips slightly parted, she lifted them to Billy for their first real kiss.

They had forgotten Kylee was waiting on the stairs. She turned and went to the top to wait for Mary, feeling that she was intruding on a moment belonging only to them.

"Billy, Billy," Mary sighed against his lips. "I do love you, I do. Yes, yes, I want to marry you!" she whispered taking her lips away.

"Speak to Poppy soon as the tobacc is tied an' sold. He'll be in a good mood then," she informed Billy, eyes wide with love and dreams then gave her lips for another kiss.

A kiss more heated than the first, more demanding and longer. Mary pulled back breathless looking up at Billy with wonder in her eyes. There was no resemblance to the bashful boy she knew. His kisses and the look on his face were that of a man in love with a woman, the childhood playmate gone forever.

Tom came in bringing the fresh smell of the dark night. The couple broke apart, blushing crimson at being caught in such an enraptured embrace.

"See you in the mornin', Billy," Mary promised, freeing herself she picked up the box that held the precious beads. "Goodnight," she whispered to Billy.

"Goodnight, darlin'," Billy said softly swallowing hard and causing his Adam's apple to bob.

Bravely he took his sweetheart back into his arms and gave her a sound kiss, unmindful of Tom's teasing gaze. Mary totally confused and embarrassed broke free from Billy's embrace. Mumbling a low goodnight to Tom she ran up the stairs glad to be out of sight and away from the older man's knowing look.

"Uh-huh! The youngin's a man, grown an' not wastin' any time. You couldn't have picked a likelier gal. I'm tellin' you one thing, brother; there better not be any triflin'. You better hear me good! You treat that one with respect!" Tom said, laughing at his brother's look of hostility.

"I know'd that Tom! I'm gonna marry her, soon as Jan'll be willin'." It was all the information he volunteered. It was none of Tom's business anyway.

Billy went to bed crawling between the corn shuck mattress and the feather quilt, fully clothed. He would dream of Mary knowing now the sweetness of her lips, the softness of her arms, and the firm roundness of her body. They were real, much more than a mere dream.

"I ain't gonna wait long." He thought to himself still warm from her closeness. Something wonderful was happening to Billy. He was feeling the first real splendor of being a 'grown man', as Tom had said.

Tom rolled a cigarette from a packet of tobacco and papers he always carried in the pocket of his shirt. He fired a stick and lit the slim cylinder and inhaled deeply. Blowing out the smoke slowly, he leaned on the mantel enjoying the quietness of the room and the last glow of the flickering embers. There were times when it was nice to be alone he thought.

Flipping the remains of the finished cigarette into the ashes, he went to bed. He listened to Billy's heavy breathing as he slept listlessly. Tom could tell by his restless turning that the young man's dreams were unsettled. The boy was indeed becoming a man. There would be no living with him now until he made Mary his bride.

Tom struggled to keep his mind on Mary and Billy. But as the cabin filled with darkness, his thoughts kept returning to Bess knowing in his heart it was wrong to covet her loveliness.

CHAPTER TWELVE

The fall heat intensified. They were deep into the Indian summer days; even the nights failed to cool. The tobacco hung dry and cracking in the drying barn. The heady aroma smothered the heavy stench of cow and horse droppings. Above all, the unmistakable perfume of over ripe persimmons filled one's mind with the thought of the puckery sweet fruit.

The morning dawned warm and still. Drying leaves that usually rustled and rattled as they trembled in the breeze hung to the trees immobile in the sultry air. A breeze was only a memory, remembered from a cool spring night. In their bedroom, tucked under the eaves of the Stewart's two-story house, the girls were already feeling the increasing humidity. The one window faced the east and was filled with a mellow sunshine.

The girls had been in the kitchen at dawn helping Bess. Thanks to their early morning efforts, lunch was packed. Baskets of goodies sat on the table waiting and ready to be hauled to the family cemetery on the hill behind the tobacco barn.

In Mary and Ginny's room, the girls gathered to ready themselves. Ginny had finished and was down the stairs on a run to help Billy load her father's wagon. Kylee was stripped to her chemise bathing her arms and neck. Mary was through with her turn at the washbowl and was dressing her little sister. Emily, distracted with the possibilities the day would bring twisted about excitedly making it very difficult for Mary to fasten her buttons.

"Emily Ann, if you don't stand still, I'll never get you done. Now stand still!" Mary demanded, pulling at the little girl's dress impatiently. "You're worse than a fly on a hog's back. I swear you're never still! We'll never be ready when Poppy is. Then you'll hear him bellerin'. You wouldn't want Kylee to hear that would you? Now hold still!" Mary gave the little girl a sharp rap on the head with her thumb and index finger hoping to quiet her.

"Ouch!" Emily exclaimed, sobbing in pain as the tears came to her eyes. "You don't have to be so cross! You're an ole' bear. I was gonna give you a kiss for your birthday. Now cause you're so mean I'll give it to Kylee."

She promptly went over to Kylee, pulling her down she bestowed a loud smack, tears and all, directly upon Kylee's lips then smiled triumphantly. The girls laughed, but Emily was not so easily reconciled. Folding her arms, she pouted gloriously waiting for Mary's apology.

"I'm sorry darlin'. I was a bit cross." Mary picked Emily up and hugged her firmly. "Let me kiss it better."

Emily instantly ducked her head, waiting for the kiss to be placed upon the injured area. Mary kissed the top of the mass of ringlets she had so tediously rolled on her finger and placed in layers.

"Now do I get a birthday kiss?"

Emily encircled Mary's neck with her dimpled arms and kissed her sister soundly on the lips.

"Happy birthday, Mary," she cooed, all smiles again and squirmed down to prance out of the room and down the stairs, all forgiven and forgotten.

"Finally that's done. Emily's always such a chore," Mary sighed pushing aside the curtain at the window, hoping for a breath of fresh air.

Kylee pulled her pink dress up over her shoulders, fastened the buttons and straightened the collar. She brushed and rolled her hair into a soft bun, pulling forward the small tendrils that crept around her face.

Mary chose a white blouse and blue skirt from the closet and put them on over her cotton petticoat grumbling because they looked so girlish. "I wish I had somethin' that looked older. After all, I am sixteen now. Kylee, I'm gonna marry Billy, if Poppa'll be willin'."

"I wanted to tell you Kylee, 'cause we're best friends now. Best friends share everything. Maybe I can fix my hair up so I'll look older, sort'a like yours Kylee. I've got to have it some way 'sides braids." Mary lifted her long hair and rolled it to the top of her head and held it for Kylee's appraisal.

"I suppose it would be proper, you're sixteen now," Kylee observed cheerfully.

"Oh well. I don't have any pins anyways," Mary said in disappointment letting her hair fall in a cascade around her shoulders. "I'll brush it down an' tie a ribbon around it."

"Now I need something to dress up this ole' blouse. I know! Oh, I wonder if I dare?" Mary said in deep thought as she finished brushing.

"I wasn't gonna wear these, but they're so beautiful. After all they are my birthday present from Billy." She reached into a drawer of the dresser where she was sitting and took out the box and opened it. "I think he would like it if I wore them." Mary explained as they watched crystal beads releasing a thousand flashing stars to dance about the walls of the sunny room.

"Oh, Mary, they are beautiful. I'm so excited for you an' Billy. Of course your poppa will be willin'! Billy is such a fine young man," Kylee said admiring the lovely beads. She was filled with happiness and pride at her new found friendship with Mary.

The day would be hot, promising to be uncomfortably humid before noon. Looking out the window they could see the vibrantly blue sky above the whiskered mountaintop. There was no sign of the dark clouds that had appeared the day before.

As they came down the stairs to join the family Jan gathered Mary in his long arms hugging and kissing her. Then he held her at arms length, eyeing her closely. There was a change in his daughter. Could turning sixteen make such a difference? Was it a brighter glow in her dark brown eyes, the carriage of her head framed with flaxen blonde hair, or the roundness of her body that he hadn't noticed before?

"Just look at you! I can hardly believe it. How can a night make such a change in a lass? Is it 'cause you turned sixteen? Is that the reason, eh Kylee?" Jan looked at Kylee with a sly wink.

"Well, my darlin' girl, it had to happen sometime. My, don't you look like your mama? An' you, Kylee, what a lovely gal you be. There ain't much that pleasures a man's eyes more'n a pair of purty women, unless it is a pair of matched dapple grays. Off with you now. Billy has the wagon waiting at the front step. We'll be right along." Her father hastened them on their way.

The girls dangled their feet over the back of the wagon talking and laughing trying to be heard above Emily's loud singing:

"Oh, I went to the animal fair,
The birds and the bees were there.
The big baboon, in the light of the moon,
Was combin' his auburn hair..."

"Emily," her mother reprimanded. "That's not a song to sing on a day like this." But the little girl continued with Kylee and Mary joining her:

"The monkey, he got drunk
An' sat on the elephant's trunk.
The elephant sneezed
He fell on his knees,
An' that was the end of the monk,
The monk..."

They all laughed at the silly song. Billy, sitting on the wagon seat beside Bess and Jan tried to turn and get a view of Mary. They had been shy at breakfast trying not to look at each other afraid they might give their secret away. Mary hadn't escaped Tom's teasing looks. She hoped he wouldn't share his knowledge before Billy could speak to her father.

Tom left early driving Ira's wagon loaded with tools for building benches and tables. As they drew close to the cemetery on the hill, the ring of the hammer echoed through the trees. Above it the sound of Tom's strong tenor voice could be heard singing as he worked:

"Rock of ages, cleft for me.
Let me hide myself in thee..."

Mary's honey colored hair floated down her back in deep waves left from the tight braids. The shining soft color incited in Billy a deep longing. He smiled with pleasure as he sighted the beads around her neck. Lovely brown eyes caught his glance and he read a promise there. His stomach began to churn and he couldn't swallow. He would have to speak to Jan soon. He wouldn't wait long. He must not look too long at the way her blue skirt hugged her hips. He turned his eyes away trying to get his mind on something else. There was the picnic to concentrate on.

It wasn't hard for Billy to think about food with the array of goodies the women were setting on the tables. Pumpkin cake and apple pie, coleslaw with vinegar and cream dressing, a tub of pickled corn on the cob, fried chicken, molasses cookies, Kylee's blackberry cake as well as a large Virginia ham, sweet potatoes and a leg of lamb rounded out the feast.

Billy supposed he could keep his eyes away from Mary for a while. Now he was finding it hard to stay away from the food. He was beginning to wonder how Preacher Andy would be able to do justice to the preaching.

A number of wagons, buggies, and horses had already arrived at the cemetery. The women had busied themselves with the food and chatting with one another. The young people gathered together to renew old acquaintances.

Preacher Andy arrived with the Jennings where he had spent the night. He immediately mingled shaking hands with everyone. Andy Baldwin set his beliefs with the hard-shelled Baptist, which had a following in the hills. Wherever Andy preached he held a crowd. Most people like his fiery way of delivering the Word.

The preacher was a small friendly looking man with receding gray hair, clean-shaven, and very neat in appearance. Laughing gray eyes became clouded with seriousness as he watched the young people. He was depressed at the amount of guns, not too well hidden, carried by some men and boys. Watching a group at the edge of the clearing he did not fail to see the jug being passed around. He had long decided the older ones certainly did not set an example for the young. He could tolerate a drink in moderation, but not on Sunday, and not at a service such as this one. Especially not in front of the women folk who took their religion with hard headed conviction.

Andy shook his head. He knew all too well how hard it was to hold to moderation. Alcohol had been his ruination until he came to know the Lord. After shaking the habit of drinking he turned to his sister Mattie for help in learning to read. He had read his Bible over and over, memorizing scripture after scripture. When he informed them he had been called by the Lord to spread the word, Ira declared he was tetched. How could a man who had spent two-thirds of his life saturated in booze claim to be called by the Lord?

"I don't know either, but it's the truth. I've been called!" Andy tried to explain.

Ira's stubbornness would not allow him to see. Andy tried to convince his brother-in-law to give up the whiskey trade claiming it was a tool of the devil and would be the undoing of the Phelps family. Ira promptly retaliated with a firm demand that he keep his nose out of his business and stay away from the mill.

Andy stayed away. When he preached at different places in the hills Mattie took the boys, but Ira stayed home. Through the years they never made up their differences. Andy sorrowed over his sister's death, but more over Ira's unsaved soul.

He tried to help Mattie's boys. Billy was bending, but Matt and Tom kept to their wild ways. He understood how it was to be young. He would be patient and pray for the Lord to touch them.

"Mornin' Mary." Tipping his hat he spoke to Mary as she passed with Kylee.

"My, what purty young things. Help the fellows, Lord! They'll need all the help you can give them this day." He thought and lifted his eyes to the sky.

The hill people were firm in tradition holding to the old Methodist or Baptist ways, claiming to be either soft-shell or hard-shell, each with their own way of belief. No matter what their differences, they all gathered to hear Preacher Andy.

He started by reminding them they were all there to remember one who had been called away to be with Jesus the year before. Rueberry was a good man who had long ago declared his belief in Jesus as his Savior. He reminded them of the man's good points and asked God's blessings on all those present. Then be began his preaching in earnest.

He assured them all that if they continued to be sinners they would surely be punished and that the punishment of sin was surely death forever. He went on to tell them that there was a promise of forgiveness for sinners in the blood of Jesus if we but come to the cross and ask. Through His grace they could be saved.

"Yes, brothers'n sisters, when we disobey the Word of God, then do we surely sin! When we lust after the flesh an' covet thy neighbor's wife an' his prize mule, then do we surely sin. We all fall short of the glory of God. We must try to live by his commandments and by the one that Jesus gave his disciples that we love one another!" He went on and on.

The sun rose high and blazed away in the center of its orbit. Stomachs became lean and still Andy preached.

"An-ah, God planned a way for us sinners. An-ah, he sent his son to die in payment for our sins," his voice rose to a high, singsong pitch. "You can only come to God through Jesus Christ!" He went on waving his arms and slapping a hand into his open palm. He promised them God's gift of eternal life if they received Jesus into their hearts. Perspiration began to form on his upper lip. He removed his suit jacket uncovering his already wet shirt.

"When brethren? When will you receive the gift? You do not buy, work, or trade for it in case some might boast, but-ah-it is a gift from Him. An-ah, it has already been paid for by Jesus' blood. An-ah, brothers an' sisters ah, when are you gonna be reborn an' become children of God an' join his body an-ah, know his love an' forgiveness? Seek ye righteousness, be ye baptized an' receive the Holy Spirit."

Hallelujahs were heard among the group. Andy was shouting, engulfed with the feeling of the gospel he was preaching. Women were crying and shouting with him. Men sat with their heads bowed telling themselves they would do better and live in the ways of the Lord, promises that would quickly be forgotten.

"We must not be mistaken an' believe that we can sin forever an' still receive his forgiveness. He will quit striven' with us. There is a point beyond redemption, a point past His forgiveness, ah, do not let yourself reach that point. Ah, be quick brothers'n sisters; accept Jesus in your heart, then will you have a real desire to quit practicin' sin. Ah, receive Jesus an' his sacrificin' blood upon the cross, ah- an', his glorious resurrection from the tomb. That we might believe. Ah, if you live by his laws, accept his blood, then receive the gift brought by Jesus, eternal life, by His grace." Andy's voice lowered as he softly added a prayer. "In Jesus' name." Then a soft but forceful, "Amen." He was finished then added in a short, "bless this food dear Lord, Amen. Let's eat!"

Billy sat on a low stump listening earnestly thinking about the preacher's words about coveting and lusting after the flesh. He ducked his head and looked at his feet. Could his Uncle Andy see into his very soul and read his desire for Mary there? He wanted the Lord to understand his feelings for the girl was not lust. Only love and a burning desire to make her his wife.

When lunch was over the singing began. Tom with his strong full tenor voice full of warmth and loud volume reached out among the crowd and flowed into the treetops. He'd sing out the line, then the group would join him repeating the words.

Billy remembered how Tom used to sing when working the fields, lifting his head and letting his voice out to the mountains. It spilled into the trees and echoed back down the hollow. That had been a few years back. They hadn't harvested the fields since the whiskey trade had become so profitable.

After the lunch things were packed away into the wagons Bess and Jan worked to beautify the grave of their infant son. Jan cleared away the dried weeds and unwanted rubbish while his wife repainted the white wooden marker. Bess thought she saw Bob Mitchell at the edge of the cemetery away from the group, hugging into the trees. Because of the events of the previous night the undiscernable appearance concerned her. When she informed Jan he assured her she had been mistaken. He was certain none of the Mitchells would dare appear at the gathering.

Bess was not convinced and kept a close watch, but she did not see the shadowy figure again and thought perhaps she had been wrong. Bob had been like her own child at one time, and she felt concern for him under Jay's influence. She was living in the past, remembering that having Bob and his brothers at the time she lost her baby son had saved her mind and helped her to live with the grief. She could never quite understand the grudge between the Phelps's and Mitchells, thinking that to hold so much hate was dangerous. Blaming some of the Mitchell's bitterness and meanness on the way the hill people shunned them.

Billy visited with Carl and some friends and relation he hadn't seen for sometime. They snacked on cookies, cakes, and pies that had been left on the tables for later appetites. He noticed the young people beginning to spread out and pair off. He spotted Mary with Ginny and Kylee following some couples down a trail leading into a wooded area. There had not been a chance all day to be with Mary. Billy followed them to a grove hidden safely away from Preacher Andy's spiritual guidance and parental eyes. Young people were gathered around a large chestnut stump. They were involved in a sport that was popular entertainment in the hills, but forbidden at church meetings. The young people would gather in a secluded spot to do their stump dancing.

It was Tom's turn on the stump. As he tapped a rhythmic tune several young men took up the beat clapping their hands and drumming their thighs in time to the tapping. Tom's trim weight and natural rhythm made the dancing easy and fun for him. As the clapping became louder Tom tapped his heels and toes faster. Composing together a fast light-hearted melody to float about the little group. Tap, tap-clap, clap-tap, tap-clap, clap, clap, twirl and jump.

The tempo increased. The hand beat became faster and faster patting in time to see how fast Tom could step. Until he became short of breath and pleaded with them to stop, he'd had enough.

Sitting down on the stump he fanned his face with a hat that belonged to a cousin. Blonde hair hung limp with perspiration and light blue eyes glowed with happy satisfaction.

"Yah-hoo, Tom. You did all right; you did all right! The best yet," the cousin complimented Tom taking his hat back and placing it on his head.

"You out did us," he patted Tom on the back.

"I could of gone longer, but I thought I had better give you all a rest. Didn't want to wear your hands out. Think I'll go back to singin'. It's easier." Tom laughed and picked up his suit coat hanging on a bush and slung it over his shoulder. He gave a wave to the group and disappeared up the path.

Billy sought out Mary standing beside Kylee engrossed with the step dancing. Cautiously he took her hand as she smiled up at him. He looked around Mary and spoke to Kylee, "Did you enjoy the preachin' Kylee an' the picnic?"

Kylee answered with a smile and a nod. She did not say but she liked the stump dancing best of all, admitting to herself, there was something special about the young man who was dancing. He hadn't seemed at all like the same Tom Phelps who had been so insolent in the wagon the day before.

"Mary an' I are gonna walk on back down to the house." Billy tugged slightly on Mary's hand.

"Ginny, tell your paw so's he'll not get mad. We'll see you all back at the house." He pulled Mary away from the group and onto the path.

"I think that's rude of you Billy. After all we'uns came together. Poppy'll be madder then a wet hen. You'll see!" Ginny called after them.

Billy and Mary walked faster disappearing into a sea of trees unconcerned with Ginny's observation. Billy only wanted to get Mary alone so he could talk to her, hold her in his arms, and tell her again how much he loved her. He needed to be near her.

The couple stayed on the narrow trail avoiding the road. Even now they could hear some of the wagons pulling away from the cemetery moving down to Pound road and heading home. Above the sound of the rolling wheels and horses hooves rose Tom's voice:

"I am a poor, wayfarin' stranger,
Left in this world to weep and mourn..."

The day remained humid and sticky making their Sunday clothing extremely uncomfortable. The thickness of the many trees only held in the heat. Mary's long blonde hair clung heavy on her neck. The damp weight had pulled out the tight waves until it hung straight down her back. Now that they were alone Billy could say nothing. The old shyness had returned. He felt nervous and awkward.

Watching closely Mary could see the tense tightening of the muscles in Billy's jaw. Knowing she was the cause filled her with a tinkling sensation, a sense of power. An attractive glow covered her cheeks. Billy's closeness was something she felt with every nerve in her body. She picked up a large stick lying in the path, very suitable for walking.

They walked slower, extending the time to be alone together and feasting their eyes on the beauty around them. The vibrant colors of the fall wild flowers reminded Mary of her mother recalling how her father teased her about the flowerbeds she tended so carefully.

Tediously her mother carried water from the well or creek. With care she fenced out the pigs and chickens. "Don't know why you spend so much time on them there flowers. You cain't eat them!" her father would josh.

"You can feast your eyes on them, Jan," Bess would retort with feeling. "Sometimes that's important, to fill your eyes with beauty."

"My eyes are filled with beauty every time I look at you. That's all the beauty my eyes need to feast on!" Jan would be quick to tell Bess. "Sides, there's beauty all 'round you woman. All you gotta do is look if'n you're a seekin'."

"I know dear. These hills are a lovely place. I know I cain't improve on what the Lord has done already. I just want to add a little of my own." Jan finally relinquished and left her alone to fuss over her flowers.

The large trees along the seldom-traveled path grew tall with wide spreading branches closing out the sky above Mary and Billy. So thick covered with bright colored leaves they refused the passage of the sun's rays. Occasionally a stray beam, by chance, would find its way through the barrier to rest hesitantly on a bed of soft chestnut twigs.

A movement of air found its way up the trail and cooled the warmth on Mary's flushed cheeks. She breathed in deeply taking advantage of the wayward breeze. Hearing the intake of breath Billy turned to look at her fully for the first time since they had left Kylee and Ginny.

"Sure is warm," Billy commented in search for words.

Mary nodded her head. Billy stopped and picked a flower from a blossoming bush at the side of the path and handed it to his love.

"I'm just goin' over Jordan,
I'm just goin' over home."

The last of Tom's song trailed out faintly to them and was lost in the dense trees.

"Oh, how purty!" Mary exclaimed and tucked the flower behind her ear.

It flamed in burnished orange against her golden hair. The bright color brought forth the dancing highlights from the depths of Mary's brown eyes.

"I'm hopin' Mary that it don't take much longer to get the tobac' stacked an' tied. It's been so dry an' it'll crumble somethin' fierce. A little moisture in the air would help. I'm wantin' awful bad to ask your paw."

"Me too, Billy, but we gotta wait. Poppy's been in a real ill mood tryin' to find a buyer for the tobac' without haulin' it down to the auction barn in Norton. He's been workin' awful hard 'cause of it. I don't want to burden him with my needs right now. If we did, he might just tell us no. I couldn't stand that! We'll have to keep ourselves busy 'til the right time comes. If we don't get some rain, that darn tobac' might hang right there an' crumble to nothin'."

"I was thinkin' that it would pleasure him more at a time when he wasn't so worried. Sides, maybe we need more time, to make sure of what we'uns are a-doin'." Mary glanced shyly at Billy from under lowered eyelids.

She watched his lips tighten and she walked faster feeling Billy increase his hold on her hand. She tried to pull herself free.

"I'm sure of what I'm wantin' to do, Mary!" Billy's voice was firm with decision.

Mary pulled away from his tight hold and broke into a run down the dusty path. She moved out ahead of him raising clouds of dust with her feet as she ran waving the walking stick above her head.

"Race you to the barn! The last one there's a toad!" she called back to him. Her long hair floated out behind picking up the breeze her moving body created.

"Hey, that's not fair, Mary! You got a head start. Come back here. What's your all-fired hurry anyways? Don't run away from me! Mary!" Billy called after her fleeing form.

He broke into a high run determined to catch her. She rounded a bend and headed for the tobacco barn. Seeing her on the path ahead he watched her bright head vanish into a dip. When she appeared again it was on the road that led into the wide doors of the tobacco barn. She slowed down and disappeared inside.

Billy stopped at the door, winded and sweating. As he entered he closed his eyes momentarily adjusting them to the shadowy light inside. Perspiration had stained the underarms and back of his once clean white shirt. The garment had worked up and out of his trousers, his shirttail hanging loose at the back restricted only by his bright colored suspenders. Opening his eyes he looked around wondering where Mary was hiding.

"Over here Billy. I'm over here in the corner where the straw is piled." Mary called in a soft inviting voice.

The barn was high and wide. It was built with up and down slats angled and spaced for letting the air circulate drying the many rows of hanging tobacco. Billy ducked under the high racks of rustling leaves. Walking between the half filled lower racks he found Mary resting on a pile of straw stacked into the corner. The barn was dark and cool.

Billy breathed a sigh of pleasure as his body began to respond to the coolness inside the big building. The barn was filled with the smell of drying tobacco. He twitched his nose in distaste. He never liked the heavy musty aroma.

"It is so hot; all I could think about was how cool it would be in here. Come sit down, Billy, on the straw beside me." Mary invited, smiling as he settled beside her.

"You know, I was thinking; Kylee told me you were teachin' her how to play the banjo an' she's been teachin' you how to read. That's wonderful Billy. After we'uns are wed, I think you'll have to teach me how to play the banjo. Is it done like this?" She questioned him, holding the walking stick close to her body pretending it to be a banjo.

"Would you place your fingers just so on the strings?" Looking down at the imaginary banjo neck she placed her fingers in just the right position, playing a game of make believe with him, suppressing the desire to kiss him. "Really, Billy, if this isn't right you must show me," she coaxed playfully.

Eyes downcast, she was afraid to look at the young man. Billy's closeness was causing a giddy feeling inside, cutting off her oxygen. She couldn't breathe freely. Was she going to faint? She would invent anything at this point in her little game to make Billy put his arms around her.

"Well, sorta, exceptin' you'd have this arm out a little further. An' the banjo would fit up next to your belly, 'bout here," he explained pushing the stick closer to Mary's waist. He demonstrated then turned radiant pink as he realized what he'd done, but continued.

"This arm would rest on the edge of the banjo head, like that," he stammered, tenderly lifting her elbow away from her body. He rested it on the head of the imaginary banjo. Reaching his arm cautiously around her shoulders he showed her the position to place her other hand on the neck. As he did so, Mary turned her face to his.

"Oh," she sighed, "I see!"

Their faces were so close. Mary placed a slight kiss without pressure squarely on his lips.

Billy, not needing further invitation, pushed her gently backwards resting her head on his arm and removing the pretend banjo. He felt her arms moving slowly around him pulling him in closer. They laughed together at the ridiculous pretense. She placed her lips on his, the game was over, and reality began. Billy returned the kiss as they moved down into the straw.

Soft, soft were their kisses. Tenderly inviting in their young innocence until Billy felt his passion rise into a burning need for her. He kissed her harder urging her to respond. Sighing, she returned his kisses with full pressure and parted lips.

With one hand she stroked the back of his head and down his neck. Her other hand moved down his back pulling his body tightly close. His head was in turmoil. Mary! Sweet, lovely Mary, was all he could think of. Breaking the kiss he raised his head to look at her. Her eyes were closed, lips still parted and moist where his kiss had touched. A streak of light played through a broken plank on the barn wall and danced across Mary's face. The silver light turned her flowing hair into shimmering spun gold. The crystal beads around her neck caught the light and fired into a million flashing sparks. The prisms bounced about the bed of straw, on the walls, then danced across Billy's face like wild fireflies.

Mary lifted her dark lashes slowly and opened her eyes, veiled and inviting. She smiled at Billy in total submission. Preacher Andy and his sermon of the day were far away, his promise of eternal life, or hell-fire, forgotten.

"I love you, Billy. I love you so much I can hardly stand it. If you don't love me, I'll die!" She closed her eyes and lifted her lips for another kiss.

He kissed her slowly and caressed her arm running his fingers along the sleeve of her blouse. As she relaxed he moved cautiously to unfasten the row of buttons at the front of her blouse. Sliding his hand into her camisole Billy discovered the wonder of Mary. He was beginning to know what the pictures in Tom's room were all about and why his older brother liked having them there.

Tarnation, he thought as he continued exploring the soft firm expanses of Mary's body, kissing her again and again. He kissed her neck and the pale sweet valley where her young breasts separated.

"Oh Mary, I gotta have you! I cain't wait another minute. Please Mary, please." His voice was raspy, his throat dry. He tried to swallow but couldn't.

As his hand moved bolder with more insistence, Mary became cautious. She held his hand gently but firmly, staying its wandering. She decided this was not the time or place. It was a possibility someone might find them. She thought too of what Polly had told her. She was not ready yet for the total experience. She should not have allowed their emotions to get this far.

"No Billy. We best get on to the house. Some one will be lookin'" for us." In a patient voice she pleaded with him.

She couldn't believe the fiery passion of bashful Billy. With a warm smile she pushed him away. Lord, forgive her; she had been

179

ready, too. "Please Billy, stop," she coaxed a little more firmly. But Billy was not going to give up.

He silenced her with another burning kiss holding her down into the straw with his body. But Mary was adamant; she pushed him away and began to button her blouse. "We'uns are gonna wait."

"Don't push me away darlin'. You're so wonderful, sweet an' lovely. You feel so good. My God, I love you!" he declared trying to push away her sustaining hands.

"No!" Her answer was definite.

Her voice was stern, not warm with desire as it had been before, chastising Billy. He withdrew his wayward hand and cradled his head on her breast.

"I love you so much Mary. I want you terrible. I don't know how I can wait."

She held him close kissing the top of his head. Mary smoothed his hair as she kissed his ear waiting for him to see her point of view.

Billy's love was great enough; he could not chance making her angry; he would wait. Only the experience was so new and sweet, he wondered how he could live another day without her. As Mary rocked Billy to and fro saying nothing, just holding him she became aware of another presence. Someone had found them. She hoped it wasn't her poppa. She stiffened in Billy's arms. The new comer was lifting the hanging tobacco leaves. A long shaft of light from the door lay across the two sweethearts.

"Well now. Ain't this just peachy? I seen you two goin' down the path headin' this way. I figured you were up to somethin'." A chilling voice came from the sea of hanging tobacco.

"I had to sneak 'round gettin' here bein' careful no one saw me. You know how this bunch feels about Mitchells."

Framed against the ball of light Mary could only see faintly. Squinting to see she made out Bob Mitchell's face, black eyes glowing with contempt from their pale mass. A thin slight mustache splashed across the boney structure of his face.

Billy rolled over when he heard Bob's voice and was on his feet in a lurch. He struck out blindly in haste at the tall figure. Moving too quickly, he stumbled. Bob was alert and waiting to take the advantage landing an appalling blow squarely to Billy's jaw. He fell back and sprawled into the straw beside Mary in deep unconsciousness.

Bob watched Mary struggling to rise. Reaching down he pulled her roughly to a standing position.

"Keep your hands off me, Bob Mitchell!" Mary told him spitefully striking his hands. "Billy, oh Billy what has he done to you? Billy! Billy, speak to me."

"He's only knocked out. Look at you. I ain't good 'nough for you? But you let this Phelps be your lover?" His eyes caught sight of the beads around Mary's neck. Reaching for them he lifted the bright band to reflect the light.

"Well now, ain't these purty? Somethin' new?" he questioned Mary. Such extravagance was uncommon to women in the hills. "They from sweet Billy?"

"Get your hands off, ain't none of your business no-how!" She pulled slightly on his arm trying to release his hold on her precious necklace.

"That's all you mean to him, a string of worthless glass beads? I could'a bought you better than that," Bob bragged.

"Don't break them, please," Mary pleaded slapping at his arm.

Bob jerked the beads firmly and the sparkling lights danced in many directions upon the barn floor. His jealousy increased thinking of Billy winning favors from Mary. His paw was right; he said you shouldn't spoil a woman. You had to be firm with them from the beginning or they would turn fickle on you. He usually disagreed with his father but now he could see he should have been rougher with Mary instead of treating her as if she was something special.

"Look at you!" Bob took firm hold of Mary pulling her across the floor into the trail of light coming through the big doors.

"You look like a common whore! Polly been givin' you some of her ideas?" he questioned in disgust, looking at her tousled hair entangled with stems of straw. "I ain't sure I want somethin' a Phelps has slobbered over anyways!"

She buttoned her blouse crooked and her long skirt hung limply to one side. Under any other circumstances Bob would have been dismayed if anyone had ever treated Mary as he was. The sight of tears rolling down her cheeks in desperation would have turned him to jelly.

All he could think of now were the weeks he had tried to convince Mary he loved her. He wanted her but abstained himself because of his respect for her and her family. Now that he found her lying in the straw with Billy, the respect was gone. Billy was out of the way, he was going to have Mary. He began moving her back into the darkness of the barn.

"You're nothin' but a bitch! All those times in the hills, I could a had you for the takin'. But no, I told myself. I thought you was a nicey-nice. I didn't want you to think less of me. Didn't want you to think I was like the rest of the Mitchells. I know now they's as good or better than you or any Phelps." Here he was acting just like his old man. His father would have been proud of him.

"I'm gonna get me a piece of what was good enough for Billy Dean! When I get done with you, ain't no Phelps gonna want you! They'll never let Billy marry anyone that's laid with a Mitchell," Bob laughed.

Mary was feeling ill. He was making her love for Billy sound dirty talking to her as if she were a tramp. Tears stung her eyes. Her anger at Bob's insinuations turned to fear as she realized fully his intent. He increased his hold on her arm.

"You're mean Bob Mitchell! I never would have married you! Let go of me, you PIG!" Mary screeched trying to free herself from his savage hold. She was trying to strike out fiercely but he held her arms firmly to her sides. She resorted to kicking but Bob's high boots protected his legs.

"I'll scream for Poppy! If he know'd how you were treatin' me, you'd be dead in a minute. He'd never let me marry the likes of you! Never! Never!" she screamed twisting to free herself.

"He'll not hear you; he's still on the hill. Besides do you think he'd be delighted to know you an' sweet Billy were a lollygaggin' in the straw. Real cozy that was, Mary. Soon, soon as I've finished with you, your paw'll be beggin' for anyone to marry up with you." His face was twisted with jealousy and he was trying to stay angry enough to complete his intent.

"I'm tellin' you Mary, Billy Phelps is a dead man! You think yourself too good to marry me? Hear me good Mary, you'll never marry him! You hear me? I know my paw. He's a mean man full of hate. He don't let anythin' or anyone get in his way." Bob held her tighter trying to move her through the hanging tobacco.

"I hate you! You don't know what your talkin' 'bout. Now let go of me!" Mary was struggling harder, frightened for Billy and wondering if he was already dead.

The dark look on Bob's face, the anger in his dark eyes, was totally alien from his usually pleasant face. There was almost a resemblance to his father. He began to swagger with new found arrogance.

Billy stirred, opened his eyes and closed them. Raising himself on his elbows he opened his eyes again trying to remember what had happened. His head was fuzzy and he thought he heard faint voices. He laid back down trying to regain a clear mind.

Total recovery hit as he heard Mary scream. He lunged to his feet. With trembling knees, he stumbled up the aisle between the tobacco racks. He heard Bob Mitchell plainly telling Mary, "If my paw don't kill him, yours will when he finds out you ware a layin' with that bastard."

"Let me go! Let me go!" Mary continued to screech.

Billy spotted them struggling against the light of the big door. Bob was attempting to lay Mary down on the floor of the walkway. Her determination to stay upright was creating a problem for Bob.

Billy was fuming. "You dirty rotten bastard! I'll kill you!" He laid a hard blow with a tightly knotted fist at the side of Bob's head.

Bob released Mary giving her a hard shove as his body flexed. She stumbled backward with force against the railing of a drying rack. The impact knocked the air from her body and she folded into a crumpled heap on the walkway.

Bob's head flipped sideways and he reached to hold the door for support, knowing what was coming. Billy took advantage of his momentary stupor and came in with another hard blow to the jaw.

Bob struck back but had weakened. His blow held no impact. He pulled back again and landed another blow forceful, hard, and solid, squarely to Billy's nose.

Billy felt the bones crunch and the blood spurted in a stream onto his white shirtfront. He retaliated with a strong blow to Bob's middle that doubled him and dropped him to his knees outside the barn door. Billy reached to pull him to his feet. Bob's eyes caught sight of a pile of fresh cow droppings at his knee. He grabbed a handful of the wet manure and slung it with force into Billy's face.

The unexpected onslaught was effective. Billy let go and staggered backward. The wet dung stung and burned his eyes. It was down his face, in his mouth, and mixing with the blood trailing across his lips. He thought he was going to be sick. He lifted his arm and wiped the mess away with his shirtsleeve cleaning his face and clearing his eyes.

Bob got to his feet. While Billy was distracted he moved in with a hard swinging blow that landed on Billy's upraised arm. The sudden jolt brought Billy back. He forgot about being ill, drew back and landed a hard strong blow to Bob's jaw.

The impact rose Bob's feet from the ground knocking him backward. He sprawled with a thud on the hot earth in front of the barn. He lay still, unmoving. The hot sun blazed unmercifully upon his upturned face. Almost instantaneously, the small black mealy bugs began to crawl across the blood oozing from the corner of his split lip. Flies zoomed in and buzzed in a swarm around his closed eyes.

Mary had her wind back and was beginning to breathe regularly again. She pulled herself to a standing position. She could see the fight going on outside the barn door. With shaky legs she managed to make it to the doorway. Clinging weakly to the doorframe she leaned heavily against it. She drew back quickly in astonishment when Bob's body landed in the dust at her feet. Hysteria struck when she saw Billy with blood streaming down his face and covering his shirt front. She began to cry and wring her hands.

"You're hurt. Oh, Billy. You're hurt bad. Oh don't die! Please don't die! It's all 'cause of me," she blurted out with a choking sob and fell against him.

Billy enfolded her in his arms trying to reassure her and calm her. It was agony to move his body but he held her close then moved her back to see into her eyes.

"I'm alright, Mary. Calm yourself sweetheart. It's only a bloody nose. It'll stop bleedin' in a minute. I ain't gonna die!" Billy assured her tenderly, and then warned her, "You'll get all bloody if you get too close."

"I don't care! I want to hold you," she told him and folded her arms around him.

Billy was trying to regain his composure. Mary was crying quietly, her head lying against his chest. His nose had quit bleeding and the blood had dried. He was struggling between hating Bob Mitchell and his sense of wrong at being engulfed in such feelings. The entire episode made him sick inside, sicker than the taste of dung in his mouth. It was certain, for his own piece of mind, he had to reconcile with Bob. There was no triumph in his victory. Fighting was against all his principles. He believed that you should love everyone, even the Mitchells. He patted Mary's shoulder tenderly.

Taking a large white handkerchief from his back pocket he dried her tears. She lifted her head and waited for him to finish. Taking the handkerchief from his hand she freed herself, and went to the well. After drawing up the bucket filled with water she set it on the edge. Tipping it Mary let the cool water run across the white material. She went back to Billy and began to wash his battered face.

"It's broke, I know it is. I felt the bones crunch." Billy related as Mary touched his swollen nose.

"Anyways, it's stopped bleedin'," Mary told him and her tears started again.

"Don't cry darlin'. Please sweetheart. I'll be fine. It'll just take a little time."

Billy walked with his arm around her to a bench built onto the fence connecting the tobacco barn with the stock barn. He sat with his arms folded on his knees and head resting on his arms trying to recover from the trouncing Bob had given him. Mary sat beside him her head leaning against his back, loving him more at that moment than she had ever thought possible and hating Bob Mitchell.

The man on the ground began to stir, raised his head and looked around. Brushing the bugs away from his face he raised to a sitting position. He remembered what had happened. There was no more jealousy or hate left in him. He would not renew the battle. He spotted Mary and Billy huddled together on the bench unaware of his recovery. Thankful for their preoccupation, he stood up shook his head to clear it, and made his way weakly to the well.

After the two sweethearts left the picnic, Ginny and Kylee made their way back to the cemetery walking slowly, visiting and meeting friends and relations. Kylee found that, through her father, she was related to almost everyone on Pound. They found little Emily playing with Carl Jennings's children. She ran to give Kylee a hug and pulled her over to where Tom sat eating his third piece of blackberry cake.

"Come on Tom, you 'member? You promised to show me how to catch a terrapin. I want one to take home for a pet. You said we'uns could walk back home an' find one. Come on Tom, can we'uns do that?" the little girl pleaded smiling sweetly. "Please Tom, you promised, an' I want Kylee to come with us, please." Emily reached up and pulled his arm down. The little minx took the last bite of his blackberry cake when she received no answer. That got his attention. Tom laughed at her teasing trick and pulled a curl playfully.

"We'll do it, Emmie. I promised, sure 'nough. A promise is a promise. Of course Kylee can come. I need to get someone to drive my wagon down the hill first. I'll tell your mommy an' poppy what we'uns are up to." As Tom talked he fastened his gaze on Kylee as he smoothed back the unruly lock of hair that insisted on falling across his forehead. Kylee quickly avoided his clear blue eyes. He walked away to find Bess and Jan.

The three, Tom, Kylee, and little Em walked down the trail stopping where the path forked and led down to Baldwin's Branch. Tom helped Emily search under large gnarled tree roots reaching from the banks across the water. Here the water eddied slowly making an ideal murky hiding place for the small slow crawling amphibians. They finally spotted one under a big root hiding in the cool shadows. It was easily caught and Tom instructed Emily on how to pick it up by the shell.

"Oh no, Tommy-kins! I cain't do that. It would hurt him!" Emily jumped up and down shaking her hands in protest.

"No Emmie. See if you hold him like this." Tom handed the unsuspecting turtle to Emily. "Put your hand around him like this." He showed her how to fasten her fingers under the edge of the shell holding it securely. The little turtle wiggled its head and feet.

"He's a little one, just right for a little girl's pet," Tom told her, smiling and watching her stretch small fingers around the hard shell.

Emily stood very still looking at the little green and orange terrapin with all seriousness.

"Is it a boy or a girl, Tommy-kins?"

Kylee waited and watched as she stood on a large smooth rock. She couldn't hold back an amused smile.

"I don't know, Em!" Tom answered her in shocked surprise but couldn't help laughing at the little girl's forwardness.

"Well, cain't you tell the difference 'tween boys an' girls? Anyone knows they're different," she declared disappointed at Tom's apparent ignorance.

She stared at Tom with large desperate eyes. "I want a boy one! We ain't got no boys in our family at all. I want a boy one. If it ain't a boy, I don't want it! I'm purely tired of just girls." Her voice was definite and large tears began to puddle in her brown eyes.

Tom looked at Kylee; they could tell she was not to be made fun of. The smile left Kylee's face and she blushed noticeably at his bold scrutiny. Kylee had only accompanied them because of Emily's childish insistence. Like everyone else she was already completely enslaved to the child's dimpled persuasion. She needn't have worried about being with Tom and making conversation, Emily took care of that, she was never silent. Tom took the little animal and turned it upside down, pretending to examine it closely.

"Yep, you're in luck, little one. It's a boy for sure!"

"Are you sure, Tommy? Let me see. Show me, show me!" the little girl demanded reaching to pull down on Tom's arm.

"Emmie, Emmie! No, no. Shame, shame! Don't you know girls don't peek at boys and boys don't peek at girls? Least ways they ain't supposed to. That's the rules!" Tom handed her the turtle, smiling with assurance.

His pale blue eyes sparked with mischief as he looked again at Kylee and remembered how angry she had become just because he had seen above her knees and saw her stockings and bloomers. He supposed that was why she had been so hostile toward him. She hadn't even spoken or acknowledged him in anyway since the incident.

When Emily insisted Kylee accompany them on their adventure it was as if Tom didn't exist at all. It was no use trying to make amends. He had tried that already. It would be better to bide his time and be patient. Surely she couldn't stay silent toward him forever. At least you wouldn't think so, living under the same roof, he assured himself.

So they walked side by side down the same path Mary and Billy had taken, not speaking, only listening to Emily's childish patter. They watched her golden curls swinging to and fro, up and down about her shoulders as she skipped down the path ahead of them.

Kylee was thankful for the evening shadows turning the heat of the day into blissful coolness. Emily's skipping feet raised little clouds of white dust around her. She cooed softly to the terrapin, calling it 'Stanley' and promising it her everlasting love and attention. Turning it upside down she watched his legs wiggle. She was trying to peek inside the shell to see if Tom was for sure telling her the truth.

Emily skipped into the barnyard in time to see Bob pouring a bucket of water over his head. Spotting Mary and Billy on the bench she ran to them. Forgetting the turtle in her concern, she dropped him in the dust. Glad for his freedom, the little prisoner moved slowly under a low bush out of sight, forgotten.

"Billy, Billy!" she cried running to him and clambering upon his lap as he raised his head. "What's wrong? You're all bloody. Oh, you're all bloody!" She threw her arms around his neck and looked into his face.

"What happened to you? Was it that mean old Bob Mitchell over there at the well? Was it?" Taking Billy's face between her hands she looked deep into his eyes. Her eyes filled with worry and concern for the person she loved best in the entire world.

"Don't worry kitten. I'm fine. Let's have a smile now," Billy said to the little girl on his knee.

Billy sat Emily on the ground and smiled at her with assurance. She clutched his hand tightly and gave him a small smile but a worried concern filled her eyes.

Bob doused the bucket of water over his head. He looked up in time to see Tom and Kylee coming down the path. Billy was rising from the bench and coming toward him. Bob's head was still fuzzy but he was not about to be caught between two Phelps's. He started on a high run through the trees toward Pound road and the safety of Tandy's Mountain.

Tom's stare followed Bob's retreating figure. Seeing Billy's battered face he tried to figure out the situation.

"There's been trouble here brother!" Tom stated, studying Billy's swollen nose and bloody shirt.

"Come back Bob, let's talk." Billy yelled after Bob, pushing Tom aside, ignoring him. "Let's work this out!"

"What's ailin' you boy? That's a Mitchell you're callin' after." Tom laid his hand on Billy's arm restraining him firmly. "You cain't run off into the hills after him. It's hard to tell how many Mitchell's are out there waitin' for you to do just that."

"I only want to talk to him."

"How many times have I gotta tell you? You cain't talk to Mitchell's! They ain't no talk in them! All they understand is killin'."

"This is my affair, Tom. I'll not have any interference. I can handle this!"

"I understand Billy, but I'm tellin' you, they only understand killin'!"

"I ain't gonna listen to that kind of talk. I'll handle it. I think I'm old 'nough to take care of my own affairs." Billy was sullen and pushed Tom's arm roughly aside.

"Okay Billy." Tom threw his hands up and backed away. "You can take care of your own business, but let me tell you somethin' brother, when it comes to Mitchells, well, that's family business an' don't you forget it!"

Kylee was brushing the dust from Mary's skirt attempting to button her blouse straight. Mary was shaking visibly and close to the point of crying again. Kylee's presence comforted her and she was beginning to pull herself together.

"One thing Billy, can I ask what's happened here? Was Bob after Mary? Did he hurt her? Talk to me, brother! Don't you think because Mary's involved here that Jan should know 'bout this?" He was noticing Mary's tangled hair and twisted skirt and thinking about Jay's threat the night before.

Tom was beginning to get riled at his brother's independent attitude. Emily ran back to Mary and Kylee full of questions and inquiries of her own.

"I'll explain it to Jan. I'm not tellin' you again! I'll take care of it! I don't want no one takin' out after Bob on a killin' spree, understand? A bunch of folk could get killed. It were only 'cause he wanted Mary. I guess if I was in his shoes, I'd feel the same way. I'm the lucky one, Mary's gonna be mine," Billy said, giving Tom a shaky smile.

"I want to be sure Mary will be safe. So yes, I'll tell Jan so he can be sure she doesn't go into the woods alone. She ain't hurt, she's mostly scared. Let's take her on to the house 'fore the rest of the folks get here," Billy declared.

The group walked silently up to the house, Kylee, with her arm around Mary. Tom and Billy walked side by side with Emily hanging on to Billy's hand, hugging his arm. She was trying in her own childish way to understand what had happened to Billy and Mary. One thing she was certain of, it was all because of Bob Mitchell.

They watched the sun sink slowly behind the big trees covering the tall hills. Through the evening air they could hear the rumbling of Jan's big wagon coming down the road from the cemetery.

CHAPTER THIRTEEN

Kylee felt sorry for Billy and his battered face during the days that followed. Watching as his bruises turned dark purple then ghastly blue and yellow spreading across his nose and circling his eyes.

Billy couldn't get the fight off his mind, concerned over the hate Bob had cultivated toward him. He wasn't happy with the outcome of the situation. He needed to have an understanding with Bob.

Tom and Matt were of one mind, get rid of all of them in one full swoop. Their father agreed but put the lid back on the smoldering kettle.

"There'll come a time Jay'll do somethin' to put his neck in the noose. This ain't the time for us to go up there an' shoot things up. How would that look with Tom thinkin of runnin' for Marshal? I understand Nell is waitin' to birth a youngin'. There's the twins an' Taynee to think about. They ain't harmed no-one. It ain't their fault they be Mitchells. I ain't aimin' on harmin' them!" His decision was definite and final.

He sternly forbade Billy from seeking Bob out for any reason. He prohibited any contact with the young Mitchell. Their lives resumed without hearing a word or threat from Tandy's Mountain.

Billy put Bob out of his mind after his fathers' decision. Mary became his only thought. He waited with forbearance for his nose to heal and his bruises to fade thinking often of Mary's soft warm body and how close he had been to having her. Visions of her soft brown eyes were before him, shining with love and sparkling with laughter. Her eyes had not been so full of happiness that last afternoon before they left to come home but were dulled with sadness at Billy's battered face.

She tenderly touched his swollen nose. Afraid for him, she reminded him again of Bob Mitchell's words. "Billy Phelps is a dead man!" Remembering the words Mary cautioned him again.

"He didn't mean that Mary. He was hurtin' 'cause he'd seen us walkin' down the path together. I was with you an' he weren't."

"It's hard to tell what he might do Billy. Jealousy is an ugly thing," Jan added to Mary's warnings.

"I reckon your right, he's hurtin' bad 'cause Mary refused him," Tom added.

"You watch yourself Billy. I'll not let Mary go to the woods without Alvin or me. Soon as I get the tobac' took care of I'm goin' over to Mitchells. Jay an' I are gonna have ourselves a talk! I cain't take a chance on that bunch of ruffians stealin' Mary. We'd never see her again, they'd see to that! I'll not chance it. We all know their kind. I'll not have them force Mary into a marriage she don't agree to. I'm worried for you Billy. The Mitchell's don't usually make idle threats. Jay has already said his piece. They'll lay low, waitin' for a good chance to get your paw too. In fact, nothin' would pleasure Mitchell more than seein' you all dead. Now you mark my words! You take care, you hear!" Jan advised, concerned for all of them.

Mary and Billy avoided any speculation with Jan about being in the tobacco barn. Jan had surmised Bob caught them on the path when they were walking home. They would leave it at that. Jan wished now he had been more concerned about the wispy shadow in the pines that Bess had seen.

As Tom and Billy climbed into the wagon to head home, Mary whispered secretly to Billy, "Come over as soon as you can. I think Poppy'll be willin' now. I love you! Be careful, you hear?" She caressed him with the look in her eyes afraid to kiss him for fear her father would see. She smiled bravely at Billy as she waved them good-bye.

Long summer days became history and the shorter fall days took their place. The tall oak and maple shed their wardrobe of red and gold and now stood bare and gray signaling the promise of winter. The hickory nuts had fallen and a cool breeze rose across the pines as the nights grew longer and colder. It wouldn't be long before life settled down to the dullness of staying inside most of the time.

The Mitchell's weren't mentioned but hadn't been forgotten. Billy had heard nothing from Bob and refrained from seeking him out. Kylee kept his days busy always finding something for him to do much to his consternation. There were the pumpkins and big yellow squash to cut in circles, string and hang among the rafters to dry. Cider to make, hogs to cure, soap making, nuts to gather, wood to stack, and candles to dip. The chore of digging sweet potatoes to store seemed never ending.

Ira had left with Matt for Carolina for the last supply of whiskey before the winter made traveling impossible. Grinding corn kept Tom busy at the mill. Kylee occasionally worked at the mill with Billy or Matt, but emphatically refused to go when Tom was there.

Kylee had become part of their family. Even Ira's irritability had lessened. Kylee tended to him patiently putting his desires and needs always first. He basked in her attention growing more attached to her each day. She never complained or scolded. She was always ready with a sunny smile, a hot cup of coffee sweetened with a touch of whiskey the way he liked it. There would be a blanket warmed and waiting for his lifeless legs.

Billy was still her favorite and the other men did not challenge his place in her eyes. Feeling a true sisterly affection for Matt she would laugh, talk and felt at ease with him. Tom, was another matter, she only spoke to him when absolutely necessary.

Kylee could not sort out her feelings for Tom. When he was home his almost colorless eyes followed her everywhere. This in itself made her nervous and irritable toward him. When he spoke to her the answer would be short and snappy. The tension between them grew making any friendship impossible.

When finished with his work at the mill, Tom would sit before the fire, his long legs stretched toward the flame. Kylee thought it strange that Tom had such long legs for his short stature. His black knee-high boots were always polished to a high sheen catching the light of the fire.

The long fall nights soon brought time for the young men to become bored as the workload lessened. Tom visited Trace's Tavern regularly seeking Polly's company. Kylee understood by now that this particular young lady was the object of a constant squabble between Matt and Tom. As brothers often do, they both wanted the same thing.

Matt's first love was cards and he began to seek out a game often. Ira had always hated the game and refused to have a deck in his house and warned his son against it. Matt, however, argued that playing once in a while never hurt anyone and refused to give up his right to seek his own pleasure. Ira would not relent in his forbidding of the habit. He had seen men die from a bullet or knife blade because of a foolish disagreement over cards. He did not want his son to wind up a victim of such a devilish pastime.

It was coon hunting time and a favorite sport of the Phelps men. After Ira's crippling illness he had not allowed himself the pleasure of hunting. He had even sold his coon dogs. At the insistence and persuading of Tom and Billy, he relented and admitted he would enjoy the company of some good dogs. He discussed the matter at length with his sons and had consented for Tom to purchase some dogs if he could find a satisfactory pair.

Kylee listened patiently to their discussion. She developed her own opinion about the matter and informed them in short terms how she felt.

"I'll not have any hounds in my kitchen!" Her eyes flashed a warning should anyone dispute her.

"Come on Kylee, they'll not take up much room," Matt coaxed.

"No! Not in my kitchen!"

"I thought you liked dogs, Kylee," Billy put in his opinion, disappointment clear in his voice.

"I do Billy, but animals belong in the barn an' that's where they'll stay." She would not be shaken.

"Now Kylee, it'll be nice havin' some dogs around. They'll keep down the snakes-n-rats," Ira explained. "I'll see that the boys make them stay in the barn as you want; if that's gonna be your wish."

"Very well, the barn then," she relented, "But not in my kitchen!"

Kylee had her mind made up. There would be no hounds in her kitchen. She knew how it was with men and dogs. First thing she knew, they would be sneaking them in behind her back to lie in front of the fire. She would not have it. She would show them. They would not sneak a single dog past her! But Kylee would retract her decision and learn the bitter aftertaste of the hasty words she would soon have to swallow.

A few evenings later, Matt and Ira left for Kentucky to deliver a load of whiskey. Tom, as usual was away. Billy and Kylee sat alone beside the fire parching corn in a large iron skillet over the hot coals. They ate the hot kernels with a little salt, savoring their warm crunchy goodness.

Outside a bitter wind blew fiercely down between the hills shaking what remained of the dead leaves from the huge maple and oak trees. It was on this chilling night that Tom brought home the new hounds. He opened the door and came stomping in bringing with him the cruel night air and two huge dogs. One was a blue-gray hound with loose skin, sagging jowls, floppy ears, and incredibly short legs. The other dog was a large Golden Retriever with warm friendly eyes. The dog stood thigh high to Tom and his arm rested fondly around the big dog's neck. The dog nuzzled the man affectionately on the leg. It was apparent the two were already close friends.

"Hi you'ins. Billy, Kylee, come say hello to Blue an' Big Boy!" Tom greeted them patting the head of the big yellow dog beside him.

"Tarnation Tom! What beauties!" Billy responded and immediately began a demolition course through the room with the smaller dog, Blue.

Their romp through the kitchen turned over chairs and benches and left a muddled heap on the floor of coats and hats from the pegs beside the door. Much to Kylee's dismay the destruction continued without restraint. The laughter and barking increased until Kylee could not contain herself any longer.

"Stop! Stop this minute! You're makin' a total mess of things. You hear me Billy? Stop this instant! Just look at this room. You get them beasts out of my kitchen. Do you hear? Do it right now, Tom!" Kylee ordered jumping up from the rocker.

Tom had scored another mark. It was apparent that he had intentionally ignored her wishes about the dogs.

"Billy!" she shouted again at the young man. Billy was ignoring her too for the first time since her arrival. Again she blamed Tom.

"I'll not tolerate such goin's on. Now stop!" she spoke sharply, stomping her foot.

Billy brought Blue and himself to an abrupt halt in front of the fire. The dog began immediately smelling out the dropped kernels of corn, gobbling them up with loud munching and chomping.

"Now Kylee, they were only gettin' acquainted," Tom explained soothingly.

His intentions had not been to anger her. He realized he had not taken her wishes concerning the dogs seriously enough. Before he could answer with an apology and remove the dogs, she came back at him.

"Get them beasts out of my house!" she demanded angrily at Tom. "If you intend to make a dog house out of this place, I'll go!" Untying her apron she lifted it over her head preparing to leave. She threw it with an emotional thrust into the rocker seat.

"Your house? Now Kylee, ain't that takin' a lot for granted? Where in tarnation do you think you'll go in the middle of the night?" Tom asked with a teasing smile, which Kylee immediately misjudged.

Still nursing her anger she failed to hear the light hearted tone in Tom's voice. Her body stiffened at his words, her lips a tight line. She had assumed a lot thinking her place was established and unshakable. Of course, this wasn't her house. Appeased, her anger spilled, she was left weak and shaken. Kylee sat back down in the rocking chair, bowed her head and folded her hands meekly in her lap, subdued.

"Of course you're right. I took too much for granted. You're right this isn't my house. I don't have any other place to go," her voice was shaking. It was the longest conversation she'd had with Tom. She was fighting back the tears and realized she was humbling herself before this hateful man and hating herself for her weakness before him.

"Now look a'here, Tom! Don't you get mean with Kylee. Of course this is her house, same as its mine an' yours. I didn't mean to tear up the place Kylee. I'll straighten everything up. You'll never know the difference. You're gonna stay right here. I'd never let you go anywhere's else. Tom'll take the dogs out, won't you Tom?" Billy requested nervously afraid that Kylee might fulfill her threat.

He would never let her leave. Never! He had been over excited about the dogs. Realizing his part in the episode he moved quickly to straighten up the mess. The blue-gray dog was close on his heels anticipating another hurdle through the room. Billy patted his head cautioning him to be quiet.

"I'm sorry," Kylee apologized weakly.

"You've no need to be sorry, Kylee. I didn't mean to anger you. I only wanted you to see the dogs. It was so cold outside an' all. Of course this is your home. I'm the one who needs to apologize. If that's what you want, the dogs'll stay in the barn." Tom thought he'd never understand women. He began gathering the dogs together to move them outside.

The big light colored dog had a different idea. He stood quietly watching, pushing in close to Tom. Sensing the friction in the room he had never taken his large soulful eyes off Kylee. As Tom moved to leave, the dog padded softly over to Kylee and lay down on the floor beside her. He put his head on her knee and looked up sadly into her downcast eyes, as he flopped his big tail loudly upon the plank floor. With super conviction he was pleading their cause, pitifully begging her forgiveness.

"Come on boy. You musn't plague Kylee. We've caused enough trouble already. Come on, out you go!" he called to the big honey colored dog. The blue gray dog stood waiting at the door.

"No, you will not take him away," Kylee declared looking into the dogs understanding eyes. She wished she could have taken back the things she had said in anger about the dogs. She patted the top of Boy's head in acceptance. In response the dog gave her a grateful wet lap across the cheek making Kylee laugh. The sound broke the tension in the room. The cold feelings were gone. She hugged the dog's neck.

"Of course you can stay, you darlin'. You'll even stay in my room if you've a mind to." She laughed again and backed away from another wet kiss on the face.

Boy was, from that moment on, Kylee's devoted companion. There was a bond between them. The dog developed a great fondness for her. However, the big golden dog had a great love and loyalty for Tom. When he was not by Kylee's side, he was Tom's trustworthy guardian.

Things were back to normal once more. Kylee was her smiling self again. Tom was satisfied, he had his dogs, but he longed for the time when Kylee would laugh with him as she had with the dog, Big Boy. He wondered if he would ever know why she hated him so badly.

The bruises on Billy's face and around his gray eyes began to turn a sickening yellow. The ugly swelling across his nose was receding. It had been weeks since he had seen Mary. He had waited long enough. The first step was a talk with his father then, he would go speak to Jan.

"Paw," Billy began slowly. "I want to wed Mary Stewart. If you're willin', I want to speak to Jan."

"Well, Billy. I hadn't thought about you gettin' married. You're only a youngin'!"

Ira sat before the fire warming his lifeless legs. "It takes a man grown to care for a wife." Ira waved his hand. "Don't talk of marryin'. It should be Tom or Matt talkin' 'bout that. You're my baby," he added looking at Billy, the love shining in his blue eyes. He was seeing for the first time the young man Billy had become.

"I'll be nineteen in a few months, Paw. You said yourself I could begin haulin' an' earn my share. I reckon it'd be 'nough to keep a wife. If you'll give me a piece of ground, or maybe I could buy it from you, I could build us a cabin. Tom an' Matt'll help me. We'uns could have it ready in a few months." Billy smiled persuasively.

"Well, I don't see no problem there. Things are slow; it'd warm up your blood poundin' a few nails. Very well son, if that's what you want. Mary's a fine girl, she'll make you a good wife an' me a good daughter-in-law," he added with satisfaction.

It was hard for Ira to believe his baby had grown into a man. Where had the time gone? He shook his head in disbelief. He was glad Billy had forgotten the incident with Bob Mitchell.

"Thank you, Paw. I'm goin' over tomorrow an' ask Jan. Yah-hoo!" Billy exclaimed. He wanted to hug his father but knew that would never be tolerated. At least he had never seen anyone hug his father, no one except little Em and Kylee.

If he didn't express his joy, he would burst. Billy took his fiddle from Kylee's bedroom, tightened the strings, drew the bow, and danced as he played. The house rang with the exuberant feelings that overwhelmed him.

Billy rose early the next day to complete his chores. He decided it was the day he should go talk to Jan. Ira and Matt had left even earlier to take the last load of whiskey into Kentucky. Ira wanted to make it across the mountain before the rain that was threatening started. Tom had ridden out on Jole' to an unknown destination, probably Polly's.

Billy's insides were in turmoil as he hurried to get ready. Kylee laughed at his haste, because everything he did went wrong. The morning was becoming cloudy and dreary and by the time Billy was ready a soft mist was falling.

"It couldn't wait until tomorrow to rain, could it? No, it had to rain today," Billy muttered as he looked out the window. He was discouraged with the weather and the miserable day made him irritable.

"Well, Matt an' Paw chanced it so I will too. I ain't waitin' another day to see Mary. I'll be back for supper Kylee. It's hard tellin' when Tom'll be back. Paw said not to leave you alone after dark. So I'll not take any chances, I'll be back." Billy's muffled voice came from inside the coat closet under the stairs. Sorting through the apparel, he pulled out a raincoat. Putting it on, he picked a hat from the pegs by the door.

"Bye Kylee," he said putting his hat on and pushing it down tightly.

Billy opened the door to leave, then closed it. He turned to Kylee sitting before the fire, hands folded watching him.

"I've gotta tell you Kylee. I'm so glad you're here with us. I'd of died if you'd left us over the dogs. I'm sorry 'bout your paw, but I sure am glad you came to us. You've become like a sister to me. I want to thank you for bein' so patient with teachin' me to read. I can read lotsa verses in the Bible now," Billy bragged. "My maw would be proud. I been thinkin' a lot 'bout them verses I been readin'. But I don't understand what happens when you die. You suppose there's any in between when it come to the reckonin' day? I always tried hard not to do anything too wrong. I sure do accept Jesus as my Savior. But I ain't ever been baptized. There's some say, you'll never make it to heaven if you ain't been baptized in water. I was gonna get baptized last summer when we went to the foot washin', but I backed out. Now it bothers me heaps, I sure don't want to burn in hell." Billy took a deep breath and continued.

"I always tried to be good to everyone. This thing with the Mitchell's plagues me to no end. For some reason, I can't believe that Jay killed my maw. Some folks say it weren't natural at all the way she died. As ornery as he is, I just don't think he'd stoop that low. I missed my maw something fierce after she died. You comin' helped that a lot Kylee."

"For some reason lately, I've had this question 'bout what happens to you when you die. Sometimes, I cain't sleep for thinkin' 'bout it. I dream 'bout my maw lots. I can see her plain as day. She reaches her hand out an' beckons for me. Kylee, when I play *Golden Slippers* on the fiddle I wonder. Do you believe that we really will be wearing them on the golden street? Gosh, I'm sorry Kylee. I've rattled on an'on." Billy shook his head in disbelief. "Why don't you tell me to shut up and get on out'a' here?"

"Oh Billy, I'd not do that. I like talkin' with you; I only wished I had the answers. I was never too much on religion. My papa always sent me to church but I never understood much of what they were talkin' 'bout. Exceptin' when they'd tell 'bout the gentle mercy an' grace an' love Jesus has for all his children." Kylee looked at Billy with affection. "I think that means even you an' me, Billy, all of us no matter what color or what religion we follow, whether you've been baptized or not. You're a fine, good man. I don't think you got anything to worry 'bout. Bob Mitchell's the one that needs to be worryin'! Now, get out'a here an' go see Mary 'fore it gets too late. An' yes, Billy, I believe if anyone will be wearin' them golden slippers, you will," Kylee concluded with a wide smile filled with promise.

Billy replaced his worried look with a wide grin. With a sudden impulse he went over and placed a kiss on Kylee's cheek. Embarrassed at his action, he turned and left in a hurry his face bright red causing Kylee to laugh at his confusion.

With his leaving, the room felt suddenly empty and cold. Kylee rose from the rocker and stirred the fire thinking to renew the warmth. The silence still hung heavy, chilling the room. The sunny happy spirit that seemed to be present when Billy was around was gone, and she couldn't regain the warmth. She recalled Mary's feeling of dread. The sudden thought put a deep depression on her. She wanted to believe it was only the dismal day that left her depressed and blue.

She would busy herself and forget this glum mood. Sitting down on the window seat, she picked up a quilt she had been piecing. It would make a nice wedding gift for Mary and Billy. As she worked her spirits lifted.

The rain was beginning a slow soft pitter-patter on the porch roof. Through the window she could see Billy leave the barn on Red, the old mule. The big red animal moved out slowly reluctant to leave the barn on such a day. Her head bobbed rhythmically with the slow movement of her body.

Kylee could see Billy hunch his shoulders into the rain. She had an urge to call him back, convince him not to go, persuade him to wait until another day, but he had disappeared into the fog that was already closing in the creek and bridge below the mill.

"Oh Billy, you come at last! I thought you never would." Mary squealed with delight as she opened the door to Billy's anxious knock. "Come in; come in quickly out of the rain. You're soaked!" She helped him out of his raincoat and hung it beside the big stove to drip and dry.

"Hurry! Off with your boots, I'll set them over at the fire." Looking at him fondly, she blushed deeply at his returned gaze remembering the touch of his hands upon her body.

The big room was warm and inviting. A low ember glowed in the fireplace at the back wall. It was the iron cook stove emanating a warm coziness that attracted Billy. A pot of shuck beans (dried green beans) and sowbelly was simmering on top. The wonderful aroma filling the room could remove the chill from the coldest day. He watched Mary set his boots in front of the fireplace. She came back and placed her hand in his.

"Your poppa home, Mary?"

"He went into Donkey yesterday to meet some buyers for the tobac'. It's all tied an' ready to load as soon as the rain stops. Poppy has been in a real good mood. The crop was better than he thought it would be. He'll be comin' along soon. Oh Billy, I thought you would never come!" Mary's voice trembled with excitement.

"I was ready to run away and throw myself at your feet. Then I thought what a shameful hussy I was for thinkin' such a thing. I have longed for you 'til I could hardly bear it," she confessed and flung herself against Billy with such force she almost pushed him over.

"Mary, Mary," he sighed and closed his arms around her, confused at the girl's boldness.

Mary kissed him hard on the lips and Billy was ready to answer the invitation.

"I've thought of you too, Mary. I couldn't wait another day. I want to ask your poppy now. You're so sweet an' beautiful. I love you so much, Mary," he whispered and kissed her again with a deeper more demanding pressure.

Mary broke away, gasping for breath laughing up at him with eyes shining with love. She called up the stairs for her mother and sisters, not trusting herself to be alone another minute with Billy.

It was late afternoon when Janice Stewart arrived home. His immense frame filled the room and the damp rain hung heavy about him.

"Well, hallo, Billy!" He greeted Billy over the heads of the three girls who were engulfing him with hugs and kisses.

"Hallo, Bess, dear," he said to his wife bending to kiss her.

"Did I hear horses Jan? Who was with you an' why didn't they come in for a spell an' dry out?" Bess questioned.

"It was Jay an' the older boys. I ran into them havin' a card game with Carl. It ain't rainin' a drop lower down the creek. Jay an' I had an understanding 'bout things with Bob. He thinks we should encourage Mary to consider giving Bob a chance for courtin'. I told him if we agreed I'd let him know. Maybe the boy deserves that much. I don't think Jay knew anythin' 'bout the fight between Bob an' Billy. Least ways, he didn't speak of it."

"Jay reckoned that was the Phelps's mule tied to the porch so he said he'd just move on. Said it was a gettin' close to Nell's birthin' time an' he'd already been gone three days. He said it was possible he was a poppa again. Nell had so much trouble when the twins were born. I can understand why he was a worrin'," Jan explained to Bess.

"Don't seem to me he was a worryin' much! Out playin' cards an' swarpin' for three days. Don't matter none, probably better he was gone, give the women folk a mite of peace," Bess stated, disgusted with Jay's wild ways. "Taynee could care for Nell anyways."

"She's only a lass, dear. A wild one at that," Jan added, thinking of Jay's beautiful daughter.

"Well, she could ride for Hail; she's only a ways up the road," Bess said in defense.

"Now, wife, you know how things are with Jay an' Hail. Hail wouldn't go there when Taynee's maw had that miscarriage an' died. He still blames Hail for her death. He loved Mae in a big way, for Jay anyway."

"Yes dear," Bess answered, "but Hail were with Mattie, remember. That was when Billy fell out of the boy's tree house. If Hail hadn't of been there to stop the bleedin', he'd a bled to death for sure. When he was out'a danger she went right on to see 'bout Mae. It was too late. She was already dead," Bess said sadly, her eyes on Billy where he sat talking and laughing with the girls.

"How did the tobacco deal go, dear?" Bess questioned looking up at Jan fondly. He stood with his back to the stove, warming and smoking a pipe.

"Things are lookin' up, Bess gal. This one guy bought the whole lot. Said he'd bring his wagons to get it in a couple a weeks. Made a good price too, dear. Left Alvin at Trace's, told him not to come home 'til he was a mind to. He's earned it, Bess, he's earned it," Jan explained, looking at his lovely wife with affection and understanding his wife's great love for her older brother.

"Well, Billy. How are things with you folks? Say your face looks real good, almost healed, huh?" Jan took a closer look as Billy came over to stand before him. Mary followed and stood quietly beside him.

He had to ask Jan now before his bravery was completely gone. He smoothed his hair back, trying to muster the courage. Bashfully Billy hung his head and stared at his stocking feet.

Mary, watching his shyness tucked her hand into his hoping to give him strength. Billy found the encouragement he needed in the pressure of her hand.

"Well, sir. Things are fine at home. Paw an' Matt are in Kentucky," he swallowed hard. The gulp sounded loud in the room and hung suspended for an unending moment on the silence that followed.

Billy felt tongue tied, awkward, and very insignificant standing before this hulk of a man. The purpose of his visit became overwhelming. For the first time in his life he felt like a stranger to Jan. His eyes began to burn and his face became hot.

"What are you doin' out on a day like this?" Jan looked closer at Billy. He sensed something in the young man's attitude not as relaxed and happy as usual. Billy seemed winded, out of breath, and red in the face. He wondered what was going on.

"I came to ask your permission to marry Mary," Billy squeaked out his desire. His throat was tight and dry; he needed a drink of water. Feeling smaller by the minute he looked again at his stocking feet.

"What?" the older man bellowed.

Billy's heart sank to the bottom of his shoeless feet. Would Jan refuse him because he'd forgotten to put on his shoes?

"You're only a boy! What have you got to offer a wife?" Jan spoke loudly, glaring at Billy.

"I love her sir," Billy declared in a very small voice. He hadn't expected such reprisal from this old friend.

"You cain't eat love!" A tiny smile started to creep in around the corners of Jan's whiskered lips. A small spark began to twinkle deep down in his hazelnut eyes.

Billy, too crestfallen to notice still looked to the floor. He wiggled his toes and squeezed Mary's hand until her fingers became numb.

"I'll work for her Jan, an' I'll be good to her, I promise. Paw said I could start haulin' with him in the spring. I'll be makin' my share. Matt an' Tom are gonna help me build a cabin." Billy glanced sideways at Mary.

His courage came back and he stood up taller. His nervousness waned; only his love for Mary mattered now. "I think she feels the same way, Sir. I can give her as much as any Mitchell," Billy added with more courage and looked Jan squarely in the eyes.

"Well, lass?" Jan questioned his daughter.

"Yes, Poppa," Mary said in a quiet coaxing voice. "Please! I'll die Poppa if'n you say no."

Her eyes pleaded with her father, it had always been Mary's brown eyes that brought him down; he was sunk again. He would have to give her up sooner or later. Billy would be a good choice. Billy was holding Mary's hand so tight Jan could see her knuckles turning white even in the dim light.

Jan's loud booming laughter filled the room. He gathered Billy and Mary into his long arms. Kissing Mary he said to Billy, "She's yours son, an' heaven help you." He released them and shook Billy's hand.

"Ya-hoo!" Billy shouted and wheeled around on his stocking feet. Could it be true? At last, Mary was going to be his.

"There's only one thing. You gotta allow proper time for courtin'. So's the ladies can get things ready, you understand, son?" Jan said and Billy stopped whirling.

"Yes, sir! Don't make it too long sir, please."

"Well, I'm figurin' if you want the gal bad enough, you'll wait. Maybe Valentines Day would be a nice time for a weddin'." Jan was serious again. "Besides, we need to keep her a spell longer."

"That's clean 'til February, gosh, Jan," Billy stammered. "But whatever you say'll be fine."

"You can come a callin' when her maw says it's fittin'. But I don't want you makin' a pest out'a yourself! Is it settled then?" Billy nodded and they shook hands again.

"Let's have supper now wife. Billy you'll stay the night. It ain't a fit time out there for man or beast."

"Well, sure do thank you Jan an' Bess, but I gotta get back. Kylee's alone. I promised her I'd be back for supper. If I ain't, she'll worry. So I'll take my leave. If I may, I'll come courtin' Mary soon as paw gets back. For now, I better get. I already been here too long. Kylee'll give up on me."

"I'm so happy, Billy. You have always been very dear to me. Now you'll truly be our very own son. You come on over whenever you can." Bess instructed, smiling at Billy.

"Oh, Mommy, Mommy, I'm so happy!" Mary's voice was soft and filled with dreams.

"We're gonna marry Billy. We'uns are gonna marry Billy. We get to have our very own boy," Emily sang excitedly jumping up and down as she clapped her hands with joy.

Mary and Ginny began planning. Billy watched Mary across the room with her sisters, their heads together in deep discussion.

"It's true," Billy thought, "it's settled, Mary's gonna be my wife."

Janice puffed his pipe encased in a smoky fog. He was beaming with satisfaction as if the entire idea had been his own. They begged Billy to stay the night, but he insisted on getting back to Kylee. Even Emily's dimpled smile and chubby arms encircling his neck couldn't persuade him.

He put on his shoes, raincoat, hat, and bade them good-bye. Taking his hand, Mary walked him out to the porch rail away from the teasing eyes of her father and Ginny.

Billy's thoughts were a happy jumble as he rode away from the house. Mary had kissed him good-bye with a sweet tender caress, unlike her fiery passion of earlier. He was puzzled; wondering if he would ever learn all there was to know about this wonderful girl. Standing on the porch she waved him good-bye. Her white apron was a bright splash against the gray dusk. Her long blonde hair cascaded around her shoulders, a golden streak, shining out through the drizzling rain. Mary threw him a kiss as he disappeared across the creek.

Leaning against the porch rail Mary peered into the dimness trying to see Billy through the rain. But he was gone; there was not even a shadow left. Standing for a moment she let the rain cool her flushed face. Then realizing she was getting wet turned and went reluctantly into the house.

Billy rode slowly his legs flopping carelessly at the mule's sides. He was deep in thought. The old mule sensing his mood was in no hurry either. They moved down the road in a slow creeping mass of blackness.

The gentle rain was falling onto the wide leafed fern forming small waterfalls and dumping rivulets of moving water onto the carpet of fallen leaves. It dripped from the tall mulberry bushes and left the still green underbrush dark with dampness. A fog began to settle in making it hard for Billy to see the road. Giving Red the lead, he let the mule pick the trail knowing she would find her way home.

The afternoon mingled with rain and fog becoming a murky gray mass. Billy couldn't tell if it was the fog mixed with rain that was causing the dark to settle in early. He was thinking it must be getting late and hurried Red along nudging her in the flank with his heels.

"Come on old' girl, let's get home an' out'a this weather. Just 'cause I didn't prod, you're a slowin' down to a crawl. Well, let's get to hurryin'. I'll sing you a little song; maybe that'll perk you up some."

> *"Goin' up Cripple Creek, goin' on a run.*
> *Goin' up Cripple Creek to have some fun..."*

Billy sang loudly, his voice hanging close to him in the heavy dampness. The fog deepened settling around the pines and drifting into the ravines and hollows. The rain slowed and became a steady drizzle chilling him to the bone. Hunching his neck down into his shoulders he tried to warm himself smiling as he thought of Mary. The thought of her soft body warmed him some.

Moisture began to drip from his brimmed hat traveling across his shoulders and down his arm then dripped from his elbows. The old mule moved along a little faster. Billy had no idea where he was. He could only see the road under the mule's belly. He was satisfied the mule knew where she was going.

He stopped singing for a moment, pulled his hat down closer over his eyes. The water ran in a stream from the brim. Thinking he heard the sharp ring of metal against rocks he straightened up and listened closer. There was nothing but the steady drumming of the rain on the wide leafed fern. He nudged Red again with his boot heel. The mule jogged on a little faster. There it was again, definitely the sound of hooves against rocks. He heard the sound of horses blowing as if winded from a hard ride. Perhaps it was a neighbor riding up Pound Creek. Who would be out on an afternoon like this, except a lovesick fool like himself?

"I say, who goes there?" he called into the rain. There was no answer. The fog was getting heavier. He could hear the horses coming in closer. "Who goes there?" he called again, still, no answer. It must be someone headed up the trail on the other side of the creek. "Perhaps we could ride together, friend."

He urged the mule to move along faster. Red jogged a few yards at a quicker pace then stopped and stood stubbornly immovable. The sounds on the trail were coming up close behind him.

The fight with Bob Mitchell ran through his thoughts, the scene on his mind as if it were just happening. Bob's threat came ringing in his ears. "You're a dead man, Billy Phelps!" The fear of Mitchell became a burning reality. He urged Red harder, desperately.

"Dog-gone it, Red, you ornery ole' critter! Get on with ya!" The horses were coming faster up the trail behind him. The old mule wouldn't budge. Looking into the fog he could discern dim shapes moving in behind him. Flinging himself from the mule he stumbled along, running frantically, struggling in the heavy mud. He moved from the trail into the wet grass. Horses rattled through the bushes behind him. His raincoat became a heavy burden. Removing it he let it fall to the ground.

In a panic he ran aimlessly, struggling through the brush, not looking or caring his direction. Low hanging branches pulled at his wet clothing. He had lost his hat and his hair hung dripping in his face. Stumbling over a tree root, he fell to the ground. Breathing hard he needed to rest for a minute to get his second wind. There was no sound in the night only the steady drumming of the rain. Hugging his body to the ground he laid still trying not to make a loud sound with his breathing.

Perhaps whoever had been following him had gone around, but then he could hear the sound of someone coming through the brush on foot. He tried to rise up but was so weak from his struggle that he fell back to the ground.

"Gotta get up, keep moving. Oh, Lord, help me." Billy raised himself to a kneeling position. Before he could pull up to stand, a shape came at him from the fog. A red-hot pain pushed through his ribs, knocking him back to the ground. The air left his body in a gush. He flexed and stretched out on a bed of wet leaves his face pressed hard against the earth. A sob wracked his body and he shuddered.

Reviving, he attempted to raise himself, but the effort was useless. The blood rose in his throat and ran from his nose and mouth. If he rested a minute, perhaps he could go on. The rain fell upon him, gently washing the blood from his face.

It seemed like he had lain in the same spot for a long time. His head began to clear and he could think rationally. There was a sound coming through the thick under brush. He could definitely hear a horse trotting along the road. It must be a dream, but he could hear someone whistling, it sounded like Tom. It was Tom. He had heard him whistling like that many times coming from the fields or from working at the mill.

He called to Tom; he must hear him. Let him know he was down here and needed him. He tried to call out, but all he could manage was a gurgle. The blood rose in his throat and ran from his lips. The whistling stopped, but now he heard Tom singing:

> *"Oh that long tail coat that I used to wear,*
> *I'm gonna wear it in the chariot in the morning..."*

He raised his head to listen closer. The night was quiet. Stillness all around, the singing was gone. He laid his head back upon the pillow of wet leaves. His thoughts turned to Mary and how lovely she looked standing with the rain sparkling in her hair as he left her. A breeze blew cold over Billy chilling his face and drying the rain as it fell. The coldness revived him for a moment. He tried to move but he was quickly falling into deep shock.

Opening his eyes he could see a bright refulgent circle forming in the darkness. Inside the light he envisioned Mary in all her golden loveliness. Her head was uncovered and the rain fell upon her shining hair. The moisture clinging to its softness causing a thousand sparks to dance and glisten in its waves. A crystal band of beads encircled her neck creating a shimmering necklace of stars radiating brilliance around her.

The bed of leaves fast became a puddle of mud turning crimson converging with the blood oozing from Billy's body. He struggled to crawl and reach the transcendent illusion. He tried raising his head to speak to her but only managed a faint sigh. The journey over, he rested his head upon her white feet and encircled her legs with his arms.

He could hear Tom singing again, faintly, the last sound in his ears as he faded into death.

"Oh, them golden slippers, Oh, them golden slippers...
Them golden slippers I'm gonna wear to walk them ....Golden streets.

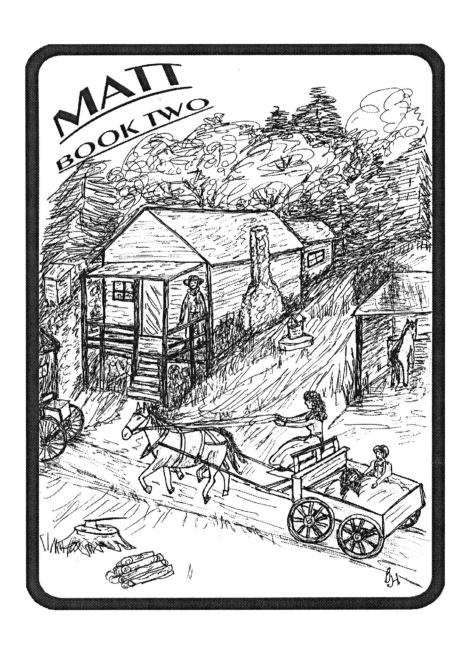

MATT
BOOK TWO

213

CHAPTER ONE

Tom hated riding through the hills after dark, especially on a fog-inhibited night like this one. Drizzle and sleet prevailed and ran in rivulets down the naked limbs of the giant chestnut and maple. A trickle of rain eased its way into his shirt collar and began a freezing journey down his spine. The chilling effect of the weather increased his longing to be home.

Feeling the dampness creeping into his bones, Tom was beginning to wish he'd waited out the night at Trace's. He had ridden out of Donkey with a strong desire to be at the mill and trusted Jole' to find the way along the dark road. He whistled softly to himself.

The soft rain slowed and the fog began to lift. Finding a path through the darkness, the silver moonlight dispersed the clouds and cast dark shadows through the gray trees. The eerie light rested occasionally upon a round-eyed owl or an opossum hanging by its tail from a limb.

As Tom rode, Polly crept into his thoughts. The rain was chilling him to the bone, but thinking of her had a warming effect. Lying with Polly Trace had always been pure joy. However, it was getting too cold to be rolling around in the straw. He had wiled away the afternoon with Polly in the top of her father's barn. Tom was certain the beautiful young woman had other admirers, but his brother Matt was his biggest concern. Some way he had to make him understand Polly was his.

"You don't have to leave now, Tom. It's gettin' late an' it's raining over Pound." Polly had told him.

Tom silenced her with a kiss. "I need to get back an' check on Billy an' Kylee."

"Kylee, Kylee, that's all you've talked about. Who is she anyway?"

"She's a cousin that's come to live with us."

"Livin' with you, how convenient. A cousin is a little close for marryin' though."

"Marryin'! Who said anything about that? Besides she doesn't even like me. She could care less if I'm livin' or dead. Probably prefers me dead. She doesn't even talk to me, unless she has to."

Tom rolled away from Polly and scrutinized the roof of the barn. He picked up a straw to chew on. A silence ensued while he reviewed Kylee's attitude toward him.

"Have you ever thought about marryin', Polly?" Tom broke the silence with the question, spit out the straw and rolled back over on top of her. He had to laugh at how ridiculous her pantaloons looked as a pillow. Her dark hair fanned out about her lovely face.

"Marry you, Tom? Marryin' you would be like saddlin' a whirlwind. Besides, I have other plans. Let's not talk about those things now." Polly looked into Tom's blue eyes so close to her. She smiled and kissed him softly, pulling him tightly against her.

Through the heavy wall of trees and breaking into his reverie rode a group of horsemen, almost running him down. He pulled Jole' up short. The riders rode on up the trail as if the devil were on their heels. The sound of the horse's hooves echoed sharply on the still night and fell hollow on the mass of dampness.

Tom strained his eyes to see, cursing the floating clouds for choosing this moment to cover the moon. Billy's fight with Bob came to mind. The riders could well have been the Mitchell's. Running around at night was a habit of theirs. He had no desire to tangle with them in the middle of the night.

The hills had been plagued with outlaws and renegades. It was not a good idea to be out alone at night. Reaching for his Winchester, he slipped it from the saddle boot and rode with the rifle cradled in his arm. He was feeling again the dismal night pressing in around him.

Tom's longing to be home became a driving force, he encouraged Jole' into a faster gait. He began whistling again softly to himself then broke into singing an old song he had played and sang many times with Billy.

Kylee waited until late wondering about Billy. She settled her mind with the thought that he had decided to spend the dismal night at the Stewart's. Banking the fire in the kitchen, she carried some coals on the shovel into her bedroom and soon had a cozy fire going. Boy promptly occupied his favorite place before her fire.

It was far past Kylee's usual bedtime, but she did not have the slightest inclination toward sleep. When the teakettle hanging over the fire began to steam she wondered if a bath would encourage her into slumber. The large oak tub hung outside at the back door. She stepped across the porch in her stocking feet and lifted it down.

Blue, unlike Boy, preferred the outdoors and had taken up residence in the barn. At this point in the night he decided to take chase after a rabbit feeding in a patch of moonlight. Kylee reached for the tub just as Blue streaked around the corner of the house and across the porch. The sudden, unsuspected movement at her heels was startling. Losing her grip on the heavy wooden tub, she dropped it with a thump on her big toe. A sudden pain shot through her body destroying her composure. Leaning heavily against the wall, she clenched her fists but could not stop the tears of agony that filled her eyes.

"Hush your mouth, Kylee, you're a big baby!" she said out loud, scolding herself for her weakness. Gritting her teeth she tried to sustain the throbbing pain that was beginning to shoot up her leg.

Picking up the tub, she carried it to her room. The desire for a bath had left her mind. She thought, perhaps soaking the injured foot would decrease the pain. She set the tub before the fire and poured in some hot water, and cooled it with water from the pitcher on her dresser. Sitting on the rocker, she laid a towel over her lap and removed her stocking. An ugly red swelling had already begun to enlarge her big toe and a bluish discoloration was appearing under her toenail. With extreme caution, she eased her foot down into the tub. A deep dark feeling of nausea overwhelmed her. Feeling faint she quickly ducked her head between her knees.

Boy, sensing something wasn't right nuzzled her elbow sympathetically. Kylee put her arm around the big dog's neck, thankful for his presence. For a reason Kylee couldn't explain, and dwelling on her agonizing torture, she had a sudden longing for her mother. It was the first time since she had been a little girl that she had thought of her mother in such a way.

When she was a child, she often encouraged her father to talk about her mother. She would coax him to tell her more about when she had been born. He would become tight lipped and refuse to talk about it, becoming even more silent about the matter as she grew older. When he did talk about her mother, he would end up staying in a drunken stupor for days of lonesome misery, so she had learned to stay away from the subject.

Kylee remembered the tender gentleness of her mother, missed her father, and wished Billy was home. She began crying, sobbing loudly. She wanted desperately for someone to sympathize with her misery.

When Tom entered the house, the dim light from Kylee's opened door fell across the floor giving a welcome glow into the kitchen. He could see Kylee huddled over the tub. Boy lifted his head, thumped his tail loudly on the floor, but never left Kylee's side. Tom knocked respectfully on the open door, not waiting for an answer; he hurried to her side.

"What in tarnation's goin' on here? Kinda late to be washin' your feet ain't it Kylee?" Tom questioned teasingly as he came into the room, seeing at a glance that something was definitely wrong.

"Oh, Tom," Kylee exclaimed surprised at his appearance. Raising her face filled with pain and tears she endeavored to dry her eyes on the towel in her lap. "I dropped this durn'd old tub on my toe. It's throbbin' somethin' fierce." her voice was still trembling from pain. She raised her foot from the water and held the toe up for his inspection. Taking the towel from her hand Tom dried the foot carefully then turned it cautiously in his hand.

"I reckon it's not broken, can't say for sure though."

Kylee looked like a small child with a big hurt. He put his arm around her gently; doubtful of how she would take any attempt he made toward comforting her.

"It'll be better in the mornin'. Let's get you to bed. Come on Kylee, lean on me," he encouraged, helping her to stand.

Stepping lightly upon her foot Kylee hesitantly put her weight on it. As the pain increased she fell against Tom thankful for his support.

Tom could see stepping on the foot was sheer agony. He lifted her carefully in his arms and laid her on the bed, smoothing the coverlet over her. He sat down on the edge of the thick feather mattress. The sweet smell of her was beginning to drift over him.

Kylee looked up at him with wide eyes grateful for his presence and thankful for his tender kindness. She encircled his neck with her arms; raising herself she kissed him lightly on the cheek, to thank him. A kiss of gratitude, butterfly soft, so slight he could have scarcely felt it. She must really be out of her mind with pain. Why was she kissing a man she hated?

Misunderstanding, Tom promptly gathered her into his arms. Placing his lips firmly on hers, he kissed her soundly. Kylee struggled to free herself, totally dismayed at his actions. Tom realized in an instant his mistake. He quickly covered his confusion with anger and pushed her roughly back among the pillows.

"What an all-fired, mixed up woman!"

"I didn't mean..."

"I'm sure as hell sorry, Kylee. I didn't mean anythin' either. Seems I'm always misunderstandin' your intentions." Tom rose from the bed and looked down at her. "And you're always misjudging mine!"

"I only wanted to thank you," Kylee offered in a shaky voice, leaning back into the pillow.

"Yah, like a sister," Tom said bitterly.

"Yes," she said, weakly.

"Forget it Kylee, I will! I'll see you in the mornin'."

Noticing the tub, he picked it up and carried it outside. After dumping it over the porch rail, he hung it back on the peg. Coming back inside, he walked over and softly closed Kylee's door as if telling her again it was finished and they should forget the incident. But he couldn't. The brush of her lips still burned sweetly.

The morning was a duplicate of the day before. Rain and dreariness caused Tom's disposition to be ornery and dismal; thinking of the night before didn't help matters.

Kylee was getting breakfast, walking carefully on her heel, and protecting the injured toe. She glanced up as Tom came down the stairs.

"I'll not be needin' any breakfast Kylee. I've got work to do at the mill. I'll have somethin' later." He put on his raincoat and opened the door to go out, then turned back to Kylee.

"Where's Billy, Kylee?"

"He was off yesterday to see Mary. I suspect he stayed the night, least ways he didn't come home," She looked at Tom directly for the first time.

"Did he ride Red?"

"He did, why?"

"Well, I see that ole mule standin' down at the barn, big as all get out. I don't see Billy nowhere's. Now, I know that old mule, she has a habit of leaving you stranded. I know, she's done it to me plenty a times. The old reprobate ain't good for nothin' exceptin' the glue factory. I better take the wagon; Billy will be needin' a ride. If I know him, he'll be headin' home. It sure ain't much of a day for walkin'. Don't worry Kylee; he's probably on the road already."

Tom was out the door and across the yard to the barn. Pulling his hat down over his eyes he hunched his body into the force of the wind and rain. Boy was close on his heels. Kylee watched until he drove the wagon out of the barn with the big dog sitting close to him on the wagon seat.

Before Tom reached the Stewart's the rain stopped; only a soft mist was falling, chilling the air and leaving the road slick on top of the already soggy mud. Tom had not found Billy on the road and he was developing an uneasy concern. The horsemen of the previous night came to mind and his apprehension grew. By the time he turned up the branch to the Stewart's a mood of oppression was upon him. He tried to lift his spirits telling himself he shouldn't borrow sorrow. He tried singing, but it didn't help. He tried harder to convince himself he would find his brother safe and sound at the Stewart's.

Mary waved to him from the garden where she was digging turnips for the noon meal. She was fighting the mud that hung to the shovel in globs making her chore slow and tedious.

Bess was on the porch sweeping away the excess rainwater. She was singing a happy song in time with the swishing of the broom. Her song stopped as she watched Tom approach.

"Howdy, Bess," Tom called as he drove the team up close to the steps.

Gorgeous Bess, her golden beauty never failed to enthrall him. She was the only woman he knew that had not been touched by the harsh life of the hills. Jan and Alvin had always protected her and the girls from the hard work and desolation of the mountains.

Tom feasted his eyes, wondering if he would ever get his fill of her loveliness. The sight of her almost dispelled his nervousness about his brother. He could not shake the hungry longing he had for the older woman. Why, why? He had asked himself many times. Why did he have this driving desire for a woman who had been like a second mother to him? She was the wife of his very dear friend. It was ridiculous, he would warn himself. It could go nowhere; he had to bury it!

"You look mighty lovely this rainy day, Bess. Reckon the rain'll ever stop?" He removed his hat and held it in his hand.

"It always does, Tom. Soon be time for snow. I was hopin' for some more Indian summer before that happens."

They watched Mary coming from the garden carrying the bucket filled with turnips. Tom hadn't seen Billy anywhere. Maybe he was at the barn with Jan. He climbed from the wagon to greet Mary.

"Hello, Mary. Ain't you the purty one this mornin'." Tom's eyes traveled over her. "You're all bubbly and happy. It seems you're just overflowing with joy."

Her large brown eyes were wide with a new happiness. Her long sleeved chocolate colored dress caused her eyes to look vibrantly dark. The pink scarf holding back her long blonde tresses stirred gently in the soft breeze. The brightness from the scarf created a splash of warm sunshine on the dreary day.

What a lovely woman she had grown into, rounding out just right in all the required places. No wonder Billy was eager to have her for his own. He noticed a little longer than necessary the way her firm breasts thrust against her close fitting dress. He stared at how the moist breeze pushed the soft wool into the cradle of her legs. He flashed her a bright smile.

"Why, Tom. Hasn't Billy told you? Poppy promised we could wed." She was smiling, flushed and happy.

"So that's why you're so shinin' bright? You're gonna be a bride. I'm happy about that, Mary. I ain't seen Billy, darlin'. I thought he was here. Kylee said he came to see you yesterday. He ain't been home. Old Red came home without him. She's always doin' that, so I came to see if he was needin' a ride." Tom glanced with troubled eyes from Mary to Bess.

"Oh, dear God Mommy, somethin' dreadful has happened. I know it!" Mary cried in dismay. "I'll never, never see my sweet boy alive again!"

They buried Billy beside his mother in the family burying place, at the top of the hill overlooking the mill, in the shadow of the cool green pines he loved so well. The day was cold, rainy, and continued to be so. The men hurried to cover the homemade casket. The casket Kylee lined with tears and the blue satin Ira had sent Matt into Gladeville to buy. He insisted that his son would have the very best to lie in.

The open grave was filling rapidly with water from the heavy rain making it necessary to drop large rocks upon the casket to weigh it down. Tom's heart was as heavy as the rocks holding the casket down into the murky grave.

"Oh, God, if I'd only known he was lyin' there, perhaps I could have helped him." Tom sobbed to himself. Hunching his head into his coat collar, he remembered his ride home that night. He also recalled vividly the riders on the road.

After searching the hills, Jan, Alvin, and Tom, with Boys help, found Billy in the narrows. They thought it strange; Billy would have never gone into the narrows. He believed the stories that it was filled with spooks and haunts.

They found Billy's raincoat and hat lying in the grass. The path of his struggle was clear, even after the rain. Down into the bottom of the ravine it led. Underbrush and scrub elm so thick one had to squirm to walk. It hadn't been hard to tell how Billy's assailant had worn him down and knifed him in the back. Boy found Billy first, lying in a puddle of mud, his head pillowed on a white stone, arms encircling the white trunk of a young birch tree.

Tom could hear Jan's big booming voice saying a few words over the grave. He had promised Ira to do the honors in the absence of a preacher. Jan was struggling to hold back the tears that were causing his voice to break. As Tom listened, he vowed to himself to tear up the hills until his brother's murder was avenged. Forgetting the pledge he made to do things Billy's way. The old hate raged for the Mitchell's; he was ready to go with Matt and kill them all.

Matt stood beside Tom holding his hat in his hand, baring his head to the drenching rain. Unashamed of his grief, he let the moisture fill his round eyes. The tears flooded over mixing with the rain and washed down his bearded face. He watched closely the grieving women on the opposite side of the open grave.

Little Emily stood pressed against Mary. Her small arms encircled her sister's legs as she sobbed loudly and remembered how Billy would lift her high and ask, "Hi Kitten, still my sweetheart?" Kylee stood close behind them head bowed in deep sorrow, one arm protectively around Ginny who was holding an umbrella over them. The younger girl was crying unabashed and openly, her fair complexion turning scarlet from weeping.

A black silk bonnet covered Mary's golden hair. She stood bravely beside her mother, crying silently, the big tears rolling down her face and off her round chin. Her mother watched her closely; afraid her daughter was close to collapsing.

The Jennings came to join the others in their grieving. Seth blew softly on the mouth harp Billy had given him. No one had the courage to reprimand him. They knew Billy would have loved the music, even if it were only a slight noise from a small boy.

Matt was totally stricken at his brothers' death. His heart went out to Mary in her misery. Wishing there was something he could do to lessen her pain. He sympathized with the deep hurt that engulfed her. He wanted to put his arms around her and hold her close, to comfort her and in doing so ease his own grief.

His watchful eyes traveled from the girls to his father sitting at the end of the grave. Jan stood behind him; the men's bodies open to the rain. Ira was a huddled mass, grieving over his murdered son.

Matt would never forget the evening they had returned to find Billy laid out on his father's bed. Devastated and stunned, Ira sat staring at his dead son, speaking to no one. His heartbreak and silent agony caused a deeper despair upon the others.

Horrified at his brother's death, Matt's hate for the Mitchell's became a searing flame demanding revenge. He was all for going to the Mitchell's and shooting up the place. Only Tom's forceful arm and stern voice stopped him.

"In time brother, in time. First things first." His desire to kill the Mitchell's was burning too. There was the task of burying Billy first. He remembered Billy's gentleness and told his brother:

"Maybe we should think of how Billy would want us to handle this. He never did cotton to killin'. We ought to see if there's anythin' the law will do. Billy would like for us to do that, don't you think?" Tom tried to persuade his brother. "We don't know it was Mitchell's. Billy would want us to be fair about this."

"What the hell you talkin' about Tom? You know they murdered Billy! There ain't such a thing as fair with them bastards! You haven't forgotten who the law is around here have you? Mitchell's will get off scot-free! You know, an' I know, it were Bob Mitchell that got Billy, with Poppa Jay proddin' just a bit. We're not gonna let them get away with that, are we?" Matt was eager for revenge and was disgusted with his brother's unresponsive attitude.

Ira sat beside his son's dead body and had something to say about the matter for the first time since he'd arrived home. "We'll get the bastards one way-or-other. I swear to that! If the good Lord lets me live, I'll see it's done. But first, can we see to buryin' Billy?"

Their father now sat huddled beside Billy's open grave, his faithful friend Hail White standing beside him. Ira pushed away the umbrella she was trying to hold over him. As a result the brim of his black hat filled with rain and dumped into his lap whenever his head bent forward. The blanket over his lifeless legs became drenched and he shivered from the wet cold.

"Let's get you to the house Paw, before you catch your death," Matt suggested to his father.

"I wish it were me lyin' there dead instead of Billy. I'm half dead anyways. I'll not leave until the buryin' is over."

"I only want to get you back where it's warm. There's nothin' more you can do here. Hail will go with us."

"You go on Hail, dear friend. See that the folks get coffee and food. They's been plenty brought in," Ira requested looking up at the woman beside him.

"You stay Matt an' see to the closing of the grave. I'll have Jan take me on down in his wagon. It will be easier that way." The matter was closed and Ira wheeled himself over to where Jan was talking with Carl.

"I will see to that, Ira," Hail promised to Ira's back. "Get your father to the house as soon as you can, Matt. We don't need his death on our hands."

"I'll see you all down at the house." Hail spoke to Bess Stewart as she drew her cape tightly around her shoulders. She walked slowly around the grave and down the hill, her black umbrella protecting her from the rain that was beginning to slow.

Matt had been puzzled at the amount of people that had showed up for the burying. He knew that Billy was well loved and would be missed, as well as the music he played. The day had been so dreary and drippy he thought people would be pragmatic and stay home. He had been wrong. Here they were gathered around in their buggies or riding horseback and carrying umbrellas. They were there to offer their last respects to Billy.

Matt watched as a young woman, new to the group walked proud and aloof across the cemetery. Her haughty bearing separated her from the rest of the mourners. She stopped in front of the Stewart women and was speaking to Mary. Matt was shocked and more than a little puzzled at this new addition to the gathering. How could Taynee Mitchell dare to show up here? He walked closer to hear what she was saying. Taynee had taken Mary's hand and was talking to the grieving girl in a soft low voice.

"I come to tell you Mary, how sorry I am about Billy. I know the Phelps's will think it was Mitchell's what killed him. I want to tell you I had nothin' to do with it, neither did Bob. I know he was jealous of Billy, but he would never kill him. Never! Billy was so good, I feel so sad about his dyin'. You, an' Billy, an' me, we was always friends. It didn't matter to Billy that our families hated each other. He always treated me the same as he done everyone else. He loved everyone. I know he loved you Mary, he told me so."

"Oh, Taynee, it was good of you to come. You shouldn't have chanced it." Mary greeted the other woman in a whisper, her voice filled with terror. "I'm afear'd for you comin' here. You should have waited an' come to the house."

The tears that had filled her eyes dried and were replaced with fear. She looked closely at her friend, and then glanced cautiously over at Ira. It was apparent he was engrossed in a conversation with Carl and hadn't noticed Taynee's arrival.

"I had to come, Mary. I think when Mr. Phelps knows how much I loved Billy; he would let me be here," Taynee surmised, holding her head high, bright courage in her eyes.

"I ain't worrin' about Ira. It's your paw. He'll kill you for sure, if he finds out you were here. Go home, Taynee, before he comes here an' shoots us all!"

"I reckon you're right. I'll go, Mary. I'll come to your house an' we-uns can talk." Bravely she held her head high and her body tensely straight. There was no fear in her flashing violet blue eyes. She bent and kissed Mary on the cheek. "I wanted you to remember they's some of the Mitchell's not full of meanness an' hate."

Taynee eyed Kylee with curiosity. She kissed Emily on top of her head and turned to leave. "Bye, Mrs. Stewart," she said to Bess as she passed.

Matt stepped out from behind Bess to block Taynee's way. With all his six feet stretched to the fullest he stood only a few inches taller than Taynee. All the things he had thought to say to insult her left his mind when he looked into her wide eyes. He was speechless.

226

"E-gads," he puzzled to himself. How the girl had changed since the last time he had seen her.

A slight smile played around the corners of his mouth as he remembered Taynee as a skinny unwashed kid with wild, tangled hair. The smile became real and widened as he recalled the homemade corncob pipe he'd offered her. He had to admit she'd had spunk and smoked the pipe like one of the boys and hadn't turned a bit green. At the time she had worn a pair of Blaine's ragged britches and a faded patched shirt. He supposed she couldn't help what she had to wear. Her mother was dead and she had grown up with three wild half brothers. No wonder she acted like a boy, she had to, in self-defense. She'd looked like a boy, walked like a boy, and rode a horse like no one he had ever seen then or since.

Surely this young lady standing before him was not the same person. There was no resemblance, except for her eyes, wonderful eyes, wide and violet blue with a slight slant to the outside corners. Her brows were black as the soot that gathered at the back of the chimney, with a sweeping curve upward. He could still feel the sharp whack she'd laid across his face after he suggested she be his girl. He had wanted her to go inside Trace's barn and lay with him in the hay. Could it have been so long ago?

Here she was now, bloomed into a fantastically, superb young woman, wearing a dress, clean and neatly pressed under her long black cape. Her face glowed with cleanliness, tight curly hair, brushed and shining underneath a black silk scarf wet from the rain.

Looking now at her dark gypsy-like beauty, he wished he'd been successful in taking her inside the barn. Dark curls of unruly hair crept out from under her scarf to hang about her lovely face. Matt could see it was curly as the tangle gut that grew around the rocks in the darkest hollows of the forest, still defying all Taynee's attempts to tame it. The sassy, rebellious gleam in her eyes was still there.

Taynee caught her breath and her face paled. She wondered about the slight smile on Matt's face. But not for long as it turned quickly into a smirk of hate. He hadn't smiled at her after that day at Trace's barn, but he had made fun of the way she had been dressed. He had been very angry when she refused to go into the barn with him for indecent activity. Taynee remembered the sharp slap she'd laid across his face. My goodness, he had grown tall since then.

"That is you, ain't it?" Matt asked, blocking her way.

"Of course it's me, Matt!" she retorted trying to make her way around him. A nervous trembling was developing deep in her middle.

"I knew it was you Taynee, but I couldn't believe any Mitchell would dare show up here!" Matt took her arm and guided her forcefully over to his father.

"Look who's here, Paw!" Matt told his father triumphantly as if he had just marched home from battle with a prize trophy.

They were finishing with the grave and people were beginning to move slowly down the hill. The rain had stopped but the sky was still heavy and overcast. The once green grass now a drab brown, preparing itself for the covering of winter snow, was heavy with moisture.

Ira looked up puzzled. His eyes were clouded with grief and unshed tears. He waited patiently for Jan to take him in the wagon back to the house. "Lord-a-mercy! If it ain't Taynee Mitchell. It is Taynee, ain't it?" Ira's voice was soft as apple butter. He looked at her searchingly. Taynee wanted to run, but Matt held her arm in a firm grip.

"Sure enough it is Taynee, Paw!" Matt answered, his eyes filled with victory. He stood tensely straight, as if waiting for his father to string up his captive to the nearest tree limb.

Ira looked at her with his well-known scowl, not in a hurry to speak. Taynee felt as if his stare had reached to the bottom of her shoes and he could see the corn on her little toe. When Ira did speak his voice was kind, not harsh as she expected it would be.

"You look like your maw, girl. She was a beauty!" Ira could see Taynee had her mother's Gypsy beauty, with tightly curled hair, skin the color of creamed coffee with a pink tint on her high cheekbones. Her lips were a deep rose color, full and sensuous. Her eyes, violet blue with a black ring around the outside of the color, causing the white's to be a bold contrast. Dark brows and eyelashes were finely shaped as if they had been painted with an artist's brush. Yes indeed, Ira thought Taynee was as beautiful as her mother, maybe even more so. He could tell she was beginning to be frightened and hurried to assure her she needn't be.

"Paw, maybe she can tell us somethin' about what happened to Billy." Matt held tightly to Taynee's arm.

"Let her go boy. We've no quarrel with this girl," he indignantly told his son turning to Taynee and commenting, "You're a brave one, comin' here at a time like this."

"Billy was my friend, Mr. Phelps. Maybe you didn't know that, but Billy was a friend to everyone, even Taynee Mitchell. I only wanted to come see him buried. If my paw finds out, he'll kill me for sure. But I ain't carin', I come anyways!" Taynee said triumphantly; glad to be free from Matt's hold, trying to rub the circulation back into her arm. "I don't know a thing about what happened to Billy. I only know I'm dreadfully sad. So sad I could kill the one who done it."

"It's right decent of you gal, right decent! But there's no need to get your paw angry at you. You better go on home now. You remember any friend of Billy's is always welcome at the mill. Any friend, even Taynee Mitchell!" Ira told her, looking significantly at Matt.

"You're kind, Mr. Phelps. I'm so sorry about Billy."

Taynee said goodbye to Ira. Giving Matt a searing look of hostility she walked quickly back into the forest. She disappeared into the trees beyond the cemetery where she had tied her horse. She moved as quickly as the wet grass would allow. Her long skirt and heavy cape left a silver trail behind her.

The faster Taynee walked, the angrier she became. Who in the hell did Matt think he was anyway? Just because he was a Phelps didn't give him the right to treat her like dirt. She couldn't help being a Mitchell, no more than he could help being a Phelps. She should have stayed away. Taynee was very aware of the curious stares her presence had drawn.

She held her skirt high and away from the wet grass, enabling her to walk faster. Her dark blue skirt was shabby around the bottom, but had been neatly patched and mended. The only pair of black stockings she owned had been darned in many places. Her badly worn boots were polished and buffed to a high sheen. She wondered if all the effort it had taken to look respectable had been noticed by anyone. Well no matter, Billy would have!

Thinking of her dear friend made her cry. She rested her head against the nose of her horse. Midnight waited patiently until the flood of tears subsided. The black horse neighed softly as if in sympathy with her sorrow. Regaining her composure, she pulled up her skirts and mounted straddle.

Rueben would skin her alive for taking his saddle. He had left early in the day with the small wagon and a lunch Nell had carefully packed. He had high hopes that Polly would accompany him on a picnic. Taynee could not understand her half brother's apparent and sudden dedication to Polly Trace.

Removing her scarf she tied it around the saddle horn. Digging her long fingers into her scalp, she loosened her tightly curled hair until it hung free and loose past her shoulders. Touching Midnight gently on the flank with the reins, she urged him into a fast gallop toward Tandy's mountain.

As she rode into the wide fenced yard, her father and two men came out of the house. Here was trouble. She had to make up a story fast. When she'd left, her father had been gone and she'd hoped to be home before he returned. He stopped her at the barn door, nodding for her to get down.

"Where you been, Taynee?"

Jay noticed her wet clothes and tangled hair. Midnight was winded and sweating. Taynee stood, face flushed, chin high.

"Just ridin', Paw." She avoided his steady gaze.

"In the rain?" The question was a mockery. He could tell from her wet locks and the winded horse she had been more than just riding.

Jay's smile was a white smirk through his dark whiskers. He hadn't failed to notice her rosy face and the way the dampness had turned her hair to shimmering satin. Her eyes flashed with rebellion.

"Well, Nell was so poorly, I rode to Hail's to see if she'd come," she lied.

"Well?" he asked, waiting for her to go on.

"She weren't home." Taynee looked at him boldly, daring him to doubt her.

"You should have know'd she'd be to Billy Phelps's buryin'. You know'd they were a buryin' Billy today, didn't you? One less Phelps to plague me," Jay muttered under his breath into his beard.

"No Paw, I didn't," she said bravely, lying again. Taynee turned to busy herself ducking her head as she untied her scarf from the saddle horn. She did not want to see the fire in her father's eyes when he spoke of Phelps's. She had heard clearly what he'd said about Billy, 'one less Phelps.'

"Come on, Jay!" one of the men called as they mounted their horses.

"You are a comin', aren't you?" the other shouted.

The men were both armed, pistols strapped around their hips over their long coats. High caliber rifles were tucked into saddle boots. They watched Taynee, not missing a thing. The youngest man with brown hair and beard gazed boldly at her. His piercing brown eyes held more than a casual interest.

Ferrell Hall was an outlaw from Tennessee, unashamed of his livelihood. He had seen Taynee during his many visits at Jay's and couldn't forget the beauty of the girl. He had plans to ask for the young woman, knowing if he had the price, Jay would not refuse him. He had to get the money soon, he thought as he watched the girl. Seeing the spark in her eyes as she defied her father made him think of the fire that must burn inside her. He wanted to be the one to fuel the flame.

"I'm comin'! I have to get my horse." Jay disappeared into the darkness of the barn.

Taynee sighed with relief. She had been saved by the men's urgency to leave.

Sitting high on his big horse, Jay rode out of the barn warning Taynee again as he passed her, "You get inside an' help your maw. Don't be worrin' your purty head about ridin' to Hail's or no other place. I'll see to fetchin' her when Nell's time comes." He gave Taynee a twisted smile of assurance she didn't believe. The men rode away leaving behind them a sharp stench of animal droppings and horseflesh wafting on the damp air.

"Sure!" Taynee mused as she watched them ride away. "You'll let her die, that's what you'll do. You'll let her die! Just like you did my maw!" She hated her father as only a child can hate a parent.

Kylee followed Mary and Ginny from the cemetery stepping cautiously on her heel; she found it difficult to keep up. She'd taken her old shoes and cut the toe from one fashioning a pair to fit her swollen foot. The moisture from the wet grass soaked into her stocking and filled the shoe with water. The rain had penetrated her worn cape and she was shivering from the cold.

She hated going back to the house. Her entire personage was filled with despair at Billy's death. The last few days had been too busy for clear thinking and the pain from her toe had become an added burden. Now that it was over the reality of Billy's death weighed heavy upon her.

First her father died, now Billy. Two people she had loved dearly were gone; it was more than she could stand. Things would never be the same now without Billy. Matt and Ira still treated her the same, but Tom was a different matter. She felt he preferred her to be miles away. There was no place in her thoughts for Tom now. Mary was waiting for her on the top step.

"I'm feelin' poorly Mary. I don't feel up to meetin' with all them folks. I'm goin' to my room. Tell Uncle Ira I'm not feeling well. I'm goin' to bed. I'm sorry Mary. I'm so terribly sorry about Billy. We're all gonna miss him." She fought the tears that flooded her eyes.

Mary smiled faintly, the misery showing in her countenance. Saying nothing to Kylee, she hugged her friend and went into the house, swallowing hard to keep back the flood of tears at the mention of Billy. They would talk later, talk of the beautiful dreams and wonderful promises of the tender love and unfilled passion. The plans were gone, all gone. Nothing was left except for their love; it would never die.

Kylee followed but went to her room and closed the door. The kitchen was crowded with friends drinking coffee and eating the food they had brought. A jug was being passed among the men, under the disapproving looks of the women.

Kylee welcomed the chance to be alone. There was still a dim glow from the earlier fire. Thankful for the slight warmth, she undressed and went to bed. She thought her dreams would be of Billy, but her troubled slumber was infiltrated with visions of Tom. She could feel the strength of his strong arms around her and the sweetness of his lips upon hers. Then, there it was again, the smirk on those same lips after he had stolen the kiss. Always, always, it was his attitude toward everything, the attitude that caused her deeper resentment toward him. It only added to her mental file of, 'hate Tom'.

CHAPTER TWO

Kylee rose reluctantly the next morning after sleeping well into the day. She was hopeful of feeling better, but her foot had become a thing of throbbing fierceness. She was managing to get around barefooted, walking carefully on her heel. She prepared a late breakfast and waited for the Phelps men to rise.

Billy was heavy in her thoughts. She missed his sunny smile and thatch of early morning tousled hair. Fighting back the tears bravely, she struggled to give herself a cheery attitude for her adopted family. Knowing their grief was deep; she wanted to be a comfort to them. However, Tom was the only one who showed up for the meal. Ira would not come out of his room and Matt was still asleep.

Tom said nothing to her as he ate and she was sullen toward him. They both remembered vividly the incident on the night of Billy's murder. Tom readied to leave the kitchen fishing his raincoat out of the closet under the stairs.

"How's the foot?" he spoke softly as his head reappeared from a sea of coats and wraps. He eyed the unfortunate toe.

It was the first time in three days he had spoken directly to Kylee. Everything had happened so fast. Tom was still in a state of disbelief. There had been no time to think or worry about Kylee's attitude toward him, so he had ignored her.

"Is it better?"

"It's still swollen some," she said, biting hard on her bottom lip.

She stared at the floor and couldn't bring herself to look at him. Why didn't he go on down to the mill? She didn't want to look at his unruly hair hanging in his face nor look into his eyes laden with grief. Eyes so light blue they always made her feel as if she was drowning. Down, down into a pool of cool water that she couldn't get out of.

Kylee watched as he buttoned his raincoat getting ready to go out into the dripping weather. His large hands with wide square palms and long strong fingers stirred a feeling inside her, hands not strangers to hard work. She remembered how gently he had felt her injured foot for broken bones. His hands had been tender on her inflamed flesh. A scary thought engulfed her; she wondered how it would be to have those strong hands caress her body.

"My God! Help me!" she pleaded silently as a warm glow filled her body. "I'm acting like a hussy! What's got into me? I don't even like this man!" She ducked her head, hiding her eyes, ashamed of the sudden outburst of feeling, knowing it would surely bring about hell fire and damnation. Hadn't the ladies from the church warned her?

Turning away she busied herself at the table hoping that Tom had not noticed the blush on her face or guessed her thoughts. Better get this nonsense out of her mind! It was if she had a fever in her head. Did this mean she was beginning to allow Tom an equal rating with the other Phelps men? Never!

Tom poured himself another cup of coffee watching Kylee's every move. Her beauty filled him with a longing and a new unrest he didn't understand. His hand shook but not from the weight of the filled cup. Desire for a woman was not a new thing to Tom, but there was more to this. Before he had finished his coffee his father wheeled into the kitchen. Tom, still in his raincoat moved quickly to pour him a cup of coffee.

"I've got to get away from this place, Tom. There's too much of Billy here. I see him in every corner. I cain't stand it another day. Killing Mitchell's is not gonna ease the pain. Besides I'm not up to chasing them bastards into Kentucky. I heard from Carl that's where they've gone, hiding out, waitin' for this to blow over. You remember what Hensely had to say when we reported Billy's murder? We didn't have a drop of evidence to prove that any of them were involved. He would not back us up in takin' out a warrant." Ira sipped his coffee appreciating its early morning goodness. "He warned we'd become the laughing stock of the county if we pressed charges against Bob, just on suspicion. We would only rile Jay into killing us all if we insisted on Bob's arrest. In that case we-uns had better sure enough find a place to hide. Well, I ain't ever took to hidin' from no one, least of all Mitchell's!"

His sleep of the last few nights had been troubled and restless. His eyes were heavy and swollen. Hensely's attitude about Billy's murder hadn't helped ease his grief. "I ain't aimin' on swearin' out no warrant for Bob's arrest, so's that polecat Jay can get off scot-free. You know what I mean?"

He drank down the hot black coffee wiping his lips with his hand in satisfaction. Looking over the cup he accepted the breakfast Kylee sat before him. "We don't really know, do we Tom, if it were Bob? Seems to me it's more likely Jay's the guilty party. He's the one for us to reckon with. He's the one that's so all fired set on killing Phelps's." He looked at Tom with burning decision in his eyes.

Ira stroked his white beard into smoothness but let his tousled hair go unattended. He continued to ponder over when and how he would get even with Jay. One thing for sure he wasn't going to get away with killing Billy.

"I know what you mean, Paw," Tom agreed unbuttoning the top button on his raincoat. It was getting warm next to the fire.

"I think Jay's gonna make himself scarce for a few days. Him an' them no good boys of his will be hangin' out with that bunch of outlaws they've been dealin' with. Carl said he had it from good source they had all headed for Kentuck. It's just as well; I ain't ready to tangle up ass holes with that bunch of outlaws. So we'll wait until we can pin Jay down closer to home. While we are a waitin', we'll take a little trip into Caroline." Ira announced his decision.

"Aw Paw; I ain't wantin' to go to Caroline. It don't seem fittin' with just buryin' Billy an' all."

"It makes no-never-mind; we-uns are a-goin' anyways!"

Deep down behind the grief in his father's eyes, Tom could see the glint of blue steel. He knew his father was not to be argued with.

As far as Mitchell's were concerned there was not a doubt in his mind, it was Jay who should pay for Billy's death. He was certain that Billy would understand now that it was positive there would be no help from the law.

"Hitch up that new team of grays you bought in Kentuck. You haven't been along with me for sometime. You can get along without Jole' for a few days."

"I'll get the team hitched an' be back for you." Tom accepted the decision and disappeared out the door just as Matt came down the stairs.

"I'm ready Paw!" Matt greeted, "are we gonna get us some Mitchell's today an' even up the score?"

Matt fastened his gun around his hips and smoothed down his black hair. He placed on his hat and reached for his coat. He was ready and couldn't understand why his father and brother didn't share his eagerness.

"Not today Matt, it's gonna wait son!"

"Wait? What the hell you mean, Paw? It was weight what broke the wagon wheel. That's what you always told me." Matt reminded his father, not believing his passive attitude.

"We ain't chasin' Mitchell's across the country. You keep your gun holstered until we get back," Ira's orders were implicit.

"Get back? Get back from where? Where you goin?"

"Tom an' I are goin' to Caroline. We'll pick up another batch of shine. This'll be the last trip before winter. You can take care of things here. You watch after Kylee too. Don't be goin' off to see Polly or lookin' for a card game. I'll not have her left here alone." Ira's eyes rested on Kylee.

"You're lookin' kinda puny girl. Anythin' wrong?" he questioned her, his voice filled with concern.

"It's nothin' Uncle Ira. Don't worry about me. I'll be fine. You worry about yourself, an' keepin' dry. I'll get your umbrella an' raincoat. We can't have you gettin' sick. I'll fix you up some vittles to take along," she told him smiling at him sweetly.

"Nag! Nag! Why is it women think it is their born duty to nag a man? But I'll take the umbrella an' the vittles, but it's not necessary Kylee. We'll be stayin' the night at Stewarts."

Ira took Kylee's hand and scrutinized the young woman closely. She wasn't looking well. He couldn't tell if it was physical or perhaps because of her grief over Billy. He knew the two had become close friends. Or was she still grieving for her father?

"Still missin' your paw, girl? I miss him too Kylee. I've missed him for a long time. Of course he told you we go back a long way. We were not just cousins; we were friends, like brothers. When our folks died we were youngins, fifteen an' sixteen. There was a lot of sickness in the hills, an epidemic of sorts. A lot of folks died. Your paw an' me was left to raise each other, an' me being' the oldest, I took head responsibility. I'll take you some time Kylee, up the branch to your paw's old place. It's still up there. It's all covered with vine, but it's still there." Ira promised.

"I should have explained Kylee, about all this business with the Mitchell's an' other things too. Seems all this hatin' started back when our folks both wanted this place. I want you to understand girl, how it is." Ira's mind wandered, taking liberties with the past. "My great grand pappy, Booker T. Phelps owned this land. It was his legally and deeded. But Rueben James Tandy came and started building on it. My great grand pappy had to run him off. Tandy took offense. He thought he was here first an' the land by law of possession was rightfully his. His family has been hatin' an' killin' us ever since."

"Old man Tandy, Jay's great grand pappy, was a hard man. They called him, 'Iron Jaw'; not only because of his ornery personality but also because of his looks. The side of his face was disfigured and was like iron. He had to talk out of the side of his mouth."

"Oh, that's sad!" Kylee offered a sympathetic observation.

"I'm sure it was, dear. I never saw him. He died long before I was born. But grandpa said he was as hard as his jaw. 'Iron Jaw' claimed that we-uns stole his property here at the mill. Now Jay thinks this place should belong to him. He aims to kill us all to get it. You would think after all these years the youngin's would forget all the hatin'. But they are still at it. Billy's dead an' I'm afear'd Kylee; this is just a new beginning. Good, dear, Billy. He never hurt no one. Why didn't they come after me? I ain't worth nothin' anyways!"

The history Ira related to Kylee was filled with tragedy and hate. He knew it would not end as long as any of them lived. Another murder had been done and he knew it had only just begun.

"Did my paw have anythin' to do with the fightin'?"

Kylee sat down in the rocker next to the fire close to Ira. She carefully covered her injured toe with her long skirts. Looking at Ira she understood the grief the man was feeling for his son. She thought that perhaps talking of other things might help him forget for a moment. Maybe now would be a good time to find out just what connection she had with the Phelps's and why she was here.

"My paw told me he had done a favor for you one time. He said you would take me into your home, because you owed it to him. Is that true, Uncle Ira? Did you let me stay because you owed my paw? What was the favor Paw done for you?" Kylee's eyes widened as she continued her interrogation.

"I took you because I wanted you Kylee. I loved your paw as a brother. We had other brothers an' sisters but they all left the hills before our folks died. Your paw an' I decided to have a business together, so we built the mill. Then the war spread over the country an' things stopped for awhile an' your paw went into the army. After the war he decided to find his fortune somewhere else." Ira scrutinized Kylee closely. "It was his decision not to come back here. I believe he done all right, from the looks of you. Your paw an' I were partners in everything, Kylee girl. He was a full partner with me in the mill. It's true; it's all legal. His share belongs to you now he's dead. So you see darlin', you ain't just a charity case, you belong here, same as the rest of us. Don't let anyone tell you different! I was waitin' for the right time to tell you. I wanted to make sure you would stay here, make certain that you would love this place the same as I do. I believe that you do. So, you see Kylee, this is your home."

Having her here was like having the daughter he had always wanted. Looking at her now he couldn't believe how beautiful her eyes were. It caused him to reflect on a girl with fire in her hair and eyes just as gooseberry green. Ira became vague; ignoring deliberately Kylee's question of what the favor was her paw had done for him.

"Oh, Uncle Ira, can it be true? Am I part owner in the mill with you all? It ain't truly possible. It's a dream, a story you made up to make me feel at home, now Billy's gone."

"Is this true, Paw or just a story you made up? You never told us a thing about it," Matt questioned in total surprise.

Matt was sitting on the stairs polishing the barrel of his pistol with the handkerchief he carried in his back pocket. He couldn't believe what he was hearing. He was as shocked as Kylee.

"I never know'd a thing about this." There was a hurt tone added to Matt's voice.

"There's lotsa things you don't know, boy!" Ira told him coming back to the present. "It's true. Kylee is owner with us in the mill. Your paw never know'd of it Kylee. I never told him, but it is the way things are. Now come give your ole uncle a kiss an' we'll be goin'. I see Tom comin' with the wagon." Ira waited with anticipation for Kylee's kiss.

Kylee stood up and moved cautiously to embrace her uncle and placed a warm kiss on his cheek. Her sudden feeling of emotion toward him was confusing and bewildering. Here was a totally new aspect to her life. After diabolically losing everything that was her father's, she had suddenly become a property owner. This really was a place for her. She did belong here.

Kylee bit her bottom lip and clenched her fists tightly. The pain in her foot was beginning to be an agony that was encasing her body. She tried to keep a pretense up for her uncle, not wanting to worry him.

Matt wheeled his father out to the long low porch and Kylee limped along behind them. The clouds were clearing and there was beginning to be a promise of dry weather. Matt lifted his father and carried him down the steps to meet the wagon. Kylee handed down the umbrella, raincoat, and black felt hat that was still damp from the rain of yesterday. She then handed the little bundle of goodies she had tied into a clean white dishtowel.

"You better tell Tom what you told Kylee an' me, Paw. He'll be wantin' to know. You take care now!" Matt told his father with brash firmness as he lifted his father up to the wagon seat. He carefully tucked the gaily-colored quilt around his legs. He looked at Tom with a meaningful glare.

"You take care of him, Tom, you hear?"

"Don't tell me what to do brother. I'm as capable of takin' care of Paw as you be. You worry about takin' care of things around here." Tom was sullen, still not over eager for this trip.

"I don't know when we'll be back son. You do as I told you. You take care of our girl. Don't be gallivantin' off somewhere's lookin' for a card game. You been takin' up too much with them no-good card playin' fools. They ain't ever gonna be your friends, they's only after your money."

"Another thing! Don't be for seekin' out Mitchell's on your own! You hear me good now!" Ira said his final word and settled onto the seat ready for the journey.

"Take care of Jole' for me Matt. Bye Kylee, take care of that toe." Tom gave her a flashing good-bye smile. Clicking his tongue at the horse, they headed for the bridge below the mill.

Kylee watched them until they took the turn into the trees and disappeared. She watched Matt cross the yard and enter the mill, then she turned slowly into the empty silent house.

Matt came to the house later in the day to find Kylee huddled in the window seat. Her knees were drawn up making a resting place for her head. She had wrapped her arms tightly around her legs. Her hair tumbled in a wild cascade around her. She was crying quietly, her body shaking with the flood of tears.

"Kylee, what's the matter?"

Her huddled body told Matt something was badly wrong. Going over to where she sat, he smoothed back her heavy hair. Finding her chin he lifted her face.

"Matt, I'm sorry. I couldn't get supper, but there's plenty of food left from what everyone brung," she apologized weakly.

"Well now, I reckon that's not the end of the world. My land girl, you look terrible. You're burnin' up with fever."

"It's my durned ole' toe," Kylee answered weakly, holding the object up for Matt to survey.

He could see that not only was the toe blue and discolored, but her foot was inflamed and swollen. A fine red line had begun extending its way up the inside of her foot and leg.

"My word Kylee, how long has this been goin' on?" he questioned, frightened at the extreme infected look of her toe.

"Since the night Billy was killed. I dropped the tub on it. I didn't think it was gonna be so bad," she explained drying her eyes on her hair.

Matt could see Kylee was sinking under the stupor of an intense fever. Her eyes were vague and her speech fading.

"I'm takin' you to Hail's, Kylee. She'll know what to do. I'll get the buggy an' be right back. We should've had her look at that toe when she was here at Billy's funeral. You sit right there 'til I get back."

In the barn he wheeled out the black rig that had belonged to his mother. The buggy had seldom been used since Mattie's death. It was still in excellent condition inside and out.

Ira and Tom had taken the big wagon. The small wagon was loaded inside the mill with meal to be delivered. He pulled the buggy outside, picked up a bucket of oats giving it a rattle, and waited for the horses to come. Picking out Dolli, he hitched the old gray to the buggy.

He found Kylee in the same dejected position as he had left her. Taking her cape down from a peg beside the door, he wrapped it around her huddled shoulders.

"Come on Kylee. I'll be careful not to hurt you," he assured her in a soft, gentle voice as if speaking to a child, "put your arms around my neck. I'll carry you out."

Placing his arms under her knees, Matt lifted her carefully. Kylee eased her arms around his neck and he carried her outside and placed her in the buggy. The sun was passing between the dark clouds, determined to resume its dominion over the blue sky. There was not much light left, the day would soon be at an end.

Guiding the team through the gate, Matt turned west from the mill toward the Gap. The road wound sixteen miles on over Pound Mountain into Kentucky. Matt drove up the road two miles to a place where Tandy's branch swirled into the main creek. The narrow wheels of the buggy were almost lost inside the wide ruts left by the big wagons that made up the traffic over the mountain. The tracks were filled with mud and water from the recent rains and Matt was concerned about the condition of the road as he turned onto Tandy's Mountain.

Kylee tried to stay awake but her eyes kept closing into sleep, induced by her rising fever. She scarcely knew what was happening. Matt watched her closely reaching and tucking her cloak carefully around her. Her head was bobbing up and down from the movement of the wagon until he became concerned for her safety. Putting his arms around her shoulder, he eased her down, encouraging her to stretch out and lay across his lap. Kylee was so thankful for the change of position that she dropped off immediately into a deep slumber.

The sun bowed out in a blaze of glory, letting the dusk settle in. The heavy trees up Tandy's road closed in the darkness and it seemed later than it was. On a high rise Matt looked back down the mountain, the same place where Mattie had stopped so long ago. He could see dimly the top of the mill. The sun was glowing red behind the tall shadows of the large oaks.

Gnarled branches were bare now except for a few brave brightly colored leaves. These hung on tenaciously, not wanting to let go of the nourishing bosom of the mother tree. Flickering gaily, they quickly caught a bit of the sun's fleeting rays.

The remains of their old tree house still perched high on a burly branch casting a dark silhouette against the setting sun. Matt recalled the time Billy had fallen from the tree house splitting his head open. He had cried for hours, afraid his little brother was going to die and certain it was his fault. Their mother had warned him many times not to take Billy into the tree house because he was too little. Mattie had been afraid such a thing might happen. They sent for Hail and she stopped the bleeding with her secret prayers and a little medical knowledge she learned from her father.

Matt always hated his position as a middle child. He felt his mother loved Billy better and that his father favored Tom. He often wondered where he belonged in the childhood triangle. Tom had always been chosen to do the adult things and he had been stuck watching Billy. If anything happened to the little brother, he was to blame. Sometimes he felt as if he didn't even belong to the family at all, and it hurt. Then they found his mother dead and there was no time for feeling his way out of the middle. He had become the constant companion for Billy and they became very close. There was still a chip on his shoulder toward Tom, but it became lighter as they grew older.

He watched the visibility of the tree house sink into an ocean of darkness and scraggly gray branches. He meditated on what his father had often told him. "Ain't never gonna cut down them magnificent oaks. If anything happens to me, don't you let no one cut them. The pines, they's beautiful, but they stay the same, never changin'. The oaks, they's different. They change into a new dress for every season, never lettin' us forget how time is passin' away from us."

Heavy darkness was setting in stretching out along the crest of the hill. The road grew steeper and was washed out in places, but the horse and buggy were traveling well. Matt breathed relief as they turned past the orchard. They had pulled the worst part of the road. They were in luck; so far there hadn't been any Mitchell's. He supposed they were still in Kentucky.

He was so concerned for Kylee that he'd left his gun laying on the stairs. There wasn't a rifle in the buggy anymore. If they happened to run into the Mitchell's they would be dead for sure. Getting Kylee to Hail's quickly was Matt's only concern. Without much thought he had headed for Tandy's Road. He breathed a little easier when he guided Dolli through the broken gate and stopped in front of Hail's cabin.

The cabin sat precariously upon the side of the steep hill, nestled into the tall pines. The porch reaching out into space was supported strongly by long poles giving the cabin some promise of safety. Under the porch Hail had stored all manner of junk, wagon wheels, old kettles, wooden chairs, etc. To the right of the house was a lean-to that housed her mule and two nanny goats; next to it was a corral where several sheep grazed. Keeping them company was a gaggle of hissing geese. Hail kept these noisy critters purposely to pluck their down for pillows and comforters.

Matt could scarcely see through the darkness that was gathering around the thick trees. A scant light shone from the windows and showered the young night with warmth that gladdened his heart. As he brought the horse and buggy to a halt, he gave a loud, "Hallo."

"That you, Matt?" Hail's voice, filled with surprise, floated out to them from the doorway soft as the udder down of a goose's belly.

"Yes, it's me, Hail," Matt called in answer, "I brung some one to see you."

"Well, get on in here out of that evenin' dampness. It ain't good for no one. It's a might chilly after that rain."

Matt lifted Kylee from the buggy and carried her up the steps. Kylee couldn't believe their journey was over. She had slept all the way and was scarcely aware of the ride. Raising herself a little as Matt carried her in, she tried to rally from the feverish sleep. She wanted to be somewhat alert coming into a strange house.

Even in her feverish state, Kylee recognized the woman in the doorway. She had been at the mill many times during those sad days after Billy's death. She had constantly been at Ira's side the day of the burial. Kylee had been too wrapped up in her own misery and sorrow to give the woman much thought. There had been so many friends and family coming and going, weeping and wailing. Kylee had withdrawn whenever possible and spent most of the time in her room.

She vaguely noticed that the woman still wore a black dress fully covered with a white severely starched apron. Heavy hair, platinum white, was pulled back fiercely across her ears into a large bun at the nape of her neck. Her skin was peaches and cream, without a wrinkle, which denied the old appearance her white hair imparted. Heavy brows were a dark contrast that arched across her face. Her lips that had once been full and sensuous were now pulled into a straight line, never relaxing. A fine shaped nose was the prominent point in her beautiful face. She looked as if she had just been scrubbed and pressed.

Matt sat Kylee on a small straight back chair. He stood close beside her. His hand rested strongly on her shoulder. The inside of the cabin looked as Hail did, neat and scrubbed. The walls were finished with wood plank and wallpaper. The kitchen area was whitewashed and neat. An impressive rock fireplace filled one wall of the small room. The plank floor had been scrubbed with a broom and sand until it was gleaming white.

Through the windows, without curtains, Kylee could see the thick pines tossing against the darkening sky. Leaning heavily against Matt, she felt an overwhelming nausea over powering her.

"It's her foot, Hail," Matt informed the woman.

Hail lifted Kylee's bare foot in her hand, turning it carefully. She pinched her bottom lip between her thumb and forefinger.

"My, it is bad youngin'. See that red line? That's blood poisonin'. First we gotta get that old blood out from under that bruised toenail. Take your coat off Matt an' scrub your hands over there in the basin. You can help me."

"You should a had me look at this when I was at the mill, child." She silently cursed the carelessness of the young. She remembered the young woman. Ira had explained she was Val's child.

"I have see'd people lose their legs for letting an infection like this wait too long," Hail continued in her soft voice, not meaning to frighten her patient.

A large black pot hung on a tripod over the grate inside the fireplace. The pungent odor ensuing from the pot finished Kylee. She headed off the chair into a deep faint. Matt caught her just in time to keep her from sprawling on the floor.

"Quickly, take her to my bed." Hail's tone was one of urgency and concern.

The bedroom was a small lean-to at the back of the cabin, nestled near the side of the hill. A single high bed was made up with quilts, muslin sheets, and large fluffy down pillows. It seemed to be ready and waiting for Kylee.

The bed had been placed close to the wall. Across the bed and half way up the back wall was an oblong window. At the side of the bed was a marble-topped cabinet with washbowl and water pitcher. A small shelf was nailed to the wall above; a leather covered Bible buckled shut with a leather strap occupied a place on top.

A large white chamber pot with a lid sat on the floor at the end of the bed. A cluster of blue daisies decorated the side. A large curly maple highboy chest completed the room's furnishings. The room was very plain with no frills of any kind. The colorful bouquet of painted flowers on the side of the pot looked strangely out of place.

Kylee was scarcely aware that Matt had carried her into the room and laid her on the bed. Coming out of her faint, and still groggy, she clung to Matt. With mounting concern she was trying to realize what was happening.

"Don't leave me Matt. I'm afraid. Take me back home. I'll be fine, I promise. Oh, please don't leave me here. She's gonna take off my leg," Kylee wailed in utter despair and fright. "I'll die for sure if you leave me!"

"I won't leave you, Kylee. I'm gonna be here to help Hail take care of you. No, she's not gonna take off your leg, I promise you that." He smoothed the hair away from her flushed face.

Kylee was crying softly. The bed felt good and in spite of her fear was beginning to relax. Hail came in with some towels and a basin of steaming hot water.

Giving Matt instructions to move the washbowl and pitchers to the top of the chest, she placed the basin on the stand. She left again and came back with a small glass filled with water and a small amount of laudanum. "Drink this child, it will help the pain," Hail instructed lifting Kylee's head to help her drink down the bitter potion.

The last thing she remembered was Hail wrapping a steaming hot towel around her leg and foot. Moaning from the intense pain caused from the hot towel, she drifted into oblivion as Hail began to scrub her toe.

She awoke in the night some time later. The pillow and bedding were wet with perspiration. She realized she was inside the quilts and in a flannel gown. Her foot was heavily bandaged and it seemed to weigh as much as her entire body. Looking out the long window at the side of the bed she could see into a wall of thick trees. The night was dark and without a moon.

The fever had gone and she felt cool. She had a cozy safe feeling as if she belonged here in this little white room. The bed held no strangeness. She relaxed and fell back into a restful slumber.

The morning dawned bright and clear but cold and without a breeze. A slight film of white frost lay upon the northwest side of the green pines. A thick layer spread under the shady side of the wide leafed ferns where the sun had yet to emerge. When Kylee awoke, she felt well and rested. She had no desire to move due to the warm comfort surrounding her. Lifting her head from the pillow she looked out the window.

The sun sifted through the tall pines causing shadows of light to play across her bed. She moved her foot slowly and for the first time in days, the pain was gone. Sitting up, she swung her feet over the edge of the bed. Sliding from the bed she stood up cautiously putting only slight pressure on her bandaged foot.

Lifting the curtain that divided the bedroom from the kitchen she moved slowly into the other room. The room was empty. Matt and Hail were both gone. She walked across the room to a small window. Jars of dried roots and leaves sat along the windowsill. Kylee could see out into the fenced yard below the house. She spotted Hail dressed in an old wool plaid jacket many sizes too big for her. She was at the chopping block splitting wood. A cocky red rooster perched in a mulberry tree behind her. It crowed proudly as the sun warmed its feathers. She watched as Hail picked up an armload of wood and headed for the house.

Kylee hurried back to bed and lay back, smiling to herself, not believing how well she felt. She pulled the covers up close under her chin. The bed felt soft and warm, but she still felt a little shaky. The floor was cold and she decided the bed was a nice place to stay. As she relaxed again, she wondered what could have become of Matt. He promised not to leave her.

Hail came in and dropped her load of wood. Kylee could hear her fussing around in the other room. Under the curtain she could see the woman's heavy shoes and the swishing of her dark wool skirt as she moved about. She was singing an old hymn as she worked:

> "I love to tell the story, will be my theme in Glory
> To tell the old, old story of Jesus and his love..."

Kylee listened and dozed. She awoke later to the smell of something wonderful cooking beyond the curtain. Before long Hail came in carrying a bowl and cup and set them on the stand next to the bed. The aroma strongly infiltrated Kylee's sense of hunger. She had a sharp pang in her middle.

"Look a here now, you're awake. Feelin' like you might eat a bite?"

Kylee couldn't believe the transformation on the woman's face when she smiled. The smile brought warmth to her countenance that denied the chill that was still in her eyes, eyes that never smiled when her lips did. They kept a vague look, hard to understand.

"Oh, yes!" Kylee answered with enthusiasm.

"Can you manage or shall I help?"

"I'd like to try," Kylee requested, "I'm fine."

"Well, sit up here then."

Hail helped Kylee to a sitting position on the edge of the bed. She pulled the nightstand over in front of Kylee and laid a towel over her lap. Propping the pillows behind her back she handed Kylee a spoon.

Inside the bowl there was chicken broth, okra, chopped greens, and a flavor Kylee couldn't recognize, perhaps a wild herb. The aroma was enticing. It was as good as it smelled and she ate it all, as a cat would a saucer of cream. She drank down the strong comfrey tea laced with honey. Her insides warmed to the repast and she felt even better.

"Thank you," Kylee said to Hail as she removed the dishes and pulled the curtain to the side of the door casing.

"I'll bring you some more tea," Hail offered, removing the stand and instructed Kylee to lie back down, propping her up with the stack of pillows. She left quietly and returned soon with another cup of tea as she had promised.

"Is Matt gonna take me home?" Kylee drank the hot liquid. "Where is he?"

Hail looked as she had the night before, clean and fresh. Her skin was fair and Kylee thought she wasn't as old as she had first concluded. She was very pretty and looked nothing like the granny woman or midwives she had seen. Her hands were large with wide palms and long fingers; they looked as strong as a man's.

"Not today child. Matt went back to the mill. He had chores to do. He'll be back for you tomorrow. I wanted to make sure the infection was gone before you went home. I'll take a look now." Hail began removing the bandages carefully. Under the bandages were layers of large wet leaves wrapped carefully around Kylee's leg and foot.

"I had to lift the toe nail. It has quit bleeding. It looks fine an' will grow back soon, good as new," Hail stated as she looked closely at the toe. The redness was gone and the swelling was decreasing. The area was still darkly discolored. Hail carefully turned Kylee's foot making sure everything was healing well.

"Thank the good Lord there is no more danger from the infection." Hail quietly gave thanks and felt a little pride in her own efforts. She looked curiously at the young woman lying in her bed. Hail was itching to talk and ask questions about her father. The young woman held no resemblance whatsoever to Val. Her desire overcame her good manners and she discreetly began:

"Ira told me you were Val's girl, but we've had no chance to get acquainted. There was not much time at Billy's buryin'. I knew your father well. Mattie, Ira, your father, an' me go back a long way. I was sad to hear of his death. I would have liked to seen him one more time. I reckon he never wanted to see these hills again. I don't reckon he missed his old home an' friends. From the looks of you, he found much happiness in Tennessee," Hail paused. She had seen the grief come into Kylee's eyes and decided to let the dead stay buried and changed the subject.

"Ira is a good man. He has been crippled for a long time. My father tried to help him but he died before he could do anything for him. We took him to a doctor in Norton, but they could do nothing. He's been in that damned chair for a long time. I guess he has a right to be cantankerous at times. But it seems he takes great pleasure in makin' everyone miserable when he's feelin' out a 'sorts. He has been good to me. I will do anything for him or his'n. I'm glad you are at the mill. You will make a difference." Hail was surprised at herself. Her tongue was wagging, like some old hill gossip.

As Hail's tongue loosened, her hands were busy rubbing Kylee's leg and foot with a smooth cooling ointment. She re-bandaged it loosely. Easing Kylee back onto the pillows, Hail lifted her legs onto the bed, fixed the covers neatly and left the room.

Kylee smiled faintly at the granny woman's retreating back. Hail had known her father. The knowledge made her feel at home. She laid back and fell to sleep.

Hail returned to the room late in the day and brought Kylee's pink gingham dress and underclothing neatly washed and pressed. Also a hairbrush and the white pitcher filled with warm water. She laid a pair of heavy knit stockings on the pillow and woke Kylee from a sound slumber. Kylee had managed to sleep away most of the day.

"You can wash an' get dressed. Put these on. They'll keep your feet warm. You wore no stockings or shoes when you came. Come out when you're ready an' sit by the fire to have supper."

"I want to go home, please," Kylee told her shyly.

"Why girl, you've no way of goin' home 'til Matt comes to fetch you. I've no buggy or team. I only have my old mule, Dr. Jekyll. You'll spend another night here. Matt will come for you in the mornin'," Hail promised as she disappeared through the curtains.

Kylee bathed her body, taking what her father had always called a spit bath. "You're okay, if you don't run out'a spit." He would tell her and they would laugh together at his joke.

It didn't hurt so much to think about her father among these people who had known him. Now the memories only reminded her of the love she had for him. The sorrow of her father's passing had been covered with the new grief of Billy's death.

She brushed her tangled hair slowly and with great difficulty. Kylee could sit on her long hair and she always braided it or put a bed cap over it when sleeping. As a result of staying in bed with her hair down it was badly tangled. She thought it would take a currycomb to put it in order.

Weak and not up to twisting and coiling the long tresses, she parted it down the middle and pulled a portion over each shoulder. Then pulling several long hairs from the brush she wound the loose hairs around each section. It would stay neat and untangled.

Kylee sat in a small rocker by the fire enjoying the bright flame and the crackling sparks flying up the chimney. Hail had lamb stew ready for supper and corn bread. It was good and Kylee was ready for the heavier nourishment.

"You stay off that foot, child," Hail ordered when Kylee offered to help with the dishes.

Kylee wished the woman wouldn't call her child. It made her feel just that.

Through the windows Kylee could see the evening dusk settling. It was tucking the inside of the cabin into darkness. The room was warm and cozy. Kylee's head nodded and she dozed. She was startled awake by a loud knock on the door.

Hail had lit a lamp and was working at the table crushing herbs. She was placing them in jars or small brown paper bags, labeling each with a pencil before she stacked them on a shelf behind the table. From there she would carry them into a room off the kitchen. The extra room was once her father and mother's bedroom but now served well for storage.

At the knock, Hail stiffened and moved reluctantly forward. She dreaded these late night callers. Usually they turned out to be a birthing but occasionally it would be a bullet or knife wound, which she hated. Sometimes these could be messy and dangerous for her. If she failed to save a life, then she was usually blamed for the loss.

Lifting the latch Hail peeked out cautiously. When she saw who the visitors were she moved quickly to drop the latch into place but wasn't fast enough. The caller shoved the door open roughly with a heavily booted foot.

Hail's cheeks grew deathly pale as she moved back into the room. The long barrel of Rueben Mitchell's Winchester pressed into her middle. His brother Blaine stood behind him framed in the doorway grinning broadly, the night a black curtain behind him.

CHAPTER THREE

"You ole' witch! I oughta bust your skull for tryin' to shut the door in my face!" Rueben growled his face ashen with rage.

"It's late Rueben; an' I don't welcome the likes of you at any time!" Hail's voice was tense, her face frozen. "Now, get out!"

Rueben laughed loudly, amused at the invitation for his withdrawal. He pushed the barrel of the gun harder into Hail's belly. Rueben, a young man in his thirties was dirty and obese. His corpulence caused him to appear even shorter than his height of five-foot-four. A soggy middle hung slovenly over his trouser belt. He wore his favorite, well-worn sheepskin jacket that reeked with an odor that made one's stomach turn. The coat was several sizes too small, even a tug of war would have failed to fasten it across his wad of belly

Rueben's reddish-blonde hair hung to his shoulder separated in dirty, oily, tangled curls. His bullish jaw was clean-shaven, sun tanned, and wind burned. A thick untrimmed orange-blonde mustache almost hid his upper lip. His blue eyes squinted as if he were always looking into the sun causing cobweb wrinkles to appear at the corners. The squinting, no doubt was caused from his extreme near-sightedness and not from the glare of the light. The little boy look of his round face denied the meanness that came to light sometimes in his eyes. Still laughing, he pushed Hail into the room and motioned Blaine to close the door.

"I ain't here cause I wanta be! Ain't no social call! When we-uns leave Hail, you're goin' with us! So get your things! Nell's havin' a bad time gettin' her youngin'. Paw sent us to fetch you. Get ready!" Rueben snarled and jabbed the gun again as he saw the hostile refusal come to surface in Hail's eyes.

"I'll go but not 'cause of your paw, but for Nell's sake. She needn't suffer on account of your paw's beastliness." Hail gave a desperate sigh, resigned to the chore ahead of her.

"Hey, look'a here, Rueb! Ain't this a likely gal? You reck-a-lect who she be?" The younger brother was exuberant; he'd found Kylee again.

Crossing the room Blaine leered closely into Kylee's face. Blaine, tall and slim, had the same dark good looks as his father. Bushy brows almost hid his beady black eyes, eyes that gleamed with perverse anticipation as he looked at Kylee.

"Can we take her with us Rueben? Can we?"

Kylee crouched into the rocker shocked at Rueben's treatment of Hail. She was frightened at Blaine's closeness, remembering his lustful looks the night at Carl Jennings and was fearful of what might happen.

"No! You cain't do that! She's too sickly to travel." Hail stated emphatically.

"Well, ain't that too bad? If she's so sickly, we'd best take her along," Blaine answered with determination. "We don't want to leave her alone, do we?" He grinned at Kylee with anticipation.

"You cain't do that! I told you, she's ailin'!"

"She don't look ailin' to me!" Blaine insisted, lifting a long strand of Kylee's hair to the firelight, caressing its softness.

Kylee sat silent, too frightened to move or speak, hoping Hail would convince them to leave her.

"Look at that hair, brother. Ain't that somethin'? It's soft as a ground hogs belly an' almost the same color. I'll bet its three feet long. Ain't she the purtiest thing?" Kylee's hair laid softly waved upon Blaine's hand shimmering in the firelight.

Kylee bitterly recalled Kenus Hall for the first time in many weeks. She was filled with a wave of anger. Pulling her hair from Blaine's hand, she tried to move away. He was not easily discouraged and began to stroke her head. She shivered and forcefully pushed his hand away.

"Stop that!" she ground out between clenched teeth, her green eyes flashing dangerously.

"Well, now. Ain't you purty when you're mad? I sure do like 'em with a little spunk! Look at them eyes Rueb. Ain't they the purtiest things?" Blaine laughed, peering close into Kylee's face. "They's just like jewels."

"Leave her be, Blaine! She'd only slow us up," the older brother ordered with authority.

"I reckon I'll just wait 'til you get back an' keep this purty thing company. Can I Rueb, can I?" Blaine hoped his brother would hurry and leave with Hail.

"You better bring her if you got your mind set. Paw'd be crackin' mad if you didn't come home! We'd better be for gettin'. If anything happens to Nell before we get back, Paw'll split our hides for sure. Come on now, Blaine! Bring the gal if you're a mind to. You ready?" he sneered at Hail.

"Get movin', witch!" Rueben motioned the gun toward the door. He backed away to make room for Hail to pass.

"Leave the girl!" Hail demanded angrily.

She hated them both and her total helplessness. She feared for Kylee in the hands of Blaine. Jay's pride toward his second son was warranted; he was a duplicate copy of his father.

"I'll carry her to the wagon," Blaine declared excitedly.

Blaine couldn't wait to get his hands on Kylee. He pinned down her arms, lifted her squirming and twisting from the chair. The smell of horses and tobacco was a permanent part of Blaine. The overwhelming odor started Kylee's sensitive stomach to churning. She was hoping to get sick all over him certain that would squelch his desire for her.

"I ain't takin' any chances on you gettin' away." Blaine informed Hail, laying his gun next to the wagon front he reached into the back for a rope. He tied Hails hands behind her back and secured them to the wagon seat. Climbing up beside her he glanced behind to see if Blaine was settled with the girl.

"Paw ain't forgot what happened to Taynee's maw. He said it better not happen to Nell or he'd make kindlin' out'a you! He reckons you're the only one that can help Nell now." Rueben whipped the mules into a high run as he talked to Hail.

"It wasn't my fault what happened to Mae. It was God's will. Sides, I were at the Phelps's, it was the same time Billy fell out'a the tree house. I couldn't leave him, it would have been his death," Hail shouted.

"It would'a been God's will!" Rueben mimicked Hail, a sneer on his fat face. "It would'a been one-less Phelps. Would'a been better if none of them damn Phelps's had ever been born."

Rueben whipped the mules harder. The team stretched out at a fast speed rocking the wagon dangerously. Rueben's thoughts were not on the duty at hand. His anger was not at Hail. His torment was always on the fact that Polly Trace preferred Tom Phelps to him.

"Slow down! For God's sake! You'll kill us all before we ever get to Nell. I told Jay Mitchell years ago to ask nothin' of me," Hail screamed, trying to be heard above the pounding horse's hooves.

Turning around as far as she could Hail tried to see how Kylee was making out. Blaine had moved her to the back of the wagon. Hail clutched her tied hands as best she could to the wagon seat frantically trying to keep herself upright.

"He's afear'd for Nell an' the little one. Paw said if Nell dies, you will too. So you better see to it that everythin' goes well with her an' the baby. Hensely couldn't come. He's off gallivantin' somewhere. So it's up to you!" Rueben answered more to the wind than to Hail.

After he informed her of his father's intent he became sullen and silent concentrating on driving the big mules up the dark road. In his own way, he was concerned about Nell and felt Hail was her only hope; he had to make her come, he had no choice.

Hail resigned herself to the situation and decided to make the best of things. She would not let her personal feelings for Jay endanger their safety. She would keep calm, silence her opinions, and pray for their safe arrival back home.

It had been many years since she had been inside the Mitchell cabin. The memory chilled her and she began to shiver uncontrollably. She must get herself together, keep her senses, and think clearly. She would harness her feelings and keep a tight reign on her tongue. It would be a hard struggle, but she could do it. Her hate and terror of Jay Mitchell was a personal thing. She had lived many years with the hope and desire to see him die. Because of her love for the Lord and her compassion for others she would do her best for Nell.

Kylee was still struggling with Blaine in the wagon bed. He had managed to unbutton the bodice of her dress and his hand was searching and demanding. Strong legs held her securely in a scissor like leg lock. With brute strength, he held her wrists behind her back with one vise-like hand. His free hand wandered over her body, laughing gleefully thinking of the pleasure to come.

Kylee was wasting no time on screaming. She was struggling, twisting, searching for a place to sink her teeth into his flesh where it would do the most good.

"Make him leave the girl alone. She's only a child!" Hail yelled, pleading with Rueben in desperation kicking him soundly on the leg to enforce her words.

"Leave her alone, Blaine! You can get at it when we're home," Rueben bellowed into the back.

"I'll get you for that, you ole' witch!" he screeched a promise to Hail.

"Well, I reckon I can wait. But I was just startin' to have fun!" Blaine's voice was gruff with passion. "I don't know if I can wait Rueb."

"My God, you're a lovely one!" he whispered in her ear holding her tighter.

His wet beard was close to her face. Knowing the dampness to be tobacco juice she shuddered and twisted her face away.

"Relax, you little vixen! Relax, you'll enjoy it!" Blaine spoke low, his smile a white slash against his black beard and the dark night.

"Paw says gals always put up a fight, even when they want to give in. He says they don't want us fellers to know that they enjoy it as much as we do. He says gals like to be coaxed a little. Hold still, you little hellion! I'm tryin' to coax you gentle like."

"Oh! Oh!" Kylee hissed, "You're nothin' but a dirty beast!"

Feeling his ear against her nose she knew it was the target she had been searching for. She lifted her head and bit, sinking her teeth hard into his soft earlobe. The warm blood oozed into her mouth.

"Damn you!" Blaine cursed her.

Taking his hand away from the wonder of Kylee, Blaine struck her hard across the face with an open palm. He tightened his hold as she moved backward from the blow. Forgetting the pleasure he thought would be his; he nursed his wounded ear with his shirttail but kept a firm hold on the young woman.

Kylee's inflicted injury cooled Blaine but the pain in his earlobe was building up a burning desire for revenge. He'd wait until they were home, then even the score.

Kylee was furious, more angry than hurt. Be damned if she'd cry. She swallowed the tears and bit on her bottom lip. Her toe felt so well that she had forgotten it in her struggle. Now that Blaine's desire subsided, the pain had returned, slight but it was there.

The Mitchell cabin sat on the hillside casting a long dark shadow into the night. Long poles supported the narrow porch and house. A dim light showed faintly in the two visible windows. A weather beaten rail fence surrounded the yard.

Their ride had been a wild one. The night, with only the beginning of a crescent moon caused the road to be dark and hard to see. A pair of spotted hounds met them at the gate with loud yapping. Hail gave a sigh of relief and a short prayer of thanks that they had arrived intact. As she prayed, her trembling ceased and she remembered the Lord would deliver her as He had so many times before.

Taynee walked the floor. She had done everything she knew, but Nell's baby was stubborn and wouldn't be born. It had been over a day since she had gone into her labor and Taynee was frantic. She made Nell comfortable and had given her castor oil as Hensely had advised her, but still nothing happened. She cursed her own stupidity and twisted her hands together nervously as she paced the floor. Thank goodness the twins had gone to bed. They were such little monsters when Nell was ill. The small soft-spoken woman was the only one that could handle the eight-year-olds. Their father spoiled them rotten and they had their way with him. Blaine and Rueben delighted in tormenting the twins and Bob never had time for them. They slept peacefully now on a pallet on the floor in the corner of the kitchen. Taynee checked to make sure they were covered, for the night would become cool before morning. Suppose Nell was going to have twins again? Maybe that was the problem. At the thought, she began pacing again.

"For Lord's sake, gal! Sit down! You ain't doin' a damn bit a good pacin' the floor like that,' her father demanded.

Jay sat beside the fire in a large black rocker with a jug of whiskey in his lap. He lifted the jug often, resting it in the crook of his elbow to take a long drink of the fiery liquid.

"You best go back in an' see if Nell needs anything," he told Taynee and settled deeper into his chair. "The boys'll be here directly with Hail. Everything'll be over before you can say *scat.*"

"I was just in there, she was sleeping. You ain't helpin' things a bit drinkin' an' shoutin' at everyone," she told him angrily, disturbed with his unworried attitude.

"Hush up, youngin'!" Jay snarled at her rising forward in his chair, fire in his dark eyes. "Don't forget this be your paw you're talkin' to! You gettin' above your raisin', Taynee gal! You ain't a standin' up in my face an' tellin' me what I can do. I'm still your paw! A man has the right to drink to another son!"

"Daughters, all their good for is trouble! Always tryin' to tell you what to do. I hate for anyone to tell me what I can or cain't do, least ways a woman!" he grumbled spitefully, wiping the whiskey from his mouth as he settled deeper into his chair.

"Now get on in there an' tend to your maw!" he ordered sullenly.

"She ain't my maw. She's Nell," Taynee spoke quietly. She hoped Jay wouldn't catch what she said. The anger was still in her voice and Jay did not fail to hear. He leaned forward again and was ready with a harsh reply.

"Makes no difference. She raised you an' treated you like her own, don't you forget it!" His tongue was thick and his speech slurred from the liquor, his coordination slowing. Jay fell back in a drunken stupor. The jug tipped over in his lap. The remainder of the whiskey spilled into the seat of the chair soaking into the soft material of his trousers.

Taynee went into the bedroom knowing there was no point continuing the issue. The jug would still be there when she returned or replaced with a new one. She hadn't meant any disrespect towards Nell, only wanted to strike back at Jay.

She loved Nell. She had been the only mother she'd known. Her mother died when she was five, then four years later Jay married Nell. Taynee had been ready for a mother. She had grown up as an unruly tomboy. She followed her three brothers everywhere competing with them in all their wild escapades. She'd learned to swim, ride, and shoot. She could hitch and unhitch a team faster than Bob, Blaine, or Rueben. She was a better shot than her father. Through it all she learned very little about being a girl. When it was time for her to become a woman she was thankful to have Nell and willing to give up her boyish ways. She began to like being a real girl, wearing dresses, helping Nell, taking baths, brushing her hair, and not cutting it short anymore. She even forgot how to swear. Nell was only five years her senior and she felt more like a sister than a stepmother.

As she watched Nell's restless turning and listened to her groaning, her concern increased. Nell had several miscarriages after the twins then it had been years without a pregnancy until now. Nell stirred slightly, groaned, and opened her eyes as she felt Taynee's presence in the room. Taynee moved to her side and smoothed her hair away from her face.

"It's takin' so long, Taynee. I don't think I can do it. If I can only see my baby an' know it's well an' healthy. Promise me Taynee, you will stay with the twins an' raise this baby. Don't let Jay ruin them like he has the other boys. Promise me! You are strong; Jay will listen to you. He never would pay me no mind," Nell coaxed weakly raising herself to look into Taynee's eyes.

"Promise me, promise me!"

Taking hold of Taynee's arm Nell shook her hard then fell back on the pillows exhausted. Beads of perspiration dotted her forehead. Taynee reached for a towel and gently wiped her brow.

"Things are gonna be fine, Nell. I ain't listenin' to you talkin' that way. Paw sent for Hail. The boys will be back with her in a bit. Things will be fine, you'll see!" Taynee promised her, smiling an assurance she didn't feel.

"You're good to me Taynee, but Hail won't come. She's hatin' your paw too bad. There's bitter feelin's between them. She won't come, you'll see. If only my maw could have been here. She came when the twins were born. This happened so fast there wasn't time."

"Hail will come. She will be here!"

Taynee knew her brothers. You didn't refuse them anything if you wanted to stay alive. Hadn't she heard them bragging about killing Billy? She shuddered when she remembered.

Mary confided to Taynee the love she had for Billy. Unknown to her father there had often been times when she visited Mary. When they were children she played in the swimming hole below Phelps's mill and in the tree house with Billy and Mary. There was a time when she had ignored the feud between her father and the Phelps's. She had watched Billy and Mary's love grow from their childhood. They talked of a time when they could all live and play happily together without fear of being caught by Jay.

Taynee loved Mary like the sister she'd never had. But the last few years Jay had begun watching her closely. He even had Rueben and Blaine spying on her. She had stopped seeing Billy. She did not want to endanger his safety. Then Bob had told them of his love for Mary Stewart.

It had been a special night, a night a few days after Mary had told her of a girl cousin that had come to live at the mill. She said her name was Kylee. Taynee remembered her family had gathered around the fire telling stories for the twins. They were all laughing and roasting chestnuts, the sort of night that didn't happen often. They were telling each other of their plans and dreams. To have Mary for his wife was Bob's desire. Taynee quickly discouraged him by announcing, "Mary will never marry you because she loves Billy."

"That's no never mind son, if you're a hankerin' for the Stewart girl, I will talk to Jan. If you want her, you'll have her! Ain't no Phelps gonna keep a Mitchell from havin' the woman he wants. You will have her!" Jay announced with confidence. Their father had been in one of his rare moods.

They had kept his love Mattie from him; it wasn't going to happen to his son. He would convince Jan of Bob's abilities. He would get Mary for his son. Jay had talked to Jan, but things had not gone the way he planned.

Because of Mary's love for Billy, he was dead. Taynee wanted to bite her tongue off. Oh, wicked tongue of fire, would she ever learn to guard hers?

So Taynee grieved for Billy and was sad for Mary. It was her quickness that had lead to Billy's death and the misery of her friend. She tortured herself with blame and wished she could run away but because of Nell's condition she had to stay. She wanted more each day to get away from her father.

She was nervous about the way his eyes always followed her watching every move of her body. She caught him peeking at her when she was dressing or bathing. It was hard to have privacy in their small quarters. At least she could scare off her brothers; they respected Taynee's threats. She was awakened often in the night by Jay's searching hands reaching for her under the covers when he thought she was sleeping. For safety she tried sleeping between the twins. Then he would catch her at the springhouse and try to place a slobbery kiss on her neck or a suggestive pat on the buttocks. She hated him and didn't know how long she could discourage him and manage to stay out of his reach.

Jay had no conscience about his desire for Taynee. He thought it was his privilege as a father to introduce her to the joy of being a woman. Taynee, with her woman's intuition and fear, felt the tainted desire Jay had for her. She became frightened at the prospect of being alone in the house without Nell.

"You ain't gonna die! You hear me Nell? Don't you dare die!" she forcefully demanded shaking Nell violently, pleading in desperation. "You're gonna live an' get well an' raise your own baby! You ain't gonna die an' leave me alone. You hear me? Don't you dare die! I ain't gonna let you! Now you just stay awake, Nell. Let's get busy gettin' you this baby!"

She was ready to try anything and was pushing easily on Nell's swollen belly. Then she heard Rueben pull the mules up sharp with a loud shout.

"Whoa! You dumb bastards! I said whoa!" The mules snorted loudly in protest but came to an abrupt halt.

Taynee ran from the bedroom and crossed the kitchen. She stood on the narrow porch waiting for Rueben to drag Hail up the rickety sagging steps into the house.

Kylee was exhausted and every bone in her body ached. She was glad when Rueben pulled the mules to a stop and the jolting of the wagon ceased. Blaine had tired of nursing his wound and relaxed. The burning desire for Kylee had cooled due to the concern for his injured ear. He dozed and lessened his grip on her.

Kylee breathed easier and slowly shifted her body weight to see if she could loosen Blaine's hold. When she stirred he quickly tightened his arms and legs around her. Kylee had lain very still trying not to disturb him until her body was tense and aching. When they stopped, Blaine rose up and looked wildly around.

"Uh-huh! We're here an' I still got you," he said triumphantly.

He unwrapped his long legs from around her and took a firmer hold around her arms. Blaine lifted Kylee from the wagon holding her backwards against his body. He dragged her kicking and screaming up the steps and into the kitchen.

Inside, the cabin was dimly lit with a bitch. The homemade light was a rag soaked with animal fat and placed in a pan and set on fire. The torch cast a smoky light around the room. The greasy odor mingling with the smell of stale tobacco and whiskey left a heavy unpleasant smell in the air.

Clothes hanging on pegs cluttered one wall beside the window. An assortment of shoes was scattered on the floor beneath the clothing. At the side of the door was a cupboard with an array of dishes and cooking utensils. On a washstand in the corner was a water bucket with a gourd dipper hanging above it. A three-layered wood bunk filled the opposite wall with a ladder at the foot. On the back wall was a fireplace and a door that led to the bedroom where Nell continued her ordeal. An oblong table with an assortment of chairs filled the center of the main room. The room had a neat clean appearance except for the remaining supper dishes on the table. The floor was scrubbed and gleamed startlingly white in the dim room.

The cabin hadn't changed since 'Iron Jaw' had built it for his Gerda. It was still strong and sturdy; however, years of neglect were beginning to show in deteriorating beams and flooring. Cracks were showing in the caulking. To keep the cold from coming in Nell had stuffed the holes with mud and grass.

Jay slept in his chair before the fire unconscious of their arrival. A small spotted dog gnawed noisily on a bone at his feet.

"We're back, Paw!" Rueben announced loudly pulling Hail into the room followed by Taynee.

Blaine followed half-carrying, half-dragging Kylee. Rueben was disappointed at his father's sleepy unconcern. He was looking forward to being praised and receiving a jug of whiskey as a reward.

"What's ailin' you, you big galoot? Why have you got Hail tied up? What's the big idea treatin' her like a mangy dog? You ain't got no decency what-so-ever!" Taynee was totally disgusted with her brother's treatment of Hail.

"Now untie her!"

"Keep your nose out of this, Taynee! I was only doin' what paw said. He told me to bring Hail back if I had to tie her up, an' that's what I done. She's here ain't she?"

"You get her into Nell an' hush your mouth," he added untying Hail and pushing her toward Taynee with a hard shove.

"Don't be for shovin' us around, you big numskull! I'll belt you a good one." She gave Rueben a hard wallop on his arm with her fist to enforce her words.

"I know who this gal be, she's the one from Phelps's. What's Blaine doin' with her?" Anger blazed in her flashing blue eyes, as she watched Blaine drag Kylee into the room. "You know better than to bring her here! Paw never said to do that now did he? You know what'll happen if the Phelps's find out she's here?" Taynee added, displeased with this development.

"Ain't nothin' gonna happen. Phelps won't find out unless you go blabbin'. She'll be afear'd to tell them after I get done with her! I brought her for me. Now tend to your own business! Get in an' see to Nell!" Blaine ordered, the hostility burning in his dark eyes.

"We-uns ain't afear'd of no Phelps's anyways!" Rueben spoke proudly. "Now get the ole witch into Nell before it's too late."

He pulled Kylee roughly away from Blaine and pushed her toward Taynee and Hail. "Take her with you, you might need her, Blaine can wait."

"Aw, Rueb! You didn't have to do that did you?" Blaine protested, disgusted with his brother's actions.

"We're gonna have us a card game! Soon as Ferrell and his cousin gets here. Wouldn't you druther have a game? The gal'll keep."

Blaine watched Kylee disappear through the doorway clutching tightly to Hail's hand. Her bandaged foot and heavy wool stockings made walking awkward. Blaine was disappointed but his love for playing cards distracted him.

"I reckon you be right Rueb. She'll keep," he smiled at his brother, pacified for the moment.

CHAPTER FOUR

Taynee looked forward to Nell's baby thinking with glowing dreams of the man she would marry and of having her own children. As she watched Hail closely and listened to Nell's moans of pain she thought perhaps it wouldn't be so glorious.

Kylee was exhausted and slumped to the floor on a pile of clothing in the corner, still weak and shaky from the infection in her foot. Her struggle with Blaine hadn't helped. She laid her head against Taynee's long cape hanging on the wall. She was relieved to be rid of Blaine's fierce hold and she only wanted to rest a moment.

Taynee was confident now that Hail had arrived. She apologized for Reuben's mistreatment, but Hail firmly assured her she could in no way be blamed. Hail woke Nell and gave her a few drops of laudanum in a glass of water to relax her and help ease the pain.

"I'm givin' you something for the pain, Nell. You won't forget to help me will you? You'll have to help if we're gonna get this child born."

Nell nodded her head. The impossible had happened, she couldn't believe it, the granny woman was here.

As Taynee watched Hail examine Nell, she recalled playing in the Stewart's barn when she was nine. She had fallen and broke her leg. Hail had set it and packed it in clay. She couldn't walk for several months because the cast was so heavy. When Hail carefully broke it away and tied on some wooden splints, she was relieved and happy. She stayed at the Stewart's until the leg was well and it had been one of the happiest times in her life. The tears came to her eyes as she remembered what close friends she had become with Mary. Now because of her careless revelation to Bob she was to blame for Billy's death and her friends sorrow.

"Quickly now Taynee, get hot water an' soap. Lots of old papers an' clean rags, as many as you can gather, but they must be clean. Kylee, come help if you feel up to it. You both scrub your hands; I'll scrub Nell. We must be clean, cain't chance infection for Nell or the baby. Now hurry; take them scissors out of my bag. Put them in a kettle of boiling water; bring the kettle back with them. Don't touch the blades." Hail pushed Taynee out of the room as she talked.

An oil lamp on the table beside the bed imparted a low scant light. Hail turned the wick up and it flickered bravely, adding more light to the room. Feeling Nell's belly slowly, Hail missed nothing about how the baby was positioned inside the mother.

"Kylee, take one of them towels there and wipe her face."

As Hail felt the baby, Nell started into a long pain. It helped Hail to feel if the baby was moving with her labor. She bowed her head and prayed. The Lord was her shepherd and He did the healing. She took time to ask His help and recited the scriptures that enabled her to trust in Him and strengthen her faith that He would answer her prayers. It was not magic as Jay believed or witches power, as he was certain she had, but Hail's unshakable faith in the Lord that her prayers would be answered.

Taynee came back with a teakettle and the scissors in a pan of boiling water as well as a bundle of clean rags and papers under her arm. Giving the pan with the scissors to Hail she filled a washbowl on the table from the teakettle. She handed Hail the basin of water and the bundle of rags. Next she passed a piece of homemade lye soap and a small brush. Hail began the task of scrubbing Nell's body. Kylee and Taynee scrubbed their hands and were waiting for instructions from Hail. As Hail scrubbed, Nell went into another pain that pushed a scream from her ashen lips.

"Oh! Oh!" Nell moaned in a weak voice. "I cain't do it any more, Hail! I cain't! I'm too tired!"

"I know, Nell. I know. The baby just doesn't want to come. Pray, Nell, pray. The Lord loves you. Pray and ask for him to be willin' for you to have this baby. It takes a heap of prayin' in this house, but if you ask, He'll hear you! Pray for the guidance of these hands that are workin' with you. We've got to do something different, Nell."

"Taynee, bring that small cider keg there by the window. We've got to get the baby to move down."

Taynee and Kylee rolled the full cider keg over to Nell's bed. The room was large and held two beds, clean and neatly made with feather quilts and ticks. Two tall dressers, full kegs of cider, and barrels of bleached apples sat against one wall. A large opened closet filled the other wall. The room was cold and filled with a damp chill.

"Here Taynee, set on the barrel an' spread your knees apart. Pull your gown up to free your knees. There now, come help me Kylee. We're gonna help Nell get this baby!" Hail said with determination.

Kylee and Hail helped Nell from the bed and carefully straddled her across Taynee's lap. Letting her swollen body hang between Taynee's spread legs, lessening the pressure on the struggling mother and child.

Frightened for her baby, Nell wailed, "Oh, Lord-a-mercy!"

"Hold her tightly now, Taynee. What ever you do, don't let her slip. Hold her tightly right there under her arms an' above her bosom. Ready now?" Hail instructed as she reached up inside Nell to help the baby.

"Push Nell! You gotta push! Push! Good, good!" she said as Nell strained and the baby began to move down.

"It'll be easier this way Nell. It'll let the baby straighten. There now, you're doin' fine. Now, again Nell, let's try again. Help me now! Hold her back a little more Taynee."

Nell gave a hard grunt. A scream escaped her lips as her water broke and the baby's head slipped through. From then on it was easy and the baby came quickly. Nell sighed with relief as the baby passed from her body into Hail's waiting hands. Hail put the baby on Nell's lap and worked quickly to cut and tie the life-giving cord.

Hail lifted the baby by the heels and spanked him sharply. There was no cry. She administered another slap and still no sound. With a finger she cleared his throat for blockage. Quickly she felt the water in the basin where Taynee had poured it. It had cooled and was only slightly warm. She quickly placed the baby in the water. He cried weakly from the shock then let out a lusty squall. Lifting the baby out of the basin, she wrapped him in a clean towel and handed him to Kylee.

Kylee looked down at the baby in awe. It was the first time she had seen a baby born. She was stunned and stupefied at what Nell suffered to produce this wiggling mass of red flesh. It was all ears, nose, and a mouth that was bellowing loudly.

"He's a fine baby," Hail said triumphantly, proud of her night's work.

She turned to Taynee, "Let's get Nell in bed; I'll get the afterbirth. Now Nell, we'll have you took care of in no time." They laid her in the bed and Hail began to knead on the woman's belly encouraging the afterbirth to pass.

"Take care of the baby, Taynee." Hail smiled with satisfaction.

The young woman rubbed the baby down with the olive oil she had warmed and readied. The baby bawled gustily in protest of her handling. Taynee washed his eyes carefully with clean boiled water and placed a drop of silver nitrate in each corner as Hail instructed. She wrapped a white cloth band tightly around his middle to hold down the remaining cord and navel.

Taynee remembered the hours of laughter and chatter with Nell as they sewed the little garments. While wrapping a small soft blanket around the baby, Taynee saw a fleeting smile cross his face. Kylee had seen it to and they laughed together. Thank God, Taynee thought, he was so like Nell, no resemblance to Jay at all.

"I swear he smiled, didn't he Kylee?" Taynee said laughing.

"He certainly did!" Kylee giggled.

The laughter was like magic. The room was alive and the struggle to give life over. Even the lamp beside the bed seemed to glow brighter inside the smoked chimney.

Kylee was overjoyed with the sweetness of the baby. For a while she had forgotten her sorrow over Billy and the death of her father. Even the struggle with Blaine seemed unimportant.

Hail wrapped the afterbirth in paper and placed it in a white chamber pot beside the bed. She padded Nell and wrapped a wide bellyband around her middle securing it snugly with three large safety pins. Moving Nell over easy she removed the soiled sheets and replaced them with clean ones. She worked quickly and efficiently.

"You done good, Nell. You were very brave an' everythin' went well. You deserve a rest. You have a beautiful baby boy." Hail smiled at Nell as she tucked a pillow behind her head.

"See for yourself, he's beautiful!" Taynee announced proudly, laying the baby in Nell's arms.

"You really are red an' wrinkled, but I love you an' thank the Lord you made it here with everythin' in place," Taynee added remembering Hail's prayers. Taynee kissed the baby tenderly. He immediately popped his thumb in his mouth and went to sleep cradled in his mother's arms.

Nell gazed at her son happy at how perfect he was, especially after the terrible struggle. She was satisfied with the reward of her labor and fell into a restful slumber.

Hail looked at the baby and turned away with a smile on her lips. Behind the smile, Kylee could not understand the look of anguish that filled her eyes. Hail gathered her things and followed Taynee into the other room satisfied with Nell's condition. Kylee followed close behind them.

In the other room a card game was in progress. The players included Rueben, Blaine, Ferrel Hall, and his cousin from Tennessee, Rob Jones. They were unconcerned with the ordeal that was taking place in the back room. Birthing was a woman's doing. The fire flickered faintly almost fading from the lack of attention. Taynee stirred it and added some wood and several lumps of cool. The men were too engrossed with their game to be bothered by her.

The cards continued with loud and boisterous talking. Dishes had been pushed to one side to make room. The players were oblivious of the clutter. Jay slept in his rocker, lost in a drunken stupor far away from the world around him, snoring loudly.

"Please Taynee, have Rueben take us home."

Hail's concern for Kylee was increasing as she looked at her paleness. Her own weariness was approaching the point of total exhaustion.

Taynee walked over to the table and stood a moment waiting for someone to notice her. When she received no response she moved in angrily. With a sweep of her arm she scattered cards, dishes, money, and whiskey jugs with a loud crash to the floor.

"Get out, all of you! Ain't none of you got a bit of respect!" she shouted at them, her face flushed with anger.

Ferrel Hall and his hollow cheeked cousin did not miss the message in Taynee's voice and eyes. They grabbed their hats lying on the floor and backed hurriedly to the door.

"We're goin' Taynee. I wasn't winnin' anything anyways. Don't get your dander up! We're gone!" Ferrel said and left with his cousin following close behind.

Taynee would take some handling Ferrel thought as he walked down the steps. He surmised she'd be worth the try and pondered over the prospect.

Rueben was angry but seeing the fire in Taynee's wide violet-blue eyes decided to wait until she cooled. Blaine however, was not so inclined. He'd been put down at every turn this night and this interruption was the last straw.

"Now just an all-fired minute, sis! What's the idea, just when I had a surefire hand? Paw! Paw! Look'a here what Taynee's went an' done!" Blaine whimpered turning to his father for comfort.

In a flash of temper Blaine jumped to his feet, pushing his chair back roughly. It toppled backward and crashed to the floor. He gave it an angry kick hitting one of the chair rounds hard with his anklebone. He cried out loudly in pain; furious at the chair for causing him such misery and angrier with his sister for bringing it on. He picked up the chair by the legs and struck out furiously at Taynee.

Kylee smothered a scream with her hand. Hail put an arm around her and backed against the bunk beds to get out of the way, fearful of what may happen.

Taynee moved swiftly away from the swinging chair. It missed her and struck the corner of the rock fireplace wall with swinging force. The rounds in the back of the chair broke and splintered into many pieces scattering about the floor. The impact of the heavy blow vibrated through Blaine's body and had a calming effect on him. He set the remainder of the badly broken chair upright on the floor next to the fireplace, forgotten.

"It's all your fault, sis. You get busy and pick up all that mess. You sure do like to start somethin'! You're gonna get your back split now, for sure!" Blaine told Taynee drained of his anger and rubbing his injured ankle.

"Hush up, Blaine! You're the one that broke it. You pick it up! You're always blubberin' about somethin'." Turning to Rueben she demanded, "Take these women home like you promised. Ain't none of you care what's happened to Nell? She could be dead for all you care!"

Rueben was kneeling trying to pick up the scattered money between the broken plates on the floor totally unconcerned with the turmoil going on in the room. Taynee and Blaine were always squabbling about something.

"Come on Taynee, you're just a bit riled," Rueben said standing up, the mess on the floor forgotten.

"Of course we care about Nell. Has she birthed the baby yet?" he asked smiling faintly at Taynee hoping to soften her mood. He peered into her face and could still see the anger there. He backed away quickly.

"It's over Rueb. Little you care! If Bob was here, he'd care. It was a bad time for paw to send him off to Kentucky. Don't know why he had to do that for." Taynee was almost to the point of tears. She was weary and exhausted from the long hours helping Nell.

"Sure, you always did like Bob the best, didn't you Taynee? Me an' Blaine you never cared a lick for. It's none of your business why Bob was sent to Kentucky."

He was glad everything was fine with Nell. No matter what his sister thought, he cared about the young stepmother in his own gruff way.

"Come on Rueb, take these women folk home. They done what you brung them for," Taynee persisted, "now take them home!"

"I'll take them! Just hold your horses!" The older brother snarled and reached for his hat. "You don't have to be so pushy. You're always pushin'!"

Jay stirred and leaned forward in his chair. He stretched and kicked the dog roughly out of his way. The dog had moved from under the chair hoping for a pat of affection but received the kick instead. The animal yelped and cowered away from the man's boots and crawled under the bunk at Kylee's feet.

Jay yawned and rubbed the sleep from his eyes. He reached to take a drink from the jug on his lap. Finding it dry he pitched it into the fireplace laughing loudly when it shattered in pieces against the fireplace wall. He took a tobacco twist from his shirt pocket and bit off a chew.

"What's all the noise? What's goin' on here?" he questioned sleepily, scratching his tousled black hair. "Somethin' wrong?"

"It's all Taynee's fault, Paw. She gets mad an' flares up cause of nothin'," Blaine hurried to tell him.

"What's this gal? I ain't listenin' to any more of your bitchin! Who's here?" he inquired, peering into the dim room, the stupor clouding his eyes.

"It's the ole' witch I brung for Nell, Paw," Rueben spoke up proudly waiting for his father's praise, "remember, you sent me to fetch her?"

"Sure as hell is, ain't it? You did come, didn't you Hail? You weren't gonna let this wife of mine die, were you now? Why ain't you in there with her?" Jay shouted at Hail.

Jay rose from his chair and came over to where Hail and Kylee stood waiting. Peering so close into Hail's face that she leaned back to get away from his ill breath and taunting leer.

"Paw, you have a little son. It's already done. Nell an' the baby are fine, thanks to Hail." Taynee told her father putting her hand on his arm trying to ease him away.

"Now make Rueben take them home. You hear Paw? Have him take them home!" Taynee was perturbed at being ignored by the men in her family and fearful of her father's hatred for Hail.

"Well I be mighty obliged, Hail." Jay smiled triumphantly leaning closer to Hail, ignoring Taynee's restraining hand.

"I oughta keep you here a spell. It's been many a year since you spent any time at my place, ain't it Hail? What you got to say about that?" His dissipated smile curdled Hail's blood.

His diabolical pleasure at her presence was more than she could stand. She looked back at Jay with burning hate in her eyes and spit at him. The spit caught him high on the cheekbone and ran down over the scar on his face.

"Why you no good bitch! I'll kill you!" he screamed in burning wrath raising his arm ready to strike her.

A stirring look of raging hate and old memories fired on Hail's face. The revulsion glowing in her eyes stopped Jay cold. He lowered his arm slowly.

"Take her home, Rueb." His shoulders sagged and he was trembling with weakness and defeat.

"Get her out'a here! Get her out'a my sight! The further away the better! I cain't bear the sight of her!"

"Oh shucks Paw! Do we have to? I want to keep this one here. I brought her for me. Rueb promised me that I could have her after they birthed Nell's baby. Now it's my turn Paw!" Blaine whined to his father looking at Kylee with lustful longing. "Come on Paw, it's my turn!"

Kylee's heart pounded so loud it began to throb in her ears. She was terrified. Jay turned from Hail to look closer at Kylee, his black eyes burning. He remembered her from Stewarts, recognizing her as the girl who had been with Tom and Billy. In an instant he realized the situation. He was quick to see Hail's protective arm around Kylee as they huddled against the bunk bed. Blaine moved over and took a strong hold on the young woman's arm trying to pull her free from Hail's firm hold. Kylee thought she was going to be sick.

Here was a way to get even for Hail's all fired uppity ways. Jay would even the score for her fiendish action toward him. Perhaps he could anger the Phelps's a little more while doing it.

"Well, now!" Jay said slowly as he chewed his tobacco and leaned back on his heels while diabolically eyeing Kylee.

"This be the Phelps gal, eh? Well, now son, I reckon as how she'd be a likely one, right enough. We cain't take her back without spoilin' her a little, now can we boys?" He was overjoyed at having an opportunity to defile one of the Phelps women. He then delighted his son by adding triumphantly, "Take her to the barn Blaine an' have your fun!"

"No! You cain't let him do that!" Hail warned.

"Ira's bunch'll kill you fur sure," Hail continued bravely with her head held high and chin thrust forward. Her silver hair was a blaze of light against the dark coverlets on the bed.

"You know better than to tell me that Hail," Jay sneered, delighted at her concern.

"Take her on boy. You ain't afear'd of no Phelps, are you? I reckon the girl ain't gonna object too much. 'Sides that'll only make it sweeter!"

"Paw, you're not lettin' him do that, ain't you got any decency at all? It just ain't fittin'. You ought to go in an' see your new son. You ought to do that, Paw. Make Blaine let the girl be! Make Rueben take the women home!" Taynee pleaded again with her father.

Jay wasn't listening. He was engrossed with his enjoyment at seeing Hail squirm.

Blaine grabbed Kylee around the waist pulling her away from Hail's protective hold. He dragged her forcefully across the room walking backwards. He was breathing heavily in her face fanning the flame of her terror and anger.

There must be some method of force to free herself from Blaine. She was not about to be drug off and be the victim of his lustful pleasure. The events of the night had shattered Kylee's nerves and she was ready to try any desperate measure. Without thinking twice, she pulled her knee up hard into Blaine's groin.

Flashes of lightening, bright globes of light, and the rack of torture suddenly pulled Blaine apart. A hot fire raced up through his body and doubled him up with intensive pain. A deep gasp ensued from his lips and he freed Kylee, pushing her roughly away. Grabbing himself at the groin, he turned to vomit violently on the floor.

Kylee waved her arms and struggled frantically to right herself as she staggered backward from Blaine's thrust. In her wild effort she stepped on a chair round rolling it under her injured foot encased in the heavy stocking and lost her balance completely. She fell backward with her full weight across the broken chair. She screamed in agony. Her head flipped back sharply striking the fireplace wall with extreme force. From somewhere far away she could see Taynee

278

trying to reach her. Total darkness engulfed Kylee as the air left her body.

"Oh my God!" Taynee cried as she saw what was going to happen. She could not reach Kylee in time to save her. Rueben had taken a firm hold on her arm holding her back from interfering with Blaine dragging Kylee to the barn.

"Let me go, you ugly beast!" Taynee shouted giving him a vicious kick on the leg.

Rueben loosened his grip on her arm. By the time she was free it was too late. The broken spokes had pierced Kylee's slight body and she lay limp across the chair, the blood oozing out slowly around the sharp spikes.

Jay stood grinning and leering at Hail, imprisoning her shoulders against the bunk with strong hands. Forcefully he kept her from rescuing Kylee from Blaine's intended rape. When he heard Blaine cry out in anguish he dropped his arms and turned with fatherly concern to help his son. Hail moved to aid Kylee but she had already taken her fall.

"Oh my God! Help her! Help her! She will surely be done for without your tender mercy!"

"Help me, Taynee. Hold the chair by the legs, don't let it slip! We'll turn her over on her stomach. Now we must be careful, we mustn't pull the spokes out too quickly. If they have pierced a vital organ she will bleed to death for sure," Hail cautioned Taynee.

They turned her over gently laying her out on her stomach. Taynee held the chair firmly while Hail's strong fingers felt about the punctured areas. Two broken spokes had gone through in a fleshy area close to her side. Hail was hoping these hadn't caused too much damage inside. Another shorter round had pierced closer to her stomach.

Hail couldn't tell for certain what had happened. It could have punctured her upper bowel, kidney, or liver. If it had, Kylee's chances would be slim. With the extent of the injury she was aware that the internal bleeding could be enormous.

"Oh my!" She breathed as she continued searching. "She's hurt bad."

Her fingers moved swiftly and firmly, but tenderly, trying not to hurt her unnecessarily. Kylee was far into unconsciousness. It was apparent she felt nothing.

"Get me all the clean towels you can find. Hurry!" Hail ordered firmly taking hold of the chair.

"Now Taynee, hold the chair again. When I tell you, pull it out fast!" she instructed Taynee when she returned with the towels. "Quickly, now pull!" She commanded and pushed the rags into the wounds as the chair came away free from Kylee's body.

Taynee stumbled backward and struggled to catch her balance. Looking at Kylee's blood dripping from the spokes she threw the gory broken chair upon the fire. It crackled and hissed as the dry wood ignited instantly making a roaring flame up the chimney.

Kylee gave a deep sigh as if relieved of a great weight. Hail worked rapidly. She pushed and tucked more towels and pieces of cloth in snugly against the holes in Kylee's body. The blood was bubbling up slowly and flowing across her clothing and onto the floor. Hail wrapped a long cloth tightly around Kylee.

"Help me, Taynee. Come, help me lift her to the bed."

Taynee was nauseous at the sight of Kylee's blood.

"No, don't put her in the bed! Get her out of here! You hear me? I cain't keep her here!" Jay blubbered.

His only concern had been for the well being of Blaine. He swore to get even with Kylee for invoking such misery on his favorite son. Blaine had recovered and only his pride was hurting. He was taking advantage of every minute of his father's attention.

Jay was triumphant when he saw the Phelps girl lying on the floor near death. He watched with glee as Hail worked over Kylee, hoping with diabolical hysteria that the girl was dead.

"You'll pay for this Jay Bird Mitchell! You wait! Sure as I'm livin', if this girl dies, you'll die for sure!" Hail warned him, her voice ice.

"Lord a mercy, Hail get her out of here," whined Jay as he realized what would happen if the girl died at his place.

"Get her out'a here! If she dies here, the Phelps'll destroy us all. You'll make her well won't you Hail? You got the power, now use it an' make her well!" His moment of triumph was over and he began wringing his hands together as if in deep torment.

"We cain't move her, Jay. If we do, she'd be sure to die. Now help me get her off the floor onto the bed!"

Hail had been kneeling beside the young woman waiting to move her. She had wrapped Kylee tightly in her cape and was watching the blood ooze through the heavy material.

"Take her out of here. I cain't bear to look at her!" Jay shouted in anger becoming more irritated at being disobeyed.

"Get them all out of here Rueben. I'm goin' in to see my new son. Now get them out! I want them out of my sight! Don't care what happens to them. Just get them out of here!" The incident was dismissed as far as he was concerned.

"But Paw. She's a bleedin' awful bad. The joltin' of the wagon'll make it worse. Let her stay until she quits bleedin', or she'll die!" Taynee coaxed her father.

"Hush up, gal. I'll see to you later!" Jay's usual hateful disposition had returned and he shoved Taynee roughly aside.

"She deserves to die. Look at what she did to your brother. Ain't you got any feelin's for him? Take them Rueben while I'm a mind to let them go." Jay's mind was made up and there was no swaying him.

"You are surely a spawn of the devil, Jay Mitchell! I've heard you a singin' your hallelujahs to him. You're a possessed man an' you're raisin' your sons in the same evil ways! One of these days the Lord'll see to it that you meet your match, then you'll be destroyed!" Hail's eyes glowed with hate as she rose to face Jay.

"Get out of my face you ole' witch! Don't preach to me, I ain't a scared of the likes of you. I've heard your threats before. Get Rueb, get!" Jay repeated waving his arms wildly.

Rueben lifted Kylee cautiously and moved quickly to the door wanting to get away from the rage and fire burning in his father's eyes. Blaine was still standing resting his head on the mantle, involved only in his own misery.

"Your time'll come, Jay. The Lord has retribution for the wicked. He promises the righteous that He will destroy their enemies. I'll just pray that He will provide me with the means to see you destroyed!" Hail spoke her final words. Her voice trembled with emotion and weariness. Yanking a pile of quilts from the bottom bunk, she followed Rueben out the door.

"You don't say! I suppose you think you're one of them righteous? Well I got news for that ole boy up stairs you ole hypocrite!" Jay's shout followed Hail out as he slammed the door behind them. He turned and went into the bedroom, the events of the night dismissed from his mind.

Taynee stood silent listening to the exchange of words between Hail and her father. She hated her father with a burning passion and agreed with Hail. She reached for the shotgun leaning in the corner by the door. Opening the door she stepped out onto the porch. She stood waiting for Rueben to lay Kylee on the bed of quilts Hail was making for her in the wagon bed.

The mules had patiently waited through the night. Rueben was preparing to jump up on the seat when Taynee confronted him with the gun.

"Back away from there, Rueb! I'm drivin', you hear? Back away!" Taynee's lovely face was distorted with fury and she leveled the gun at Rueben.

"I said, back away from the wagon! I mean it! I'll let you have it right between the eyes with both barrels!"

Rueben could see the pale tautness in her face and he recalled one day when they were children. He had caught a little possum with the intentions of making a pet of it. Taynee knowing his love of cruel tormenting decided she was not going to let it happen to this animal. She held Jay's big shotgun (the same gun she held now) on him, demanding that he free the unfortunate animal. Not about to be put down by a girl, he refused. Taynee pulled the trigger; lucky for Rueben the big gun kicked her shoulder soundly. The severe pressure knocked her to the ground and the shot went wild. Her brother, however, was seeded in the shoulder with buckshot, but nothing disastrous. Rueben had a few days of misery but nothing compared to the anguish from the taunting banter he received from his father and brothers. The incident had taught him one thing, never to argue with Taynee, not when she held the gun.

"I didn't want to take them anyways, only Paw said for me to do it. I'm glad to have you take them," he told her backing away and relinquishing his duty with fervor.

Taynee laid the gun in the wagon bed, climbed upon the seat and took the reins in her hands. She gave a glance back at Hail to see if she was settled with Kylee in the back of the wagon.

"Are you ready, Hail?"

Hail answered with a nod of her head.

Taynee slapped the big mules sharply on their rumps and headed them out onto the road. She could see the breaking of dawn around the top of the dark trees. A shaft of brightness filtered through the black branches of the tall pines. The crescent moon had faded into the dawn and the early morning sun was leaving a silver ribbon upon the road. Taynee was grateful for the splash of light that would help her see through the heavy thickness of tress that lined the road leading to Hail's.

CHAPTER FIVE

Matt finished his chores early, hooked up the buggy and headed for Hail's to bring Kylee home. The morning dawned cold and foggy. An occasional ray of early sunshine escaped but could not find a nesting place through the mist. Breath from the horse's nostrils created puffs of white clouds on the chilly air.

He pressed his luck and chanced another trip onto Tandy's Mountain. He drove into Hail's yard quietly because of the early hour. He didn't want to wake Kylee if she were sleeping. He thought it strange there was no smoke coming from the chimney. Hail was usually an early riser.

The sun appeared above the hills and began its journey over the heavy timber. The remaining dawn settled around the cabin in a smoky fog. Streams of unsettled sunshine warmed the scrawny gray branches of the tall trees turning them into glistening silver spears. White frost shimmered on the still green fern. A gleaming layer transformed the brown and yellow bushes into interlacing patterns of gold and silver.

"Hallo!" Matt gave a loud call as he climbed from the buggy and tied the horse to a post.

Hail's old gray mule Dr. Jekyll brayed an early morning greeting in return. There was no answer to Matt's anxious knock. He walked the length of the porch. He could see no activity looking through the windows so he went inside. The cabin was cold with a quietude that sometimes settles in vacant places. Feeling the dead ashes in the fireplace he concluded they had been cold for some time.

"Now where could them women be?" He puzzled.

It was too late in the fall for Hail to be picking herbs. That was springtime work. The ground was too frozen to be digging roots. Hail had no buggy to carry both women and Dr. Jekyll was under the lean-to barn.

He went outside and studied the tracks in front. He deducted someone had needed Hail's medical help and had come for her in a wagon. She had taken Kylee with her not wanting to leave her alone. The Mitchell's were the only other family on the mountain. The cold began to creep through his black leather, blanket lined jacket chilling his bones. If they did not show soon he would check out Mitchell's no matter what the consequences.

Picking up an armload of wood from a stack under the house he returned to the kitchen. He thought, perhaps the women would like the cheerfulness of a warm fire if they returned soon. The fire snapped and cracked then blazed away happily. It warmed the chilly room and helped Matt think rationally about the wagon tracks in the yard. He remembered hearing that Nell Mitchell was close to having her baby. Perhaps that was the explanation of the situation. His conclusion made him uneasy.

He heard the rumbling of wheels and from the sound decided it was traveling fast and hard. He was on the porch when they rolled into the yard on a wild run.

The mules were lathered and frothing with foam from the hard drive. Taynee guided the wagon into the yard handling the team like a muleskinner. Feeling her strong pull on the line, the mules snorted loudly.

"Whoa!" she ordered forcefully bringing them to a smooth stop next to Matt's rig.

Taynee had no time in her thoughts for Matt. He was leaning into the porch rail, the sun spilling around him, and his breath fogging the early morning air.

Hail shouted and waved her arms, "Get down here quick, boy!"

Matt's heart sank. Something dreadful had happened. From his place on the high porch he could see into the wagon bed. Kylee was lying with her head in Hail's lap, her face a pale splash against Hail's dark skirt.

Matt ran down the steps two at a time. In his haste he stumbled on the bottom one and caught his balance on the run. He met Taynee at the end of the wagon and they glanced fleetingly at each other.

"My God!" What's happened?" His concern for Kylee took precedence. "She's not dead is she Hail? Tell me she's not dead."

Kylee lay deathly still, not a moan or groan escaped her lips. Her face drained of all color.

"No, Matt she's not dead. Take her quickly into the house. She's been bleedin' badly. Carry her gently," Hail cautioned him.

Matt lifted Kylee carefully. There was no movement, not even a flicker of an eyelash. He carried her into the cabin and once again laid her upon the bed in the back room. He felt as if he were sleep walking or repeating a bad dream. The two women followed close behind him, Hail making certain Matt was careful to lay the injured woman flat on her stomach.

"Are you goin' to tell me what's happened Hail or leave me guessing?" Matt asked laying Kylee as Hail instructed.

"Tell Matt what happened, Taynee. I'll to see to Kylee and be out when I'm finished," she addressed Taynee and gently but firmly eased them from the room. She closed the curtains behind them.

Hail moved quickly to remove Kylee's blood soaked clothing. She ducked her head through the curtain. Taynee and Matt were standing silent before the fire. Matt absently poking at it turning the logs and making sparks fly.

"Fetch a basin of warm water Taynee. Bring it to me quickly. That bar of lye soap too, an' a jar of whiskey," Hail gave orders to Taynee.

"Hurry now," she added.

Taynee handed her the soap and whiskey then turned to get the water. Hail was frightened at Kylee's stillness. She could see her breathing slowly with extreme difficulty. Taynee brought the water and some towels and Hail began her task. She shuddered at the gaping holes left in Kylee's body by the chair spokes.

The wounds were closing together, the bleeding slowing. It was good Hail thought. She hoped there had not been too much damage inside and that the internal bleeding minimum. The spokes seemed to have missed any vital organs.

"Thank God," she murmured.

Kylee was cold and Hail worked rapidly. She filled the holes with a yellow powder from the shelf above the nightstand. She padded the wounds with thick folded bandages and wrapped a long white cloth tightly around her body turning her carefully. Sighing heavily as she watched the blood seeping through the whiteness.

She put a soft flannel gown on Kylee then covered her up warmly. While bathing her face and smoothing her hair she was startled to find a laceration at the left side of Kylee's head. The hair was stiff and matted with blood. She recalled the young woman's head striking the fireplace with dreadful force.

The new discovery filled Hail with new appalling concern. Picking up the basin full of bloody towels and water she slid back the curtain and moved into the other room. Passing the two standing at the fireplace she filled the basin with clean water and rags then returned to Kylee without saying a word.

Back at Kylee's side she bathed the head wound carefully. The bleeding had stopped but the area was swelling. Hail wet a towel in the basin of cold water and laid it over the swollen area. She mixed some whiskey and water in a glass and began to spoon the liquid into Kylee's tight lips. Perhaps the shock of the liquor would revive her. Kylee swallowed and stirred slightly and moaned, but still did not open her eyes.

Hail could hear Matt and Taynee talking in low voices in the other room. She changed the towel on Kylee's head with a clean one. Kneeling beside the bed she began to pray repeating quietly and reverently the scriptures she believed would stop the bleeding. She had done everything she knew for Kylee. It was up to the Lord now. If it was His will, He would heal her.

Taynee and Matt had stood for a long time saying nothing, each fully aware of the other's presence. When Hail came out and went back in to Kylee without saying a word they knew she was greatly concerned. Matt stopped his preoccupation of stirring the fire and spoke to Taynee.

"Well Taynee, tell me what's happened! You been standin' here with your mouth closed long enough. Now if the cat ain't got your tongue completely, maybe they's enough of it left to tell me what happened to Kylee," he inquired forcefully, his voice soft but gruff, almost to the point of being rude. Why was it when you wanted information from a woman you had to coax it from her?

Taynee still shaken from the events of the proceeding day and night began to tremble. She pulled herself together enough to tell Matt in a shaky voice what happened, not softening any of the involvement Blaine or Jay had in the night's events.

"I don't care what you do to them or what you say. I'm stayin' here until Kylee's well. I aim to make it up to her for what's happened, if I can. I'll help Hail take care of her. No one will talk me out of my decision. My mind's made up! Sides this is Hail's place. She'd be the one to tell me I'd have to go."

"Do as you will, Taynee. I reckon Hail could use your help. But you got to think of Nell; she will need you too. Your paw ain't gonna take you staying here lightly. We was told Jay was in Kentucky. He goin' to be gone awhile?

Matt's first bitterness toward Taynee was tapering. He thought her pledge to help Kylee commendable. Didn't sound much like anything a Mitchell would bother to do. He waited for Taynee's answer concerning her father, but she offered nothing.

"I can't do much here. Think I'll go to the mill an' do up the chores then ride into Gladeville. Maybe I can get Hensely to come take a look at Kylee. I'll tell him what's happened. Perhaps he'll be willin' now to arrest a few Mitchell's." Matt's trust in Tanner Hensely was very limited.

"That would be good Matt. Kylee's wounds aren't as bad as I first feared. The bleedin's stopped, but she is still unconscious an' not comin' around. This worries me." Hail offered coming into the room in time to hear Matt's announcement.

"Maybe Doc Tanner Hensely can leave his duties as Marshal an' favor us with some of his medical know-how. He's always comin' to borrow my father's medical books so he can doctor more. But I know mostly what he's doing is robbin' people an' usin' them to his advantage. He's good at it all as long as it profits him. Don't know why he wanted to take up Marshalin' unless it was to cover up his renegade ways. Don't understand how he's kept from gettin' hung long before now," Hail added puzzling the situation.

"I hear he won't please Ira in any way. He hates your paw as much as Jay does. Ain't that right, Matt?" Hail questioned the young man watching him closely.

"You can hear most anythin' if you got big ears." Matt smiled softly at Hail to let her know he meant no disrespect.

He was aware that Hail knew more about Hensely than he could ever tell her. It was true there was no love lost between Hensely and his paw. Matt also knew that the Marshal spent time at Hail's cabin. Some said courting was his intentions. Matt did not agree and respected the woman too much to ask. He was convinced Tanner's visits were only to catch whatever bit of news Hail might drop concerning his father. Matt could have told him he was barking up the wrong tree, Hail would never say anything that might harm her dear friend, Ira Phelps.

"I'll look in on Kylee an' be on my way. I'll take the wagon back an' pick up Jole'." He peeked in on Kylee and left the cabin.

Taynee watched Hail through the doorway as she knelt beside Kylee's bed. She knew the woman would be praying while keeping a close watch. She thought it wouldn't hurt to add her prayer too. She had never known how to pray but reckoned there was no set pattern. Maybe the Lord hadn't completely forgotten her; after all, things had gone well for Nell and the baby. Kneeling down beside the little rocker she began her prayer in a whisper:

"Please God," she reckoned you ought to say please, "see to it that the girl gets well. I'll never doubt you again. No matter what Paw says! You can do anything you want with me, but let her live, an' thanks about Nell an' the baby. Please see that they get along while I'm not with them."

Her prayer was earnest and sincere. The experience humbled her and the tears filled her eyes and deep sobs shook her body. She began to tremble, exhaustion overcame her and she slumped to the floor.

"Please, please, God, don't let her die, let her live!"

Taynee couldn't understand her desperate concern for this strange girl. It wasn't just because her family had threatened Kylee's life; there was a deeper unexplainable concern.

"If You let her live, I promise You Lord to stay with her an' take care of her until she's well. I promise You! Amen," she added softly, her prayer finished.

"I swear I'll stay with her until she's well!"

Taynee stood, picked up the poker, and stirred the fire. Her tears had dried. Once over they had brought a calm upon her. She watched the fire blaze and the bright sparks whirl cheerfully up the chimney.

"My paw can go straight-ways to hell!"

Matt again chanced a ride down Tandy's Mountain without any confrontation. He completed his chores and saddled Jole' and rode to the Stewarts. To his surprise he found out that Mary and Jan had accompanied Ira and Tom on their journey. He told Bess and Alvin of the events on the mountain and rode on to Gladeville.

The Mitchell's, he was certain, had been responsible for Billy's murder and now Kylee was lying on her deathbed. Confident that his father would agree with him under the circumstances, he urged Jole' into a fast gate. The big horse surprised Matt stretching into a stride that gave him a graceful easy ride. He wanted to make it to Gladeville before dark if possible. He was hoping to find the marshal in his office. Donkey was only a landmark on his journey; there was no reason for slowing down. Stopping at the top of a hill, he took a short break for himself and the horse then was on his way again.

It was well after dark when he rode into Gladeville. Gas streetlights glowed dimly, scattering scant light upon the darkened streets. Matt drew little attention from the few late citizens stirring about. He was no stranger to the town and knew where he was going, the U.S. Marshal's office behind the courthouse square. He was in luck, the lights inside were still burning and he could see Tanner through the window at the marshal's desk.

Under a dim lamp the Deputy was lazily playing a game of solitaire. He looked up reluctantly as Matt entered. They made their social greetings and Matt explained why he was there. He received the reaction he should have expected.

"Well Matt, I'm alone here. Marshal Snow's in West Virginie an' the other Deputy's off. I'm sure enough too busy to ride that far to look at a girl. I'm sure Hail can take care of her. Far as you explained, she's definitely in a state of shock that could last for days, even months. Ain't nothin' I could do for her that Hail cain't do. When I get up that way I'll drop in an' take a look at her. They's a chance she'll be up an' about in a few days," Tanner diagnosed.

"You really cain't expect me to consider runnin' down the Mitchell's for any reason in this case. Sounds like an unfortunate accident to me," the Deputy marshal added unconcerned and watching the red anger mount on Matt's cheeks.

"Damn-nation, Hensely! You've done nothin' about Billy's murder an' he's dead enough!" Matt was steadily losing his control and the fury began to darken his blue eyes. Exasperation tightened the corners of his thin lips. It was evident he had ridden all this way for nothing.

"What did Marshal Snow have to say about Billy's murder?"

"Well now. I reckon he said the same damn thing about Billy as I did Matt. If your paw was to file a complaint an' take out a warrant, I'd have to serve it. But you damn well better have some evidence to back it up, or a witness. An' then make up your mind who you're gonna charge."

"What kind a witness do you expect in the middle of the night in the narrows where we found Billy? A haunt or hoot owl?" Matt questioned in disgust. "You know as well as I do it was Bob Mitchell that killed Billy with Jay proddin' just a little."

"That's not necessarily so," Hensely retorted. "You never showed me no evidence what-so-ever to prove such a theory."

Tanner flipped the cards in exasperation scattering them in wild confusion on the desk. Why couldn't the Phelps bunch stay out of his hair? He stood up, anger mounting bringing a twitch to his lips.

Tanner Hensely, average height, was slender in stature except for a slight paunch that hung like a small soggy wad of dough over his belt. His black hair salted with gray neatly cut and combed back severely. A graying mustache was very precisely trimmed. Thick gray eyebrows were startling on his dark swarthy face with dark eyes that held no warmth for Matt.

He polished his deputy badge with the sleeve of his neatly pressed suit coat. Walking to the gun rack on the side wall he reached down his gun belt and strapped it around his hips.

"How come you're in town on this business yourself, Matt?" Hensely questioned slyly. "Ira isn't with you, is he?"

"He's in Caroline." Matt answered heatedly before he thought, then added quickly. "He's probably home by now."

What a stupid outburst, of course the deputy picked up on it. Taking out a sack of tobacco and papers he nervously rolled a cigarette regretting his hasty answer. What could he do to cover up? He had fallen right into Hensely's trap.

"If I was to arrest Jay on suspicion of murder in Billy's case it would never stick. Like I told you an' your paw, Jay would be out in a twinkle. You ain't got a bit of evidence against him or Bob. It's only a hunch on your part. No proof what so ever, like I told you. As for this gal, I cain't see what kind of a charge you are wantin' to bring against them. It seems to me the girl was at Jay's on her own free will. Looks as if she were just askin' for trouble." Tanner scratched the top of his head as if in wonder.

"Seems to me Mitchell's bunch just want to be left alone. They ain't comin' in here a wastin' my time demandin' I arrest someone or other. They seem to think things are bein' run fair-an-square." He looked at Matt hard, picked up his pipe from the desk, struck a match on his boot heel and lit it.

"Fair-an'-square? What do you call fair an' square? Hail an' Kylee were kidnapped. They were took to Jay's by force by Rueben an' Blaine Mitchell. Now what was fair about that?" Matt was growing short on patience. In desperation he could see his cause was futile.

"Ain't nothin' I can do, Matt. Get out of here an' quit wastin' my time. I might take a notion to put you in jail for bein' pushy with an official of the law." Tanner warned him impatiently.

"I can see how things are around here. Looks as if the Mitchell's have been around with a pay-off," Matt said his temper mounting.

"It's sure as hell easy to see how the pig is greased. I reckon I ain't gonna get a thing done around here about Billy or Kylee."

"Are you accusin' me of takin' a pay-off, Phelps? You better slide in easy. I ain't about to listen to any such accusations from the likes of you," Tanner added becoming more impatient. Hensely walked over to where Matt was standing his ground firmly. He looked him squarely in the eye, his face livid with rage, black eyes flashing a warning. Matt picked up the signal.

"I've had my gut full of you Phelps's, ridin' around like you were God-almighty Himself. I know my job! Now get your ass out of this office! Don't come back unless you got a legitimate reason!" Hensely growled at Matt.

With the demand he lifted his thirty-eight pistol from the holster. He pulled the hammer back and aimed it at Matt's mid-section. Matt received the message and backed out the door giving the marshal a final look, a look that stated clearly it wasn't over yet.

When Matt left the office it was well past midnight. He headed for the nearest tavern, but not for a room. He needed a card game to settle his nerves.

Hensely let the hammer down on his gun and slid it easily back into the leather. Sitting down in his chair at the desk he picked up the scattered cards, shuffled them, and began a new game.

"Ye Gods! What a hot-headed youngin'!" He muttered to himself. "Reckon I'll have to ride up the mountain an' take a look at that gal. I need to see Jay anyway. But I ain't goin' this minute! Sides, I reckon this be as good a time as any to see if I can arrange a little surprise for Ira Phelps on his return to Pound."

CHAPTER SIX

Taynee was good as her word staying at Hail's to help care for Kylee. The day after Matt left, early in the morning while things were quiet, Taynee hitched up the mules and headed toward the Mitchell cabin. Her intentions were to see how her family was doing, leave the wagon, and bring back her horse Midnight.

She found Nell and the baby doing fine with Rueben and the twins helping. Jay had gone to Kentucky and taken Blaine with him. Taynee bathed the baby, changed the bedding and straightened the house. She tied up a few things in a bundle and promised her family she would be back to help.

"You mean you ain't stayin', Taynee? You better not leave again. Paw ain't liked it a bit, you bein' gone," Rueben warned her.

Contrary to what his personality showed, Rueben was good with Nell and the younger boys. Sometimes his moments of tenderness surprised even himself. Carefully he hid it under a gruff tempered exterior. He was always trying to prove he could be the person his father wanted him to be.

"I ain't comin' home yet, Rueben. You tell Paw I'll be stayin' until the girl's well. I'll be back tomorrow to do the wash. You have things set up an' the hot water ready." Taynee had no intentions of being disobeyed.

"You don't have to be so all-fired bossy, Taynee! If Paw were here you wouldn't be so uppity. You could ask a fellow decent like."

His eyes filled with a hurt look, but that was Taynee, she could be sharp.

"Good-bye, Rueb," she told him paying no attention to his remarks or the look in his eyes. She kissed the twins who had been at the fire popping corn, took a handful, and said her good-byes.

"You two, be good you hear?" Taynee cautioned them and was out the door.

Kylee's injuries were not as severe as Hail had first suspected and were beginning to heal nicely. She could get her to swallow liquid, but that was all. Kylee had not rallied from her deep unconsciousness. Her continued sleep baffled Hail so she reread her father's doctor books daily to see if she had missed something that would help her find a solution to Kylee's slumber.

Matt and Taynee's paths had not crossed. When he came to Hail's, Taynee would be at home with Nell. Matt never stayed long. He would sit with Kylee and hopelessly wish there was something he could do. He helped Hail with her chores but would soon become bored and leave. He brought the news from Hensely and assured them they would receive no help from him.

Tom and Ira had not returned and Matt had a nagging worry about them. He was anxious for their return and impatient to get at the task of getting even with the Mitchell's.

The mill, the store, and visiting Kylee had kept him busy but he began to have some leisure time. He strapped on his guns and checked the Winchester in Jole's saddle boot then rode out to begin stalking Jay. He rode Tandy's Mountain and hunted the forest around Mitchell's place.

One day after a long ride along Tandy's road and around the orchard he rode up to Mitchell's cabin. Thinking he saw Blaine go into the barn he rode boldly into the yard. He called for him to come out with no thought for his own safety. Nell hearing his shout came to the door with the baby in her arms. She called out to Matt that the men were gone and had no idea when they would be back, maybe not for days.

"They're gone sometimes for long spells, even weeks. Please don't hang around here Matt. I'm afear'd for your safety, an' ours. I'm sorry about the girl, but it weren't my fault. I don't want my youngin's hurt," Nell pleaded shouting down the steps into the yard.

"I reckon it ain't no fight of yours," Matt answered sullenly and rode away disheartened with his failure.

Several days later, Taynee rode up the road from Hail's slowly, her mind on Kylee. She couldn't believe how the girl slept. It was far beyond her comprehension. She decided that Nell was well enough that she could stop these everyday journeys. Today would be her last. She was pleased to find that Bob had returned home. He was thin and his solemn seriousness troubled her.

"Don't worry Taynee; you go ahead an' stay at Hail's. I can do what's gotta be done for Nell, all the heavy stuff. It'll be an excuse so's I don't have to go with Paw. He said you better be gettin' home soon cause he figger's you been gone long enough. I don't think he'll come to Hail's an' get you. I reckon you got nothin' to worry about." Bob smiled assurance. "He ain't a carin' what happens around here, he's too busy robbin' folks."

Taynee noticed the shaking in his hands as he put the dish he was drying into the cupboard. Bob had always been Taynee's mainstay, helping her with the chores inside and out, easing the burden of the tedious life on Tandy's Mountain. He was always gentle and kind to her and Nell.

When Jay was home, Bob stayed out of his way. His father tormented him constantly about being old enough to ride with real men. Bob had no desire for the wild life his father and brothers lived. He had tried at times to pattern himself after his brothers to please his father. The pretense was so distasteful he would find any excuse to be left behind. Taynee felt sorry for her half-brother and knew he was hurt and ashamed over what happened to Billy. She approached him with the subject.

"Bobby, you ought to tell Marshal Snow what happened in the narrows." She watched him closely.

"Tell? What's to tell? I wasn't there," he answered with a display of confidence. He turned to hide his eyes from Taynee. He realized she would read the guilt deep inside.

"Sides, Snow's always gone. Hensely'll do what ever Paw tells him to." Bob's voice was muffled.

He remembered all too well that night and the few preceding. His father had wanted him to ride into Gladeville with him and his brothers.

"I don't think the time is right. Nell is about ready to have her baby. Her and Taynee might be needin' me." Bob tried to convince his father to let him stay home.

"Oh sure! You love any excuse, don't you Bobby? Wall, stay here an' play granny-woman. I thought it was time we made a plan to see there was nothing in the way so you could have Mary Stewart for a bride. That's still what you want ain't it?"

"Sure Paw, but it ain't the right time. I'm figurin', may the best man win. I ain't wantin' anythin' to happen to Billy."

"That's a puny plan, son! It ain't gonna work. I'll convince Jan but first we gotta do somethin' about sweet Billy. If you ain't got the guts for it, I'll see it gets done. He's just another damn Phelps," his father promised him in disgust.

When they had returned that stormy night, three nights later, Rueben and Blaine came to the house alone. They had woken Bob from a sound sleep to tell him their paw wanted his presence at the barn. He had, they informed him, a surprise.

"We done it, Bobby. We got Billy. We got him good! We chased him into the narrows an' got him. The knife slipped up between his ribs, slick as all get out. The job's done son. Mary will be yours. Ain't gonna be no one find him, not in the narrows. We just gotta keep our mouths shut, you understand? You can't tell no-one until you an' Mary are hitched." Jay bragged, extremely pleased with himself.

"Aw Paw, why did you do that for? I didn't want him killed. I tried to tell you I didn't want him killed!"

"What are you sayin'? Of course you wanted him killed! There was no other way. Now Mary will marry you, I promise you. There's gonna be a weddin."

"No Paw, there'll be no weddin', not now. Not for me anyways. Do you think Mary will have anythin' to do with me after this? She'll guess what happened knowin' the way we feel about Phelps's. She'll hate me more than ever now."

"Why you snivelin' boob! You'll get ready to court Mary! You got no choice. Jan gave me his word he'd give you a chance. He's expectin' it! Now, you get your mind made up."

"No, Paw. I won't!" Bob argued.

Here it was again, the defiance. Why were his two offspring, Taynee and Bob, always defying him? It angered him. He would have their obedience! He made a fist and struck Bob hard on the jaw knocking him to the floor. Reaching for the bridle hanging on the post behind him he laid the heavy strap, without mercy, across Bob's back. He'd make sure Bob told no one about what happened in the narrows.

"When you get up from there, you snivelin' coward, get your things together. I'm takin' you to your grandma's in Kentucky. When I decide to bring you back, we'll see who's gonna marry who." And the strap fell again and again.

"You know an' I know! Don't pretend with me!" Taynee's voice brought him back to the present. "I was in the barn that night after Billy got killed."

Taking his shoulders, she turned him to see into his troubled eyes. She also was remembering that fatal night. It was one she would never forget either.

She had been awakened and drawn to the barn by Jay's loud voice. Bob was lying in a huddled heap on the straw in the corner. The strap in Jay's big hand fell regularly on the young man's back. His shirt was in shreds and his back cut and bleeding. She put her hand over her mouth to keep her scream from escaping. She knew it would be useless to interfere. Jay finally stopped and leaned against the post breathing heavily. She listened to her father telling her brother:

"You're a damn snivelin' coward! That's all I can say for you. Someone had to do your killin' for you so's you could have your woman. Well, Billy's dead an' you're still defyin' me. Make up your mind Mary Stewart will be a Mitchell! Make up your mind, you no-good cowardly whelp." Jay sneered in contempt at the boy on the straw.

Taynee slipped into the shadows as Jay went by. She moved quickly to help Bob, thinking he was dead he was lying so still.

"Now don't you be playin'. I don't know nothin'." she continued, gently prodding the young man. "You never did tell me what happened that night."

"They wanted me to go with them Taynee an' kill Billy, but I couldn't. The thought made me sick. You can see why Paw was mad. I was a big boob. I could fight Billy, sure, I did. I busted him good. But I couldn't kill him in the dark. Knifin' him in the back when he couldn't see. No-ways, Taynee!" Bob shook his head.

"It weren't my style. Maybe I could have killed him face to face at the right time, but not that ways. Sides Billy weren't too bad a guy, not the kind you'd jump an' knife in the back. I was burnin' jealous of him that was for certain, but I didn't want to kill him. It didn't set right with me. Was I wrong, Taynee? Was I?" He looked at Taynee, the haunting memory of the fatal night deeply apparent in his dark eyes.

"No Bobby, you weren't wrong!" She patted his shoulder hoping to reassure him, hating to see the sadness in his eyes.

"You can see how it is. I cain't tell, ever! Paw'd kill me for sure if I did! He hates my guts already! I couldn't tell! You can see why, cain't you?" His eyes pleaded with her to understand.

"Sure Bobby. I know how it is. I'm goin' now. I won't be back until Kylee's well. Paw'll have to understand. It's my duty. If you need me, send the twins over to fetch me."

She kissed the young man on the cheek and was gone anxious to be back with Kylee. She urged Midnight into a high run cutting across the bend in the road down a horse trail and up toward Hail's.

Matt sat on a propensity of rock above the trail stubbornly waiting for a Mitchell to appear. When he spotted Taynee moving along at an accelerated speed, he mounted Jole' and rode out from behind the rock abruptly into her path. She tried to ride around him but he wouldn't allow it. She pulled to a quick stop beside Jole'.

"Why'd you stop me, Matt? This is Tandy's Mountain. I've a right to be here, you don't," she said with contempt dripping in her husky voice. "Now let me by!"

300

"I been waitin' here to kill your brother an' your paw for what they done to Kylee an' Billy!" he said fiercely, his piercing dark blue eyes looking her over, wondering how she'd accept his declaration.

"Well you ain't gonna catch them waitin' here!" she informed him, giving him back look for look, her usually candid eyes dark with disdain.

"That's for sure! I ain't seen hide nor hair of them, the slippery bastards!" His voice softened, as he became absorbed in Taynee's beauty.

"In the first place you're in the wrong spot. They're somewhere on top of Pound Mountain makin' whiskey to run your paw out of his Kentucky moonshinin'. Only they don't bother to go to Caroline for it. You can kill all of them. See if I give a damn! I'm sick to death of all this hatin' an' killin'." She tried to push around him without slipping down the hill. "It ain't gonna quit until one side or tuther's all dead!"

"I know Taynee, I know."

His blue eyes began to shine with a warm light of discovery as she guided Midnight to move around Jole'. She rode without a saddle, her skirts and bloomers pulled high on her bare shapely legs totally unconcerned with the frosty chill in the air. She hugged her knees tightly into Midnight's rib cage for warmth. Matt's eyes narrowed as he watched her closely as if doubting what he saw. Through the years he had forgot about Taynee until she appeared at Billy's funeral. He realized again what a beautiful and desirable young woman she'd grown into.

She sat tall, straight, and tense holding the reigns securely in one hand while the other hand nervously buttoned and unbuttoned the top fastener on her worn blue wool shoulder cape that had belonged to her mother. Aware of his deliberate sweeping scrutiny, she felt her cheeks burning with high color. Delighted with her apparent confusion, a fleeting smile crossed Matt's bearded face.

Anger flooded Taynee. This arrogant Phelps was making fun of her again. Motivated into action she pushed around Jole' and whipped Midnight into a high run. She rode like the wind, her black hair a shining streak floating behind her.

"What the hell Taynee? Wait up. Come back here! What in tarnation's the matter? What'd I say? I ain't gonna eat you!" Matt shouted after her.

He spurred Jole' into a fast run following the black horse. Midnight loved the chase and stretched out far ahead of Jole'. Matt could not begin to catch her. Stopping in defeat he turned around and rode back down the hill toward the mill. He was not thinking too highly of Tom's wonderful Jole' Blonde's speed.

Taynee pulled up at Hail's. Tying her horse, she raced up the steps breathless from the whirlwind ride. She hurried into the cabin, head held high and face flushed scarlet from the cold.

Hail was startled at her sudden entry, wondering what caused the girl's haste. She was like a wild deer, breathing fast, eyes glowing.

"Oh my, it's cold!" Taynee offered breathing deeply, catching her breath. She hung her cape by the door and moved to warm her hands at the fire watching the door for Matt, but he never came.

It was not until the next afternoon that he made an appearance driving the buggy. Hail greeted him at the door to take his hat and coat. Matt declined her hospitality.

"I'm not stayin' Hail. I've come to take Kylee home," he told her decisively. "Paw an' Tom ain't home yet. I'm lonesome. I'm takin' her home."

"Matt ain't you worried about your paw an' Tom? I think it would be better if you left Kylee here an' went lookin' for them. It ain't like Ira to be gone so long at one time."

"Well, they got Jan an' Mary with them an' I suppose they are just visitin' an' enjoyin' the trip. Paw's tryin' to forget about Billy. He said he didn't know when he'd be back. I expect there's nothin' wrong. I wouldn't know where to look anyways," Matt told her, concealing his concern about the travelers.

"You cain't take care of Kylee. It wouldn't be proper. She's not able to care a lick for herself. She has to be cared for like a baby. She needs women's care," Hail informed him shocked at his decision.

"I don't know if it would be wise to move her. I ain't gonna be responsible if your insistin'." She shook her head wondering what she could say to change his mind.

302

"You can come on down to the mill, Hail, an' care for her. You've stayed down there before. It would please Paw." Matt followed the invitation with a teasing smile.

"You needn't worry about anyone taking care of Kylee. I'll be goin' with her." Taynee announced coming from the bedroom. She had been feeding broth to the sleeping girl, forcing the liquid down a spoonful at a time.

"You cain't go!" Matt told her gruffly and decisively.

"If she goes, I go! I promised my Lord I'd stay with her as long as she needed me. She's still needin' me. You wouldn't want to make me out a liar, would you?"

"I don't know, Taynee. It could make trouble. Paw might not welcome you. Sides, if your paw finds out you're at the mill, it could start a full scale war!" Matt said, walking over to where Taynee stood waiting in the curtained doorway.

He stood close to her, very aware of her lithe, willowy beauty. He remembered how the muscles vibrated in her bare legs as she sat stately upon Midnight's back when they met on the road. Taynee's five feet-ten inches made her almost as tall as most men. Standing in front of her now, Matt could see almost directly into her magnificent vibrantly violet-blue eyes. A loud throbbing began in his head removing everything from his mind but the loveliness of the young woman before him.

"If you let me by, I'll get the gal ready." Hail's voice came as if from far away, but forceful and demanding, bringing Matt back to the duty at hand.

"I don't want to cause any trouble, but I'm goin' anyways!" Taynee stated and pushed Matt aside.

"I'll not believe that your paw wouldn't welcome me," she stated as she crossed the room, remembering Ira's words the day of Billy's burying. "He told me any friend of Billy's would be welcomed at the mill."

They wrapped Kylee snugly in down quilts and laid her carefully on the seat in the surrey, her head in Matt's lap. He urged the horse to step lightly to ease the bouncing of the wagon. Taynee followed riding Midnight.

When they drove into the yard at the mill the big dogs greeted them with loud barking. The twelve days of Kylee's absence had been long and they were overjoyed at her return. Matt carried her with great tenderness up the wide steps, the dogs jumping happily at his feet.

Taynee followed slowly thinking back to when she was a child and of the daydreams she'd had of being a princess and living in the big house. Now she thought remorsefully, it would be the castle for a sleeping beauty. How long, how much longer Kylee, before you awake?

Boy, with a dog's sense of knowing something wasn't right, pushed in close. He whined and nuzzled Kylee's hand coaxing her to pet him and almost caused Matt to fall. Matt had to speak sharply to the big dog to get him out of the way. Carrying Kylee into her bedroom, he laid her upon the bed. Her slight weight scarcely dented the thick feather mattresses.

Matt started a fire in her fireplace and soon the room was filled with cheery warmth. He was satisfied now that Kylee was home. He knew she would soon recover. She would awaken and be back with them.

Much to Matt's relief the other Phelps men returned one evening just before dusk. He told Ira and Tom everything that had taken place during their absence.

Tom quickly put the blame on Matt, angry because he had taken Kylee to Hail's. "You asked for trouble when you went on Jay's Mountain."

Matt was perturbed with his older brother for not understanding his urgent concern for their young cousin. The old bitterness reared its ugly head.

Ira put the blame where it belonged, on the Mitchell's; his desire was only to settle the whole thing. The long trip away from home hadn't lessened his grief over Billy's death. He was certain that the only thing that could ease the pain would be to kill the Mitchell's.

This time it was Matt dragging his feet. Due to his recent evaluation of Taynee, his usual fiery disposition had mellowed. Taynee's presence had eased the urgency to kill the Mitchell's. Having her in their home caused Matt to arrive at a conclusion. God had created this beautiful woman for one reason only, to pleasure his eyes. He attempted to calm his father.

"Easy, Paw. We're sure as hell gonna even the score, but shouldn't we see to gettin' Kylee well first?"

Ira was not so easily pacified and he turned his anger in force on the one Mitchell close at hand. The fact that she was there to help with Kylee did not soften him. He could hire a woman to come in and care for her. "Taynee, I think it would be best for you to return home. Your bein' here troubles me."

Taynee was bent over the seething embers stirring a pot of rabbit stew for their supper. She straightened at his words. Laying the ladle on the table she turned to face the head of the Phelps household.

"Very well, Mr. Phelps. I'll leave, but I would have you know I made a vow to the Lord to care for Kylee. If I don't keep it, He might not take it kindly. But so be it, let it be on your head," she said softly but definitely.

Taynee had taken her vow to care for Kylee as a sacred oath, not to be broken. As much as she wanted to stay, she would not humble herself further before these men. Why couldn't they just forget she was a Mitchell? She had misjudged Ira's acceptance of her presence in his home. She stood tall and proud, head high, facing the men.

Ira was trying to understand Taynee's burning desire to care for Kylee. His hostility subsided. He admitted to himself there was no way she could have stopped her family's actions. Recalling her look of real sorrow at Billy's burying, he softened even more. He lifted his hand to detain her. He would let her stay. It would be a thorn in Jay's side. Before long it would begin to throb.

"Wait Taynee. You'll be stayin'. I guess the good Lord know'd we'd be needin' you." He smiled reassuringly at her.

Taynee happily hurried back to finish her chore of setting supper on the table. But Ira had a warning to add:

"I think you ought to know, now that your stayin', when the time is right, I'm gonna kill your paw." His words were cold and unrelenting. "He will come Taynee; he will come sure as you're standin' there. He'll bring Blaine an' Rueben, an' he will come. I'd venture to say it won't be long."

Taynee bowed her head as she resumed stirring the stew. She felt no remorse at what he told her. "The sooner the better!" she muttered to herself bitterly.

Matt explained to Ira what Hail had read to him from her medical books concerning Kylee's illness.

"The books explain that the deep unconsciousness Kylee's in is called a coma. It can happen when somethin' awful happens that's a terrifyin' shock to the persons system. It's a way to shut out the things that are too horrible to remember. Hail thinks Kylee's sleep is somethin' she chooses because she doesn't want to recall what happened. It's Hail's opinion that we need to fill her days with love an' carin' an' talkin' an' singin'. We might persuade Kylee it would be a happy occasion for her to wake up an' resume her life with the folks that love her."

"You mean she could wake herself up if she wanted to?" Tom questioned in a puzzled voice.

"That's what it says in the book. Some last for months or longer," Matt answered enjoying his new found knowledge. "Sometimes even a year."

"Well, we ain't waitin' no year for that to happen," Tom announced decisively. "We-uns are gonna start persuadin' her first thing in the mornin'."

Ira wheeled up to the table satisfied with his decision to let the Mitchell girl stay. He was glad to be home, the trip had been an ordeal. Then, even worse, he had come home to Kylee's illness. He was almost too tired to eat. There had been too many weary nights since he'd lain in his own bed. Across the table Matt was asking:

"Well, how was your trip, Paw? How come you were gone so long? I'm sure glad you're back. I've been tendin' to all the work around here an' seein' about Kylee. In between I tried to find a Mitchell to kill. Didn't have any luck at that. Sure have missed Billy around here." Matt immediately regretted the mention of Billy when he saw the unrequited grief dull the bright blue of his father's eyes.

"It's a long story, Matt." Ira's voice held weariness. He hadn't wanted to talk about this. There was too much to tell. He felt he wasn't up to the project but Matt was insisting.

"Well when we stopped at Stewarts, Mary was taking things pretty hard, moping around, mournin', an' grievin' over Billy. The buyers had come an' hauled the tobac and Jan wasn't too busy. He got it in his head, him an' Mary was goin' with us. Mary would spend the time while we were lookin' for a wagon, a team, an' some whiskey with Bess's folks that live there."

"We got the wagon an' a team of worthless horses, we couldn't find any mules. We found some super good whiskey. We loaded the wagons with supplies for the store an' covered up the shine. When we got back into Virginee an' headed over the mountain into Gladeville on the old road, by golly, you'd never guess what happened." Ira was receiving a new spurt of energy and was beginning to enjoy telling the events that had taken place.

"Well, we was relaxing an' havin' lunch when a couple of strangers came down the road, no one I had ever seen before. We got to exchangin' stories, chewin' the fat as fellows do. As we was a gabbin' they was a tellin' us they had met some other folks up the road. Turns out the 'other folks' they had met was a deputy Sheriff out of Gladeville waitin' on the road for some whiskey runners. By golly, yes sirree! We found out quite by accident that Hensely was a waitin' on the road for us!" His father continued with the story.

"Right there an' then we knew we had to do somethin'. We had come too far to turn back. There was no way around him, or over him, or under him. We had to out-smart him. Every bit of that super shine is buried back there on the mountain. We hid it good. Jan an' Tom rolled a big rock over the spot. They brushed up all the telltale signs. I don't believe anyone, not even someone as good as Hensely could find that whiskey. We split up the iron an' store supplies between the wagons an' went on our way at a good pace." Ira took time to light a pipe and motioned for Taynee to refill his cup with a little whiskey to sweeten it and continued.

"We-uns was maybe two or three miles on down the road when sure enough sittin' right there in the middle of the road with his back up men, was the Deputy Sheriff. There he was big as life an' twice as ugly, sittin' there grinnin' like crazy. He was certain he had caught us-uns red-handed with the goods. They was surprised all right. Tanner was madder than a busted hornet's nest."

"Well, we thought we was off scot-free but it was our turn to be surprised. Hensely had other plans for us. You know what that damn fool done? He escorted us back to town an' locked us up, ever jack-nab one of us, Mary too, tighter than the hubs on a wagon wheel. He called it detainin' us while he had time to find the evidence," Ira paused and stroked his whiskers then went on.

"There we-uns stayed while they spent days searchin'. They never found nothin'. Jan demanded his rights to see a lawyer. His plans were to charge Hensely with false arrest because of Mary bein' a minor. The Sheriff got a little nervous an' let us go. He done a lot of hollerin'. He wasn't pleased! No sirree, he wasn't pleased! He was redder in the face than ole Billy-hell. He thought for sure he had Ira Phelps. He didn't like it at all because we-uns had got the best of him. I'm still tryin' to figure out how he knew when we would be on the way back from Carolina. That's how it's been Matt." Ira stopped talking long enough to sip his coffee.

"We'll rest the whiskey a spell, until spring. It's too hard diggin' that ground right now. Tom had to use a pick. Besides, Hensely will be watchin' that mountain pretty close. Another thing, he's not gonna be any happier when he finds out Jan an' I talked Tom into runnin' against him for the marshal's job. Ain't that so, Tom?" He sighed wearily, finished his coffee, and pushed himself away from the table.

"Things will look better tomorrow, Paw. I found out Jay's makin' whiskey somewhere on Pound. He's gonna be deliverin' into Kentucky. Thinks he'll take over our territory there, with Hensely's help. Looks to me like their plan is to push you out of any business in these parts." Matt informed his father.

"So that's what Jay's been up to? Keepin' hisself out of sight, is he? Well, we'll just see about that. Makes the cheese a little more binding, don't it, boys?" Ira looked at Matt with no merriment in his eyes. He wheeled over and peeked in on Kylee for a moment. Wearily he went into his room and closed the door.

"You sure that's what Jay's up to Matt?" Tom questioned his brother.

"Taynee told me an' she oughta know. Go ahead, ask her."

"If that's the way it is, on top of everythin' else, we're sure as hell gonna tear things up in these here hills, the sooner, the better! Right, brother?" Tom asked looking to his brother for an answer reaching across the table for a handshake to seal the agreement.

"Makes my mind up for sure to run for marshal." Tom smiled.

"That's a good thing, brother!" Matt agreed and accepted Tom's handshake. Perhaps Tom would forget he had blamed him for Kylee's run-in with Blaine. It would be good for his brother to make a stab at Marshal Snow's position.

"I don't think we oughta just sit on our hands just because I'll be campaigning. We're gonna do everythin' we can to aggravate the Mitchell's," Tom promised.

Matt was happy with the decision. He would do everything in his power to influence a few votes. He knew Hensely had the same idea and wouldn't take kindly to Tom being the competition.

The winter days were upon them, bleak and cold. The hours passed slowly and the weeks seemed long. There were many hours spent at Kylee's bed. Ira sat holding her hand watching and waiting and singing softly to her.

Tom read stories out loud from the books on the mantel. He thought, perhaps if Kylee heard a familiar story or a lesson she had taught Billy, she would respond.

Taynee would sit nearby, listening closely. She loved the stories Tom read. She was becoming an accepted part of their days. She hoped she would never have to go home. There was no sight or sign of Jay and it seemed that he had forgotten her.

One blustery day with the sun shining brightly Taynee rode home to see Nell and the baby. Hoping that Jay would be gone, she took the chance. She was in luck; her father and the two older boys had gone to Tennessee.

"Weeks ago," Nell told her, "on business. They don't plan on comin' back 'til spring. He's madder than a hornet about you bein' gone. It would be best Taynee if you came home before he does. If you don't, I'm afear'd of what might happen when he gets back."

"I can't, Nell. You're all doin' fine now Bob's home. I'll have to chance it. Kylee's no better," Taynee announced her decision firmly.

Taynee reassessed the situation. The baby was growing fat and Nell was like her old self. Bob was taking good care of them, the old spark back in his eyes. She thought perhaps there was nothing to worry about for a while longer. She returned to the Phelps's relieved that her father would be gone for a while.

Christmas came and it was hard to be filled with joy remembering their concern for Kylee. On a snowy Christmas Eve day the Stewarts arrived in their sled. They were bearing gifts and goodies for everyone making the season happier with their love.

Tom and Mary brought in a scraggly pine tree and with some effort it turned out to be quite nice. They popped corn and made long white strings to drape about the branches. Bess strung some dried red berries that she picked with Emily and crossed them in and out intertwining the white corn.

Jan and Matt made molasses taffy and they all had a taffy pull with much laughing and talking. It was a happy time for Taynee. She had never had such a Christmas. Mary looked happier and she wondered if she should ask her if she would consider Bob as a suitor. She decided it was not the time or place.

Christmas day Taynee made dinner of ham, sweet potatoes, chick beans, and corn bread. Afterwards in front of the fire Emily sat curled upon Ira's lap stroking his long white beard and thinking about Billy.

"I want Tom to play us a tune. I want to hear a tune! Please Tom," Emily begged looking at Tom and entwining herself around his heart with dark eyes that engulfed her face.

"Not this time kitten. How about if we all sing some Christmas Carols?" Tom still missed Billy and the music brought back too many memories. So he led the group with his high tenor voice into, *'O Come All Ye Faithful'* followed with *'Holy Night'* and *'Jingle Bells'*, and others. Emily was pacified.

Christmas was over and Jan prepared his family to leave assuring the Phelps's they had a wonderful time. But they had left Uncle Alvin alone long enough. They all kissed Kylee goodbye. Mary's brown eyes clouded with sadness and she could not hold back the tears when she said goodbye to Kylee.

January came and went. February brought Valentines Day, which would have been Mary and Billy's wedding day. It was March and spring was on its way and still Kylee held her slumber.

Hail was a regular visitor, riding down the mountain on her old mule, Dr. Jekyll. She was still concerned for Kylee. She urgently told Ira that if Kylee did not respond by the time spring came they should take her to the hospital in Norton. He was reluctant but agreed that would be best for the young woman. One consolation to Hail was the fact that Kylee's wounds had healed with no apparent complications.

Spring arrived and carefully hidden under a grouping of rocks where the warm earth first released the frost, a swelling began in the ground. The Jack-in-the-Pulpits came sneaking forth. Matt was glad the long winter was over. He took long walks among the forest glades. He gathered a bouquet of beautiful small blossoms for Kylee's room. He hoped she would open her eyes to see their wonder before they faded.

Creating things to occupy the winter days, Tom had been teaching Taynee to play the banjo. She had become very proficient with the strings. The music helped fill the hours beside Kylee's bed. She would pick a tune and sing the songs Tom had taught her over and over. Once again the happy sound of music filled the house.

One spring day Matt opened Kylee's window to a balmy breeze. He placed a small bowl of blue violets on the windowsill thinking how much they were like the color of Taynee's wonderful almond shaped eyes. Taynee sat cross-legged on the foot of Kylee's bed strumming the strings of the banjo and humming an old ballad she remembered her mother singing. Recalling the words, she began to sing.

> *"Black is the color of my true love's hair,*
> *And his face is wondrous fair..."*

Early that morning she dressed Kylee in a lovely new bed sack that Ira bought in Gladeville. It was made of soft dimity and trimmed with ruffles of fine lace that encircled her neck and cascaded down over her breast. It hid her flannel gown beautifully. The only color on Kylee's pale face was a dark splash of brows and heavy lashes. Plaiting Kylee's hair carefully Taynee tied the ends up to the beginning of the heavy thick braids behind her ears with pieces of white yarn. The auburn braids lying across the green of the sack blazed with soft lights. Amazingly a shade of rose appeared on Kylee's cheeks.

Kylee was like a doll Taynee had never had and she groomed and fussed over her constantly, keeping her bathed, clean, and sweet smelling. She kept her room neat, fresh, and filled with happy talk and laughter. Kylee would moan and mutter, but she never moved an eyelid. Taynee waited, knowing some day, if she kept trying, Kylee would wake up.

Taynee stroked the strings of the banjo lovingly and resumed her song...

> *"Black is the color of my true love's hair,*
> *And his face is wondrous fair..."*

Matt stood at the window resting his elbow on the sill looking out and watching the wonders of spring. The oaks and maples in early foliation were eager to display their new greenery. The flowering trees were budding profusely, anxious to spread their blooming fragrance upon an unsuspecting world.

A sudden sweet stirring of air filled the room. The ring of the banjo filled Matt's heart with sadness as he thought of Billy and how he had loved to play his fiddle. How wonderful everything had been before his death. Turning his eyes on Kylee, his sadness deepened. Then he saw a stirring of her hand on the coverlet. He looked closer; there it was again. Moving away from the window, he learned closer. Kylee moaned weakly and stirred, only a whisper of movement, but it happened.

"Kylee," Taynee whispered in wondering surprise.

"Play, Taynee. Don't stop now. Softly, very softly." Matt knelt beside the bed saying in a hushed voice. "Kylee, are you awake? It's me, Matt. Please Kylee, wake up."

Taynee touched the strings gently, and hummed softly deep in her throat. Kylee's eyelids fluttered. She opened her eyes and stared past Matt and Taynee, unseeing. They heard her sigh deep inside and in the same instant she closed her eyes to sleep again.

"Oh please, don't go back to sleep Kylee. Please stay awake," Taynee pleaded as the tears flooded her tremendous eyes.

"It's no use, she's gone again. It happened, it's a start. It'll happen again, you wait an' see, Taynee. It'll happen again. I know it will," Matt told her hopefully reaching to squeeze Taynee's long fingers resting on the banjo strings.

"Maybe Matt, just maybe the banjo will help us bring her back again." The music had broken through to Kylee, if only for a moment.

The days were getting longer and the nights shorter. It seemed to Ira there weren't enough hours in the night to get his body rested. He was short tempered and irritable. To add to this, he was awakened early one morning by a racket coming from the front of the house. He hurriedly pulled on his pants lying on the foot of his bed. Pulling himself into his chair, he wheeled himself onto the porch. He found Matt with bar and hammer tearing apart the existing railing.

"What in tarnation you up to, waking a man from his rest? This isn't somethin' we talked about is it, Matt? Have I missed somethin' here?

"No, Paw. I'm afraid the idea was mine."

"Well, tell me now, what kind of idea is it?"

"You know Paw, an' I know, sooner or later Jay is gonna be here after Taynee, an' us for havin' her here. I can't seem to raise anyone off their dead ends to go find him. I'm thinkin' one of these days soon we're gonna find him at our front door step. I'm gettin' ready! This old railing looks good enough but it's no protection what so ever from a rifle or a shotgun blast. It's coming down. I'm buildin' us a fort!"

Tom stuck his head out the door smiling. Taynee peeked out from behind him. Tom waited for an opening to tease his brother about his project.

"What's all the noise? You'd wake the dead."

"Matt thinks we need a fort. He thinks we're gonna fight Indians." Ira informed the two heads at the door.

"No Paw, Mitchell's! Their worse than Indians!" Matt declared. "Can't seem to get anyone excited about anythin', you all got lead in your butts! I can't even get to the bed to see Kylee. Tom's always right there. You'd think he was the only one that cared."

"Now that's not true, Matt." Tom's smile disappeared, the teasing was forgotten, and the old anger surfaced.

"Looks like you'd get on down the road an' see Polly instead of hangin' around here all the time. You lost your hots for her, Tom?"

Matt laid down the bar and stood up. Tom moved out onto the porch, Taynee followed. Polly was still a touchy item between the two brothers.

"Ain't no business of yours Matt. Besides I like the company here." Tom looked at Taynee admiration in his steel blue eyes.

"Move over, Taynee, let me by." Matt threw the hammer down and headed for the stairs, challenging his brother. "I'm ready if you are, there'd be more room on the ground."

Tom deliberately stuck out his foot to trip his brother as he moved for the stairs. Ira had other ideas and just in time wheeled his chair between the two hotheaded siblings.

"I'm sorry, but not today, boys! There's work for you in the barn, Tom. You get busy on finishin' this wonderful project you've started Matt. Either build somethin' worthwhile or put it back together the way it was."

"I will, Paw," Matt promised and moved over so Tom could go down the stairs. "I'll build my fort."

To Matt it was as simple as that. When the old railing was down he replaced it with a log wall. Tom had no interest in the log wall; there were fences to mend and roofs to repair. He needed to ready the store and mill to reopen after the long winter. Then there was always Kylee to sit with.

Taynee was always there to help Matt. He found himself being more aware of her presence each day. He was amazed at the sudden tingle when their hands met as Taynee handed him a nail. He thrilled at the touch when a wisp of hair crossed his cheek when she held a log in place for him to fasten. He was concerned about the deep serious look in her eyes when they talked of his reason for the wall. Matt realized this young woman was taking up a permanent place in his heart.

Three feet high he built the wall. It would be high enough to hide a man and look good too. When the barricade was up and Matt was not busy elsewhere he took up watch behind it. He was ready for Jay when the time came. He knew he had to kill him. It was the only way he could keep Taynee and avenge Billy's death and Kylee's illness.

CHAPTER SEVEN

The following days passed uneventfully except for a rash of sudden warm rain. The smell of the wet earth and the new budding greenery reminded Ira that it was time to plow and ready the earth for planting. Tilling the soil was something Ira hadn't done for many years. The land had lain fallow and overgrown with foliage. For some sudden reason he wanted to see the ground in crops.

Maybe if the market were to improve he could hire some help. He would put aside moonshining and give Jay and Hensely no competition. The illegal trading was becoming risky. Besides, it had become a strain on his faltering weak body and a grind on his taut ragged nerves. With Tom running for marshal it would be best if they were legal in all aspects.

Tom and Matt weren't too happy with the prospect of plowing and planting. The mill and store were enough trouble but if it was what their father wanted they would comply with his wishes. So it was decided Ira and Matt would go to Gladeville for seed and supplies.

"While we-uns are there, we'll get us a room for a couple of days an' see if we can find out what Tanner has been up to. We'll find out if he's still lookin' for our whiskey. Maybe he's forgot about it by now. But knowin' Hensely, I'd bet he hasn't! The ground is thawed an' when the time is right we-uns'll make a special trip to dig it up!" Ira told them with excitement in his voice.

A grin traveled over his face lifting his white grizzled eyebrows to a lofty height. Blue eyes gleamed at the possibility of out-smarting the Deputy Marshal, Tanner Hensely. He gave them a sly wink.

The morning Matt and Ira left for Gladeville dawned warm and sunny. The spring rain had turned the world into an emerald fantasy. Tom made a bed for Kylee on the porch swing in the path of the warm sun, then carried her outside. The air was gentle, sweet, and refreshing. A wisp of breeze stirred the dark curls of hair around Kylee's haggard face.

Taynee was frantic. "What are you doin'? You want her to die for sure out here in all this damp air? Take her back into the house this minute!"

"I'm bringin' her outside, Taynee. Maybe a change'll do her some good. We've tried everythin' else. Get the banjo; we'll play her a tune. Mixed up with this beautiful day, who can tell what might happen?" He added hopefully, as he watched the look of dark disagreement coming to light again in Taynee's blue eyes.

"She's been lyin' in bed too long Taynee. We ain't wantin' no crown of feathers formin' in her pillow, do we? You know what that means don't you? If a person lies too long in bed an' that happens, it means they're a dyin'. Now we'uns ain't gonna let that happen, are we Taynee? I'm gettin' her out of that bed." Tom said trying to convince her.

The sunrays drifted down touching Kylee with a tender warming caress. Her auburn brown hair, a soft mass framing her emaciated face rested in one enormous braid over her shoulder and across her breast. Her invalid pallor was a ghastly white contrast in the golden afternoon sun. Tom tucked a bright colored quilt around her legs and body. Then he sat down on Matt's new porch rail waiting for Taynee to bring the banjo. Boy quickly took up his customary place beside Kylee, his head resting on her knee.

"I'll play Taynee, you sing somethin'." He strummed the banjo and Taynee began singing. Her sweet high alto voice rang clear and sharp on the still air.

"Oh where have you been,
Billy boy, Billy boy?
Where have you been,
charmin' Billy?

Oh, I've been to seek a wife;
she's the joy of my life.
She's a young thing an
cannot leave her mother..."

Watching Kylee as they sang they both saw a butterfly flutter of movement. They were tense with the possibility that the music was working. They waited trying not to move in on Kylee with a sudden joyous action that would frighten her. Taynee continued singing softly with Boy thumping his tail contentedly.

"Can she bake a cherry pie,
Billy boy, Billy boy?
Can she bake a cherry pie,
charmin' Billy?
Yes, she can bake a cherry pie
Fast as a cat can wink its eye.
She's a young thing an
cannot leave her mother..."

The old childhood song saddened Tom as he thought of Billy and gazed upon Kylee's illness. Again the bitter hate for Mitchell's burned inside him. There again, he saw a twitching in Kylee's hand and a fluttering in her eyelids.

"Please Kylee, please open your eyes. Come on darlin', wake up!" Taynee coaxed softly.

Tom stopped strumming, the silence falling hollow on the bright day. The two were elated with anticipation as they watched Kylee. Then, filling the quiet spring afternoon and lying heavy upon their ears came the clatter of horse's hooves across the bridge below the mill. Thinking that perhaps it was Matt and Ira returning, Tom quickly crossed the porch with thoughts of encouraging them to hurry. As the riders came into view, he recognized them instantly. He flew into action leaning the banjo against the door casing. He gathered Kylee up in his arms in one quick swoop.

"Get inside Taynee quickly, it's your paw!" The urgency in Tom's voice spurred her to move quickly. She ran to open the big door for Tom and stood out of the way as he carried Kylee into the kitchen and laid her on the window seat.

"Oh my God! I knew they would come sometime, but why now? Why? Oh Kylee, you're awake, you're awake!" Taynee exclaimed with joy as she looked into Kylee's vague eyes. She knelt down beside her, the men on the road forgotten.

"Stay with her Taynee," Tom told her, his voice chilling cold. He lifted his rifle from the rack over the fireplace, grabbed a handful of bullets from a metal box on the cabinet counter and shoved them in his pocket. In a split second he was back on the porch. Tom knelt down behind the barrier as the three Mitchell's rode boldly into the yard. He crouched lower behind the porch wall thankful for Matt's forethought. He watched the men approach. They rode slowly with long coats tucked behind their holsters freeing the guns for fast action. He cautioned Boy to be quiet and remain on the porch.

Jay and his two sons had spent the night at Trace's Tavern. They had completed the night playing cards and drinking. Blaine was in a fowl mood because his luck at cards had gone sour. Rueben was drunk, sullen, and irritable because his father wouldn't let him leave and go home. He had no interest in cards and Polly had refused to spend any time with him causing his annoyance to increase when she told him to, "Go wash your hair and take a bath. You smell worse than a boar pig."

He had slapped her with his hat and promised her, "Okay for you Polly, you'll not see me again."

"That don't break my heart Rueben Mitchell. You better never hit me again or I'll kill you!"

Rueben stood beside the tavern door waiting irritated while his father settled some business with Trace. Jay completed an order for moonshine to be delivered as soon as it was ready. The deal was made and with a pocket full of money as part payment they left the tavern. They walked into the morning sunshine eyes squinted from the sudden brightness.

Even with the sun in his eyes Jay hadn't failed to see Ira and Matt pass on a direct course through town. He was quick to draw the conclusion that the men were headed for Carolina. Taynee came to his mind. She had been gone too long. It was high time he did something about bringing her home. He'd let her stay at Hail's, but this thing with the Phelps's was going to come to an end. If his business in Tennessee with Ferrell had not taken him away for the winter he would have brought her home by now.

Tom would be the only one left to care for the mill. It would be the time to rid his world of the most hated Phelps and get his daughter back. With two Phelps's gone he shouldn't get too much repercussion. When they rode into the yard things around the mill seemed quiet enough.

Alert to Tom's fast movements Boy remained at his side watching attentively the approach of the three men.

"Steady Boy, steady. Let's not get excited yet. We'll see what they're up to first. We're a little out numbered," Tom cautioned the big dog softly, patting him gently to calm him down.

"Hold it, Mitchell! That's far enough!" Tom shouted from where he crouched behind the wall watching them ease their way up the curve in the road to the steps.

Tom had the advantage as long as they stayed on their mounts. If they decided to rush the house, it could be a different story. It was possible they could kill him, Kylee, and Taynee too if she refused to go with them. He would have to convince them they had no chance to get past him. He fired a warning shot over their heads.

"Hold your fire, Tom! I've only come to fetch what's mine. She's tended that gal long enough. Mitchell's belong on Tandy's Mountain. Now send her out! That girl asked for everythin' she got! We were not to blame in any way for what happened to her. Send Taynee along an' we'll be on our way, peaceful like. However you want it to be. Should have killed that gal when I had the chance. The whole things Hail's fault for bringin' her to my place." Jay's loud voice thundered across the yard. It was Jay's way to blame Hail for anything that happened in his life.

"Taynee's not goin' anywhere an' you're trespassin'. Now leave before I fill you all full of holes. It's pay back time for Billy and Kylee," Tom yelled back his answer. Boy hunkered down nervously, his hackles bristling.

"I'm comin', Paw! I'm comin'! Hold your fire, please, Paw! I don't want anyone to get killed cause of me." Taynee called to the men in the yard. She ran from the house, crossed the porch to stand behind Tom waving her arms at her father.

"Get down, Taynee. You ain't goin' anywhere's," Tom instructed pulling her down beside him and holding her arm firmly.

"He'll kill you too Taynee. He's not gonna let any of us live," Tom whispered a warning.

"There's three of them Tom. If you let me go, he'll leave you an' Kylee alone."

"No, darlin' girl, that's not the way Jay does things." Tom held her arm tighter.

"Paw, you ride on home. I'll get my things an' come along as soon as Ira finds someone to care for Kylee. No need for anyone getting hurt here. You know it were Blaine's fault what happened to her. We owe it to her, Paw. We owe it to her to see that she gets well." Taynee pleaded with her father.

"I don't owe nobody nothin', least of all Phelps's. Now get on down here Taynee! Get your butt up behind Rueben; we're goin' home. If you don't come down now, gal, when I do get to you, you're gonna be sorry! You thinkin' you're a Phelps? Well, gal, ain't no Mitchell gonna be a Phelps! Send her down Tom or I'll come get her!"

Pulling his pistol Jay stood up in his stirrups as if to dismount. He was only trying to spot Tom and Taynee over the porch wall.

"Don't un-sit your horse Jay. I'll kill you before you hit the ground! Ride off! I'll let you go without anyone gettin' killed."

"I'll kill them all if you say so, Taynee," Tom whispered turning to look into Taynee's fantastic blue eyes.

"Taynee stays here!"

"Well, listen to Tom. Thinks he's the big man now, don't he Paw? He says Taynee stays here! You ain't gonna let that happen are you? It ain't gonna be hard to get one puny Phelps. We just gotta rush him. Come on, Paw!" Blaine challenged his father with a sardonic grin. He was growing anxious waiting for his father to take action.

"Come on now sis. You're always causing trouble," Blaine growled getting a dig in at his sister.

Tom peeked over the porch rail at the horsemen in the yard. Jay sat tall and erect on his big bay horse, leaning forward slightly. His dark and forceful eyes squinted to focus in on Tom. The sun was beginning its path to the West laying a bright streak between the trees striking Jay in the eyes.

Rueben was sitting on a big black mule and was behind Jay two or three yards as if waiting to make a hasty retreat. He was still pouting and nursing his wounded pride at Polly's denial. His heart wasn't in this, not caring one way or the other if Taynee was at the Phelps's or not. Then he remembered that Tom was a favorite with Polly. While his paw was in the mood he might as well help him get rid of the competition. Rueben closed in the distance between himself and his father.

Blaine inched his black Morgan forward getting closer so he could make his pistol count. He wasn't to certain about firing his rifle from the back of a horse that was twitching nervously. He was well aware that Tom had the advantage hiding behind a barricade three feet high. He wondered when they had built that little bit of strategy.

Tom could see Blaine moving forward slowly. "You feelin' lucky Blaine? You comin' to get Taynee? Come on! Come on an' get her!"

"Hush Tom. I'll go; it's time I went. You can get Mary to care for Kylee." Taynee was desperate. She couldn't let Tom get killed because of her.

"I'm not gonna let you go." Tom detained her forcefully.

"We been lucky Paw ain't come before now, Tom. I think Kylee is awake. You need to be in there seein' to her. You don't need to be gettin' killed. What'll happen to her if you get killed an' she's here all alone? They's been enough killin'! I ain't afear'd to go." She lied, trying to keep her voice from trembling. She felt a terror of returning home remembering what happened to Bob for disobeying their father. She tried to stand up, but Tom held her firmly.

Blaine, angered by Tom's prodding spurred his horse in closer then dismounted and ran for the stairs yelling as he closed in. "Come on out you chicken livered bastard, you yellow coward! Why don't you come on out where I can see you? You're hid up behind that damn wall. That's a coward's hiding place."

He fired as he ran. The rounds went wild hitting the door casing shattering Tom's banjo. Taynee pulled free from Tom's vice-grip and stood up.

"Go back, Blaine! Go back!"

Tom rose slowly, stepped out in full view. Blaine halted at the bottom of the steps surprised at Tom's sudden appearance. He stopped firing his pistol, took better aim, and foolishly took a second before pulling the trigger.

Tom calmly pulled up his rifle, all the hate for the Mitchell's, his grief for Billy, and his anger over Kylee's long illness was in the shot. He squeezed the trigger. The rifle shot caught Blaine square in the chest. The impact of the bullet moved the tall man backward. His pistol shot went wild, whizzed past Tom's head and embedded in the porch roof. Dropping the gun, Blaine clutched at the fire in his chest.

"Why, you son-of-a-bitch! You've shot me!" He sputtered, his eyes bulging in astonishment. The breath left his body with an exorbitant rasp and he fell forward to lie sprawled across the bottom step.

"That's one for Kylee. Now we need one for Billy. You're next Jay," Tom declared calmly kneeling back down behind the wall.

Boy's dog sense swelled with hate when Tom stood up to confront Blaine. There were invaders in his domain threatening the people he loved. In a spurt the dog was down the steps and began an attack on Rueben. Jumping up and biting at his pant leg, the dog tried to find a place where it would be possible to get teeth into flesh.

Rueben struck out sharply with his quirt, whipping the dog back. Boy nipped at the mules' heels causing the big animal to begin a series of rotating bucking. The mule was trying in vain to land a hoof in the middle of Boy's head. The dog's attack made it impossible for Rueben to help his father.

Jay had been ready with drawn pistol when Tom appeared but Boy's onslaught on Rueben's mule had also upset his big horse. To miss the mule, the horse sidestepped and Jay's shot went wild.

Rueben's mule began to buck, head down, neck arched turning in circles. The mule brayed loudly and was slinging snot as it whirled. Jay finally quieted his horse and urged it toward the porch firing his pistol as he went. The bullets thudded loudly into the logs where Tom crouched.

The big yellow dog would not be discouraged. But Tom's stern voice reached out. With grim firmness he demanded the dog return to his place on the floor beside him. Boy returned reluctantly and lay with his head stretched between his paws watching every move. He was ready to leap at the first signal, a low growl escaping from his curled lips.

"Stop it Paw! Stop it! I'll go Paw, I'm comin'!" Taynee sobbed loudly as she knelt beside Blaine very aware of the bullets thudding into the porch wall.

She thought she would be glad if they were all dead. She knew now as she looked at her dead brother, it wasn't true. A memory flashed before her of the times she had followed her brothers through the woods. They were just kids, Rueben, Blaine, Bob and tag-along Taynee. Tears flooded her eyes and over-flowed down her face. Turning Blaine over she cradled him tenderly in her arms rocking to and fro, crying quietly. It was all her fault, first Billy, now Blaine.

"Oh, dear God. Is this the price I must pay for stayin' with Kylee? I was only keepin' my promise. Please, God this killin' must end. For God's sake Tom, don't kill them all! Please don't kill them all!"

"Stop it! Stop it Paw! See what all this shootin's caused? Blaine's dead! See here, Paw, Blaine's dead. See what all this hatin's done? First Ira's son, now it's your son lyin' here. Who's next Paw? Rueben or Bob? Why couldn't you have just waited for me to come home? No! You had to ride in here spreadin' your hate all over, gettin' folks killed." Taynee sobbed louder shouting up at her father as he rode up.

As Jay slowly realized the full impact of what had happened he turned into a limp useless mound. Shaking visibly he holstered his pistol, held his horse steady, and looked down at his dead son in his daughter's arms.

"Now hear me, Paw. Blaine's dead because of you comin' here. It's all your fault!" Taynee gazed wide-eyed in shocked horror at the blood oozing from her brother's body.

"Hush up Taynee! It weren't my fault. It were a Phelps what killed your brother, don't you forget it! You should have been home when they took the girl from Hail's instead of comin' here. If you had been home where you belonged, I'd a never come to this hateful place to fetch you. Blaine wouldn't a been killed. Now, who's to blame?"

Jay was trembling uncontrollably in sudden devastating grief. Looking at his son clutched in Taynee's arms he began to sob loudly, blubbering incoherently. Rueben finally settled his mule and rode up beside his father. He tried to make out what he was saying and wondered why he wasn't on the porch killing Tom.

"Look a here what's happened Rueb. Blaine's dead. You get down an' hand him up to me. Will you do that, my boy?" Jay blubbered, crying quietly now. Big tears cascaded down his bony cheeks, the driving urge and burning hate gone, only a broken sniveling lump of a man left.

Rueben dismounted expecting a volley of bullets from Tom. He would obey his father. Lifting his brother in his short strong arms he handed him up to his father and laid him across his lap. Taynee followed to help.

"Who's gonna be next, Paw?" She deliberately stood between Tom and Jay controlling the line of fire.

"Tom'll be next, gal! Tom'll be next for killin' my son! I'll get him, you'll see! He's gonna die before we leave here."

"You take Blaine an' Taynee home." Rueben told his father.

Rueben pulled Taynee roughly over to his mule and helped her up on the saddle. Blaine's high-spirited Morgan had taken off for parts unknown when the scent of blood filled its nostrils.

"I'll see to that Phelps bastard! I'm comin' Tom! I'm comin' to get you!" Rueben shouted in a fierce thundering voice.

Tom had remained silent and restrained. He didn't have the heart for another killing. He would let them take their dead home because of Taynee. He would allow them that consideration. He wanted them to leave so he could see to Kylee.

"No Rueben. They's been enough killin. Paw, tell him no! You don't want to get another son killed do you? Come on; make him go home with us!" Taynee pleaded leaning from the saddle to take hold of Rueben's coat collar in sheer desperation.

"Tom's got you pinned. He'll shoot you both before you ever get to him. Please Paw, let's go home an' take Blaine before Tom kills us an' buries us all in Phelps's cemetery." Taynee dismounted but kept a tight hold on Rueben's collar pulling him toward their father. Looking up and hanging onto Jay's saddle, she pleaded with her father. Her violet-blue eyes filled with misery and fear that she had failed to convince him. But Jay agreed, frightened at the thought of Mitchell's being buried in Phelps ground. The desire for revenge had left him.

"Let's go home, son. There's no point in it now. We've got Taynee. There will be a time an' place for us to even the score. I done told you! Come on now, we're takin' your brother home," Jay ordered and like always with head bowed, Rueben James II meekly obeyed.

"We ain't done with you yet Phelps! We'll meet again!" Rueben yelled at Tom as he mounted the mule.

Rueben pulled Taynee up behind him. She clutched him tightly around the waist as they rode up to their father waiting for him to lead out. She received a cold deadly stare from him and a promise.

"One thing you need to know, smart-aleck-missy. There'll never be a Mitchell buried on Phelps ground!" With that statement Jay rode out ahead of them.

Jay was patting Blaine's back in a loving gesture. He had always been proud of his second son, with his dark good looks and cruel personality. Jay was happy with the knowledge that in every way he had been a replica of himself. Now he had been shot down and he would not forget who was responsible! He would take care of the Phelps's in his way. There would come a time when he would rid Pound Mountain of the whole damn clan. He would take care of Taynee too. Her time was coming. For now, he only wanted to take his son home. Everything else could wait.

Taynee looked back and could see Tom standing on the steps watching them leave. Would she ever see Matt again? It had become very clear to her that he was a very important part of her life. She was certain nothing could come of it as long as her father was alive. She felt a deep concern for Kylee. She had opened her eyes when she left her lying on the window seat. Had she stayed awake or had Kylee returned to her sleep world?

As the riders galloped away Boy followed barking loudly at their heels until he quietly lay down in the middle of the road. The big dog watched their retreating forms, on guard in case they should decide to return.

Tom held his fire in consideration of Taynee and her safety. He was thankful for her unrelenting care of Kylee. He wondered if there would ever be such an opportunity at the Mitchell's again. Staring at the ugly splotch Blaine's blood had left on the bottom step, he felt no remorse, only triumph.

"There's Blaine for what he done to you, Kylee. I won't rest until I get Jay for you, Billy," he promised under his breath.

He heard a sigh behind him. He turned to find Kylee struggling to pull herself from the floor up the door casing next to where his broken banjo lay.

When Kylee first awakened she was staring into a beautiful girl's wide excited eyes. The lovely girl with the black hair jumped up and left her side. Kylee could not grasp the situation. She was in her new home at the mill; she recognized that much. She remembered hearing banjo picking and singing. Then the music stopped and she heard gunfire. She had the urge to stay awake and see what was happening. There was loud talking and boisterous threatening voices that brought back the dark despair. Closing her eyes she hoped to return to the beautiful dream world, away from all the noise and shouting.

Her eyes were shut but she could not return to her shining world. There was only darkness behind her closed eyelids. She must have slept for a long time, remembering only that there had been many dreams. Surely they were only dreams because she realized most of the people were only fantasy.

First there was a gorgeous woman with flaming hair who claimed to be her mother. She kept insisting even when she had shown her the tintype of her real mother sitting on the dresser. There had been brothers and sisters to play with, a reality Kylee had never known. Then the most beautiful dream of all, the one she had never wanted to end. While in a deep sleep, a handsome prince with golden hair had kissed her and she was awakened, just like the fairy tales she had read to Billy. Then he lifted her upon his giant steed; a horse so bright in color she couldn't tell where the horse ended and the sunshine began. They had ridden together in a world of glowing stars into an emerald green valley shrouded in a warm mist. Huge silver trees were draped in soft golden moss and vine. With shining grass so wonderfully soft, it was like walking on a cloud. She floated through this sparkling world with her wonderful prince. He was always there to kiss away any darkness that overcame her.

She laughed and talked in this resplendent fantasy with her father and Billy. Billy carried a golden violin with silver strings. The music he played was as light and airy as the fluttering of angel wings. Then the music began to sound earthly and harsh. She wanted to wake up and see what had changed her beautiful dream.

With her eyes closed, she tried to bring back the exquisite fantasies; all she could see was blackness. She recalled going to Hail's and the terrible ride to Mitchell's. She remembered her and Taynee laughing over Nell's baby. Then the struggle with Blaine and the fall that had sent her into the dreadful blackness that had possessed her. Then the bright dreams that brought her out of the darkness into a lovely valley. She wanted to sleep forever. Kylee could only see blackness and realized with sudden terror that if she didn't open her eyes she would never wake up. She would be doomed to stay behind this black wall shut off from all the people and the life she had grown to love. She opened her eyes quickly; lifting her heavily lashed eyelids up in one sweeping movement. She was determined not to let them close again. She stared out the window seeing but not comprehending what was happening in the yard.

She realized the person at her side had been Taynee, now she was gone. The shooting and loud talking outside increased. Kylee rolled off the window seat onto the floor. She pulled herself slowly, weak and shaking, across the floor to see out the door. Tom and Taynee were kneeling behind the porch railing. Suddenly Tom stood up and she could see Blaine coming toward the stairs. When she saw him coming in long strides across the yard, a moving giant, and surrounded by bright spring sunshine, she was back in the Mitchell's cabin. Blaine was running to catch her. She was falling, falling and would be pinned underneath him.

"No, please no! Don't hurt me, please don't hurt me!" Kylee whispered under her breath lifting her hands with palms open as if to push him away.

Kylee filled with horror and terror at seeing the man again was reliving what had happened to her at Blaine's hands. The experience was real to her. She fell back against the door casing weak and trembling. Deep in shock, but with eyes wide open, she watched the scene in the yard. She saw Tom shoot her assailant as he came up the stairs firing his gun. The loud noise of the shots brought her back and she realized she was lying on the floor. Then it was quiet and she could see Tom standing with his back to her.

She heard the horses moving away and Boy barking. She wondered why she was on the floor. What was the shooting about? She could remember nothing. Try as she might, she could only remember Matt taking her to Hail's. Her toe had been infected and Hail had made it better. She looked at the toe. The toe was healed and the toenail had grown back.

That must have been a long time ago. It was spring now and the day was warm. It had been fall and a cold day when they had gone to Hail's. She looked around, where was Matt and Ira? She remembered with sadness Billy's death. Looking at her hands she realized she was terribly thin. She must have been ill.

Tom's shattered banjo lay on the porch floor. Kylee vaguely remembered hearing music. Tom was standing there with his back to her. As usual he was ignoring her. Why didn't he come help her up? She clutched at the doorframe trying to rise up, but fell back. A long sigh escaped her lips as she fell back to the floor.

Tom stood on the step and watched the Mitchell's ride out slowly and make the turn on to Pound Road headed for Tandy's Mountain. He heard the sigh and turned to find Kylee lying on the floor looking at him. There were shining stars in those wide green eyes that he waited so long to see.

"Kylee, oh Kylee, how did you get out here? Thank God, you're awake!"

Tom lifted Kylee in his arms. Her weight was slight and he carried her easily into her room. It felt so good to hold her in his arms.

"I'm so happy you're awake. I'll take you back to bed. You need to rest. We can talk later," he told her laughing with joy at the thought of being able to talk to Kylee again. Her sweet lips were so close. In his extreme happiness he bent and kissed her firmly on the lips. Amazed, Kylee pulled away looking at him with terror in her eyes.

"Don't do that! Don't ever do that again! Please put me down."

Tom had been impetuous again. He had moved in without thinking. Would he ever learn? He could tell by her cold stare there would be no forgiveness. He laid her carefully on her bed and pulled the coverlets up around her. Kylee was really awake. So many things had happened since he had taken her out of the bed that morning.

He left the room and went back out on the porch. Tom could always do his thinking better outside. What could he do? Kylee would never let him care for her. He had fixed that. He picked up what had once been a fine banjo. The head was split and the neck broken in two.

"Well, if that ain't a sick sight. Don't know if I can fix you or not, but what the heck I'll give it a try. Thank, God at least I'm alive to do it." Tom said more to the banjo than to God for sparing his life.

He lifted his head to the sound of hurried hoof beats coming across the bridge. He picked up his gun from where he had laid it.

"Tom, Tom!" Hail called as she rode into the yard. She jumped down and tied Dr. Jekyll to the stair railing and ran breathlessly up the steps. She saw the blood splotch on the bottom step. She could see the dry splinters laying about the porch floor left from misplaced bullets hitting into wood.

"I heard the gun shots back a piece as I came from Bess and Jan's an' hurried. I was afear'd somethin' terrible had happened," she said breathlessly.

"Am I glad to see you Hail. Thank God for little favors! Hurry on inside. I have a lot to tell you. You couldn't have come at a better time."

Hail's arrival had proven to be a blessing. Kylee in her weakened condition needed continued care. Two days later Ira and Matt returned from Gladeville. They were delighted at Kylee's recovery but not surprised at the incident with Jay's bunch. They were thankful that the three of them hadn't been killed. Matt was certain they were saved because of his wall. There were no regrets for Blaine's death.

Kylee's recovery was rapid. Much to Ira's delight Hail stayed on to care for her. Then one day she felt that Kylee's progress was far enough advanced that she could take her departure.

Matt and Ira had learned nothing at Gladeville concerning Hensely or the buried whiskey. They brought back the farming supplies and Ira was eager to start planting.

Matt spent the warm spring evenings on the porch talking with Kylee. She wanted to hear repeatedly what Taynee had told him of the incidents that led to her illness that terrible night at the Mitchell's. He carefully left out the sordid details about Blaine's intended rape, afraid that if he became too explicit it might send her back into the dreadful slumber.

She was bewildered at the terrible scars on her side and appalled when Hail told her about the fall over the chair and felt sorry she had no recollection of Taynee and her kind devotion. She also felt sad at not remembering the long hours Tom had spent at her bedside reading, talking, and playing his banjo. She could not remember Hail being there, or Matt, or Ira's watchful attention. She vowed that someday she would repay them all for their constant vigil.

Kylee tried hard to bring back a memory of anything that happened after Hail made her foot better. There was nothing between eating lamb stew and Tom standing on the porch at the mill.

She made an effort to tell Tom of her appreciation. Every time she began he would turn her off with, "Don't bother me, I didn't do it for thanks." There was no understanding. After all he had been so loyal to her when she was ill. She had forgotten about the kiss when he was carrying her. Why was he still holding the same old insolence and bad manners toward her as before?

Unknown to Kylee, Tom did not trust his feelings toward her. He could not risk being too close; afraid he might move in too quickly and be turned away again. He could not chance another icy reprisal from her. So he treated her with an indifference that left Kylee puzzled. Tom watched from a distance the roses bloom again in her cheeks and the dewy brightness shining once more in her green eyes. He was so delighted to see her become her happy beautiful self again, yet he knew he would never be allowed to hold her loveliness in his arms.

Ira was certain they had not heard the last of Blaine's killing. He waited tense and ready for whatever might happen.

Tom and Matt finished plowing the twenty acres on the side of the hill and the forty-two acres across the stream behind the mill. They were ready for planting and were resting before starting the tedious job. Matt decided to give the mill a spring house cleaning with Tom's help. They lugged out rolls of sacks Ira kept for the ground meal from the top floor. They swept, cleaned, stacked, oiled, and polished the long heavy shafts and gears that turned the grinder from the water wheel. The day had been warm and was steadily growing hot and sultry. Beads of perspiration formed on their faces. As they worked Tom sang and Matt whistled. Their happy songs reaching across the yard to the house:

> *"Said a little red rooster, to a little spotted hen*
> *Ain't had a little tail since I don't know when.*
> *So ruffle up your feathers, and lift up your tail*
> *I'm gonna get a little if I have to go to jail..."*

At the end of each song, they would laugh and shout, "Ya Hoo!" Then begin another ditty. They had no idea the shady songs were reaching Kylee's ears where she sat on the porch with Ira. The pale roses in her cheeks became a little more in full bloom as she listened.

Kylee was mending, a duty that had been sadly neglected during her illness, thinking silently of Billy as she worked. Ira was sitting close to her diligently trying to balance the books from the mill and store. He pointed out to Kylee while doing so that he intended to turn the job over to her as soon as she was well enough. He told her where the records, bills, and correspondence were kept in the store at the side of the mill. He also informed her that he had been putting money for her share in the mill profits in his bank in Gladeville.

From under the shade of the sheltering roof they both heard the thudding of horse's hooves on the bridge below the mill. Together they watched the single rider approach the house. He rode easily holding his mount to a trotting gait raising a cloud of white dust behind the horse. Their curiosity grew as Deputy Marshal Tanner Hensely rode through the gate and up the drive.

Riding up close to the steps he pulled his horse to a stop. He sat without saying anything, took off his hat and scrutinized the inside. Taking a handkerchief from his back pocket he wiped the sweat from the inside band of his hat. The contemptuous silence between the two men was adversely removed when Hensely announced the purpose of his arrival.

"I have a warrant for Tom's arrest Ira!" Tanner said with a twisted grin, very satisfied with himself.

The marshal wiped his handkerchief across his graying hair before replacing his hat. Deliberately he moved his stylish suit coat away from the big thirty-eight at his hip. He rode with a black medical bag strapped behind his saddle. Shifting his weight a little he waited for Ira's reaction. They wouldn't dare kill a U.S. Deputy Marshal, Tanner consoled himself.

"What's that you're sayin'?"

Ira wheeled his chair away from the small table holding his bookwork and pushed closer to Matt's wall. So, this was Jay's retaliation. It wasn't what he expected.

"I don't reckon there be anythin' wrong with your hearin' Ira. You heard what I said! Now, you tell Tom to come on along peaceful like. Let's have no trouble. You can plead whatever case you got in court."

He was fully enjoying the performance of his duty. Carefully he avoided the blue blaze of Ira's eyes. He looked toward Tom and Matt coming from the mill.

"Now just a damn minute, Hensely!" Ira retorted, his white beard sticking out in agitation. "We got a right to know what kind a warrant you got there!" Ira pulled his frosty brows lower over the pale blue glare of his eyes.

"Tom's bein' charged with the murder of Blaine Mitchell," Hensely said loud and bluntly to the point. He handed Ira the warrant then looked at his fingernails closely. He had said all that was necessary, but added. "There be witnesses, Ira. I hope you-uns don't plan on givin' me any trouble."

"Witnesses! You got witnesses you say? Now whom may that be?" Ira's voice was deadly calm. "Any them witness's say anythin' about ridin' in here on my place an' threatenin' our peace an' quiet? Don't a man have the right to protect what's rightfully his any more? I believe the law still allows you to protect your own life an' them you love. That's exactly what Tom was a doin'!"

"You can state your case in court," Hensely told him, unconcerned with any protest Ira might make. "That's your right. So get a lawyer. You can afford the best!"

"Don't you worry none, Deputy. He'll be the best!"

Tom and Matt were puzzled at Deputy Hensely's arrival. They drug the rolls and sacks back into the mill, closed up and headed for the house. Tom brushed the dirt from his trousers as he walked and also buttoned up his shirt where he had bared his chest to let an occasional breeze cool his body. As they strode in closer they could hear enough of the conversation to surmise that Tom was being arrested.

So this then, was the answer? He hadn't quite expected such retaliation from Jay. A knife in the back, in the dark was his way. At least now they could see what was coming. He would go willingly. Matt however was not so easily convinced.

"That's purty damn good! You never done one son-of-a-bitchin' thing about what happened to Billy! You wouldn't take a warrant out against Jay. You wouldn't take any of your precious time to come up here an' see about our gal. No thanks to you, she's well now as you can see. You never done a thing about that damn Blaine for kidnappin' her an' almost gettin' her killed. She was only protectin' herself from gettin' raped by them bastards. You don't have to go Tom! You don't have to go!" Matt was still angry about Hensely's uncaring attitude where his family was concerned.

"You keep your nose out of this Matt! You could make things a heap worse. Anythin' you might say could be held against Tom," Hensely informed Matt tryin' to keep his temper. "You better tell Matt to keep his nose out of this Ira," Hensely advised. "My business is with Tom."

Tom stood silent, hands in his pockets eyeing Hensely and not resisting in any way. He waited for Matt to simmer down smiling to himself at Matt's quick outburst.

"You know Marshal, he's right," Tom offered calmly. "As far as Blaine goes, it was him or me. It's as cut an' dried as that. So I guess we will just have to prove it. I've got no choice. I'll have to go, right Paw?" Tom questioned his father as he climbed the stairs to stand beside Ira.

"Right here an' now, as I see it, we've got no choice, son. Matt an' I will be right behind you. We'll find a lawyer an' get bail set. We'll stop at Stewart's, let them know what's happening an' send Mary to stay with Kylee. I promise you'll not spend anytime in jail," Ira informed Tom while ignoring Tanner's instructions to quiet Matt.

"There'll be no bail for murder, Ira," Hensely promised.

"Don't look so sad, Kylee. Everythin' will be fine, you'll see. Trust me," Tom said softly moving toward her.

Kylee had stood up totally surprised when she heard Matt's declaration. She had never been told of Blaine's sadistic intent. Hearing the statement aroused a memory of terror somewhere deep inside. She moved to meet Tom touching his arm shyly and looking deep into his eyes.

"I'm sorry Tom," she spoke quietly her eyes filled with concern.

"Don't be sorry, Kylee. It was no fault of yours. Blaine got what he deserved." He wondered if he had misjudged again too soon the tender warmth in her eyes. He went into the house and returned with his coat. He offered his hand to his father for a shake.

"Cain't undo what's been done, Paw. But I've no regrets! I'd do it again. He needed killin'. It were him or me." His voice was strong and steady.

"I'll get my horse, Marshal," Tom said at the bottom of the steps. "I'll meet you down at the gate. I ain't gonna try anythin', just meet me there," Tom added when he saw the look of warning on Hensely's face.

Matt followed close on Tom's heels as they walked with long strides to the barn. As Tom saddled Jole', Matt was urging him to head for the trail behind the mill. Hensely would never find him.

He could be safe into Carolina before anyone could tell where he'd gone.

"Come on Tom, take out the back. I'll go with you. We can hide up somewhere. We'll kill all them son-of-bitchin' Mitchell's then this whole damn mess'll be over!" Matt begged his brother.

"No, Matt. This has got to end! We got to stop doin' things this way. We gotta have some sorta law besides the bullet. Somewhere we need to stop all this hatin' an' killin'." Matt helped him saddle Jole'. "If it hadn't been for all this hatin', Billy would still be alive. Look at what's happened to Kylee. Mary's still grievin' an' Blaine's dead, bastard that he was. It's gotta stop someplace. Maybe it'll stop with me, an' everyone will start doin' things accordin' to the law. I'll be glad to go!" Tom said with sincerity swinging easily up into the saddle.

"Stay away from them card games, an' Polly!" He warned Matt smiling down at him and offering his hand for a shake.

"How in the hell do you tell a Mitchell to stop hatin'? They ain't gonna stop hatin' us Phelps's as long as they's any of us left!" Matt hung on to the handshake reluctant to have Tom leave.

"You know they want to kill us all!" He called after his brother as he rode out of the barn. "Go ahead Tom! Run on out there! You're afear'd to make a break for it! You're a stinkin' coward. Yeller-bellied coward!"

He took off his hat and threw it on the barn floor in exasperation then stomped on it in anger trampling it beyond recognition. He couldn't accept what appeared to be Tom's total admittance of defeat.

"Get back here feller!" Matt called Boy after the dog followed Tom and Jole' out of the barn barking loudly.

"Go back feller, you cain't go this time!" Tom commanded the dog. Boy returned reluctantly and settled down on his haunches at Matt's feet.

Kylee watched Tom and the Deputy ride down the road. The midday sun made short shadows of men and horses as they moved slowly beyond the mill and across the bridge. The wall of green trees soon engulfed them and she could see them no more. Dark shadows deepened in her eyes and she was lost in her own devastating concern for Tom knowing there was nothing she could do to help.

CHAPTER EIGHT

Taynee's return home had been miserable and her unhappiness was affecting the entire family. She seldom talked to anyone; even Nell and Bob were ignored. Bob was concerned because Taynee was their happy light, bringing sunshine and purpose into their lives. She could even make Jay's drunken stupors a little more bearable.

Jay was one to augment his own misery until everyone around him was in the same dark despair. Since they had buried Blaine, he had slipped further into his slovenly ways satisfied to sit in front of the fire and drown his grief with drinking. He had no interest in making whiskey and Trace was nagging him for the product that had been promised. If anyone dared to suggest that he change his habits, the war would rage. The family treaded lightly trying not to rile him.

Even Taynee, who before had often dared to go against him, was submissive so as never to anger him. She gave into his every whim, placating his fiery moods. She played with the baby and did her share of the work, maybe more, so that Nell could have more time with the children. She tried to leave the house whenever possible wanting to stay away from Jay's drunken hostile stare. Much to her surprise there had been no retaliation against her for being at the Phelps's. She tried not to think about what could happen if her father sobered enough to remember that she had disobeyed him. She was anticipating one of his violent rages, knowing in his warped mind that he secretly blamed her as much as he did Tom for Blaine's death.

She was afraid to ride too far. If Jay found out she was riding into the forest, he would accuse her of going to the Phelps's to see Kylee. She used the orchard as an excuse to stay away from the house, although it was late into the growing season for pruning. She would take the twins to help her trim the branches and gather them to burn. They would take a lunch and make a day of it. Jay promised her she could have any money she acquired selling the apples. He hated and ignored the orchard and it usually went begging.

Taynee had plans, if she could make enough money, she could leave and never come back. She promised the twins a share and they were more than willing to help. It also kept them out of Nell's hair. After a hard day in the orchard, Taynee would complete her duties helping Nell. The full days and her unhappiness at being home were beginning to take its toll. She ate little, became thin and irritable until Nell threatened her with spring tonic.

"I know what you need. A dose of sulfa an' molasses. Don't shake your head at me! It's what you're gonna get an' lot's a sassafras tea. I'll get the molasses, you fix the tea!" Nell ordered with firm authority handing her a bag of sassafras.

"Aw, Nell!" Taynee objected. "That's for youngin's. Give it to the twins."

"It's for any one what needs it. An' you need it! If you don't take it down without fussin', I'll get your paw to give it to you," Nell said, smiling wickedly.

Nell lifted the big spoon filled with the bittersweet potion. Taynee opened her mouth wide at the threat of Jay and swallowed the medication that was supposed to cure her of all ills. Gulping a mouthful of hot tea, she swallowed hard to keep from being sick.

"You're gettin' a dose everyday until you start perkin' up. I've had enough of that long face of yours. You hear me?" Nell threatened her and Taynee nodded her head and tried to smile bravely.

"Another thing. You been workin' too hard. I think it's time you spent a little time to yourself. I want you to go down the mountain an' spend a night with the Stewart's. They'd be glad to see you. I'll fix it with your paw. Sides, he's gettin' ready to take the boys an' go to work on the still. It's about time he started perkin' up too! It just ain't proper to grieve forever. April's most over an' he's still mopin' around. The way you an' him's been acting with your long faces an' sullen mouths, it'll be a pleasure to have you both out'a the house."

"You hurry back 'cause I'll miss you," Nell added and gave Taynee an affectionate hug.

It was just what Taynee had hoped for, a chance to ride swiftly down the mountain with the spring breeze blowing through her hair. She always loved the tall stately pines growing at the side of the road. The evergreens had always been her friends. As a girl, she watched the squirrels in the long branches and searched for bird nests. She would carefully count the eggs and wait to see how many hatched. She confided all her pent-up emotions to the tall trees.

She ran barefooted across the yard to the barn to saddle Midnight. Her happiness at the thought of getting away exalted her into song and she was singing happily as she entered the barn. Her joy was short lived as Jay met her inside carrying an armload of tools to load in the wagon.

"Where you headin' Taynee?"

"Nell wanted me to go down to the Stewart's." A nervous trembling began in her middle.

"That's so? Well you can change your plans because I'm takin' Rueben an' Bob and the twins with me. Nell'll need you here. We're leavin' in a bit. I reckon you'll have to put off your trip to Stewart's. When you do go down there, you might convince Mary to reconsider her decision about marryin' Bob," Jay suggested with unusual kindness.

"I will Paw. Could I take a short ride back on the mountain? I'd not stay long an' be back before Nell needs me."

"Well, we won't be loaded for a spell. I reckon it'd be agreeable. Don't get any ideas about leavin' permanent. I'd only come an' get you! I been aimin' on tellin' you. I had an offer for your hand, a good-one. He'll be a good man for you. Soon as I see Tom Phelps hang for murderin' your brother, we'll have a weddin'! I've promised you to Ferrell Hall. How do you like them apples?" Jay leaned forward to leer closely into her face.

She backed away shaking her head, no. Ferrell wasn't such a bad sorta guy, but Taynee would never approve of his wild ways. It would be just like living with Jay; her lips tightened.

"You needn't shake your head at me girl! You're ripe for the pickin'. It's time you was wed!"

Jay licked his lips and wiped them dry with the palm of his hand. He glared at Taynee with a sadistic glitter in his eyes, the look she tried hard to avoid. It was that flaming glare that made her want to ride deep into the wooded forest where her father could never find her.

She saddled Midnight and urged the mare into a swift run, loving the sweet breeze caressing her face and the silence of the big trees. She rode swiftly, the wind blowing her hair into a fan behind her. Her skirts flying high, floating back to free her legs to an occasional shower of sunshine that was coming through the intense branches. She was thinking about Jay's promise that she was to marry Ferrell Hall, then turned her mind and thoughts to Matt.

Lately Taynee had been thinking a lot about Matt. He had been helpful and considerate to her while she was tending Kylee. She found herself enjoying every opportunity to be with him while she was at the mill. Matt's new attitude toward her denied the earlier pessimistic appraisal she'd made of him. Thinking of him now, she wondered if she would ever see him again. She absently rode toward Hail's. She would rest on the rock where she had found Matt sitting that day so long ago and spend a few minutes sunning and dreaming of Matt.

Matt had been sitting on the rock since morning, dreaming of Taynee. He was also thinking of the futility of Tom's situation. The thought made him angry at his helplessness. The lawyer his father hired promised them they could only be patient and wait. Matt did not trust the judicial system; he wanted to reap his own vengeance on Jay. His brother warned him not to seek out the Mitchell's. So he spent much of his time riding and discovering the many wonders of spring. He would ride to Hail's and help her pick herbs and dig roots. Then he'd ride down the mountain to the Stewart's and spend time with Mary, talking about Billy, then back to spend time with Kylee.

Then there were times like today when he would just sit and wait, hoping for a glimpse of Taynee. The mill was dull and boring and Matt missed her terribly. Even Kylee's smiles couldn't fill the empty hollow in his heart. Plowing and planting didn't help either.

This yearning he felt for Taynee was new and a feeling that couldn't be denied. His thoughts dwelled often on the round firmness of her tall willowy body, her full lips and the bright flash of her wonderful eyes.

When he spotted Taynee coming up the trail, he couldn't believe his luck. He was delighted. He mounted his horse and rode out to meet her afraid that she'd ride past him. He waved for her to stop and rode up beside her and clutched hold of Midnight's reigns. He wasn't taking any chances of her running away this time.

"What the hell Taynee. You're always runnin' away from somethin'."

"I have lotsa things to run away from!" She gave him a troubled look.

"Not me, Taynee! Don't run away from me," he told her softly, his look melting into the dark violet of her eyes.

"No, not you Matt, Never you! But if my paw saw us together, he'd kill you for sure. I don't want that on my conscience too."

Looking to the ground she tried to avoid his eyes, afraid he would read the longing she had for him. She had never thought it possible that she would find him at the rock.

"It'd be best if you let me go!"

He rode in closer to her, feeling the warm flesh of her bare legs next to his knee. He felt the little pulse in his temples throbbing wildly.

"I know Taynee, but he ain't gonna find out. I know a place where no one'll find us. If you'll come, I'll take you there." He waited for her answer.

She nodded in agreement and Matt gave her back the reins. He turned his horse and guided them down a trail past the big rock. They continued down the mountain and deep into an intensely wooded area onto a section of Tandy's Mountain that belonged to Hail. Here the pines grew thick, tall, and straight. The branches spread upward, pledging their undying love and devotion to their

Creator. Taynee caught her breath in awe. It was the most beautiful place in the world.

Matt guided her into a circle of trees, where rays of sunshine pierced the thick branches and flooded the ground in a pool of fused light. Taynee caught her breath as the intoxicating beauty and quietness of the place filled her with deep reverence. She remembered her experience with prayer and the possibility that there was a God.

Matt helped her down and pulled her close to him before her bare feet touched the ground. She pushed him slightly and playfully.

"It's good to see you, Matt," she told him laughing, their bodies so close they seemed to breathe at the same time.

"Tell me about everything at the mill." She watched every line in his tanned handsome face trying to absorb everything about him so she wouldn't forget.

"How's dear Kylee?" she questioned him, pulling away and looking at him.

"She's up an' about now, Taynee. She's gettin' stronger each day. Beginnin' to look like her old self, but she cain't remember anything that happened at your place. She was awake when Blaine was killed, an' she cain't remember that either." Matt thought how beautiful her eyes were and wondered why they were standing and talking. He watched her soft lips smiling at him and could wait no longer.

"Come back here where you belong." He pulled her back into his arms.

"Stop it Matt! Stop it right now," she pleaded pouting her bottom lip but making no effort to free herself.

"I cain't stop Taynee, dear heart! I have wanted to hold you in my arms since I laid eyes on you at Billy's buryin'. In fact, I think it's been since you was a straggly kid in boy's breeches. I think I have loved you since then. I've been waitin' all this time for you an' never knew it. Now, I got you I'll never let you go," he promised pulling her close and kissing her slowly, tenderly.

The kiss was filled with all the longing he had been feeling for her. Then he kissed her harder with desire and demand. She sighed heavily, filled with the flame Matt's kisses aroused in her, and then she broke away from him. Taking his hand she pulled him to where a spot of light was flooding a bed of soft pine needles. She settled herself on the warm ground and pulled Matt down beside her. He laid his battered hat beside them on the ground.

"Please Matt, let's talk. Sit down beside me. I cain't think when you're a kissin' me so." Giving him a sweet smile she drew her knees up and hugged her arms around them. Her eyes were clouded with a sultry look filled with love and desire.

Matt knew he had waited all his life for that look and settled himself at her knees. He loved her violet eyes surrounded with long black lashes. Her skin was warm honey brown and he had to touch her. Reaching out, he laid the back of his hand lightly against her cheek stroking the velvet smoothness.

She caught his hand and laid the palm against her cheek feeling the ridges of calluses. She turned her head and kissed his fingers tenderly.

"Why are you sad, Matt? Your eyes tell me you love me, but there's sadness too. Is it because our families hate each other? I don't care, I love you!"

"Oh my God, Taynee. Do you think it'll ever end? Will we ever be able to raise a family in the middle of all this hate? I feel especially sad because your paw took a warrant for Tom, now he's in jail in Gladeville. There ain't nothin' I can do. If I killed your paw an' brothers, they'd hang Tom for sure an' me too." Matt laid his head against her knees.

"Oh Matt, I'm sorry! But they'll have to let Tom go. He was only defendin' himself. It was him or Blaine, it's as simple as that," she assured him stroking his black wavy hair.

"I don't know sweetheart. Tom's lawyer said that Jay an' Rueben were witnesses. They've declared Tom killed Blaine deliberately in cold blood. There's no one to say different."

"There's me, I seen what happened!" She bent and kissed the top of Matt's head.

"You'd testify for us?" He looked up at her searchingly with disbelief. "We couldn't let you do that, it's too dangerous! Your paw'd kill you for sure."

"I'd take the chance, to save Tom's life. Then I'd leave this mountain an' never come back!" Thinking of Jay, Taynee shivered. But she wouldn't let them hang Tom even if her father killed her.

"If it comes to that darlin', I'd take you away from here. Far away! Now, that's settled! Have we talked long enough?" Matt smiled at her mischievously, his eyes filled with anticipation. He pushed her back gently to the ground.

Taynee could see the tall pines forming a wall around them. High above a small round patch of bright blue sky shone through. The long shafts of light penetrated the deep shadows and created soft lights on the ground. The little grove was dim and cool. The pine needles made a soft bed underneath them. An overwhelming glow possessed Taynee.

They were the only people in the world. Her eyes wandered from Matt's dark hair to his heavy brows then down to his thin finely shaped lips, almost covered with dark beard and mustache. She pulled him down to her. His eyes smiled seriously as he kissed her, coaxing her lips to part. Softly, softly he kissed her until she sighed and he felt her relax in his arms. He kissed her neck and shoulders gently easing her dress down until he could kiss the cool flesh above her breast. She breathed deeply as he kissed her lips again. His hands were wandering and demanding. Taynee was eager for each caress. The flesh on her thigh was warm and vibrant to Matt's touch.

"I love you. I love you, Matt."

"I love you too, Taynee. Say you'll marry me. I'll take you away from your paw. Soon as Tom's trial is over, we'll make plans. Do you love me enough to do that, Taynee, my darlin'? You're so sweet. I love you so much."

His hands explored the wonders of her body. Why did women wear so many clothes, he thought to himself still marveling at Taynee's beauty, her long legs and smooth skin.

"You promise we'll run away Matt? Promise?" She felt his urgency to complete their love.

"We'll go west Taynee." His mouth was dry. "Oh my God, you're wonderful!"

He ran his tongue across his dry lips and kissed her again. The need for her was a searing flame he couldn't control. She lay waiting, hoping he would hurry. As he laid his body over upon hers, he felt her stiffen. Undeniably she refused him and pushed him away.

"No Taynee. I'll not wait! Don't push on me like that! What's the matter? My God, don't pull away, Taynee! Taynee!"

"Stop it Matt! Stop it. I heard something. I did. I heard something. There it is again." She began to tremble. Matt complied with her wish and freed her.

"Someone's watchin' us, I know it, I can feel it. Oh Matt, I'm so sorry. I wanted to, really I did. I wanted to with you, because I love you. But I'm frightened. I fear for both of us. It could be paw," she whispered with terror in her voice.

Taynee rose from the warm pine needles and began to straighten her clothing. She was trembling and her hands were shaking uncontrollably. She looked searchingly into the shadows of the pines.

"It's nothin', Taynee. Listen. The sound you heard was the trees swishin' together. See, there is no-one, sweetheart." He comforted her looking up at her with eyes filled with disappointment. "If it were your paw, we'd both be dead!"

He was aware that Taynee would never be free of her terror of being caught with him. He understood her fear and knew they would not recapture the beauty of the previous moment as long as Jay was alive.

"You're not angry with me, sweetheart? Please don't be angry with me," Taynee begged, unhappy with the way things had gone.

Matt rose, smoothed his hair, picked up his crumpled hat and put it back on his head. His emotions were under control and he took Taynee back in his arms, kissed her tenderly and assured her:

"I could never be angry at you darlin'. I love you. Promise me that you will always be my love. I'll let you go now, but promise me you'll meet me here again, soon. Promise?" He helped her up on Midnight. "I'll wait for you everyday at this same time."

"I'll come whenever I can. I promise. I love you," she whispered against his lips and was gone.

Matt lay back down on the soft bed of pine needles. He stretched and put his arms behind his head looking at the patch of blue sky above him. He thought of all the wonders of Taynee and how close they had been to being one. A small breeze blew through the tall pines and Matt felt a chill. Without Taynee lying beside him, the grove turned suddenly cold and empty.

Taynee and Matt met many times in the weeks that followed. They treasured every moment as if it would be the last and their love deepened as the days went by. He had never believed it was possible to love a woman so much.

Taynee also marveled at the wonder of love. Still afraid Jay might catch them, but throwing caution to the wind and spending every moment she could with Matt. Their meetings were always sweet and tender, their lovemaking passionate and demanding; their bodies craving to know the fulfillment of their love. They promised each other to abstain from their desires and wait until they were married. Taynee was always ready to withdraw their vow, longing to give herself fully, but Matt was the one to curb the passion and wait.

"It won't be long darlin'," he promised her, "as soon as Tom's trial is over, I'll be to get you. We'll get away from your paw. A long way away."

"I'm willin', Matt. Don't you love me enough?" She teased him wickedly.

"Oh my God, girl! Do I love you? How can you ask? It's because I love you that we're gonna wait."

"I know darlin'. I was only teasin' you. I love you more for not takin' advantage of my shamefulness. But my body longs for you so. I don't see how I can bear it!" She kissed him passionately and lay her head on his chest satisfied to be held tightly in his arms.

Tom's trial was not far away. Jay and the boys had returned from the still. As Nell promised, Taynee was to have her day and night to spend at Stewart's. She planned to take her mother's wedding dress that she had carefully saved through the years. Mary would help her remodel the gown. It was too short and the lace was badly in need of repair. She knew the Stewarts could be trusted to keep her plans a dark secret from Jay. The joy of her visit was complete when she found Kylee spending some time at the Stewart's also.

Kylee and Mary were going to leave in a few days for a shopping tour with Bess in Gladeville. Ira insisted Kylee needed some proper attire for the trial. He absolutely refused to let her wear the pearl gray suit with the still visible dust streaks.

Ira had arranged with Bess to bring the girls into town a day early. They were thrilled and excited about spending a night in a real hotel. Jan full heartedly agreed with the plan and had allowed Mary a sum of money to buy a new ensemble as well. He thought that perhaps the diversion would be a good change for both girls.

Kylee and Mary were overjoyed at Taynee's appearance. She told them in a hushed voice of her plans. They were ecstatic and began to work immediately on the wedding dress in the privacy of the girl's bedroom. After a night of fun and laughter they had to work quickly the next day to finish with the dress.

Taynee was so excited she could scarcely stand still. She wiggled and twisted to see herself in the long mirror as Kylee pinned and adjusted the wedding gown.

"You'll be sorry if I stick you a good one," Kylee warned her firmly. "Now stand still!" she added with a smile to lighten her words.

"Maybe I'll know then if I'm dreamin' or not. Just look at that beautiful day!" Taynee ducked her head to look through the window under the eaves.

"When it seems the good Lord has forgotten me, He showers me with joy. Look at you Kylee darlin'. That's proof enough that He loves me! Then He up an' gave me Matt for my own. Now look at this beautiful day that He made especially for me. We'll trust that He'll make everything fine for Tom." Taynee's voice saddened a little as she thought of Tom.

She smiled confidently at Kylee and breathed deeply of the sweet air coming through the opened window. The sun found a path through the curtains as the breeze blew them apart, warmed Taynee's bare feet. She curled her toes and hummed a tune contentedly, then began to sing...

"Twas in the merry month of May
When flowers were a bloomin'.
Poor Willy on his deathbed lay
For love of Barbara Allen.
He sent his servant into the town
Into the town she dwelled in.
Saying my master dear has sent me
Here if your name be Barbara Allen.

Taynee's voice was sweet and low as she sang softly the old English ballad Tom had taught her while Kylee was ill.

> *They buried Willie in the old churchyard*
> *And Barbara in the new one.*
> *On Willie's grave there grew a rose*
> *On Barbara's a green briar.*
> *They grew an they grew to the old church wall*
> *An they could grow no higher And there they tied a crew of knots*
> *The rose bush and the briar!"*

Taynee thought she understood how one could die for love but felt much happier about living for it.

Kylee was letting the hem down on the dress. Mary was working on a new veil from a piece of lace Bess saved for such an occasion. Ginny sat on a small three-legged milk stool making tiny rose buds from satin ribbon to sew on the dress and veil.

Emily sat cross-legged on the bed beside Mary rolling the remaining ribbon and fastening the rolls with pins. She joined Taynee in her humming and singing. They were all talking and laughing at the same time, happy to have Taynee with them and elated at how well Kylee looked.

They talked of Matt and Taynee going west and felt a little sad that they would be leaving. They mentioned Tom's trial, dreading to think of what could happen. Seeing Taynee and feeling a deep warm affection for her caused Kylee to have a tingling in her mind. Somewhere, vaguely, there was a slight recollection of the night Nell's baby had been born.

"How is the baby, Taynee?"

"Oh Kylee, you remembered. Matt said you couldn't remember nothin'. The baby's beautiful." Taynee laughed in surprise remembering the scrawny red newborn of so many months ago.

"If only I could remember what happened the day Blaine was killed. I could help free Tom. But I can't remember anythin'," Kylee said, brooding over her lost memory, but hopeful after remembering about the baby.

"Oh, let's not speak of those unhappy things. It'll spoil this perfect day. There now Taynee, the veil is done, see how beautiful you are." Mary placed the misty veil over Taynee's head.

Speaking of killing brought back the painful memory of Billy's death, a memory that was still very clear in Mary's mind. Through the heavy tears inside her heart, she smiled bravely at Taynee and thought how absolutely lovely she was and secretly envied her just a little for having the wedding gown and her happiness with Matt. She had vowed in her grief that she would never allow herself to love again.

They all sighed in appreciation at Taynee's magnificent beauty. The color was high in her cheeks, the veil a snowy white against her raven black hair. The white of the gown and veil caused the dark splash of her brows and thick lashes to show up vibrantly. The dark violet blue of her eyes glowed with happiness as she gazed at herself in the long oval mirror. She was wonderfully amazed and impressed with her own beauty.

"Oh, I have never looked like this. It must be the veil." She breathed softly as if talking to herself. "This lovely person cain't be me, I'm so happy, I cain't believe it! I only hope nothin' happens to spoil it."

A cold chill stood the goose bumps at the nape of her neck at the thought of what could happen if Jay found out about her plans. There it was again, spoiling her pleasure, the fear she had for her father.

Emily bounced up and down on the bed excitedly. "You're like a fairy princess. You're a princess. Really you are Taynee! I'm gonna be just like you when I get big." The dream widened Emily's brown eyes as she gazed in childhood fantasy at Taynee. The little girl had never seen anything so magnificent.

"Thank you all. You are all dear friends. Perhaps I'll not see you again before we-uns leave. But I promise you, we'll come back an' see you all. Maybe then things'll be different between our folks." Taynee carefully rolled the precious dress back into a bundle.

"I gotta be goin'. I'll have to ride hard to be home before dark." She kissed Emily and hugged her tightly, then told the other girl's good-bye and hurried down the stairs.

Bess was setting a pan of corn bread to cook on the iron stove as Taynee came through the kitchen. She hugged the girl and warned her to be careful, thinking of the risk she and Matt were taking. Bess sent with her a greeting for Nell and a gift for the baby wrapped in a bright piece of cloth that was tied with shiny ribbon.

Taynee's legs flopped carelessly against Midnight's flanks. She rode slowly, not worried. Her thoughts were miles away from the green world of trees and bright blooming spring flowers around her. She was unaware of the blue Virginia sky and the song of the birds; she sang her own happy song...

> *"Near a quiet country village*
> *stands a maple on the hill.*
> *Where I sat with my Geneva long ago.*
> *We would sing love songs together*
> *As the birds had gone to rest*
> *As you linger there in silence*
> *Thinking only of the past*
> *Let your teardrops kiss*
> *the flowers on my grave."*

She clutched the wedding dress tightly under her arm. The brightly packaged gift sat between her knees. When Matt came for her she would be ready to go with him and marry him, have his children, and live happily ever after. Away from Jay! She added to her thought visions of fulfilling her wifely duties.

She rode up the road from Stewart's around by Hail's. She noticed that Hail's mule was gone and went on by. She hurried past the orchard to home. Darkness was creeping in steadily as she rode into the barn. Her hopes that Jay would be gone were short lived when she saw his big bay in the stall. She fed and watered Midnight then tucked the wedding dress high in a corner under the eaves. She took the baby gift and started out the door. Through the doorway of the barn she could see lights from the house glowing faintly into the already dark night. A long shadow carrying a lantern moved across the doorway and she froze.

"What took you so all-fired long, Taynee? Wasn't you supposed to be home before dark?" Jay's voice was soft, not filled with anger as she thought it would be.

"You didn't stop no where's else did you?" He reached and pulled the wide door shut. The barn grew light as the lantern glow blazed higher.

"Ridin' slow, Paw. The day was so beautiful. I come by Hail's but didn't stop, her mule was gone."

"Maybe you'd like to get away for good. Maybe that's what the Stewart's are up to, huh girl?" He lifted the lantern high letting the light fall around her.

"No, Paw!" she assured him. "I'm not wanting to get away."

She moved backward trying to think of a way to get around him and escape through the door. His eyes glowed in the light of the lantern. Taynee could read, hiding deep within what her fate would be. The night she found Bob in the barn flashed before her. She ducked her head so her father could not see her fear.

"I'm sorry I was so late Paw. Please let me by. I have a present for little J.B. I want to take it in the house." Taynee told him, biding time. She felt him soften a little at the mention of the gift and she looked up.

"It's from Bess," she added trying to force a smile and hoping he would let her by as she pushed the gift toward him.

"It'll wait. You'll not leave again without my say, Taynee girl! Nell should have never let you go. Long as you're under my roof, you'll do as I say!" Jay took the gift and set it on the ledge of a stall. He grabbed Taynee's arm and twisted it behind her back then pulled her close to hold her firmly. He reached to hang the lantern on a hook above their heads.

Taynee shrank away from him and he felt her withdrawal. He tightened his hold and reached for a bridle strap hanging from the rafter. His anger flared as he felt her trying again to free herself from his hold.

"Disrespectful youngin'. Trouble with youngin's today, they ain't got no respect! Well, when I get done with you, you'll be a little more respectful!"

"Let me go, Paw! I promise not to leave again!" she pleaded loudly. "Don't whip me, please Paw! Don't!"

Jay ignored her and gave her a savage push against the wall. Before she regained her balance, he raised his arm and the bridle fell with a smashing whir against Taynee. It wrapped around her body and fell away leaving her worn dress torn and in shreds biting sharply into her tender flesh. As the bridle hit her again, she screamed and fell upon the straw in the empty stall.

Jay reached to pull her to her feet, her dress and petticoat gave under his hold and he yanked viciously. He reached and lifted her up to stand before him. Dropping the bridle, he became engrossed in another pleasure. Ivory skin, glowing through the patches of torn attire, enticing him to further rage and he began tearing at her clothing.

"Please Paw, don't! No Paw!" She tried desperately to hold her dress together.

Jay fiendishly ripped at her clothing until she stood naked and exposed in the flickering lantern light. Humiliation was complete and she cringed into the shadows trying to cover her nakedness with her arms. Her mind could not comprehend the horror that was happening. Jay reached for her and pulled her up tightly into his steel-like frame. He ran his hands down over her naked body feeling the smoothness of her skin.

"See now, ain't that nice?" His breathing was becoming labored, his face a livid mass behind his dark beard. "You needn't act like that girl. You're gonna get married soon. I promised you'd be a willin' wife." He planted a slobbery kiss on her neck.

Taynee's body was taut, every nerve frozen. She tried to bring her mind to the point of resisting and fighting back. A sob rose in her throat and she began to struggle.

The first shock of the attack was beginning to wear off. A fluttering of her old fight returned and she pushed hard against Jay. Biting, scratching, and kicking, but with her depleted strength it was no defense against him. Her sudden reprisal only aroused him into burning, flaming, ecstatic determination.

"Damn it youngin'. I said for you to be willin'!" He pushed her roughly down upon the straw and dropped his bulk of body heavily on top of her. Jay's huge hands burned against her chilled flesh and she became more determined to free herself. She twisted and exerted herself trying to squirm from under him.

Jay's desire for Taynee was no longer a sneaking, slithering, aggravating breeze. It had become a raging hurricane that he could no longer control. He lifted a clenched fist and struck her hard on the jaw. Her head jerked back, the struggle was subdued. She could feel his wet beard on her face and his heavy breathing close to her ear. The smell of whiskey and tobacco mingled with his unwashed body reactivated the fight in her. She renewed her struggle and tried to keep consciousness. She felt a scream rise in her throat but it was silenced by another thudding blow.

The lantern swayed crazily above Jay's distorted hideously grinning face as he hit her again and again. The struggle was ended and the blessed darkness floated in around her. The night outside was clear and warm. A barn owl hooted incessantly into the darkness. The pines were silent, their long branches not stirring in the calm night. Jay staggered from the barn, his arms hung limply to his side. He leaned heavily against the doorframe letting his head rest on his chest. His lust for Taynee quenched. He stood for a moment as if undecided about what he should do. Getting his second wind, he turned into the barn but not to help the girl. He saddled his horse, mounted it, and rode into the night.

CHAPTER NINE

Matt sat alone on the courthouse steps. A warm, easy drenching rain had started in the night lasting long enough to cause the day to be hot, sticky, sultry, and totally uncomfortable. The humid dampness enticed all manner of crawling and flying insects to aggravate and torment one's body. One wandered into Matt's boot. He tried to discourage the little pest from traveling any further by poking at it with a piece of broken tree limb. He only succeeded in prodding his foot sharply. He abandoned the pursuit and threw the stick across the walk into the grassy square.

His flashy striped pants were topped with a plain dark suit coat. A standard white shirt was beginning to show wrinkles and soil from the two days of being away from home. His attire was new and sporting but he still wore his misshapen hat.

As Matt looked across the square his thoughts were filled with Taynee. She was on his mind as overpowering as the warm spring rain. Under his breath and solely to himself, he sang...

> *"There's a cabin in the shadow of the pines*
> *and a blue-eyed girl is waiting there for me.*
> *I know she'll be my wife an we'll live a happy life*
> *In a cabin in the shadow of the pines."*

He became suddenly silent. He missed Taynee and wanted to hold her in his arms and feel her body close to his. For some reason there was sadness in thinking of her. He wanted this trial to be over. He wanted to get her away, far away from her father.

Taking a long brown tailor made cigarette from his coat pocket he rolled it between his fingers slowly before lighting it. He turned his thoughts to Mary and Kylee and how happy they looked that morning. The shopping spree was just the medicine both girls needed and with Bess's supervision they had done well. Ira and Jan had ridden to town with Matt leaving both places in the capable hands of Uncle Alvin. Ginny and Emily Ann were staying over with the Jennings.

Matt watched Ira where he sat in his wheel chair in front of Hail. She was perched carefully on the edge of a weather beaten bench that was still damp from the recent rain. They sat talking under the shade of a white blooming dogwood, its sweet fragrance flooding the air. As Matt approached the couple he could hear them talking in low voices, emerged in a conversation he knew absolutely nothing about.

"Now look a-here, Hail. What's got into you all of a sudden? You weren't to know then, an' ya promised never to ask. That was the deal then, it still stands! I ain't gonna tell you. It would only cause you unrest. You said you didn't want to know nothin' about it for fear Jay might find out. Nothin's changed as far as he's concerned. You still cain't risk him a-knowin'!" Ira puffed his pipe and watched Hail closely.

"I know Ira, but I'm wantin' to know. I gotta know for my own piece of mind. Times a gettin' away from both of us. We ain't gonna be here forever!" Her anxiety was apparent as she looked at Ira with pleading eyes. "I have a little savings, I could do some good with it. Perhaps make life a little easier."

Coming to town for anything other than medical supplies was a luxury Hail did not allow herself. She had been delighted when Ira offered her the use of the buggy Matt had taken from the barn. She wore a jaunty black bonnet trimmed with black ribbon and white silk camellias. Her black silk dress had close fitting sleeves and a long rustling skirt. The soft bodice gently hugged the curve of her body. The dark color was very becoming with her platinum white hair. Hail was completely unconcerned with her compelling attractiveness. Any vanity or desire to be noticed had faded from her mind long ago.

Ira thought her silver hair only added to her beauty. It accented her black finely arched eyebrows and thick eyelashes. Her small features looked as if they were cut from fine alabaster. Her eyes, he thought, were penetrating, soul reaching, and undeniably the most beautiful he had ever seen. They still had the power to stir his heart as they pleaded with him now. He remembered when the roses had bloomed in her cheeks and her hair had been the flame of an age-old penny. He looked to the ground, away from her penetrating look. Afraid if he looked at her another minute he wouldn't be able to deny telling her what she wanted to know.

"I ain't worryin' about Jay anymore! I've been afear'd of him too long. I'll not be scared off by him again!"

"It doesn't matter. We'll speak of it no more!"

The look in his eyes told her to drop the subject. Taking his watch from his pocket, he eyed it closely then looked up as Matt came up to them.

"It's time to go back in Matt, wheel me over. I sure hope that lawyer I hired has something new a-goin'. So far all he's done is look purty. I reckon I know I'm payin' for all them fancy duds he's a wearin', ruffled shirt an all!" Money wasn't the object. He'd spend all he had to free his son and beat Mitchell and Hensely.

As the second session of the trial progressed, Kylee sat nervously twisting her handkerchief. She kept having these little inclinations of memory that were taunting her. They had been teasing her since she remembered Nell's baby. She had been trying to piece the puzzle together. When Matt had arrived in town, she talked to him about it. He tried to help her again by telling her everything Taynee had told him. She wanted to testify for Tom, but when she informed him, Matt flatly refused to let her take the stand. He was afraid for her. If she took the stand and could only remember vaguely what happened, the cross examination might send her receding back into absolute amnesia.

She sat listening to the court proceedings and watched Rueben and then Jay's beastly faces peering at her from the witness stand. Jay's face was so much like Blaine's. She couldn't believe the exact resemblance. As Jay talked and grinned in his best manner, she suddenly remembered.

She could hear Taynee crying. "He's dead, Paw! You've got Blaine killed! See what you got done, Paw?" She heard again the bullets thudding into dry lumber and the squealing of frightened horses.

Putting her hands over her ears she ducked her head trying to shake the terrible memories that were coming to light in her mind. In a terrifying moment she knew she could recall out of the darkness of her mind, anything she wanted to. Turning to Matt sitting beside her, she whispered her decision in his ear. He transferred the message to Tom's lawyer.

Mr. Allen, the city attorney from Norton was elated. At last he had something to work with. Tom was still telling her, 'no' and shaking his head. It didn't matter; her mind was made up.

When Kylee had her chance to take the stand, circumstances changed for the better. She told them every incident that led up to the shooting. She convinced the jury of the despicable characteristics that incited Blaine to charge the house, calling Tom out so he could kill him. Kylee made it clear that Tom had only defended himself and the women. She explained the long illness that had compelled Taynee to be at the Phelps's home to care for her.

The jury took a long look at her. Her sad green eyes were drowning in the pool of her pale face and surrounded by curls of auburn hair. The jury decided it was truly a miracle that she had recovered at all. They acknowledged the fact that Jay had the right to demand that Taynee return to her home, but agreed that it didn't give him the right to charge the Phelps's home. It was the jury's unanimous decision that Tom had no other choice but to kill Blaine and brought in a verdict of self-defense, and Tom was free to go.

Jay was distraught; his face was blue with rage. He sprang to his feet and cursed the judge and jury. Threatening them with retribution and warned them they had not heard the last of this case. He shook his big fist in Ira's face and shouted...

"You've won this round, you miserable cripple! You had to hide behind a woman's apron strings, you damn son-of-a-bitch! I don't know why I've allowed you to live this long. You ain't no good to any-one! You cain't even stand on your own two feet! You cain't even crawl, you're less than a snake! I'm tellin' you this, you better listen good! I'm gonna see all you Phelps bastards buried! The state of Virginie ain't big enough for the both of us. I'll see Tom Phelps burn! I'll scatter his ashes across the Blue Ridge! You remember this, I'm goin' to rid Pound Mountain of the likes of you-ins!"

"An' you, you old witch! I'll see that you burn too! This is all your fault. I'll get rid of you yet!" Jay hissed at Hail, his eyes burning with insane anger and hate.

Marshal Hensely wasn't happy at the turn of events either. He'd been certain they had Tom pinned good. He hadn't counted on Kylee's testimony. She was a pretty one he mused; no wonder the jury was captured.

A new moss green suit accented her lovely green eyes and brought the flaming high lights to the surface in her reddish brown hair. Her shining curls were covered with a matching flat styled poke bonnet trimmed with lace and velvet braid. It was tied under her chin with a silk bow. If anyone had told Kylee it was her look of delicate pale purity that had captivated the jury, she would have never believed it. She had little confidence in her own beauty.

Matt was overjoyed with the turn of events and openly hugged his brother and kissed Mary, Bess, and Kylee. He placed his battered hat on his head while he shook everyone's hand. He stayed close beside Tom as if afraid he would vanish. Jan pumped their arms until Matt feared they would come loose at the sockets.

Tom's happiness at his freedom was immeasurable. He returned his brother's hug and shook his father's hand hard. He knocked off Matt's battered hat playfully.

"Looks like you could have at least bought a new bonnet for this big event, the girls did. Well, don't matter, it does have personality." He kissed Mary on the cheek and gave Bess a friendly hug and saved his warm looks for Kylee. He looked at her for a breathless moment, wondering if he dared, then took her boldly in his arms and kissed her full and hard on the lips. To his amazement, Kylee didn't pull away and he held her tighter.

Matt picked up his hat and tossed it into the air. "Ya-Hoo!" he shouted excitedly.

Kylee's face and neck turned a soft pink as Tom released her, but kept his arm boldly around her waist. As they walked out into the sunny day Tom looked around at the green of the grass and the blue sky. With wide eyes he gazed at the flaming mass of flowers blooming beside the step. Breathing deeply of his precious freedom, he made a vow...

"Jay Mitchell might scatter my ashes across the Blue Ridge, but he ain't never, never gonna see me spend another day in jail. Not as long as I live!"

The trial was over, they were all back home and things were beginning to return to normal. Ira was weary and spending the days recuperating. Tom planted and hoed the corn, then planted more winter onions. He wanted to spend every possible hour outside where he could sing loudly, his voice vibrating through the heavy corn stalks.

Kylee sorted through her newly bought treasures, not believing her good fortune. She took a minute to run and kiss Ira and thank him again for his generosity, bringing a wide smile to his tired face.

Matt was totally ignored and he was glad. It was time for him to make his plans to steal Taynee.

The afternoon was beautifully warm, a soft blue haze hung about the hills. Spring was in its glory and Matt's heart sang as he left. The grove was empty and Taynee didn't come. Matt was not going home without seeing his sweetheart. He threw caution to the wind and rode to Mitchell's. As he approached cautiously there seemed to be no one around, but he had to be careful and not endanger his chance of getting Taynee away safely. If it had to be, he would fight the entire clan. He had not forgotten to strap on his guns this time.

Taynee was despondent as she prepared a cold lunch for her family. Nell, the twins, and Bob were hoeing the corn on the steep hillside behind the cabin. They would be hungry and tired for a mid-day rest. Jay and Rueben had gone to run a batch of whiskey off at the still. Taynee was glad; she always was when they were away. Setting the food on the table, she looked in on the baby playing happily in the crib that Rueben had built. She smiled at him as she kissed him fondly. He promptly delighted her with a smile and a happy giggle.

"You're such a darlin'! Who'd ever think you was that same scrawny youngin' born that awful night?"

She went back through the kitchen, and on her way picked up the churn and went to the springhouse to get the cream. The day was becoming sultry and inside the springhouse was cool and refreshing. She filled the churn and carried it outside ducking to miss the hams hanging on the rafters above her head.

Moss clung to the damp rocks along the edge of the stream coming from the hill above the springhouse. In the shallow swirls of the water grew beds of green velvet watercress that was getting old and going to seed, the color of Kylee's eyes, she thought. She was glad the trial was over. She heard it was Kylee's testimony that turned the tide for Tom. It gladdened her heart that Kylee was recovering her memory and that Tom had been freed.

Jay was not so glad. When he returned home he was in a burning temper, swearing he would even the score with the Phelps's. She sat the filled churn in a spot of sunshine to warm before she started the task of churning the butter. She chose a large smooth rock close to the wall of the springhouse and sat down. She laid her bruised and battered face against the coolness of the wall. She sighed with misery. It was sheer torture to change any position of her body. The flies hummed about the churn lid, but she was totally unconcerned.

She could never meet Matt again in the grove. Knowing what happened to her at Jay's hands made any happiness between them impossible. Her father would never rest until all the Phelps's were dead. She would not endanger Matt's life further.

Loud talking was coming from the yard. Taynee could hear the twins talking to someone. Raising her head she listened closely wondering who it could be. She had heard no sound or commotion of a rider coming in.

"Where's Taynee, youngin's?" There was no mistaking Matt's voice. Her body stiffened.

"We-uns have been in the field with Maw an' Bob. If she's not inside, she must be at the spring house gettin' some milk for our dinner."

She listened to his footsteps start around the house and cross the yard. He must not find her. There was no way she would let him see her battered face. She must find a place to hide.

Stepping across the small stream she hurried around to the back of the springhouse. Here the grape vines grew wild and entangled over a tree that had fallen into the slant of the hill. The vines encased the log and formed a cool room like shelter underneath. The twins had built a playhouse inside the gathering of thick vines. Their playthings an old quilt, broken bench, and several wooden buckets lay scattered about.

Squeezing into the sheltered arbor, she knelt on the ground, scarcely breathing, hoping Matt would not find her. She decided to never see him again. He must not be put in any further danger. How could he love or want her if he were to find out what happened. Bowing her head, she covered her face with her hands. The tears ran between her long slim fingers and fell to the ground and were immediately swallowed up by the dry dusty earth.

CHAPTER TEN

"Taynee, Taynee. Where are you sweetheart?" Matt called. "I've come for you! Come on now get your things. Taynee, answer me!"

He opened the door to the springhouse and closed it. Taynee waited, breath stilled. He must not find her. Matt spotted the churn and felt certain that Taynee was somewhere close. Perhaps she walked up the hillside. Then he discovered the hide-a-way and peeked inside. He was surprised to see Taynee crouched upon the ground in a huddled position rocking to and fro, her face clutched tightly in her hands.

"No Matt! Go away! You cain't see me. I mean, I don't want to see you! Never! Go away! No, don't touch me, leave me alone!" she told him in a muddled voice from between her closed fingers. Matt ducked into the shelter and knelt beside her.

"Taynee, why are you hidin' from me? What's wrong? What's the matter darlin'?" He attempted to pull her hands down.

"Leave me be, Matt. Go away! Go away before Jay and Rueb get back! Go!" she shouted from behind her cupped hands, pushing him away with her shoulders. "I hate you! I hate you!"

"I'll never believe that! When I go, I'm takin' you with me!"

"I cain't go with you, Matt, I cain't never go with you!"

Matt lifted her from the shelter, stood her up and put his arms around her, not understanding why she refused to look at him.

Taynee couldn't stand the pressure of his arms around her bruised body. Without thinking, she dropped her hands to push him away.

Matt was appalled as he looked in shocked surprise at her battered face. A large reddish cut puffed her top lip out of all proportion. One eye was bloodshot, black, and still almost swollen shut. A large bruise ran from her cheekbone to underneath her chin. Visible at the opening of her dress, cradled between the gentle swellings of her white breasts was a great purplish spread of discoloration.

As Matt looked upon Taynee's reason for hiding her face, he wanted to cry. Most of all he had to hold her, comfort her. A great compassion filled him and he loved her more at that moment than he had thought possible.

Great tears filled Taynee's eyes and rolled down her bruised cheeks and dropped from her chin. Matt could stand no more and he gathered her tenderly into his arms. He held her gently, smoothing her hair, rocking her with an easy to-and-fro motion, loving her, and not wanting to ever let her go. He pushed her head to rest lightly upon his shoulder. He waited for the tears to stop.

"Jay found out about us an' whipped you?" he asked her and felt the nod of her head. "You are comin' away with me, love. You go right now an' get your things. I'm takin' you with me, now!" His mind was made up. Jay would not have a chance to lay a hand on her again.

She pushed away and looked at him with great sad eyes trying to absorb everything about him. His black hair and blue eyes, she would never forget. The gentle love she could see plainly in his face made her heart break. Knowing what she had to do for his sake, she had to send him away. Raising her head proudly, defiantly she told him firmly...

"I cain't go with you Matt. I should have never led you to believe I would. I really don't love you. Besides I'm promised to another. Now please go away an' leave me be!"

Taynee pursed her lips tightly, making the cut vibrate with pain. How could she convince him of her sincerity? Trying hard to hold back the tears, she pushed around him and walked toward the house.

All the color drained from Matt's face. She was lying, all those days in the shady grove, the promises, and the plans. He remembered with a deep burning how she begged him to love her to the fullest. He recalled the shining love in her eyes, then the flash of disappointment when he denied her and told her they would wait.

Taynee was putting on an act, trying to convince him to leave, and sacrificing herself to save him. He walked rapidly around in front of her blocking her way on the narrow path.

"Get out of my way!" she hissed at him through clenched teeth, her eyes narrowing to slits.

"I'll be back tomorrow for you Taynee! I'll let you think this over until then. I know you're lying. If you feel the same when I come back, then I'll go west without you. If you're goin' with me, be ready! I ain't carin' about your bruises, I love you girl! Oh my God, how I love you!" His eyes filled with tender compassion.

"No Matt, don't come back, please! Paw'll kill you for sure!"

"I don't care! Let him kill me! If I cain't have you, I'd as soon be dead!" His voice shook to the point of breaking at the thought of losing Taynee.

"Oh, Matt!" she cried and fell into his arms sobbing. She could stand no more. "I cain't send you away! I cain't! Hold me, kiss me darlin'. Careful now!" She tilted her face and Matt kissed her bruised lips tenderly.

"I'll be back to get you, darlin'," he promised against her parted lips.

He wanted to kill Jay for laying a fist on Taynee but he knew it would only endanger their happiness, so he would let it go.

"No, don't come here, love. I'll meet you at the grove," she cautioned him, her eyes bright with the old flame. "Tomorrow," she whispered and brushed a kiss across his lips then turned and ran down the path.

Matt watched Taynee disappear into the house, his heart pounding triumphantly and about to explode with love. He ran stretching his long legs into wide strides. Matt crossed the yard and disappeared into the distance to his horse in seconds.

Matt was elated as he told Kylee of his plans while she set supper on the table. Ira sat looking into the fire silently, listening to what his son was saying. He waited patiently for him to finish then turned his chair around.

"Where do you think you'll go to get shed of Jay?"

"I don't know Paw, but we will! We aim to go out west an' find us some gold. They say it grows on bushes out there. Side's they's other opportunities; maybe we could even find a place an' build a gristmill. No doubt they raise corn out there. They gotta have their meal ground. That's one thing I'm good at," he bragged to his father.

"It sounds too easy to me. Gold growing on bushes?" Ira smiled whimsically at Matt. "That mill idea sounds more dependable to me."

"If you find any of them gold bushes, you let us know! Paw, Kylee, and me, we'll come west an' share it with you, won't we Paw?" Tom joked with his brother and winked playfully at Ira. It was about the most ridiculous thing he'd ever heard of, gold growing on bushes.

"Just be sure you take your guns an' plenty of bullets 'cause I hear there's wild savages out there. I heard the cowboys are worse than the Indians. So be sure you're well armed. You might like livin' in the west, at least it'll get you shed of Jay." Tom's lighthearted banter had started as a joke. As his eyes rested on Kylee, his heart filled with desire and he was dead serious when he finished.

Kylee bowed her head, not returning the look. She lifted a pot of early garden stew from the fire and set it on the table.

"Well, I wish you good luck," their father said as he pushed up to the table.

Ira was hungry and the stew and corn bread Kylee set on the table urged him forward. Looking at Matt, he shook his head as he dipped out the stew onto his plate. His favorite stew was filled with fresh spring vegetables. It was laced with dumplings, chicken, and thickened slightly to make rich tasty gravy.

"No boys," he went on his eyes filling with sadness. "I reckon I'll never get out west. I wish to be buried right here. I'm aimin' on takin' my final restin' place right to the side of your sweet Maw an' Billy. I never want to leave these blessed hills. You take care an' be watchful for Jay. If he finds out what you're up to, your lives'll not be worth a plugged nickel. When are you leavin'?"

"Tomorrow, Paw. We'll go into Kentucky first, stay with Uncle Hatler and Aunt Reva. We'll have them help us get wed. They'd probably like doin' that."

"Yes, I like that plan. Eat your supper now," Ira said and closed the subject.

The next day Matt readied to leave. He put his belongings in a tightly rolled bundle and tied a feather quilt and pillows into a bedroll. His father wheeled out of his bedroom holding a tin box on his lap. He opened the box and lifted out a packet. There was an empty bottomless look in his pale blue eyes as he prepared to tell his son goodbye.

"This is yours Matt. I want to give it to you before you leave. I reckon as how we cain't talk you out of goin'," he asked Matt once more. When Matt shook his head, 'no', Ira continued. "You always been a good boy, Matt. An' you've grown into a fine man. You done your work well. Sometimes I'd have a little problem gettin' you to do it, but you done it well. I've been grateful for what you've done for me since I've been crippled up. I was goin' to tell Billy too before he married, but it's too late for that now. I suppose Tom'll be leavin' next."

He was wondering how long it would be before they were all gone. Perhaps he could talk Kylee into staying and taking care of him. But looking at the thickness of her hair and the loveliness of her eyes, he knew someone would want to marry her too.

"This here is rightly yours now that you made your choice to leave the mill." He handed Matt the packet.

"Perhaps you'll not find any of them gold bushes. Maybe this'll come in handy. Be careful; don't let it get stolen. It could help you start your mill an' make life a little easier for Taynee. God only knows she's never had much so far, Jay has seen to that. God bless you! Don't get too big or too rich to ask for His blessin's on you. Don't forget to thank Him for the ones you've already had." Ira made the longest religious speech Matt could ever remember, but he knew why when his father added.

"Your maw would a wanted you to be a God fearin' man. Don't forget that. Be gone with you now." He shook Matt's hand firmly hating to let go. He turned his hand loose and wheeled over to look out the window.

"Thank you, Paw," Matt said huskily. A great wad rose in his throat choking off his words and stifling his heart. He was beginning to feel the pangs of saying goodbye. Lifting the packet, he could tell by the heft that it held quite a sum. Shaking Tom's hand, he gave his arm a tight squeeze.

"Take care, Tom!" Matt said goodbye to his brother.

"I still say you oughta buy a new bonnet. That one's a te-total disaster," Tom teased, trying not to think about Matt leaving, so he fastened his steel blue eyes on the hat.

"Dog-gone, I'm gonna miss you Kylee." Matt turned to Kylee standing beside Ira's chair. He grabbed her and kissed her soundly on the lips. "You're a sweetheart an' have been a joy to this house. I'm gonna miss you!"

"I doubt if you an' Taynee'll have time to miss anyone, lest of all me. She's gonna make you so happy, you'll soon forget all about us." She laughed. "I'm powerful glad you're takin' Taynee away from here. There's bad feelin's between her an' her paw. The sooner she gets away, the better!"

Kylee hugged Matt tightly, biting hard on her bottom lip trying not to cry. She didn't want to send him away with tears to remember. She smiled bravely at him, and bid him goodbye and instructed, "Tell Taynee we truly do love her!"

Taynee grew anxious and was visibly nervous as the day progressed. Jay and Rueben had returned, drunk and sullen. She was doubtful of getting away. If she didn't go soon, Matt would come storming in to see what was keeping her and get himself killed. Nell had taken the baby and gone to the hills to gather herbs and Bob and the twins were at the orchard. She breathed a sigh of partial relief when Rueben left for Donkey with the excuse of finding a card game and hoping that Polly would change her mind about him and allow him a visit. Taynee was disappointed when her father refused to go with him. If only he'd fall into a drunken sleep, she could sneak out and be on her way.

Jay recognized Taynee's restlessness and noticed that she kept an unusually watchful eye on him. There was a strange uneasiness about her that he felt needed watching. He felt no pangs of guilt at the sight of her battered face. The girl had finally become obedient and respectful. There were no more heated reprisals. He would keep her that way. He must be careful not to bruise her face again. They would soon be planning her marriage to Ferrell Hall.

He felt it would be wise to keep a close watch on Taynee this day. Pulling a jug of whiskey from under little J.B.'s crib, he pulled the cork. He sat down in the rocker before the fireplace, the jug in his lap.

Taynee waited until Jay had fallen into a deep sleep. She was quiet getting her bundle of clothing out from under the bunk bed where she had hidden it. Picking up her shoes from under the table, she slipped out the door without a sound.

The barn was dim inside and she strained her eyes to see. She stretched and reached the gown from the rafters where she had tucked it for safekeeping. Tying her bundle across Midnight's rump, she put on her shoes and laced them up snugly and climbed to the horse's back. Tucking her wedding gown securely upon her lap, she rode swiftly from the barn. She was confident no one had seen her. When they missed her, she would be across Pound Mountain, safe into Kentucky with her darling Matt.

Matt waited for a long time at the little grove. The sunset glowed vibrantly in red and gold, and then it was gone. Shadows grew long and blended into gray. Nervous and restless, he was afraid it would be dark before they could get away. He was about to head for Mitchell's when he heard the sound of steady hoof beats on the hard earth.

Taynee rode swiftly into the grove with her wedding dress tucked into her saddle. She pulled Midnight to a short stop, dismounted and rushed into Matt's waiting arms. She was breathless and her face flushed from the ride, but her blue eyes were bright with love.

"Lordie, I'm glad you're here. I was beginnin' to fear I'd have to come for you," he told her, kissing her.

"Let's hurry an' get away. We'll ride the cut-off. I know where it takes off on the other side of Tandy's road below the orchard. It cuts across the mountain an' comes out over at Pound road comin' up from the mill. I know all the short trails on your paw's mountain. There are some of the biggest old nut trees there. The ground hogs are fatter than pigs. I been huntin' there lotsa times. My paw would a skinned me if he'd a known. I was always careful to watch for your paw," Matt rattled on trying to calm and assure her that all would be well.

"I think he's got his still up the mountain somewhere, but I ain't never been able to find it. I know the trail blindfolded. It'll save us some time. We'll head up to Singin' Springs below the big rocks after we come onto Pound Road an' spend the night there. Tomorrow we'll be safe into Kentucky an' away from your paw!" Matt told her, visibly nervous, his hands shaking at the thought of having Taynee for his own and away from the fear of her father.

As he talked, Matt helped Taynee back up on Midnight. He mounted his horse and led them onto the trail. They urged their mounts into a fast run, riding swiftly to Tandy's road and crossed below the orchard.

Evening shadows were beginning to gather. Matt wanted to get as far as possible before daylight was completely gone. Fording Tandy's branch, they took the short cut to Pound road, maintaining their speed. Darkness was settling and Matt worried about losing Taynee on the narrow winding trail. He stopped and dismounted to wait for her to catch up to him.

"Come ride with me, Taynee. We-uns are almost to the road. We can ride double easier. We'll slow down an' not ride as hard now it's getting dark. I want you close to me."

He lifted Taynee and sat her sidesaddle on his horse. He untied their bundles and tied them on Midnight, then jumped up behind Taynee sitting on the horse's rump. He folded his arms snugly around Taynee then pulled her tightly to him. She wrapped an arm around Matt's waist and held onto Midnight's reins firmly with her hand. In the other arm she clutched her wedding gown tightly.

Taynee laid her head on Matt's shoulder resting her body into his. He bent and kissed her often. They traveled slowly, the increasing

SHADOW OF THE PINES

shadows making it hard to see. Taynee watched the outline of Matt's face against the darkening night. Over the black outline of trees, she could see the beginning of glowing light. The moon was coming up slowly like a great lantern, fusing the night with light. It soon became as day, filled with the bright resplendent glow.

Matt was watchful as he guided the horses. As Taynee watched the handsome profile of his strong well-shaped face etched against the moonlight, she suffered a pang of doubt. Had she done the right thing, running away with Matt? If she told him about Jay's vicious attack on her, would their love be strong enough to survive? Would he still love her to the fullest and not be disgusted to touch her? Would it be possible to give herself without terror and repulsion, and not push him away? How could she ever forget what happened? Should she keep the terrifying experience a secret?

No, she must tell him and trust in his patience and understanding to help her forget. She would wait until they were safely into Kentucky, but before they married, she would tell him. If she told him now, she knew Matt, he would return to avenge her and get killed. If he would decide not to marry her, then he could go on west without her and she'd just crawl in a hole somewhere and die of a broken heart!

Smothering the sob that rose in her throat, she let it escape in the form of a long sigh. Matt held her closer, kissing her dark mass of curly hair. The night was silent except for the breathing of the horses.

A sudden rush of peace filled her heart, an assurance that their love was strong enough and together they would surmount any problem. She would never be doubtful again. The pine boughs tossed in the slight breeze against the mellow moonlight. She was happy beyond reality, her thoughts rose to the top of the tall pines. The soft swishing of the trees created a lullaby high in the branches persuading her into a happy enraptured slumber. She was awakened abruptly by a harsh voice.

"Stop right there Phelps. Put the girl down! You dirty sneakin' bastard! You think you could get away with stealin' her, did you? It'll give me great pleasure to kill you!" A shot followed Jay's loud shout. The bullet exploded across the still night. Matt felt Taynee stiffen in his arms. Blood was spewing from a wound in her head. It spilled onto his shirtfront soaking through to ease its way down his chest. The surprise was complete. Matt had let his guard down taking for granted they had fooled Mitchell.

"My God Taynee, you're hit!"

There was no answer. Her eyes were staring blank. Matt realized the blood making a path down his chest was his own. The high-powered rifle bullet had passed through Taynee's head and exploded in Matt's shoulder. With quick steady movement, Matt guided the horses up the hill into a place of safety behind a large rock. How had Jay found out about them? He had no time to figure that out.

"Come on out, you yeller bastard! Tryin' to get another Phelps in the back, in the dark, like you got Billy? You're afear'd to come out in the open. You have to hide somewhere. You ain't got no guts at all!" Matt yelled contemptuously through the night.

"You've hid yourself good, but you ain't got us yet! You've missed your chance Jay. You've missed!"

Matt pulled the horses close in behind the sheltering rock. He slid off his horse holding Taynee with one hand. Then carefully he lifted her out of the saddle. Sitting her on the ground, he let her rest against the big rock. He stared in shock at the bullet hole in her head. He sat down beside her cradling her in his arms and rocking her gently.

"You'll be all right, sweetheart. We'll be on our way soon as I kill your filthy paw!" he promised her, but her violet blue eyes stared at him without seeing. "Lie still darlin', I'll cover you up so you won't get a chill."

Matt stood up and freed his Winchester from the saddle boot, leaned into the rock and looked cautiously over the top. Listening keenly, he strained his ears for a sound that might reveal Jay's position. There was nothing to penetrate the silence. The horses stood patiently where Matt tethered them. His shoulder was beginning to throb and was bleeding slowly.

Midnight with her animal sense recognized someone she knew and lifted her head and gave a loud whinny of friendliness. Jay was waiting for a sound to position them and was quick to fire, shattering the rock at Matt's head.

"You should have known better than to try an' get away with one of mine! I got her back once an' I'll get her back again. I'll kill you both an' take her back dead." The loud voice was cold, demanding, and final. "I'd rather see her dead than layin' with a Phelps! You're comin' home with me now, Taynee!"

The bright florescent moon had created day of the night and the tall pines cast long shadows upon the earth. A night bird fluttered over Matt's head and Jay carelessly aimed into the trees. Jay's shot belched flame and Matt fired wildly at the sudden flash of light, his shots falling against an empty target.

Jay guided his horse quickly to a new hiding place, firing as he went. The shots from his rifle hit high in the tree over the rock, showering branches about Matt's head and feet.

"Why in the hell don't you come out, you sneakin' coward, an' fight like a man, which you ain't! You got to hide up like the stinkin' polecat you are!" Matt yelled as he fired at a shadow he thought moved in the trees across the trail.

"Damn you! Damn you! You've done killed Taynee." Matt fired, emptying his gun.

He picked up the sound of hoof beats pounding up the trail. Perhaps he had scared Jay off. There was no return of gunfire. All was quiet on the night. Maybe Jay was planning a sneak attack. He would have to watch closely.

Matt gathered a handful of bullets from his saddlebag and loaded his gun. He waited for a long time leaning against the rock, scanning into the shadows. He bent occasionally and tucked his coat around Taynee, making sure she was protected against the night air.

Growing weary of his vigilance, he slid down on the grass and sat next to Taynee, waiting and listening. But the only sound in the night was the faint moaning of a slight wind gathering in the top of the trees.

Matt sat with his legs stretched out and his back resting against the rock with his rifle across his lap. He had no idea how late it was. His legs became stiff from the dewy dampness that was gathering on the grass. The bullet hole in his shoulder began to throb with a nagging pain. He sat until the golden rays of the morning sun pushed through the protection of the night. The moon waned and left only a faint silver replica hanging in the baby blue Virginia sky.

Only now had he accepted Taynee's death. He must get her home. He stood up. His body was becoming stiff and Matt knew it was time to move. He was certain that Jay had run off. Perhaps he was wounded, maybe there was even a chance he could be lying dead somewhere. His only concern now was for Taynee. He lifted the dead girl upon the saddle, holding to keep her from toppling and climbed up behind her. Matt's wound bled slowly and his shirt was soaked with the sticky ooze, his shoulder stiff and painful.

He guided his horse down the trail until they came to Pound Road. Then he turned back toward the mill. The road they would have taken to safety into Kentucky lay vacant behind them without a traveler or passer-by.

The last silver light of the moon converging with the yellow morning sun caught light to the white bundle still clutched in Taynee's arm. Matt held Taynee close as he kissed her cold cheek, tears falling slowing upon her blood soaked raven black hair. Giving the horse its lead, they rode with an easy walking gate; Midnight followed close behind as they traveled wearily down the road. Moving slowly they rode into a mist of early morning fog that was gathering along the creek. The softness closed out the bright golden sun, making a perfect covering for the travelers moving slowly down Pound Road.

TOM

BOOK THREE

379

CHAPTER ONE

Jay was not asleep, as Taynee surmised. There was no need to hurry so he waited for her to ride out through the gate. His big bay, Siler, would soon overtake her little black gelding Midnight. There was no doubt in his mind; she was headed for Phelps's mill. Well, he would put a quick stop to that.

Everyone had deserted him. Rueben was off to Donkey and Bob would be worthless as a helper. Bob's obtrusive attitude was beginning to wear on Jay's nerves. Feeling sorry for himself for having such a wayward brood, he thought of Blaine. Thanks to Tom Phelps, his son would never ride by his side again, eager to do his bidding. Taynee made a mistake running to the Phelps's. He brought her home once; he could bring her home again.

There was going to be an end to her running away. He would fix her good this time. She would not have another chance. He'd had a belly full of disobedient youngins. He would marry her off to Ferrell Hall and ship them both off to Tennessee!

Taynee was still a Mitchell and she would act like one. As he rode to catch his daughter, he was surprised things were not as he predicted. She was not on Tandy's road and she was not at the Phelps's either. There had not been time for her to hide her horse. He searched around the place carefully and took no chance that anyone might see him. He was used to hiding from the Phelps's, that was, until Boy got his scent.

He hadn't been able to ride by on Pound road lately without him taking a nip at his heels. Damn dog, it would spot him every time. Jay thought it was about time he marked a bullet for that dastardly dog; he'd better leave before Boy's barking brought out the whole clan.

He would have to backtrack and find Taynee. Was there a chance he had been wrong about his daughter? Perhaps she had only decided to visit Hail. Had she only gone for a ride after all? If so, she would be back home when he got there. He smiled grimly to himself. For some reason his deductions did not fit the picture Taynee had presented with her silence and sneaky ways.

As he rode by the orchard, he met Bob driving the small spring bed wagon. The eight-year old twins were riding on top of a pile of little green apples they had thinned from the trees. This allowed room for the fruit to grow to a bigger size. The discarded apples would be fed to the pigs. They were disgusted with this work duty that was all Taynee's idea and now she had deserted them.

"Golly, Paw, what are you doin' here? Thought you were at the house. We-uns just seen Taynee ride by," the twins called to him from atop their perch.

"She's out ridin' around with that Matt Phelps while we-uns are doin' the work in the orchard, all because of her," one of the twins complained. "We-uns better hurry, it's gettin' dark."

Bob cautiously guided the horses onto the road, deliberately ignoring the presence of his father and warning the boys with a frown to be quiet.

"We saw them turn onto the old Orchard road. I thought we-uns were a hatin' them Phelps's. How come she's a gallivanting around with the likes of him? Matt was at the house t'other day askin' all kinds of questions about Taynee. They didn't see us when they went by 'cause we-uns were up in a tree. What's gonna happen to her, huh, Paw?" the other twin questioned their father who was following behind the moving wagon.

"You sure she was with Phelps?"

So she had met Matt somewhere in the woods. He looked up at the twins, so much alike; he never bothered to tell them apart.

"You say they was a ridin' the Orchard road?"

"Yeah, they sure was Paw," the twins answered simultaneously.

"I'll show you what happens to a Mitchell when they's a lollygaggin' around with a Phelps!" Jay told his young sons with a thin smile.

He turned his horse around with a jerk and headed for the road below the orchard. Taynee had hornswoggled him again. She met Matt somewhere while he was searching for her down the mountain.

Hail! That was the only answer. She must have met him at Hail's. That old witch had helped them get away. With all the vast territory for Taynee and Matt to meet, it suited Jay's venom to blame Hail. She would do it he reasoned, just to snicker him!

"I'll tend to that old hypocrite later! Right now I'll see to Taynee an' Matt Phelps!" He would have to ride hard to make up for the time he'd wasted. It was dusk and before long he wouldn't be able to see a dad-blamed thing.

The twins watched the dark figure of their father from their perch on top of the moving wagon. They watched until he disappeared into the dusk and thick trees.

"Why'd you have to tell him you'd seed Taynee with Matt for? You know what'll happen now, don't you? He'll find them an' kill them both. That's what'll happen!" Bob told the twins. He gave the team a sharp whack. The boys looked at each other, their eyes wide and faces clouded with regret for having informed on their half sister.

Jay came upon Matt and Taynee riding double and moving slowly down the trail. He followed them closely, waiting until they came into a place on the trail Jay knew well. The hill leveled some and he could ride down around them and be on their broadside and get a clear shot at Matt. If Taynee didn't want to come with him, he'd leave her dead too. Jay rode quietly and cautiously down and around them, then back up through the trees until he found the exact place he wanted for his ambush. The moon appeared above the trees, a yellow orb, showering the night with golden light.

Jay heard the horses slowly picking their footing on the narrow trail; dark forms against the backdrop of moonlight were a perfect target for Jay's waiting bullet. Jay aimed for Matt's head, but his horse moved backward a step steadying itself on the incline of the sloping hill. Matt quickly guided them to safety behind the rock and returned fire.

A bullet tore a hole in Jay's shoulder. The blood began a trickling path down his chest and into the hollow of his armpit. Feeling the wetness of his own blood, he became frantic and fired a volley of bullets at random over the rock where Matt and Taynee were hiding. Jay fired from the back of his horse, cradling his long Winchester rifle in his arm. He snuggled it against his side, firing at random. With the other hand he held tightly to the reins trying to keep his mount under control pulling the bit sharply into the horse's lip.

The gunfire and yelling was making his horse extremely nervous. It pranced tensely pulling against the reins. Jay tried to settle the nervous animal enough to guide it across the path and rush the runaways.

Jay heard Matt loud and clear call out that Taynee was dead. He had a pang of sorrow that it wasn't Matt. If he could quiet his damn horse and get it across the trail, Matt would be dead too! A volley of bullets followed Matt's loud shouting. A bullet belted Jay's saddle horn tearing it away from the base and shattering it to pieces and creasing the horse's neck. The smashing impact completed the horse's fright. It couldn't be controlled now, with his head stretched forward and nostrils flared, it bolted into wild flight.

Up the hill and onto the trail it fled moving at a frantic speed, hooves striking in rapid rhythm upon the hard earth. Back toward the orchard it sped. Jay was clinging desperately to what was left of the saddle front trying desperately to keep seated on the rapidly moving horse. He was cursing the runaway beast; his screeching fell unheard upon the night.

A low hanging branch struck him sharply knocking off his hat and opening a large laceration in his forehead. The blood flowed in a river over his eyebrows filling his eyes and impairing what little vision he did have. There was no way he was going to control Siler so he hung on tenaciously hoping the animal would run itself out and not dump him off. The horse stretched into long strides up the mountain. They forded Tandy's branch below the orchard on through the trees and headed straight for the road leading to Hail's.

The horse slowed to a fast walk. It was breathing hard and pulling its head up and down in fast jerking movements, the air leaving its body in great gushes. Jay held tightly to the reins. His exhaustion from the frantic flight was beginning to overcome him. The blow on the head had caused his head to throb incessantly. A lightheaded giddiness was beginning to overtake him. He must keep consciousness and get his bearings.

Pulling out his shirttail, he tried to wipe away the blur in his eyes. The night was bathed in an illuminating light. Stars twinkled dimly fading in the florescent wonder of the full moon. The brilliant light revealed plainly the big rock at the side of Hail's road.

Jay realized where he was and wondered if the old witch would be home. Perhaps tonight lady luck would be on his side for a change. Perhaps he could persuade Hail to fix up his wounds. His shoulder was bleeding badly, soaking through his shirt and drenching his black double-breasted sack coat. Feeling the cut on his head his fingers came away wet with fresh blood. Terror filled him.

"I'm gonna die! That old witch, Hail an' Ira's bunch'll get their wish! It would pleasure them no end if I were to drop right here in the road an' die!" He mumbled, trying to guide his spent horse into Hail's gate jerking at the reins unmercifully.

"Well, I'll fool them all! They ain't seen me belly-up yet! I'm gonna live to see them all dead!

It had always been to Hail's liking, a moonlit night like this, when she could cook her herbs out in the open. It kept the obnoxious odors and intense heat outside. She absently stirred the pot she had set up over an open fire in her yard.

The daylight night had been wonderfully warm and still without a breeze. The warmth of the night and the light of the magnificent moon made it an ideal time for her work.

She had always been a lover of the night. As the sun went down, her tangled thoughts would clear. It was the days with shining sun and tall shadows in the pines that muddled her brain and made her thoughts hard to face. At night she could lose her bitter memories in troubled sleep.

In the daytime she watched the flowers blooming gaily and listened to the sweet sound of bird songs. It was then she realized fully the futility and emptiness of her hopelessly lonesome life. In the searing light of day, with her eyes wide open, it was easy for her to recall the deep scars of the past. She watched the children play and observed the courting of the young. As she helped their babies being born, the bitter memories flowed.

Many times when she had been a young woman, her father had promised her that time would heal all wounds. When she needed to forget, he hadn't been around to assure or comfort her. Time had not eased the hurt nor bitter pangs or the burning memories of a shattered life.

Stirring the herbs, she allowed her mind to wander into the past. Thinking she was alone, she muttered and talked out loud to herself confiding her many emotions to the bright rays of moonlight.

"Jay Bird Mitchell is a wicked, wicked man! I know he does the devil's bidding. I hate his evil ways an' the way he's guiding his sons. I feel sorry for Taynee an' Nell an' the wee-ones. They'd be better off if someone would destroy him. It'd be a blessin' to them, an' to me, if he were dead! If I had him here, I'd put him in this pot an' boil him 'til his hide slipped off like a scalded tomato! Then I'd stretch it in the sun to dry where everyone that he'd hurt or tormented could see. They'd know he was dead an' couldn't hurt anyone, no more, no more!"

"Oh Lord, help me. Help me find a way to destroy that fiendish man! In your goodness an' mercy, help me out'a my misery!" She prayed as she often did. "I want so bad to see him suffer as I have. Oh Lord, Lord, is there no way I can suffer that man? Please, Lord! Please take away this dark hate that lives in my heart. It is only my love for you, Lord Jesus that has kept me from killin' that black-hearted man!"

"I know your Word says that if you think the crime or lust in your heart, you're guilty the same as if you'd done it. I cain't forgive him for what he's done! I can never, never do like you say in your Word. I can never love that dastardly man like a brother!

That wicked man, he's got to be destroyed before he destroys us all!" She continued stirring the mixture in the pot, swirling the wooden paddle vigorously.

The mixture gave forth a musty odor filling the night with an ominous smell. As a result of the rapid movement of the paddle, the boiling liquid spewed over into the hot coals of the fire. Sparks flew high releasing a thick white smoke progressing skyward. Hail moved back quickly, safe from the spilling liquid, lifting her arms high.

"Lordie, I better watch what I'm a doin'."

Jay rode up the road just as the cloud of steam and ashes floated upward. Hail stood framed against the moonlight, arms raised, head back, looking toward the sky. Weary and desperate, his head throbbing as if a herd of horses were tromping through it. His black tangled hair, wild and disheveled hung about his shoulders. Agony and pain marked his face; deep torment stalked his eyes. A path of blood left a trail of sticky ooze drying to his grizzled brows.

He could hear Hail muttering through the white fog. Even in his weakened condition he thought he was aware of what Hail was up to. He would never be convinced differently. She was collaborating with witches. She was calling up help from the depths of darkness; she was going to get even with him. She would destroy him.

Mae had told him how witches conjure up means to drive a man mad. He was certain that was what Hail had been up to. She was planning such a fate for him. She warned him she would get even, make him crawl in the dirt and see him destroyed. That was why everything he set out to do failed.

She was responsible for his darling Mae's death. Hail had hated her. Blaine was dead and Tom Phelps was rambling around scot-free. Taynee was dead now too, disobedient youngin', she deserved to die! Hail had helped them get away and if he hadn't killed Matt, he would still be wandering around to torment him.

It was all Hail's fault the disappointments in his life and the fact he was sitting here right now half dead. She was the only one who could break the spell. He had to talk to her, get her to remove the hex she'd placed on him. He teetered dangerously in the saddle, close to toppling from his spent mount. There was no one else. He had no choice but to make her help him. He was not going to die yet. She would have to use her powers to make him well.

"Hail, Hail," he called weakly, "I'm needin' your help. Help me, please, I'm a dyin'!"

He was hurting badly. Pain increased in his head and shoulder. He must hurry and convince her before he faded. He was even ready to cower and beg.

Hail turned and spotted the slow moving blotch; she was filled with terror. Recognizing the black apparition to be the earthly form of Jay Mitchell she flew with winged feet to the safety of her cabin. Inside she dropped the latch securely into place. She moved quickly to the kitchen window and peered out to see what her early morning visitor was up to.

"What the hell's the matter with you, woman? I told you I'm needin' your help! I'm bleedin' somethin' fierce. Come help me into the house! You gotta stop the bleedin' or I'll die." The exhausted man mustered what strength he could into his weak body while forcefully urging a few more strides from his exhausted mount.

Earlier in the day Hail had been digging postholes to make a larger gate opening. Jay, anxious to reach Hail, urged his horse in desperation, spurring it unmercifully in the flanks. The horse reared in protest and came back to the ground hard, dropping a fore leg into one of the postholes. Jay, dizzy from his ordeal and unnerved by the sight of Hail only had a slight hold on the reigns. He was tossed over the horse's head somersaulting to the ground with a thud. He lay flat on his back, the breath leaving his body.

Jay lay still, the fall only stunned him. He rose up in disbelief; he had never been thrown from a horse before. He raised his body up trembling and weak but managed to slowly climb the stairs. Clinging to the rail with shaking hands he pulled himself along. His English-style spurs clanked loudly as he drug his feet across the porch floor. In one last vain attempt to convince Hail to help him, he pounded on the heavy oak door.

"Let me in you old witch! I'll kill you if you don't open this door! Do you hear me? I'll kill you! Damn you, let me in! You gotta help me. I'm bleedin' to death!" He screamed louder and pounded harder on the door.

Jay was filled with agonizing fear but could not persuade her. Somewhere back along the trail he had dropped his rifle, probably when the branch hit him. He lifted his big Colt pistol from the holster that was strapped low around his hips. Backing away he fired several times into the heavy door, the bullets thudding loudly into the hard wood.

"I'll not let you in Jay! I'll never let you in! You might as well ride on. I'll never help the likes of you. My prayers are answered, I'm gonna watch you die! You'll not scare me with your bullets." Hail yelled with a force of courage she did not feel. She stood to one side of the door where she thought she would be safe out of range. Her back was pressed against the wall and her fists clenched tightly.

"I'll get you for this, you old witch! I'll show you an' them damn Phelps's you love so well! You love them all, don't you? Well, I ain't dead yet!"

Jay stumbled and swayed as he stomped back across the porch. Clutching the railing he staggered down the stairs to his horse. The animal was breathing in great wheezing gasps, pulling its head up and down with each intake of air.

"By damn, Siler, you gonna die on me? Look a there, you've broken your leg in that blasted hole that witch dug for you. Ain't nary a bit good to me now," he announced to the injured horse and once again he lifted his pistol.

"Phelps's an' Hail. I'm gonna see that they die! You, you old bastard, we done a lot a ridin' together, but it's done, you're dyin' on me. You ain't a bit of good to me now! Looks like your time's come!" His voice was gruff with fondness for the horse and his eyes filled with tears.

Putting the gun barrel to a vital spot behind the ear Jay pulled the trigger. He killed Siler with the one bullet that was left in his pistol. The huge beast screamed in agonizing pain and fell to the earth raising a great cloud of dust. He was now released from his misery.

Jay dropped his pistol back into place and moved across the yard faltering and dragging his feet. The effort drained his remaining strength. He fell to the ground in a sprawling heap of muscle and brawn. His long angular body filling the space between the wagon tracks in the yard.

Inside the cabin Hail watched Jay struggle down the stairs, a toiling mass of black underneath the gray shadows of the porch roof. She gasped in horror, watching wide-eyed as he killed the horse. Hail could see him dragging himself slowly across the yard until he fell to the ground.

"Yes, yes, grovel in the dirt. It's where you belong!" She was still afraid to leave the safety of her home as long as he was lying there.

Hail patiently kept watch from the window, eyes staring out into the night. The night passed and Jay still didn't move. Hail thought that perhaps he was dead. "Joy of joy's, could he finally be dead?" She would wait a little longer.

A clear glow began to appear across the dark shadows of the pines, eliminating the golden light of the full moon. Hail bravely lifted the latch and peeked cautiously out the door. To her utter dismay, Jay was struggling to raise himself, failing; he fell back to the ground.

With increasing determination, he at last lifted his long lanky body. Bent and drained of all energy and struggling to keep his balance he slowly made it to the well. Hail backed into the house and again dropped the latch.

Leaning against the wall in total hopelessness she thought her prayers still weren't answered. It was time she did something about that horrid man. She would just forget her faith and kill him while he was too weak to get away. She moved to get her gun then regretfully remembered it was resting against the split rail fence where she had been digging. She had forgotten it until now. She bitterly cursed herself for such carelessness. She had failed again.

Jay groped at the bucket hanging at the well. He pulled up some water and poured the cool liquid over his head. He washed the dried blood from his face and eyes. The blood that was oozing from his wounds had stopped. He supposed that meant he was going to live after all. Shaking his head, he tried to refresh his mind of the events of the night.

The early morning light was spreading in shafts of pink and gray across the sky over the trees behind Hail's house. Jay thought about the blanket of rose-colored clouds that would be drifting in around his house and barn. A pressing desire to be home flooded over him.

He supposed it would be no use to try once more to persuade Hail to have a look at his wounds. The cool water and his rest on the ground had refreshed him. It rejuvenated his strength and filled him with his old drive. He had no desire to hassle with Hail any further.

He looked with regret at the dead horse. Going over to the mound of flesh and with extreme difficulty he removed the saddle. He would show the stubborn old witch that he was not about to walk home.

"I'll borrow that dumb ol' mule!" He'd saddle Dr. Jekyll and be home for breakfast.

Damn Hail, damn her to hell for not helping him. He could be lying in her bed now, recovering instead of struggling to get home. In a moment of recurring memory, he recalled Hail's beauty when she was young. If she wasn't so ornery, he could still desire her. "It's been a long time, eh Hail? A long time we've been hating each other," he grumbled. There was no remorse for the years past, only anger because she had refused to let him in. Why couldn't she forget the grudge she had held for so long and treat him decently?

A glorious dawn was beginning to lighten the yard. Hail kept the old mule in her lean-to of a barn and that was where Jay was heading. Carrying and dragging the saddle, he lifted it with determination onto the old mule's back and strapped it in place. Leaning heavily against the animal, he put his foot in the stirrup and lifted himself into the saddle. He rode toward the heavy mist that was forming in the road ahead. Turning in the saddle he shook his fist at the house, certain that Hail was watching him.

"Damn you Hail. I hate your guts! Your time is comin'." He lifted his head and shouted at the house.

If the old hellion had let him in, perhaps they could have patched up their differences. It might have been nice; he smiled wickedly to himself. Prodding the mule with his spurs, he urged the reluctant beast into a swinging trot down the road. Hail watched them disappear into the hazy dawn.

Hail knew Jay's angry gesture was meant for her. She was glad when he faded into the morning mist. Lifting the latch, she sighed with a heavy weariness and went out into the early morning. The world was bathed in a pink lemonade hue and she was drifting in the unearthly light as if in a dream. She was trying to convince herself that the night hadn't really happened.

She was still shaking but relieved Jay was gone. Ignoring the dead horse, she crossed the yard, looked into the pot of herbs and covered it with a lid. Picking up the relic of a gun that had belonged to her father, she returned to the house and again dropped the latch.

She hoped Jay would have the consideration to send Dr. Jekyll back home. After washing her face and hands, she brushed out her hair and plaited its heavy thickness into a wide single braid. Lying down upon her bed fully clothed; she covered herself with a quilt and fell into a sound sleep.

Rueben settled himself on the top step at the Mitchell cabin, hair and beard matted and tangled from a short night's sleep. His visit with Polly had been disappointing. As usual, she refused to have any part of him, even after he bathed and was sporting a freshly ironed shirt. Nell had taken special steps with the shirt because he was going to see a girl. She felt happy that Rueben had finally taken it on himself to go somewhere without his father.

But Polly was not amicable and shunned him virulently. He could not understand her hostility toward him. Rueben thought with his new cleanliness she would be more than willing. He rode home, pouting and sullen. He tried to understand what it was that Polly wouldn't accept. Was it because he was so short? His lack of height sure didn't shorten his desire for her. He had to make her understand that he would even marry her. He knew she was lying around with Tom Phelps and that thought didn't sweeten his disposition.

It was late in the night when Rueben arrived home in the drenching light of the moon. He went to bed only to be awakened at an early hour by the twins. They insisted that he come help them unload the apples into the pig lot. They wanted to take the wagon back to the orchard.

Rueben was in no mood for work detail and angrily chased them out of the cabin. Unable to go back to sleep, he went out to the front step to bask in the warm morning sunshine. The jug of whiskey by his side was a sure cure for a hangover caused from his heavy drinking the night before.

He was about to pull on his boots when he looked up to discover his father slowly crossing the yard on Hail's old mule. Picking up the jug of whiskey he hurried barefoot to meet his father, pulling the cork as he ran.

Jay slid cautiously from the mule and snatched eagerly at the jug. Taking a long drink, he let the fiery liquid flow freely down his parched throat. It lay hot and burning in the bottom of his empty stomach. The clear liquor spilled over onto his tangled beard as he released it from his lips. After taking another long drink, he handed the jug back to Rueben. Wiping the back of his blood streaked dirty hand across his whiskered mouth, he gave a loud belch of satisfaction. Taking in a deep breath and releasing it slowly he grinned in appreciation at his son.

"You're a good son Rueben. That was just what I needed. It's been one hell of a night." Jay put his arm around the young man's shoulder and leaned his weight against him. They moved slowly up the stairs.

"I'm gonna tell you Rueb, they's one less Mitchell. Your sister, Taynee's dead. I think that bastard Matt Phelps is lyin' dead beside her. They was runnin' away. Thought they'd fooled the old man. But they was the ones what got fooled. I left them fer the varmints back on the mountain. The next one is gonna be that son-of-a-bitch that slipped from under the gallows. He thinks he's off scot-free, don't he though? But I'm gonna see him swingin' from the highest tree in the Cumberlands for killin' your brother," Jay promised, letting the tears fill his eyes as he began to sniffle. "I'll get him, you'll see." He patted Rueben's shoulder and freed himself of his hold. Staring into his son's face he was shaking violently.

"Promise me, promise!" Jay's black eyes were wide and distorted with rage. "Promise me, if anything happens to me, you'll see to its doin'," Jay screeched. Then his voice quieted, trailed off, his body sagged heavily against the door casing.

"You ride now an' fetch Hensely. I need him to take this bullet out'a my shoulder. It's a burnin' something fierce. I don't know where you'll find him, but find him! Hail wouldn't do it for me. She's gonna die for that! The old witch! I'm gonna see her burnin' in the hottest fires of hell for refusin' me. It ain't gonna be long!" His voice wandered and drifted. Rueben had to bend close to hear what he was saying.

"I'll do it, Paw. I'll do it for you. I promise you that! Right now I'll go fetch Tanner. He'll fix you up. You go on an' get in bed. I'll be back 'fore you know it." Rueben nervously tried to convince his father he was capable and deserving of his trust.

Rueben helped his father into the house. He sat down on the top step and finished the job of putting on his boots, then hurried to the barn, saddled his mule and rode to town. Tears were close to the surface; he was worried about Jay. If there was anything in the world he loved it was his father, and Polly Trace.

Since Blaine was killed, he had received more attention from Jay. He had been given important things to do like riding to town for Hensely. Now, he had been trusted with killing Phelps, should his father die. To Rueben that was the utmost proof that his father loved him best of all.

Chapter Two

Tom rose early as the pink haze was beginning to lift, giving way to a warm day filled with glorious sunshine. He yawned and stretched rippling the tight muscles across his broad chest and forearms. Running strong fingers through his tousled hair, he rumpled it into an even greater state of disaster. He moved sleepily over to the dresser and poured out a small amount of water from the pitcher into the washbasin. He splashed the cool water over his face and hair rubbing it down across his chest covered with soft curly golden brown fuzz. Then he doused his underarms thoroughly where the hair was darker and longer.

The water was refreshing and made him catch his breath, really snapping him to his toes this early in the morning. He ran a stubby black brush across his ash blonde hair laying each wave into regimental order, except for one unruly curl that always insisted on lying stubbornly across his forehead.

Rubbing a hand across his square jaw he felt carefully into the deep cleft of his chin. He decided he could wait another day without shaving and gave a sigh of relief to be free of the dreaded job. He playfully splashed Boy with a sprinkle of water as he lay sleeping at the foot of the bed. His pale blue eyes twinkled with affection as the big dog acknowledged his teasing gesture by stretching and yawning until his jaws cracked.

"Well, come on you lazy whelp, let's take a walk. I cain't seem to get enough of this place since I got turned out of jail. Funny how a cell can change the way you think a whole bunch!" Tom scratched behind the big dog's ears thoughtfully.

"Makes you even think about women differently. More appreciative, sorta. I ain't even been cravin' a visit to Polly's for quite a spell. An' you know what feller? It's gonna get kinda lonesome around here without brother Matt. I been thinkin' seriously about askin' our Kylee girl to marry up with me! Now what do you think of that?"

The dog wagged his tail excitedly at the mention of Kylee. Only the heavy braided rug on the bedroom floor muffled the loud joyful thumping of his tail, declaring his approval.

Boy had been filled with extreme delight at Tom's arrival home. The dog would not let his lord and master out of sight, waiting patiently as Tom pulled on his britches over summer weight drawers. He tucked in a faded blue shirt leaving it unbuttoned to the waist anticipating a cool breeze.

As he passed Kylee's bedroom door he could hear her moving around inside, humming a tune to herself, getting ready for the day. He went on outside into the bright morning sunshine. The noisy harmony of birds singing showered the atmosphere. The bright morning caused him to think sadly about Billy. He missed the happy times they had shared together playing their music. Now Matt had taken off across the mountain and he was missing him too. There was only one thing left to do. He would crowd his thoughts so full of Kylee there would be no room for anyone else.

It had fallen on his shoulders to stay with his father and run the mill. It was beyond his comprehension that he would be the one. He had always been the renegade, the restless one. Anyway, if he were to be the stay-at-home, maybe, just maybe, he would think stronger about the Marshal's job. Pick his party preference and let his intentions be known.

"Sure be good to go coon huntin'. What do you say Boy? Won't be long either. You'd like that wouldn't you, feller?" Tom aimed his question at the dog as he walked down the steps and across the yard.

With long strides, he covered the distance to the gate. He proceeded along the road and across the bridge. He stopped at the cornfield behind the mill to admire the corn crop that he and Matt had planted. He proudly acknowledged the tall stalks, the leafy foliage, and long ears already tasseled with golden brown silk.

"It's gonna be ready for the last hoein' before I am. Sure is a lot of them bothersome old suckers growin' around the bottoms," he complained, noticing the many green shoots growing in abundance around the roots of each stalk.

The greenness of the added growth reminded Tom of the way Kylee was beginning to blossom. Her strength was back and her manner toward him direct and open. It was as if what happened at his trial had uncovered a pathway for him. They were comfortable with each other now, talking and laughing and making each day a pure joy to be alive.

He noticed each new leaf on the stalks were the same spring green as Kylee's beautiful large eyes. He thought how the pink was beginning to glow through the thinness of her cheekbones. How beautiful were her long heavy lashes. She knew when to lower them at just the right moment to make Tom's heart flip. Delicately arched, reddish brown brows raised quickly to give a warning when she was angry.

"Golly," Tom sighed.

How quickly he was discovering all the womanly ways that were the wonder of Kylee. He was yearning for further knowledge with thoughts that did not stop at her eyes or full red lips. He started to dwell often on the definite roundness of her breasts and the delightful curve of her hips.

She had become dreadfully thin and bony during her illness. Given time, she would fill out again, the deep hollows in her cheeks would disappear. The dark circles still apparent around her lovely eyes would fade. Thank God she had not lost her abundance of auburn hair as people often did when they became ill. Her hair reminded Tom of his mother's, thick and beautifully long. Kylee was small too, like his mother. It had been a long time since they buried his mother, but he still missed her.

After Billy's death and the weeks in jail, Tom began to reflect on the Bible. This for him was strange. He began to remember all the Bible verses his mother had taught him. The verses were the first things he had learned to read and his mother had made him go over them repeatedly. He was not sure he understood what they meant but it seemed they had given him hope and courage many times. He had strayed far away from the righteous path his mother had encouraged him to take. He found himself returning to prayer often when Kylee was ill. Out of love for his mother and the things she had taught him, respect, compassion, and honor, he would put a lid on his burning desire for Kylee. He would treat her with respect and wait until they were married, if she would have him.

"Let's get some breakfast, old buddy." Tom said to the dog close at his heels. "I don't have any control over my thoughts any more. Things I haven't thought about in years keep pushin' in from all sides. Cain't bring myself to spend full time a hatin' them low down Mitchell's. That's gettin' bad! I better not let Paw find out." He went on confiding to his faithful companion as he continued to look at the rows of tall corn curving around the hillside.

His stride became longer, his walk faster as he headed back to the house, the dog close on his heels. As they entered the kitchen, Kylee was at the fire cooking breakfast. She had a bright blue scarf tied around her long shining tresses, holding them back safely from the fire and food. She was singing happily as she worked. Then turned and stepped a little clog dance around the table as she set on the plates for the morning meal.

"*Roosters crow in the Sourwood Mountains,*
Ho-hum, come a teedle-dum-day.
I got a gal in the Sourwood Mountains
She won't come; an' I won't fetch her,
Ho-hum, come a teedle-dum-day."

Kylee looked up as man and dog entered. Her face flushed from her efforts at the fire and from being caught in the foolish dance. She gave them a warm smile of welcome. The smile filled her face and her jade eyes glowed with happiness.

It was so easy for Kylee to be happy these days. She was feeling so well and extremely glad about her new understanding towards Tom. The grief over Billy's death was fading. His memory, along with that of her father's, was becoming something she honored and cherished.

Tom smelled the side pork cooking long before he reached the house. He was hoping Kylee would have biscuits and gravy to go with it. Tom returned her smile and more, a deep look of longing crossed his eyes. He hoped her old attitude toward him would never return.

Tom's smile grew until it engulfed his face deepening the laugh lines at the corners of his mouth and defining the crows-feet around the outside edges of his pale blue eyes. It increased as he watched Kylee lift a pan of golden brown buttermilk biscuits from the iron oven at the side of the fireplace. It was Tom's opinion that she could make the best biscuits and gravy of anyone, dismissing none! It was certain they had made no mistake taking in Kylee. As Tom washed his hands, his father wheeled into the room and settled himself at the table.

"Well Tom, you ready to finish up the grindin'? They's a few bushels of old corn that needs to be tended to."

"We'll save a little for replantin'. There's a few bare spots in that patch behind the house. If we don't get it planted soon, it'll be too late. It won't make nothin' exceptin' fodder. You slept in long enough. That millstream's fair to bustin' the dam. If we don't let some water down soon, it'll be spillin' over them walkways you boys fancied up for your maw, so she could walk around the pond an' watch the frogs jumpin' off the lily pads. I gotta admit it was a nice idea. Them flower beds you built for your maw sure purtied up the place. I was glad it was you youngin's that was a doin' it an' not me," Ira grumbled into his beard more to himself than to Tom or Kylee.

Ira had to admit the flowerbeds had been badly neglected since Mattie's death. Starting on the breakfast Kylee set before him, he tried to put thoughts of Mattie into the back of his mind.

"I'll be ready Paw, soon as I finish breakfast. Is it all right if I finish eatin'?" Tom turned a teasing smile toward his father.

He could see his father was in an ill mood, probably still brooding over Matt's leaving. When his father started to reminisce about his mother and days gone by, he was impossible to live with. Tom knew he would be a bear to get along with all day.

"Well, get busy on it then, times a wastin'!" Ira told him irritably, and then his mood warmed as his eyes followed Kylee.

Again his memories had a place for a girl with fire in her hair and eyes as green as rain-washed fern. Lips so finely shaped made a man want to kiss them as soon as he laid eyes on them. Better not think too long on these things, he would not be able to keep back the tears and the longing. Ira pulled a large handkerchief from his pocket and blew his nose loudly.

"We-uns should have talked Matt into staying. Lord knows we are gonna need him after all the plantin' you done. Gonna make more work on you, Tom. Maybe we could find us a hired hand. It's a lot of work for one man. We can afford it son, we can afford it."

"No reason to let the crop go beggin'. Sides we need someone to be around the mill when we-uns are gone. I don't like the idea of leavin' Kylee alone. Cain't never tell when them scabby Mitchell bastards might take a notion to come snoopin' for Taynee. They might get the notion she's back here again." Ira explained with a far away look in his eyes.

"I'll talk to Trace about it. He'd probably know if there's anyone around that would be trustworthy an' needin' a job." Ira pushed away from the table. "I'll head on over to the mill. They's some things I can get started on. They'll be someone around to see if we have anything new in the store. If they do, I can take care of them."

"Soon as you get Kylee's water barrel filled an' the fire goin' so she can start her wash, you go on an' let some water out of the dam," he rambled on, wheeling out the door. "Them mules need shoes too. We have a busy day ahead." Ira left the kitchen and crossed the porch. Kylee watched him through the window as he wheeled down the ramp. Tom followed close behind him.

Kylee was quick with her chores inside, gathering the dirty laundry and out to the back yard to set up her wash. Tom already had the barrel filled. The battling board was set up and the tub filled with clean water. Pails of water lined the bench under a large heavily blooming rhododendron bush. He had lit the fire and disappeared.

The day was beautifully warm and still, bright sun and clear blue sky as far as she could see above the barrier of green trees. Kylee put her washing to soak in the tub of cool water. She pulled down a split oak bucket from a nail on the back porch railing, and walked toward the forest behind the mill. Beyond the huge oaks that lined the millpond grew a grove of mulberry trees. In the exact spot where Mattie had been found years before, the huckleberries grew thick and abundant.

Grapevine and ivy grew heavily entangled around the trunks and branches of the tall oaks. Proudly and serenely the trees reflected their magnificence in the mirror like clearness of the millpond. Kylee walked slowly and cautiously along the top of the dam looking nervously at the smooth water pushing eagerly against it. Carefully she lifted her skirts, holding them safely away from the splashing water.

"Now where do you suppose that young lady's headin' for?" Ira questioned Tom as they watched Kylee cross the path along the top of the dam.

"I haven't the slightest, Paw. She's probably goin' to pick huckleberries."

"Well, you better go after her. Warn her it's not safe to cross the dam when it's so full of water. That water pushes so hard on that wall, I'm always afear'd it's gonna give way. It's old, Tom. It could happen anytime. We wouldn't want our gal to be on top if it did. You run catch her; tell her to go back down the hill an' cross the bridge. It'd be safer. Hurry up now, we-uns have work to do!"

Tom followed Kylee across the dam, watched as she disappeared into the heavy foliage along the path lined with large trees. Then he caught the swing of her as she climbed upward along the hill, her long hair switching freely back and forth across her hips, catching the interlaying shadows of dark and light along the path.

She stopped under a wide spreading mulberry tree and hung the bucket on a low hanging branch. Underneath the tree grew a number of huckleberry bushes clustered together.

As Tom watched her begin to fill the basket, he recalled how jealous he had been of her attention to Billy and Matt. He had even been afraid that Matt was trying to win her favor. But it had been Taynee Mitchell for Matt all along.

Kylee smiled to herself as she thought how pleased Ira would be to have a pie. As she worked, she hummed then began to sing out loud, softly to herself thinking she was alone. *"Huckleberry pie, an' a huckleberry puddin', gave it all away to see Sally Goodin'!"* She sang louder remembering what Uncle Ira had said about noise scaring away the snakes and bears.

Tom came up to her on the path watching the curve of her breast as she stretched to reach a handful of berries. He moved in close and gave a low whistle and opened his arms. Startled, she turned, gasped in fright, her song hushed. She fell, as Tom had planned into his waiting arms.

"Oh my goodness, Tom. What a start you gave me. I didn't see you. I been watchin' so close for snakes an' bears," she exclaimed breathlessly as Tom held her closer. "Uncle Ira says them bears like these berries near as much as he does. He said them sneaky copperheads like to hide underneath where it's cool." She gasped again for air. "You're holdin' me so tight I cain't breath. Turn me loose. I might faint." She closed her eyes as if she were about to swoon. Kylee knew better, she had never swooned in her entire life. But Tom's nearness was making her feel giddy.

Tom could feel the pounding of her heart and the pressure of her breasts moving slowly with her labored breathing. But he did not release her. She felt so good in his arms; he wanted to keep her there forever. He hadn't touched her since the trial. In fact, it had been a long time since he had touched any woman. It had been too damn long!

All his good resolutions to wait for Kylee faded and drifted into oblivion. His heart pounded, his need for her, demanding fulfillment of his desire. He must have her now. The last time he'd had a woman was when he was with Polly, the night Billy was murdered. It had been a while. He needed a refresher course.

Kylee was pushing gently on his chest, trying to release herself. Instead of letting her go he lifted her chin and placed a long, soft kiss upon her lips. She accepted the kiss still twisting against him, trying to free herself. Tom loosened his hold slightly, enough so she could breathe deeply and return the air to her body.

Tom smiled down at her. Gosh, she was little, he thought. It was not the old teasing smile but one of gentle persuasion. Kylee was caught up in the look and before she could stop herself had lifted her arms to encircle his neck. The cloudy, sultry look in her eyes was all the invitation Tom needed.

Kissing her again with slight pressure, he could feel the tenseness of her tightly closed lips. Gently, easily, he touched them with the tip of his tongue, back and forth with a soft sweeping stroke until she relaxed with a sigh and parted her lips. He lifted his head pulling back just enough and she followed his lips eagerly. Wanting more, she stood on her tiptoes to reach his lips. Disappointed when Tom pulled away, she breathed in deeply; her eyes still closed from the long stirring kiss, then opened her eyes to look at him with half-raised eyelids.

He said nothing and did not kiss her again, as she wanted him to. Taking her hand he led her to a grassy spot between a mulberry tree and a large maple. Pulling her down with him as he dropped to the ground he cradled her head upon his arm. The softness of her long thick hair drifted in an auburn cloud upon the grass.

He kissed her again tenderly and could feel the small pulse at his temples throbbing wildly. He raised his head and looked at her closely. Dark lashes lay across her cheeks, lips red and moist from his kiss and slightly parted.

"You sure are lovely Kylee. I'm wantin' you bad. Please be willin'," Tom pleaded. He was rubbing his hand up and down her cool white flesh caressing her arm. His voice sounded low and heavy, muffled as if from drink.

Kylee opened her eyes and looked up at him in quick surprise. She liked the kisses. But if she understood him right, he was expecting more.

Seeing her shocked look, he thought perhaps he was moving too fast. Better not make his old mistake and get too aggressive.

"You shouldn't be walking alone in the woods, Kylee. You're not well yet," he cautioned as he relaxed his hold on her trying not to put her on the defensive. He gently caressed her arm then fumbled with the buttons at the neck of her dress and began to ease it down from her shoulder.

"I'm fine, Tom. I'm getting better every day." She swallowed hard, her voice small and shaky.

She felt weak in her stomach. A rush of butterfly wings fluttered, scraping against her insides. If he kissed her again, she would never be able to keep her head. Yet, she wanted his kisses. It was the first time she had been kissed by a young man, except for a friendly peck from her cousins. She was finding this experience quite pleasant. In fact, the kisses made her light headed and woozy.

"I'm out in the sun a lot. See how brown I'm gettin'?" She held up a slim arm for his appraisal. At the same time she was trying to ease his hand away and move out from under him.

Each day she had been pushing her sleeves up to let the warm spring sun brown her arms. But a harsh circle below her elbow cut the golden tan short.

Tom could not stop the vision from flashing before his eyes of what her body would look like without any clothes. He anxiously worked at her buttons and finally exposed the white smooth swelling of her breast. He knew he couldn't wait much longer and bent to kiss the exposed area at the opening of her dress. At the same time he moved his hand to push up her skirts with firm determination.

"Sure Kylee. You do have lovely skin. Let's see more of it," he told her with a teasing twinkle covering up the rising passion in his eyes. He gulped hard trying to swallow the large knot in his throat.

Kylee gave a shocked gasp, but managed to say, "You like my skin?"

"Oh, my God yes, Kylee. Yes! But you are still a little pale."

He had pulled her skirt and petticoat to above her knees and was pushing her bloomer leg an inch higher. As his hand reached closer to its target, he felt Kylee pulling away. He kissed her harder than before, trying to subdue any refusal, pinning her body under him securely.

"No, Tom. No!" she whispered, freeing her lips. Why was he fumbling with her clothing? She twisted to free herself from under him.

"Please Kylee, lay still. I've been wantin' you for so long. Ever since you came to us. When I go to bed at night, you're all I think about. Then after the trial I thought you felt the same way. I'm not waiting any longer!" Tom kissed her eyelids and the upper swelling of her breasts.

Kylee again felt the swarm of butterfly wings soaring up inside, engulfing her into submission as she returned his kisses.

In a flash of memory, she remembered the talk she and Mary had at the springhouse. This was going to be something more than sitting on a man's lap. She was not going to get with child before she was married. Tom hadn't said anything about marrying. He hadn't even said anything about love. She was frantic and began to struggle again, this time in earnest. Pulling her dress together, she tried to hide her breasts while pushing his hand forcefully away from the inside of her legs.

"What are you doin', Kylee? Lie still. I won't hurt you," he begged. "Don't push me away. Stop pushing. It'll be nice, sweetheart."

Kylee had a twinge of memory of Blaine's words on the same subject. "Girls like it too, as much as we do." Oh, there was that terrible memory.

"Stop it right now, Tom! You hear me? Right now, let me go! I ain't lyin' still for you, or no one else."

In a spurt of energy, driven by sheer desperation, she pushed hard against Tom's chest. With resisting force and a desperate need to free herself she rolled Tom over to the ground in a surging movement.

Tom was determined also and was not willing to be denied. Holding her securely about the waist, he fastened his muscular legs in a wrestler's lock around her, rolling her over on top of him.

"Now Kylee, honey, calm down. Let's talk this over, please," Tom coaxed, looking up at her, his blue eyes pleading and filled with dancing fires. The look did not move Kylee.

Tom's severe leg lock brought back vividly the terrorizing night Blaine held her in such a way, back to the past she had forgotten. She was unnerved that Tom would treat her so and began to cry hysterically.

"Ain't nothin' to talk about. Now let me go! You're a pig just like Blaine was. You're a beast, that's what you are, a beast! You men are all alike!" Kylee pushed hard on Tom's chest, tears of desperation flooding her eyes.

Her breasts were dangerously close to Tom's face and he could see down the inviting pathway of her bosom. Forcefully, he lifted his eyes away. Looking at her, he saw the tears streaming down her cheeks. All the color had drained from her rosy face. He saw beyond her lovely tear stained face into the thickness of the mulberry tree. A thick branch spread over them in all its green glory. There curled in among the bushy green leaves hanging its head in their direction was a large black snake. It hung there suspended, entranced, round beady eyes watching their every move.

Tom stiffened. For a moment he envisioned an incident long ago when he was a young boy. On a sunny day he had been hunting, lying in a grassy spot and waiting out a ground hog hole. The warm sun had made him drowsy and he had dozed. Then he was awakened by a strong odor in his nostrils. He parted the bushes to see if the little varmint had appeared from its lair. His sleepy eyes rested instead on a mulberry tree covered with black snakes.

In their interlocking mating ritual, they had not left a bare spot on the tree. An obnoxious smell hung heavy around them and had drifted out upon the air. It was their repulsive odor that had awakened him. The memory clouded Tom's mind as he watched the snake above them. Then he remembered the Bible story in Genesis of the serpent. He was remorseful.

His eagerness for Kylee cooled and he was extremely sorry for his behavior. Lust had claimed his desire for her, which had not been his first intention. Loosening his hold on Kylee, he slowly released her trembling body. He watched the snake slide away down the tree trunk and slither off, unconcerned.

Kylee pulled herself to a standing position and attempted to straighten her clothing. Pulling her long skirts into place, she fastened the buttons on her bodice hiding her full firm loveliness. Struggling to straighten her collar he could see her fingers visibly shaking. Tom watched the tears falling on her hands. Finished with the buttons, Kylee turned and ran quickly down the path.

He had made her cry. Why had he let this happen? She would hate him even more than before. He had been so used to Polly's passionate acceptance that Kylee's determined refusal had stunned him. He had not intended for this to happen. He was ashamed and sorry but did not move to detain her or try to apologize. He leaned back on his elbows and watched her go, saying nothing.

For once he was at a loss for words. Suddenly he understood why he felt so sorry. Without a doubt, he needed very much for

Kylee to return his love. The most important thing in his life, at this moment, was for this fresh, lovely young woman with her soft gentle personality, to be his.

At first she had returned his kisses, almost eager and willing. But he had frightened her with his passionate insistence. Hating himself, he had to undo what he'd done, hoping she would forgive him. He would do anything to make amends.

Standing up, he called down the path but she had disappeared. He would go find her and beg her forgiveness and ask her to be his wife. Seeing the basket swinging on the limb, he thought to fill it. It would help him apologize. Taking the basket, he began picking the biggest plumpest berries he could find.

The mid-morning sun was moving toward the middle of the sky as if in a hurry to get to the other side. Even in the thicket where Tom was picking berries, the heat was beginning to close in. In the east, a gathering of dark clouds appeared to spoil the beauty of the blue Virginia sky. The leaves on the enormous oaks fluttered silently turning their silver undersides out to shimmer in the bright sunlight. A menacing stillness hung heavy upon the air. A skinny amber tinted cloud passed between sun and earth, casting a long shadow across the mountain. Tom felt the uneasy quietness and for a moment wondered about the snake. He erased it from his mind, but had a feeling of impending dread he couldn't shake.

His father would be bellowing for him loud enough to shake the trees by now. He wasn't worried. His only concern was to find Kylee and make amends. She would be washing at the back of the house, which was where he was headed. The basket was filled to capacity with plump berries. Tom, satisfied that Kylee would be pleased, hurried down the path.

The water in the barrel was scalding hot and Kylee filled the empty tub at the end of the battling board. Lifting a shirt from the tub of cold water she pounded and thumped as her temper mounted. As she worked, her tears dried, only searing anger remained. She had to admit that Tom had been a persuasive lover. How could he have treated her so? He had even enticed her to return his kisses. She had enjoyed it too!

Feeling the silence in the air she wondered if the Lord were preparing some kind of doomsday because of her very unladylike manner. Well, her behavior might not have been on the clean and pure side, but her laundry was going to be! She plopped the shirt into the tub of hot soapy water then back out onto the battling board. She began pounding it vigorously.

Admitting she had behaved shamefully, she thought about what could have happened if Tom had been a little more tactful, confessing to herself that it might have been nice. She really liked Tom a lot. She had even forgotten the incident in town so long ago. So many things had happened in her life since then, it seemed trivial.

She looked at the shadow the cloud was casting across the hill when she saw Tom coming into the yard. What could he want of her now she thought bitterly? Hadn't he done enough already? She ducked her head closer over her work.

"Kylee, I finished pickin' the berries for you." He held out his peace offering hoping she would accept it with one of her beautiful smiles, so that he could apologize.

Her anger was keen and growing steadily. Kylee's only thought as he moved closer was revenge. The old hate for him was back in her heart. Lifting the shirt, heavy with soap and water, she turned and struck him brutally across the face.

The swishing blow so startled Tom that he dropped the basket of berries. Blue-black fruit scattered about their feet. The homemade soap strong with lye burned his eyes and stung his face. The rough edge of a broken button caught him sharply on the nose making a small gash that started the blood spurting.

"Why, you little vixen!" Tom was furious and his temper soared. Losing control and without thinking, he raised his arm and struck her hard across the cheek.

The moment the shirt struck, Kylee's anger was gone. Tom's blow devastated her. Great gushing sobs shook her slight frame. Degrading remorse and shame filled her. What had gone wrong? This had started out to be such a wonderful day. She turned and ran toward the steps leading to the back door. Then she saw Matt turning into the lower gate.

Matt was sagging wearily, almost to the point of falling from the saddle. He was holding Taynee cradled in his arms. Kylee's troubles and tears were forgotten. An overwhelming concern for Matt and Taynee took their place.

"Oh dear Lord! Tom, its Matt an' Taynee!" Lifting her skirts to free her legs Kylee fled across the grassy yard. In a moment of panic Jay Mitchell came to her mind. She had a chilling premonition and knew the girl in Matt's arms was dead.

"Come quick! Hurry, somethin's wrong, somethin' is terrible wrong!"

Tom was bathing his face and eyes in a clear bucket of water, trying to wash away the blood coming from the slash on his nose. The water helped but he knew the burning would continue for some time. He raised his head and reached for an old shirt to dry his face and clear the blur from his eyes.

As the water refreshed him, he felt no remorse for striking Kylee, she deserved it; he consoled himself. In fact, she deserved worse! He only wanted to apologize and tell her how sorry he was, to comfort her and tell her how much he loved her. He would have done anything to make amends. She hadn't given him a chance to explain, just reached out and whopped him a good one. No woman had ever treated him in such a manner. What had gotten into his head to even consider marrying such an all-fired-mixed up woman? It was very clear how she felt about him.

Hearing Kylee's urgent call, he flung the shirt onto the battle board and went on a high run. Passing Kylee in the middle of the yard, his powerful legs closed the distance to the riders in an instant. Everything else dropped from his mind.

Matt was hunched over Taynee, his body sagging with weariness. Only the need to get Taynee home had kept him on the horse. Tom caught Taynee as she slipped from Matt's hold, releasing her thankfully, into Tom's waiting arms. Matt slipped slowly from the horse's rump onto the ground.

"Catch him, Kylee. Quick, he's hurt!" Tom urged when he saw the blood on Matt's shirtfront.

"My God, man. I was afear'd somethin' like this might happen. It was Jay? It had to be Jay. I know it! Ain't no one else so damn low down!" Tom declared without waiting for Matt's answer.

Matt welcomed Kylee's shoulder to lean on. He was weary; the night's events had drained him physically and mentally.

"I never thought we'd make it Tom. It seemed a far piece. I sure am powerfully glad to be home. He caught us up on the cut-off to Pickett Rock. Taynee's dead Tom, she's dead." Matt told them weakly.

"We were surprised all right, but we give him some fight back. I think I hit him. I heard his horse running through the trees. I didn't take time to look. I just wanted to get Taynee home. If Mitchell ain't dead, he's hurt bad, I'm sure of that. The murky bastard, he caught us in the dark like he did Billy. He don't know any other way. There ain't a decent bone in his body, an' now he's killed Taynee."

They walked to the house, Tom carrying Taynee, and Kylee supporting Matt with her slight body. The wedding gown still clutched in Taynee's arms slipped unnoticed from its wrapping to trail in the dry dirt. Their blood had fallen on the bundle seeping through to stain the gown's creamy loveliness in large dark splotches.

Matt leaned heavily on Kylee. It was good to be with this gentle friend. Laying his head over on her soft sweet smelling hair, he thought of Taynee. He shed his last tears for his sweetheart while he walked with Kylee's arm around him. Soon his love and grief for Taynee would be pushed into a deep corner of his mind. His heart and thoughts would fill with a deeper driving hatred for Jay Mitchell.

CHAPTER THREE

"You'll live Jay. That bullet in your shoulder was really in there. But there it is!" Hensely said triumphantly dropping the bloody bullet in Jay's hand.

"That cut on your head will leave a scar, but I sewed it up the best I could. It should heal up fine." Tanner Hensely talked as he continued to dress Jay's wounds then turned to Nell.

"You keep them dressin's cleaned an' changed. That's what's important now, keepin' them clean. Cain't chance no infection. You watch close now. You stay off your horse Jay, you hear? Ridin'll start that bleedin' quicker then scat," Tanner warned Jay as he washed his hands in the basin of water that Nell set out for him.

"I ain't got no horse. Had to kill him. The scabby old bastard! He done me good though. Guess I'll have to use Blaine's Morgan, it finally came home." Jay informed the doctor-deputy.

"Well, that Morgan's a find horse. Where's Taynee, Nell? She's always around helpin' you." Hensely watched Nell closely as she deftly rolled up the remaining bandages.

"None of your damn business where Taynee's at. That's my business! Keep your nose in its place." Jay snarled, still hurting from Hensely's probing for the bullet.

"I weren't pryin' Jay. I was lookin' to come to the weddin'. Ferrell said they'd be gettin' married soon." The marshal assured him, talking as he put his tools away. Rolling down his sleeves, he buttoned the cuffs and put on his black coat. Picking up his bag he

411

reached for the rifle he'd left leaning against the head of the bed. He started out the bedroom door.

"You're sure in a hurry, Tanner. How come you're in such a hurry? I been wantin' to have a talk with you. Have you found out a thing about Will Tackett? When's he gonna let go of that land on Pound? I want that piece a land. I want it bad. It took me long enough to get him to leave without killin' him. I knew I had to let him live or else I couldn't get a deed for it. That's what I want Hensely, is a deed."

"Now you're a law officer. I cain't see how come you cain't find him. You could force him to sign that deed over to me," Jay continued.

"Well Jay, I thought you'd bought it. I'd heard rumor that it were already sold." Tanner stopped in the doorway to turn around and look at Jay.

"You damn well know I cain't do any business with Will. He hates my guts! Ain't no way I could deal with him. If we met face to face, I'd have to kill him before he killed me. Far as I know, that land is still up for grabs. No one around here has bought it, or I'd a heared. Someone's told you wrong! Ain't no one else gonna have that land. It's gonna belong to Mitchell's! It joins my mountain an' I'm gonna have it. You better see what you can come up with to see it gets done!" Jay's voice was growing weak but he rose up in bed to look with a blaze of black eyes at the deputy.

"Now, Jay. I don't want to get my neck into no land dispute. But I'll see what I can find out. I'll do that much," Tanner said coming back into the room to look down at his patient.

"I know Ira wants that land too. It's rich in lumber an' coal. You don't think he's gonna let a deal like that get by him? Will would let him have it because they's kin. I gotta stop him from gettin' it. They're already squattin' on land that belonged to Tandy's. My great granddaddy built the first cabin on that land. I'm gonna get it back!"

"You gotta be durn careful in a deal like this. If we go too fast you're gonna have Phelps on top of you like a dog on a bone. Let's take it slow Jay. Election time's comin' up. Some of the folks are gettin' restless. I want Snow's job. I cain't chance losin' the votes.

I've heard rumors that Tom Phelps thinks he's gonna try for the job too. Now we cain't let that happen, can we?"

"I'll handle the Phelps's. You don't think I'd let a little thing like that cripple cut me out'a this land deal do you? You're gonna need money to campaign for office, so's I'll get the boys workin' on Pound road. I think if we'd work at it a little harder, we could make it worth our while. They's more wagons goin' into Kentucky with freight for sale. They are loaded with money when they come back through. While I'm at it, I'm gonna get rid of every last one of them damn Phelps's!" he told Hensely looking up at him with a greedy twinkle in his eyes.

"You better get some rest, Jay. You're luckier than hell that the bleedin' stopped. If you go gallivantin' around like you've been known to do, it could start again. If it does, don't send for me 'cause it'll be too late!" Hensely warned. "I'm headin' back for town. I'll be back to see how you're doin'. We-uns'll talk more about this when you're back to yourself."

"I'd appreciate that Doc, surely would." Jay nodded his head weakly in a faint show of gratitude and closed his eyes. His face was ashen and grim against Nell's clean white pillow sham.

Deputy Marshal, (Doc) Tanner B. Hensely, lifted his arm in a good-bye gesture to Nell and the twins, then left. He had a far away glint of riches and power sparkling in his eyes.

Jay slept. His harrowing ride, the ordeal with Hail, and Tanner's probing for the bullet had drained him. He slept the rest of the day and through the night. When he awoke his body had stiffened and his wounds were throbbing fiercely. Unconcerned with his state of agony, he rose and dressed, trying to smooth his snarled, tangled hair and beard into order. He was undisturbed by the blood matted in his curly black hair and whiskers. Even his dark grizzled brows were knotted with the dried sticky substance.

His black eyes were sunk in his swarthy face. His lips pulled tightly in pain, stretching the skin taut as a banjo head, across his bony cheeks causing the deep scar on his upper cheek to stand out vibrantly. Not heeding the Deputy Marshal's warning, he pulled on his boots and fastened his spurs.

Nell sat on the other side of the bed engrossed in nursing the baby. Her heavy mouse-colored hair hung in one thick braid down her back. She lifted her head when Jay came around the bed and fastened his black eyes on his baby son. The troubled glint in his eyes softened some.

"Taynee's dead, ain't she? Why Jay, why? She was your own flesh an' blood, your only daughter. How could you have done such a thing? How could you?" Nell bravely questioned her husband trying to choke down the sobs that rose in her throat.

She had overheard Jay telling Rueben that he had left Matt and Taynee for the varmints. She was shocked and grieved. Large tears flooded her brown eyes as she thought how much she would miss the lovely stepdaughter. Oh the pity of it, the horrible uselessness of the whole thing. She mourned for Taynee and shuddered at the brutality of her husband. Who would be next? If Bob didn't shape up and begin to comply with his father's wishes, would it be him?

"Nell! You know I never allowed no meddlin' from my women! I know how much you loved Taynee. How you took the little vagabond an' changed her from a wild gypsy taggin' the boys to a real young lady. I appreciate you grievin' for her. I cain't feel no sorrow for her, not after what she was tryin' to do. I owed it to Great Grandpap Tandy to see her die. I'd a never let one of mine make it possible to breed a Phelps whelp! I know you will never understand that. So's I'll just forget you asked me. You hold your tongue woman! Take care of my little son. Things'll be just fine, understand?" Jay warned in a harsh demanding voice.

She nodded her head and looked down at the dark head and eyes that were beginning to look so much like his father's. There was a new fear growing in her mind. She could take no chance on Jay's anger turning on her. She must hold herself in his good graces. She must live to raise her sons, the twins and the baby in a different path than Jay had raised his older sons. She would shower her little ones with so much love they would have to grow up different.

The tears had dried on her cheeks. She could no longer taste their saltiness on her lips.

"You think you're well enough to be…."

"Nell, I'll have no meddlin'! I'm goin' now to fetch Taynee's body back here. We'll bury her by her maw an' brother. Her grandfolks are buried there too. She never had cause to hate them like I did. We'll bury her on the hill where she belongs along with Blaine an' the other Tandy's an' Mitchell's!"

"He is a mighty handsome tike, Nell. He does look like me, doesn't he?" Jay peeked at the baby in Nell's arms then looked over at the twins snoring away contentedly in the opposite bed.

"I'll tell you one thing Nell; sometimes it's as if I ain't got no choice about what I do. It's like Hail told me, I got a devil tormentin' me. A ridin' on my tail! The only thing I know is it's been with me since I was a youngin'. Ever since I had to hide out in three feet of snow to get away from Grandpappy's strap. That was after I got big enough to run faster than he did. I learned how to clean possum an' cook them over the fire to keep from starvin' to death when he'd run me out of the house. Then I got smart an' learned that I had to be meaner than he was to survive. I know'd if I was gonna get big enough to get away from here, I had to harden my heart." Jay confessed about his childhood.

"Then one day I was a backin' old Sally out'a the stall, that big old mule weighed over 1500 pounds. Well, Grandpap came up behind her, an' made it easy for me. I hated that old man so much an' I know'd I wasn't taken any more beatin's from him. All the mean things he done to me came before my eyes. I backed that old jenny up right over the top of him, a stompin' an' a snortin'. The mule had no choice, she kicked him against the wall then tromped him to death. But I didn't have anything to do with Grandma's death. I swear it! After she fell down the springhouse steps she wouldn't let me take care of her, she just lay in bed an' died. I was so happy them old folks were dead that I sang a hallelujah to the force that done it. I promised him my life for getting' rid of them hateful people. That black one from the pit is still ridin' my tail." Jay stared past Nell at the wall.

"Then, there came a time Nell, I know'd I'd made the wrong alliance. I tried to break away from my black hearted ways, but it was too late. I know there's a better way, but I ain't felt no forgiveness from God. He ain't gonna listen to me. He ain't gonna listen! I've done too many devilish things. I'm doomed to listen to that whirrin' in my head that never lets me rest." His confession continued.

"You gotta teach the youngin's different! You hear me, Nell? You're their only hope. They gotta be raised with God on their side, out'a the reach of that black destruction. On that path there'll never be no golden shore. You payin' attention woman?" His wide eyes turned on Nell; she felt their fire.

"It's too late for me, but they're young. They gotta be taught better no matter what I say, don't listen to me, teach them right. You know what's right Nell, I've heard you a prayin'. Don't pray for me. It's too late to restore a soul charred black by rape an' murder. I ain't humblin' myself before Him. But you pray for the youngin's."

"You gotta know I cain't be free of this burning desire to rid these hills of every last one of them bastardly Phelps's. I want to see every one of them on their knees beggin' for mercy. I have a sworn pledge to do it! It's been too long comin' about. Great Granddad Iron Jaw said as long as there was a breath left in a Tandy we shouldn't allow a Phelps to live. The wormy bastards! I ain't been faithful to that vow. But they's a makin' it a little easier each day for me to kill them!" Jay snorted provoking himself into a burning rage.

Snatching his hat from a peg by the bedroom door, he stormed from the house leaving Nell with a deep sense of sadness and a new understanding of the driving fury within him. She felt it would not burn out until he was dead. If he killed all the Phelps's, there would be something else to torment him. She only hoped there would be a way to keep Jay's bitterly tainted and twisted loyalties from influencing her boys. She felt even a deeper pity and fear for Bob and Rueben after what had happened to Taynee.

Burying Taynee as soon as possible was imperative Ira insisted. He was certain that if Jay could sit on a horse that he would be looking for Taynee or her body. If she wasn't where he'd ambushed the runaways he'd know where to find her. He expected Mitchell to storm the mill with Hensely and some of their outlaw friends and demand the girl. He wanted her safely buried in the family cemetery next to Billy. She had almost been his daughter-in-law. During the time she had spent caring for Kylee she had become like family. Jay's brutality toward her had cinched Ira's decision. Looking at the still visible purplish bruises about her neck and face he swore that Jay would never have her.

Hail came to doctor Matt's wounds assuring him they were only minor. The angle of the bullet that had hit Taynee slanted. It had entered her temple, passed through her head, and creased Matt's shoulder leaving a deep flesh wound. Hail cleaned and stitched the ugly ragged gash the best she could assuring him it would leave a beauty of a scar.

"You're luckier than tarnation it didn't shatter that collar bone. You'd a had a real problem then," she told him with an encouraging smile.

She helped Kylee wash and comb Taynee's curly black hair. They were careful to hide the gaping hole the bullet had left. Kylee washed the wedding dress but the bloody splotches were stubborn and left dark stains. Matt was not to be swayed and insisted she be buried in the gown. So Kylee pressed it carefully and they hid the ugly marks with garlands of flowers. Kylee tenderly dusted her face and neck with flour she had lightly browned in the oven. It turned out to be almost the color of Taynee's creamed coffee complexion and it successfully hid the hideous bruises. Then she covered her with the misty wedding veil.

Matt stood staring at the beautiful corpse, not crying, not talking, just holding her cold hand. His staring dark blue eyes were not fired with hate for Jay now but shadowed with grief. He looked at his beautiful bride-to-be in unbelief. He felt alone with the emptiness and the deep, sensitive love he would always have for her.

Tom saddled Jole' and rode to Stewart's to inform them of Taynee's tragic demise. They hurried to the burial and were stricken with grief at her unnecessary death.

Kylee and the girls cried as they talked about the happy time they had remodeling the wedding dress. They remembered Taynee's happiness and joy. The Stewarts left immediately after they put the coffin Tom had hastily built into the ground. Ira was content and satisfied that Taynee was safely away from Jay's clutches.

"She ain't no safer in the ground than she'd be on top of it," Hail insisted. With her unique ability to analyze Jay she surmised he would rob the grave. She sharply told Ira so looking at him with a flash of emerald eyes.

"Now, Hail. I don't reckon even Jay, the black hearted scoundrel that he is, would do such a dastardly thing. I think you are wrong about that, dear friend. He's too afear'd of haunts to tamper with the dead." Ira assured her in a mild manner smiling through his white beard.

"I don't intend to sit up with the grave to find out!" He added sternly.

"Maybe," was Hail's one word answer agreeing with him for the moment.

Hail harbored her own opinion. If Jay had not permitted Matt and Taynee to run away it was certain he would never allow the girl to be buried on Phelps land. For him, that would be a total disgrace. When it came to getting something he wanted he was not afraid of anything, even haunts perhaps.

Hail had so enjoyed the use of the little buggy at the time of Tom's trial that Ira made her a present of it. He insisted that her friend Mattie would have liked for her to have it. Besides, he added, it was small payment for her loyal friendship. If Kylee wanted one, he would buy her a new one. Hail accepted the buggy and horse graciously and was very grateful for the gift. Riding Dr. Jekyll had begun to be a burden on her body. Lately the old mule had been a Mr. Hyde more often than a Dr. Jekyll. There were many places on the mountain she could not attain with the buggy, then she would take her old dependable friend, the mule.

Dr. Jekyll would not accept the horse. The mule would slash at the little gelding viciously with his hooves as if the horse were intruding on his domain. For the horse's protection Hail tethered it behind the cabin, otherwise, there was no doubt in her mind that Jay would have taken the horse. She hoped he would have the courtesy to send the old mule home. But there was not a courteous bone in Jay's body. So she settled her mind on not getting the old mule back.

She left the mill driving the buggy with a plan running through her mind. As she drove the familiar road past the Stewarts and up the mountain to her place she devised a scheme to save Taynee. She would wait until dark the next evening to put her plan to work.

Hail waited patiently for night to come. Taking feather quilts and a pillow she loaded the buggy. Familiar with spending nights in the woods when traveling a long way to tend the sick, she knew exactly what to take for an outing. The night was brightened by what was left of the waning moon. Familiar with the road her journey was no problem. The cemetery was on the hill behind the Phelps place and away from the house. It sat alone and reserved in the shadow of the tall pines.

She unhitched the buggy and hid it well among the trees and shrubs, close to Taynee's grave where she could hear anyone coming up the hill from Pound road. She tied the horse farther up the mountain in a dense thicket. Here the horse had plenty of feed and would not be apt to neigh and give her hiding place away to anyone approaching.

While Hail was on her vigil at the Phelps cemetery, guarding Taynee's grave, Tom and Matt were completing a duty of their own. With Ira's team of grays, chains and pulley, the young men pulled Siler away from Hail's yard. Rolling the dead horse into a ravine they covered it with stones. They had no concern with Hail's absence, accepting the possibility she was away on a mission of mercy.

Three nights and three days Hail waited making friends with the squirrels, groundhogs, birds, and fireflies. Boy and Blue had discovered her hiding place but the dogs soon became discouraged when she refused to pay any attention to them. Kylee came and put flowers on Billy and Taynee's graves and left unaware of Hail's watchful eyes from within the buggy. On the fourth night of her vigil she was convinced that she had been wrong. She might as well go home before one of the Phelps men discovered her. She would never live down their teasing about her weird choice of a camp sight.

She started up the hill to get the horse when she heard the definite sound of wagon wheels. It was coming fast shaking the earth and disturbing the serene silence of the night. Even the fireflies darted for protective cover under the broad shelter of the wide leafed fern.

Sheltering herself in the buggy she fumbled with the buttons at her bodice front. Why did there have to be so many when she must hurry? Quickly she slipped out of her dress exposing a startling white camisole and under skirt. Hail had long ago given up the uncomfortable fashion of stays and corsets, partly on the advice of her doctor father and partly because it felt so dog-gone good.

Hail had spent many years traipsing about the hills tending the sick who needed her and digging herbs and roots for medicine. Soon to be forty, she was trim, buxom, and very pretty. Hastily she pulled the wire pins and combs from her heavy long platinum hair. Shaking it free she let it cascade in a wispy white cloud about her shoulders. Climbing from the buggy she immediately covered her ghostly appearance with a dark quilt. Behind the white wooden marker on Billy's grave she crouched down breathlessly waiting.

CHAPTER FOUR

There was little evidence of a shoot-out where Jay had left Matt and Taynee. He had heard Matt clearly shout that Taynee was dead. He found where they had sat by the rock and then mounted their horses. In the thick plush grass and heavy ground cover it was hard for Jay to find a trail. He speculated that Matt headed for the mill with Taynee's body.

Damn Phelps's, they would bury Taynee Mitchell as if she were one of them. Well, he would see about that! They needn't think that he would ever stand still and allow a Mitchell to take her final resting place in a Phelps cemetery. Never! After they buried her, then he would get his daughter. While they weren't looking he would find the new grave and bring her home where she belonged, with her own people.

"Aw Paw. I ain't much for robbin' graves, least ways after dark. I'm scared of graveyards. They's got boogers there. Anyways that's what you told us. You said that the witches meet there. I ain't wantin' to meet up with no witches." Rueben's refusal was not definite. "Are you gonna make me Paw?" A fear of haunts and ghosts overshadowed Rueben's love for his father.

"Yeah, I'm gonna make you! Your brother Bob wouldn't be a bit of good to me. I ain't gonna let no boogers get you. Side's, you're too short an' ugly! When they see'd you, they'd turn you loose in a hurry. You'd scare them to death," Jay teased.

Jay found Rueben at the barn sitting on a bench in a small clearing on the side of the hill. Above his head, stretched on the log wall of the barn hung several raccoon skins drying in the sun. The skins would be tanned and the leather used to make horse gear such as harnesses, lines, and a variety of strings and laces.

Rueben spent the morning splitting staves with a froe and mallet. When Jay found him he was sitting before a wooden vise that held the staves securely. He whittled and shaped each one to fit into a butter churn he was building for Nell.

Rueben's chosen profession was that of a cooper, if only his father would give him time to pursue it. He loved working with the wood, creating objects not only useable but things of rare beauty. He felt a warmth and satisfaction from working with wood that he had never found with any human. With his love for wood and the talent of his hands, he built things of intricate beauty. Furniture, pails, tubs, toys, hand carved and finished. He was a craftsman in his trade, unequaled in the hills.

Jay sat hunched down on his haunches watching his oldest son with awe. He wondered where he ever acquired such ability. It amazed him that such a dirty rough-hewn character as Rueben could produce such things of artistry and durability. As they talked Rueben worked piling up the shavings at their feet.

"We-uns ain't got time for that no-ways Paw. That beer's near lost its cap. You know better than me that means cookin' time. If we don't get right at it, that whiskey's only gonna be middlin! That mash'll be spoiled for sure." Rueben was proud of his whiskey making ability.

He knew well that his father would never allow anything but perfection in his whiskey. By the time the whiskey was made maybe his father would forget this crazy notion to bring Taynee home. After all it didn't matter, Rueben thought, where one rested in the ground.

"Why didn't you tell me it was ready?" Jay questioned rising from his haunches.

"Well, you've been laid up Paw. I checked it yesterday 'n it's ready for sure. I was gonna take Bob an' get at it tonight just as soon as I got this churn done for Nell."

"Then we're gonna do it! You got them barrels charred an' ready?"

"Sure's hell do Paw. They's loaded an' waitin'. I got the wood split an' piled for the furnace. The thumper an' coolin' barrel is all set up. I'm tellin' you Paw, it's ready to go!" Rueben informed him impatiently.

Rueben had been working for a long time in the early morning sun. His fair complexion was turning a fiery red. His orange blonde hair heavy with sweat lay plastered against his forehead and hung about his neck in damp curls.

"Then what's holdin' you, a wild cat hangin' on to your shirt tail? Get your bedrolls an' some vittles to take with us. Let's be gone! We-uns'll take Bob along, whether he likes it or not. He's got by with sluffin' off long enough! When we's finished up we'll hide them kegs an' the still real good. Then we're gonna head on down with that empty wagon an' pick up your sister! That's right, Rueb! Now don't twist your face all up like that. What if it froze that way? You make up your mind that we're gonna do it!" Jay declared stubbornly, his voice determined.

He glowered at his son with black fierceness in his eyes. The red faced young man, not inclined to argue with his father, straightened his face to simulate a smile.

The days and nights it took the Mitchell men to cook off their whiskey went quickly. After the whiskey had been proofed to Jay's specification and taste, it was time to disassemble the still. When everything had been satisfactorily cleaned and hidden, Jay allowed each one a jug of the finest. From then on, whatever they drank, they paid for. It was the ground rule.

"If I let you have all you wanted there wouldn't be a bit left for Trace or takin' into Kentuck. You'd lay around heftin' a jug until ever bit was gone. I wouldn't be able to get a thing out'a you-ins. All the work would go a beggin'. Let's have us a few nips, then we'll be off to fetch your sister," Jay told them with a twisted grin. His sudden loquacious mood surprised his two sons.

The fire was all that was left of the camp. The bedrolls and empty sugar sacks were piled in the bed of the wagon. The whiskey kegs had been buried at the side of the hill and deftly covered with dirt and limbs. The still was buried safely along side of the kegs.

They sat for a long time at the fire listening to Jay's chatter. Bob was sullen and silent, bitter toward his father because of Taynee. He found no place in his heart to forgive him.

As Jay talked, he drank. Bob watched the flickering flames of their dying campfire. Thinking of the fiery sparks that appeared in Taynee's violet eyes when he told her what had happened to Billy. He would never forget the beautiful sunny smile that often engulfed her face. Nor her tall willowy body and long legs and how she would spurt past him when they were racing on Tandy's road by the orchard leaving behind her a flash of black hair.

"Bet you cain't catch me. Bet you cain't find me either!" she would challenge him.

She had been right. He could never find her hidden high in the branches of a gnarled old apple tree. But she would always give herself away giggling because of her triumph over him. Jumping from a tree she would pin his frail body to the ground and wrestle with him playfully. She would tickle him until laughingly exhausted he would have to admit she had beat him. Then they would sit together on the old split rail fence eating green apples and confide in each other their special dreams. Taynee's was to grow up beautiful and marry a very special sweetheart and have babies, lots of babies, maybe a hundred. Bob's was to get to be a man so he could leave Tandy's Mountain and never see his father again.

He could still hear her screams; a smile touched his lips as he thought about the time Rueben had cut her hair. Taynee's tightly curled black hair had been impossible to keep combed and the matted mass was an invitation to nesting vermin.

After her mother Mae died it fell on Rueben to care for the little half-sister. Bob wasn't much older so Rueben had his work cut out for him. He had to care for the two little ones and try at the same time to keep Blaine out of mischief.

Rueben threatened Taynee with the currycomb or the scissors. She chose the scissors and once started, he wouldn't let her change her mind. Every time a cloud of black curls fell to the floor Taynee would wail as if a banshee were on her tail. Regretting her decision when she saw her closely cropped head, she cried for a week because she had to comb her own hair. Bob decided then that all women were fickle.

Bob had felt jealous and left out when Nell came and took Taynee under her wing. As he looked back, he remembered how they all had grown to love their new young stepmother. He would have to help her even more now that Taynee was gone. Thinking of his sister and how much he was going to miss her, a lump rose in his throat. He quickly washed it down with a swallow of whiskey knowing well that his father would consider any such show of feelings a display of weakness.

He would go with his father to move his sister's body and say nothing. He was not afraid of the dark or spooks; he had his own opinion. Bob accepted Taynee's love for Matt and her affection for the new girl at the mill. With the hatred she held for their father, he felt she would rather stay on Phelps ground.

"Now boys, that's good whiskey. You done good helpin' me. I'm gonna give you a little somethin' extra for doin' such a good job. I'm gonna give you each a jug to sell for some pocket money. You can take a visit to Polly."

"I'm thinkin' Bob ain't had any experience. I think it's about time he learned what having a woman is all about," Jay teased the younger man.

"Look at him. Look at that long face. That's the way it's looked ever since we got Billy out'a the way so's he could spark Mary. But I guess he's forgot about her. Leastways he ain't been tryin' to see her, that I know'd of. Yep, I think he's forgot about Mary an' needs a trip to see Polly. That'll stir his blood up. She's a whole bunch better than a spring tonic. Nell's likely to start givin' him some if he don't perk up. What do you say boy? Ready for a trip to see Polly?" Jay questioned Bob with a glint of almost sadistic quality lighting his dark eyes.

"Paw, don't send him to see Polly. I'm a hankerin' for her myself. I'm wanting' her for my very own," Rueben informed his father.

"What's that boy? She ain't gonna be nobody's. You should know that Rueb. She ain't never gonna be one man's, not even Tom

Phelps." Jay leaned his head back and his howling laughter filled the treetops.

"Tain't so, Paw! Tain't so!" Rueben mumbled and hung his head.

"I ain't forgot about Mary, Paw. I just don't think she's wantin' any part of me cause of what happened to Billy." Bob patted Rueben's shoulder comforting him.

"It's okay Rueb. I ain't wantin' to go see Polly," he told his brother, knowing how it was to want someone that didn't want you.

"I don't want any extra Paw. You can give mine to Nell for a pair of shoes she's needin' badly. Can we be on about our business at the grave? Let's get it over with so we can go home." Bob cradled his jug in the crook of his elbow and took a small drink. He'd had just about all of the whiskey he could take for one night. Not being a heavy drinker, he was concerned with his ability to handle himself.

"You're right, Bobbie. Let's hitch up an' be about our business," Jay stated in a civil manner. Bob could see behind his father's twisted ambiguous grin to the cruelty in his black eyes reflected in the dying embers of the fire.

Bob felt his father hadn't forgiven him for what he thought was cowardice on the night Billy was killed. He would never be able to kill a man like that, in cold blood. He had a feeling that Mary had it in her mind that he was the one that murdered Billy. He was convinced that she would never believe anything different. There was never going to be a chance for him with her. He was certain her warm brown eyes would never smile at him the way they had for Billy. With a sudden rush of longing, he supposed he would never quit loving her.

"Aw Paw, do we gotta? Let's wait a bit longer," Rueben stalled, his voice muddled with liquor.

"We-uns is goin' now! If we wait any longer you-ins won't be a smittin' of help. Sides, we better get goin' while that moon is still up. You won't like it a bit after it goes down behind that hill an' all them trees. Then you won't be able to see a dad-blamed thing. Now get your butt off that log! Let's be about our business!" Jay ordered Rueben in an angry impatient voice as he began to cover the fire by kicking up the dirt with the side of his boot.

Bob had the team hitched and ready to go. He was standing in back of the wagon holding the lines and waiting for his father and brother. Jay climbed onto the seat and took the reins from Bob. Rueben was up beside him in a drunken sullen mood making sure his jug of whiskey was safe between his knees. Bob laid down in the back and promptly fell into a drunken sleep, pillowing his head on a stack of empty sugar sacks.

Hail crouched low behind the wooden marker at Billy's grave. She waited patiently as she listened to the rumble of the wagon as it moved in close. She dared a peek as Jay guided the team up the slight slope that escalated up to the top of the hill.

So, Jay had survived Matt's bullet and he was here for Taynee's body, just as she surmised. The Phelps family-burying plot had been planned out on the crest of the hill. It overlooked the house, mill, and giant oaks. It was nestled in a magnitude of large maple, pines, blossoming dogwood, and carpeted with plush grass and laurel. It was a place of peace and solitude.

The moon shone in at just the right angle. It would intensify the shadows around the headstones and shrunken graves giving light in just the right areas to accentuate Hail's dramatization of a ghostly sentinel.

She watched Jay drive in and waited for him to circle the team then back the wagon into position. He stopped at the foot of the new mound of dirt that was gleaming in the moonlight. The stillness intensified as Jay and Rueben climbed down and stood looking at the grave. The two men began talking in loud voices as if they were trying to ward off any ghostly appearances. Jay's voice was harsh and demanding while Rueben's voice was sullen and muted from his intensive drinking.

"Fetch the shovels Rueb an' wake up Bob. We-uns are gonna need his help diggin' an' gettin' that casket out'a the hole," Jay ordered his son who was standing by his side swaying and shaking with fear.

Jay looked up taking inventory. It was the first time he had been in the Phelps's cemetery. Then his eyes caught the mystical apparition weaving and swaying, darting and floating up from the white marker near the new grave. Closer and closer came the white drifting specter. He was beside himself with intense terror, convinced and certain that Taynee's spirit had risen from the grave to avenge him. Thinking only of himself and the necessity to be removed from this place, he moved as if lightening were at his heels. He clambered into the wagon, gathered the reins, and gave the mules a sharp stinging wallop on their rumps. Whistling and snorting in loud protest the mules stretched out into a fast swinging run. The wagon shook dangerously as it bounced in haste down the steep rocky trail of the road.

As Rueben lifted the shovels from the side of the wagon bed he saw the ghostly sight at the same moment Jay had. Stunned, he dropped them back into the bottom of the wagon. Sudden panic rendered him immobile and silent. His legs wouldn't move which left him leaning into the wagon. His mouth dropped open in a gasp and stayed that way. Trembling uncontrollably, he tried to call his father and remind him not to leave without him, but no sound came.

Jay swiftly pulled out, the abrupt movement sent Rueben sprawling to the ground. Striking his head sharply on the protrusion of an old stump, he was sent reeling into momentary unconsciousness. He laid stretched flat on his back in the tall laurel vine next to Taynee's grave.

Rueben returned slowly to consciousness laying in a half-drunken stupor. He stared blankly at the sky sprinkled lavishly with stars. The lopsided three-quarter moon was barely visible behind the whiskered trees along the crest of the mountain and would soon disappear.

He began to stir remembering vaguely what happened. Rising on his elbow he took a hurried look around. He listened intently as he heard the moving of wheels coming slowly, satisfied that his father was returning for him. He rolled over and tried rising to a standing position. Making it to his knees, he lifted his head to see a buggy coming out of the shadows beyond the graves. He froze, realizing in an instant that it was not Jay and shrank back into the protective cover of the vines.

Edging by him, the buggy was close enough to reach out and touch. He recognized the driver of the black horse and rig. There was no doubt in Rueben's mind that the occupant of the surrey was

Hail. He would know that mass of platinum white hair in the darkest night. Unaware of Rueben's presence Hail passed and moved on slowly down the hill.

Rueben waited in the intense shadows of the graying night. He hunched on his knees in a mass of soft grass and vines too terrified to move, certain if he did Hail would appear and call up the spirits from the graves. Down the hill he could faintly hear the barking of a dog. He realized if he didn't get the hell out of there, the Phelps's would discover him when it became daylight. With driving will, he raised to a standing position, his body aching and stiff from being hunched to the ground for so long. When he had his legs and senses together he broke into a jogging trot. His short stocky body moved with surprising ease down the hill toward the safety of Tandy's Mountain and Jay.

The day dawned warm and humid making it impractical to build a fire simply for the solace of one's mind. Jay sat huddled in his favorite chair rocking to and fro as if he derived some portion of comfort from just being in front of the unlit fireplace.

He arrived home in the early hours exhausted and disturbed. He was totally unaware of the fact that he had abandoned his eldest son. His only concern had been to put as much distance between himself and that ghostly apparition as possible. Without unhitching the team, Jay ran for the cabin and found a remote corner in the bedroom and curled up in a heap of long arms and legs on the floor like a frightened child. He fell into a troubled, haunted sleep until Nell disturbed him.

Bob was awakened from his whiskey-induced sleep when Jay started his mad dash down the mountain, the wagon rocking and rolling dangerously. His only alternative was to hang on to keep from being dumped from the wagon. He had not eaten much; they had sampled and proofed the whiskey, then started drinking the finished product. As a result, he was not on good terms with his stomach. When the wagon came to a rollicking stop in the Mitchell yard, he could control it no longer. Jumping from the wagon bed, he leaned over the split rail fence that circled the yard and lost the stinking fuming mass inside his stomach.

Too ill to think out what had happened, he watched with blurred vision his father's mad dash for the house. Rueben was nowhere to be seen. Staggering weakly to the well, he doused a pail of water over his head. He washed his face and dried it on the tail of his shirt. Having compassion for the team left in harness he unhitched them. In the barn he gave them a measure of fodder. Picking up his hat out of the back of the wagon he went to the house and to bed.

Nell woke early because of the baby nuzzling at her breast. After nursing him, she rose and dressed trying not to disturb Jay curled in the corner of the bare floor. She felt a deep burning sadness for her husband and his dark despair that was caused from an unhappy mistreated childhood. She wanted to help him in some way but had learned not to pry or force the issue. Since his confession to her it was easier to understand his disturbed state.

Lovingly she put the baby in with the twins, Teaberry, and Dewberry. She demanded that the latter get up and help with hoeing of the garden before the sun became too hot. The other one was left with instructions to care for the baby. She promised to be in soon and feed them. They went quietly out of the house unaware that their movements disturbed Jay from his restless sleep.

Jay sat in his rocker wiggling his bare toes and contemplating putting on his heavy boots and finding himself a drink of whiskey. He had finished running off fifty gallons of the prettiest clear corn whiskey in the state of Virginia or Kentucky. And here he sat with his mouth as dry as a cotton ball. Looking around for Rueben he spotted Bob asleep on the bottom bunk bed. He was sprawled flat on his back fully clothed, his mouth open wide and snoring loudly. Picking up a boot Jay flung it at the snoring mass. Bob startled awake, bolted upright to a sitting position and struck his head sharply on the bunk above.

"What the hell did you do that for Paw? I waren't doin' nothin'!" Bob complained rubbing his injured head cautiously.

"That's the trouble. You weren't doin' nothin'! Now get your butt up out'a there an' fetch me a jug of that whiskey out'a the back of the wagon. Be quick about it!" Jay snarled, his black eyes burning balls of fire sunk in dark circles.

"While you're at it find out what your brother's up to. If he's out there whittlin', tell him I'm wantin' him now!"

Bob made it off the bed and started walking unstable, still half-asleep to the door. He met Rueben coming in carrying a jug of whiskey. Bob backed away and let Rueben take the whiskey to their father.

"There you are boy. I sure need that drink!" Jay said lifting the jug and letting the fiery liquid flow into his throat. He was in such haste that it ran from the side of his mouth and down his whiskered chin.

"I got somethin' to tell you Paw. You ain't gonna believe it! It took me all the way to figure it out. You ain't gonna believe what I'm gonna tell you!" Rueben was talking fast and breathless. His hazel eyes flicked with brown were wide and staring.

"What you talkin' about, all the way here? Where you been Rueb?"

"You run off an' left me on the mountain at the Phelps grave yard, remember? That's what I'm aimin' on tellin' you about. That haunt we-uns see'd weren't no spook at all! It was only that old witch, Hail!"

Jay rose from the rocker with fire in his eyes and hunkered down to see into Rueben's face.

"What are you tryin' to tell me? I remember I did take off in a fright. I'm sorry boy, but you got home all right. Now, you're a sayin' that it was Hail at Taynee's grave, playin' spook? Is that what you're a sayin' boy? Well, speak up then," Jay encouraged calmly with a twisted grin playing at the corner of his whiskered lips.

"I see'd her plain as all get out, white hair an' all. Drivin' that purty little rig like the one that belonged to Billy's maw. She came right across them graves like she was at home there." Rueben was talking so fast he was becoming red in the face and short of breath again. He continued excitedly.

"Well, I was a comin' on home a runnin'. What do you suppose I come onto? Right there cross Pound road, where the road takes off to come to our place. Croppin' grass, big as all git-out, was Midnight. Well, I straddled that horse big as you please an' come on home," Rueben told his father triumphantly as he took a long breath.

"So's that's the way it is? Ira's a givin' that witch presents." Jay's lips tightened into a thin line. A jealous glint came to light in his eyes as they narrowed to slits and looked vacantly past his son. He had a vague recollection of seeing the buggy under Hail's porch.

"That's right, Paw. That's right," Rueben assured his father satisfied with the news he brought.

"I'll tell you Rueben, we gotta do somethin' about that heckler. She has stuck her nose into my affairs for the last time! Somethin' has gotta be done about that old witch an' tonight's the time!" Jay snarled from between his clenched teeth, determined to take care of Hail.

"Now Paw, you're tired an' been a drinkin'. Hail ain't no witch! She's just a good ol' midwife. Didn't she fix things for Nell an' little J.B.?" Bob asked from where he stood at the door listening. He needed to calm his father, knowing too well that threatening look.

"I said, she be a witch!" Jay yelled at Bob.

Jay went over to where the young man stood. He struck him forcefully with the open palm of his hand. Bob reeled backward and caught his balance against the wall. He knotted his fist as if to strike his father, but turned instead and went out the door.

Bob stood for a moment trembling in anger as he clenched and unclenched his fists. In the shadow of the porch roof he waited for the desire to strike back at his father to subside. Then he went on down the steps and around the house to work off his anger helping Nell and Dewberry hoe the garden.

Inside Jay was telling Rueben his plan. "I'm tellin' you son, I gotta get rid of that old witch! If you'd a seen her callin' up the spirits from the fire like I did, you'd know what I'm talkin' about. I aim to get rid of that heckler tonight! She has interfered in my life for the last time! Send that old mule home, it's ate enough of my grass, I don't want nothin' around to remind me of her. I'll get that miserable person out of my life once an' for all!" Jay promised as he sat back down in his rocking chair lifting the jug. He prepared to fill the day with drinking and waiting for night to come.

CHAPTER FIVE

Hail stood leaning on the porch railing her long silver hair cascading in a cloud around her shoulders. She loved the cool of the evening but hated her desperate loneliness. The charade she played with Jay had been a diversion that helped pass the days. She only hoped her efforts had discouraged him from any further attempt at robbing his daughter's grave. She was confident that her little act had convinced him to stay away for awhile but sooner or later he would return. Jay wouldn't give up on anything if he wanted it bad enough.

Thinking of Taynee made her sad. What a waste of such a lovely fresh life. It wasn't fair that she was dead and her father was alive. That horrible man still lived!

Looking up she gazed with wonder into the star spangled night. A heavy cloud closed in the east of the sky moving in fast to cover the glorious wonder of the stars from her view. With it came a soft breeze that lifted her hair and cooled her face. The slight stirring of air held a touch of moisture. She moved back from the railing, untied the belt that held her robe together at the front, wrapped it closer then retied the belt. Sighing with weariness she looked with regret at the coming rain. Smoothing her hair back she gathered it together over her full breasts. The silver mass was a startling white against the early night. She began plaiting it into one thick braid. As her hands worked her mind wandered.

Oh, how beautiful were the pines she thought. Ever green, no matter how the tragedies of life came and went. The evergreens remained the same, dependable, straight, and stalwart. Somehow they seemed to bring a peace to the troubled turbulence that stormed in her mind.

She recalled how Taynee loved the pines. She was always begging her to take a picnic lunch into the forest. When Kylee was ill it was pure joy for Hail to have the two girls in her home. Although Kylee slept day and night, she began to feel a binding affection toward her. And Taynee, well, that young lady always held a place in her heart, ever since she was a snot-nosed kid running wild and tagging after her brothers. She would miss Taynee and her numerous visits and willing ear. She always listened intently to Hail's tales of her early life in Richmond, Virginia and how she came to meet Jay. Tonight the memories flooded her mind like the flutter of bird's wings.

Hail's father had inherited the faith healing powers from his mother. To further his healing abilities they sent him to college to study medicine. After a few years he decided to become a naturopath. He met and married a young lady of considerable wealth and social standing.

When the War Between the States broke out, having no sympathy for the North and opposed to slavery also, he refused to pick sides. His wife agreed with his stand as a conscientious objector. Willingly she gave up their home and belongings. Taking her twelve-year-old daughter, Hail, she went into hiding with her husband. They decided to go west and headed for Pound Gap and the Cumberland's.

Hail told Taynee many times of the experiences they had crossing the war torn battleground that Virginia had become. They helped deserters from both sides. Her father doctored and made well the wounded that had been left behind. They became friends with families left without fathers and husbands, the homeless, and destitute. In return the people they befriended helped them on their journey and kept their whereabouts a secret.

On a farm road near Polaski they met up with Jay, his wife Sarah, and their two small sons, Rueben James, and Blaine. They became aware of their mutual intentions, to hide from the armies. Jay promised Dr. White that there was no place in the world more remote than the Blue Ridge. Desperately in need of money, Jay persuaded him to buy a portion of Tandy's Mountain.

Hail grew sad thinking of her mother and sweet Sarah. She remembered clearly the tender gentleness of her mother and how the humidity and dampness added to her fatal deep rasping cough. Neither her father's medical knowledge nor the healing secrets of faith could save her. Her mother longed for the sea breeze and the beautiful home and things she left behind in Richmond. But if they returned she knew for certain that her husband would be hanged for treason. Giving up her desire for life she mourned herself into the grave. Her father and mother both lay to rest now side by side on the slope of the mountain behind the cabin.

Since her father's death, Hail's life had become one of bitter loneliness. Moving back to a town was a horror she would never consider. She still remembered too well the panic and terror of the war torn cities. For her, they held no glamour. Enough! Enough! Enough of memories and dwelling in the past! She turned and went inside, crawled into bed and fell into a restless dream filled sleep.

Her dreams were of Kylee and when she lay ill. Then she was a little girl running barefoot among the shadows of the pines, her happy laughter rippling through the tall trees. Then she was huddled on the ground in the cold, all alone and helpless. She was reaching with outstretched arms crying for Hail to come help her. Hail would run and run holding out her arms to enfold her into their safety. Then Jay would come between them. Rising up from the blackness was a dark figure blocking her. Here he was, as always, interfering in her dreams. But then, he was there also in the reality of life jumbling up her mind in every waking moment of the day.

A heavy clap of thunder brought her suddenly awake. Her entire body was wet with a cold sweat. Realizing she had been dreaming she returned to sleep and dreams. There again Jay leered at her laughing triumphantly. He reached out toward her with a torch trying to set her gown on fire. She awoke again, this time with an extreme feeling of panic. Somewhere beyond her dreams was the braying of a mule. Was Dr. Jekyll back? Then underneath the loud sound was the unmistakable neigh of a horse in panic. The sounds were real. She was dreaming no more!

Smoke! Quickly she rose to check the fire or a lamp she might have left burning. Aghast, she fell back onto the bed as a spurt of flames traveled up the door curtain and encased the doorway blocking her way. The leaping flames hissed and roared into the room. Flying sparks spewed around her falling on the bed. Slow to catch fire, they lay in smoldering spots upon the covers. A hideous odor of burning feathers converged with the stifling fumes of smoke. The patches burst slowly into flaming spears surrounding her and began to move creeping up the walls reaching toward the window. The dry logs and planking crackled loudly as the blaze intensified. The room became encased with fire and smoke.

Filled with terror Hail tried to keep rational and free herself before the smoke overpowered her. If she didn't get out, she would become a suffocating mass of humanity. She would turn into a pile of burning rubble along with her home. She had to get out! Large pieces of burning rubbish embedded in the wide braid hanging down Hail's back and hissed loudly as it burst into a searing flame. Screaming in agony Hail snatched a pillow and slapped it at her head until the flames died. She was fast losing her control and becoming irrational with pain and fear. Her flannel gown began to burn in spurts from the flying sparks. From somewhere far away she could hear screams then realized they were her own. The smoke was filling her lungs and she was gasping in coughing wheezes trying to get her breath.

"Get out! Get out!" her driving voice screeched. "Hurry, hurry. Get out the window!"

To get out of the burning building was imperative. She snatched the Bible from the shelf above the smoldering bed and began pounding at the window heedless of the flying glass. She jumped from the window onto the vine-covered hillside. Her gown was burning in flames around the bottom and on the sleeves. With enough presence of mind left to think survival, she rolled over and over in the soft ground cover. As the flames subsided she began to pull herself away from the flaming inferno. She struggled to free herself from what would surely be her fiery grave. She was in increasing pain and unable to hear the loud cursing upon the still night. The screeching voice rose above the crackling of the fire and filled the night.

"Damn you to hell, you old witch! That's the last of you! You'll not heckle Jay Bird Mitchell no more! No more!"

The only street in Donkey was short, dusty, and folded into silence this sultry day of early May as Tom rode in. The morning promised to become hot before his errands were done. Jan Stewart had given Ira a lead on a man looking for a job and it was decided that Tom would be the one to look him up. When he inquired at Traces he found out the man had taken Polly into Gladeville.

"They'll be back before evenin', Tom. Polly just had to have a new gown. Claimed she didn't have anything exceptin' rags. You know how gals are? They're bound to have their own way. I wasn't about to let her go alone; there's been too many incidents with outlaws on the road lately. Doesn't seem that Tanner's too concerned. I've heard that Talt Hall's workin' the area. That alone was a warnin' to me. So I trusted Simeon to take Polly over to Gladeville so's she could do her shoppin'." Trace informed Tom reaching across the bar to pour Tom a drink as he talked.

"I'd say the man seems to be a fair sort, about thirty five, I'd say. Clean an' proud of the way he keeps himself. You wouldn't have any problems that way. Been helpin' me around here an' Ben over at the livery some. Knows a lot about blacksmithin'."

"Sounds like someone I'd like to talk to. Paw's lookin' for a hand to help with the crops an' other things around the place. There wasn't enough to do; Paw had to add to it by plantin' corn an' tobac. He thinks he's gonna make a plantation out'a the mill. He's been workin' our heads off. Thinks it's helpin' us forget about Billy." Tom paid for the drink.

Tom looked at Trace thoughtfully, his vibrant blue eyes earnestly serious. Behind the blue ponds of ice Trace could see almost a twinkle of mirth and laughter at Ira's attempt to make a crop business at the mill.

"There's a more suitable way isn't there Tom? He could sell some of that timber off that piece I heard he bought from Will Tackett. Seems to me that would be more practical. Ira ain't in need for money anyways, is he Tom?" Trace inquired, polishing some glasses that were draining on a bar towel.

"There ain't no practical for Paw when it comes to that piece of ground. There ain't no explainin' the things he does sometimes. That property is already took care of. I don't think anyone could get a hold of a stick of that timber." Tom answered his question, but avoided any speculation about Ira's money situation. The hint of laughter deep in the pools of blue was beginning to spark a touch of disappointment. Tom was disturbed at his failure to pick up the hired hand.

"Have you gave any more thought, Tom, on puttin' your bid in for Marshal Snow's job? Ain't anyone said anything about runnin' against Hensely. You know he's a wantin' that job pretty bad, enough to kill for it. We ain't never gonna get any decent law in the hills if that happens. He'd probably put Jay in for his deputy." A look of disgust crossed Trace's face and he watched Tom closely.

"I haven't gave it too much thought, Trace. I been a thinkin' that deal with Blaine might hurt my chances. Folks don't want a murderer protectin' them."

Trace laid his head back and the laughter rolled. "That's a laugh. That's the funniest thing I ever heard. If that would lose you the election, Hensely would never make it. The way everyone sees it Tom, that was something you couldn't help. At least you're honest. That's more than I can say for Tanner. I think the folks would feel better about the situation Tom, if you were married. Ain't it about time you were settlin' down?" Trace caught his breath and looked at the younger man seriously, thinking about Tom's attention to Polly.

"I know Ira's a good Republican. He'd give you plenty of help. That's what we need, more good strong Republicans!" Trace informed him.

"Well, I'll think more about it. Right now time's a wastin'. Reckon you could send that man, you said his name's Simeon, on up to the mill? That is if he's interested in the job." Tom changed the subject back to getting a hired hand.

"Sure Tom. I think he'll be a good man for you. Only one thing I forgot to tell you, he's a Negro. Would that matter to Ira? Could be he's a hidin' from the KKK. You know Tom we-uns ain't had many of them colored folks up here. They don't seem to like the mountains.

We don't know much about the hardships an' tribulations they put up with." He leaned closer over the bar to look into Tom's face.

Trace saw the starch come into Tom's backbone. A sudden cloudiness covered the blue of Tom's eyes making his expression hard to read.

"Why didn't you come out an' say so in the first place, Trace?"

"I reckon I don't think about Simeon bein' a different color then we-uns. Maybe I had the wrong idea when I thought it wouldn't matter to you-ins. It's for sure most folks got their minds plum set against him," Trace went on cautiously setting down the glass he had been drying.

Backing away he rubbed his thick mustache with the back of his hand smoothing it away from his full upper lip. He watched the man from Pound Mountain with careful scrutiny. He wouldn't agree for Simeon to go anywhere if he weren't treated right.

"I don't know, Trace. Paw's purty bull-headed about some things. Don't really think he'd have any cause to turn a man down 'cause of the color of his skin. He sure don't do anything cause someone else does or doesn't. I reckon he'd let him prove himself. He'd have to stay away from the women folk on the mountain though." Tom's blue eyes narrowed in thought.

Trace looked at him with a peculiar light in his eyes. The whiskey red on his cheeks and nose deepened and spread across his face.

"I reckon it's left up to the women some, Tom. If they keep their place, I reckon Simeon would respect that," Trace growled, looking at the other man with hostility. "Trouble with most men, they's twisted with their thinkin'. They's sure every black's out to get him a white woman. Thinkin' that way makes a white man dog-gone cautious. In fact, it makes them imagine all kinds of things."

"Well, all I can tell you is, send him on up. He can talk to paw. Would you do that, Trace? I gotta head on out. I want to get back on the mountain before dark. I have to go across to Ben's an order some iron an' other things we need to come up on the supply wagon. I got a letter of Kylee's an' one for paw to go out in the mail. I'll see you Trace. Tell Polly I'll be by again. She better stay at home an' quit her gallivantin'." Tom smiled and with a lift of his hand was gone.

Tom walked out into the bright sunshine. He was thinking seriously about the conversation with Trace. Blinking his eyes he tried to adjust them to the startling change of light. He crossed the street to the livery to finish up his business. A magnitude of bird songs filled the day as he rode out of town. He pondered over the notion to stop at Jennings, but canceled the thought. He let Jole' set the pace. The blonde horse nibbled at the tender grass at the side of the road. The dream of being sheriff ran through his mind. He didn't know if he could handle the job and please the people or not. One thing he knew for sure, he was definitely on the side of law and order, a thing that had been pretty much alien to these parts.

By the time he reached the turn off to Hail's, before reaching the Stewart's, the day was beginning to gray. A rose hue settled around the sun spreading to the tops of the trees that whiskered the mountains. Tom shared his saddle with a box of medical supplies that he held securely between his knees. He assured Ben it would be no problem to ride around by Hail's. He would spend the night and deliver the package. It would save her a trip to town. He hadn't seen Hail since they buried Taynee. He remembered her dramatic insistence that Jay would never let Taynee rest on Phelps land. Much to Tom's surprise, there had been no sign of Mitchell's, as far as he knew.

Tom was amazed at the color of the forest and was in wonder at the entanglement of new growth. There were groves of young trees and large quilt patches of budding rhododendron that would be alive with lavender blossoms when June came and would stand twice his height. Running carpeting of crepe myrtle and colorful wisteria that covered the ground and tree trunks alike were encasing rocks and sheltering fallen trees as it grew.

He felt a reverent awe for the beauty of the mountains. The vibrant green of new foliage caused him to reflect on Kylee's beautiful eyes, misted with tears that day under the mulberry tree. She had very carefully avoided any contact with him since. They had ingeniously kept their hostilities hidden from his father. Besides Tom knew whose side he would be on.

Ira spoiled the young woman with parental blindness. He could have done no more for her if she had been his own daughter. Just today he sent a letter to the mail order house for a sewing machine for Kylee. A sewing machine, of all things! Tom almost swallowed his tonsils thinking of such an unnecessary extravagance. He recalled the lectures he still listened to because of Jole'. His father had also bought her a horse, a little red sorrel mare she promptly named Tempest because of its spirited nature. Kylee immediately convinced the horse that she was boss and the horse obeyed her every whim.

Cautiously, he rubbed the small cut across his nose where the button had struck. A hard irritating scab was forming over the top. If he would not pick it, perhaps it would heal without leaving a scar. An old ditty Ira used to sing came to mind, 'it'll never get well if ya pick it'; he smiled to himself.

Man, the little hussy sure has a temper. Who would have thought it of such a mild mannered person as Kylee? Might just as well quit thinking of her. As far as she was concerned, he didn't exist.

"We'd better quit day-dreamin' old girl. Guess we've taken it easy long enough. It'll be dark before we reach Hail's," he said out loud to his horse looking to the sky.

Above his head through the thick trees the rosy dusk was turning a dismal purple. Large fluffy amber clouds floated in the sky tinged with purple and gray. The soft shadows around the pines were dispersing a harmony of darkness in the forest glades. Fused with the darkening colors around the clouds, the grimness emanated the promise of a storm.

"That looks like a shower comin'. If Polly had been at the tavern, we'd a spent the night there. Maybe all I'm a needin' is a bit of warm flesh. Sure need somethin' to get me out'a these dull-drums." Tom confided out loud to Jole'. But his inward feelings were still in turmoil over Kylee.

He watched the purple and gray engulf the amber clouds until the dusk was more than a promise of night. Rolling into the darkness was a low rumble of thunder behind the mountains. A sheet of lightening brightened the black around the tall pines. Patting Jole' on the neck he comforted the horse from the impending storm and urged her into a swinging trot.

"Sure as shootin', we're in for a storm. You take it easy. Everythin'll be fine. Easy! Easy!" He cautioned the big mare softly, holding the reins firmly as he urged the horse into a slow trot up the mountain.

Tom found Hail lying in the dense underbrush behind the heap of smoldering rubble that was the remainder of the cabin. A definite odor of fire had filled his nostrils as he rounded the bend that led to Hail's. He was certain the interplay of flashing lights in the sky above the trees was not caused from the storm alone. The rain had started in raging sheets of water. The deluge did not come in time to save the cabin, but had prevented the mountain from being engulfed in a flaming forest fire.

Hail felt the rain in her face as she lay in a bed of wet vine, her father's Bible clutched tightly in her hand. She had escaped the blazing inferno through the window by breaking the glass and hurtling herself upon the ground. Crazed from pain and terror, she crawled through the dense brush away from the burning mass until she succumbed into intense shock and lay in a crumpled heap on the ground where Tom found her.

She faintly heard someone calling her name. In her state of shock, she was too weak to move or call out. She needed to cough but her throat was too parched and dry. Her gown smoldered in puffs of smoke as the rain doused the flames with sharp hissing, soaking what was left of Hail's garment. Her silver hair had burned to crisp chunks that dropped off in globs from her scalp. Her brows and lashes were seared. The drenching rain made rivulets down her charred face leaving burnt red streaks of skin. She could hear someone calling her name again. She tried to answer but only a rasping groan came from her cracked lips. Her body was an endless weight as she tried to raise herself. Calling upon the mercy of the Lord to save her, she fell back exhausted and trusted her fate to Him.

When Tom rode up to the still burning cabin his first thoughts were of Hail. He prayed to God that she had not been trapped in that flaming inferno. Then above the rain and the crackling of the fire, he thought he heard a moan.

"Oh Lord, let it be Hail," he prayed out loud.

The glow of the remaining fire spread a wide range of light and Tom began his search for Hail. He found her lying in the heavy wet vines, her gown still smoldering. The puffs of smoke enabled Tom to find her. He was shocked and frightened at the blackened heap of humanity lying in the grass. The torrents of rain had drenched the outside of his suit jacket but the inside was reasonably dry. He wrapped it carefully around the unconscious woman. Tom could see her struggling to breathe and hoped he could get her home before she gave up.

When the rain started, Ira began a list of complaints, claiming the dampness caused his moveable parts to ache increasingly. He said goodnight to Kylee and went to bed. Matt, in a sullen grieving mood had saddled his horse earlier in the evening and ridden to Stewart's to spend the night. He longed to visit with Jan and Alvin. Perhaps talk them into a card game.

Depressed with the rain and dismal evening Kylee had gone to her room and prepared for bed. Settled deep in her pillow she listened to the thunder and watched the play of lightening flash through the window over her head until she drifted off to sleep. She was awakened suddenly in the night by a loud thumping on the front door.

"Hurry, someone! Matt, Kylee, open the door! Hurry!" Tom yelled at the house kicking the door sharply with the toe of his boot.

Hearing the urgency in his voice, Kylee rose quickly, put on her robe and hurried to the front door. There was no recognition of the crumpled, disfigured bundle in Tom's arms.

"It's Hail, Kylee. There's been a fire. She's burned badly."

"Take her to my bed." Kylee ordered calmly, her voice firm. "What happened? How could such a thing happen?"

"Her cabin caught on fire. Could have been from the lightnin'. I'm thankin' God I came by in time. She must have jumped from the window." Tom told Kylee as he tenderly unwrapped the wet jacket and dropped it to the floor. His wet clothing left a trail of water and was dripping a puddle on the rug at the side of Kylee's bed.

"She's burnt real bad Kylee, but she's still breathin', isn't she?" Tom questioned and laid his ear down on her chest hoping to catch a fragment of movement. Kylee pulled him back gently.

"We need to take care of her. Quickly Tom, get the water boiling. Dump the box of tea into the big kettle and pour the boiling water over it and let it steep while I undress her. Bring it to me. Hurry now! I'll get some strips of cloth. We'll make her comfortable as we can. She's still breathin'. Perhaps her strong will an' faith will keep her goin'. Hurry now!" She pushed Tom out the bedroom door.

Kylee covered Billy's old raincoat with a sheet and stretched it underneath Hail. She began carefully cutting away the charred and drenched gown. At this point she pushed Tom aside.

"Go change into something dry. You're soaked to the skin. You'll sure catch your death, now get! I'll get her gown off. When I do, she ain't gonna want no man gawkin' at her. Sides, you're drippin' all over the floor." Her voice was tender but set with decision.

"What's the matter with you Kylee? I ain't gonna be gawkin' at her! I want to help." Tom had about had it with this bossy woman.

"I can do it. If I want you, I'll let you know. I can handle her. They ain't nothin' to her, know-how." She picked up the drenched jacket as she spoke and handed it to Tom easing him out the door. Then she remembered what he'd been through this night. She smiled at him warmly. It was the first time since the day under the mulberry tree.

"You have done your part. You saved her life. Now, let me get her well."

Tom was weary. The night's event had shaken him. Hail had always been one of his favorite people. He had been more than concerned at the way he found her. There was a deep dark nagging in the back of his mind. He felt there was more than lightening responsible for the kindling of the fire. There was not a sign of Mitchell as he brought her down Tandy's Mountain.

Kylee's sudden smile removed the chill from his body and set his heart pounding. Could it be possible that she had forgiven him? He felt hope for Hail and a deeper, and this time a carefully guarded, longing for Kylee.

CHAPTER SIX

The rock fireplace was beginning to crumble. It was gray and somber above the wet mound, the remainder of Hail's home. The black pot hanging over the outside fire pit was the only tangible thing left. The murky heap was a grim reminder of the fate Hail had so narrowly escaped. The rain had been complete in making a soggy mess of the ashes. Underneath the mulch, as Tom stirred the rubble with a long stick, the fire still smoldered. His lips tightened as he lifted the rim of the wheel left from the buggy that Hail stored under the cabin.

He searched in vain for some sign that would tell him what had caused the fire. Or some evidence to indicate that a person had started the blaze. Still cultivating the idea in his mind, that Jay was to blame. But he could find nothing. Once the fire had started, the wind served as a giant bellows and fanned it into a raging inferno. The rain had been merciful, a lifesaver for Hail. It had come too late to save the cabin or the lean-to of a barn. The animals had scattered into the woods. Tom became discouraged looking at the ruins. He turned to stare at his brother. A cloud of anger stormed his pale blue eyes.

Matt sat on Hail's chopping block waiting for Tom. He was absently stirring the wood chips at his feet with the heel of his boot. As he stared across the road into the thick trees, his thoughts were on Taynee. How wonderful their meetings had been in the grove lower on the hill. Thoughts of her soft arms around him and the touch of her long fingers on the back of his neck caused his heart to thump. Everything about her had been wonderful. The soft petal smoothness of her full red lips was a thrill he would never forget. He loved everything about her. Most of all, he loved the deep blue violet of her magnificent eyes that told him with a sultry glance of her undying love. The desire for her once again became a throbbing pain. Waiting for Tom and dreaming of his sweetheart made him vow to himself that he would never love again.

But Matt had not yet learned that life has a way of healing our wounds. The young are made for loving, not grieving. Time would fill the gap left from Taynee's death and Matt would love again. Perhaps it would not be with the fiery passion he'd felt for Taynee, but a tender consuming love; turning the memory of his first love into a cherished event of youth. Now the grief was too new, too real, too deeply felt. The agonizing loss was too much to endure. Right now the only thing that helped smother the ache in his heart was cultivating his hate for Jay Mitchell. He found himself nursing the hatred with venom. It was the only thing that made his life worth living. From somewhere across the yard Tom's voice broke into his reverie.

"Come on Matt, you ain't been nary a bit a good to no one lately," Tom called to his brother. He walked over to an object lying in the long grass and found it to be Hail's box of medical supplies. With his concern for her, he forgot that he had dropped it there.

"You don't understand, Tom. There ain't no understandin' in you," Matt answered, standing up and stretching, but still gazing off into the trees.

"I understand one thing. You gotta snap out'a this broodin'." Tom understood his grief but not his lack of cooperation. "They's other things to live for."

"There's only one thing for me to live for now, that's to kill Mitchell's!"

"We-uns'll see to that. But first things first! Let's get Hail well first. She's in purty bad shape, Matt. A time will come for killin' Mitchell's, soon!" Tom promised, coming up to him and placing a hand on his shoulder in a brotherly gesture. "I'm sorry about Taynee, 'Bub', real sorry."

For some reason the old nick-name, 'Bub' came easy to Tom's tongue. It was the first time he'd used it in a long while. A new closeness developed between them since the trial. Tom felt it and so did Matt. The desire for the old conflict was lessening and a new warm affection was growing. There was a bond between them drawing them closer together. Perhaps it was losing Billy that had made them realize how important brothers were.

Tom watched Hail as she recovered slowly. Her head had been seared bald, eyebrows and lashes gone. Her face was scarred hideously along the hairline down her cheeks and across her chin and neck. Strong lovely hands had been exposed viciously to the flames. They were burned so badly that Kylee feared there was no possible way to save the flesh on her fingers.

Kylee very tenderly spread the burned areas with the wet tea leaves, a technique she learned from her father. Holding them carefully in place with long strips she tore from old shirts or sheets. Remembering Hail's faith, she knelt and prayed. She felt a calming peaceful quietude and knew her prayer would be answered, certain with new found faith and sureness that Hail would be healed. When the leaves dried and had drawn the fire from the burns, Kylee replaced them carefully with fresh wet ones. This would preserve the precious moisture beginning to form on the surface of the burns. After days of stripping the fiery burns they began to whiten and blisters began to appear. Kylee stopped the ritual and left the burns exposed.

As the liquid began to ooze, she carefully spread the areas with blackstrap molasses. For the first time in a long while she remembered the day her father told her the news that he had promised her to Kenus. The thick brown syrup formed a protective coating to hold the healing liquid under the skin. Kylee watched closely as the moisture from the syrup absorbed into the skin and the air began to dry the blisters. Then she began to bathe Hail letting the clear warm water run freely over the burns and rinsing away the dried molasses. Each day Kylee changed the bed, washed and dried the bedding so there would be fresh linen for the next day.

Hail soon rallied from her unconsciousness and silently cooperated with each step of nursing Kylee performed. After washing away the last of the sticky syrup, Kylee covered Hail's naked body with a soft cotton sheet, leaving the burns to heal in the air. When the dry scabs began to form, she smoothed on a mixture of eucalyptus oil and warm mutton tallow. The lanolin from the tallow and the healing oil softened the brown scales and kept them from cracking and bleeding. The long process took days. The days grew into weeks.

Then one day Kylee dressed Hail in a soft flannel gown and hoped that after days of relentless struggle she would be willing to have company. But Hail, knowing the horrible extent of her burns covered her head with the blanket and emphatically refused to see anyone. No amount of coaxing could convince her. She was ashamed and horrified at her disfigurement; frightened at the nightmare she had become and wished out loud that she were dead.

"Now Hail, I ain't gonna let you talk that way. It ain't no good! You're alive ain't you? I ain't gonna let you speak such things. How do you think Tom would feel if he heard you talkin' that way? After he saved you an' all! Do you want him to feel that it was all for nothin'?" Kylee reprimanded her. "The good Lord didn't aim for you to die yet. He has work for you to do." Kylee continued encouraging her with a bright smile.

"The Lord is punishing me for hatin' Jay so fiercely. If you want the Lord's forgiveness, you must be forgivin'. Only Kylee, I can't find it in my heart to forgive Jay for his dastardly meanness. We are not supposed to judge no one, not in our heart or mind. I have been his judge for a long time an' I want to see him dead!" Hail told Kylee through cracked and blistered lips.

"I will never believe He would punish you for hatin' someone as hateful as Jay Mitchell. The folks here abouts need you, Hail. Who would take care of the birthin's, an' hurt animals, an' the youngins if anythin' happened to you?" Kylee comforted her as she watched Hail cover her head with the bed quilt and turn her face to the wall.

"Who would want the likes of me around? I'd scare the little ones to death!" Hail's muffled voice came from under the cover. Sobs of despair wracked her slight body. Her eyes burned from the burning scalding tears she could not shed.

"I want you! You'll stay here with me. It's my turn to care for you." Kylee remembered how Hail had made her foot well.

She pushed back the quilt and kissed the top of Hail's scarred head. She fluffed up the pillows and gently eased her back against the softness. Kylee straightened the coverlets and would not let the woman recover her head.

"You are a sweet child an' have the heart of an angel. I am not deserving of such attention." Hail smiled weakly. Her eyes filled with a deep happiness as she looked at Kylee. She knew life would go on in spite of her ugliness and hate for Jay, but she continued to confess to Kylee.

"I am not worthy, Kylee. I cannot be a vessel for the healing powers. I have lived my life without forgiveness or mercy. Everyday has been filled with bitterness an' hate. I have had the desire everyday an' night to kill Jay Mitchell. God's word tells us if we live with the desire in our hearts to do the deed, it is as good as done. My father passed the power to me. I was to cherish it an' live accordin' to His word. Keep it safe so I could pass it on to my son. The Lord has taken that away from me. I'll never have a child least of all a son. Oh, He is punishin' me for my wicked thoughts an' deeds! If you don't believe me, just look at me! The secrets of the healin' will go with me to my grave."

"That ain't so, Hail. It's Jay Mitchell who's gonna be punished. Besides you ain't goin' to your grave for a long time!"

Hail grew stronger each day but still refused to mingle with the family. Kylee tied a bright red cotton scarf around her scarred head, gypsy style and hoped she would change her mind. Instead Hail took up with the animals of the forest. They didn't care how she looked she told Kylee. She created a world of her own deep in the shadows of the pines. She told herself she had forgotten Jay. But he was always there, a black shadow lurking in her subconscious during the days and haunting her sleepless nights with dark dreams.

Simeon appeared riding on a freight wagon. Ira hired him even after Matt's return. He was confident they would be in need of an extra pair of hands.

"What's your name?" Ira questioned the man.

"Simeon Niger, sir. Simeon Niger, Ezekiel, Nicodemus, Jonah, Luke, Elias, Zachariah, Jacob, Isaac." The string of names was his answer.

"That's a name?" Ira was stunned. "That sounds more like an affliction to me."

"Yes, sir. My mom told me they was all from the Bible an' I should respect each one! All them ten names was 'cause my pap had a whopping bad temper. She said I was bound to come by it naturally. She had a plan, when I'd get mad she figured I could start sayin' my name. By the time I got to the end I'd forget why I was mad. Kinda like countin' to ten," Simeon explained seriously to Ira with a wide grin that occupied his face.

"You look to be plenty strong, Simeon Niger, strong enough to do what I'd need you for. If so, the job's yours."

Simeon became an accepted part of their days at the mill. Kylee's sewing machine, along with bundles of fabric arrived much to her surprise and joy. The air was filled with the sound of the treadle as she sewed. New curtains for the kitchen, dish and hand towels amazingly piled up. Sheets and pillow coverings developed that had been desperately needed. Ira was always willing to see that she had anything her heart desired to keep her sewing. She even invited Mary to come share her wondrous gift. The girls sewed and talked, laughed, giggled, shared secrets, and developed an undying friendship.

Hail wandered the forest alienating herself from the family until Kylee became angry at her complete withdrawal. She scolded her soundly and insisted she must at least take the evening meal with them. Hail finally, to please Kylee, consented. She tied her bright scarf around her head and prepared to be part of a world of staring eyes.

The family was delighted at her appearance. Matt and Tom told her how glad they were she had decided to come back to them. They chided her unmercifully for staying away and preferring the company of animals to theirs. Hail only looked at them with wide eyes, eyes that silently pleaded with them to not stare at her scarred face. She slid down in her chair wishing for a hiding place and sorry she had listened to Kylee's insistence. If she got through this meal she would return to eating in Kylee's room.

Ira smiled fondly at the woman. He waited for Tom and Matt to quit talking then addressed Hail who was crouched down in her chair trying to hide behind Kylee. A deep lingering affection spread flashing blue lights in his eyes.

"How come you're all hunkered down behind Kylee, Hail?" His voice was warm and tinged with a hint of teasing. "I'm aware of what you're lookin' like. It don't bother me a speck! Sit up here; let's get a better look at you! Hunchin' down in your chair like that's gonna get your cornbread all wadded up in your middle. We have been friends too long to let looks come between us. Ain't that so, boys?" Ira looked seriously at Hail's scarred face. His voice became firm and his blue eyes filled with deep compassion for her misery. The boys nodded their heads agreeing emphatically.

"I know all about bein' different. It gets easier as time goes by. You begin to get used to it. You ain't got nothin' to be afear'd of Hail. I want to take care of you! I've been a hankerin' for you a long time, Hail. Now we are both crippled up an' lonely. The lonely's the worst thing. I ain't much of a man to offer a woman, so I never asked before. Thought maybe you'd not have me. I didn't want you to take me out of pity. Didn't want you to be burdened with a cripple, you bein' so sweet an' all. Any man would a been darn proud to have you! Could you find it in your heart to take a chance on me now, Hail?" Ira questioned her, the twinkle back in his eyes.

"Financially, I'm well fixed," he went on. When he received no response from the woman, he continued, "but you know that, Hail. We could take care of each other. You could help me spend some of my money instead of me leavin' it for the youngin's to squander. Every pot needs a lid Hail. I been without one too long. You're just as beautiful to me now as you ever was. Beauty's only skin deep. It's that old ugly that goes to the bone, if you let it. We ain't gonna let that happen, are we Hail?"

"We could build your cabin back. That is the boys could with Simeon to help. Quicker than scat they could do it. But I ain't never gonna let you go back to livin' on Tandy's Mountain where Jay can get to you again. We both know, don't we Hail, it was Jay that set

451

your house on fire. You hear me woman? I'm a talkin' at you?" His tenderness toward her was turning to exasperation at her uncaring attitude. He leaned forward across the table in agitation.

Hail finally raised her clouded gooseberry eyes to look at Ira. He saw the hostility there and wondered if he had spoken in haste and been too demanding.

"Oh Ira, how come you waited 'til now when you're a feelin' pity for me, how come?" her voice was acid bitter. "I'd been so happy to have known sooner. It never mattered to me how you was! I couldn't push myself on you, that wouldn't be proper. You think now that I can believe you'd want me just for me? The way I look I'd always know you were only feelin' sorry for me. I don't think I could ever believe that you wanted me because you had love for me. Sides, I can never be at peace anywhere as long as Jay's alive. That wicked man has got to be destroyed! I'll not promise anything until it's done."

"I promised to get rid of that no good bastard for you a long time ago, the offer still stands. I want him dead too, for you an' for me!" Ira told her bitterly. A deep longing fired in his eyes as he looked at Hail.

"I cain't never be happy long as he lives!" Her eyes were jade spheres, drifting in a pond of unshed tears.

Hail looked directly at Ira a deep love, long hidden, shining through the water barricade. They were far away in a world of their own. A deep memory they shared together remained unmentioned, still secret.

Tom, Matt, and Kylee's presence at the table was forgotten as far as Hail and Ira were concerned. The three listened and watched in stupefied silence.

The burns on Hail's thin hollow cheeks and body were healing but the dark scabs were dry and ugly. She insisted it would be better to wait for them to fall off naturally and rubbed them diligently with tallow and oil. She was aware that the odor of the mutton tallow was not a rare perfume. The area behind the scabs showed red against the pallor of her skin. She continued to converse with Ira.

"It's been most twelve years since dear Mattie died. I could have been helpin' with the boys. It's too late now Ira. I ain't any good to no one! Not even myself. Oh dear God, I just want to die!" Hail's words came out in a stifled sob as she pushed her chair back from the table and ran out the door, down the stairs, and across the yard. She ran around the millpond and disappeared into the mass of trees.

Tom jumped up intending to follow her. Ira reached to detain him with a touch of his hand.

"No son, let her go. She'd not take lightly to your meddlin'. She needs some time." His eyes followed Hail's disappearing form and bright scarf. He was not encouraged by her attitude and felt a stone weight in his heart.

"How come Paw, you never let her know how you felt? Maw was dead. We sure could have used a woman around here. I'd a welcomed Hail," Tom questioned his father accusingly, remembering with regret the years without a mother.

"What you talkin' about son? I was grievin' for your Maw! I never had a thought about another woman. I had no idea Hail cared for me. We were only friends, dear friends. Besides, she swore to your maw an' me that she'd never wed no man. She was so beautiful with her silver hair an' sad lovely eyes. She didn't want to share her lonely life with anyone. I was gettin' more crippled up each year. Who'd a thought anyone so lovely could want to share a bed with the likes of me? When she was young, she was the most beautiful woman I had ever laid my eyes on, with her flame hair an' green eyes. She could a had any man in the hills at that time. She only had eyes for one, but that was not to be. Then she got to be so dog-gone independent after her father died. Now it's too late! Let that be a lesson to you son. If you want something or someone let it out, go get it! Don't wait until it's too late!" Ira thought of the years after Mattie's death when he had longed for Hail silently.

Taking his father's advice seriously, Tom looked at Kylee with desire deep in his eyes wondering if there was any way he could get her to return his look. He wanted to make her realize that time was getting away from them. But she only avoided his eyes and was turning her understanding smile on Ira.

"She must love you a lot, Uncle Ira. Give her a little time. Wait until she's well. Things will look different to her then. She's been through a lot. You'll see. You both need someone an' have lots of years to share ahead of you. I'll stay right here an' take care of you both!" Kylee promised sincerely.

She felt Tom's stare and became nervously uncomfortable as he kept his eyes fastened on her. She backed away from the table and began clearing the dishes, hoping to divert his penetrating gaze. He continued to watch her with clear, piercing blue eyes. His unwavering gaze completely unnerved her. Picking up an egg basket on the counter, she went out to the hen house to gather eggs.

The summer heat had become intense and Ira hoped for rain, but there were no signs, even the dew was scarce. He watched the tips of the corn turn brown and the tobacco leaves curl thinking perhaps he had chosen the wrong year to plant a crop. So concerned over Hail's recovery he had put off any whiskey deals. Perhaps they could be saddled with a crop failure. He decided they had better at least pick up the whiskey they had buried, but not forgotten. He announced his intent as the family sat on the porch enjoying the cool of the evening.

Hail, unconcerned, rocked to and fro on the porch swing watching the darting fireflies. Simeon sat on the bottom step away from the group as he respectfully thought was fitting for a hired hand, least-ways a Negro. The only reason he was there at all was because 'Mista Ira' had insisted he join them. Simeon's place was a room they had built inside the mill which was where he spent most of his spare time.

Tom perched lazily on the top rail of the porch. Matt sprawled on the floor leaning against the house. He sat close to where Kylee sat on a bench next to Ira, whom she had grown to adore. Matt watched her closely as she reached to kiss her uncle affectionately on the cheek and pat his head fondly. Ira waited until they were all quietly busy with their own thoughts to spring the plan on them.

"It has gotta be done! We-uns are gonna get that whiskey out'a that hole on the mountain behind Gladeville. Heard a bit of news in town when Matt an' I was a pickin' up Kylee's sewin' machine. Talt Hall has been arrested in Tennessee. They're a bringin' him back to Wise County to stand trial for the crimes he has committed here abouts. Hensely'll be busy guardin' him. He won't dare take his eyes off that one. 'Sides, they was in cahoots, thicker than molasses in January, everyone knows that. Tanner ought to be in there with him. While Hensely's busy, we'll slip by him an' get our 'shine out of that hole. They'll all be occupied with the trial," Ira spoke thoughtfully, scratching his chin under his beard.

We-uns'll take that whiskey on over Pound into Kentucky. We gotta be sly about it. Snow has brought in some federal men, that he's pretty friendly with, but they'll be interested in Hall's trial. We are gonna divert their interest with a party." Ira leaned forward in his chair, the twinkle in his eyes brightened at the prospect of outsmarting the revenuers.

"It's been most a year now," he went on, "since Kylee come. She ain't see'd nothin' but sickness an' dyin'. I'm sick to death with it all. I know she is too. I'm gonna show her how we-uns can throw a shindig!"

"Billy's gone, God rest him. Tom ain't got no banjo, them bastard Mitchell's shot it up. So's will hire us some music makers. We laid the corn by an' done the last hoein' the other day. Only thing now, is watchin' it grow. Ain't time for diggin' sweet taters. It's way too early for makin' cider an' sulfurin' apples. I'd say it's time for havin' a party. The fourth of July is a good time as any," Ira rambled on, slapping his legs with an open palm and stroking his long white beard with satisfaction.

"The beans are strung an' hung to dry. The cucumbers picked, the jams an' jellies are in the jars. Kylee's been so busy carin' for all of us; she's had no time for pleasurin'. We-uns are gonna throw her a party. I want to see some happy faces around here! It's time we all quit grievin' for Billy. He would like us to have a party! Matt, I'm sick of seein' your face dark as doom's day. Maybe a party would perk you up some. Tom, you an' Simeon get the wagon ready with the false bottom. When you pick up the whiskey you can hide it between the floors. On top we'll fill it with decorations an' fixin's from Gladeville. I reckon the Walker brothers will be more than happy to play for our party. They live at the bottom of the mountain almost where you have to pick up the shine. You can spend the night with them, Tom. You can have them sittin' up there on top, a pickin' an' a grinnin'. No-one'll suspect we're a haulin' whiskey. You give

455

them boys a few drinks an' they'll be willin' for anythin'!" Ira said excitedly, his blue eyes glowing purple in the faint light coming from the kitchen window.

"Well, what do you think boys? What do you think?" Ira questioned his sons, pleased with his idea, and had forgotten Hail and their problems.

"Yah-hoo! Let's do it Paw! Let's do it!" Tom shouted jumping up.

Taking his father's wheel chair, he pushed it into a fast circle giving his father a whirling ride, almost toppling him out. Ira laughed, pleased with his son's enthusiasm, but fearing for his safety and demanded for Tom to stop. Tom put the chair back and tucked the blanket around his father's legs.

"It's the best idea you've had in a coon's age. Beat's the heck out'a hoein' corn an' tobac. A party is just what we need." Tom laughed. He felt good at the prospect of a diversion. He sang a song and stepped a dance, making a tune with his feet.

> "There was an old hen,
> She had a white foot.
> She built her a nest in a mulberry root.
> She fluffed up her feathers
> To keep herself warm.
> Another little drink won't do ya no harm..."

He reached for Kylee's hand and pulled her up from the bench, caught her in his arms, and twirled her around not letting her feet touch the floor. He continued his song as they whirled. Kylee clung onto him frantically, surprised at the sudden fling. Around the porch they went and back. Their onlookers clapped their hands and laughed at the dancers.

"It'll be great, Paw! We ain't had a party in, for-ever. When do we start?" Matt questioned, always the one to dive in headlong.

Kylee laughed breathlessly looking up at Tom. She then realized he was holding her very tightly. Their bodies were so close their hearts were as one making their own thumping rhythm. Kylee tried to pull away stretching her feet to reach the porch floor. She ducked her head and lowered her long eyelashes to cover up the joyous light in her pixie green eyes. She looked up at Tom again allowing him a glance, a veiled look, and then turned her head away in a quick movement. Tom felt her body trembling under the pressure of his arms as he held her. He caught the upward look, heavy with an emotion that puzzled him. It didn't coincide with the way she had been treating him lately. There was no mistaking the longing there. In the same instant it disappeared behind a veil of caution. He held her for a fleeting moment but she would not look at him again.

Feeling her pushing on his chest insisting to be released, he let her feet touch the porch floor and freed her. Standing in silence, he watched her open the screen door and disappear into the house. The moment of happiness was gone. He moved rapidly past his father and down the steps toward the barn. The three remaining on the porch and Simeon on the step, watched his receding back. Curious glances followed Kylee's moving shadow in the kitchen with open mouths and questioning eyes.

Jay's wounds healed without any complications, even with the intensive amount of riding he had been doing. Along with Ferrell Hall, they had organized an active band of outlaws. The young man was disappointed at the news of Taynee's death. He was curious, but Jay offered no explanation.

The outlaws were well organized and worked on a cooperation basis with Talt Hall, their ringleader. Talt had outlaws coursing the southern range of the Blue Ridge Mountains, including Kentucky, Virginia, and Tennessee. Hall was sly and cagey. Although the robbing and murders were rampant, the law had not been successful in catching him until he became careless and over confidant of his ability to fool them. He was finally detained in Tennessee. His reign as bandit king had ended. Jay was confident he could fill his shoes, at least on Pound Mountain.

The shipping of goods over Pound Mountain was becoming a steady business and the drivers on their return trip carried a tidy sum. Often drivers and wagons came up missing. It was supposed that the drivers had been murdered and probably buried, the wagons and mules taken back into Kentucky and sold. It was indeed handy to have the law, in the form of Tanner Hensely, on their side. If they could, in any way manage for him to get the position of Sheriff, it would be even sweeter. The Kentucky law was too far away.

'A real sweet set up', Jay thought. But better still was the fact that the operation was going to help him get rid of Ira Phelps and his bunch, soon. Soon! Ira would sooner or later make a trip into Kentucky. He knew it, and he would be waiting. Some way he would find out exactly when.

It hadn't taken the people of the hills long to figure out the outlaw band working Pound Mountain was tied in with the Kentucky bad man, Talt Hall. Although they hated and feared him, they often allowed him to stay in their homes. They all breathed a little easier when they found out he was in custody. They figured that Jay would take up where Hall left off. It would be a bad time in the hills.

Hensely was blind and deaf where the bandits were concerned. They paid him a neat sum, even recruited his help. He cautiously warned them that he had to be careful, as election time was coming and he could not afford to be found out. When Hall was brought to Gladeville to stand trial for crimes committed in Virginia, Hensely became even more cautious. There was no way he could help free Talt. Federal agents were all over the place. Jay and Ferrell would just have to lie low for a while.

Jay and Rueben were cooperating with Hensely's orders to keep out of sight. They spent a few days at home with Nell and the family. Ferrell was holed up in a cave on top of the mountain, close to Picket Rock with two other men. Jay became bored with his stay at home. He thought about heading back up the mountain to reactivate his life of crime, no matter what Tanner said. He was crossing the yard to find Rueben to tell him of his plan when Ferrell rode up. He informed Jay that he'd been to the Gladeville jail to visit his cousin, Talt Hall.

"You never said before, Ferrell, that the man was your cousin."

"Never thought it mattered none Jay. Wasn't first cousin's no ways. So I figured it didn't make no never mind," Ferrell retorted. He was still unhappy over Taynee and had his suspicions about Jay. For some reason, although they worked together, he could not bring himself to like the man.

"I was fixin' to head up to the rock, figurin' you was there. I cain't handle this standin' around. Figured we could stir up some sorta activity," Jay informed the younger man.

"Well, Talt's wantin' to see you, Jay. He has a business proposition for you. He wouldn't tell me what it was. Said it took face-to-face dickerin'. So's you can head on down to Gladeville."

Jay rode by Hail's without a sideward glance at the pile of rubble. Myrtle and wisteria vines had already entwined the desolate chimney. Plush green groundcover almost obliterated the mound of ashes. Having no idea Hail had survived the fire, he was satisfied the heap of cinders was her burying place. So satisfied with his new occupation, he had forgotten his driving urge to return Taynee's body to Mitchell ground. He had even forgotten the horse Tom Phelps had stolen from him. The only thought he had for Phelps's was how soon he was going to kill them all. As he turned onto Pound road he met Janice Stewart riding a big bay. Jay drew up his Morgan and spoke sociably to his neighbor.

"Mornin', Jan."

As Jay looked into Janice's nut-brown eyes a storm of memories came surging forth. The bitter hate for the Phelps's rode high on the torrent. Mary's refusal to marry Bob surged forth as runner-up.

"Runnin' into you couldn't have happened at a better time, Jan. I've been wantin' to see you," Jay announced and steadied his horse.

"Well, now Jay. I live in the same place. I reckon you'd a been welcome," Jan answered with a sardonic grin, not overjoyed at being cornered or having to be neighborly with Jay. "What was it you wanted to see me about?"

Jan took a cigar from his vest pocket, bit off the tip, and wet it with his tongue before putting it into his mouth. He struck a long match with his thumbnail and lit up. He was deliberately stalling, not particularly interested in whatever it was Jay had to talk about. He supposed it was Mary. He puffed in satisfactorily on the smoke, stretched his tall body up to sit straighter in the saddle to relax his back. His reddish crop of hair was covered with a fine wide brimmed white hat. The black hat that was popular in the hills had never been a favorite with Jan.

"Well, I guess you've heard Jan, that I'm wantin' to get my hands on that piece of ground that belongs to Will Tackett. I ain't been able to track him down. Thought you could help me out. Everyone but the Phelps tribe knows that land, by rights, ought'a be mine, 'cause its next to my place." It still irritated him that Stewart would not pressure Mary into marrying Bob.

"I can sure enough tell you where to locate Will Tackett if you're meanin' that strip of prime timber land on top of Pound?" Jan shifted his cigar, knowing full well what he meant.

"That's the one, Jan. I know'd Ira's wife was a cousin of yours. It was Baldwin's what had that land first. But you're a fair man, an' fairs, fair!" Jay smiled a crooked grin showing wide perfectly shaped white teeth.

"Well Jay, if you want to find Tackett you'll have to travel a piece. He went west some months ago. That strip of land now belongs to Mary. It was a gift to her from Ira. She's got the deed, all legal an' proper. It wouldn't be wise on your part to trifle with it."

Jan removed the cigar from his lips and held it between his long fingers as he talked and looked at Jay straight in the eye with bold fearlessness. The friendly twinkle that was usually alive in Jan's eyes was now clouded.

"Why, you damn bastard! You an' Ira done that to snicker me didn't you? You did that so's I couldn't get my hands on it! I reckon you'll sell all that timber to the Northern furniture bigwigs, an' the mineral rights too. You'll all get filthy rich! That's the deal ain't it? Ain't it?" Jay bellowed standing up in his stirrups. He was holding on the saddle horn with one hand while the other hand rested lightly on his pistol that was strapped around his long frock coat.

"There'll not be one piece of that standin' timber cut down to sell long as I'm alive!" Janice Stewart's red beard stuck out in agitation with the set of his jaw. He leaned forward in the saddle. Never! Never! He would never back down to Jay Mitchell.

Jay eased back down in his saddle, took a twist of tobacco from his coat pocket and bit off a chew, trying to calm himself when he saw the fire in Stewart's eyes. He'd back off, there was a scheme coming to life in his twisted mind.

"I'll bid you good day, Jan. I'll be talkin' to you on this matter another time. Would it be a good time for Bob to come courtin' Mary? You promised to give the boy a chance. I'm holdin' you to your word, Stewart!" Jay said in a quieter manner. But the skin on his high bony cheeks stretched tight in determination.

"It's like I told you Jay, if the lass is willin', yes. But I'll tell you one thing; you better keep him off the road! I'd never allow Mary to marry-up with an outlaw, even if she saw fit to accept the lad! She could not take another death in her life at this time. Bein' dead is where he's headin' if he's followin' up with you. I'll be seein' you Mitchell!" Jan tipped his hat. He settled his immense body into the saddle and spurred the big bay into a swift trot away from Jay leaving him red faced and fuming.

Jay sat watching Jan's receding back, thinking how easy a target he would be for his big thirty-eight. Him and that damn Ira Phelps; they had out-smarted him again. It would be the last chance they'd get! Pretty slick how they had pulled that land deal off right under his nose. He'd let him ride on for now, but there would come a time! He'd get rid of Jan along with the Phelps bunch. Then he'd see that Mary and Bob married. The land and timber would be his after all to do with as he pleased, but first things first. He would see what it was Talt Hall had on his mind. He watched Stewart turn off the road and cross the creek and disappear into the thick trees.

The heat of the day was beginning to bother Jay. He rode up to the Gladeville jail at the back of the courthouse. He dismounted, unbuckled the belt and holster from around his hips, and removed his coat. Rolling up the coat, he tied it to the back of the saddle then re-strapped the gun around his hips before he went inside out of the blazing sun. It took a moment for his eyes to adjust to the dimness inside the jail. Tanner was nowhere around. The skinny-faced deputy guarding Hall showed Jay to the cell and informed him he had exactly ten minutes.

Talt Hall was called 'the Kentucky bad man' because of his many heinous crimes. A small insignificant looking man, Jay thought, until he turned his gaze upon him. The blaze of dark eyes burned an impression on Jay's mind, one that he wouldn't easily forget. Jay expected a man of greater stature. It was the first time he had met

461

the man. All their dealings had been through Ferrell. Talt Hall was a soft-spoken, mellow mannered man. He spoke low and only when he had something of importance to say. When Jay told him who he was, he softly asked if it was possible he might have some tobacco on him. When Jay handed him a twist from his pocket, he bit off a chew and put the rest under the pillow on the cell bunk. Then he calmly stated his business with Jay.

"I'll not waste your time, or mine." Looking Jay straight in the eye, he recognized him as a man not to be trusted. But his business could be done with no one else.

"Thank you for the tobac. I understand you have had dealin's with a man on Pound Mountain by the name of Phelps." He waited for Jay's answer. When he received only a cold stare, he continued.

"I have a cousin who is looking for a girl who might be stayin' with the family. If you know of him, say so!" Talt's dark eyes flamed. He held little store by the old adage, 'honor among thieves'.

"I know of him, an' the girl," Jay growled. He was caring little for this small unimpressive man.

"You will be working close with my cousin. I promised to get the job done for him, but as you can see, I'm gonna be a little tied up," Talt laughed. "You'll find him at the hotel across the street. Just ask the clerk for Kenus Hall. He'll give you the room number. Kenus is expectin' you." Talt sat down on the bunk and dismissed Jay with a lift of the hand. The matter was closed. It was the first and last time Jay ever saw him.

Kenus sat on the edge of the bed in his hotel room, irritable, and increasingly uncomfortable. He had been determined to find Kylee but had not bargained on such a long trip. He was not going to let her get away with running off and disappearing. In his business, he had too many contacts and knew too many people. It was her father's promise that she would belong to him and he intended to have her.

When he found out Aggie and Dolf had been receiving mail from Kylee from Wise County, Virginia, it was clear what he had to do. He had seen his cousin Talt at a friend's home in the mountains at Stoney Gap. He sat stone silent, his Winchester laying threateningly across his knees. Kenus understood his outlaw territory covered into Virginia and Kentucky and that Talt would be the help he needed to find Kylee.

Talt had received the information from Ferrell of a girl that could be the one he was looking for. But before they could get the job done, Talt had been arrested. Ferrell refused to be the one to take Kylee back to Tennessee. Kidnapping was a criminal offense and he would not risk it. Kenus would have to come for her himself.

Kenus had been holed up in this hot hotel room for days. He had been waiting on Ferrell who was as slow as a terrapin in making the arrangements to steal Kylee. He was prepared to pay a handsome reward for her. Kenus was certain Talt's neck was due to stretch on Virginia hemp. He had done too many bad things to get off any other way. At least he had kept his word to help him find Kylee Bentley.

Kenus had agreed with Ferrell that Jay would be the one to get the girl from Phelps. As he waited for this Mitchell person to arrive and make their plans, he thought of how close he was to having Kylee. It had been a long time. He'd waited almost a year. The net was closing in. His passion for Kylee had never cooled. He still desired her for his bed and could not pacify himself with any other woman. Licking a wet tongue across dry lips, he breathed in deeply. Breathing was becoming difficult in the stifling room and thinking of Kylee didn't make it easier. The sight of her firm breast thrust against the tight fit of her cotton dress was a picture always on his mind.

He rose from the side of the sagging bed and went to the window. He could feel the rivulets of perspiration run from under his armpits and down his sides. The curtains hung limp at the open window. A swarthy, somber man with a black hat and beard was tying a black Morgan horse to the hitching post in front of the hotel. Dark hair was curling from underneath his wide brimmed hat and fell almost to his shoulders. Kenus could tell by looking down on the man that he would tower above his six feet.

Could this be the man Ferrell and Talt had sent? For a moment, watching the foreboding looking person, his dreams of Kylee diminished. He wiped the sweat from his forehead with a white handkerchief and ran it backward across his receding hairline. He closed his eyes and again thought of Kylee. He was brought back to the reality of the hot hotel room by a loud knock on the door. He moved slowly to open it to Jay Mitchell.

CHAPTER SEVEN

At the mill events were moving along swiftly, much to Matt's liking. The party would be held in the bottom of the mill. The rock and mortar walls and floor kept the large spacious room dry and mercifully cool from the hot July sun. Wide double doors used to drive in team and wagons were propped open wide. Tom, Matt, and Simeon spent long hours sweeping and stacking to make the room clean enough to be approved by Kylee's watchful eye.

The flow of water through the big wheel had slowed to nothing. It was just as well; the loud creaking and noise of the grinder would not drown out the music. A variety of lanterns, all sizes, were hung on a rope between the mill and barn. They would effectively light the circle drive and shower a faint light into the yard and back across the millpond. Jole' and Daisy watched across the fence unconcerned with the commotion going on inside the mill.

Tom and Simeon left the work to Matt and prepared to leave for Gladeville to bring home the Walker brothers and the buried whiskey. As Tom was hitching the team of big grays to the wagon Mary and Ginny arrived riding double on an old mule. They brought with them their best frocks, carefully wrapped. They came to spend a few days and nights before the party and to offer their help with the fixin's.

Their merry laughter and happy voices made it almost impossible for Tom to leave. It had been a long time since he had spent any time with the Stewart girls and he was reluctant to say good-bye. He

465

departed with a sullen mood, reminding his father that it was Matt's turn. But his father was unsympathetic and told him he knew where the whiskey was buried and he would be the one to go.

Hail was disgusted with the whole bunch and was quick to tell them so with fervor. "Dancin's a sin! You'll all get drunk, mark my words, an' fight over some worthless hussy, you always do! I'll keep the dogs company, they's got more sense."

Turning away, she headed for the quiet peacefulness of the forest glades, heedless of Ira's warnings not to stray too far from the mill. He was concerned that Jay could be lurking somewhere. He had been seen at different times spying on the place. He worried that if Jay found out she was alive he might succeed this time in destroying her.

A few days later Tom and Simeon returned. Loaded under the wagon's false floor were jugs of whiskey wrapped and padded with burlap. Tom had tediously dug them up from their hiding place. On top were decorations and supplies. Sitting above the load, their happy music ringing into the hollows and through the trees, rode the Walker brothers. Their attire was dark suits, ruffled white shirts and ankle high patent leather dance shoes. Derby hats perched jauntily on their heads. They were the essence of style.

The happy ring of their music and loud laughter drifted into Kylee and Ginny baking cookies in the kitchen. Their rollicking music had even touched Tom and he was no longer in the sullen mood he'd left with. His face flushed and filled with an easy smile as he added his strong tenor to the singing. Simeon, relaxed and at ease with the group, graced the song with his rich deep bass.

Mary met them at the mill doors. Inside, she had been helping Matt build a stand for the music and a table for refreshments. She abandoned Matt to help Tom string the bright red, white, and blue streamers. The Walker brothers entertained them as they worked, allowing Tom at intervals to pick a rollicking hoe-down on the banjo. He sang loudly:

> *"I went down to Ole Joe Clark's,*
> *Standin' in the door.*
> *Shoes and stockin's in his hand.*
> *Feet all over the floor.*

Fare-thee-well, Ole Joe Clark,
Fare-thee-well, I say.
Fare-thee-well Ole Joe Clark,
I'm gonna leave today..."

The spirits soared as they all joined in the song. The young men laughingly, in good humor, teased the girls. Mary watched the bright streamers ripple in the breeze and Tom watched the happiness growing in her brown eyes. The unhappy shadow left by Billy's death was almost gone.

"What a wonderful idea Uncle Ira had, having a party," Kylee thought humming to the ring of the banjo coming through the open doorway. She talked with Ginny about the trip they were going to take into Kentucky to deliver the whiskey. Ira had decided that Jan and Bess, along with the girls, should accompany them, and Kylee would go too.

Ginny chattered and Kylee marveled at the change that had taken place in the girl. The chubbiness was gone, replaced by the firm rounding of young breasts that were definitely not girlish. The red of her hair, not so much like Jan's anymore, but taking on a golden bronze, almost the color of Tom's horse, Jole'. It laid across her shoulders and down her back in a mass of tiny corkscrew curls. Her attitude had completely changed. Where had the shyness gone? She chattered all the time. Her eagerness for the party and the trip had brought a definite glow to her amber eyes, bringing out the gold flecks to sparkle like hidden treasures. Kylee wondered what secrets were veiled behind those shining yellow spheres. Even the hem of her skirt had been lowered to hide the shapely curve of her ankle.

"It'll be such fun, Kylee! We-uns are gonna stay two nights, Mommy said, with our cousins on the Kentucky River. It's so beautiful over there. I've been there before. You'll love it Kylee! You'll stay with us, Mary said so. While the men get their business done," Ginny informed Kylee rambling on.

"Poppa said I could ride with him on the wagon seat. I love my poppa. I just love him to pieces! You know, Kylee, how much you can love your poppa?" Ginny paused with the question looking at Kylee with wide serious eyes.

467

"Yes, I know!" Kylee answered with only a trace of sadness for her father. It didn't hurt any more to think of him. The thing she remembered was the silly old hat he had always worn and his deep gentleness. Always, she would remember his tender kindness toward her. Except that one time, when he told her she was to marry Kenus. Now Kenus too had been forgotten, completely.

"Oh, I'm sorry, Kylee. I'm terrible! I forgot what happened to your paw. I'm so sorry about that. I'd die if anything were to happen to my poppa. I'd just die!" Ginny exclaimed with girlish enthusiasm. Tears of dismay clouded her eyes at the thought of life without her big, booming, wonderful father.

"That's all right Ginny. It don't hurt so much anymore. I'm happy here with Uncle Ira, the boys, an' all my dear friends."

Kylee lifted her apron, wiped her hands and took a moment to hug Ginny. The young girl's cheeks were pink from the fire they had kept hot to heat the oven. Kylee's eyes flashed happy green stars as she watched Ginny running a slim finger across the cookie dough and licking it clean as she relished the spicy goodness.

"Here, take these cookies out to the mill. I'll bring some milk. Let's do it before we put the next batch in," Kylee instructed Ginny handing her a plate filled with warm cookies.

Kylee hurried her out the kitchen door following with an empty pitcher she would fill at the springhouse and a handful of blue enameled cups. They passed Hail and Ira sitting close beside each other on the front porch. The usual bright patchwork quilt covered his lifeless legs, even in the heat of the day. Ira puffed his pipe, a look of complete contentment on his whiskered face. The two of them sat moving their heads in time with the merry melodies coming from the mill.

Ira begged Hail to sit beside him. He even convinced her to hold his hand. Occasionally he would give her hand a squeeze. Once he had been so bold as to lift it and kiss the palm of the scarred claw. He was afraid she would leave his side when he felt her pull away. Patting her hand, he reassured her that he would behave himself.

"Gee, Uncle Ira. Are you sure you're gonna be ready to make a trip into Kentucky after all this partyin'? It sure does take a lot of fixin's for such a shindig," Ginny good-naturedly chided him.

Ginny offered them cookies from the plate, smiling sweetly at Hail but avoiding looking directly at her. She still could not look openly at Hail's face. She gave a sigh as if she were weary from the extreme job of cookie making.

Kylee gave her uncle a kiss on top of his head and tucked the pitcher under her arm. She patted Hail's scarred head with affection. Hail bestowed a sweet smile on her. Kylee gently but encouragingly gave Ginny a shove toward the steps.

The party began as most parties do, slowly. Then as the night wore on and the big room filled with music and dancing feet, the party became intense with gaiety. The news of the Phelps mill party traveled quickly. Everyone was eager for a celebration, tired of hoeing corn and tobacco or tending to chores. They came with music in their hearts and their feet. They danced, sang, ate, and drank. The banjo, fiddle, and occasionally the dulcimer rang merrily above it all.

It seemed to Tom that each tune became louder and faster as the night moved on. The older women dressed in dark silks trimmed heavily with lace could be heard saying how shameless the young women were. Showing every inch of anklebone and flipping their skirts higher than necessary about their legs making sure the men had plenty of view to occupy their gaze.

"I'll swear, it ain't like it were in our days," one dowager declared. She puffed her pipe slowly as she spoke to an older woman. "Young men ain't no better than the girls make 'em be. If a girl is gonna let a boy have privileges, he sure is gonna take advantage. Then he'll expect all the other girls to follow the pattern! Sure invitin' the boys to be bold, showin' their ankles an' swingin' thar hips. Look-a-there, ain't that? I swear, ain't that Polly Trace?"

"It is! It surely is!" Grandmother declared chewing her tobacco contentedly as she peered through the field of dancers. "I declare, she has a nerve comin' to a respectable party, but then I hear'd Tom Phelps has a sweet tooth for her."

"I bet he don't know a thing about what I heard. You know, I heard she had publicly become..." the other lady was eager to tell of the indecent things she had heard concerning Polly. "We-uns

ought'a demand she leave town. We ain't never had one of them kind
in our town before!"

"I know, it's disgraceful! An' we-uns are lettin' her get away with
it! I say, ain't that the Negro what's workin' for Ira standin' over
there in the shadows? I swear I cain't hardly see him at all exceptin'
for his eyes! Hope he don't come over this way. I'd die! What in the
world would you say to him anyways? Heard he worked a spell for
Trace. It's been said he was seen sportin' Polly around here an' there.
Did you ever hear tell of such a thing? But she strikes me as bein'
that kind. Wouldn't matter what color a man's skin was as long as he
was a man, with money! She's dark enough; she could be one herself.
What do you think Etta? Trace takin' up with him an' all?"

The two grew quiet as Matt swung Polly around the dance floor
to move in close to where they were sitting and stopped. There was
a definite telltale look of guilt upon their faces and a tight shutting
of their lips. They had been talking about Polly, or him! He hated
hill gossip and these two were known to be the busiest.

"Evenin' ladies," Matt offered politely to Cousin Etta Baldwin
and Grandma Mullins.

Somewhere high on the family tree hung the bloodline that
connected the Baldwin, Mullins, and Phelps. Matt only knew they
were kin and everyone on Pound River and up the branches called
Sarah Mullins, Grandma.

"Have you all met Polly?" Matt inquired teasingly. A delightful
twinkle fired his round blue eyes. A mischievous arch lifted his dark
brows. The twist of his finely sculptured mouth looked to be in
danger of bursting into roaring laughter.

Polly said nothing, only tightened her lips and Matt could hear
the impatient tapping of her toe. Her eyes were a glow with angry
fires. Polly was very aware that she was not a favorite with the hill
women. She cared little.

"Matt, darlin'," she cooed. "Let's finish our dance." And she
planted a kiss on Matt's cheek to shock the older women as she
pushed her full bosom hard into his chest.

"Why did you do that? You know I was acquainted with them
two old tongue-waggin' biddies!" Polly accused as she drug Matt
back onto the floor and out of hearing range.

"I'm sorry Polly, truly. But I just couldn't help myself. I had to see the look on their faces when we stopped in front of them." Matt put his head back and laughed with delight at his prank.

Jan and Bess arrived with Emily Ann. The little girl immediately captured Tom. She would not be appeased until he had whirled her a half dozen times around the floor. Jan danced with Mary and Ginny, both at the same time, creating their own little circle of toe tapping fun. Bess found Kylee behind the long table laden with food. Depositing her roaster full of fried chicken, she offered to help Kylee serve the food and coffee.

Tom felt a small tugging pang of jealousy when Polly arrived and pulled Matt onto the dance floor. For a fleeting second, he wondered why he hadn't been chosen.

"Oh well," he comforted himself, "that's what you need, Bub, old feller, a hot blooded wench to get your mind off Taynee."

He couldn't deny that Polly was beautiful. Her dark loveliness was a flaming glow under the dim lantern light. The flickering lights made a bright splash of her yellow dress, the color of buttercups. A superbly voluptuous body swayed with an easy to read invitation in Matt's arms. Tom's face began to burn watching Polly. He turned his gaze to Kylee.

It was like a cool breeze after a hot wind and he glared at Kylee. She was a vibrant beauty in her own right, attired in a green water-grain taffeta dress she had made. Taffeta Ira bought in Gladeville because it reminded him of Kylee's green eyes. It caused her eyes to be shimmering pools of the same color. Tom was reminded of how he had hesitantly asked Kylee to dance only to be turned aside with, "I'm too busy, Tom, servin' the food." He sullenly retorted that people could serve themselves and that the party was for her. She only squelched him with a hostile look and he moved away.

He danced Emily around the floor watching Polly and Kylee with a feeling of despair at his failure with them both. He turned his gaze from the young women to Bess and there it stayed, and there rose the desire to dim all desires. The one he knew was wrong beyond all the rest, but could not be denied.

Here again was the aggravating longing for Bess Stewart. As he stared at her she raised her head. For an unknown reason she felt

Tom's eyes upon her. He looked at her beyond the dancers and into her very soul. The searing burning stare captured her gaze. She could not turn her eyes away. As their visual path locked, it was as if they were all alone. Tom could not fight his desire for Bess Stewart. He could feel his very being rising above the moving bodies into a dream world. He took Bess's hand and pulled her up into his arms, kissed her and felt a soaring whirring wind lift him above all reality. He lay with Bess as he longed so much to do. He made passionate love to her; a thing he knew would never be possible.

Bess forcefully pulled her eyes away, feeling the magnetism that had pulled their thoughts together. She could not allow this game with Tom to become a reality. Not even in her imagination could she allow it. It was wrong, terribly wrong. Jan and the girls danced up and Bess was glad for their appearance. Quickly she latched onto Jan's arm and whirled him away, across the room and away from the pull of Tom's sultry look.

Tom decided his dream of Bess had to become a reality. He could deny it no longer. He felt the desire in her too. His enchantment was being broken by Emily's pull on his arm attempting to recapture his attention. Her toes were tapping in time with the music. Tom picked her up smiling apologetically and deposited her firmly on Ira's lap. She sat happily stroking Ira's long beard. Tom pushed his way through the sea of dancers to Jan and Bess.

"Sorry Jan, would you share Bess with me for a dance?" The trembling he felt inside was rising and beginning to throb in his throat.

"I will finish the dance with my husband, Tom," Bess informed him.

"Go ahead Bess. Give Tom a dance. I'll dance another round with the girls. Maybe Kylee will honor me," Jan laughingly relinquished his wife.

"Please Tom. Don't look at me so!" Bess looked to the floor.

"I will not keep you long Bess, but you feel this as I do. Somethin' has got to be done. I promise you one thing. One of these days you an' I are goin' to have a hands on affair. None of this eyes across the table will work anymore. You know this an' so do I! There will come a time an' place."

His eyes held a promise not a threat. Their eyes met and he could see seriousness in Bess. Was this a promise? But no, she was whispering softly.

"Passion burns hot as fire Tom. When the fire goes out all that's left is a pile of ashes, cold as clay. It's the low burning ember that lasts and lasts. From this ember you can warm yourself forever an' ever. Passion is what we are feelin' Tom. The long lastin' ember is what I have with Jan. Get this out of your head! It can only hurt us, an' Jan. I can't allow that to happen. No matter what we feel, we have to bury it!" Bess was adamant.

The desire was gone from Bess's eyes. Only a deep sadness remained. She pulled herself away from Tom's embrace and hurried across the floor. Tom turned to take his father a drink and find a jug for himself. Still shaken from his passionate encounter with Bess, he would attempt to wash it away with the fiery liquor. He knew Bess was telling him the truth. Their desire for each other could never become a reality.

Tom found a place outside away from the lantern light and off in the shadows at the corner of the barn. He perched casually on the top rail of the barnyard fence. He smoothed Jole's soft nose, as he talked to the horse in a low voice. Taking long drinks from the jug he proceeded to get as loop-legged as possible in a short time. He decided he could keep his emotions under control and returned to the party to find Matt still dominating Polly.

Kylee was still at her post serving food. Simeon was pouring the coffee supplied from the iron stove in the store. Tom walked boldly over to Matt and Polly as they huddled together embraced in a waltz. Tapping his brother on the shoulder he pulled Polly into his arms and whirled her away leaving Matt standing in the middle of the dance floor.

It had been a long time since Tom had held Polly in his arms. He admitted she fit there nicely as she pushed herself indecently up to him as they danced. And he, indecently, loved every minute of it. Still with the burning desire for Bess fresh on his mind, he was eager to block it with another means of fulfillment.

He felt the soft firmness of Polly's full breasts pushing against his chest. Here was something to get your mind on, something real, not a dream. The heady sweet smell of her perfume filled his head with a light giddiness. Mixed with the high proof homemade whiskey he had been drinking, his head began to spin.

"Let's get out'a here," Tom whispered gruffly in his partner's ear, "I need some air."

Taking Polly's hand he guided her through the dancers, out the wide doors, and up the path to the edge of the millpond. Tom paid little attention to how far the dark waters had receded down on the rock dam from the intensive drying heat. Any other time he would have been concerned. The filling of the millpond was the source of power to run the big grinder inside the mill. He loosened his collar and unfastened the top button on his shirt. He removed his suit jacket and carried it over his arm. Arriving at a grassy spot under a big oak he spread the coat and sat on it pulling Polly down beside him.

Matt had allowed Tom to pull Polly away without restraint. He moved over to the table of food and teasingly convinced Kylee that Mary could take care of the serving. He danced her away.

Kylee had not realized she had so many cousins. In one-way or other almost everyone had been related to her father. As the night progressed she enjoyed the dancing. The Virginia-Reel was fun and the circle two-step. The La-Souvian left her panting and breathless. Her cheeks began to burn and her feet were throbbing as she followed her partner's every step. It was becoming hot in the crowded room. Most of the men had been drinking heavily and she swore the perspiration was half alcohol. She was warm and sticky herself.

Watching Tom dancing with the pretty dark haired girl called Polly gave her a twinge of jealousy. She thought to herself that the young woman was a little plump and her lips too red to be natural. She remembered her from the day she met Billy, the same day Tom had carelessly showered her with dust. What a long time ago that had been! How much her life had changed.

She noticed Tom's face glowing red from his heavy drinking. The music was becoming faster and the men were doing more stomping than dancing. She saw Tom leave with Polly, but why should she care? She became more involved with the dancing until she could feel the perspiration running down her back. The strong smell of animal odor came through the doors mingling heavily with the smell of whiskey and human sweat. Her head was jumbled with noise and confusion. She begged Matt to take her out for a breath of fresh air and they pushed through the wall of dancers.

Outside the night was ready to drop the morning dew. The slight moisture touching Kylee's warm brow felt cool and refreshing. Matt held her elbow and guided her up the path around the millpond. At night the pool was ebony dark catching the reflection of the twinkling stars and new developing yellow moon. Darker shadows along the bank cast from the huge oaks sheltered the water from all other reflections. Matt was delighted to share the serene beauty with the lovely person walking beside him.

Faintly the music drifted above their heads. The happy sound dimmed by the steady burr-rump of the frogs and the sharp stiletto of the crickets. They watched the gaily-lit lanterns swinging slightly in the breeze causing shadows to dance among the trees and skipping sparks between the lily pads. Above the music and the sounds of the night rippled the soft swishing of Kylee's beautifully ruffled taffeta skirt.

"Did you like the dancin' Kylee?" Matt questioned.

"Yes! Yes! An' you?" Kylee answered in a soft voice as if she were trying not to disturb the sound of the night.

"Well dancin' never was my best thing. But I sure do like the music. I've missed Billy an' the music him an' Tom used to play. I never could make any music myself, but I sure did like to listen to them. Taynee got so's she could play the banjo right smart when you were so sick. I liked listenin' to her sing a powerful lot. It's been lots a fun seein' all the cousins. They all liked you Kylee."

He let go of Kylee's elbow and took her hand and tucked it under his arm. They walked along in silence enjoying the beauty of the night. Kylee was satisfied to be quiet, thinking Matt's thoughts were with Taynee. She laid her other hand gently across his arm wanting him to know she understood and sympathized with his grief.

Matt watched Kylee from the corner of his eye in the dim light. Her auburn brown hair was piled high on the crown of her head in thick twists and swirls. Long curls lay upon her shoulders and bounced up and down as she walked. Kylee could not have guessed at the time how far away from Taynee his thoughts were as he looked down upon her. With deep tender brotherly love his thoughts were on the young woman beside him. Grateful for her presence and the unselfish care she gave them all.

As Kylee and Matt left the mill they passed men and boys standing on the outside drinking and smoking while they enjoyed the fresh air. They nodded, winking at each other knowingly as the young couple passed.

"Any one what's got a daughter better be for keepin' an eye on her this night," one of the men declared and they all agreed with a nod of their heads.

"If it were me," another one remarked, "I'd keep a special close watch on them Phelps scalawags!"

"Oh Tom, I have missed you," Polly sighed softly as Tom stretched out beside her. Her voice was soft, husky, and full of promise.

"I have missed you too, babe. Boy, have I missed you!" Tom met her warm, moist, parted lips in a passionate kiss reaching and searching for her skirts. "I was sorry you were gone when I came by."

"I wondered why you hadn't been back, darlin'. Oh, darlin'!" she breathed heavily reaching and trying to help Tom lift her skirt. At the same time she freed her breast to cup Tom's hand around it. Polly was fumbling and pulling on her skirts trying in her way to encourage her partner to hurry.

"I ain't been lonesome, mind you," her voice was muted and soft velvet. "Oh please hurry Tom! It's been so long since I been with you. The yokels around here ain't nothin' compared to you, Tom darlin'. Oh, I cain't wait! Please Tom, get on with it, darlin'!"

Tom stifled her pleading with a searing kiss. He felt her relax in his arms. He was in no hurry but was beginning to wonder if he would have to send out a search party. He was certain Polly wore a dozen petticoats besides bloomers and hose under her dress. He wanted to have time to enjoy every inch of her luxurious body. Somewhere, it was there under all those skirts. Why did women insist on wearing so much clothing? It must be fearfully hot on days like this one.

Polly was not going to be delayed any longer. She was wiggling and twisting, pushing her body against him. Tom laughed at her eagerness.

"Take it easy Polly. Relax! There's plenty of time."

Polly let out a long sigh anticipating the pleasure to come and was quiet in his arms. She enjoyed having Tom make love to her. She would calm her eagerness. They were very quiet lying in the grass enraptured in their progressive love making. The night was satin still around them and they melted into its smooth softness.

The long summer grass hid their bodies well, a huddled glob, not yet to the point of hard breathing, when Matt and Kylee stumbled upon them. Kylee gasped in astonishment, surprised at their presence on the ground. Matt was startled and caught himself in time to keep from stumbling over the pair. He recognized the couple on the ground immediately.

Matt knew there was no shame in Polly. She filled her need wherever and whenever it pleased her. He remembered how Polly had enticed him with her body while they were dancing. She was up to promoting just such an incident. Matt was embarrassed and sorry that Kylee had seen the two on the ground enraptured in each other's arms. Protectively he put his arm around Kylee's waist to draw her back away from the pair.

Tom rolled back surprised at being discovered. He staggered unsteadily to his feet. The moment of unrelieved passion and his over indulgence had pushed him into a state of obnoxious drunkenness. His body was weaving dangerously threatening to topple over as he tried to keep his balance and straighten his clothing.

"Good Heavens Tom. Ain't you got any decency?" Matt questioned his brother, angry and shocked.

"Who you callin' not decent?" Tom answered in a slurred voice, in quick defense of his actions.

"Don't you know there's folks all over the place?" Matt retorted in exasperation at his brother's apparent uncontrollable drunken condition.

"Tain't none of your business, Bub!" Tom was upset and sullen at having been caught in the middle of such a personal moment. He was not too drunk to realize it was an embarrassing situation and hid his feelings under a blanket of anger.

"I see you're out with your girl, ain't you?" Tom asked indignantly, looking at Kylee's face, a splash of white against a mass of dark hair. "Ain't you found the right place yet?"

Over her head he could see a pink dawn beginning to break around the tops of the thick trees. Tom hadn't missed Matt's arm placed intimately around Kylee's waist, a place that was off limits to him. He gave his brother a hostile look. He was drunk all right, but not too drunk to see what was going on between those two.

"We take your spot?" He insolently questioned Matt.

"Damn it, Tom. Knock it off! I ain't wantin' any trouble tonight. Now make yourself respectable an' go back to the dancin'." Matt reached down as he spoke and helped Polly to her feet. A polite gesture Tom had failed to apply. He was quick to see the offered courtesy and promptly took offense.

"Keep your hands off my woman." Tom's tongue was thick and his speech slurred. With a hard shove he pushed Matt roughly backward.

"You bet I can be respectable!"

"Damn it Tom. Cut it out! Behave yourself. Let's not have a fight tonight," Matt coaxed. Catching his balance from the shove he staggered backward. He kept from falling into the millpond releasing Kylee as he did so.

Tom was unreasonably drunk and stubbornly angry. He was beyond the point of being talked out of anything. Swinging out his fist he caught Matt squarely on the jaw stunning him for a moment.

"You're drunk Tom. Let's go in an' forget this," Matt pleaded as he caught his balance.

Matt knew Tom had been drinking heavily all evening. He didn't want to have a fight with his brother over Polly, a year ago perhaps, before Taynee, but not anymore. He shook his head trying to clear it from Tom's blow. Any other time when Tom was sober his punch would have carried more weight and it would have flattened him.

"I ain't drunk, you chicken-shit! You never could get the best of your big brother." Tom swung out and hit Matt weakly on the arm.

The slur and the blow angered Matt. He reached the end of his patience. He drew back and threw a hard punch square on his brother's jaw. Tom reeled back and fell against one of the oak trees.

Polly turned and ran to the mill. She was going to get away, knowing full well how the fights between these brothers ended. It was best to let them battle it out. They would be friends again after a day or two. Venturing too close would be complete folly.

Kylee was not so wise in brother fights. Her cousins back home never fought in her presence. She tried desperately to find a place to get in and stop them.

"Stop it Matt! Stop it Tom! You're awful. Stop this minute! Do you hear me? Stop it, I said! I'll fetch Jan. I will, then you'll both be sorry!"

They ignored her completely. Her threats went over their heads. They were too engrossed in battling each other. Tom, tired of interference, shoved her roughly out of the way. She stumbled backward, lost her balance, and fell in a tangled pile of skirts into the shallow millpond.

Matt and Tom fought on unaware of Kylee's plight. They fought hard but Matt had the advantage. Tom was weakened and slowed from his drinking. His returned blows became fewer, slower, and with lessening force. It was hard to see in the waning darkness and Tom's eyes were beginning to blur. Matt landed a hard left on Tom's jaw. It sent him reeling backward to land with a splash between the lily pads beside Kylee who was struggling to raise herself from the pond.

Matt graciously helped Kylee up to the bank. Then he turned to his brother sprawled in the shallow water. He pulled Tom up, lifted him out, and laid him under a tree to sleep if off. He put his arm around Kylee and helped her walk to the house. Her crisp taffeta gown held no rustle. The water-grain pattern was soaked water-grained. Again she was fuming inside; furious at Tom for ruining the beautiful party dress she spent hours making.

Chapter Eight

Polly sat beside Mary on a roll of meal sacks tied into a tight bundle exchanging secret thoughts. Polly expressed her sympathy again at Billy and Taynee's death. Blaine, she remarked, deserved what he got. He was so mean and ornery he should have never been born. Rueben was going to join him if he didn't quit pestering her. She couldn't stand his squinting eyes and bad breath, she confided in Mary.

Polly had a rare beauty with honey colored skin, smooth as silk, and accented by dark brows and black eyes. Her lips were full, almost thick. A small nose, sharply pointed, added a look of elegance to her round face, framed with a mass of ebony ringlets. A yellow chiffon scarf was folded, pressed, and tied closely across her forehead holding the many curls at bay. A small yellow rose was fastened over her left ear. She watched closely for Matt and Tom to appear. When neither of them showed, she decided to find Simeon and persuade him to take her home. She rode up the mountain with the Jennings family, but they had left the party early. She promised Carl she would find a ride home or spend the night with the Stewarts. Her popularity with the hill families was nil. In fact, other than Tom, she suspected Mary was her only friend. Polly's attraction to men and her sexual permissiveness did not win her any popularity contest with the women.

The dance lasted until dawn. The remaining guests loaded sleeping children and left to beat the golden sunshine and do the chores waiting at home. If possible they would all head to Gladeville to participate in the 4th of July celebration. They couldn't miss that or the campaign speeches for the coming election in the fall.

Polly found Simeon feeding the horses and mules, doing his early morning chores. Ira had told him to take the day off, deliver the Walker brothers back home, and enjoy the celebration in Gladeville. But he was to have the wagon back early the next day before they left for Kentucky on the fifth. The situation was right for Polly to have a ride home.

"I don't know, Miss Polly. It wouldn't look right for you to be ridin' with a bunch of men, especially when one of them is a black man. I'd best ask Mista Ira first," Simeon informed her cautiously.

"I've ridden with you before, Simeon. What's different now?" Polly questioned with a look of confusion.

Ira agreed to let her go with the men, knowing there wasn't much that could damage Polly's reputation. She needed a way home and he told them to be on their way. With the Walker brothers asleep in the back of the wagon and Polly sitting beside Simeon, they headed down the mountain. Boy and Blue sent them off with loud yapping. It was the middle of the day when they drove up to the tavern steps. Polly and Simeon chattered to each other most of the way, Polly telling him of things that had taken place at the tavern since he went to work for Ira. Simeon, in return, told her tales of his life before he came to the mountain.

"Ain't much ta tell, Miss' Polly, 'ceptin' my life was good when I was a lad before the war. My pap an' mam were slaves on a big plantation in Louisiana. My pap served in the Confederate Army, right along side his master. They took care of each other an' came home together. We lived on the plantation just like before the war. The Mista gave us our freedom but we chose to stay on with him. My pap was a man of the Lord. He believed in the Word, he did. My mam and pap are dead now an' the young uns' married an' raisin' families. My mam always hoped I'd be a preacher in memory of my pap. I'm hopin' I will be some day. I been nigh onto eight years workin' my way to Columbus, Ohio. Goin' to get me a job in a factory, go to school an' learn to read the Lord's book. Someday I'll be the most fired up preacher they be. I'll go back an' help my people. My people need so much help, Miss' Polly," Simeon hesitated, slapped the mules on their rumps and spent a minute tending to his driving.

"The folks in the north gave us freedom, then forgot us. The folks in the south thinks we's trash an' want no part of us. So what are we free from? Free to be treated worser than dogs. Folks treat their dogs with respect an' kindness, not us. What is there for us to do? There's no place to turn. I ain't wantin' no sympathy, just understandin', that's all any of us wants. An' understandin' that we're free to have some of what this country has to offer. We jest want an understandin' that we's folks too, that's all!" Simeon glanced at Polly, taking his eyes from the road. For some reason, he could talk freely with this young woman. He found that he could say things he hadn't dared to relate to anyone, except his mother. Polly didn't make him feel as if he were inferior or that he was a black man getting out of his place. What had gotten into him, laying his soul bare to this white woman? He must be touched in the head. She'd have no compassion for his problems. He turned his eyes back to the road and was silent, almost apologetic for wasting her time.

Polly looked at him, a black stormy sea showing under her heavy eyelids. She glanced down at his big hands, wide palms with long, strong fingers. His fingers caressed the reins as if in love with the big dapple-grays pulling the wagon.

"Now, Mista Ira has been real kind to me. But I get the feelin' he'd like me better if my skin wasn't so damn black," Simeon remarked, looking over at Polly with a wide mocking grin.

"Soon as I help Masta Ira get the crops in, I'm headin' on into Kentucky, then Ohio. I might even go to Detroit. Sure gets mighty lonesome travelin' alone. But I meet lots a folks, good an' bad. You an' your paw have been some of the best, Miss Polly!" Simeon looked down at the ground under the horse's hooves. He was afraid she might read what he felt in his heart, a feeling even black men could have, but weren't allowed.

Polly watched the road ahead, winding and turning in and out of the trees. She became drowsy from the movement of the wagon and the long night of partying. Looking at her hands folded together in her lap, a sudden shock filled her. She turned them over slowly.

She had the same startling white palms as Simeon Niger with the definite pink around the fingernails. She hid her hands in the folds of her skirt. But she could still see how creamy dark her skin looked against her yellow party frock.

"Why I'm most as dark as you be, Simeon! People don't stop an' think that we's all the same. The color of your skin isn't important. They's some folks I know that's blacker on the inside then you be on the outside! There's no amount of white wash that could change them!" Polly declared turning an understanding smile on the black man. "But, I believe Simeon, you should be a preacher if you'd like. Our Lord an' Savior died for us all, not just a special few, or just a few with a certain color of skin, or certain occupation, but for us all!"

Simeon was thinking strong on what Polly said, thinking about her skin being almost as dark as his. He helped Polly down from the wagon at the tavern steps in Donkey and made sure she arrived inside before he drove away. He drove on through Gladeville, filled with people celebrating, and pulled to the side of the road in a shaded area. Here a crystal clear spring swirled around the roots of an age-old chestnut tree. Simeon guided the team in close and let them drink.

He was weary and needed a moment to rest. He untied the lunch Hail had put together for him and was happy for the biscuits, cheese, and slices of ham. Best of all was the big piece of apple pie inside a square blue dish. He ate with relish, then needed a drink. He climbed from the wagon, cupped his hands and drank his fill of the cool water. As he was climbing back into the wagon one of the Walker brothers peeked over the edge spreading his mouth into a wide yawn.

"Where are we-uns?"

"We's just out'a Gladeville. I'm fixin' to take you on home," Simeon told him laughing at Walker's sleepy disheveled look.

"Ain't gonna let you do that. Wasn't there anything goin' on in town?"

"Yes, suh. There's a bunch a people an' fire crackers goin' off all over the place. I come on through an' found a place to rest a minute," Simeon explained settling himself on the seat and lifted the reins.

"Wal, don't bother yourself about takin' us on home, Simeon. Take us back into town. We're gonna find us a shindig! Come on Hap, wake up! Let's find us a shindig an' some whiskey." The man shook his brother roughly, attempting to wake the sleeping musician.

"I'll drive you on back. I can tie up at the other edge of town. I need to take me a nap, don't think the firecrackers could keep me awake. Besides I need to rest the team a spell. Think I'll go on back an' spend the rest of the night at Trace's." Simeon's voice was slow and tired. He would be glad for a chance to lie down.

The musical boys straightened their attire, smoothed their hair and beards, and tapped on their derbies. Simeon stopped on the main street while they jumped out. They lifted their instruments and headed off up the street. Simeon drove on and pulled over to the edge of the road leading out of town and stopped. He crawled into the back of the wagon, stretched out his body and was immediately engulfed in slumber. He lay flat on his back, snoring loudly, with his mouth wide open. His ragged straw hat covered his face, discouraging the flies and other flying insects. He was brought back to reality by the feel of cold steel on his neck just behind his ear. The slight pressure encouraged him to wake.

"Move slow, nigga! This trigger is a might touchy. Just lay still an' explain what you're a doin' here with Ira Phelps's favorite team an' sleepin' in the back of his favorite wagon. You running out on him? Maybe stealin' his wagon an' team?" Tanner Hensely asked over the edge of the wagon, standing on the hub of the wheel.

"Maybe you're a plannin' on diggin' up some whiskey that's hid here abouts? Explain yourself, nigger!" He demanded in a louder voice. The cold steel moved deeper. Hensely removed the man's straw hat and threw it on the wagon floor. Simeon lay taut, not moving a muscle, with his round eyes open wide.

"No suh, Mista Marshal, suh! I ain't a movin' til you tells me to. I was thinkin' though suh, it'd be better if I sat up. I can explain better sittin' up. They's a possibility I could swallow a fly an' couldn't talk at all." Simeon attempted a jest, even if he didn't feel like joking. His voice was calm, but beads of perspiration popped out on his forehead and upper lip, signaling his nervousness.

"Who gave you the right to think? Never saw a nigger yet that could think worth a damn for himself. But go ahead an' sit up, carefully! Don't make any sudden moves or you're a dead nigger! They's the best kind any ways!" Hensely backed the thirty-eight a few inches from Simeon's neck but still held it threateningly close.

"Now that you're sitting up, tell me exactly what you're a doin' here! It better not be a lie. I can tell when a nigga's a lyin'. His eyes get all bulgy an' he starts slobberin', slobberin' somethin' fierce!" Hensely told him in a cold voice that froze the Negro's blood on the hot July day. "I cain't stand a slobberin' nigger, jest as soon kill him dead!"

"I's just a doin' an errand for Mista Ira, suh. Givin' the Walker boys a ride to their place, like he told me to. Nothin' more, nothin' more, suh! You find the Walker brothers. They'll tell you I'm tellin' the truth." Simeon tried to keep his voice calm.

The perspiration began to form in rivulets and wash down his dusty face. His tightly curled black hair flashed blue sparks fired by the blazing Virginia sun. He held his full lips tight, not quivering, and not slobbering as Tanner had suggested.

Simeon knew he had to move cautiously using respect and humility with every word. He learned to do that well through the years. Sometimes even that didn't work, especially with some of the black men that had risen to power by kissing white politicians behinds. They especially like to see their fellow black men suffer and cower at their feet as if it made their black hides white. Simeon was thinking fast as he watched carefully for Hensely's next move and trying hard to keep the growing hostility from showing in his eyes.

"Well now, I think I'll take you on over to jail. We got a place for the likes of you. Climb down an' walk ahead of me, slow like. I'll tell you where to stop. I'll send a deputy to care for the team an' wagon. In fact, I'll just send a message for Ira to pick it up. Meanwhile, I'll put you in safe keepin' for a spell!" Hensely told his prisoner as they walked down the street filled with people. "Keep your hands above your shoulders and fasten them at the top of your head. We'll have ourselves a little talk later. Maybe you'll have more to tell then." Tanner promised as he shoved Simeon in the cell and locked the door. He left with a sidelong glance at Talt Hall in the neighboring cell.

Outside, firecrackers split the sound of scuffling feet, rustling petticoats, and children's laughter. The neighing of horses and dogs barking added to the noise. The heat was intense spreading along the streets and walks in rippling waves, then embracing the spurts of dust, as a lover holding them close to the ground and making it almost impossible to breath.

Simeon had walked ahead of Deputy Marshal into the jail and listened with discouragement to the clanging of the cell door. He had a feeling of certainty that he would be there a long while. From somewhere above the noise, heat, and dust came the ring of a banjo and the high-pitched notes of a fiddle.

"The Walker brothers found their shindig," Simeon thought. "I should have kept them on Pound Mountain. Then I'd be there too, sitting on the edge of the mill pond skipping rocks across the wide spots of water between lily pads all decked out in their bright blossoms of pink and gold." Simeon held his head in his hands breathing a heavy sigh. He had a dark feeling of impending disaster and knew with total helplessness, he could do nothing to prevent it.

Tom woke to find himself stretched out in what had, at one time, been his mother's flowerbed. His faithful dog, Boy, was lying beside him. He had worked hard to rock and fill the bed with dirt at the edge of the pond. Now it had grown over with grass and vine. He had no recall of how he arrived there, but knew he had to get himself up and into the house. His clothes had been wet but were drying and sticking to his skin. The chiggers found every open spot on his body, around his neck, face, hands, and the calf of one leg where his pant leg had pulled above his dark socks and low dance slippers. The little insects had embedded themselves in a row along the edge of his garter and the top of his sock. Already, they had aggravated him into irritating itching that could drive a man crazy from digging at his skin to release the tiny pests, which only imbedded them deeper.

As he walked across the yard, he discovered the numerous tender spots on his body. His jaw was aching and there was an open cut on his bottom lip. He remembered vaguely being with Polly. Then the memory increased. Kylee and Matt had stumbled upon them. He had fought with Matt and wound up in the millpond. That was as far as the memory went. He must have said something pretty nasty to Matt, nasty enough to cause a fight. There was no doubt in his mind; he was the one at fault. It would probably be the end of what was beginning to be a better relationship between them. Well, if Matt wanted to poke him in the nose over Polly, he could take it. A warm flush covered his face; he was embarrassed, remembering that Kylee had seen him with Polly.

There was no one about. Only the streamers and burning lanterns remained. Horses and buggies were gone. Everyone must have left while he was asleep on the ground. He missed saying good-bye to friends and relatives. They must think he was a real washout. The house was still and he assumed everyone had retired. He went upstairs, removed his damp clothing and went to bed with Boy's head resting on the coverlet beside him.

He woke later in the day, sullen and miserable. There was a heavy buzz saw grinding in his head. He remembered more about what happened as the day progressed. He met his brother at the bottom of the stairs and Matt sociably offered his hand in a peace making gesture. Tom was surly and would not accept. He was certain that Matt was only gloating because he finally whipped him. It was the first time Tom had taken a beating and defeat was not sitting too well. Besides, he was feeling terribly ill, possibly he thought, from his intensive drinking.

Matt was sorry about the fight. He felt victory had been his, due to an unfair advantage. Tom had been far too drunk to fight. He had a quirk of conscience every time he looked at Tom's battered lip.

Ira kidded them good-naturedly about their bruised knuckles and faces, but did not question them about the cause. He watched them closely knowing it would work itself out. Meanwhile, so there would be no renewing of the disagreement, he kept them both busy working.

Tom felt they had all turned against him and went about his work, nursing his aching head and speaking to no one. He greased the wheels on the big wagon and readied Ira's bedroll and the personal things he would need on the trip. He was sorry he wasn't going with them.

Kylee was more distant to him than ever and he didn't blame her. An old bitterness filled him as he thought of Matt being with her and Bess on the trip. Right now, while his head was busting and his body aching, he was going to make a vow to forget this sinful coveting of beautiful Bess. It was that desire that caused him to get so drunk and drove him into Polly's arms.

When he saw Kylee laughing and talking to Matt on the porch, even holding his hand and looking up at him intimately, he felt worse. Well, if she could make Matt laugh like that again and bring the happiness back in his eyes, he would give her up too. Maybe he would have to settle for Polly. He would like to be on sociable terms with Kylee even if she did like Matt the most. But Kylee would give him no chance to apologize for his indecent conduct. Every time he came close to her she would move away quickly as if he had the plague or something worse. If she hated him so badly, he would spare her the embarrassment of having to look at him or talk to him. He would stay completely away from her.

Kylee's thoughts however, were very different than Tom surmised. She only appreciated Matt's kindness to her. She enjoyed his company as she might have a brother or her cousin, Jesse. Again, she was angry with Tom for his insolence and vile manners. A deep compassion filled her when she looked at his bruised face. She hated Matt, a little, for hitting him so hard. She was afraid, every time Tom came close that she might give in to the urge to put her arms around him and comfort him. She longed to hold him close and tenderly touch his face and tell him how sorry she was he had been hurt.

Kylee knew she could not allow such weakness or give in to such a display of emotions. She would move quickly away if Tom were around. Maybe he wanted her to be like Polly with no conscience about lollygagging around in the grass with him. Well, he could just think again! She recalled a time under the mulberry, when she had almost given in to such indecency. She hated Tom for being with Polly and Polly for being with him. Well, he could take his little hussy and jump in the lake! She would have to cover her grin when she remembered it was Tom and her that landed in the pond. Then she would die a little inside longing for his hands upon her. She wanted desperately to be the one to lay beside him in the sweet grass, even as Polly had done in complete submission. Touching the flame on her cheeks, she knew her thoughts were indeed shameful, and she didn't care!

Kylee was not going to let the fight or her confused feelings about Tom dampen her happy excitement for the trip into Kentucky. With joyful anticipation, she took Val's souvenirs from the worn valise and put them in a drawer and packed the things she would need. The old piece of luggage reminded her of Billy's bashful awkwardness when she first met him on the porch at Trace's Tavern. She remembered how his cheerful smile never failed to warm her heart. There was no holding back the rush of tears. Oh, how very much she missed him! How different her life had become. She could only slightly remember her life without Uncle Ira, Hail, the boys, and her dear friends the Stewarts. There were times when she still thought about her mother and how her father always refused to talk about her. She had asked her Uncle Ira if her father had ever written to him about her mother.

"No Kylee, he never. You must forget about those things. There's lot's a folks who never got to know their mother, or even their father. Remember your father, that's enough. Let's not talk of the past. You got your whole future ahead of you. It's no good worryin' about what's been. This is your home now, it's always gonna be. Now give me a hug an' let's think on other things. Let the dead be dead," he would tell her with a far away look in his eyes and again dismiss the subject.

His attitude did not still the uncontrollable sadness because she had no memory of her mother. Kylee sighed heavily and finished tucking her things into the valise, wishing she could tuck the nagging longing away inside too. She looked at the tintype of her mother on the dresser. Even it was beginning to fade.

Ira stayed up late, hoping Simeon would come before he went to bed. He wanted everything ready to start out when Jan arrived in the morning.

The women retired early. Hail was still sleeping in the big bed that had once been Billy's. Kylee tossed restlessly on her pallet in front of the small fireplace. She was over tired from the pressure of the previous night. Her days work had not been easy, this combined with her growing excitement for the trip caused a sleepless night.

Matt and Tom sat with their father watching fireflies darting about as they listened and waited for Simeon to show up. They spoke nothing to each other and addressed their conversation only to their father.

"Simeon should have been back by now Paw. He said he'd try to be here before we went to bed. Musta got to celebrating an' decided to make it in by mornin'." Matt stood up and ran his fingers through his brown slightly curled hair and stretched. "I'll be up an' get the mules hitched an' Kylee's horse saddled. Everything's ready. I reckon you'll want to leave soon as Jan gets here. If I know him, it'll be daylight. Goodnight Paw, Tom." Matt nodded and cautiously addressed his brother, expecting no answer in return.

"Night!" Tom answered sullenly as Matt walked by him and into the dark house.

At least it was an answer, Matt thought.

"If Simeon don't show up before we'uns leave in the mornin', you look him up Tom. You was goin' into Gladeville anyways. Get a hold of Daniel Fletcher. He's the Republican you need to talk with. Tanner Hensely's not gonna be too happy about you runnin' against him for Snow's office. But that's sure as hell too bad! I'm glad you decided to do it, son. I was a little displeased because you didn't stick around closer to the party last night an' do a little more jawin'," his father commented.

"Damn it, Paw. Them folks all know me. Most of them are family anyways. I think I can count on their votes. I'm concerned about the money, Paw. It's the money what buys the votes." Tom was wishing he had stuck closer to the party too. He was still sick and miserable.

"Shaw! Money's no problem, son. We got the money. What we ain't got, someone else has. Folks are so tired of the bullshit Tanner's been gettin' away with. They'll be rarin' to back you! Jan an' Carl's already promised their support. All the folks on Baldwin Branch'll back you. Money's no problem, Tom. I'll make a good bundle on that 'shine in the wagon. We'll sink it all into your campaign. Only thing, they's not too much time. You should of been in town today shakin' a few hands an' kissin' a few babies. Ain't no time like the fourth of July to further a political career." Ira was confident his son would be the next County Marshal.

"I'd like for you not to leave Hail for too long unless Simeon's back. Jan was a tellin' me he'd had a talk with Mitchell. Jay was a trifle riled when he found out I bought that piece of ground an' deeded it to Mary. Jan said Jay was plumb bent out'a shape. If he gets wind Hail's still alive he'll try somethin'. It won't be safe for her to be alone," Ira continued.

"Cain't talk her into goin' with us. Tanner's gonna be tied up with Talt's trial. Jay'll be snoopin' around for some mischief to get into. Them two are closer then a mama possum an' her little ones, hangin' on to each other with all their might. Folks are sick to death of it! They's ready for a change. Snow's still dumb to what's goin' on, blinder then a bat! You know Tanner an' Mitchell ain't gonna like bein' pushed out'a the way. Ain't gonna like it a bit." Ira rolled his chair over to the door then turned to look at Tom with ice blue eyes.

"I don't think Simeon would run out on me. He sure enough seemed a nice sort. It's hard to tell 'bout a black, though. No one around seemed to know much about him, even Trace. One way or tuther, I ain't aimin' on lettin' a damn nigger snicker me out'a a good wagon an' team. If he's left the country, I'll find him. I'll find him! He'll wished he'd never see'd Pound Mountain!" Ira declared and rolled into the house.

The Stewart's arrived the next morning with the dawn. Jan's big wagon was loaded with their belongings, bedrolls, cooking utensils, and a supply of food. Ginny and Jan sat high riding on the seat. Emily sat sleepily between them unusually quiet for the four-year-old. Mary was behind them riding a roan mule, straddled like a man. Bess rode Jan's big bay sidesaddle, as was the custom for females of an age, her skirts pulled modestly around her legs. She preferred the easy gait of Jan's horse to the roughness of the wagon seat. Her beauty looked so fresh and golden in the early morning. The black riding habit she wore only added to her translucent loveliness. She wore a plain bonnet with the neck ruffle protecting her high rolled hair from the onslaught of dust that would surely be on the road. The dark color of her attire would prove to be uncomfortably warm as the day wore on. But hidden from her viewers was the fact that she cheated when dressing and lessened her undergarments, one petticoat and no stockings. The others were tucked into her bag for later use if protocol demanded.

Tom managed to give up the comfort of his bed to come down and say good-bye. His head was splitting and he had a nauseous churning inside his belly. Even after all his vows to forget Bess, he could not keep his eyes off her incredible beauty. She wisely avoided his gaze, knowing well if she allowed one look, she would again be locked in the passionate pull of Tom's blue eyes. Jan had always been a perfect husband in every way. She was totally happy with him and never thought of anyone else. But she could not ignore this drawing surge that flooded her being when she sensed Tom's feelings. She was glad Tom was not going along on the trip.

Kylee was ready and waiting when their friends arrived. Ira was on the porch waving them a greeting. The early morning sun shifted streamers of light through the tall pines on the east hill behind the house. Matt breathed deep of what was left of the cool dawn freshness knowing it would soon give way to a blazing Virginia sun. He finished adding their gear to the already loaded wagon and was hitching the mules. Simeon had not returned with Ira's prize team of grays. Kylee's horse, Tempest, was saddled and waiting.

Matt drove the wagon around to the steps, lifted Ira into the seat and helped Kylee up sidesaddle on her horse. Between the loud talking and spurts of laughter he was trying to remember if he had forgotten anything they might need on the five-day trip. As Matt lifted Kylee onto her horse, he thought how dewy fresh and pretty she looked in her new dark blue riding skirt. She chose a soft white blouse because she felt it would be cooler. Long tresses were wrapped at the top of her head with a wide coil of braid leaving the rest to hang in a long switch down her back. A pink silk scarf was tied loosely around her neck adding a splash of bright color.

Matt climbed up beside his father. The small caravan of two
wagons with teams, two saddle horses, one mule, and eight people
were on their way. Hail and Tom waved them good-bye encouraging
them to hurry back. They wished them a safe journey but doubted
they had even heard; they were so anxious to be on their way.

Kylee was ecstatic over the beauty of the mountains. Fields of
rhododendrons were reaching over their heads, standing regimentally
straight in rippling colors, and not stirring in the increasing heat.
Everywhere the heavy ground cover encased rock and tree trunks
and in the middle of it all grew large groves of pines, dark green and
magnificently beautiful. They stood apart from the numerous wide
leafed trees. In the valley behind them spread the illusive smoky
haze. The hills were faced with plush green grass and patchwork
squares of various colored wild flowers. The dogwood had shed
their bright spring blossoms. The big spreading chestnuts were
beginning to form small green nut pods and dropping their twigs
in soft-blanketed circles on the ground.

Bess was enjoying every mile of the road but was getting tired
riding sidesaddle. They stopped for lunch, then traveled on to the
Gap to spend the night at the top of the mountain at a place called
Singing Springs. After the evening meal Jan and Matt, with the
help of the girls, gathered bunches of chestnut twigs and then piled
them together for beds.

Kylee was surprised how soft and comfortable the twigs were.
She could not resist teasing Matt and Jan and declared to them that
she could feel every rock under her bed. Mary told her she must
truly be a princess to feel the pea through all the padding. The
conversation fired Emily's imagination and she coaxed Mary to tell
a story. Mary's story triggered a series of stories from each member
of the family; some causing hilarious laughter to rise through the
night into the tree branches. Jan finally insisted they must get to
sleep or they would be too tired to finish the trip into Kentucky.

They traveled across the mountain, down into the rolling hills
covered with dense forest and on into the Kentucky River Valley.
Jan's sister lived at the mouth of a branch joining the river. A wide
plush meadow surrounded the small log cabin. The house was little

but spotlessly clean and neat. There was a large kitchen and two bedrooms filled with children and furniture. Excited to have company, Aunt Dorie and her family made room for everyone stuffing every available corner and empty space. Backward and shy at first toward Kylee, but with Mary and Emily's help they were soon at ease. A wonderful warm hospitality made them all comfortable.

Dorie, a buxom woman, tall of stature like her brother, was so glad to see them. She cried and laughed at the same time. The women busied themselves with visiting and household things. They picked vegetables, berries, cooked meals and sat on the wide lawn sewing, and tending to the children. Their female chattering covered many areas from sick relations, new members to the family, herbs, new patterns for sewing, and quilt making. The conversation came around to an Uncle Lee Acres who had been robbed and murdered at Pound Gap. This caused them all to reflect on the increased number of bandits on the back roads.

Evan Acres, Dorie's husband went with the men to sell Ira's whiskey and buy a new brood mare for Jan. Bess was so concerned over their conversation about murder and robberies that she confessed to Dorie her worry about returning home.

"Don't you worry none, Bess my dear. They'll not waste time on a family. They's usually too poor to chance the risk. You'll be safe as if you were at home in your own bed. Mark my word, they'll not risk tackling a bunch the likes of what you're travelin' with!" Dorie assured her. "They's safety in numbers. You remember that."

Bess was calmed. Her sister-in-law's optimism eased her concern until the day before they departed for home.

Jan came in carrying a small tin box. He went into a bedroom minus giggling children and chattering young women and motioned for Bess to follow him. Setting the tin box on the bed he looked at Bess with deep seriousness darkening his brown eyes. He informed her of the box's contents and other things of importance.

"I found a honey of a mare, Bess. She'll be ready to foul about the same time you'll be, late in January. My dearest-dearest girl, I want to tell you," and he took Bess in his massive arms and kissed her Dresden cheek, "How very happy I am about the little one. I hope this trip won't be too much for you. We'll rest more goin' back."

Jan held her at a distance to look at her with wondering love. He renewed his delight at Bess's early pregnancy and the possibility the child might be a son.

"Oh, shaw Jan. I'm fine! I have never felt better. What's in the box?"

"In the box is a sum of money. It's Ira's from the sellin' of the whiskey an' some other debts that were owed to him on some past deals. We don't dare leave it in the box, too hard to hide. We want you to sew it into the hems of your petticoats. You have enough betwixt you to hide all of it well. If you have to wear a few more, make it so's it will not be noticeable."

"Oh Lord a mercy Jan. Do you know what you are askin'? That's invitin' outlaws. It will be a danger to all of us. We cain't endanger the girls. Don't ask it, please, dear!" she pleaded with Jan her eyes wide with concern.

"Oh, blast it woman! Them road bandits'll never stop a family. They'll have no idea we have money. It was all done secret an' quiet. They's after rich men travelin' alone or freight wagons returnin' to Virginie with payment from supplies. No one knew Ira was travelin' with whiskey. Besides, the ringleader, Talt Hall, is off the road an' in jail. Things'll be quiet on the mountain. We couldn't have picked a better time, dearest." Jan tried to ease her fears.

"Anyone that knows Ira knows his business is whiskey. One of these days they'll get him. They know he travels with money, lots of money!" Bess argued.

"You got no cause to worry, woman. Hide the money like I told you! Besides, they usually don't kill anyone unless they refuse to give them the money. Just remember, if by any chance we get stopped, we'd give them the money an' that would be the end of it. Nothin's gonna happen, dear. We're leavin' before sun up tomorrow. Want to get as far as we can before it gets too hot. This heat's gettin' to be a bear cat!" Jan left with the command, leaving Bess with no other alternative but to obey him.

As Bess opened the box her concern increased. Inside was a large sum of money, all in bills. Over two thousand dollars lay stacked and waiting to be sewn into the women's petticoats.

Bess could not subdue her growing concern. It did not lessen as they journeyed into the mountains. The great fear for their safety only added to her weariness. The tension of her mind and body began to show on her usually gentle nature. She was beginning to find herself being cross with everyone, even Emily.

The little girl carefully stayed as far away from her mother as possible and attached herself with clinging tenaciousness to Mary. Mary laughed at her little sister. Emily tried not to aggravate her mother. She teased Mary into stories and adventures along the road, seeking out squirrels and beetles or any sort of crawling creature. Mary could never understand Emily's fascination with such activities, but went along to keep peace with their mother.

Jan and Matt tried to cheer Bess, assuring her constantly that everything was going as planned. They reminded her that they were getting closer to home each hour, one more night on the trail and lunch about noon the next day, close to Singing Springs. She knew well, a few more hours from the spring and they would be at the mill.

Even with the cheerfulness around her, she could not erase the fear and concern over the hidden money. Deep apprehension gnawed at her very being and left her with a dark foreboding attitude. She had a black dread that her loved ones were in grave danger.

The night on the ground was filled with dreams of her children when they were small, and of the baby son they had lost. She dreamt of Jan as a young man when he was courting her. Then he was making love to her, but there was a twist. The face on the man was always Tom's. Then she saw herself drowning in a pool of black water, swirling down through a whirlpool to the bottom filled with darkness. Someone would reach out to pull her back and the face at the end of the arm, smiling with longing, would be Tom's. She wrestled with the dreams through the night, until she could stand no more and rose before dawn, weak and sweating from the struggle.

She smoothed and straightened her clothing. After brushing her golden hair, she rolled it into a large bun at the nape of her neck pulling it carefully over her ears. As she rolled and twisted she made a promise to herself. She would shake the dreadful fear and make their last day more pleasant.

Tom's pale transparent skin stretched tight across his cheeks leaving a haggard look. His usual bright eyes were clouded and dark circles remained. He managed to shave, then ran his long fingers across his smooth jaw. He walked outside and sat on the bottom step. He was thankful for the coolness of the early morning; it would be short lived as soon as the sun appeared above the green trees. Tom patted Boy's head as he sat beside him on the step. Tom reached down and picked up a stick and threw it for the dog. Tossing the stick game seemed to be the extent of Tom's ambition.

The days since his family's departure had been sheer torture for the young man. He hadn't felt well the morning he'd bid them good-bye. There had been a deep churning in his stomach. He was certain it had been caused from something besides moonshine. Before the sun climbed to noon, he became violently ill. A high fever raged, causing a series of convulsions. Deep internal churning in his lower intestines still kept him from eating anything solid, but he was getting better. Hail tended to him diligently, never leaving him for more than a few minutes at a time. She bathed him to cool him, spooned broth and herb tea into his burning lips, and gave him regular drops of paregoric. The tranquilizing medication kept him resting but probably resulted in the transparent look of his skin. She knew if this malady did not burn itself out in twenty-four hours, Tom would be in trouble. The fever broke and the twitching stopped and he finally rested.

Hail breathed a sigh of relief and lay down for a few hours of sleep. She thanked her God that He had seen her through another illness. She had a suspicion that Tom had swallowed some of the unmoving water in the millpond. She hoped Kylee was all right. The motionless water could be filled with a variety of germs, causing numerous disorders from dysentery to typhoid. Thankful that Tom was on the way to recovery, she would warn them all not to swim or bathe in the still water. The stream was drying from the intense heat with barely a trickle to feed the pond. The iron door was closed and no water moved, leaving it still and stagnating.

Tom got tired of the stick game, much to Boy's disappointment. He decided to resume his duties. He walked to the barn to feed the stock and see Jole'. Simeon had not appeared. He wondered if he was strong enough to sit on a saddle. The only way to find out was to try. Hail became distraught when he told her of his plans.

"You're not well enough to do that, Tom! You should still be in bed. There's no way of tellin' if this thing is over. You could drop off your horse along the road somewhere and lay there an' die. Ain't there no way to talk you out of such foolishness?" she coaxed him, knowing too well by the set of his jaw that his mind was made up.

"I'm gonna find out about Simeon. I need to see what's happened to paw's wagon an' team. You been carin' for everything here anyways. I guess you can handle it another day. If I get too weary to make it back tonight, I'll get a room at Trace's," Tom stated, watching Hail closely waiting for a reaction. It was not long coming.

"A room at Trace's? Now Tom, you ain't well enough for such shenanigans! I ain't no dumb-bell! I know what a room at the tavern means for you, a tumble with that wench of Trace's. Polly ain't the kind of gal you should be thinkin' about at anytime! You ought'a be findin' a nice girl an' plannin' a home of your own. You're getting at an age Tom. You should be doin' that, instead of horsin' around wastin' your manhood on the likes of Polly. I'm tellin' you, you better give up that plan! You been too sick!" she told Tom, patting him gently on the arm.

A restrained smile played around the corners of her scarred lips. The scabs on Hail's burns had dropped and the scars had turned white. She rubbed them each day diligently with a slice of cucumber dipped in heavy cream. Her skin was becoming soft and pliable and she was learning to accept her disfigurement.

"I swear men are all alike! There's only one thing on your mind, sick or well! It won't make no-never-mind what I say. The scriptures are clear tellin' men it's better to cast thy seed upon the ground than into the belly of a whore," she added, peering into Tom's face and seeing a hint of a twinkle deep in his clear blue eyes at her bold statement.

"No! It won't matter Hail. Maybe that's what I need to put myself back in order. An' Polly's not a whore!"

"Well, it ain't Polly you be a needin'. I listened to you a rantin' an' ravin' while you was sick. It weren't her name you was a callin!" She was aware of the widening of Tom's eyes and the look of immediate shock that surfaced.

"You wouldn't be a payin' too much attention to what a sick man was a rantin' an' ravin' about, now would ya Hail? At least you ought'a tell me who it was I was ravin' about!"

"That's all I'm a sayin'. But I will tell you this much, you're a scalawag, Tom Phelps! You ain't really got your mind on Polly. All she did was get you dumped into the pond. Oh, I heard how it was between you an' Matt. I heard how come you wound up takin' a swim early in the mornin'. I told you, didn't I, how you'd all get drunk an' fight over some worthless wench, an' you did! Didn't you?" She sat down in the rocker by the window watching Tom button a starched collar onto his clean shirt. "Bye Hail. You old sweetheart! You might as well give in an' make your mind up to marry Paw!" He advised her, giving her a kiss on her scarred cheek.

"I guess I can say my piece too, see'ins how we're a buttin' our noses into each other's business." Tom buttoned his cuffs and ran his finger around the collar. He knew he was going to be uncomfortable, so he took it off.

"That's none of your business, Tom! You're too young to make your own decisions. But I'm old enough to know what I'm a doin'." She grinned lifting her chin.

"Stars an' garters, Hail! You cain't lay that malarkey on me! If you an' Paw had a know'd what you were a doin', you'd a been together a long time ago." His voice was not teasing anymore and Hail was silenced. Tom went out the door leaving the coolness of the house. He walked into the heat of the already blazing sun, Boy at his heels.

Tom wanted to make it to Gladeville before noon. He would find Dan Fletcher and put in his bid for the marshal position and see if anyone had seen Simeon Niger. He ignored Trace's and rode on through Donkey. It was not in him to push Jole' too hard and he spent more than a time or two resting at the side of the road. But strange as it seemed to him, by the time he reached Gladeville, he was feeling better. He was beginning to crave food for the first time in four days.

Everything was quiet in town. The courthouse square and the streets surrounding it were filled with horses and buggies. The courtroom was crowded with spectators. There was no longing in Tom's heart to view Talt Hall's trial; it brought back the bitter memory of his own and the circumstances leading up to it.

Court was in full session and the jail was locked up tighter than a drum. Tom found no one who might have seen or heard of a black man driving a team and wagon. He found out that Republican Advisor Fletcher was in the courtroom. He gave up and headed back to Donkey and Trace's. Hail was right. He was going to see Polly, hoping that when he arrived there, he could find a bowl of rabbit stew and a biscuit.

He walked into Trace's still thinking about food, but asked for Polly. It was dark outside and a full moon replaced the sweltering sun. The vibrant yellow glow cast long shadows into the wide street.

"She's in the kitchen, Tom. She has other things to do around here besides layin' up with a different man every hour!" Trace slammed a glass down on the counter and watched stupefied as it shattered onto the floor.

"Well, you've always let her do pretty much as she pleased ever since she was knee-high. No reason for you to change your attitude now, is there, Trace?"

Trace shot Tom a hostile look, his eyes stating clearly for him to mind his own business. Changing the subject, Tom asked if he had seen or heard anything of their hired man. When he got a sullen shake of the head, he asked Trace for a room and a jug of his best whiskey.

"Ain't seen hide nor hair of him since he brung Polly back from your place." Trace handed him a jug and key, then went on about his business of cleaning up the broken glass.

"Wal, I guess he sure enough, hornswoggled us! He's disappeared out of sight, takin' our team an' wagon with him. No fault of yours, Trace. We'll talk about it later," Tom added.

Tom went on around to the kitchen to find Polly, glad to be away from the smell of gas lanterns and tobacco. He found Polly washing dishes from the evening meal. Her sleeves were rolled up past her elbows and beads of perspiration covered her forehead. The kitchen was hot and sticky and Polly was not too happy with the chore. She sloshed the water and rattled the dishes loudly, hoping to irritate her father. Perhaps then he would be aware of her anger because he made her do up the dishes and tidy the kitchen. When she had enough money she would hire a girl to do these dirty chores.

Tom came up quietly behind her. "Lawsey, Tom! You don't care how you catch a body!" Polly said in shocked surprise, her dark eyes unenthusiastic at seeing him.

"An' what a body!" He said putting his arms around her waist. What was wrong? Why wasn't she delighted to see him? "I have a jug, you gonna come share it with me?"

She turned in his arms, her hands still wet from the dishwater. A warm sweet look came from her sultry eyes. A smile touched her lips as she noticed the fading bruise on his chin and the slight swelling still in his bottom lip. Tom gave her body a squeeze and kissed her warm cheek. Polly lowered her eyelids and her smile grew.

"It's good to see you, Tom. I have to finish this darn kitchen first." She picked absently at the top button on his shirt.

"Hurry up, its number six." The greasy smell of dishwater was bringing the churning back into Tom's stomach. He had forgotten about food. Letting her go with a charming grin, he left the kitchen.

The hall above was dim, lit from one light at the top of the stairs. The room was reasonably clean. The wallpaper was smeared in a few places where someone had attempted to wash away the numerous specks of flies. Pale pink rosebuds were still discernible on the gray-blue background. A thought was running through Tom's mind. Trace was sure letting the place go to the dogs. All he thought about anymore was making money.

Underneath the limp lace curtain at the window hung a greasy shade pulled almost to the bottom. Someone had tried to pull it farther down succeeding only in ripping it away from the roller at one corner, leaving a three-corner tear.

"I shouldn't be doin' this. I should have listened to Hail," he mused to himself, lighting the lamp on the dresser. Uncorking the jug, he took a long swig of the fiery liquid and sat it on the stand next to the bed. Feeling the burning moonshine hit the bottom of his empty stomach added to the churning. He knew it was not going to sit too well on his already weakened condition. Dismissing the thought, he took another long drink.

"I ought to find a card game an' forget Polly for tonight," he muttered to himself.

Tom was having a hard time keeping Kylee from walking through his mind. Why should it bother him? Why was he having guilt feelings for wanting Polly? As if he were being unfaithful to Kylee. Why did he feel that way? Kylee hated him. She was probably having a wonderful time with Matt. He was convinced she wasn't worrying about him. Would it be the same after tonight, after Polly? Would he still want Kylee as much as ever?

His mind rested on the two together. Matt's arm around Kylee's waist. The thought of his brother touching her was too much. A sense of jealous anger filled him. He pulled his boot off and threw it with force at the door. Taking off the other boot, he threw it beside the other one that had come to rest on the floor. He removed his shirt and hung it on the bedpost then stretched out on the bed.

It was a long time before Polly showed up. He had almost finished the whiskey and was about to sleep when she knocked on the door. Pushing it open slightly, she peeked in to see if Tom was asleep. He motioned for her to come in. When she moved into the room she brought with her the scent of a heady perfume. She pushed the door shut and stood leaning against it eyeing Tom closely with sultry brown eyes. She had changed into a dress of vibrant red satin, cut low in front exposing a good deal of her full breasts and the valley between. Her black hair was held back with a red silk ribbon tied at the top of her head. Countless curls bounced about her shoulders with each movement. The curling iron steeped many times in a lamp chimney, Tom thought was quite a bit of work.

"What took you so long?" he questioned going over to stand in front of her. "You didn't have to do all of this for me, it's nice though, you look wonderful. I swear you are the most beautiful woman, Polly."

"It's nice to see you, Tom. I'm glad you come. I'm sorry I was so long."

Placing his hands on the door behind her shoulders, he bent to kiss her. She turned her head and pushed him away.

"Come on Polly, you took forever. What's ailin' you now? I was thinkin' we could finish what we started the other night." He backed away and stood looking at her, waiting for an explanation.

She stood quietly, gazing with joy at his handsome face. He had a square jaw beginning to show some signs of a beard, growing always first in the deep cleft of his chin. His blue eyes were as heavily lashed as a woman's and darkened with anticipation. His fully sculptured lips smiled teasingly at her, reminding her of a little boy waiting for a piece of candy. Seeing Tom always filled her with a happiness she couldn't explain, and she always loved to be with him.

"Sure Tom. I'm willin', but there's something I'm gonna tell you first. This time it's gonna cost you!" She took a box of cigarettes from a pocket in the side of her full skirt. Polly put the tailor made between her lips, struck a match on the door and lit it letting the smoke out slowly. She scrutinized his reaction closely.

Tom watched her handling the thin cigarette. "Not rolling your own anymore? Comin' up in the world, aren't you? Cost me? What are you talkin' about?" He realized the rose tint on her cheeks was rouge and the red of her lips painted. The fancy dress purposely cut indecently low. Watching the slow movement of her breasts, he was enraptured again with her voluptuous beauty.

"That's what I mean Tom. You gotta pay same as the rest." She puffed the cigarette and wondered how Tom was going to take the news. "Things have changed since you was here last."

Tom let his head back and laughed loudly. He backed away and sat down on the bed still laughing. "You mean you're gonna be a whore an' start sellin' what you've been givin' away?" He stopped laughing and looked at her seriously, watching closely as her irritation began to show.

"Might as well. It's a way to get what I want. I'm gonna get enough money to leave these damn hills. Instead of lying' around for nothin', I decided I might as well make what I was doin' pay off. A body has to be sensible about things." She shrugged her shoulders.

"But takin' money, Polly. That makes it a profession! It'll never end." Lifting the jug he took another drink and handed it to Polly.

Not that it mattered to him. He was aware that he hadn't been Polly's only admirer. "How come you decided this?"

"When I found out there were men with money willin' to pay for a little pleasure. Instead of takin', an' takin', an' never givin' anything in return." She looked at Tom with sadness in her eyes.

"I never thought about it like that, Polly. If I'd a knowed you needed money, I'd give you as much as you wanted. I thought you had a feelin' for me."

"I do Tom. But it weren't any use, were it? I weren't never gonna be anything to you but someone to lay around with whenever it pleased you."

There was huskiness in her voice and Tom thought a little despair underneath also. Looking in her eyes, he saw the hopelessness too. His glance traveled down to the fullness of her breasts and her slim waist. There was no doubt in his mind she had the body for it. He recalled his first experience at becoming a man. They were both young teens and Polly already developed into a woman. She was wise beyond her years in pleasuring a man. He had been a green kid, eager to follow her lead and anxious to learn. It had been a beautiful experience and what she said was true. Whenever he desired a woman, there was always Polly. A smile teased the corners of his mouth as he remembered the disappointment and anger when he found out he was not her only lover.

A realization filled him. He knew one man would never do for Polly and he was sad. Listening to her declaration to join the oldest profession, he knew it could be no other way for her. Running his wet tongue over his dry lips, he took a deep breath. Yep, he reckoned he'd pay her this time.

"You had any customers yet?" he questioned, watching her reaction closely. Seemed he was making it a practice of butting into other people's business lately.

"I reckon that ain't none of your business, Tom." Her look was hostile.

"How much for how long?" He asked, reaching into his pocket for his money. He surveyed his wealth and waited for her answer.

Sultry eyes watched him closely. "Nothin'!" she informed him thoughtfully. "Like old times for the night Tom. Make it like old times. Like we was kids again, an' there were just me an' you."

"I don't want any more hand-outs! I aim to pay for what I get," his voice was scratchy and harsh. "But it won't be like old times. It'll be like I say, understand, Polly?"

"Anything you say, Tom," she said moving away from the door. She moved to the foot of the bed and stood waiting his command.

"Well, sweetie. I always wanted to see you with your clothes off. All the times we've been together, I never seen you without all them damn skirts. I've never seen no woman naked, exceptin' in pictures, then only partly. I aim to lay back here an' get my fill of watchin' you take your clothes off."

Laying back he stretched his full length upon the bed making sure she noticed the muscular hardness of his well-formed body. Polly slowly unbuttoned the tiny buttons down the front of her dress, deliberately taking her time and watching him closely with heavy eyes. Tom took another drink and wiped his mouth with his hand. He leaned back and fastened his hands behind his head tensely waiting.

"Come on, Polly. Make me want you bad enough to pay for it," he challenged, anticipation turning the corners of his mouth.

Polly was down to her petticoats. Shoes and stockings came next. She unlaced her corset and hung it over the bedpost. She lifted her chemise over her head and revealed her dusty rose flesh. Her breasts were firm and smooth and thrusting forward with round brown nipples that tantalized him. Tom caught his breath. My God, he thought, what a beautiful woman!

Polly blew the light out on the stand. Reaching through the curtains, she gave the blind a tug pulling it from the roller, letting it fall. She dropped her drawers in a heap on the floor. The pale yellow rays streaming through the window drenched her body with moonlight, a golden statue standing before him in all her naked loveliness.

Tom was impressed, aroused, and anticipating what was to come. She walked slowly toward him as she swayed her hips and rotating slowly, then pushing upward with a suggestive motion. He reached out for her, he was ready, but she eluded him. He had named the game. She was going to play it to the fullest. For once he was going to beg.

"Oh, not yet Tom. You're only half-ready. It wouldn't be worth anything yet!" Her voice was a husky whisper in the shadows filling the room.

Tom smiled, she knew how to make him sweat, this lovely vibrating yellow goddess of love, swaying and twisting in the moonlight. He watched the golden lights bounce from every lush spot on her perfect body until he could contain himself no longer.

"Now, Polly. Now!" he begged. "I'm ready! I'll pay you whatever you want. Come here!" And he opened his arms for her.

She came to him laying herself across him fully, pressing herself down hard against him. As his eager arms encircled her warm flesh she kissed him softly, but holding back. He could feel her soft tongue caressing his top lip, back and forth, teasing. He could stand no more. He rolled her over sinking her naked body deep into the feather softness of the bed.

Tom kissed her with great tenderness afterward. He reached and pulled the bright colored comforter over her naked loveliness. He was unable to look at her without wanting her again. The many waves and curls of her hair made a dark circle upon the pillow. A lingering ray of moonlight touched a spark in its mass then danced away. Two ebony pools of darkness watched him from the depths of the bed. He got up and found his pants in the shadows.

"Anything Polly. Anything you ask, it was worth it. I'll pay whatever you ask," he said softly, a note of sadness in his voice.

"I told you, Tom, it was for free this time, for old time sakes. It was the best ever. You'll be back."

He couldn't see her face clearly against the pillow, but he knew the rouge burned red on her cheeks. He'd bet she was smiling, satisfied with herself.

"I wish you luck, Polly. Success an' everything you want. I hope the choice you've made will prove profitable, if not satisfying. You're a lot'a woman, Polly," he sighed. He leaned against the door and pulled on his boots. The thought crossed his mind that this was the first time he'd ever made love to Polly with his boots off. Tom reached for his shirt and sat down on the bed beside her.

There were no regrets where Polly was concerned. She had always completely fulfilled his desires. That was all it had been he knew that now. Suddenly he wanted something more from life. Hail was right. He thought of Kylee and he was ashamed for being here. Without doubt, it was his last visit to Polly! Taking some gold pieces from his pocket, all that he had, he scattered them on the pillow beside her head.

"Good-bye Polly. Thanks for what you've been to me. I'll not be back, but I'll see you around." With the statement he smiled, his white teeth flashing in the scarce light. He picked up his jug of whiskey and was gone, closing the door silently behind him.

Polly lay for a moment, savoring the night. Tom had always been an ardent lover, demanding, but gentle. She had taught him well. She smiled to herself as she thought of the very willing pupil he had been. For her there would be many men, but never anyone like Tom. She loved him as much as she could any man. The tears started. She felt she was losing something, knowing all too well, that Tom would not be back. It may be a struggle for him, but she was certain he would never visit her again.

Most of the enjoyment of being with Tom was the fact she needed him. Polly would never need him again, but there would be times she would want him desperately. She dried her tears on the corner of the quilt. She was never one to waste time crying. You had to look at things practically. Rolling on her side and raising on her elbow, she picked up the coins Tom had dropped. She counted them slowly, letting them fall one at a time on the softness of the pillow.

Downstairs the card room was dense with smoke. The heavy smell of wet tobacco juice was prevalent. Gas lanterns gave off a yellow glow to the room and everyone in it. Tom sat down in a winged-back chair and tilted it against the wall absently watching the card game in front of him.

"Hello, Tom, you old son-of-a-gun," a friendly voice addressed him through the haze.

"Well, how in tarnation are you, Alvin? You takin' good care of things for Jan?"

There was the drop of moisture on the end of his nose. His watery yellow eyes peered close at Tom in the dimness. Tom was afraid the drop would fall on him and he leaned back closer to the wall.

"Sure is lonesome up there with the gals all gone with Jan. Sure has been hot, ain't it? Sure could use some rain. The tobac's burnin' up. Thought you went with the folks, Tom." Alvin's drawl was slow and halting.

"No, I stayed with the place. I gotta be gettin' back. Wanted to meet the folks at noon at the Gap."

"You ain't headin' back to the mill now, are you Tom?"

When the younger man nodded his head, Alvin was quick to add, "you better wait until mornin', Tom. You're in no shape to ride tonight. Be mornin' before too long anyway," Alvin advised him reaching to steady Tom's chair.

"Thank you for your concern. I appreciate it, Alvin. I ain't hardly drunk nothin'. I'm fine as frogs hair." Tom rose to prove his statement. He was still carrying his jug and swaying dangerously. Alvin took his elbow and guided him helpfully through the door.

"Thanks for the help, Alvin. But I told you, I'm fine!" Tom pulled his arm away and walked stiffly down the stairs leaning backward to keep from falling headlong.

Boy was waiting for him curled underneath Jole's belly, his head resting on his paws. The horse stood waiting patiently for Tom's return.

"Friends! You're a man's real friends!" he told them solemnly, giving both an affectionate pat and lifted himself into the saddle.

The sweet fresh air cleared his head some but not the churning in his stomach. He rode in no hurry, the jug sitting between his knees. He sang softly to himself:

"Oh, my pretty quad-roon,
The flower that's faded too so-on..."

The moon gave daylight vibrancy to everything. Tom rode in the light spots, lifting his head and letting his song out free and easy:

"My heart's like the string on my banjo,
All broke for my pretty quad-roon...
Her form was exceedingly fair..."

"Oh, was it ever fair," he said to himself thinking of Polly, then continued his song....

> *"Her cheeks like the red rose in June,*
> *And her ringlets of dark glossy hair,*
> *Were the curls of my pretty quad-ro-on."*

Tom's usually clear and resilient voice was slurred from drinking. Boy would take time to howl a few bars at the moon in appreciation of Tom's fine rendition. "Tarnation Boy. You sound as awful as I do. Sure a good thing no one's around to hear us! Sure would make 'em sick! It makes me want to puke." He spoke out loud to the dog as he rode slowly through the dense trees with the help of the moon and Jole's horse sense.

He took the short cut behind Trace's up the mountain. It would come out on Pound road just before getting to Baldwin's Branch. The whiskey only added to his condition and weakness. He was beginning to shake in the saddle. He was not going to be able to ride far. He breathed in deeply of the heavy green of the forest and the smell of wild flowers opening to catch the early dew. He found himself comparing the fresh sweetness to Polly's overly aromatic perfume. As he thought back on the night's event, he was glad it was over. Feeling sorry for Polly made him have a pang of conscience as if he were deserting her. He could have married her but was certain that would not have been the answer for Polly or him, perhaps she was wiser than he thought, her decision had solved the problem. Dismissing it from his mind he began to concentrate on staying in the saddle. The swaying motion of the horse was adding to the queasiness in his weak stomach and he was becoming ill. He pulled up on the reins.

"Tarnation, Jole'. You're movin' like a damn rockin' horse." He sat for a moment trying to gather his composure then slipped slowly to the ground on his knees. Violent retching racked his body.

"Oh God, I'm sick! Never again! Never, never, never! No sir-ree!" Picking up the jug that had fallen on the ground beside him he threw it with what force he could muster into a tree. The jug shattered and the contents washed down the trunk into the ground. The strong mash odor was heavy in his nostrils. He was sick again, leaving him drained of all strength. He hoped his fever would not return. Laying his head on a moss-covered log, he fell into a drunken sleep.

Boy watched with sympathy as his master retched violently. When Tom at last fell into a deep sleep the dog laid his head on his arm. The animal watched him closely with sadness in his large eyes. The dog lay next to him not stirring. He never took his eyes from Tom and patiently waited for his master to revive.

CHAPTER NINE

The trial of Talt Hall had become a community event. Most hill people felt the Kentucky bad man was long past due for the hangman noose. They had come from miles around to hear him receive the sentence.

The Deputy Marshal, Tanner Hensely, appeared to take his responsibility of guarding Hall seriously. But his mood was hostile at Snow's prolonged absence due to a sick relative. He was feeling the pressure of being tied to Gladeville and the trial.

Hearing the undertone of gossip that Tom's intentions to run for Marshal were true had not improved his disposition. There was a nagging insistence to head for Pound and see what was happening on the mountain. It was taking Jay too damn long to get rid of the Phelps bunch. One thing for sure, it had to be done. He was not going to stand by and watch Tom Phelps fill Marshal Snow's shoes. He was going to take him out of the picture, permanently!

He arrived at the jail before dawn to get the prisoner ready for the courtroom. His attention centered on the black man in the opposite cell from Hall. Hensely rattled the cell door to get Simeon's attention.

"You aimin' to rot inside this jail, nigger? You ready to tell me the truth about what you were doin' with Ira's wagon? You was tellin' the truth about it being empty. It was empty as hell!"

"No sir. I ain't wantin' to rot here, no sir. I sure don't want to do that. It were just like I was tellin' you, Mista Hensely, Marshal sir. I was doin' what Mista Ira told me to do. Deliverin' them Walker boys wherever they were wantin' to go. If you'll find them, they'll tell you. That was all there was to it. I'll bet Mista Ira was madder then all get out, Marshal sir, when he had to go into Kentucky without his wagon. He was lookin' for me to have it back home," Simeon declared, his nervousness visible.

"You say Ira was goin' into Kentucky?"

"Yes sir," the Negro replied.

"When was that gonna be?" the Deputy Marshal appeared unconcerned and examined his nails closely.

Simeon's eyes set deep in dark hollows and glowed black in the dim light of the cell. It was apparent he was tired of his stay in jail. There could be no harm in telling Tanner of Ira's trip into Kentucky. The deputy had no jurisdiction there, and Ira would be rid of the whiskey by now and on his way back home. There was no way the information could hurt anyone, at least that's what Simeon innocently thought. It was his only chance to be freed.

"He was a leavin' the next mornin' after you arrested me, sir. Yes sir, he's gonna be madder than all get out when he had to leave without that wagon." Simeon tried to stay calm and not appear too anxious with the possibility of being free. The past four days had been long and weighed heavily on his nerves.

"How come you never told me anythin' about Ira goin' into Kentuck?" The Deputy Marshal raised his lowered head to look square at the black man with a freezing glare.

"Well, sir. You never asked me nothin' about Mista Ira's where abouts. I'd a told you for sure! You only ask about the team and wagon." Simeon stood closer to the cell door, mentally preparing an attempt at explaining the oversight.

Hensely reached through the bars and clasped the black man's shirtfront pulling the collar up tight around his neck. The nervous sweat began to form along the top of Simeon's upper lip.

"Listen good, nigger! I'm aimin' on knowin' Phelps's where abouts! If you don't be tellin' me, you'll be right here until doom's day! You know about doom's day, coon?"

Simeon nodded his head emphatically at Hensely's question.

Hensely's tobacco breath spewed into Simeon's face, the brown juice beginning to show at the corners of his mouth and along the edge of his freshly trimmed mustache. His narrow brown eyes held no mercy.

"I ain't knowin' much about where he be now. He never confided in the likes of me much. I only knows he was intendin' to head for Kentucky the day after the fourth."

"When's he comin' back? Tell me, tell me!" Tanner's desire to have Ira and Tom Phelps was suddenly becoming a flaming priority.

He would as soon kill the black as bother with him. But that would never do. U.S. Marshal Lorenzo Snow would never hold still for murder in the jail. That would surely bring about retaliation. There were too many bigwigs buzzing around the jail and courthouse. He had to watch himself and see to Talt's hanging. Handling himself well under pressure would be good politics. People would begin to think twice before they believed he'd had anything to do with the outlaws on Pound. If there was any chance he could arrange to permanently get the Phelps's out of his hair, he was going to do it. It would be a perfect time while everyone was involved with Talt's trial and Snow was out of the picture. And he could get the Bentley girl for Kenus at the same time. He gave the man another shake.

"Who was traveling with Ira?" the Marshal continued to interrogate the Negro.

"Miss Kylee, an' Mista Matt, an' Mista Jan Stewart. Mista Tom was gonna meet them at the top of the mountain when they came back across. Some place they called Singin' Springs."

"When, you idiot, tell me when!" Tanner was burning with the possibility of being late.

"I can't 'member sir. I can't 'member."

"Your black hide better 'member if you know what's good for it!" He pulled Simeon's collar tighter to reinforce his words.

"Let's see. I reckon today." Simeon thought hard, mentally counting the days. "Yes sir. It'd be today! That's when, today about noon. I 'member now."

Hensely let the Negro's shirt front drop. He smiled his best political smile at Simeon showing his gratitude while smoothing his shirtfront.

"You done told me the truth?"

"Yes, sir! I wouldn't lie to no Deputy Marshal, Mista Hensely, sir! Now can I get out?"

"We'll see. We'll see." He turned and left the desperate man clinging to the bars in utter hopelessness.

Kenus took his leather suitcase from under the bed, set it on top, opened it, and began filling it. He was tired of this waiting game. He'd heard nothing more from Mitchell or Ferrell. With no interest in watching Talt's trial, he wanted to go home. He had made up his mind he would have to leave without Kylee. A knock on the door stopped his work. To his surprise it was the Deputy Marshal.

"Thought you'd be on your way to court!"

"In time Hall, in time. I got other business on my mind. Looks like you're readyin' to leave." Tanner stated, looking around, noting the half-packed suitcase and Hall's clothing laid out on the bed.

"I was."

"Well, you can be for changin' your mind. Get your guns if you got any, an' come with me. You might be able to bring back the virgin you been a huntin'." Tanner winked an eye and watched Kenus closely. "You're gonna have to pull your part of the load."

"That's no problem," Kenus said excitedly, strapping on his shoulder harness. He checked his pistol for bullets and shoved it into the holster. "I'll need a horse though."

"There's one a waitin'. Let's be goin'. We have a far piece to ride. We gotta look up Jay. I wanna be on the mountain before noon. Snow'll be in this afternoon. The other deputy can handle things until then. I'll be back before the trial's over."

"You're leavin' the trial?" Kenus couldn't believe it.

"They's nothin' I can do exceptin watch Talt squirm. His fate's sealed. It's Phelps I'm wantin' to do something about, while I got a chance."

Far back on Pound Mountain on the Kentucky side stands a gathering of rocks, a protrusion defacing the green of the scenery. The high rocks jutting from the mountain made an ideal sentinel place. Positioned behind the large rock one could see for miles down both sides of the mountain. It was an ideal place to watch the approach of horse, men, or wagons entering the Gap. Looking up at the protruding rocks, it was easy to understand why Confederate General Humphrey Marshal used it as an observation point. He would station his sentinels around the clock to observe the activities of the northern advancement until Union General James A. Garfield drove them out of the Gap. New trees, pines, and green undergrowth had long erased the activity of the armies. But the rocks remained, ever somber, ever ominous.

The dawn dropped a trace of dew turning the rocks to a glistening silver and chasing the shadows from their surface. The air was still and clear. At the lookout watch in these rocks, now called Picket Rock, Jay Mitchell could see far down the mountain. From this vantage point and with the help of a high-powered scope, he could watch Pound road between Kentucky and Virginia. On either side of the mountain nothing escaped his watchful vigilance.

He lifted his head from the scope and sniffed. In the air was the promise of rain. Some moisture would be a welcome change from the intense heat. He rubbed his left knee cursing the painful rheumatism. The pain always increased with the threat of a storm. Nights sleeping on the ground didn't help.

Jay stared down the mountain, unconcerned with the beauty around him. He only wanted to see the movement of a wagon that would prove promising. The valley lay mysteriously quiet and the intense blue-green of the hills stretched for miles before him. It was seldom one could see so far. The smoky haze that usually shrouded the valley and crept into the hollows resting along the slopes was absent this day.

Jay never tired of outlaw activity. His boys rode by his side, and life was complete. Even wildcatting whiskey was forgotten. He wanted nothing more. Nothing was missing, except Blaine. Soon he would see Tom Phelps answer for that. Paying for Hensely's protection and blind eye didn't sit well with Jay. But even so, he made a fair profit.

517

It was worth it to have his freedom on the mountain. He heard a movement climbing the side of the rock. He lowered the scope as Ferrell walked up beside him carrying his hat in his hand. Leaning against the rock, the younger man looked out over the mountain.

"Lovely mornin'," he offered as a greeting, smoothing his tousled hair and putting on his small brimmed hat.

"Yes, it is for sure. You suppose anythin'll come by today, Ferrell? You sleep in long enough. Them yah-hoo's of mine still in the sack? It ain't mornin' no more, it's most noon. See where that sun's at?"

"Somethin'll show up sooner or later. I seen a few people go by into Kentucky while you an' the boys was a visitin' Nell. But weren't anything that looked promisin'. Looked to be a family of sorts, so I let them go by. They was a bunch of them," he stated giving Jay a wide grin through his heavy beard. He looked back across the trees to the horse trail below them.

"Say, look a there Jay. Ain't that someone headed this way?" He looked closer into the trees. "There. There they are! Sure as shootin', someone's comin' up the holler. They are still down there a ways. Take a look, Jay, see if you can tell who it is."

Jay focused the scope and caught a fleeting glimpse of the horsemen as they wound in and out among the thick trees. Sure enough they were going to have company.

"I'll be damned if it ain't Hensely," Jay exclaimed handing the scope to Ferrell to take a look.

"It sure as hell is! I'll be damned if it ain't cousin Kenus ridin' with him. What you suppose they got on their minds ridin' all the way up here? Talt's trial goin' on an' all. Don't look like Hensely could be leavin' town at a time like this."

"You wouldn't think he'd be checkin' up on us now, would you? Let's get down to camp. They'll be there before long. I could see 'em whippin' their horses good," Jay answered and left the rock.

Tanner rode into camp first, Kenus close behind. Pulling their horses to a stop, they dismounted saying nothing at first and reached for the jug Jay offered them.

"Good news! Good news, Jay!" Tanner wiped the whiskey from his graying mustache with a snowy white handkerchief. "Good whiskey, we needed that! We've had a hard ride. You ain't seen nothin' goin' by on the road today, have you now? I was hopin' we weren't too late."

Jay shook his head. "What do you mean by that?"

"We passed no one on the road. I finally squeezed it out'a that nigger. Ira will be at the Springs at noon, headin' for the mill. If I know Ira, he's been in Kentucky sellin' whiskey. That damn nigger didn't have much to say about that. It don't matter no-how. I figure it would be a good time while everyone's thinkin' about Talt's trial to get rid of them Phelps bastards. Admit it Jay, you want Ira dead as bad as I do. Let's get it done!" Hensely demanded and took the jug from his partner in crime.

"The Bentley girl is with them, we'll get her for Kenus. He can take her away from here. We'll kill them all. Dead men tell no tales, we don't want no one left livin' to talk about it. They'll be carryin' a wad a money too, Jay. I ain't interested in that, you can give my share to the boys. But I want Ira an' Tom dead! He gonna pull his weight on this job, Jay?" Hensely nodded toward Bob who was tying his bed into a roll. He was getting ready to hang it on a tree limb safe from snakes and crawling insects.

"Of course, he's a Mitchell, ain't he? Don't worry about Bob, Tanner. I'll see to it he does his part. How come you brought that furiner? He gonna carry his weight?" Jay sneered, watching Kenus drain the jug of whiskey.

"Janice Stewart is with Ira, I cain't help that. The only one I want left livin' is the Bentley gal. Kenus came to take her home with him. He's payin' good for her safety. So don't let anythin' happen to her!"

"I want my money before we start. Are the boys with Phelps, both of them?" Jay stretched his hand to receive the money Kenus was counting.

"Matt's ridin' with Ira and Tom's meetin' them at noon. When they reach here, they'll all be together. That's the way it'll be. Let's make sure none of them but the Bentley gal lives. Let's take the scope an' get on the rock or they'll get plum away from us. We've jawed enough!" With that command, Hensely started up the path, Kenus and Ferrell close behind.

"I'll be right along Tanner," Jay promised, excitement growing inside him. "You hear boys? The time has come; we'll get us some Phelps's today! It couldn't be sweeter. We'll get 'em all, an' Jan Stewart too. Then Mary'll be yours, Bob. You hear me, boy? You been listenin'?"

"What's the matter, boy? You're lookin' kinda pale. You gettin' the worms? Maybe Rueben's cornbread ain't settin' too well on your stomach. We-uns knows he ain't the best cook in the world. You should have a smile all over your face," Jay laughed.

"But Paw, Jan's been our friend, a good friend!"

"I been a tellin' you boy, killin' Jan's the only way for you to get Mary. We'll take care of it, don't you worry! We're gonna take care of this!" He patted Bob's shoulder with assurance, ignoring his son's declaration.

"I want no more sass from you! Be ready to mount up when we spot the wagons." Jay's eyes were beginning to glow with anticipation. "You forget they're gonna pay for Blaine! I'll have my horse back. That bastard Tom Phelps thinks he's gonna be ridin' it forever! Matt'll be sorry he stole Taynee. We'll bring her body back to Mitchell's buryin' place were she should be lying, instead of beside Billy Phelps!" Jay picked his hat up from a log and jammed it angrily on his head.

"Yah-hoo, Paw! Yah-hoo!" Rueben shouted and jumped in the air slapping his soiled sweat streaked hat against his thigh. "Sure is sweet, Paw! Sure is!"

Bob grew sick thinking of what was going to happen. There was nothing he could do to stop it. If he rode out to warn them his father would kill him. There was no way he would listen to his pleading. He hated the outlaw life. He still dreamed of a time when he could stand up to his father and declare his plans for his own future. Each time they robbed a wagon he hoped his father would let him go home.

Jay had no such intentions. His goal was to make a man out of Bob and he dragged him along on all the raids. Bob had learned to carry a gun without total repulsion and could even fire it into the air to scare the muleskinners. His father was beginning to think his lessons were working.

Bob had let his hair grow to his shoulders. His beard was long and had finally filled in to hide his chin. He was handsome with a refinement his father lacked, probably a flash back from his great-great-grandfather, "Iron Jaw". He would never forgive Jay for Taynee's death. Dark sad eyes were filled with loneliness and hostility toward his father.

Rueben, on the other hand, loved the rugged life. He swaggered and boasted of each accomplishment that pleased his father. He enjoyed having money in his pocket and promised himself to save enough to become rich. Then he could win Polly's love. If it was money she wanted he would get it. At least she would share her bed with him. It would be easier after Tom Phelps was out of the picture.

"It won't be long until them Phelps's are all dead! They'll torment us no more!" Rueben declared jubilantly to his father.

Jay lifted Bob's gun from the holster as he went by and shoved it into his own belt. Jay warned him with a glance not to protest. He couldn't chance him turning on him. Jay mounted his horse and motioned for his sons to move out ahead of him to where Tanner, Kenus, and Ferrell stood in the crevice of the tall rocks watching the road winding between the trees below with Jay's scope.

Ferrell looked glum. He was all for the robbery, but he wanted no part of murdering these people. It still irked him that Jay would not talk of Taynee's death, only informed him Matt Phelps was to blame. Perhaps if that were true, then they deserved to die. Thoughts of Taynee clouded his eyes with sadness. He listened with mixed feelings as the three older men planned the kidnapping of Kylee and the massacre of the Phelps clan.

"Kill the teams; we can't chance anyone pullin' ahead. Don't kill that Palomino Tom Phelps will be ridin', that horse is mine!" Jay was emphatic.

It had been Ira's decision to have his caravan moving before dawn to take advantage of the early morning coolness, and then stop for breakfast later. Bess still held the dread she felt around her like a cloak. Smiling through her fear, she tried to not let her concern show through to the others. The hem of her petticoat filled with bills weighed heavily against her ankles. The bulky burden was a constant reminder of the possibility of outlaws.

"Bess looks as if she could use a few minutes away from that horse. I'm ready for a bit of breakfast anyways. Spread a blanket for me son. Think I'll have a nap while the women folk ready things. No need to unhitch the team. Lead them on over to the creek an' let them drink," Ira told his son on the wagon seat beside him.

"Tell the gals not to ramble off too far; they need to stay close to the wagons. Soon as we pass under Picket Rock, we'll be ready for a break again. Perhaps we'll meet Tom by then. He always did enjoy the ride up the Virginia side of the mountain. Said it was his favorite spot in the whole world." Ira scanned the huge outcrop of rock barely visible from where he lay on the blanket Matt spread out for him. He took a long drink from the jug of whiskey beside him, lay back and fell into a sound slumber.

Jan's wagon was behind Ira a quarter of a mile. Bess, Mary, and Kylee straggled along behind. He had not pushed his team too hard up the long grade of the mountain. The young mare he had purchased was tied securely to the back of Ira's wagon. Matt untied her and tethered the horse close to the stream.

Jan pulled his wagon up close to where Matt was letting the horses drink. Jumping out, he lifted Emily into his arms as Ginny climbed down stepping on the wagon wheel. Emily was unhappy with her father and sat sullen and close to tears between her father and sister. She was broken hearted because of a sharp reprimand from her usually tolerant parent.

Emily had been riding in the back of the wagon content and happy. She was singing and rolling around on the bedding and had become too energetic jumping and flipping about. She was kicking her heels and turning somersaults until Jan became concerned for her safety. The slightly loaded wagon bounced around considerably on the steep rocky road and he was afraid she would topple overboard. He scolded his little girl for being rowdy and made her sit quietly on the seat between he and Ginny. Jan gave her a tight hug as he lifted her down.

"You're not still mad at your ol' poppy, are you now, little one?" he questioned his pouting daughter. Her eyes filled with forgiveness and she shook her head, kissed him soundly, and squirmed free of his hold and ran to play.

Jan slid a wooden chest that held the food and utensils to the back of the wagon letting it rest on the tailgate. He turned to help Bess from her horse as the younger women rode up. He kissed her affectionately and held her close for a moment inquiring how she was taking the ride.

"I'm fine Jan, really. I'll have a bit of vittals together in a little while."

"I could do it Bess. You could lie down an' rest."

"I never heard tell of such a thing, lyin' down in the middle of the morning! I never done that in my entire life. You lie down, go on now!" Bess demanded and gave her husband a push. "Over there long side Ira. I'll have plenty of help from the girls." She smiled at her husband, thankful again for this big generous and considerate man.

Jan lay down beside Ira careful not to disturb him. He enjoyed a pipe and snoozed, glad to stretch his long body out in a flat position. He watched Matt check the harnesses on the big teams. He laughed to himself as the young man playfully teased the girls, lifting Mary's long flaxen braid to tickle her nose. He kept a close eye on Bess noticing the fatigue showing in the droop of her shoulders.

Bess thought how good it was to be away from the back of her horse. She enjoyed fixing the food for breakfast but looked with discomfort at the tall rock high on the mountainside. Could she see if anyone were hiding in the dark crevices? She thought she had seen a movement of shadow fall across the gray outcrop of stone. She comforted herself that it was only the long shadows of the morning or the movement of a bird fluttering over the top. She turned back to her work.

Emily was trying hard in her own small way to be helpful, but was only managing to get underfoot and terribly in the way. Ginny spread a cloth on the back of the wagon and pushed her roughly aside.

"Run an' play Emmie. Mommy doesn't need you to be botherin' her!"

It was apparent to Emily that she was the only one with any energy left to enjoy the excitement of the trip home. She was finding it impossible to understand why everything she did was wrong.

"Oh you don't know everything, smart aleck, carrot hair!" Emily retorted with venom, sticking her tongue out to reinforce her words. She knew that referring to Ginny's copper colored hair, as carrot would infuriate her.

Emily hurried away safely out of her sister's reach, flipping her head, bouncing her sunny hair with its own shinning highlights of burnished orange. She skipped away into a patch of bright flowers and busied herself by picking a peace offering of love for her mother. She sang loudly so everyone was sure to hear:

> *"Flies in the buttermilk shoo-fly-shoo,*
> *Flies in the buttermilk shoo-fly-shoo,*
> *Skip to my Lou my darlin'."*

The root of a huge oak formed a bridge across the creek flowing close to the roadside. The swirling water underneath had washed away the dirt around the gnarled tentacles. It was on this tangled mass of tree root that Kylee and Mary chose to sit. They dangled their feet in the cool water and ate their breakfast of pickles, cold ham, and corn bread.

Kylee suppressed a desire to jump into the cool water and blissfully hide her body from the heat. She listened to the musical sound it made against the many rocks on the bottom. It splashed and whirled merrily along its way to the Kentucky valley.

The trip had been a pleasant diversion but she missed Hail and Tom and was glad to be going home. In fact, her thoughts rested often on Tom. Her dreams had been filled with his handsome face and silver blue eyes. She remembered the touch of his searching hands under the mulberry tree. She wondered if she would ever again feel the ecstasy that swept through her from Tom's kisses before he became forceful and demanding. Watching the swirling water around the root she thought of Tom's bruised lip, swollen and discolored, and the storm of hostility that darkened his blue eyes. The thought of seeing Tom at the top of the mountain caused her heart to pound. What a silly woman. She was wasting her time thinking about a man who obviously preferred someone like Polly Trace.

"We better get our feet out'a here. I see poppy wavin' his arm an' here comes Em. Reckon they're ready to move out," Mary said as she dried her feet on the hem of her shirt careful not to disturb or dampen the bills in her petticoat hem.

Emily skipped across the road to the stream edge still singing her happy song and eating a cornbread sandwich. Her apron pocket was filled with bright flowers she had picked, stuffed there, and forgotten.

As their journey progressed Mary and Kylee trailed behind the wagons leading Tempest and the mule. They talked and exchanged secret thoughts and enjoyed the large patches of wild flowers at the side of the road. The young women inhaled deeply the heady aroma of the persimmons beginning to ripen. They stopped to watch a passel of baby possums playing at the bottom of an old tree.

"Them possums love them 'simmons the best in the world. When they get good an' fat, they'll be in someone's pot," Mary laughed. "It's been a lovely trip Kylee. It's been such fun having you with us. Billy an' I talked of goin' into Kentucky together again. We had been with Ira a few times when we were youngins but that was a long time ago. Oh, Kylee! You can never know how I have missed him! I loved him so, more'n anyone knows." Mary looked at Kylee her wide eyes filled with sadness.

"Mary, stay at the mill with me. Stay for a long time. We'll sew an' go to the forest with Hail to hunt roots and ginseng. It would be such fun! Please," Kylee begged.

"I really would like to Kylee, but Mommy needs me now. I haven't told you yet, but she's gonna have a baby. Poppy says she's not doin' too well. He says we gotta be real careful an' watch over her, mostly 'cause of her age, she's most forty. He says that's the dangerous time for women to be child bearin'. But he is wantin' so much to have a boy. He tried to talk her out'a makin' this trip but she had her heart set on it. There was no changin' her mind." Mary's voice was hushed and worried.

"What happy news, Mary. Of course we-uns'll help her all we can. She'll be fine Mary, you'll see. Hail will keep a close watch on her when she finds out. It will give her somethin' to think about an' help her forget her own unhappiness."

How fortunate Mary was to have such a wonderful family. She was lucky too, having Uncle Ira and the boys, Hail, and the Stewarts for her dear friends. She thought of Taynee and Nell's newborn baby that night so long ago. She remembered the laughter they had shared at the baby's fleeting smile. She felt empty at the memory of beautiful Taynee. Her thoughts were miles away and Mary's voice was going on and on, chattering like a blue jay.

She was telling her of the history of the springs where they were to meet Tom. The very place where they had laid their bed rolls on the piles of chestnut twigs and shared their stories on the first night of the trip going over the mountain. It was a wide place in the road and a wall of rocks seemed to hold back the extreme steepness of Pound Mountain.

"Years ago," Mary was saying, "a missionary and some Jesuit priests were massacred at the springs by some Indians. The legend says that their blood covered the rocks where they fell. Right then an' there a gush of water spewed up through the rocks. Kinda like it was tryin' to wash away their blood. The water comes up with such force that it makes a whistlin' sound. You remember, Kylee, it kept us awake? That's why they call it Singing Spring. Everyone stops there to have a drink of the cold water. Someone even carved the word 'rest' on the flat rock where you have to kneel to get a drink. That sun's most to the middle of the sky. I reckon we better be for hurryin', it's only around the bend. We can see the top of those big ol' chestnut trees." Mary looked up into the sky.

"Up there," Mary pointed, "is Picket Rock guarding it all."

Matt was guiding his team toward the opening in the rocks. Jan's wagon and Bess's horse followed then disappeared around the curve ahead of Mary and Kylee. Kylee wondered if they were falling too far behind. On their left was a steep embankment. From the mass of vine and bushes she could hear again the tinkling music of water flowing over the rocks.

Mary's chattering voice stopped. Above the tinkling stream she could hear the whistling sound of Singing Springs. Through the water symphony came the thundering blast of rifle shots and the horrifying screams of her mother and sisters.

Matt pulled into the wide spot between the rocks and chestnut trees. His mules caught the first volley of bullets. Their big bodies crashed to the ground in a fog of dust and gravel. A bullet struck Matt. He pitched over the side and lay still under the storm of dirt and the blaze of bullets. Ira had been hit twice in the body and lay prone over the wagon front.

It was too late for Jan to whip his team into a run to get around Matt. No time to warn the women who were following. A bullet whizzed into his ribs and out through his stomach splitting it open. He straightened and pitched over the wagon side. As Jan sprawled on the ground another bullet hit him in the leg. His team was hit. The big horses pawed the air and crumpled in a heap to the dry earth toppling the wagon as they fell. Ginny was tossed screeching to the ground. She was silenced as the breath left her body and she lay unconscious. Emily bounced high off the seat and fell screaming under a crashing pile of dying horseflesh crushing her small body instantly.

The shrill whistling and whizzing of dying horses mingled with the blasting of rifle shots filled the mountaintop. Bess's mare reared high as a bullet struck it in the head. It fell to the ground throwing Bess into the rocky wagon tracks of the road.

As the outlaws had planned, the horses were down. Ira and Jan were close to dying; Ginny was unconscious and Bess prone on the ground, stunned. Matt lay motionless, deathly still; his face turned to the earth. The firing of the Winchesters continued, striking loudly into the wagons and ricocheting from the hard surfaces of the rocks surrounding them.

Kylee's horse, Tempest, and Mary's spirited mule reared high, pulled free, and plunged headlong up the hill through the thick trees. The sudden action threw the young women off balance and into each other. They slipped over the steep embankment and losing their balance rolled into the tangled brush at the bottom. The blasting of the rifles and screeching of the horses covered their screams.

The gunfire stopped. Only the heavy whistling and snorting of the dying horses could be heard. The dust was settling around the fallen animals, covering Matt, and changing Emily's golden curls to ashen gray. Into the scene of carnage rode the outlaws, arrogant and forceful. Their faces were hidden behind bandannas and Winchesters hung in the crooks of their elbows. Pistols were strapped close at hand around their hips. Some of the men dismounted and walked cockily and boldly among their victims.

Jay came to Jan lying next to the toppled wagon bed and nudged him roughly with his boot. He was breathing slowly in long irregular wheezes. Jay walked around Bess's dead horse to where she lay and bent down to roll her over.

"This one's still alive. Tie her to a wagon wheel Rueb," Jay ordered going back to Ira's upright wagon.

He stood for a moment staring at Ira's prone body lying across the wagon front. Jay pulled him from the wagon and dropped his body on the ground close to where Stewart lay.

Rueben finished tying Bess securely to a wheel as he had been instructed then turned back to receive further orders from his father. He stood looking down at Jan lying on his belly and bleeding badly from his stomach and leg.

"Should I put a bullet through his head?" Rueben asked his father as he watched Jan struggle to pull himself to his knees.

"No! Put a rope around his neck. Ira's breathing too, let's hang them both. We'll make sure they ain't gonna breathe no more!" Jay said gleefully. He pushed Jan back to the ground with his foot then rolled Ira over with the same foot. Ira stared up blankly and identified his assailant.

"Hidin' your cussidness behind a mask now-a-days, Jay Bird?" Ira struggled to make his voice heard while gasping for breath as the blood rose in his throat and ran from his lips. He would know that voice and those eyes coming from the darkest pit of hell. Blood was flowing from his body. He knew he was dying.

"Think your smart as hell, don't you? You damn cripple! Understand well who has the upper hand here! I have finally rid Pound Mountain of you bastardly Phelps! Reckon I'm glad to have you know, before you die, that it was Jay Mitchell what seen to your dyin'." Jay pulled his mask down and stood triumphantly looking down at his long time enemy.

Bess regained her rationality only to find she had both hands tied securely to a big wheel on Ira's wagon. Her mind was clear now. She filled her lungs with long hard breaths realizing fully that what she had dreaded was happening. She spotted Emily's body pinned underneath two thousand pounds of massive horseflesh, the colorful flowers from her pocket settled in the dust.

"Oh, my poor little one, what have you done to her? Let me go to her, let me go!" She sobbed struggling to free her hands so she could rescue her little girl who was beyond help.

"Oh, Ginny, Ginny, where are you? Are you dead, too? Have they murdered you all? Oh Jan, Jan, what's happenin'? Are we all goin' to die? I told you I was afear'd!" Bess screamed and fell into violent crying and wailing. She looked wildly around to spot Jan. She spotted Ginny lying on a bedding of soft chestnut twigs. She screamed, "I told you, Jan! I warned you! I warned you!"

"If you're out for a hangin' Jay, get on with it! Let's be done with this before someone comes." Hensely encouraged Jay handing him two circles of rope with hangman's nooses already tied at the ends. The curls of rope always hung ready from his saddle horn.

"Yeah Jay, hurry up an' be done with it! But first make 'em tell us where the money is. Let's get this over with Jay!" Ferrell added nervously.

"Where's the money, cripple? I know you got it somewhere, now where is it?" Jay shouted at Ira.

"Oh, my babies! Let me go to my babies!" Bess was screeching.

"For hell sake Rueben, shut that woman up! Tie this across her mouth." He untied the bandanna from around his neck and tossed it to Rueben.

The whistling and screaming of horses, blood soaking the ground, and the smell of death, none of it bothered Jay. But Bess's mournful wailing was beginning to unnerve him. He turned back to Ira.

"Answer me, you damn cripple! I know you're carryin' a bundle! Now tell me where it is!" Jay demanded loudly.

Ira was on the brink of death and stared at Jay blank and vacant. He knew he was dying and he wasn't about to give Jay the satisfaction of having his money.

Getting nowhere with Ira, he turned to Jan, "The money, Stewart! Where's the money!" Jay questioned, reinforcing his words by pushing the end of his rifle behind the big man's ear. "Tell me or I'll blow your head off!"

"Be damned!" Jan said with what strength he could muster while struggling to think of a way to save Bess and the girls.

Jan raised himself to his knees clutching at his opened gut and trying to push his insides back. Looking around he could see no sign of Mary and Kylee. He hoped they had escaped and would keep themselves well hidden.

"Have mercy on the women folk, for God's sake, Jay. They've harmed no one." Jan was dying and would stoop to beg for the women he loved.

"The women, of course." Jay mused coldly, his voice filled with contempt.

Jay walked slowly over to Bess. Resting his rifle against the wagon he reached for Bess's clothing. With a few savage rips, he bared her body to the stares of the men.

Bess glared at Jay with large brown eyes, free of tears but filled with pride and hate. She would not give this hateful man the satisfaction of her tears.

Her skin was milky white, breasts firm and round from her early pregnancy. Jay was stunned at her pale beauty and stood silent, feasting his eyes on her.

"My God, Jay! If you got any feelin's for yer own wife, leave her be!" Jan's head was almost touching the ground and he was trying to stay alive to save his wife. Trembling and weakness filled his body. Terror for his wife's fate spurred him to stay alive.

"I'll tell you where the money is if you'll spare the women. Bess is with child. I'll tell you if you'll let her go." Jan tried to raise himself on an elbow but his strength ebbed.

"Well?" Jay threw Bess's clothing on top of her and turned to Jan, "Talk Stewart, we're listenin'."

"If you'll free the women," Jan whispered.

"Course we'll let them go, we've no quarrel with your women."

"In the women's petticoats, in the hems." Jan's words were garbled and he lowered his body letting it sprawl out on the soft twigs.

Jay separated the petticoat from Bess's clothing. "Get the girls, Rueben!"

"I'll get it," Ferrell stated firmly as he put his rifle in the saddle boot and dismounted.

Taking a knife from his pocket he lifted the blade and cut the money from the unconscious Ginny's petticoat paying little attention to the girl's prone state.

"Look Jay. Ain't this a pretty sight?" Ferrell stacked the money in his hand and looked at it gleefully.

"Yeah, sure is. Look a here, it matches this!" Jay grinned and took the money from the young man's hands and stacked it together with what he held from Bess's petticoat.

Jay turned back to Ira and Jan dying on the ground. He handed the money back to Ferrell. There was something else more important to him than all the money in Kentucky and Virginia.

"Hang onto it Ferrell, we'll divide it later," Jay told him calmly.

Tanner fit a hangman noose over Jan's head, then Ira's. He threw the ropes over a strong branch of a chestnut then deftly tied the ends, one to Rueben's saddle horn, the other to his, then stood waiting.

"Hang Stewart, Tanner! Hang him, hang him!" Jay screeched.

Hensely smacked the horse's rump with his hat and Jan swung free of the ground, his death assured.

"You ain't won yet Mitchell!" Ira struggled to prod Jay once more before he died. He paused to get his breath. "Tom'll get you for this!" Ira managed to gurgle out the rest of the statement. Staring up at his friend swinging on the limb above, his eyes flooded with tears of grief.

"My God, forgive me Jan! I had no intentions of gettin' us all caught up in such a thing," Ira muttered feebly.

Jay was irate and kicked Ira sharply upon his lifeless legs. Getting no response his anger mounted until the veins in his neck rose. Reaching down with both hands he grasped Ira by the shirtfront and lifted him until he could look into his eyes. Ira's lifeless legs hung dangling free above the ground, the hangman's rope still around his neck.

"You son-of-a-bitchin' snivelin' coward! You think I'm afear'd of one puny Phelps? I'll get him before the sun goes down, now die!"

Ira looked him straight in the eyes, his life fading and blood oozing and dripping from his body. He hacked enough saliva and blood into his mouth to spew into Jay's face.

Jay was beside himself with fury. A cruel insane smile curled his lips. He let go of Ira's shirt and let him fall into a crumpled heap at his feet. An instant calm swept over Jay and he slowly wiped the bloody spit from his face with a shirtsleeve. He motioned for Tanner to hang Ira. He was done with them, certain of their dying. Walking with long strides over to where Ginny lay in the tall grass along the road; he lifted her and listened for her breathing.

"She's still alive, Rueb," Jay announced, dropping the girl back to the ground.

Rueben turned from watching Hensely securing the hanging rope around a young dogwood tree. He grinned trying to swagger as Jay did. There was, in spite of his sandy complexion, a startling resemblance to his father.

"That's Ginny, Paw. She sure got to be a pretty one, didn't she?" Rueben bent to stroke the girls flaming hair.

"Take her to the bushes!" Jay laughed wickedly. "Use her an' don't leave her livin'."

Ginny began to stir; Jay's rough handling of her shocked her back to consciousness. Her eyelids fluttered. Rueben was quick to cover her mouth with a strong hand silencing any sound that might escape. He lifted her and carried her into a patch of tall rhododendron bushes beside a big rock.

"For God's sake, stop Paw! Have you gotta kill 'em all? You told Jan you would spare the women." Bob pleaded with his father.

Bob and Kenus sat their horses at the edge of the road with no intentions of dismounting. Bob wanted no part of the murders or the money. Kenus cared little either way, just waited for Kylee to appear.

"What's the matter with you, boy? You know we can't leave anyone for a witness. You want us all to hang same as Ira an' Jan?

I see you're still a fraidy cat. Thought you'd got over that. When you gonna grow up boy? You must have a yellow streak a foot wide. You're maw must a had a sweetheart hid somewhere's. Can't see any of me in you at all. If you're a man of any sorts, come along an' prove it! Have a go at this lovely one." Jay spoke straight at Bob. "Word to a dead man don't mean nothin'!"

He was sick and tired of Bob's opposition. He was going to give him one more chance or he would leave him dead with the Phelps's. He looked down at Bess. Her eyes above the gag were wide with shock and horror. Fear for Ginny and bitter grief for little Em, Jan, and Ira, clouded her dark eyes. Jay always thought Bess a strikingly beautiful woman but his preference lay with dark beauty such as Mae's and perhaps Polly Trace.

"Come on now, get over here. Bess ain't gonna mind." Jay reached and untied the bandanna knot at the back of Bess's head. "Well Bess, you're a lovely one. We'll give Bob a chance to become a man, won't we now? She's a little beyond your age, but that ain't gonna matter. The best tunes are played on old fiddles, ain't that right Bess?" Jay laid his head back and laughed loudly pleased at his little joke. "You'll change your mind after one kiss. Them lips were made for kissin'. What you say, son?"

Hensely was done with the hangings and satisfied with the security of the ropes. He walked over to where Ferrell sat on a big rock, unconcerned with Jay's preoccupation of Bess and the hangings. He was entertaining himself with shuffling the money he held, admiring the crisp new bills and mentally adding up the amount in his mind. He concentrated on what he would do with his share. The extreme heat was already drawing hordes of flies to swarm about the dead horses and splotches of blood Ira and Jan's bodies had left upon the soft chestnut twigs.

"Let's get out'a here, Ferrell. Let Jay finish his business. I'm sick of it! We can meet him back on the mountain," Hensely said, forcefully rubbing his hands hard with the large white handkerchief he'd removed from around his face as if trying to wipe the death from his hands.

Kenus rode up to the rock where Ferrell sat talking to Hensely, leaving Bob to listen to Jay's sick instructions. "Where's the Bentley girl, Tanner? I ain't seen hide nor hair of her. You promised she'd be here. I want that woman! I ain't had no part of these killin's. I only want the woman." Kenus demanded angrily. "I wanna get out'a here before someone shows up!"

"I wondered how come you was takin' that nigger's word. You can see the Bentley woman ain't here!" Ferrell added.

"I plum forgot about them gals. I saw Mary an' that gal of Ira's through the scope. They were comin' along behind, walkin'. I'd a sworn it was them. You couldn't mistake Mary's yeller hair. They musta run an' hid in the bushes. They can't be far," Hensely declared.

"That Bentley girl's a small one with a heap of hair. We'll find them, Kenus. I'll see if I can spot where they left the road. I'll get my horse. You come along. That nigger was right about one thing, we found Ira and Jan, but I ain't seen nothin' of Tom," Tanner muttered to himself as he scrutinized the grass at the side of the road.

Tanner Hensely was well known for his tracking ability. He had formed and led many groups to track down men wanted for many things from stealing to murder and had even looked for lost children. He had guided men of means and money to hunt bear and deer. He was good at the tracking game. He had no doubt he could find the two women.

Hensely was still carrying his handkerchief in his hand wanting to get it wet and wash his hands and cool his face. The perspiration ran down his cheeks and was lost in his heavy sideburns. He was hot and uncomfortable. The rocks along the side of the road served as a conductor for the sun's rays. The numerous trees captured the heat and held it to the road. Tanner felt as if he'd had a blast from a furnace and was beginning to feel ill. At the creek, he took off his hat and laid it in the grass. Dipping the handkerchief in the water, he lifted it and laid it over his head letting the water soak his hair and run down his face. He replaced his hat over the wet handkerchief. He lifted a handful of water and took a drink of the clear clean liquid. He was feeling better and climbed onto the horse Kenus had guided down the steep bank.

Kenus sat watching, fidgeting in his saddle and twisting from side to side, he wanted to get on with finding the women. He let his horse drink and figured he had waited long enough.

"Let's get on with this Hensely! I'd like to get into Kentucky before it gets dark. I'll have to find a place to spend the night with the girl," Kenus told Tanner unable to hide the look of anticipation crossing his face.

"Right! Look here. You see where they tumbled down the bank after their horses ran away? See there, see them tracks? They's clear as a bell. They crawled along the creek here." Tanner showed Kenus the tracks he discovered.

They followed the path Mary and Kylee made. Tanner dismounted and examined the grass and vine closely.

"Look here, one of them tore her dress." Hensely lifted a piece of cloth from a branch of mulberry bush.

"See how the grass is layin' down all along here? They came from up there on the bank. They probably stood up there behind that big chestnut an' watched everything that went on. We gotta find them for sure. If they get away an' tell the whole story, we're in a heap of trouble! Let's get on with the job," Hensely added fearfully.

Back at the scene of carnage Jay continued to coax Bob into the rape of Bess. "Come on Bob, what's the matter with you anyways."

Bob turned his face away. He had seen all he could stand. He wanted to vomit. His insides were rolling and tossing. He watched Ira and Jan swinging from the tree and the horror of Emily's crushed body. He sat cowardly on his horse doing nothing as he watched Rueben drag Ginny away.

"If you ain't got the guts for this boy, I'll see to it. But you're gonna watch an' see how it's done. If you move that nag of yours one inch, I'll blast you both!" Jay pulled his gun as he spoke and lifted the hammer back. He laid it on the ground beside Bess's head within quick reach of his hand.

"Oh God a mercy," Bess moaned. "Bob, please make him stop. If you ever had love for Mary, stop him. Please! Please! I'm beggin' you! I nursed you at my breast after I lost my babe. I loved you as if you were my very own," Bess screamed. "No! No!"

Jay's body was a weight on top of her. There was nothing she could do. Her hands were tied. It was no use to plead to Bob, he was too afraid of his father. She tried to bounce her body and kick Jay off. Her struggle only delighted him more. Closing her eyes, she blocked out Jay's leering face. Her struggles stopped, she lay still and hoped the pain that was filling her body would stop her breathing so she could die.

All of her family was dead except for Mary. She prayed Mary and Kylee had escaped this nightmare. Large tears rolled slowly from the corners of her eyes.

Jay looked upon Bess's ravaged body with fiendish coldness. Her struggles to resist him had ceased. She was like death itself, pale and cold. Fastening his clothing he reached for his gun and fired into Bess's head. Turning around he fired the remaining bullets in his gun into the dead bodies of Ira and Jan ripping them apart at the groin.

Rueben walked from the bushes, his face gloating, and proud of his deed. He was unconcerned that his fat rough hands left Ginny lying lifeless in the grass, her flaming hair flowing upon a pillow of lavender blue daisies. Her legs were broken and twisted in a pool of her own blood. Jay grinned proudly at his son. He put his arm around Rueben's shoulders. They walked over to Ferrell where he sat counting the money.

Bob leaned from the saddle and spewed vomit on the ground; he could hold it no longer. When he was done he wiped his mouth on his shirtsleeve then guided his horse into the thick trees. He was expecting a bullet through the back and hoped it would come soon, he would be better off dead. He had turned a deaf ear to Bess's pleas. She was the woman who made his life possible as an infant. He watched as his father raped her and had done nothing.

He watched the whole terrible mess and didn't let out a sound. He stared in shock and horror at Ira and Jan's purple swollen faces and bloody bodies. He held back the scream that rose in his throat. The terror of his father was far greater than his compassion for these people. He knew his father would allow no interference and made no move to protest. He understood now why his father had taken his gun and set Kenus close to guard him.

Never, in the farthest recess of his mind, had he imagined it would be so terrible. He could have ridden to warn them, but he hadn't. So now all that was left for him was making excuses and trying to pacify his cowardice.

He could not look back on the scene of carnage. He wanted to scratch his eyes out that he might never see again. Even if his eyes were sightless he knew it would never erase the sight of little Emily's mangled body or Bess's large eyes pleading with him. Behind the darkness would always be the sight of Ira and Jan's distorted faces. Whenever he looked upon a sparkling stream or saw patches of wildflowers or smelled the fragrance of paw-paws ripening on a mountaintop, he would see again the hopelessness in Bess's eyes and remember he had done nothing.

Bringing his horse to a stop he lifted his eyes to the sky and prayed for his father's destruction. He prayed, as the tears burned his eyes and washed down his bony cheeks, that some day his father would meet a death worthy of these heinous murders. Oh blessed day, he would then be free of this cursed man and the hold he had on him. He rode into the dense forest wanting a place to hide deep in the never changing shadows of the pines.

CHAPTER ONE

Kylee had lain still for what seemed to be an eternity. Sitting up, she brushed the dirt and grass from her face and tangled hair. She could see Mary lying farther down beside the stream. Struggling up the bank she realized the shooting and screaming had quieted and now she heard loud talking and shouting. The voices were muddled and unfamiliar.

"Oh, I can't believe this is happening," Kylee murmured.

Hiding herself behind a large tree she peeked cautiously around the trunk filled with terror and unbelief at what she saw. She covered her mouth tightly with her hand holding back the scream that wanted to escape. She heard Mary climbing the embankment behind her. She must not see what was going on in the road. Never must she see what happened. There was nothing, absolutely nothing they could do. They would only wind up dead and there would be no one to bring help. She must manage some way to get Mary and herself around the outlaws.

"What's happening, Kylee? Let me go!" Mary demanded as Kylee put her arm around her and pulled her back down toward the stream. Mary kept struggling and pulling away, trying to crawl back up the bank. Kylee was desperate. Mary's effort more intense.

"Why, Kylee? Why are you keeping me from going to my folks? I want to go to them. What's happening? What's happened?" She fought with determination.

"You can't help them Mary! We must get away! We must get help! Come with me now, we must get away!" Kylee whispered trying to keep her voice low, hoping not to attract attention.

"I'm going up there! I know they're all dead. They've killed them all, haven't they?"

"Come on Mary!" Kylee had to do something. She knew she must resort to drastic means. She had to silence her. Bringing her arm back she brought it forward with all the strength she had left. She made contact with Mary's jaw and knocked her out cold.

Moving quickly she lifted Mary around under her arms and dragged her into the cover of heavy brush. Her thoughts had no time to dwell on snakes or the possibility of all manner of crawling creatures hiding in the shade from the heat.

Thick branches clutched at their hair, tore their clothing, and scratched their faces as she worked her way backward pulling Mary with her. She couldn't have been imagining. She was certain she had seen Kenus Hall sitting on his horse in the shadow of the trees next to a younger man. There was no mistaking his stature or neat attire. There was only one reason she could think of that could have brought him here. He had found her.

She remembered Tom was supposed to have met them at the springs. Had the outlaws ambushed him too? Was he dead? She began to cry. What she had seen beyond the tree was a nightmare. She would soon wake up and hear Emily singing, 'Skip to My Lou My Darlin', and all this would be washed away. But what she heard were horses coming and she realized she was awake and what was happening was real. Mary was beginning to stir. Kylee knew she must find a place to hide them. They were leaving a prominent trail along the edge of the stream. The bank was growing smaller and the stream wider as it flowed east down the Virginia side of the mountain.

A sudden thought came to her mind. From somewhere in the past she remembered her father telling her how the bears built their winter dens behind and under a fallen log. She must be very careful and hurry. Could she lay Mary down for a minute? She had to risk it. Through some dense brush she saw what she was looking for.

Two fallen trees, one lying over the other making a cave-like hollow covered with branches and leaves.

She must be very careful not to break any branches. She crept through toward the logs. Carefully, very carefully and quietly, she hollowed out a place behind them with her hands. She could hear the horses coming crushing the brush and undergrowth as they moved slowly and occasionally stopping as if listening.

Cautiously she reached through the brush and pulled Mary through to hide her behind the big logs in the hole she made. They were safe! With new horror she saw the definite path Mary's body had made. Back she went through the bushes. Underneath, next to the ground, she discovered a dead limb. It pulled away easily and silently.

Hurriedly she swept the deep grass brushing it to a standing position and backed through the bushes to where Mary lay. Climbing over the logs she laid down on top of Mary pushing their bodies into the soft earth. She placed branches over them and pulled the low hanging bushes in close around them.

When Mary began to stir, Kylee covered her mouth with a hand holding back any sound that might escape. Mary looked wide-eyed into Kylee's eyes directly above hers. The light was dim in their hideaway and the space small. There was a possibility of Mary starting to struggle, but Kylee's body weighed heavily on top of her.

Kylee signaled with a finger across her lips warning Mary with her eyes not to move or make a sound. She hoped they were as safe as a mama bear and her cubs during a winter storm.

She felt the trembling of the earth. The horses were coming faster, probably at a trot. Through the latticework of branches and leaves she could see the front legs of a horse moving in closer. Then a stirrup and a man's boot and leg so close to Mary and Kylee she was afraid they might be discovered or stepped on. They remained still and silent; afraid even their breathing might be heard.

A volley of shots rang out rattling the leaves lying close to Mary's face. The riders reined their mounts in sharply. Kylee could have reached out and touched a hoof.

"That must be Jay. You think something's wrong?" Hensely asked Kenus turning in his saddle.

"I couldn't say. That's one man that's purely trigger-happy. I didn't have nothin' to do with them killin's. I only wanted to get the Bentley girl. I've waited a long time to find her. Ain't no one gonna put any blame on me! Looks as if them girls got plum away. It's my guess they seen everything. They've high-tailed it to get help. If that's what's happened, there ain't gonna be no place in these here mountains for you-uns to hide!" Kenus warned the deputy.

"What the hell you worried about Kenus? Ain't no one could tell who we was with our faces all tied up."

"Can you be sure Tanner? I ain't too well acquainted with you, but I could recognize your voice even behind a mask. I wouldn't chance it! I'd be for leavin' these hills for damn sure! I'm goin' to get my money back from Mitchell an' head for Kentucky an' home. I'll forget about the girl. Bad as I want her, she ain't worth gettin' hung for."

Kylee had been right; it was Kenus she had seen. She heard a horse thunder through the brush, then the one that stopped so close to their hiding place moved away and followed slowly. Could they move now? Should they chance being discovered? Perhaps they had better remain hidden a while longer.

"Shh! Shh!" Kylee warned Mary in a low whisper after a few minutes elapsed. "Don't talk Mary." Kylee removed her hand from Mary's mouth.

"We will make sure they're gone before we move. We can't risk them comin' back an' findin' us. Believe me Mary; they could, then what chance would we have? They'll keep tryin' to find us, especially 'cause they know we know who they are. They'll keep tryin' to find us! We gotta get home an' have someone hide us, Mary. We gotta get to a safe place. They's one chance Mary. Maybe Tom is still comin' up the mountain. Let's think on that," Kylee's words came out in a rasping whisper.

"I must go to my mommy an' poppy, Kylee. They've killed them all, haven't they? Haven't they? Tell me! Tell me, Kylee! I know they're all dead."

Kylee nodded. Why should she lie to her? There was no one alive as far as Kylee could tell from where she watched from behind the tree. Ira's standing wagon blocked her view of Bess. But she had seen Ira and Jan hang and she could see Ginny lying still on the ground.

Mary's eyes stared wide and filled with shock and horror. Large tears began to fall. Slowly they rolled from her eyes and fell into the loose dirt underneath her.

They lay still until their bodies began to ache. Kylee rolled away from Mary so the other girl could breathe freely. The only sound Kylee could hear was the lyrical music of a mocking bird and the far away tinkling of the stream. It seemed they lay still for an eternity, but they must not move!

Over the end of the log Kylee saw a new shadow. An easy movement, scarcely visible, but Kylee saw the black snake slithering slowly over the log. She opened her mouth to scream but the snake moved on across and away from them. They had waited long enough. She moved the branch away and parted the brush. Still visible above the treetops was Picket Rock. If they kept the sun behind them, they would be going east and they would come out at the mill.

Pulling Mary along with her, Kylee followed the stream until she could see the road above them. Thinking it would be safe now and easier to walk on the road where they could make better time and maybe, please God let it be so, maybe they would find Tom.

"Let's go back Kylee. Let's see if maybe someone might still be alive. Surely they wouldn't kill little Emily and Ginny. I want to go back, Kylee. Do you hear me? I want to go back!" Mary screamed pulling back on the hand Kylee held tightly.

"We can't go back! Don't you understand, Mary? We can't go back! They'll kill us too, then where would we be? We gotta keep goin' until we find someone or get to the mill. Come on now, save your breath an' run! Mary run!" Kylee stammered breathless.

Mary's tears had dried leaving white streaks down her dirty face. She wasn't crying but whimpering, trying to comprehend that her family was gone. Resentment was building toward Kylee because she wouldn't let her go to the people who were her life.

Kylee tried to comfort her friend as they stumbled along. The road was dry and powdery from the long summer days without rain. She was trying hard to cope with her own realization that with the dead were Uncle Ira and Matt, and maybe Tom. Their feet sank deep into the soft dust raising small white puffs as they ran. It wouldn't be dusty long. Kylee could see a dark cloud rising over the mountain covering the valley with a large shadow. The rifle shots were gone, the screams were gone, and the hills and hollows were deadly silent. The only thing to be heard was the pounding of their feet and Mary's desperate wailing and pleading with Kylee to return to Picket Rock.

The noon sun was hot on Tom's face. He awoke to the buzzing of bees and flies singing in concert above his head. Boy listened to the swarming musical without concern, waiting for Tom to awaken. Jole' stood patiently cropping grass and not straying from the moss covered log where Tom's head rested.

Boy gave a low warning growl, lifted his head, and eyed the approach of a horseman. Kenus and Tanner had ridden by early while the dawn was still young and the morning had scarcely begun. Their galloping horses had not disturbed the dog. They had stayed on the trail and gone quickly by. Everything had been peaceful and serene except for a low snore escaping Tom's drunken sleep. This person rode slowly and off the road toward their grassy spot. Boy was alerted and on guard should this intruder prove to be a threat to his master.

The continued low growl brought Tom to a sitting position. He stretched and ran his fingers through his ash blonde hair. Cautiously he felt growth of stubble on his jaw with the back of his hand. He yawned and scratched a chigger that cunningly buried itself underneath the skin of his forearm. He reached to playfully pull Boy's ear.

"What's the matter, feller? Someone comin'? I sure ain't ready for company, but it's time I got up from here. Tarnation!" Tom squinted toward the sun. "It looks to be about noon. We was supposed to meet Paw on the mountain at noon. Never make it now, but we'll ride on up an' meet 'em anyways," Tom said, still scanning the sky above the trees and spotting the forbidding dark cloud moving up toward Pound. He reached and pulled a twig from a low tree branch, chewed the end to pulp and began brushing his teeth.

"Upon my word 'n honor, if it ain't Uncle Andy. Sure ain't the time for me to be seein' him. Quiet Boy!" Tom demanded as Andy guided his big red mule toward him.

Tom rose, straightened his clothes, and reached a hand of welcome to the preacher.

"Tom, what the heck are you doin' here lyin' in the grass? I thought it was you when I saw someone spread out on the ground. Tain't no spot to be a snoozin'. Them chiggers'll eat you alive." He looked around with an experienced eye and sized up the situation.

"You been out swarpin' again, Tom?"

Tom didn't dare lie to his Uncle Andy. He'd be damned for sure, lying to a preacher.

"I reckon," he answered.

"Been to see Polly, I suppose?"

"Tarnation, Uncle Andy! Reckon you know how I feel about Polly."

"You mean you got intentions of marriage? Someone ought'a wed the gal an' settle her down."

"No, not exactly." Tom's ears began to burn.

"I'm tellin' you Tom, as a friend, not as a man of God, you better change your ways! I have warned you before about loose women." The preacher paused then added in a quieter voice. "But you don't take heed."

"Now I'm tellin' you as a man of God, it is time you took some hard fast steps toward the Lord Jesus. Confess Him as your Savior, be baptized, be saved Tom! Your dead mother'd be wantin' it. If you want to be with her in the Lord's kingdom, you better be preparin'." Preacher Andy looked his nephew hard in the eyes.

"You better be headin' toward the straight an' narrow, they ain't no in between. You better be turnin' back Tom before it be too late an' you reach the point beyond redemption. The Lord's not goin' to strive with you forever!" He continued to preach.

Tom picked up his fallen hat and smoothed his hair then reached for Jole's reins. He listened to his uncle out of respect, not interest and nodded his head in agreement.

"You be right! You be right. You got any food on you Uncle? I'm sure in need of a biscuit." He added out of hunger but really trying to change the subject.

"You keep sayin' that Tom, because you have respect for me, but you're not actin' on my words. You're hearin' me talkin' but you ain't listenin'! Billy was a good lad, he was curious about the Lord. I slacked my duty not seein' to his baptizin'. I have regretted that. Come to the Lord, boy! Pledge to follow Jesus today. Accept him as your Savior an' be saved. Be blessed by His saving grace. Do it Tom before it be too late. I reckon I got a corn bread an' a piece of side pork." He handed a small packet to Tom but it had not deterred the preacher.

Preacher Andy removed his black hat and hung it on the saddle horn. Taking a small New Testament from his pocket he readied to give Tom a complete sermon.

"You gotta begin Tom, at the foot of the cross where Jesus died for your sins. He had compassion, son. He'll forgive you, if you ask. You gotta ask an' have faith as if it was already done!" The preacher's sermon continued.

"Not today, Uncle Andy. Not today! I'll talk to you some other time. Sorry, but I gotta meet Paw on the mountain. I'm already a little late. It's been nice seein' you. Come by the mill an' we'll talk," Tom said his good-bye and lifted himself in the saddle. "Thanks for the bread, it saved my life."

Tom was not ready in mind or body to listen to a sermon and definitely not for baptizing. Smiling weakly, he waved good-bye and spurred Jole' into a high run. He was taking no chances on his uncle following him. Besides he was in a hurry. He had no time for preaching!

"I hope it won't be too late, Tom! Man does not live by bread alone. It's Jesus that'll save your life!" Andy's loud voice followed him up the road. A look of dismay and total failure was apparent on his skinny face. He closed the Testament, then lifted his head. A song followed Tom up the road rising above the pounding of Jole's hooves:

"Amazing grace, how sweet the sound,
That saved a wretch like me.
I once was lost, but now I'm found.
Was blind but now I see....."

Andy was hoping Tom's blind eyes would be opened and that he might see before it was too late. He gave a deep sigh of failure, "Oh well, I'll leave it to the Lord. He has mysterious ways, His wonders to perform!"

Jole' was moving fast up the mountain. However, Preacher Andy's song found Tom's ears. He spurred the horse again wanting to move out of hearing range. Always he liked to sing the old gospel hymns but he had never been one to take their message seriously. He patted Jole' on her neck and slowed her down. Tom was not feeling too well and the jogging of the horse only added to his discomfort.

His head was a ball of fuming disorder and throbbed with every movement of his body. Riding with his eyes closed he tried to gather his wits together. He had eaten the corn bread and bacon too fast and his stomach was beginning to churn. He tried to think of Kylee to get his mind off his sick stomach. He remembered her feelings toward him the morning she left the mill and that just made him sick at heart.

He welcomed the small breeze coming with the thundercloud. The cool air dispelled the trailing heat waves that had lain upon the road. The refreshing caress soothed Tom's head and he began to feel better.

When he met the folks he could rest and eat something light. Maybe he would lose this feeling of weakness that was causing his hand to shake visibly. What he needed was a cup of Hail's chicken soup.

But the trail he traveled came out above the mill at Baldwin's Creek. He would have to back track to the mill. There was no time. He rode on out to Pound Gap with no idea of what waited for him at the top of the mountain.

Chapter Two

The last twenty-four hours had been a living nightmare. Tom kept shaking his head trying to rationalize the past events. The words kept ringing in Tom's ears, "Can you pay for an operation such as this injury might require?"

"I can pay. See to it that he gets the best doctor there is! He's my brother; I don't want him to die."

Tom counted and stacked the required amount on the white counter. Feeling the strength draining from his body he leaned heavily on the counter edge. Hoping his body and mind would stay in tact until he had Matt taken care of. He watched his brother, pale and inert, lying on a hospital gurney in the middle of the corridor.

He met Mary and Kylee on the road tear stained and tattered. Dismounting from Jole', he put his arms around Mary who was at the point of hysteria. He attempted to calm her. Holding her firmly he patted her shoulders and tried to hear above the loud sobbing what Kylee was trying to tell him.

"Oh, my God, Kylee! It ain't so, tell me it ain't so. I must hurry on to the rocks. Take Mary an' go for help. Get on Jole', you can ride double."

"No, Tom! No! I gotta go back to mommy an' poppy. I want to help them," Mary screamed.

"Don't go to the mill, it's too far. Ride up Mullins Branch an' tell Aunt Lizzie. Be quiet Mary, listen to me."

"Have her send her men folks. We'll need teams an' wagons if the horses are dead as Kylee said. You understand, Mary? Send Aunt Lizzie!" Tom further instructed them as he put Mary on the saddle and Kylee behind.

"Hurry now! You gotta get help Mary!" He said as he handed Kylee the reigns.

Taking his rifle from the saddle boot he slapped Jole' sharply on the rump making sure the gallop was fast enough to discourage any idea Mary might have of sliding off.

Tom went on a long stride run up the mountain. Cautiously he approached the area where the big rocks lined the road. He moved in steadily between the big trees. Everything was ominously still.

The outlaws had moved out abandoning the search for the two girls on Kenus's advice. He convinced Jay that waiting for Tom would only be folly. Anyone could show up on the road, a traveler or a freight wagon.

Even with Kylee's tearful description of what she had seen happen, Tom was not prepared for what he found.

He let his father and Jan down and straightened their bodies. He covered them with one of the blankets he found scattered on the ground from Jan's overturned wagon.

Tom untied the ropes that bound Bess's wrists to the wheel of Ira's upright wagon. He found her dress underneath and slipped the torn garment over her head. Pulling it down over her body and tenderly tucking it around her stocking clad legs. There was no way he could hold back the tears that crowded his eyes.

Beautiful, beautiful, Bess. Kneeling down he cradled her in his arms stroking her golden hair caked with dried blood. He tucked in the wire pins that had slipped loose and carefully pulled a strand across the bullet hole Jay's gun had left in her forehead. The love he felt for her would never cease. He would always think of her with a burning unfulfilled passion. At times throughout his life it would rise to run rampant in his thoughts. He understood fully now it could have never been a reality. What she had told him was true, someday he would find the slow burning flame that would warm him the rest of his days as it had been with her and Jan. His love for her would always be the secret of his heart, revealed to no one.

"Oh God, why did it have to end in such a way?" He rose and laid Bess's tattered petticoat over her head to discourage the flies that were coming in swarms.

It was impossible for Tom alone to lift the weight of the team of grays from Emily's crushed body. He would have to wait for help to come. He assumed Matt was dead when he found his body on the far side of Ira's wagon. Searching the area for Ginny, he found her body in the shadow of a big rock, her neck bruised and battered. He carried her back to the wagons and laid her beside her mother, pulling the corner of Bess's petticoat across her face as he straightened her clothing.

Tom's tears were dried. His eyes narrowed to slits of hate and grief, teeth set together tightly, and his face a sculpture of stone. Lifting Matt under the arms he fastened his arms around his chest. He dragged his brother slowly to where Jan and their father lay under the blanket. Grief and sorrow overwhelmed him and he began talking to the man in his arms.

"Oh God, this can't be happening," Tom muttered holding Matt firmly. "I was wrong, Bub. My stubborn bull-headedness wouldn't let me tell you how sorry I was about the fight."

"God, if you are a God of mercy an' grace, how could you let such a thing happen? How could you? I've lost all my family. First Mama, then Billy, now Paw an' Matt. The Stewarts are gone too. Dear lovely Bess, an' Jan, an' little Em. She was only a child. Lord, how could you? Ginny was so young, so young."

How was he to go on? Then he remembered Kylee and Mary. He took a stronger hold on Matt. From deep inside Tom came the shock and horror. Looking to the sky a screeching cry escaped his lips.

"Help me! Help me, Lord! Help me to find the ones what done this! I swear to you, as you be my witness, I swear, I'll kill the ones what done this! I swear it!"

"I'll see them die as my paw an' Jan did! I swear it!" He vowed loudly to the silent trees and ominous rocks.

Releasing the cry had shaken Tom. He became weak, stumbled, and almost dropped his brother. Taking a tighter grip around Matt's chest revealed a heartbeat. The beat was so slight at first he thought it had been caused from his own trembling. Then he was certain it was there, faint but steady.

Placing Matt on the ground beside his father Tom knelt and laid his head on his brother's chest. There it was, a distant murmur, but definitely a heart beat. Matt was alive! Tom found no apparent wound but there was dry blood in Matt's hair and on his shirt collar at the back of his brother's head. It was apparent to Tom that Matt had taken a bullet in that area. He had felt a whisper of breath touch his cheek.

"Matt! Matt! Speak to me! Can you hear me?" Tom pleaded.

But the brother was deathly silent. Not a twitch of muscle to indicate life.

Tom found Matt's hat lying in the grass at the side of the road. He covered the younger man's face with the battered old hat. A slight grimace toyed at the corner of Tom's mouth as he remembered the day Hensely served the warrant. Tom sat down on a rock to wait watching Matt closely. Above the drone of swarming flies came the sound of rolling wheels. Help was coming. He would get Matt to Hail. She would keep him alive. The outlaws had made two mistakes. They had let Mary and Kylee get away and had failed to make certain everyone was dead at the rocks.

With the aid of long poles Tom helped the men lift the fallen horses from Emily's body. Then with Matt carefully resting in the back of a small wagon belonging to Aunt Lizzie, he started down the mountain. Friends and relation would bring the others.

Easing the team into an even gait, Tom kept the wagon rolling as smooth as was possible on the rough road. Above the rumbling of the team and wagon he could hear the crying and wailing of the women over the dead.

To his surprise he found Kylee and Mary still riding double on Jole' coming up the road slowly. He guided the wagon close in beside them and pulled to a stop demanding to know what they were doing coming back up the mountain.

"What are you doin' here? Aunt Lizzie said they had sent you on to the mill to let Hail know what's happened." Tom jumped from the wagon. "Come on, get in the wagon. Hurry now! Be quick! I have Matt in the back. They didn't kill him Kylee; he's still alive. But I have to get him to Hail. They's no need for you to go back. They's nothin', nothin' you can do. Now come on! You're goin' with me. Climb up on the seat!" he demanded sternly, clearly nervous about the delay.

"I ain't goin' on without my mommy an' poppy! I ain't a goin'! You can't make me." Mary screamed and slid from the horse's rump. Her silken hair dulled from dirt and leaves hung in streamers around her face dusty and streaked with sweat.

"It's no use Mary, they're all dead! You can do nothin' for them now. We gotta help Matt, he's still livin'. Come on now, get up in the wagon like I told you," Tom ordered, forcefully holding her arm.

"No! No! It can't be! Not mommy an' poppy an' my sisters! Not all of 'em! I don't believe it, Tom! You're tellin' me fibs! You know you're a lyin'. Now come on lets go get them!" Mary screeched at Tom pulling herself free from his hold. She broke into a fast run up the road.

"Come back Mary! The Baldwin's an' Mullins are bringing your folks. They'll be at the mill most as quick as we-uns will."

Mary was no match for Tom's swift stride. Catching up to her he picked her up bodily and ran back to the wagon. He placed her firmly upon the seat. Kylee stood waiting and holding Jole's reins as if glued to the spot.

"Get in the wagon Kylee," Tom told her gently as he tied Jole's reins to the back of the wagon. "Hang on tight to Mary; I don't want to stop again."

"I tried to make her understand, Tom. There ain't no understandin' in her. It's dreadful what's happened. She can't accept what we're telling her. She told me she'd walk back up the mountain by herself. I couldn't let her go alone so I brought her back on Jole'. I'm sorry Tom, I couldn't stop her," Kylee apologized, eyes wide and filled again with tears.

"Is it true, Matt's a livin'? He looks awful dead to me." Kylee fastened her arms securely around Mary.

"I ain't blamin' you Kylee. You done the best you could. We'll help her all we can." Tom climbed onto the seat and started the team out slowly.

"I'm so sorry, Mary! So sorry!" He looked at the young woman sitting between him and Kylee, quiet now, eyes staring blankly at her folded hands.

"Oh Lord, help me find a way to help her understand. Lord, help me find a way to kill the ones that done this thing." He prayed under his breath.

"They's all dead, Mary, my paw too. Maybe Matt has a chance to live. We gotta get him to Hail."

"I don't believe you!" Mary said emphatically and turned to Kylee, "If they's dead, it's all your fault! I told you we should a went to help them. We should of helped them! Now they's dead, all cause of you!" Mary yelled through a clash of thunder spreading across the mountain. Mary broke loose and struck Kylee fiercely across the face.

Kylee was stunned but closed her arms again firmly around Mary. Holding the younger woman close and rocking her with the movement of the wagon, she comforted her dear friend as her tears of grief and compassion fell upon their dusty garments. Mary's eyes were dry staring ahead at the road, her tears not shed.

Above the thunder rolling over the hills, Tom could hear the wind stirring a ripple through the trees. A flash of lightning left a blaze of gold in the sky in front of them. Rain was only an unfulfilled promise. Sultry, sweltering heat was reality, drawing flies and vermin in swarms hovering close to the earth.

Dark thoughts clouded Tom's mind as they rode in silence, brooding somberly as he listened to Kylee's quiet crying. He cursed bitterly to himself, blaming his long stay with Polly for his late arrival on the mountain. If only he had left the booze alone he could have been on the road earlier. There would always be the torturing possibility he could have been there to help them. He must do everything possible to keep Matt alive. His only thoughts were to save his brother.

Hail discovered a small wound behind Matt's ear and presumed a small gun such as the one she had seen Rueben Mitchell carry made it. Assuming the bullet was lodged somewhere close to the base of the cranium and probably pressing on a nerve causing his unconsciousness, it was too risky for her to try and remove. Without proper tools and technique it could surely cause his death. She would not attempt it and encouraged Tom to take Matt to the hospital in Norton. With Tom's help they fixed a bed of feather ticks and down quilts, as many as she could gather to absorb the shock of movement from the wagon.

"I can't make you any promises Tom, that's a dangerous wound. But I heard my papa talk about men with this type of wound from bullets or shell fragments. Sometimes they could be helped, sometimes not. He ain't bled much, just a might in his hair an' on his shirt collar. What there was has stopped." Hail talked as they readied Matt, moving him as little as possible.

Kylee helped Mary down from the wagon and they stood watching. Kylee's tears had stopped. Her thoughts were of Matt and she prayed silently for him to be allowed to live.

They listened as Tom described to Hail the carnage at the rocks while she washed the blood away with lye soap and water. Then she carefully tied a clean cloth around Matt's head. Not that it would help, she had explained, but it would keep the flies away and the dust out.

"It's hard to believe, Tom. It's terrible, just terrible! All the horses too? To do such a thing a body would have to be tetched. You an' I know that could only be one person, or persons, the Mitchell's!" Hail emphatically stated as she settled Matt's head gently between two thick pillows.

"You're right as rain Hail, that's for sure!" Tom stated as he munched a sandwich of ham and biscuit Hail brought out to him. She insisted he eat something before he started his journey. He washed it down with a cup of coffee black as a moonless night. He handed the cup to Kylee and climbed onto the wagon seat.

"Hail, stay with Kylee an' Mary! Someone has to see to the buryin' of our folks. Whatever you do, don't leave the girls alone. Whoever done this thing will be layin' for them. Kylee said they know who was on the mountain an' witnessed what happened. They'll be comin' for them. Guard them carefully Hail. I'll send some help from Marshal Snow." Tom lifted the reins.

"Wait Tom, you'll need some money. It takes lots for hospitals. Mary an' I have some sewed into our petticoat hems. Get Mary's,

Hail. She ain't in no condition for doin' anything," Kylee said and began crying again.

"I seen them take the money out'a Ginny's petticoat. They probably got what was in Bess's too. I couldn't see around the wagon. But the one man what drug Ginny away was shaped like Rueben Mitchell," Kylee sobbed. "They all had kerchiefs over their faces."

"The two that came after Mary an' me, I'm certain one was Deputy Hensely, the other one I couldn't mistake his voice, it was a man named Kenus Hall. He came clean from Tennessee. He was lookin' for me. He spoke of Jay shootin' too much. He must have meant Jay Mitchell. How did Kenus know I was with Uncle Ira? How come they know'd we-uns were on the mountain at that time? How come, Tom?" Kylee questioned, completely puzzled.

She ripped the bills from her petticoat, dried her eyes and blew her nose on the hem, hoping she could keep back the flood of tears that crowded her eyes again. She must get herself together. Hail was going to need her. Mary would be no help to anyone. She felt a deep compassion for her friend and again put her arm around Mary's shoulder.

"I'm afear'd Tom. They'll sure come after us. They won't be satisfied until they kill us too." Kylee sobbed in fear.

"Hensely? Are you sure, Kylee? Could you have been mistaken?" Tom looked into the moisture filled eyes peering up at him.

Kylee slowly nodded her head, "It was him!"

"Sure, it fits! I see it all now, a way to get paw an' me out of his hair an' pin the whole damn mess on Jay. Exceptin' he didn't figure on anyone escapin'. I'm goin' now Kylee. When I get back I'll sure see to gettin' even with them all! Who is Kenus Hall?" But he didn't wait for an answer.

Tom tucked the money in his pocket and drove away in a cloud of dust. The rumbling of wagons coming down Pound road filled his ears. He didn't look back. He drove through Donkey without a sideways glance. At Gladeville the mules were tiring and needed a rest. Tom thought it better to refresh the team rather than take a chance on them quitting before the trip ended. It gave him the time he needed to report the massacre.

He found United States Marshal Lorenzo Snow deeply involved with paper work. He sat mumbling to himself over Hensely's absence at such a time. It was hard for Snow to believe the deputy's part in the murders. He promised to send someone immediately to the Gap. Tom had no choice but to leave the investigation in the Marshal's hands. As he left he could hear Lorenzo still muttering to himself about what the hills were coming to. Talt was sure going to hang and now there was this mess on Pound.

The intense mountains gave way to lesser rolling hills and occasional wide stretches of farmland. Tom had been relieved when his journey was about to end, glad for Matt's sake. The trip from the mill to Norton had taken fourteen hours. It was good that most of it had been at night saving them both from the blazing sun. The intense traveling had been hard on Tom and he was concerned for the brother who was close to death.

Only after the skinny attendant had the money locked securely in the hospital safe did he agree to send for the doctor. Quickly and efficiently he delivered Matt into the hands of a nurse who wheeled the gurney away down the hall.

The doctor arrived in what seemed to be hours but was actually only a matter of minutes. The night clerk was explaining to Dr. Richards about Matt's condition but could not get his mind away from Tom's disheveled looks. A two-day beard, no sleep, and to the point of exhaustion, he was not his usual, neat as a pin, person. After an introduction Tom shook the doctor's hand.

The clerk was still talking as the doctor removed his coat and hat. He told him that Matt was one of those ignorant hill people, apparently a victim of one of those century long feuds that were known to rage in the Cumberlands and Blue Ridge. He was puzzled that they had made the trip to bring a patient to see a real doctor. It was his opinion they still believed in faith healers and granny women. He babbled on as he led the doctor and Tom down the hall to where the nurse had taken Matt.

"What do you think we are, Douglas?" Dr. Richards asked as he carefully examined Matt, his voice soft and warm with the slur of the Deep South. "I claim to be an educated doctor; I have a piece of paper that tells me so. I learned a lot in the war, was only twenty-two and in the middle of college," the doctor talked as he thoroughly examined Matt.

The nurses had bathed and dressed Matt in a white hospital gown. They put him in a bed and one nurse was busy fussing with the sheets when they entered. She stood now waiting for further instructions.

"But I'm telling you boy," the doctor continued to inform the clerk, " It has a lot to do with faith. Yes sir-ree, I'm a faith man myself. Right now I'm breathing a prayer asking for a bunch of help with this fellow. Yes sir-ree, I need all the help the Man up there can give me." He turned away from the bed with specific instructions to the nurse to ready Matt for surgery.

Tom liked the doctor immediately, an average looking man in his middle fifties, with a clean-shaven face, and large capable hands. His hair was thinning and gray at the temples. He had pale skin, indicating he spent most of his working and waking hours away from the sun. His dark eyes were hard to read, the slight twinkle of mirth was almost hidden behind a wall of deep seriousness. Tom was satisfied to turn Matt's fate over to him.

"Get yourself a room at the hotel across the street," Dr. Richards advised Tom gravely. "It will take two or three hours to get the bullet. Touchy business, have to go slow. The time it takes will depend on where the bullet's lodged. The hole looks to have been made with a small caliber gun at a distance. Might have been the reason it didn't kill him right off. Can't say for sure until I go in. If the surgery can be done without endangering any vital nerves and the bullet hasn't gone too deep or done too much damage, I think I can save your brother's life."

"What happens if you can't get it?"

"He'll die on the operating table. If I can find the bullet and he lives, there's always the possibility he could be an invalid," the Doctor responded.

"Do the best you can doc. I'm use to invalids. My paw was one. I took care of him. Reckon I could care for Matt. I just want him to live, he's all the family I got left," Tom's voice shook with concern and weariness.

"I better get on with it then. You do as I said. Get you a room and some rest. Soon as I finish I'll send someone for you. There's no need to sit here and wait. You're condition looks a bit shaky." Dr. Richards advised noticing Tom's paleness and sunken eyes.

"You been sick?"

Tom shook his head no. He didn't want no doctor fussin' over him.

"You must take care of yourself. Your brother will need lots of help." The doctor patted Tom on the shoulder. He shook his hand and left him standing alone in the white entry hall of the small efficient looking hospital.

Tom found a stable for the team and wagon then rented a room in the hotel across the street from the hospital. He felt uncomfortable in the confining quarters of the small room. He washed and cleaned up the best he could and regretted not bringing a razor and some clothes. The bed was inviting but he was unable to sleep. Horrible scenes from the big rocks at the Gap filled his head. A pain began in his empty stomach and was gnawing through to his backbone. The biscuit and ham had grown lean. The growling in his innards was not going to quit.

Being alone in the room was not good. His thoughts dwelled on his father and the Stewarts then the revenge he would take against their murderers. The law could take care of Hensely, but Jay Bird Mitchell was his! Leaving his dark thoughts in the room he returned to the hospital to concentrate only on Matt's survival.

A warm golden morning filled the streets as he crossed to the hospital. Buggies and horses were moving slowly as if reluctant to start the day.

There was coffee available but breakfast, a pretty nurse informed him, was only for the patients. He would have to go to a cafe. With Tom's winning ways, he talked her out of some scrambled eggs and a slice of brown bread lavishly spread with molasses. It was just what he needed. He felt his strength and capability to rationalize return.

He brooded over Mary and Kylee. He must return home as soon as possible. Taking their lives would be a necessity for Hensely. If Kylee identified him and his part in the attack his hanging would be assured. It would be the end of a good thing for him. The outlaws had not bargained for anyone getting away.

Tom sat down to wait on a bench near the door. He watched the people coming and going as the early morning hustle of the hospital increased into the full swing of the day. He was unaware that he had lain over on the bench and had fallen into a sound sleep.

Concerned with Tom's comfort a nurse carefully tucked a pillow under his head. An easy shaking of his shoulders interrupted his sound slumber.

"Mr. Phelps, Mr. Phelps, wake up. The operation is over. The doctor said for you to come," an elderly nurse told Tom as he opened his eyes. Tom followed her to a room at the end of the hall.

A high hospital bed occupied most of the space in the small room. Dr. Richards waited close by as the two male attendants made Matt comfortable. Then he hurried them both out of the room. He stood for a long moment with a stethoscope to Matt's chest listening closely. Tom waited, looking at Matt who was pale and still, his head swathed heavily in bandages. He had been to Norton many times but had paid little attention to the hospital. Now here he was standing at the foot of a bed waiting to see if his brother would live or die.

The doctor lifted the stethoscope and turned to Tom. Tom's heart skipped a beat. He held his breath waiting. The doctor looked worried, the operation had been long. What did this mean?

Doctor Richards smiled at Tom. "It could be a long time before he wakes up. The anesthetic will keep him resting for a while."

"Is he all right? Is he gonna live?" Tom asked after getting his breath again.

"I'm certain he will live. The bullet was lodged against the cranium, but had not pierced the skull so it was removable without any complications. I will not be sure about the movement of his legs, maybe for days. Sometimes these things take time. Now, the important thing is for him to rest."

"Thank you doctor, I'm grateful that he's alive. When can I take him home?"

Doctor Richards looked at Tom with extreme shock showing clearly in his face.

"Home? Where's home?"

"Pound Mountain, other side of Donkey."

"Really now? You must realize it will be weeks before this young man could stand such a journey. He has just undergone a serious surgery. Such a trip would surely be fatal. If he stays he will get well. You must not even consider moving him." The doctor was emphatic.

"You can leave anytime," the doctor continued remembering Douglas's referral to a hill feud. He assumed the man wanted to return to avenge his brother lying on the bed. "Your brother will have the best of care here. Patients usually recover faster when some of their family is with them, but I'm certain if you want to leave he would do nicely without you. You could return for him in a few weeks."

"I'll not leave him if he can't go with me. I'll not leave until he can travel. I wanted him to live that's why I brung him. I'll not leave him now." Tom's decision was made. He would stay. Everything else would have to wait, at least a few more days.

"Good, good. It's better that way. We'll let him rest for now. I'll be back to check on him later. You get some rest and come back this afternoon. Maybe he'll be awake then." Dr. Richards shook Tom's hand.

Matt was going to be all right. Tom felt like shouting. Hope amid all this horror. Matt was alive and soon, very soon, Jay Mitchell was going to die!

Ira and the Stewart family laid for viewing in the big room at the Phelps's house. Their caskets had been built quickly, sanded and polished to a high sheen by many loving hands, then lined with satin or velvet. Little Em's had been carved with garlands of wild flowers that she loved so well.

The news traveled fast in the hills and the curious came. They came from miles around, Kentucky, Virginia, and even a few from the hills of North Carolina where Ira was well known. They came weeping and mourning the passing of their friends. As they grieved, they cursed the ones that had committed such fiendish murders and pledged any help they might give that would lead to their capture or death.

Kylee wondered where all the people came from. She moved as if in a nightmare. Hail had been a pillar of strength and took most of the responsibility, forgetting for a while, her scarred face and hands.

The scars on Hail's cheeks, chin and across her forehead were fading some, but the deep rivers of scar tissue that covered her head, neck, and hands would never decrease. She pulled her sleeves down to cover most of her hands and sewed a high ruffle around the neck of her black dress. She replaced the bright colored headscarf with a black silk and lace cap that hid her scarred head in an attractive manner.

People came and went. Kylee remembered none of them afterward. They buried Ira next to Mattie, Billy, and Taynee in the Phelps cemetery on the hill and then moved to the Stewarts for their burials.

Uncle Alvin sat beside Mary on the top step of their home waiting for the coffins that held their family to be moved up to the cemetery. Alvin held an arm firmly around Mary's shoulders. It was as if he were trying in some small way to impart a visage of strength, even he didn't possess. His eyes were laden with grief. The little drop of moisture that usually hung at the end of his nose, by some means of dehydration, had disappeared almost completely. Only a few beaded dewdrops glistened in the sun.

They sat unaware of the commotion around them. Mary didn't realize the many condolences that were offered to her. She momentarily acknowledged one person standing at the bottom of the steps. She jumped to her feet.

"What are you a doin' here? Why ain't you out catchin' them black hearted bastards that killed my folks an' Uncle Ira?" Mary screamed out at Marshal Snow.

"You know it were them Mitchell's! They was furious 'cause I wouldn't marry Bob. They killed Uncle Ira cause of Blaine. Don't you see it had to be them? They're the ones! They wanted to kill us all! But we fooled them! Kylee an' I got away! Now, get out'a here! I want them all hanged! I wished I could kill them with my bare hands!"

Mary shook. It was the most she had said since she saw her dead family in the wagons at the mill. She had only answered questions with a nod or a shake of her head. She nervously clenched and unclenched her fists.

"Now Mary, you know I have been gone for a few months. You're talkin' about things I know nothin' of. But I'm gonna find out. Tom was cleared of that charge against him when Blaine was killed. There was no evidence to prove anything about Billy's death," the Marshal spoke gently to Mary, understanding her outburst had been stimulated by her grief.

"No, there wasn't no evidence because they hid it. That bastard that was your deputy was supposed to be the law when you weren't around. He was the one that made sure it was all twisted to suit him an' the Mitchell's, because they paid him. You can bet your life he's a settin' right in the middle of this whole thing. My poppy an' Uncle Ira knew what they was up to. My poppy was gonna see that Tom got elected when you retired. They wanted us all dead so no one could interfere. If you don't see to their hangin', I'll see to it you're never elected for anything anywhere! You hear me? Never! Never! I want them dead like my folks are dead!" Mary continued to scream and ran down the steps and pounded Lorenzo on his chest with clenched fists.

"Now, Mary," Snow held her wrists staying her hands. "It's natural you're upset. Let's see to your folk's buryin', then we'll take care of this matter. I have people workin' on it now Mary, all over the hills they are lookin'. We are gonna talk more of this after the burying." Marshal Snow was deeply hurt over what had happened. He had known the Stewarts since Mary was born and he felt their deaths deeply.

How had Hensely managed, right under his nose, to get such a hold on Pound Mountain? He couldn't pin down where the whole stinking business started. It was his fault; all this had been possible because of his blind trust in Deputy Hensely. He had a lead on Hensely and Kenus Hall. When they were brought back, there would be a hanging for sure. But there was nothing definite against the Mitchell's, only the hatred and feud that had been going on for years. He put his arms around Mary and comforted her.

"I'm sorry, Mary. I can do nothin' to bring back your folks. But I can promise you a hangin'. I'll see that you an' the Bentley girl are looked over. No ones gonna harm you! Soon as we get your folks buried an' you get rested, we are gonna get a grand jury together to hear your stories. It'll make it easier to bring these animals to justice. Until then, please Mary, for your safety an' your friend, talk to no-one about this. No one, understand?"

But Mary understood nothing; she was back into her deep dark depression. The vacant look was back in her eyes, the fire gone. She was limp and exhausted. Lorenzo sat her back down beside Alvin.

"Take care of her Alvin. Take good care of her." The marshal rode his big white horse up the trail to the cemetery to help with the opening of the graves.

Mary sat with folded hands resting in her lap. She looked blankly across the yard. The sound of metal upon wood touched her ears. Suddenly her heart beat with joy. Her father was there somewhere in the yard splitting staves. The sound filled the air with a never-ending melody as he would swing the fro with a sudden sweep of his strong arms. A shrill whistling rang through the trees, danced across the hills, and occupied the earth with its happy work song.

"Poppy! Poppy!" she cried. The vision was so real that Mary jumped up to run to her father. Uncle Alvin caught and held her firmly.

"No, no lassie that is not your poppy. It's only the Baldwin boy splittin' wood to make coffee for all these folks. There now, there now little one," he comforted her, pulling her back down on the step.

Mary laid her head on his shoulder and closed her eyes hoping the dream would return. But it was gone. Gone forever, vanished, never to appear again. The realization that her father was really dead brought a deep shadow of desperation, a dark burden of grief she could not cope with. A fine thread dangled between Mary's sanity and the dark shadow beyond.

Mary sat cross-legged on the ground between her mother and father's grave refusing to move. Hugging her arms around herself and rocking to and fro, she comforted herself. She sat there the rest of the day and through the night.

Kylee waited patiently beside her. Mary would move in time, she told herself. She knew how hard it was to leave someone you loved under a mound of cold earth and Mary's grief was multiplied. Kylee was torn between her own sorrow and her concern for Mary but she would stay as long as Mary sat there.

Then the rain came. It was as if it had waited until they had buried their dead. The cool drizzle came around midnight then turned into a steady down pour. Kylee reminded Mary to cover her head with her shawl and in a whisper suggested returning to the shelter of the house. The grieving girl shook her head and continued her rocking.

The morning dawned gray and bleak. The rain slowed at times then would start again with renewed force. In the early morning it gave way to a deluge that threatened to wash the young women down the hill. It came in huge welting drops pushing giant leaves from the old oak trees and skinning the bark from the young ones. The drops pounded on the loose dirt piled high on the new graves depleting the mounds to puddles of mud. The murky dirt ran in rivulets into the long grass and down the hill. The immense drops drove into the muddy ooze creating jump-ups that splashed unmercifully onto their huddled figures.

"My goodness Kylee, we're getting' all wet aren't we? What are we a doin' out here anyways sittin' in the rain?" Mary spoke slowly, still in a daze.

Kylee lifted the grieving girl to her feet and guided her cautiously down the trail. Carefully she eased Mary along, keeping her moving, afraid her friend might change her mind and return to the graves. Suddenly in shocked realization, Mary stopped and turned to stare at the muddy mounds, her eyes filled with dark misery.

"They are all gone, Kylee. They are all gone, aren't they? An' Billy too. I ain't got nothin' to live for. Nothin'! Oh dear Lord, I wish I were dead too! I just wish I were dead!" Mary declared, admitting to herself for the first time that her family was dead, gone from her forever.

"Oh dear Lord, strike me dead, strike me dead!" she wailed, but there were no tears. She turned and pounded her fists against a nearby tree moaning and screaming.

"I just want to die an' be with them. I just want to die! Oh, Lord, help me!"

Exhausted from her ordeal Mary clung to her friend and rested her head against Kylee. Their wet hair fell free from the restraining pins and combs tangling together and dripping moisture onto their already wet clothing. The rain slowed as they moved down the trail. Wet brush and dripping leaves created a deluge of their own.

Hail waited for the hordes of people to disperse. She gave Alvin definite instructions to keep a close eye on Kylee and Mary when they came down from the graves and to be suspicious of any strange movement around the place. Now that all the people had come and gone she felt sure someone might try to move in on the young women. She was certain they were in imminent danger and advised Alvin strongly against drinking anymore.

"I must go back to the mill Alvin, an' see to the chores. I'll be back before dawn. See that the girls get some rest when they come down. Mark my words now! No more drinkin', or I'll have your hide!"

She had this nagging in the back of her mind about Simeon and wondered if maybe he had brought the wagon back to the mill, however, there was no sign that he had been anywhere about the place. She turned the chickens, geese, and pigs loose to forage the best they could. They would survive in the forest. Daisy II would be dropping her calf soon so she needn't worry about the cow. Things would go on while they were gone. She rode Jole' during Tom's absence. Unsaddling the yellow horse, she turned it into the pasture with old Red. She gathered some things together for herself and Kylee including raincoats and umbrellas, knowing the rain would become more than a threat. She carefully put away the lace cap and again wore the bright scarf. Sitting down on the window seat, she slept until long after midnight.

Hail stretched and yawned wanting more sleep but it would soon be dawn and she was due back at the Stewarts. Large hard pellets of rain started as she walked to the barn. Taking the small wagon Ira had used for his ground corn she hitched up Jole' and Red, the mule. She was aware the two made a strange team but they would have to do. The warm hard rain turned to a cool drizzle as she crossed the bridge below the mill. A gray light was misting across the trees beginning to fill the world. It would be daylight soon.

She found Alvin passed out, far-gone into a drunken stupor on his corner bunk. Kylee and Mary were nowhere about, not in the bedrooms or outside. Angry with Alvin and fearful for the young women, she shook the small man rattling his teeth. Receiving only a low grumble she dropped the brandy soaked mass into a mound on his bed.

Panic filled her; she should have waited for the girls to come down from the cemetery. The cemetery, of course, she would start there. Past the tobacco barn and up the wet path filled with mud and slimy leaves she ran. Sliding dangerously as she went. The rain stopped and only a soft mist was falling. The dark clouds tossed about by a mild breeze let through patches of sunshine revealing a moisture sodden world.

Hail met the young women coming slowly down the path. Their black attire an earthen hue from the moisture and mud splatters. The two fell upon her overjoyed. Hail was relieved to find the young women and they resumed their walk. They walked three abreast clinging to each other with Hail in the middle, her bright headscarf a splash of berry red against the dark green leaves.

"I'm near sick to death worryin' about Matt an' Tom. It's been nigh onto a week since they left an' nary a word of any sort. If Matt were dead Tom would have been back with his body. If they fixed Matt up, an' he lived, you'd think they'd be back by now. Either way, they'd been home. I feel it in my bones Kylee. Somethin's gone wrong. Somethin' just ain't right. I ain't trustin' Matt another minute to them city-fied doctors. The only thang they know how to do is use a knife, an' they believe in usin' it too. They don't hold back one minute." Hail was silent for a moment and they could hear the big drops falling from the leaves and dripping into the puddles on the ground.

"Now I don't dare leave you-uns here, so I'm takin' you with me!" Hail said with her mind made up.

"Takin' us with you, where Hail, when?" Kylee questioned.

"Hush an' listen. Can't trust Alvin one minute. Oh, he'll do the chores then have his nose in the jug until he crawls clean in. Ain't trustin' Snow neither. That bunch of outlaws will be lookin' for you here or at the mill. The safest place I could think of would be in the city. I ain't wantin' to be there, but we're goin'. While I thought you two were safe in bed asleep I went to the mill an' took care of things there. I hitched up old Red an' Jole' to the little wagon, I'm ready to travel. Soon as you've changed to some dry things an' ate a bite of breakfast, we'll be on our way!"

The murky storm was not over; a slow drizzle was beginning as they left the house. Mary sat bravely between Kylee and Hail, she realized little of what was taking place, letting them guide her like a puppet.

Kylee sat on the outside holding a large black umbrella over their heads protecting them from the rain. She became increasingly concerned and nervous for Matt. When she came to Virginia a year ago, she came through Norton. In a panic she remembered how far the journey had been and prayed for Matt's well being. They rode silent and still, eating on the way, and stopping only when their bodies demanded. They were wishing for their journey to end. They were a constant moving object and often the only ones on the road as they traveled south to Norton, to Matt and Tom.

The days Tom spent beside Matt's bed seemed an eternity. Along with the deep anxiety for his brother's health, he fought an urgency to be back on Pound Mountain looking for Jay.

Matt's recovery hadn't been as swift as Tom would have liked. The first three days he remained unconscious, not moving or opening his eyes. Then on the fourth day he moaned a lot and opened his eyes occasionally, but recognized no one. The doctor kept insisting that these things took time. But Tom could tell by Dr. Richards's nervous attitude that things were not going as well as he had expected.

"That you, Tom? Where's paw? Where am I? What's happened?" he asked weakly and raised a hand to feel the bandages on his head.

"Tarnation Matt, you're awake. We've waited a long time for you to wake up. You've been bad sick 'Bub'. I brought you to Norton to the hospital. The doc here operated on you an' you're fine now. We'll be takin' you home, soon," Tom explained. He took his brother's hand and stood close to the bed squeezing it tightly.

"I can't remember anythin' Tom. I don't even remember gettin' sick," Matt spoke slowly, his voice dragging.

"That's enough visiting for right now young man. You can talk later," Dr. Richards interrupted and then smiled broadly as Matt moved a leg. "You rest now; we'll be back and talk to you later. You missed supper but if you feel like eating, I'll have the nurse bring you some food."

"I am feelin' a little hungry. I think I'd like that."

"All right, we'll go and see about it. Come along Tom." The doctor put his hand on Tom's shoulder and moved him out of the room.

"It's happened Tom, it's happened. He's out of the woods now! Yes sir! He will be fine now. I saw him move a leg and he lifted an arm. That's progress! Now, if we can get him to take on some nourishment we've got it whipped. Yes sir, we've got it whipped!" Dr. Richards explained and shook Tom's hand still holding on to his shoulder.

"He does have the ability of speech and movement. Now it's only a matter of time before we'll have him up and about. If you need to go Tom, it would be all right now. I want your brother to stay here for another week at least, but there would be no need for you to stay. You could come back for him, say in two weeks just to make sure." He was glad to see a spark of happiness in Tom's clouded eyes.

"You have this other business to take care of."

"Thank you, Doctor. I'll be leavin' now I know Matt's all right. I will send someone for him in a couple of weeks. I'll be back to check on him before I go."

"That'll be fine Tom." The doctor watched Tom's quickened step down the hall. There was a purpose to the stride, a straighter line to the back.

Tom felt good about Matt. He could leave now and not worry. He would have Carl Jennings or one of the Mullins men come for Matt. He would be in good hands. His pace quickened at the thought, soon; very soon, he would be on Jay's trail.

He stopped stark still halfway to the front door and stared in shocked surprise at the three women talking to the clerk at the front desk. There was no mistaking Hail with her bright gypsy scarf, nor Mary's flaxen hair. The small one must be Kylee. She looked almost like a child with her hair half rolled up and the rest hanging almost to her knees.

"By damn, it is them. It is!" Tom reassured himself and hurried his step. "Kylee, Mary, Hail! I ain't a dreamin'! It is you-uns."

Mary fell into Tom's arms weary from her journey and filled with overwhelming joy at seeing him. Kylee and Hail followed her and embraced the young man with hugs and demands to know about Matt. The rain stopped before they reached Norton and a gentle warm wind had dried their clothing and hair.

"Matt is just fine, just fine," Tom answered getting his breath and recovering from their onslaught. "He still has a long way to go. Today he moved an' opened his eyes. He knew me an' was askin' questions about paw, but we ain't told him nothin' yet."

Looking at Mary he was concerned with her paleness and the vacant look in her eyes. He guided them down the hall to Matt's room. He kept his arm lightly around Mary's waist to keep her moving.

Dusk was creeping through the narrow window by Matt's bed filling the room with a dim yellow light. The bandages around Matt's head and the white sheets and pillows absorbed the yellow glow giving everything, including Matt's face a golden hue.

"He looks terrible ill," Kylee whispered as they stood staring at Matt's sleeping figure.

"You musn't stay long." A middle-aged nurse told them following them into the room. "We mustn't tire him. Too much company will do just that!" A slight frown crossed her face. She turned on the gas light on the wall above the bed to a bright flame.

The light dissolved the yellow fog and the room was again gray and white. Hail stood rigid offering a silent prayer, her lips moving slowly. She was giving thanks for Matt's recovery and praying for a way to see Jay Mitchell die.

Matt opened his eyes, "That you Tom?"

"Yes Matt, it's me. Look who's come to see you? It's Kylee, an' Mary, an' Hail too. But the nurse said to only stay a minute, we don't want to tire you Bub. I'll let them say hello to you, I've talked enough." Tom backed away from the bed. Kylee moved in and kissed Matt's cheek. Matt smiled at the soft touch.

"Kylee, you're so beautiful. But where's Paw?"

"We'll talk of that later, right now here's Mary to say hello. I'm so glad you're gonna get well, Matt. I love you." Kylee added sadly and pushed Mary gently to the bedside.

"Oh Matt, you look so terrible sick. Please get well; promise me you won't die. I couldn't bear it if you died too!" Mary laid her head on Matt's shoulder and clung to him, she wanted to be sure he was alive, to feel the life in his body.

"Die too? What's she talkin' about Tom? What ain't you tellin' me?" Matt felt a tremor of memory, horses squealing, flying dust, stomping hooves, and whistling bullets. A slight awakening, he knew something terrible had happened. Feeling the trembling of Mary's body he raised an arm and held her close. From somewhere deep inside he realized she was in deep sorrow and he comforted her patting her shoulder and smoothing her silken hair.

"What's happened Tom? What's happened I should know about?" He questioned over the head of the grieving girl on his chest.

Tom raised Mary from the bed. "We'll talk of it tomorrow, Bub. The women have come along way. They need some rest. We don't want to over tire you either. You rest now, we'll be back tomorrow."

A very pretty nurse came into the room. She informed them impatiently that they would have to leave. Her attitude was authoritative and not to be refused, but she met her match in Hail.

The mid-wife stiffened her back and lowered her body into a small rocker beside Matt's bed. From there she took up watch over Matt until he left the hospital, much to the exasperation and ill temperament of the nurse. Hail refused to relinquish.

Dr. Richards only laughed at the guarding gypsy angel, as he called Hail and told the nurses to leave her be. He gave strict instructions for them to see that Hail had her meals when the patient did. He also suggested in a diplomatic manner that a folding cot, now in the hall, would do nicely for her a bed. He explained to the shocked nurses that her presence would only hurry Matt's recovery. The matter was settled.

Tom arranged for the women to have his room. He gave them the key and told them emphatically to always stay together. He warned them against taking up with strangers and above all, not to walk about the streets unless Hail was with them.

He felt confident that Jay or Hensely would not look in Norton for Mary and Kylee, Gladeville, maybe. But it would be too risky to extend a search this far. He felt certain that faces of the outlaws would soon appear in all the newspapers and on wanted posters. The outlaws would hide even farther into the mountains, making it almost impossible to find them, among the many rolling hills, plunging ravines, and slashed hollows. Mountains and hollows alike were forested with a variety of big trees and tall shadowy pines that would cover their tracks.

Tom looked older, Kylee thought. Maybe it was the new collarless shirt he purchased or the dark corduroy suit that was very conservative attire, not at all like Tom.

"Stay together at all times. I can go now that you-uns are here." Tom informed them and divided the money he had left after paying two weeks advance for the room. "If you spend this wisely it should last until you take Matt home. The room is paid; all you'll need is to eat an' pay for the livery. I'll take Jole', an' Red, an' the little wagon you brung. You'll have the bigger wagon to bring Matt back home in. It'll be more comfortable." Tom instructed them as he rolled his dirty clothing into a bundle and tucked it under his arm.

Mary sat on the bed; hands folded submissively in her lap and watched Tom closely, "I want to go with you, Tom. Take me with you. I could help you find those bastards that killed my folks. I could cook for you an' I wouldn't get in your way at all, I promise. Please let me go. They have killed everything I had to live for. If you'd let me go with you, it would give my life some purpose."

Tom placed the back of his hand against her cheek. "No Mary, I travel too hard. Please do not ask. You have Matt, an' me, an' Kylee, an' Hail. We are goin' to be your family now. An' you have Uncle Alvin too. Thank God for the miracle that saved you an' Kylee. We'll all stick together. I'm depending on you to see that Matt gets well. Then you can help take him home. I promise you, I'll see to killin' them bastards what killed your folks. I promise you, Mary, God as my witness, I'll see to it! I must go now."

Mary lifted her cheek for Tom's kiss then offered him a slight sad smile. Taking Kylee by the arm Tom guided her through the door, closed it, and sat his bundle on the floor. There in the dim light of the hall he looked at her long and hard, not speaking, just looking into the jade pools that were Kylee's lovely eyes. She returned his stare, not bashful anymore, and looked deep into his light blue eyes, so much like Ira's.

She noticed the scar across his nose turning white and fading. The mark was slight but she felt a pang of remorse for having hit him. Then she saw the pain, grief, and hate shadowed deep in his eyes. Shadows that told her all else was forgotten in his life. Her heart filled with a great compassion and love for him. Laying her head upon his chest she folded her arms around him and hugged him close. Feeling him swallow the sob that rose in his throat she understood why he didn't speak but stood silently holding her.

Tom stroked her shining hair, loving its sleek softness. Fleetingly he thought of Polly. He vowed when this thing he had to do was done, he would tell Kylee everything about Polly. He would beg for her understanding and forgiveness.

"Oh Lord a mercy, how I need you Kylee dearest! Promise me when I come back you'll be waitin'. Promise me!

"I will Tom, I will." Kylee promised with her head still held to Tom's chest.

"There are so many things I want to tell you. I have no right yet. So until I do, take care of yourself. Take care of Mary too. Hail will be busy watching over Matt. So you will have to see after Mary, she is in no condition to care for herself. I'll trust her to you, Kylee." Kylee smiled up at him through a new surge of tears.

"Don't let anythin' happen to you, Tom. Please, we all need you. I will pray every day for your safety." She tried to give him a brave smile through the flood, wanting him to remember her smiling and not the tears.

Tom thought how beautiful her green eyes were shining with moisture like dew on the lily pads early in the mornings. He kissed her then lightly and tenderly, released her and picked up his bundle from the floor and was gone. He walked across to the hospital for one last look at Matt and a short chat with Hail. He reassured her with each word that he would soon see to Jay's hanging.

Hanging, Hail informed him, was not good enough. She wanted to see Jay burn in the hottest fire hell had to offer.

CHAPTER THREE

"Damn, I ain't seen Tanner for days. I think he traded over from keepin' the law to breakin' it. We's been too busy gettin' ready to hang Hall to worry about the likes of you." The young deputy stated when Simeon asked to see Deputy Hensely.

"I'd like to talk to the regular Marshal then. They's a regular Marshal ain't they? Ain't he the head of things? Why ain't he been around?" To Simeon Niger the time he had spent in jail was already a considerable wedge out of his life.

"They ain't got no right holdin' me. I ain't done nothin'. Ain't I gonna have a trial or nothin'? Can't I even see a judge?" Simeon was nervously wondering if he was going to rot there, as Deputy Hensely had promised.

"You gotta be out'a your head nigger. There's no judge wantin' to see the likes of you. Like as not, they'll hang you on some trumped up charge when all this other stuff settles down. What, with Hall goin' to hang an' the Phelps an' Stewart families murdered at the Gap, Marshal Snow has been up to his ears without worryin' about your black butt! Now, don't bother me any more! There ain't nothin' I can do anyways. Just be glad their feedin' you, even if it's only grits an' beans. At least it's something. I've seen them starve blacks in jail, to death! Yeah, clean to death. Until they shriveled up an' died!" His loud laugh followed him down the corridor.

"What are you sayin' about them folks got murdered? What you talkin' about?" Simeon stood up and yelled after the deputy. "Come back here an' tell me what you was a sayin'." But the man was gone. He heard the door to the cellblock slam shut.

Simeon sat back down on the bunk, clenched his fists to the side rail until his knuckles turned white. He knew without a doubt it was his friends that had been murdered. The deputy had said families. Were they all dead, all of them, he wondered?

"Oh my God, let it not be so." Simeon sank his head in his hands and wept for his friends and the utter hopelessness of his situation.

The next morning Simeon awoke tired and desperate. His sleep the preceding night had been tossed and ragged. He was flat on his back staring at the bunk above him when Marshal Snow appeared at his cell door.

"Simeon Niger, if that's your name. I can't find any reason why you're in jail, exceptin' it says here you stole a wagon an' team belongin' to Ira Phelps. No one has reported such a theft. It appears to me if you had a stole it, you wouldn't a been drivin' it right through town big as all get-out on the Fourth-a-July. I can't see no reason to bring you up to trial. It's costin' the county to feed you. What do you have to say?"

Lorenzo Snow was a skinny man, tall and lanky. People often misinterpreted him as being weak. It was far from the truth, he was strong and full of vigor. His weakness was that he was good natured and trusting. Trusting to a fault as proved to be the case where Hensely had been concerned.

"Now I guess you don't know about Ira an' the Stewart family. They was murdered up at the rocks some days back. It was purty dreadful. It has the whole county tore up. There was five of them killed in cold blood. The men were hung an' their bodies riddled with bullets." Snow scratched his head under his black hat.

"Don't see how you could of had anything to do with it, bein's you was in jail. Don't suppose you have any idea who might a done such a terrible thang? Huh?" The Marshal peered through the bars at the man lying on the bunk. "Them outlaws had to find out from someone just when them folks was gonna be at that spot, at that time. That's the way I see it anyways. You got any ideas who might a told such a thing?"

Simeon rose from the bunk shaking his head vigorously with his eyes opened wide.

"They didn't get Tom an' Matt. It's my opinion," Snow continued and rubbed his jaw carefully, "if they get an idea who informed on their folks, well, that person won't stand more chance than a snow flake in hell!"

"No sir! I don't know nothin' about nothin'. Mista Ira was my friend. I sure am sorry to hear about that, sir," Simeon answered nervously, smoothing his hair. "Yes sir, Mista Ira was good to Simeon Niger. Mista Tom an' Mista Matt too."

"Well, them Phelps's will be out gunnin' for anyone they think had anything to do with them killins." Lorenzo looked closely at the black man.

In his mind, Snow couldn't connect this man with the murders. He could see no reason for keeping him there. He was going to turn him loose. Perhaps, he wondered, could Simeon's being in jail have anything to do with Tanner's plans? Had he in some way used the Negro for information? He opened the cell and motioned for Simeon to follow him to the front office.

"I think if I was you, Simeon Niger, I'd get my butt out'a this county. Mitchell's ain't too fond of anyone connected with Phelps's. You'd be wise to leave that wagon an' team up at Ben Hardman's in Donkey. Get yourself clean over Pound Mountain an' lost somewhere." He handed Simeon his hat and belt from the desk drawer.

"If I had my way they could bury that town up there. All it's been good for is trouble." The Marshal tossed his hat on a peg and sat down at his desk.

"Parley, take this man over to the stable an' get that wagon an' team. I don't want to see him here again. You better do as I've said Simeon! Don't take off with that team an' wagon. Tom Phelps will sure have your hide. If he don't, I will!"

Snow realized he had made a big mistake trusting Hensely to clean up Pound Mountain. Now he wanted no part of the mess. Well, he'd find a good man and deputize him and give him the job. The Phelps's were well liked and had a lot of relations on the mountain. Everyone would be in sympathy with Tom. Perhaps he would be the

BARBARA JONES HARMAN

one to become Marshal when the time came for him to retire. He
was hoping it would be soon.

Simeon breathed deep of the hot summer air. He would never,
never again take his freedom lightly. The grass and trees were still
dark green from the recent rain. What a blessing for the crops.
But then again, too much rain this time of year washed the dirt
from around the corn and tobacco leaving the roots exposed to the
blistering sun. The insects were twice as intense after a heavy rain.

He was sad about Ira. The Marshal had indicated that Tom and
Matt survived. What about the young Miss Kylee? Was she among
the dead? He had better be on his way. If Matt or Tom found out
he had been in jail at the time of the massacres it wouldn't be long
before they put the pieces of the puzzle together. He had known
everything about the trip to Kentucky.

Oh, dear God. He was the one responsible for his friend's deaths.
Like the Marshal said, he had better scoot out of this county. There
was no excusing his little talk with Hensely. Phelps would kill him
for sure. He would leave the wagon and team with Ben, say good-
bye to Polly and Trace and be on his way. If he took one of the big
grays he was driving, it wouldn't be like stealing. Mista Ira owed
him some wages. Would that be considered fair?

Jay's frantic endeavor to hide from the law was beginning to wear
on his nerves. He understood that Virginia and half of Kentucky
had a manhunt out for Tanner Hensely. Kenus Hall had split to
Tennessee after demanding they return the price for the Bentley
girl. Ferrell took his share of the money and was long gone. Tanner
had warned Jay to find a hiding place.

"Damn it Jay. We let them women get away! We don't know what
all they seen. I'm not gonna take any chances. I have no family, I'm
headin' west. You have a family Jay. I understand your not wantin'
to leave. But hide yourself an' them boys good! Wait for this thing to
blow over. If those gals seen you or your boys at the rocks, the law
won't take their eyes off your place," Tanner continued to warn Jay
and give him instructions on what to do.

580

Jay hadn't dared to return home. But it was Tom Phelps that kept him close to Pound Mountain. He still wanted Tom dead. If he understood anything about Phelps, he was certain that Tom would be looking for him. Tom hadn't been with the Phelps wagon and Jay knew Ira's promise could come true, that Tom would get him. He had to get Tom first. There would be no hiding place for him even in the dense forests of the Blue Ridge, anywhere in the Cumberlands, south or north. Tom knew the mountains as well as Jay. He had heard rumors that a crowd had gathered at the Phelps's mill to view the bodies and help bury the dead. There would be no chance now to get the women.

Jay was concerned with Bob's restlessness. He was aware of his nights filled with nightmares when the young man would scream out in his sleep. He expected at any time that Bob would leave and ride for home. It was an action Jay could not allow. Bob's horror over his father's crimes and his grief over the Stewart's was a known fact to Jay. He could not chance Bob's returning home. He kept him under close surveillance, never letting him out of his sight. Not only did he have to watch Bob, but every bush and tree that Tom Phelps might be hiding behind.

There had been no sign that Tom was anywhere on the mountain. He supposed he was busy burying his folk. Well, there was no one left to bury Tom, except him. He had to find out exactly where Tom was and what he was up to. He could trust Rueben to be careful and not be seen by the law. Trace would hide him and tell him what was going on. Trace knew everything that was happening on the mountain. Besides, he would have no problem convincing Rueben to go. It would give him a chance to see Polly.

It was not hard for Rueben to sit and be patient. He filled the time with whittling. He sat on a log sheltered by a wide spreading chestnut tree carving a small figure. Scraping with a sharp blade from his pocketknife and carefully blowing away the wood dust. He polished the figure with his fingers until he had fashioned an animal of shining beauty. Jay took the carving from him and turned it over in his hand.

"What sorta animal is this, Rueb boy? I never seen a horse with a horn in the middle of its head. I've seen a heap of horses an' mules but never like this one."

"I can't tell you Paw. Maybe it's not a horse. Maybe it's some kind of goat or somethin'. I only know what I saw. I saw it in a picture on Polly's kitchen wall hanging over the water bucket. Trace said it was her favorite picture. He said she liked it 'cause it was different, like she was. I don't know what he meant but I only know Polly's the most beautiful thing I ever saw. I made this for her." Rueben declared and took the carving back from his father and tucked it safely in his shirt pocket.

"Well, that's nice Rueb, real nice. How'd you like to take it to her?" his father suggested, patting his son on the shoulder.

His son was delighted that his father trusted him with an important mission. Also he was instructed to kill any Phelps he might run in to.

Much to Rueben's disappointment he could find no one around the Phelps mill. The stock and chickens had disappeared. Even the big water wheel was silent. But the dogs were there and they encouraged him to be on his way. He went on past the Stewarts without a remorseful thought of Ginny's battered body, only an increasing excitement that he would soon see Polly again.

"You better head on back up the mountain, Rueben." Trace advised him when he appeared boldly at the tavern. "You're lucky there's no one about. You know they just buried the Stewarts an' Phelps's tuther day. Did you have any part of that, Rueb? The law's been checkin' here every day, sometimes twice. Folks ain't gonna stand for those murders. I ain't gonna hide no fugitive! It's thought that your paw was responsible for them killin's. That true, Rueb?"

Rueben stuck out his bottom lip at Trace. "I ain't tellin' you nothin', Trace. It ain't for you to know. Ain't no one got any proof we-uns killed anyone. Now, I want to see Polly. My money's as good as any." He proudly showed the bills that were part of his share from Ginny's petticoat. He'd show Trace he had money, but he wasn't going to pay Polly a cent for lying with him.

"Come on Trace. Paw said you'd hide me an' tell me where Tom Phelps is."

"I can't do that Rueben. I ain't seen Tom for days. It's up to Polly if she wants to see you. She's in the last room to the left. Take your chances."

Trace was seriously contemplating sending for Snow. But the Federal Marshal had asked for all this by trusting Hensely. Trace had accepted Hensely's blind eye in many cases of illegal moonshining. He felt he owed Hensely one. As far as the Mitchell's were concerned he didn't know what he felt. He did know that the law wanted Jay for questioning. There had been no positive identification to connect him with the crime. The only thing he knew for certain was Jay's well-known hatred for Phelps. Knowing in his heart that the Mitchell's were the ones responsible for the raping and murder of the Stewart women, Trace decided he would not harbor Rueben Mitchell. He was deep in thought wiping down the bar and seriously contemplating what action to take when Simeon Niger walked through the door.

"Simeon, good Lord man. Where have you been?" Trace put down the bar towel and reached to shake the black man's hand.

"I been in jail, Trace. That damn deputy stuck me in jail for havin' Mista Ira's wagon an' team. He was a thinkin' I stole it. I been there ever since the day I brung Miss Polly home. I just got out. Mista Marshal Snow said he couldn't see no evidence to keep me. So's I brung back Mista Ira's wagon an' team. Marshal Snow told me about Mista Ira an' the Stewart murders. I feel very sorry about that. I need a horse bad Trace. Walkin' in these hills is mighty tough on foot. You reckon if I took one of them grays that Mista Tom would understand? I had some wages comin', you suppose that'd be fair?" Simeon looked seriously at Trace.

"I reckon Simeon. I could square it up with Tom."

"I'd like to say good-bye to Miss Polly. Could you have her come down? It wouldn't look right for me to go to her bedroom. I sure do thank you for gettin' me that job with Mista Ira an' all. I liked workin' for them. They was nice folk," Simeon said sadly. He smiled gratefully at Trace and offered his hand, his smile a white slash against his ebony skin.

"I'll take the wagon over to Ben's an' tell him good-bye. I'll come back to see Miss Polly, then I'll be on my way." Simeon turned to leave when there came a frantic call from upstairs.

"Paw! Paw! Come an' get this bastard out of here!" Polly's angry voice came from the hall above. "I ain't never gonna have anything to do with this trashy pole-cat! I don't care how much money he has!"

Across the street Ben Hardman had cooled his forge, sorted and stacked the various sizes of mule and horseshoes. He hung them in meticulous order on the back of a cupboard door. He closed the door and set the padlock. Things had been pretty quiet since the murders in the big rocks at the Gap. If it weren't for a few freighters Ben would not have bothered to open. Even the freight business had slowed. Skinners were concerned with the amount of robberies on Pound. They were holding off until the mess was cleaned up or Snow could supply them with protection or, they told him they would supply their own. Even Trace's had been surprisingly quiet. Ben closed the big doors at the front of the livery. Inside the tall building the forge was cooler than the surge of heat coming from the dusty road. Two gun blasts from the tavern sent Ben on a high run across the street.

Usually gunfire in the small village wouldn't have disturbed him but with the events on Pound and deputies all over the place, it was cause for concern. Then while locking up the doors, he thought he recognized Rueben's black mule and the Phelps wagon and team outside Trace's tavern. That combination in itself was a certain pattern for trouble. He passed young Mitchell as he was coming down the stairs on a high run.

"It weren't me, Ben. They ain't gonna pin this one on me! It was that damn nigger. He's the one that shot Trace. It were his fault! All of it!"

"That damn black! He's got my gun. I'll be back to get it," he muttered a promise to himself.

Mounting the big mule he rode into the heavy tree cover behind the tavern. Here he could hide and see the front steps. He would watch and wait.

Rueben Mitchell always carried a small derringer tucked into a holster buckled around his shoulder then hidden under his brown summer weight long coat. Rueben always wore a second gun strapped around his hips.

Ben found Simeon standing in the bedroom door holding a small gun in his hand. Polly sat cross-legged on the floor cradling her father in her arms, sobbing loudly.

"I can't do that Mista Trace. Don't ask it. You be quiet an' save your breath. It wouldn't be right for Miss Polly to be travelin' with the likes of me."

"I ain't leavin' you Paw! Simeon'll go for help or we will take you. That's what we'll do. We'll take you to Gladeville. You just lay still an' save your strength," Polly pleaded rocking her father gently to and fro. Her tears were streaking the black from her eyes and washing a definite path through the rouge on her checks.

"Polly, Polly, it ain't no use. I'm done for. I'm dyin'. You gotta accept it!"

"Hush! Hush now! Go quick Simeon. Get a wagon an' horses. Hurry now! Hurry. We are gonna take papa for help."

"I got the Phelps wagon an' team at the front steps Miss Polly. Let me get a hold of him. I can carry him easy." Simeon offered throwing Rueben's derringer on the bed.

"It ain't no use, Simeon, leave me be. Leave me an' get away with Polly. Go! Take Polly with you! They'll blame this damn thing on you, Simeon, even if you was trying to take the gun from Mitchell when it went off. You know they'll take any chance to hang a black. Folks here about will never let Polly stay here doin' what she's doin'. I hear'd rumors they was gettin' ready to tar'n feather her. They'll see to its doin'. Long as I was here I could protect her. But I'm dyin', I know it. You know it's gonna happen. Now leave me, an' go!" Trace struggled to force his words.

"We're takin' you Paw! I ain't leavin' here without you!" Polly's tears were dry and a new forcefulness was in her voice.

"Wait a minute, please Polly, wait a minute. They's something I must tell you, then we'll go. I promise, we'll go then. But in case I don't make it there's something I must tell you now." The color was leaving Trace's face and the brightness in his eyes clouded. He was struggling to keep breathing with long hard gasps. A pool of blood was forming under his body from a chest wound and filling Polly's lap. His usually rosy face was ghastly gray.

"I have always loved you girl an' respected you as a good father should. Haven't I girl?" He asked watching Polly nod her head. "I let you have your way about this thing you was doin'. It were your choice. God forgive me. I should have kept a firmer hand on you. But things sort a got out'a hand after your maw died. I gotta tell you about your maw, Polly. It's right that you know. I was gonna tell you if you ever decided to marry. I could see that wasn't gonna be your choice so I let it ride. Now you gotta know."

"No one ever knew, Polly. Your maw an' I were never married. We was gonna but after the years went by, it didn't seem important. I loved her just as much. Your momma would want you to know what I am gonna tell you." Trace coughed slightly and lifted Polly's hand to lay it next to his cheek.

"I found your ma lyin' on the back step of the tavern I owned in a little town in Alabama. She was in love with a black man and they had been seein' each other. You know well, white folks would never allow that. When them folks found out they had been sneakin' out together, they beat him to death an' went lookin' for your maw. They would a done her the same way because she was pregnant with a black man's baby. When I found her she was near death an' a few months away from her birthin' time. She was so in need of help an' so lovely an' pitiful; I couldn't help but fall in love with her. I knew what would happen if the child was black. There was a chance it would be. I sold my business and moved here. She said she would leave after her baby was born an' go north. She didn't want to cause any trouble for me. I couldn't stand the thought of bein' without her. I loved her so much I could not think of letting her go. What ever happened, we would chance it! When you was born, Polly, you was so light skinned we knew there'd be no problem. I was buildin' this tavern. Your mama was a hard worker; even helped me put the roof on. Your mama was never too well after you were born. When she died it was you an' me. I was busy finishin' this place. I guess I neglected you, Polly. You done as you pleased, it was easier for me that way. I never worried about tellin' you. I just let you pass as white. But now you can go north with Simeon. He can take care of you. It won't matter to no one. Now go! Take her man, an' go! I'm puttin' her in your hands," were Trace's last words.

"Take him to the wagon Simeon, we're gonna find help. When he's well, we'll all go north. That will be the thing to do. We will wait until he is well." Polly's mind was made up. She was not concerned with the fact that she was part black. The color of a person's skin had never been an issue to Polly. It was the character that mattered, what was inside that counted. She looked up at Simeon. To her, it never mattered that Simeon was black; she liked him for the gentle person he was. She turned her father over to his care. She always loved Trace as a father, what he had just told her did not change that.

Simeon lifted Trace easily in his strong arms. For the first time he noticed Ben standing in the doorway.

"Bring some of the quilts, please Mista Ben. We'll get him comfortable as possible." Simeon spoke with the utmost respectability afraid the man in his arms was already dead.

"Take care of the place until we get back, will you Mista Ben?" Simeon asked as they hurried down the stairs.

"Sure, Simeon, sure thing. I can do that. Don't look like there's much hope for Trace though." Ben voiced his opinion working quickly to lay the quilts out on the back of Ira's wagon.

"I'm goin' on ahead. I'll tell Snow that Mitchell was here. We'll have help waitin' for Trace." Ben ran to the stable behind the livery. He saddled a horse and was gone down the road leaving a cloud of dust behind him.

"Come on Polly, what's takin' you so long?" Simeon called into the tavern. He glanced around. No one was on the street, he couldn't blame them, the sun was blazing hot.

"I'm comin'! I had to change my petticoat it was all bloody. I had to put on a dress, I couldn't just go ridin' in my corset cover an' drawers." She settled herself on the wagon seat, turning to keep a watch on her father.

"I think he's dead Simeon. Oh dear, I think he's dead," Polly sobbed as she looked at Trace's lifeless body and ashen face.

Simeon started the team out slowly then encouraged their gait into a smooth rolling trot down the road to Gladeville. The dry dust rose in a cloud around them and settled on Polly's yellow voile dress turning it to the color of clay. A shot whistled through the trees,

then another. Simeon pitched into the wagon bed. He sprawled
backward on top of Trace's body, dead instantly.

Polly reached for the reins and walloped the team into a high
run. But the team with the heavy wagon behind them was no match
for Rueben's mule and he was soon abreast of the wagon. He caught
Polly in his arms. He fastened his arms tightly around her body and
held her firmly, attempting to lift her onto his lap. Twisting with
determination Polly tried to fasten her feet under the wagon seat.
Her struggle was futile. Rueben succeeded in pulling her over onto
his knee, holding her securely. The team ran swiftly down the road
unattended. Soon they ran themselves out and stood breathing hard
and lifting their heads up and down in the middle of the road.

Rueben's expert horsemanship allowed him to keep his big mule
moving at an exhilarating speed at the side of the wagon. After he
had Polly safely on his knee he pulled his mount to a slow gallop.
Polly was still struggling, trying to loosen herself from Rueben's
hold. She kicked and squirmed trying to free herself of the abductor's
strong arms.

"Hold still, you cheap whore! You had no right to refuse me,
Polly! My money's good as any!" he yelled at her. "I wanted you to
come with me! I was even considerin' marryin' you. But you thought
yourself too good!"

"You're a fiend, Rueben Mitchell! You killed my paw an' Simeon.
I know you killed some of the Stewart's too. I know you did!" Polly
screamed above the wind created by the moving mule.

"You ain't never gonna touch my body! Never! I'd kill myself
first!"

Rueben guided his mount up the mountain onto a trail that led
to the Gap and Kentucky where his father waited. Polly increased
her struggle and Rueben was becoming concerned that he might
drop her. Pulling the mule to a stop he wrapped the reins around
the saddle horn. He was tired of this game, drew the gun at his hip
and shot Polly through the head. She flinched, her struggle ended.

Rueben spurred the big mule and rode on up the mountain
behind the big rocks. Before descending into Kentucky he stopped
again. The blood still oozed from the bullet hole in Polly's temple.
He began to cry, blubbering and wailing like a baby. He took a large

white handkerchief from his back pocket and wrapped it carefully around her head covering the wound. He used his teeth to help tie the knot.

"I didn't want to kill you, Polly. You're so beautiful an' all. You shouldn't have fought me. You shouldn't have!" He sobbed as he lowered her to the ground.

Dismounting he unwrapped the reins and let them hang loose. He took out his pocketknife and began to dig at the base of a large stately pine. The earth was soft and pliable from the recent rain. Loosening the dirt with the knife then scooping it out with his hands, he made a deep hole in the earth. The skin on his fingers split and began to bleed. When the hole was deep enough he lifted Polly and laid her in the shallow grave covering her with the loose earth and pine needles. He took a limb and carefully brushed away any telltale signs around the spot.

Rueben raised into the saddle, then had an after thought. Sliding to the ground he took the carving from his pocket. He pressed the wooden animal into the dirt at the head of Polly's grave.

"I done this for you, Polly! You shouldn't have refused me. But you always did! You shouldn't have Polly. I loved you, Polly," Rueben sobbed. He took off his hat and bowed his head as if to pray. "I loved you, Polly! You wouldn't have me. Now ain't no one gonna have you. Not no one!"

Rueben again straddled the mule and rode on across the mountain. The tears flooding down his face were not all for Polly. Some were because he had failed to complete the mission his father had sent him to do, he had not found out where Tom Phelps was. As Rueben crossed into Kentucky the mountains became high and thickly forested with trees. He rode in and out of the deep and narrow ravines and over the steep hills on to where Jay and Bob were hiding. Without looking back he left Polly in her shallow grave with a wooden unicorn for a head stone. She was sheltered underneath a spreading branch of a tall pine.

Tom rode out of Norton after dark. He made the necessary arrangements at the livery and left with a heavy heart. A threatening rain cloud hung above the town causing the night to be even darker.

A cooling breeze was moving in from the north bringing with it a splattering of rain. He was glad he had borrowed Matt's hat from the other wagon. He pushed it on tighter upon his head and bent into the burly breeze.

His thoughts matched the night, sinister and foreboding. He knew the days he'd spent with his brother had given Jay a long head start. He would be far into the mountains by now. Jay could quickly lose himself in the densely wooded draws that made up the Blue Ridge. The best place to start his search would be at Marshal Snow's office. His life held only one purpose now, to kill Mitchell's and see Hensely hang.

At dawn he stopped for a moment under a tall oak remembering how his father loved the colorful oak trees. A night like this was hard on both man and beast. He shook the water from the borrowed hat and put it back on his head. The rain had stopped and the sun was coming up pink and orange across the treetops. He could feel the increasing thickness of the trees. He would be in Gladeville long before noon. Outside of Gladeville Tom stopped the team. He pulled out a small cloth bag of tobacco and papers from his shirt pocket and expertly rolled a cigarette. The heavy rain clouds dispersed and the glorious sunshine was drying out the earth. The extreme heat was raising columns of steam from the heavy grass and leaves. The storm was finished and Tom was certain it would be the last for the summer. The remainder of July, August, and September would be unbearably hot. He would be praying for a cooling rain. The sweltering humidity would bring out every crawling creature imaginable to add to his aggravation in the miserable heat.

"I'm a heap glad Matt is goin' to be alright. Yes sir, a heap glad! I'm not too happy about the women folk bein' gone though, Tom. We have a Grand Jury almost ready for them to appear. I was about to head up the mountain an' tell them to come in Monday," Marshal Snow explained.

"You'll have to put it off until they get back. I don't think it'll be too long. They're safer there than they would be here abouts. What about Mitchell?"

After a welcoming handshake Tom and Lorenzo Snow stood talking in the Marshal's small office. The round stove in the middle of the room was still hot from an earlier fire. A coffee pot sat on top next to a small dishpan of dirty cups, the room extremely warm.

"We had some leads on Hensely. I have trackers out looking for him now. He's pretty clever but it's just a matter of time, Tom. We've had no sign of Jay, nor any positive proof they were at the scene of the crime. We have to see what we-uns can make out of what the girls have to say."

"Sorry, but I ain't waitin'!"

Tom arrived in Gladeville shortly after noon and found the town quietly settling in from the unbearable heat. Marshal Snow's information was not very satisfying. Tom was eager for revenge. He had already waited long enough.

"I'm wantin' to bring whoever is responsible for this to justice as much as you do Tom. But it takes time. The rain has made it hard to do any trackin'. I haven't seen it rain so hard this time a year for a long time. Usually comes toward fall. That spot up there's so close to the state line they're havin' all kinds of disputes about which should be the one to prosecute. But we-uns are the closest county seat, guess it's settled for us. You know, Tom, them fellers has got a lot'a territory to hide in. Up there a ways at the point of the mountain you can see four states. I'm tellin' you boy, that's a lot of territory, an' Pound Mountain's the roughest," Snow raved on and on.

"Tell me about it Snow. That's my home up there. I know it like the back of my hand. If Jay's in there, I'll find him. It might take awhile, but, I'll find him! That is God's country. I love it. I've made it my country too! I want it to stay just like it is. I want people like Jay out of it!" Snow could see the blaze of hate in the man's eyes.

"Hail said you helped bury our folks. I be obliged for your kindness." Tom attempted a grateful smile, but the bitterness inside him pushed it aside and it was cruel and twisted.

"It was the least I could do. I needed to keep an eye on things anyways. I never seen hide nor hair of anyone we was lookin' for. I thought maybe out of curiosity some of them outlaws might show up. You know Tom we gotta keep this man hunt on the side of the law. Things are gettin' pretty sticky about crossin' the state lines. It takes all kinds of paper now to bring a man out'a one state an' into another. You need to do this according to the law, Tom! If you run out an' make a murderer out of yourself, you'll be the one in jail. What good would that do you? Or your women folk?"

"I'm gonna kill Jay! I have no intention of bringin' him back, that's a promise!" Tom's lips tightened to a thin line.

"Let's talk this over, Tom. Don't be creatin' another problem," the Marshal requested, wanting to keep Tom's revenge within the law. "Sit down an' have a cup of coffee. Let's talk this over." "Thank you. I'll take the coffee, but I'm in no mood for Sunday-School!" Tom drank down the coffee hot and black. He tipped his hat to the Marshal and was ready to leave.

"Now Tom. I'm tellin' you, we uphold the law here!"

"That's a laugh. Right now you're lookin' for what you've called the law, for murder an' robbery!"

"I'll admit things got out'a hand. But that's gonna change! Hensely will pay for his crimes!" The Marshal's eyes began to flash with the statement.

"I was gonna tell you Tom, we had your nigger field hand here in jail for a spell. He was caught with your wagon an' Tanner thought he'd stole it. I wasn't aware of the situation 'til after we'd buried your folks. With Talt's trial an' all, it's been a hell of a mess around here Tom. One hell of a mess! Tanner's got me so messed up I still can't tell if I'm comin' or goin'. If things had a went the way he'd a wanted, he'd probably a been Marshal by now."

"Simeon was here in jail?" So that's what happened to the black, there had been a reason he hadn't returned. "He had a right to the wagon. He was doin' a job for paw."

"I released him this mornin'. I sent him on up to Ben's with your wagon an' team. He ain't been gone more'n a few hours. Seemed a coincidence that we had him in jail right at the time your folks got murdered. Did he know your folks were goin' to be in the Gap?" Snow planted the suggestion.

"Damnation for luck. Of course he knew! Of course that's how Hensely knew. He got it out'a that black. Damn! Damn! I'll kill that nigger for sure!" Tom threw Matt's hat on the desk scattering papers in a white storm to the floor.

"Now Tom. He was an innocent informer. You can't kill a man for just sayin' somethin'," Snow argued.

"I got a right, Lorenzo! I got a right! Lord knows I got a right!" Tom gritted out the words and clenched his teeth. All trace of gentleness gone, body tense with frustration and determination, his hands clenched into tight fists.

"I reckon you ain't gonna listen to me." Snow could see Tom was beyond reasoning. He bent to gather up the scattered papers. "Heaven knows I could use your help Tom. But I want it to be accordin' to the law. I'm gonna appoint you as a deputy. Then you can bring these men in. We'll try them accordin' to the law."

"I ain't wantin' no deputy badge. You can't make me, can you?"

"No, I can't make you, Tom. But it's your duty as a citizen in a matter like this. It'll make your job easier. People'll be encouraged to talk to you an' tell you things. Most people are respecters of the badge." Snow watched the young man closely. He took a shining badge from the top desk drawer. He polished it slowly on his shirtfront. Holding it away he admired the gleaming surface, playing a performance for Tom's benefit.

"I don't know Lorenzo. They's lots a responsibility connected to that badge. I know some people don't think so, but I figure if you took that badge you'd be beholdin' to stand up for what's right. I'll pass an' wait until this business is over," Tom declared as he eyed the bright badge.

For just a moment he weakened considering becoming a law abiding citizen and promise not to kill anyone only in the line of duty. Snow could see the weakness and he pinned the badge on Tom's coat front.

"Repeat this oath Tom. You'll be fully deputized. Then you get out there an' bring them murderers in. It'll be your duty," Lorenzo recited the oath for Tom's benefit.

"I'm gonna kill Mitchell! He'll not get off scot-free! I'm gonna kill that son-of-a-bitch with or without your say. The badge ain't gonna make no difference!" Picking up Matt's hat, he slammed it on his head and went out the door.

Deputy Parley Akers walked in as Tom walked out. He tipped his hat to Tom and shut the door from the swarming insects. He went to the stove and poured himself a cup of coffee then hung his hat up and scratched the top of his head thoughtfully.

"That Tom Phelps?"

"That's him. Hot headed ain't he?" The Marshal smiled.

"Seemed to me from what I see'd he was a might cold hearted. Wouldn't even give a handshake. No manners what so ever. He ain't overly sociable either."

"Never you mind, Parley, don't matter none. He's gonna bring in Jay Mitchell an' maybe some of them others what killed his folks." He supposed it didn't matter that Tom didn't repeat the oath. He was still wearing the badge.

"We'll just give him time, we'll just give him time," Snow muttered mostly to himself. He picked up Tom's empty cup and stuck it in the pan of greasy water. Opening the stove door he spit a stream of tobacco juice onto the dead ashes.

"I'd like to lay you odds, you'll never see any of them alive if he finds them," Parley stated. It would be a while before the young deputy would forget the revenging fire in Tom's eyes.

Tom hurried Jole' and Red anxious to be in the hills and hoping he would find Simeon in Donkey. He had cooled down some since talking to Snow. He was certain the black man had not intentionally informed on his family. Flopping the reins he tried to coax more speed from the odd team. Red wanted to be stubborn. She'd had all she could take of this team and wagon game. Plowing was her thing. This racehorse beside her who didn't know 'gee' from 'haw' was a different story. Jole' felt Tom's insistence and moved along with increased speed leaving the mule no other choice but to keep up. Jole' also was anxious to be free of the harness. He met Ben on the road with his horse coming on a fast run. Tom guided the team to the side of the road to let the rider pass. He recognized Ben's horse and waved him to stop.

"Tom, I'm glad to see you. How's Matt?"

"He's gonna make it Ben. It'll take time for him to be himself again. Where you headin' in such a hurry?"

"It's a terrible thing Tom. Rueben Mitchell shot Trace. Simeon an' Polly are bringin' him in your wagon. I'm goin' on to Gladeville to see if I can find someone to help Trace an' tell Snow about Rueben bein' in Donkey. Means Jay's not far back on Pound, I'd bet. I'll talk to you later, I'd better be goin'," Ben told Tom hurriedly and with a wave of the hand was down the road at a hard gallop.

A few miles from Donkey Tom found the wagon in the road with Simeon and Trace lying in the back. Making sure they were dead he covered them with his raincoat. He would send someone back after them when he reached Donkey. He wondered about Polly. Hardman said she was with Simeon. Was it Rueben who had shot Simeon? Had he stolen Polly? Of course, he'd shot Trace. That had to be the answer. Mitchell had stolen Polly.

Rueben would have to steal her. She would never go with him willingly. Rueben had always coveted Polly, but she had always ridiculed him, shunned him, and cursed him for his slovenly ways. No, she would never go with him willingly! If they had Polly, there was another reason to find Mitchell's.

There was no one around the tavern. Tom found Polly's blood soaked petticoat lying on the bed beside the small derringer. He was worried. He stuck the gun into his belt. He gave the bad news to Dee Jones's wife. He told her to send Dee after the bodies and have Ben keep his wagon and team until he came for them. He was again on his way.

Tom stopped at the Jennings to tell Carl of Simeon and Trace's murders and of Polly's disappearance. He told him of Matt's progress, and asked if Carl had heard anything of Mitchell.

"Haven't heard a thing. I don't know, Tom, what these hills are comin' to. We've had killin's before but not like Ira an' Jan's families. Now this! You say there was no trace of Polly? She weren't around the tavern or maybe hidin' in the woods?"

"Nary a sign Carl. She could be hidin' on the hill in the trees. Will you get some men together an' look for her?"

"We sure will Tom. If she's there, we'll find her. I ain't seen hide nor hair of any of the Mitchell's, Tom. The truth is, if I had, I'd a killed them myself. Always said it was them what was responsible for Billy. Anyone what's got a bit a sense knows they was the ones what done them murders at the rocks. I sure am sorry about that, Tom. They's probably headed into Kentuck. But folks over there are riled up too. They ain't gonna get no one to hide them, either side. They'll just have to make it in the hills."

"Feel free to bury Trace an' Simeon at our place," Tom offered shaking Carl's hand. "I'd like them to have a decent burial."

Carl sent Tom on his way with a warm smile assuring him he'd watch out for his women folk when they came back. He wished him good luck and gave him a strong pat on the back.

"Oh, my, Tom looks just dreadful. So much older than when we see'd him at the party. Hate an' grief has a way of leavin' terrible hardness on ones face," Nettie Jennings remarked as she watched Tom drive away. "On a face as handsome as Tom's, it's fearsome," she went on watching the wagon disappear into the trees.

"Pity the man that he turns that storm of hate onto." Nettie shook her head and smoothed her hair back from her tired face.

"No!" she added as an after thought, "That black hearted one deserves no pity!"

At the Stewarts, Alvin was diligently working in the tobacco and was surprisingly sober. Tom took time to visit the graves and could not hold back the tears when he noted the smallness of little Emily's grave. He remembered again Bess and Ginny's bruised faces and broken bodies, Ira and Jan riddled with bullets swinging in the tree, their faces purple and distorted, their bodies blasted apart at the groin.

Tom grieved for the dead and again vowed a quick vengeance! He stopped at the mill long enough to turn Red loose, saddle Jole' and change into more durable clothing consisting of a dark shirt and pants held up by a wide belt and suspenders. The pant legs were tucked into a sturdy pair of work boots. He chose a light corduroy jacket, a rifle and pistol, and a supply of ammunition for both. He slipped a wide bladed hunting knife into a built in sheath on his boot for skinning and cutting, then tucked the small derringer inside his belt. He rolled some corn meal, salt, coffee; salt bacon, a cup, skillet, and coffee pot inside a bed roll then strapped it across Jole's rump. He had friends in the hills, but did not want to be dependent on anyone.

He rode to the cemetery and laid a bouquet of flowers on Ira's grave and said his last goodbye to the father he dearly loved. Boy followed him to the cemetery and would not be turned back. Finally Tom conceded. The big golden dog followed at Jole's heels ready to perform any service for his adored master. They rode out together, man and beasts ready for however long it might take to find the ones that murdered his father and the Stewarts.

CHAPTER FOUR

"Ninety-nine, one-hundred," Kylee counted diligently. Patiently she brushed her long tresses as her father had taught her. Mary sat by the window sorting through a stack of books she had borrowed from the matronly woman who owned the hotel.

Kylee could not believe the change in Mary. In the two weeks that had passed she was her old self again, but Kylee could detect an undercurrent and that worried her. Mary smiled often and laughed a lot. There was an older and wiser look on her face, yet her large brown eyes still held the sadness and grief. Now she went by herself, running back and forth often between the hospital and hotel. She spent most of her time beside Matt's bed listening with enthusiasm as he read aloud to her all the magazines and books she could bring him. She remembered as she listened how excited Billy had been when he had learned to read. She understood now as she became involved with every character in the stories. She imagined herself in each exciting adventure. In doing so she had pushed the reality of her dead family into the back of her mind and lived in a world of make believe.

Matt was her hero, a prince in shining armor. Her world revolved around him. She watched as he grew stronger each day thinking how different he was from Billy, older and more mature. She could think of Billy now without sadness, just a deep sense of peace at having loved him. But Matt needed her now. She had someone to depend on her, someone that could belong to her. The young man in the hospital bed became her entire reason for living. Morning, noon, and night revolved around Matt.

Matt waited for each visit. He was grieved and outraged when Hail told him what happened at Picket Rock. Kylee explained how she and Mary escaped. Matt was thankful his life was spared so he too could avenge their families. He yearned for a speedy recovery so he could return to the hills.

Mutual grief tied the bond between Mary and Matt. Mary refused to talk of the event and would leave the room when Matt spoke of revenge so he carefully avoided the subject, satisfied to coax a smile on her lovely face with a story or limerick. He could not stand the dark shadows that clouded her eyes and the pain that came to surface on her face. He kept the burning desire for retribution inside and worked on the driving insistence to get well.

But Matt's recovery was not as rapid as he desired. He had movement of his right arm and leg. The left leg and arm would not cooperate with his urgency to be up and about. Dr. Richards held him in the hospital insisting a few more days would show a difference.

"These things simply take time. Often a great deal of time. You will see, you will see. Be patient a little longer," he encouraged them as he worked Matt's leg up and down.

The days passed and they waited. Kylee watched Mary stacking the books in a neat pile and smoothing her skirt getting ready to visit Matt. She had become a woman in the last weeks, a woman with a quiet tenderness and compassion. But Kylee could still see the lines of pain etched around her lips even through the smiles.

Touching her golden hair, Mary made certain the Gibson girl roll was pinned tightly in place. She picked up the books in one arm and turned to Kylee.

"You comin' now, Kylee?"

"Yes. Wait until I finish my hair. Remember Tom said we musn't go out alone."

"Well, we haven't, have we?"

"No, not often anyways."

Kylee rose from the bed and hurried to twist her hair. Wrapping the long coil in circles about her head she pinned it snuggly into place and finished by pulling tiny curls around her forehead and ears.

Kylee watched with concern, as Matt became Mary's sole purpose for existing, afraid she might become too involved. She was aware that Matt was far from being well. If anything should happen to him, could Mary handle the shock of another loss? Shaking her head she assured herself that Matt was going to get well, then thought she was only borrowing trouble. Dismissing the thoughts from her mind she decided to turn them to being happy for the change in Mary and for Matt's recovery.

The weeks at the hospital passed slowly for Hail. The money Tom left was growing short and she was becoming restless. Hail hated the city with its snippy ways and noisy hustle. There were so many horses and buggies that made it dangerous to cross the streets and hordes of people always going somewhere, always in a hurry. She hated their stares of horror and pity at her scarred face and their open curiosity at her colorful headscarf. To look more in style she bought a small poke bonnet trimmed with daisies and ribbon to tie over her gypsy scarf.

Taking refuge in the hospital she refused to leave its shelter only under cover of night, then only for a few moments to get a breath of fresh air. She missed the sweet smell of the broad leaf ferns and the melodies the breeze played in the top of the big trees. She was homesick, her spirits lagged, and her appetite waned. Suddenly one day at the end of two weeks she made a firm announcement to Matt and the two young women sitting on the edge of his bed.

"We're goin' home! I don't mean tonight or tomorrow, I mean right now, this minute."

Failing to have the courtesy to ask anyone else's opinion Hail hustled off to find the doctor. She told him firmly of her decision to take Matt home. Dr. Richards was thwarted by her stubbornness and relinquished with a smile on his lips and a frown of worry on his brow.

"I can't make you stay if you're of a mind to go. I am certain Matt could stand the trip now. I will however, encourage you to wait until tomorrow. The trip is too long to leave at this time of day. We will have him ready and you can leave early in the morning. Allow me that much," Dr. Richards requested in a soft persuasive voice.

Before dawn the next day they were ready and waiting at the hospital door with the team and wagon, anxious to start their journey. Dr. Richards sent them on their way with a firm handshake to Matt and definite instructions.

"You work that gimpy leg, Matt. Don't let it get the best of you. You have been lifting your arm a little more each day and it will come back in time. You will be ready to handle a sweetheart, when the time comes," he assured Matt as he watched Mary fussing over his pillows and mattresses on the wagon bed.

"Besides you have the best nurse in the state," he added with a twinkle in his eyes, looking fondly at Hail as he helped her to the wagon seat.

"You must remember to stop at the hospital and see me when you come back to town," he said to Hail. "Let me know how Matt is getting along and how things are coming about on your mountain."

He squeezed Hail's scarred hand and sent them on their way with a smile. Not only was Matt's surgery a success but the guarding gypsy angel, as he fondly referred to Hail, had become a very dear friend. He was reluctant to see her leave, but watched them drive away down the dark street as they left before the sun had risen.

The day promised to be hot. August would be ushered in with heat waves and blazing sun. They were glad to be going home. Matt rambled on about joining Tom. Mary bowed her head and watched the road slipping away from the back of the wagon.

The last days drug by slowly for Kylee and she had found herself thinking often of Tom. A depressing longing to be back at the mill filled her. Perhaps he would be there. The thought perked up her spirits and she was more anxious than ever.

Matt began to sing, happy to be well and delighted to be going home. He sang the old gospel hymns Billy and Tom had sung. Kylee and Hail joined in the happy songs, cementing the bond that was growing between them.

They stopped at Gladeville, but things were quiet. Snow was gone and the deputy was not giving out any information concerning

Hensely or Mitchell. He assured them that Marshal Snow would be to see them now that he knew they were home.

They spent the night at the Jennings to give Matt and the horses a chance to rest. Donkey was quiet and Trace's tavern was barred up, silent and cold. Carl informed them about Trace and Simeon, and Polly's disappearance. After a nights rest they were on their way again.

Mary's depression deepened as she listened to Matt's prattle about joining Tom. As their journey proceeded into the intense mountains she knew so well, her face became a frozen mask. She was back again into the world she had drawn away from. The fantasies drifted away and again she was vulnerable to the heartbreak of reality.

Matt could see the change in her and was sorry he had brought up the subject to join Tom. He wondered if it was a wise choice to bring Mary back. She seemed so on top of the situation at the hospital. Now he could tell it had only been a game. The loss of her family was still a thing she was going to have to cope with. At the turn off to the Stewart's Matt suggested:

"I am gettin' terrible tired Hail. Let's go on to the mill. Let's keep Mary with us. Let's not stop. It would be best, don't you think? Ain't no good for Mary to be there. Alvin would be in the fields all day. It would be best for Mary to be with us. We can let him know we are back. He can come see us. Perhaps he can tell us something of what is happenin'."

It was dreadfully quiet at the mill. The big wheel was silent on the shaft, the water low against the dam wall. The magnificent oaks reflected their greenery in the spaces between the lily pads as if nothing had happened. No matter the tragedy, their life circle went on.

Mary felt the emptiness of the big house and huddled even closer to the tailgate of the wagon hoping she wouldn't have to get out, but it was inevitable. Kylee ran into the house and brought back Ira's wheelchair. Now the problem for the three women was to get Matt out of the wagon and into the chair.

"Well, we'll just have to work this together. I can scoot to the gate an' get on my good leg. Just hold me now, give me your shoulders. There, there, I'm on my foot. Now help me get that damn gimpy leg out of the wagon."

"Can you get your bad arm over my shoulder, Matt? I'm shorter." Kylee wondered as they lifted, pulled, and twisted until they had Matt safely into the chair.

Mary held and moved Matt's unmovable leg into the chair. She quickly pushed Kylee and Hail out of the way and pushed Matt up the ramp into the house.

The house was cool and refreshing after the heat of the day outside. Evening was moving in and the tall pine branches cast long shadows across the house. Nighttime came early in the mountains underneath the heavy blanket of thick trees. Inside, the house was easing into darkness.

Kylee lit the lamps and Hail built a fire. They soon had cornbread cooking. Mary stood close to Matt, her arm around his shoulder waiting to fill any need he might require. Her lips were drawn in a tight line across her lovely face.

"Matt, the doctor said you was to start resuming a few chores each day. So now you can begin," Hail announced placing the coffee beans and grinder on the table close to Matt's elbow. "You help Mary," she ordered with definite authority.

"I'll go out an' unhitch the team," Hail added.

Kylee tied on her apron and went to the springhouse. She found the salt pork was gone and supposed Tom had taken it. The shelves were bare. She thought to herself that must change. She went to the garden before darkness completely closed in and picked some green onions, kale, and corn. The weeds had taken over the garden. That too must change, she told herself.

On the way back to the house she finished filling her apron with green apples from the old apple tree. Their supper was good, corn on the cob, fried apples sweetened with brown sugar, kale cooked tender and generously seasoned with herbs, pepper, green onions, and cornbread finished their meal.

Kylee thought about Billy and their first cornbread and smiled to herself at the memory. What happy times she'd had with Billy. Then she grew sad as she watched Matt manipulating Uncle Ira's wheelchair. Oh, she would miss them, but she must be thankful that

Matt had lived and she and Mary survived. She must have faith that Tom was alive somewhere out there on the mountain. "Oh dear God," she prayed, "keep him safe."

Matt sat watching the women putting away the dishes. He missed his father and promised himself he would not become a permanent fixture in the wheel chair.

Hail stirred the fire into a small blaze and sat the coffee pot next to its heat. The night was still warm but the cozy feeling of the fire drew them together. They sat in a half circle silently watching the glowing embers, each wrapped in a world of their own thoughts.

Mary sat on the floor next to Matt's feet, her head resting on his knee. He absently wound a strand of her flaxen hair around his finger. What a lovely color it was in the flickering firelight and how pretty it was that day at the spring, the sunlight dancing happily in its golden sheen. Matt decided not to think about what had taken place at the rocks, he couldn't remember any of it anyway. He would instead think of the wonder of Mary sitting at his feet making his life complete with her love. He thought of how it had been with Taynee and a warm peace engulfed him. He would remember her with devotion and cherish the memory, but he would fill his life now with loving Mary.

Mary watched the flames as they danced about, remembering sitting around the fire at home with her family. Suddenly the memories came in a flood. With them, for the first time since her family was buried, came the tears. She cried quietly hoping no one would notice.

She remembered the night Tom and Billy arrived with Kylee. Billy had brought her the beautiful beads. She could hear again the ring of the banjo and fiddle. She could hear in her mind little Emily clapping her hands and singing to the happy music, her curls bouncing as she tapped her feet and whirled around the room. There was the day in the barn and Billy's handsome face and the wonder of his hands upon her body. Oh, the beauty of that moment. Then she remembered the meanness when Bob Mitchell came in. Her mouth tightened into a grim line then softened as she thought of happier times. How could she ever forget the happiness shared when they were remodeling Taynee's wedding dress? Mary knew by the blush on Ginny's cheeks of her dreams for a handsome sweetheart, now that would never be. She would always remember the beauty of her mother. How tenderly she cradled her in her arms when Tom and her father brought Billy's body home from the narrows.

"Oh mommy, mommy," Mary sobbed silently to herself.

How could she stand the memory of her father? She remembered the joyful twinkle in his eyes as he told her of the child inside her mother's body? It tore her apart to remember her big booming father with laughter like thunder rolling through the house when he was happy. But she would remember now, with sorrow and joy, the feel of his strong arms around her making even the saddest things in her life bearable. She could feel his love like a cloak around her giving her the strength she needed.

The tears came in a deluge falling in a flood on Matt's knee. It hurt so much to remember the sad and happy times that had been the wonderful life with her family. But now she knew the memories would always be there to comfort her. Life was never going to be the same without her dear ones. At least now she could think about them and remember the love they'd had for each other.

Matt felt the tears and heard her sobbing. With his good arm he lifted her from the floor to his lap. He kissed away the tears and held her close until she quieted and lay sleeping on his shoulder.

Tom rode out of the dark places deep within the dense hollows into the light spots on top of the mountain ridges. He rode through the rain and into the sun. He rode places far and wide, through Kentucky, Virginia, and areas of West Virginia. He watched summer give way to the beautiful colors of fall, but saw no end to his searching.

Somehow Jay always managed to elude him. Friends and strangers were anxious to help but they had seen nothing of the Mitchell's. It was as if they had dropped from the face of the earth. Tom did not tarry in one spot long. He was on a death hunt and would not falter or linger. The people of the hills talked with respect of the wandering searcher of Jay Mitchell and his faithful partner the big dog, Boy.

If Tom tired of the hunt, Jay Mitchell also grew weary. He heard that Phelps was searching for him. He would have to get Tom before he got him, but Tom had a protector; that damn dog.

Jay knew well that if he approached Tom the dog would be sure to warn him. With his canine partner he could kill them all in their sleep. He had to plan a strategy. To kill the big dog was imperative.

The fall days still held the heat of summer but frost covered their bedrolls often in the early morning. Jay sat hovering close to a small fire warming his hands from a chilling wind that was blowing in from the east.

"I'm goin' home, Paw!" Bob announced from the other side of the fire with homesickness in his husky voice. "I'm tired a runnin'. I ain't afear'd. I don't give a blue damn about the law. I didn't do anythin' to none of them folks. I'm gonna take my chances."

"You're out'a your cotton-pickin' head boy! We're about to get Tom Phelps settin' in our laps, an' you're talkin' 'bout leavin'? You've never been over excited about us bein' together, I know'd that. You're a stayin'! We're a family, an' that's that!" Jay yelled at the young man and closed the subject.

"Damn weather. It's gonna storm, I can tell by the way that wind's a howlin'. My damn knuckles are a achin' something fierce." Jay rubbed his hands together attempting to eliminate the painful rheumatism.

"I'm goin' home, Paw!"

"We left Ira an' Matt, an' the rest dead at the rocks. We're gonna leave Tom the same way! Now you want to chicken out on me? Not in a duck's butt, you ain't! The law'll pick you up for sure. You're talkin' crazy!" Jay's eyes were a blaze under his dark brows.

"I don't care if they put me in jail. I never cottoned to what you done to them folks. Stealin's one thing, but you didn't have to kill them. You went too far, Paw. I'm goin'! Ain't you carin' how Nell an' the boys are doin'? We've been gone most three months an they could be needin' us." As he spoke Bob's lips set in a straight line, his jaw firm with decision. He found new courage in his defiance of his father and rose to saddle his horse.

Bob's desire to go home was not a sudden thing. He had lain awake many nights yearning for the sight of Nell cooking over the fire. He was glad that Mary and the Bentley girl had escaped. He had outgrown the longing he had for Mary, knowing it could never be. He had never forgiven his father for Taynee's death and these new atrocities chilled his blood.

Bob pulled the cinch tight on his saddle. "I'm tired of sleepin' on the ground and eatin' half raw possum every meal. We don't dare show our mugs in nary a town, twixt here an' Tennessee or Kentuck. Ain't no one cares 'bout seein' us come. We cain't even buy us a decent jug of booze. If we're gonna have to live the rest of our lives like this, it ain't worth it!"

Jay followed Bob to his horse. Taking hold on his shoulder he spun him around violently.

"You ain't goin' no-where's! I can't risk you a blabberin' your lip on us. Now hit the sack!" Rueben stood watching; anticipating what would happen if Bob were to disobey their father. He was clearly disappointed when Bob went obediently to bed. Rueben settled totally into the rugged life, he had no other ambition. There was no remorse or consciousness over the murders and rapes on the mountain, not even a twinge for Simeon and Trace, only twisted pride when his father told him he had done the right thing. They deserved what they got for the way they treated him. But Rueben had never told his father about Polly, that was his secret. He mourned in his own way for his beautiful love, lying in her lonesome grave.

Bob rose stealthily in the early morning and led his horse deep into the trees before he mounted and rode east. The wind grew stronger with the breaking of day, tossing the high branches of the trees in a wild uncontrollable dance against the murky sky. The shrill noise the wind wove among the branches covered well the sound of his leaving.

Tom's sleep had been restless. He thought he heard the sound of horse hooves in the early morning. Boy bared his teeth in a low growl. He was reluctant to leave the warmth of his bedroll. The wind chilled him to the bone. There was definitely a horseman on the trail riding swiftly across the crest of the mountain. Without doubt, Tom thought, headed for Pound Gap. He quieted Boy and hurriedly put his gear together and curiously rode out to follow the hasty rider.

Nell was overjoyed to see Bob, but concerned with his presence at the house. Looking at his thin face she felt a deep sorrow for the dark shadows in his eyes. He seemed older, more of a man. But how could she tell with all that hair and beard, slightly curled and uncombed. Wild was the word Nell was searching for, wild and unkempt.

"You get the tub boy, I'll heat the water. I'll not have you in the house lookin' like that. Looks as if you haven't seen a tub of water since you left here."

"I haven't Nell, I haven't. Nor a home cooked meal neither," Bob informed her with a smile.

"Why'd you come home for? You know'd the law's lookin' for the three of you. They want to question you-ins 'bout the murders at the Gap. They ain't got no certain proof that any of you were there. They know'd for sure Tanner Hensely was there. That Phelps girl an' Mary Stewart got away an identified Tanner. He'll sure hang when they find him. But Marshal Snow said they just want you-ins for questionin'. He checks in here regular. So's soon as you get a bath an' some vittles, you better be on your way again."

Nell filled three kettles and sat them on the fire, one on a trivet and two close to the hot coals. She laid a piece of wood on the fire and stirred it into a flame.

Bob thought how good it was to see her. Her ash blonde hair was rolled into an attractive bun at the nape of her neck with wide soft waves pulled forward around her forehead. It was funny maybe he had been away too long. He had never thought about Nell as being attractive, but darned if she wasn't down right pretty.

"I come home to help you Nell. You an' the boys need someone."

"We've managed. We've got by."

The twins stormed through the door. Suddenly Bob was engulfed in arms and legs as they took him down on the bunk bed in a two to one wrestling match.

"Help, help! Tain't fair two on one's, polecat fun. Let me up, let me up!" The young man pleaded with his assailants, playfully gasping for breath.

"Well, you give in an' say we beated you," the twins said simultaneously as they released their victim. "We was out sloppin' hogs an' seed you ride up. We-uns unsaddled your horse an' put her in the barn. Where's Paw an' Rueb?" Teaberry asked.

"They didn't come with me this time fellars," Bob began to explain but was cut short as the door flew open with a bang of Tom's heavy boot.

He stood filling the doorway, his Winchester held firmly aimed at Bob lying on the bed. Boy, as always, beside him with teeth bared in a silent snarl waiting for his master's command.

"Come in Tom an' close the door. That wind's a bit chilly cuts through to the bone." Bob invited calmly and slowly raising himself from the bed.

"You askin' me in to kill you, Mitchell? Because that's what I'm aimin' to do!" Tom announced pushing the door shut with the heel of his boot.

"You can kill me Tom, if you're intendin'."

Nell smothered a scream and closed the door to the other room where little J.B. was sleeping then gathered the twins in her arms and held them close as if to protect them. Watching wide eyed and reading the hate in Tom's face she was fearful of what would happen.

"I never harmed any of your folks, Tom. I swear it!" He returned Tom's gaze steadily, not backing down. "I couldn't stop them. What could I have done? They'd a killed me too!"

"That's your say so?" Tom said bitterly.

"For God's sake, don't kill me here in front of Nell an' the boys," Bob requested, hearing the click of the gun hammer as Tom let it down into firing position.

"I'll tell you where Paw's at. Then you can turn me over to the law or take me outside to die. But please Tom, not in front of the boys. They are innocent of all this. I don't want them to remember me dyin' like this." Bob was resigned to his fate.

"Law, hell! I aim to see you die like my paw died with your groin ripped apart!"

Nell pulled the boys in closer, covering their ears with her hands.

"What the hell you talkin' about? Paw hung them that's the way they died."

"The hell you say? Don't stand there an' pretend you're innocent an' tell me you couldn't do nothin' about that neither. Jay had to commit the last outrage toward my paw an' Jan cause of his hellish hate for my kin."

"I knew nothin' about that! I swear to you as God's my witness. I never knew of that. I ain't wantin' to die, Tom, but I ain't afear'd of it either. I'd as soon be dead as to live with the nightmare I seen," Bob confessed.

The calm composure of the other man caused Tom to hesitate. There was a ring of truth in his denial. Bob's eyes were fearless and filled with misery and did not waver from Tom's steady gaze. Tom realized in that moment that he could not pull the trigger. He could not kill this man in cold blood. For the first time his eyes strayed to Nell and the boys watching, their eyes wide with terror.

"I'm waitin' Mitchell. Tell me everythin' I want to know! Everythin'! What happened to Billy an' Simeon an' Trace? Don't tell me you don't know. I want to know where Polly is too!" Tom demanded.

"It were Paw what killed Billy. He wanted me to do it, but I couldn't. It's the God's truth! I couldn't do it! He thinks I'm a snivelin' coward. I don't care any more. Trace an' Simeon were Rueben's crime. I don't know nothin' about Polly. I ain't seen or heard anythin' about her," Bob continued his confession.

"What about your paw? Tell me where Jay's at!"

"You know where the point of the mountain is, back toward Kentuck?" Bob waited for the nod of Tom's head.

"North of there is a mountain like the back of a hog. Paw calls it Razor Back. That's where I left him. You can't tell about paw though, he might move. He'll be so mad 'cause I left, he might even come to kill me. He sure ain't gonna be happy when he finds out I'm gone."

"I reckon there be no point in killin' you or takin' you to jail. You'll have enough hell of your own to last forever," Tom said before leaving the house.

As Tom rode away from Mitchell's place he had no time to worry about the unfortunate people whose life had been darkened by their father. At least his memories were of a father who loved him. Then he remembered his father too had left a heritage of hate. The thought didn't change his determination to see Jay die and if he was going to make another trip into Kentucky he was going to the mill to see if Matt had made it home from the hospital. He wanted to fill his eyes once more with the reality of Kylee, beautiful Kylee, with her shining hair and gleaming eyes, eyes as green as the utmost branches of the tallest pine. There was no one now to stop his journey down Tandy's Mountain.

Matt's health grew better each day but his total recovery was slow. The movement of his arm was gradually coming back. He could lift his leg on his own and bend his knee. Hail worked with him diligently. She took his therapy totally upon herself and seriously to heart. She was confident with constant persistence the young man would be himself again.

But Matt was anxious and wanted to be off searching for Jay Mitchell. He hated to admit his health was not going to allow such a thing for some time. He grew more concerned for Tom each day and inquired of everyone coming by the mill if they had seen or heard of him. There were a few who knew of the lone searcher of the Mitchell's. They talked with respect of the young man with the big yellow dog as a devoted companion. At least with the bits of information Matt and the women surmised that Tom was alive and well. Each hoped that one day they would see him ride into the yard.

Hail and the girls harvested the corn, picked the apples, dug the sweet potatoes, and gathered squash. They went each day into the forest and gathered nuts and roots. They preserved, dried, and stored everything in sight. Hail was satisfied their well being through the winter was assured.

After their arrival home, along with caring for Matt, Hail took over running the place like a top general. They rounded up the stock, Daisy II had delivered her calf, and there was fresh milk and butter. They could only find one pig and supposed the other had been stolen. The porker was in prime condition and would be ready to butcher when Tom got home. The chicken and geese had done well and had stayed close to the cornfield and garden.

Alvin visited and brought them two young sheep and a baby goat. He helped them store in wood and haul coal from the bank at the side of the hill. He was looking well and apparently had put aside his drinking habit. With help from neighbors and relations, he told them, he had harvested the tobacco and it was drying in the big barn. Mary was delighted to see him and hugged him constantly. He tried to persuade her to go home with him but she declined telling him regretfully that she needed more time.

Kylee watched the green fade from the hillsides. New patches of red and gold appeared each day until the world around the mill was a blaze with vibrant colors. The days grew shorter and the nights longer and always filled with thoughts of Tom.

She had been counting the days since they arrived home, hoping each day for a sight of Tom. One blustery day, sixty-eight days after they had left Norton, Kylee was scrubbing the front porch. With a long handled broom she swept the water across the dry boards. Lifting her head she listened to the wind moaning through the top of the giant oaks behind the mill. She sang a song of her own, a song that matched her mood, *"Near a quiet country village stood a maple on the hill."* Swish, swish went the broom in time with her song. She raised her head thinking she heard a horse coming. Her song stopped along with the swishing of the broom. The only sound was the beating of her heart.

Tom was dead weary when he rode into the yard. He saw Kylee standing on the porch with her feet bare and her hair hanging loosely over her shoulders. Her skirt and petticoat were pinned high above the ankles to keep them away from the splashing water as she scrubbed.

Tom reined Jole' to a quick stop, dismounted, and went on a high run across the yard and up the steps. Kylee stood wiping her hands on her apron waiting for him to come. She was holding her breath and not moving; afraid this would only be another dream.

He lifted her up pressing her close. Her feet swung free off the floor, arms tightly encircling his neck. He said nothing, stood getting used to the feel of her in his arms while looking deep into her eyes. Holding her closer he kissed her softly at first then with full realization that he was really home, started kissing her with increased pressure.

"Kylee, Kylee," he breathed close to her lips and kissed her again softly. "Oh, how I have missed you." He searched her eyes for the spark of love he longed to see.

Kylee pulled away from him laughing and catching her breath. He put her down slowly loving the feel of her body as he lowered her to stand again on the floor. She took his hand and pulled him into the kitchen. Matt sat in front of the fireplace cracking nuts. Mary was sitting beside him peeling apples to bake a pie.

"Tom, Tom, is it really you?" Mary squealed jumping up almost toppling the bowl of peelings in her lap to the floor. She kissed him warmly and encouraged him to give her his coat. Taking Matt's battered hat Tom was wearing, she hung it on a peg. Tugging at Tom's hand she guided him over to Matt.

"What has happened? Tell us everything!" Mary demanded, eager to hear the news she longed for.

"I'm sorry Mary. There's nothin' to tell. I needed to come home for a sight of you all! But I'm not givin' up yet, Matt." Tom addressed his brother and offered his hand, a puzzled look on his face. "I sure am glad to see you! You look great. But why are you sittin' in Paw's chair?"

"What are you doin' wearin' my hat?" Matt questioned his brother hoping Tom would know it was a jest. "I had to have Mary buy me a new one."

"Well, that's one way of gettin' you a new hat. Now what about Paw's chair?"

They explained to Tom everything concerning the stay at the hospital and Matt's condition, assuring him that Matt was going to be fine. As they talked and laughed, happy to be together, the door opened and Hail came in.

"Tom. I saw Jole' in the yard. I knew you were home. Oh, I'm so glad to see you." Hail greeted Tom shaking his hand and not missing the look of fatigue in his eyes and on his face.

"Hail, it's good to see you, you ol' peach!" Tom said pinching her scarred cheek.

"You mean ol' prune, don't you?"

"No! You'll always be a Georgia-peach to me!" he laughed. "I'm glad to be home. I have thought every minute about you all. I needed to come home. I'm glad you're all here an' well."

"Sure didn't cotton to that city. Cain't see what anyone sees in the likes of them. What's took you so long Tom? Tell us. Tell us what's happened with you." Hail encouraged.

"It's slow goin' in them hills. I ain't see'd hide nor hair of Mitchell's. But I know where Jay is now. I'm headin' back out in the mornin'," Tom explained and continued by telling them of his visit to Bob Mitchell.

Kylee took time to smile often at Tom as the three women prepared the evening meal. Tom was happy to sit before the fire, his long legs stretched out and crossed at the ankles. She listened as he told them of his search for Jay. He didn't seem so filled with hate, she noted, but a cold forcefulness was in his voice. It chilled Kylee. She worried about what sort of man this vendetta would turn him into. She was sad thinking about Tom leaving again.

Tom seemed older. It must be the beard and long hair, so different from Tom's neatly trimmed and groomed look. His boots were badly scuffed and bits of dried mud hung to the soles. Kylee suppressed a smile remembering his bandbox appearance the day in Donkey so long ago. Some day she would tell him all about her presence there.

Tom toyed with the idea of going to Gladeville to see Snow, but canceled the idea when Matt informed him the marshal was in Tennessee. This was disappointing news. There was no evidence the law was any closer to closing in on the murderers. Matt told him there were other members of their family looking for Hensely. And there had still been no sign of Polly Trace.

Tom left early the next morning before anyone had risen. He had a clean change of clothing, a warmer coat, a fresh supply of food, and Matt's old hat. Spurring Jole' into a fast run, he headed up Pound road toward Singing Springs, Boy close on their heels.

The pines were changing slowly into the darker green as the sap drained down preparing for winter. The brown grass was an appropriate underlay for the bright colored leaves that would soon lie upon it.

Up the hillsides Tom rode, down into the dark hollows, forded the creeks and into the dense forest. Quickly he traveled living with the hope that his search would soon come to an end.

The lonely rider became a tale around the firesides at night. Many would remember the young man with the bearded face and ice blue eyes, eyes that looked at them and beyond, not seeing them at all. The memory of him and the faithful dog lingered long after he passed. He was the faithful searcher of the man who murdered his family.

So intent was he upon his journey that he failed to see or hear the silent rider that followed him on an old red mule. The lone rider had no intentions of being discovered, always keeping Tom in her sight and knowing Boy would not give away her presence. Her woolen headscarf was just another bright splash among the colorful leaves and gathering darkness among the pines.

Tom combed every inch of the Razor Back Mountain where Bob said Jay was hiding. He found evidence of campfires but nothing definite to tie Jay to the area. It was coon-hunting time and hunters could have made the fires. But he was not discouraged and was persistent in his search. Tom moved on north, still hopeful. He moved into a densely wooded area and detected the definite odor of smoke. He dismounted and crept in on the camp holding Boy down with a gentle demand to be quiet.

It wasn't Jay. The camp was occupied by a still and numerous new glass fruit jars appearing to be empty. A closer look told Tom they were filled with crystal clear moonshine. Lying beside a depleted pile of split wood was a bearded man sleeping sound and snoring loudly, obviously wearing off a beauty of a drunk. Tom patted Boy's head cautioning him to remain silent. He moved in without a sound, picked up a jar, unscrewed the lid, and took a deep sniff of the clear liquid. He held the jar to his lips and took a long swig. A shot whizzed through Matt's old hat and thudded into a tree.

"Damn thief, thought I was asleep, didn't you? Put the jar down slowly then reach for the sky. I'll wait 'til you sit the jar down, then I'll kill ya. I don't want to spill nary a drop of that prime shine," the old moonshiner commanded.

Tom obeyed and sat the container back down slowly next to the neat line of jars. He raised his arms high above his head. "Easy Boy!" he ordered the dog.

"You're a stealin' Athel Barnum's shine and that's dyin' time," the man said, still lying on the ground but definitely aiming the gun at Tom's head.

"I take it you're Athel Barnum?"

"That's right! Before I kill you. I need to know who to notify that you're dead."

"Phelps, Tom Phelps."

"You a stranger in these parts. Ain't no Phelps I know of around here. You sure that's your real name?"

"That's right. Tom Phelps, from Wise County, Virginia. I'm huntin' a man known as Jay Mitchell. If you'll let me turn around, I'll show you my badge. I'm a legal deputy. You wouldn't want to kill no deputy would you now?" For the first time Tom was glad for the badge.

"How do I know you won't snitch on me bein's you're the law an' all? I could kill you an' bury you. No one would be the wiser."

"I wouldn't do that. This is Kentucky, isn't it? I got no authority here. I only want to know if you might have seen the man I'm lookin' for. He's travelin' with a short man with red hair."

"You don't say? Turn around!"

Tom turned around to face the man on the ground. Athel Barnum rose on an elbow.

"Now, ain't that a co-incidence. A few days back when I was runnin' off my first batch, a big guy an' a little guy with red hair stopped by. The little guy was a ridin' the biggest mule I ever saw. They was wantin' some shine. Wal, I was willin' to let them have a few jars, but they weren't aimin' to pay me. Damn them! They stole my shine! Didn't pay me nary a dime! That was purty damn stinkin' if you ask me!"

The man on the ground took a drink from an almost empty jar resting at his elbow. The Winchester didn't waver. Tom stood very still, he knew if Boy were to advance it would be sure death for the dog.

"If you'll pay me for what shine they stole, an' that jar you nipped on, I'd be obliged to let you go. I ain't got nary idea where them thieven' bastards are at now. If I didn't have to stay with this still, I'd went after them an' killed them myself." The man laid down the rifle and moved to rise and fell back to the ground.

Boy growled menacingly.

"That your dog? He's friendly ain't he?" The old codger said sarcastically.

"Yep, when I tell him to be. If he'd had any notion you aimed to kill me, he'd a had your throat." Tom patted Boy's head.

Tom was willing to pay for the whiskey. He figured it was worth the money to find out that Jay was somewhere in the area. As far as the jar he'd nipped on, he left it sitting with the others. The sip he'd taken convinced him he was through with booze. He turned leaving the man still lying on the ground drinking freely of his prime shine.

A few nights later the weather turned gray and bleak. Freezing drizzle rousted Tom from his bedroll early. He rose to build a fire to warm his cold body. The humidity, heavy and murky, held the smoke close to the ground making it difficult to get a fire going. By daylight a thin blanket of soft wet snow lightly covered the bright colored leaves on the ground. By afternoon it melted in the warm sun. The moisture softened and muted the dry leaves.

At a high point on a long ridge Tom again sniffed the definite odor of camp smoke. It was mid afternoon and a glorious sun was filling the area with splashes of light. The breath of man and animals hung suspended on the air telling Tom the temperature was dropping. He dismounted slowly, quietly.

Thankful for the dampness on the leaves and ground he tied Jole' to a bush then checked his guns. The Winchester was in the saddle boot and the pistol strapped around the outside of his long coat. The day was eerily still. The long branches of the tall pines were unmoving. A smoky fog rose about the trunks of the barren trees and Tom could smell the soggy dampness. The quietness hung heavy about him. He could hear his own breathing and Boy's heavy panting. Afraid they would be heard, he tried to curb his excitement and breath easier.

With Jole' secured safely Tom moved in slowly with cushioned steps. Low muffled sounds of voices came to his ears. He moved cautiously and crouched in behind a big tree, his rifle ready and a hangman's noose hung over his shoulder. Could it be possible that his search was coming to an end?

Rueben's mule was tethered to a small dogwood, still saddled. Jay's Morgan was cropping grass next to a grove of elms. He spotted Jay on the other side of the smoking fire, stirring it impatiently with a stick trying to encourage a blaze. By the looks of the camp they hadn't been there long.

The two were sitting beside a small fire each smoking a pipe. They were alone and seemed to enjoy the stillness about them. Jay took a drink from the jar between his feet, wiped the back of his hand across his lips and handed the whiskey to his son.

"Take it easy now, Rueb. We's about got that shine gone, we cain't backtrack an' get more. So's let's make it last."

Jay's beard had grown almost to his belt. His hair hung in tangles about his shoulders. A dusty sweat streaked black hat covered his mass of hair, the brim almost hiding his dark eyes.

Rueben was even more unkempt and had settled completely with satisfaction into his slovenly ways. His reddish blonde hair was almost gray from dust and filth. His squatty structure and heavy growth of beard and hair almost engulfed him making him appear more like an ape than a man.

Rueben unbuckled his belt and hung it with his gun and holster over a tree branch. He'd given up wearing his shoulder holster but had often wished for the smaller gun he'd left behind at Traces. His plan was to stretch out and take a nap. But his father had other ideas. Jay put his arm around the young man's shoulder and pulled him over to the edge of the hill.

A long stretch of valley lay before them filled with tall chestnuts, hickory, gum, sourwood, and maple. The tall stately pines shone green rising above the graying branches of the bare trees. Rueben could not understand his father's sudden interest in the beauty of the country.

"Well, Rueb boy, how do you like Kentuck? It's plum beautiful ain't it? Look here boy, you see?" Jay waved his long arm in a sweep indicating the vast expanse before them.

"If we built a cabin right here, we could set off an evenin' on the porch an' look at our land down there, it will all belong to us. I'd see to that. Wouldn't be no damn Phelps's to take it away from us." Jay knocked the ashes from his pipe on his knee. He stuffed it in his pocket and replaced it with a chew of tobacco.

"I been thinkin' hard about havin' somethin' for Nell an' the boys. Yeah, Bob too. Even if he is a chicken-shit bastard! He's still my son. Least ways he didn't run off an' side with the enemy like your sister done. That was purely un-loyal, Rueb boy. It hurt me a lot what she tried to do," Jay sniveled and wiped a sudden rush of tears from his eyes with the finger of his free hand.

"We wouldn't have to run anymore son. Phelps ain't gonna spend any time or money lookin' for us here. If they'd leave us alone, I reckon we could forget about them. We'll bring Nell an' the boys up here when all this dies down. We'll be free of them moldy bastards. What do you say, Rueb? What do you say about that?"

"Yah, yah, I reckon Paw. If you've a mind to." Rueben answered clearly not interested in settling down.

He shrugged his father's arm away and turned back to the fire. Taking another drink from the jar he set it back against a log and put another piece of wood on the fire. He watched the smoke lay in a fog about the camp. Stirring a pile of leaves with the toe of his boot and trying to find a dry spot underneath, he prepared to lay out his bedroll for a nap.

Jay forgot his dreaming and came back to the fire. Aimlessly he turned the reluctant blaze with a long stick raising more smoke and ashes.

"This is it Mitchell! Don't move! I'd advise you to drop your guns!" Tom's voice rang harshly from behind a wide tree.

The rising column of smoke marred Jay's vision. He dropped to the ground unholstering his gun and firing toward the sound of Tom's voice. With quick agility he rolled away from the fire.

Rueben bent over his bedroll was slower to react to Tom's command. When he realized fully the impact of what was about to happen, he turned to run for his gun. Tom's bullet caught him well into the left thigh high above the knee. The impact spun him around knocking him to the ground.

"Drop it I said! This is far as you're goin'!" Tom ordered again.

Jay was trying hard to see Tom's hiding place, peering into the forest of trees from where he lay on the ground. He was firing wildly, the bullets thudding high into the trees splitting bark. If he could keep Tom talking he could get to his horse.

"What's the matter Tom? You afear'd to come out where I can see you? You're plum afear'd to show yourself! Wal, if you want my gun come get it," Jay shouted.

Jay rose from the ground into crouched position and began easing over to the clump of elm where his horse was pawing at the earth restlessly. Jay straightened and reached for the reigns.

"Whoa, whoa, easy! Dumb horse!" Jay muttered under his breath. He'd never have a horse to compare with his old friend Siler. The horse lifted its head and bolted.

At the same time Tom's bullet hit the gun in Jay's hand spinning it away into a covering of leaves. Tom fired again hitting Jay high in the shoulder tearing into the scar tissue of his old wound. Jay fell to his knees moaning in pain.

Growling menacingly, Boy was tensely alert. The big dog was ready to spring into action at a command from his beloved master.

"Steady, Boy, steady! There's time. Keep your eyes on that one on the ground. Good dog!" Tom ordered Boy as he walked out into the clearing. Every muscle toned for revenge now the time was at hand.

"Keep that dog away from me, Tom Phelps! Keep him away!" Jay pleaded in terror of the big dog.

Boy moved close to Rueben eyeing him threateningly. The man lay very still.

"I reckon you got cause to hate me Tom, but have pity," Jay begged seeing the hangman's rope hung over Tom's shoulder. He was reading the message of sure death on Tom's face.

"Now Tom. You ain't aimin' on killin' us in cold blood are you?" Jay whined, eyeing the gleaming badge on Tom's coat front.

"That be a badge Tom? If that be a badge, you're beholdin' to take us back to the law." Jay continued to plead.

A cruel smile played around the corner of Tom's mouth. Jay pleading for mercy was indeed sweet music to his ears, but with the whining of his voice came the memory of the horror and carnage at the Gap. He was eager to see this man die.

Boy was still guarding the younger Mitchell. Warning him with a show of canine fangs what would happen if he dared move.

"If you're aimin' on movin' Rueben, I'll drill a hole in you big enough to jump my dog through. You better stay put!" Tom ordered.

Rueben had no intention of moving. He was in total misery. He nursed his wounded leg tenderly with his coattail while watching the big dog closely and blubbering like a baby because of the misery he was in.

Rueben looked around frantically seeking a means of escape. He spotted a movement in the trees. He looked closer staring into the shadows not believing what he saw. He began to babble and sputter. Tom ignored him and deftly tied the hangman's rope to Rueben's saddle horn and threw it over a limb above Jay's head.

Jay looked up at the rope and began crying like a baby and mumbling incoherently. The saliva was running from the corners of his mouth and down into his black beard. He too had seen the unmistakable shadow in the pines, a weaving ghostly figure moving from tree to tree then back into the shadows. He recognized for certain that fleeting figure, remembering it from Taynee's grave. Jay feared that shadowy aspiration far more than he ever had Tom Phelps.

Jay grabbed Tom's leg begging and blubbering incoherently, "Don't let that ol' witch get me, she's come to get me Tom. She's come back from the fire to reap her vengeance on me!"

While Jay clung tightly to his leg, Tom dropped the hangman's noose over his head. He paid no attention to the other man's gibberish.

Boy had been seriously watching Rueben but when Jay put his hands on Tom the big dog was on the older Mitchell in an instant. The dog grabbed Jay's ankle between his strong jaws and held on viciously. Jay let go of Tom, stopped his crying and screeched. "Get that beast away from me!" Jay tried to shake his ankle free but Boy had his teeth firmly into the pant leg and flesh.

"Turn him loose, Boy, he's mine!" Tom sternly demanded.

The big dog backed away, sitting on his haunches snarling and waiting for Jay's next move. Jay rolled over and rose to his knees.

"You're not aimin' on hangin' me, are you Tom?" Jay's struggle with the dog brought back some of his calmness. He began to realize he was about to be hanged.

"I ain't deservin' of such treatment. You already killed one of my boys. Now you know Tom, you got no right to do this. This here's Kentuck. You got no rights here. They'll hang you, sure!" There were no tears now, Jay was pleading in earnest.

Tom walked over to untie Rueben's mule. His eyes watched Jay without faltering, his face expressionless and frozen, as he held his rifle steady on its target. In a deathly cold voice without feeling or warmth Tom informed Jay, "I reckon it's more then you did fer my folks, but I'm gonna let you make your final peace with your maker, if you can."

"What kind of gibberish is that? You know I ain't a God fearin' man." Jay's ankle was throbbing fiercely.

"I'm givin' you a chance to ask the Lord to forgive you of your hellish crimes, Mitchell. It'll be your last breath."

"Ask God to forgive me? Like Hell!" Jay spat on the ground.

"The devil take you Tom Phelps! You're a mad man! You can't win over a Mitchell. You're too soft! You're too easy! Right now I'll bet you ain't got the guts to hang me. You're too God fearin', like your maw claimed to be, but I fixed her so's she couldn't steal anymore of Mitchell's apples," Jay sneered.

"I taught her who owns Tandy's Mountain. Phelps's thought they could get away with stealin' everythin' that was mine. I was glad to hang that snivelin' cripple that was your paw, he deserved to die!" The words stuck in Jay's throat as the rope tightened.

Tom slapped the mule's rump sharply with Matt's old hat. Jay swung, his feet swinging searching for ground. He grabbed frantically at the rope around his neck. The job was complete, his neck snapped, his eyes popped from the pressure. Jay was dead.

The hanging was too easy. Tom thought to finish the job the same as Jay had done his father and Jan. But he had no stomach for the final outrage. Boy snarled loudly at the swaying figure. The thought to finish the job raised nausea in Tom's stomach. He grabbed his mouth and ran to the path where he left Jole'. Before he reached his mount he became violently ill. The only thing he could see before his eyes was Jay's distorted face and protruding eyes popped from the sockets. He vomited on the ground.

He found Jole' where he'd left her calmly cropping the brown grass along the narrow trail. Reaching for the reins he prepared to put his foot into the stirrup. The mare flared her nostrils in distaste. Eyes bulging, Jole' flipped her head up in immediate disobedience. Tom tightened his hold.

"What's the matter, girl? You ain't never acted like this before. Whoa!" he coaxed patting her neck and trying to calm the horse. "Let me get my foot in the stirrups. Whoa, whoa!"

Jole' was having no part of his soft talk. She jerked her head up and away from Tom's hold, freeing the reins. Attempting to get a firm stand on the steep hillside, the horse's rump swung around giving Tom a sharp whack pushing him down the side of the hill.

Tom tried desperately to get his boot heels into wet leaves and soft earth. Losing his footing completely he began a sliding course down the mountain. Struggling to keep up right, he grabbed for tree limbs and bushes, anything to get a hold of. All eluded him, slipping from his grasp or flipping out of reach as he skidded by.

His toe caught a protruding tree root. He plummeted headlong rolling over and over as he hurdled to the bottom of a deep gully. He came to rest violently against the trunk of a tall chestnut. The air left his body as he crashed into the big tree.

Flat on his back and unable to move he stared up through the gray branches at a blue patch of sky. He lay there for a moment trying to get the breath back into his lungs. Closing his eyes he drifted into unconsciousness.

He opened his eyes to gaze into a bright cloud forming in the patch of blue. He began to tremble and shake violently. The cloud opened and a shower of silver sparks rained upon him piercing his body and burning into his flesh. He lifted his arms to protect his face. As the sparks diminished he lowered his arms.

He could see his mother standing before him. They were back on Tandy's Mountain. Plain as day he saw her rubbing her swollen belly in satisfaction. Instead of an apple in her hand she held the Bible. She was smiling at him just as she used to. In a sweet gentle voice she read verse after verse from the Book. The silver sparks rained around her in a shower then stopped and disappeared and her voice drifted away. He wanted her to go on reading to him. He opened his mouth to speak to her but no sound came. The cloud faded, the sparks disappeared. The violent shaking stopped, his body was calm. All that remained of the dream was a bright patch of blue sky above him. He closed his eyes again.

Tom woke hours later. The bright blue sky was beginning to darken. He had no memory of the dream or the rain of sparks or his mother's voice. But strangely he was remembering verses from the Bible. Full realization came to him of what he'd done. He remembered Uncle Andy's warning about going beyond the point of redemption.

"Oh, my God, have I gone too far?" He thought of Blaine and now Jay. Rolling over into the soft chestnut twigs he rested his head on his arms for a moment. Rising to a kneeling position he covered his face with his hands. He rocked to and fro, his entire body filled with remorse. "I took Your vengeance into my hands. Well, there be no forgiveness for me. He needed killin' Lord. He needed killin'." But he felt no comfort. "What have I done? What have I done? I've killed another man. Is there no forgiveness for me? Oh my God, my God, is it too late? Is there no forgiveness for this sinner? Have I become less than Jay Mitchell?"

He remembered then the verse from the Bible that his mother had taught him. One stood above the rest. "Ask an' believe as though it already happened, an' you shall receive." This verse calmed him.

"Lord in Thy infinite mercy an' grace have mercy upon this sinner. I have sinned against you. I took vengeance into my own hands. Humbly I ask your forgiveness. I need your forgiveness. As my mother taught me to do, I am askin' your forgiveness." He lowered his hands and clenched them into fists resting them on his knees.

"Oh God, God, give me a sign. I need to know if I'm forgiven," Tom begged loudly. But there was nothing. No sign. No voices. Uncle Andy's words rang in his ears, "You must come to the cross to be forgiven."

He thought of Jesus' death upon the cross, the blood He shed, the stripes He wore. The tears came flooding Tom's eyes and he grieved for Jesus' suffering on the cross. He felt the tears falling on his hands. As they fell he felt a peace engulf him.

"Oh Lord, thank you for your suffering for me. I know it was for me. Help me to be worthy of your forgivin' grace. Thank you! Praises to Your Holy name, Jesus, Amen."

There was a gentle nuzzle at his elbow, he lifted his head, it was Boy. He hugged the dog around the neck and leaned his head on the softness of his faithful friend. Tom felt weak, shaken, but somehow filled with inner strength. Looking up the mountain he could see the definite path his body had taken down the hill. He knew what path he wanted his life to take now. There was no denying what he had done. Jay was dead. There was no undoing it. But he could make up for things he'd done. He knew in his heart all would be forgiven.

Kneeling under the barren chestnut tree, he looked up to a shining light coming through the gathering darkness in the sky. Tom pledged his life to his Savior, Jesus Christ. He had been made whole and was a new man. His life would never be the same again.

It took awhile to reach the crest of the mountain. Jole' was waiting around a bend on the trail; she whinnied with delight at seeing the two friends and nipped at Boy playfully. Tom mounted cautiously, still puzzled at her strange behavior and feeling the pain in his muscles and ribs. Taking in a deep breath made him moan as he felt the excruciating pain around his side and back. Then he remembered rolling into the trunk of the chestnut tree with extreme force. The thudding blow had taken his breath and spun him into unconsciousness.

The smell of smoke came faintly to his nostrils. He could see a dark gray ribbon above the green pines. Having no desire to return to the scene of the crime, he guided Jole' down the mountain.

Tom made up his mind. Having confessed his sins to his Lord, he now had to reveal the crime to man. He hoped his punishment would not be too severe. He would bring Snow back and they would take Jay and Rueben's body's home. He was anxious to be home with a warm fire and the people who waited for his return. Over Pound Gap, to Virginia, down into the soft haze that shrouded the valleys, and into Kylee's loving arms was where he headed.

Tom left Jay hanging and swinging free. Rueben lay in a pool of his own blood. He managed to raise himself cautiously determining if there were any broken bones. Moving slowly, careful not to start the bleeding in his leg again, he pulled himself along the ground into the dense trees. Under a thick bush he covered himself with a mound of wet leaves and decided to hide and wait for darkness to come. He was afraid to show himself in the few hours of daylight that remained. Peering through the cover of wet leaves he scanned the area. He had not forgotten the fleeting figure in the shadows hiding among the trees. He remained tensely still, watching, and waiting.

CHAPTER FIVE

Things were busy around the mill and had been moving at a rapid pace since Tom's departure. Tanner Hensely had been apprehended and brought back to Gladeville. A Grand Jury was formed. Kylee and Mary testified to his identity. Tanner spilled the beans on all concerned implicating Jay, his boys, and Ferrell Hall. He was not about to take the rap alone. He did, however, exonerate Bob Mitchell, telling the jury of the young man's refusal to have any part in the killings. He told how they planned, along with Kenus Hall, to kidnap Kylee. Hensely was behind bars and scheduled to hang three days before Thanksgiving.

Snow assured Kylee that Kenus would never dare show his face in Virginia again and promised both girls they would be safe. Lorenzo received news that Ferrell had been hung in Kentucky for another crime, taking him out of the picture. If Tom Phelps would bring in the Mitchell's, the case would be closed. He would have felt better if Hail had been at the mill. Her strange disappearance on the day Tom left baffled them all.

Matt grew stronger each day. He could manage to leave the wheel chair for extended periods. During these spurts of independence, he would aid himself with a hickory cane Alvin had carved for him. He had full use of both arms and used them often to hug Mary. He longed to ride out and find Tom but knew it would be futile without some knowledge of his brother's whereabouts.

Mary watched over Matt like a mother hen. She took him into her heart and filled the empty void with her love for him. An hour never went by that Matt didn't tell her how lovely she was and begged her to say when they could wed.

They all assured themselves that Hail's disappearance was only temporary. She had taken Red and would be back when she took a notion. Kylee watched the road constantly. She felt as if she knew each stone and every ounce of dirt. The pines were in their winter shades of green, the oak and maple gray and dormant. At times a flurry of snow would perch upon the bare branches. Her thoughts were often on friends who were gone. She thought of Uncle Ira with love and tenderness. She tried to keep Mary and herself busy so their thoughts would not rest too long on the past.

Kylee decided one day to change Hail's few belongings into Uncle Ira's bedroom. Matt was able to make the stairs to his bedroom which helped greatly. This change would give the two young women more room and Hail the privacy her age demanded. They thought the change would please Hail and hurried to finish the job before the woman returned.

Kylee cleaned the walls and scrubbed the floor and braided rug. Mary washed and ironed the curtains and hung out the bedding. Together they carried out the feather ticks to air. Kylee boxed Ira's books and records then Matt moved them to the mill.

"Why don't you sort through that stuff, Matt? Perhaps there's some we can burn," Kylee suggested as she handed him the boxes.

Matt said solemnly, "Not yet Kylee. I've no heart for it. I'll wait until Tom comes home."

But to appease her, inside the store with a warm fire going in the round heater, he began sorting through a stack of old letters. He discarded and burned the ones he thought were no use to keep.

Ira's room was ready for Hail's belongings and Kylee began gathering them. They were slight, only a few things she acquired since the fire. Kylee had a pang of regret that Hail had such few worldly possessions. She picked up Hail's Bible pitted and marred from the fire. Kylee had seen it many times sitting on the dresser next to the tintype of her mother. She paid little attention to it. The corners of the pages were curled and worn from the intense handling. Most every family had a Bible, not only for consolation and comfort, but family records, marriages, births, baptisms, and deaths were all diligently recorded on the center pages.

Kylee turned the Bible in her hand and thumbed absently through the yellowing pages. The leather strap had burnt through in the fire and had long been discarded. She discovered some old letters that were tucked away in the back. Kylee was intending to tuck the letters back and close the Book when something about the writing on the envelopes caught her eye. Something held her interest, the slant of the 't', or the indiscernible 'h', or maybe the 'a' that always looked like 'o'.

Drawn to the letters, she looked at them closer. They were addressed to Hail. She was certain she had seen that writing somewhere before. Without thought she sat down on the bed and opened a letter.

"I've no right to do this, no right at all!" But an urge deeper than mere curiosity drove her on. Scrawled without capitals or punctuation, the first letter began:

my darling

> *it is so lonely without your lovely face all i see here at the mine is coal dust an dirty miners i wonder why i have not received a letter from you i know you have written an i will get them all at once the work in the mine is hard with long hours i miss you an ira an mattie i am hoping now soon i'll have enough money to come home then we can finish the mill an then o happy day we can wed til then my darling you are my only love*
> > *i love you always*

val

She couldn't believe what she was reading. She opened the other letter.

my darling

> *i can not believe the news you wrote in your last letter tell me it isn't true there is no way i will believe you don't love me if it is your wish i will release you from your promise i will not return i will respect your wishes if you should change your mind i'll be by your side if there is ever*

anything you want or need i will see to it i will never love anyone as i
have loved you you will always be my love
broken hearted

val

There was no mistake the letters in Hail's Bible were from her father. She was certain of the writing. She dropped them on the bed, jumped up and opened the second drawer of the dresser. She lifted out the little chest that held her father's letters.

Carefully she spread out the crumpled letters. Apparently they had been handled many times as if the receiver had read them over and over. She hurried through each of them. One was of love and longing. Kylee could make out the words of promises to become a bride.

The second letter was so tear stained Kylee could barely make out the words. But she could read enough that she surmised it was the one telling her father his sweetheart didn't love him any more and had a new love, but both signatures were the same. The first one was signed, 'I remain always your darling, Hail'.

Why hadn't Uncle Ira or Hail told her that Val was Hail's sweetheart? Why would it have mattered for her to know? She felt a new closeness to Hail. It made her feel warm inside to know her father loved Hail before he loved her mother.

Kylee carefully replaced the letters tucking each one carefully back in its resting place. She could not get the letters out of her mind. Thinking about what circumstances had caused them to be written. If Hail had found another sweetheart, what happened to him? Hail never married, why? Well, time for answers when Hail returned.

Then one day the matter of the letters became even more entangled. Mary and Kylee had been washing and trying to dry the clothes in a cold wet snow. Matt was in the store going through Ira's endless letters. He came into the kitchen closing the door behind him hastily, shutting out the freezing breeze. The cold air hung about his clothing and his face was flushed from the bitter temperature. The kitchen smelled strongly of lye soap and wet clothes.

"Kylee, I think this will interest you. I thought you better take a look before I burn it." Matt announced handing her an envelope. He remembered when Ira received the letter from his cousin Val, never letting anyone look at the contents.

"I'll go on out an' help Mary gather them clothes." Matt offered and went back out into the freezing weather.

Kylee wiped her wet hands on her apron, glad for an excuse to rest a moment. She lifted and smoothed back the wet tendrils of hair hanging about her neck and sat down at the table.

The letter was addressed to Ira Phelps, Wise County Virginia. Immediately she recognized the letter as the one her father instructed her to mail so very long ago. She took out the letter and read it. It was precise and to the point. It definitely was Val's writing, no capitals or punctuation.

dear cousin

> *i am going to ask you for a favor there is no one else to turn to i done you a favor once i have never regretted taking the child you brought me but now she has no other place to go i think it would be fitting that she come to you she has always been good and obedient you will have no problems with her that way nan and i loved her just as if she were our own nan is dead and i am dying i want to know kylee will be with some one who will care for her properly if hail is still living on tandys mountain there is no danger of her knowing that kylee is anyone other than my daughter i will leave that to your discretion to keep the secret safe it dont matter now but i have longed to know who the childs father was now it doesn't matter it's to late i am very glad you brought kylee to us we have loved her as if she were our own i turn her back into your hands i would have liked to see you one more time dear cousin but it is to late please wire an immediate answer she will need some money dear friend if it is possible for you to do so*

> *your cousin val*

The writing was hurried and scribbled; the sentences ran together with no capitals, beginnings, or endings. The drops still showed on the paper where Val's shaking hand had splattered the ink.

Kylee read the letter hastily then turned back and read it again, slowly. What the letter implied was clear. Val was not her real father. The mother she worried about remembering was not her real mother at all. She was just an adopted child with no real parents what so ever, she belonged to no one, not even Uncle Ira. What did Hail know about the whole thing? She knew something. Val said Hail was not to know that she was anyone other than Val's daughter. But she wasn't Val's daughter, or was she?

Kylee was indeed befuddled. Where were the answers to come from? Why hadn't Uncle Ira told her about this? Hail was the only one left with the answers. She stared at the letter on the table, hands folded in her lap. Hail was the only one to tell her who her parents were. She would just have to wait. But what if she didn't return? Perhaps she would never know the secret. She folded the letter and tucked it into her apron pocket.

Matt walked with his arm around Mary's waist. The day dawned gray and chilling with a promise of rain or snow. The road was already muddy caused from the light layer of snow that had melted and crusted from the freezing temperature, leaving the earth underneath slick and soggy. The two early morning strollers didn't seem to mind. It gave Matt an excuse to hold Mary closer to keep her from sliding. She responded by snuggling closer to keep warm.

Matt said he needed some fresh air and insisted that Mary go walking with him down the slippery road. Mary had taken time to pin her petticoat hem carefully up over the skirt of her brown dress to catch the mud splatters. The underskirt was easier to wash than the heavy wool skirt.

Mary sensed Matt's nervousness, realizing the cold weather and storm brewing brought worry for Tom's safety. They wondered if the length of time he'd been gone meant something serious could have happened, Matt worried endlessly.

Matt liked the feel of Mary's hips under his hand. She walked with a little swish. He pulled her closer so he wouldn't miss a single sway. She had parted her hair and tied it with bright pink ribbons on either side of her round face. The clean smell of rosemary and soap hung heavy about her hair. Matt bent his head to lay his cheek on the softness. Taking a long deep breath he let the clean sweet smell fill his senses. Oh, how he loved her!

"Mary, Mary my love. Let's get married, today. I don't want to wait another minute for you. We could ride into Gladeville and get Judge Barnes to marry us, we'd be back tomorrow."

"I do want to, dearest, but I want Kylee, Tom, an' Hail to be with us and Uncle Alvin, he's all the family I got left. It wouldn't be right if he weren't willin' for us to marry. Don't you think that would be the proper way?" She hugged Matt tighter wanting so much to share his bed. But it was important to hold her respectability. It was the way her father and mother would have wanted it. For a moment the sadness was back in her eyes.

"Oh Matt, I do love you so much! I'm wantin' you terrible-ee. Do you think I'm shameless for tellin' you that?" Mary's voice was husky and sultry. She thought of the things Polly told her about pleasing a man and was certain she would have no problem there.

"Well, I know a few that would think you was a terrible hussy for just thinkin' such a thing, let alone sayin' it out loud. Knowin' how you feel makes the waitin' worser. I'm wantin' to take you right here in the mud," Matt teased.

"That would be a dirty trick," Mary laughed.

"If that's the way it is an' you won't marry me until Tom gets home, I'm goin' lookin' for him," Matt's voice was dead serious.

Mary turned silent, the laughter gone.

"If he ain't home in a couple of days, I'm goin' after him," Matt said definitely. "It's been too long Mary, most over a month. Winter's not far off. I'm afear'd for him. Hail ain't back either. It ain't like her to stay off so long in one stretch."

"If you must go, I'll not keep you." Her voice was sad but resigned.

Matt turned to Mary so he could see into her eyes, "You understand how it is don't you?"

"I do. I'll pray for your safe return every night an' day. As for Hail, you can't tell nothin' about her. She might be at the house when we get back," Mary reasoned, lifting her face for a kiss.

Matt kissed her tenderly, savoring the sweetness of her lips, cool from the bitter day. He released her and resumed walking. He stopped to watch a fat groundhog trying to get inside a hollow log. Picking up a muddy rock he rubbed it clean on the leg of his britches and threw it with force at the log. It hit with a thud and the little critter withdrew its head and scurried away into the tall grass.

Matt watched without concern the rider coming down Pound road. He couldn't distinguish the rider through the snow that was beginning to swirl. Then he recognized Jole' as Boy came bounding out of the trees, jumping on his chest, licking his face affectionately, and almost knocking him over with surprise. Matt scratched his ears and patted his back.

"Tarnation, Mary, it's Tom!" Matt let the dog down and ran to meet his brother. He was slipping dangerously on the muddy road. "Damned if it ain't."

He offered his hand to Tom, "God, it's good to see you! I was about to come lookin' for you."

"Matt! Doggone, you're lookin' the best ever!" Tom greeted with a pleased grin, delighted to see his brother in such good health and shaking his brother's hand firmly.

"Can't say the same for you Tom. You look plum starved an' tuckered! Come on; let's get you to the house. Kylee won't be too happy with me at all if she finds I was keepin' you out here jackin' our jaws!" Matt laughed.

Tom was dirty and shaggy with a heavy beard. His hair was untrimmed and hanging around his shoulders. His skin was brown from wind and sun and stretched taut against his cheekbones, his light blue eyes sunken into dark circles. He dismounted and handed the reins to Matt watching Mary coming on a run.

"I've been in that saddle far too long. Think I'll stretch my legs," he stated and hugged Mary tightly as she threw herself into his arms.

"Tom, Tom, it is you! Oh, it's so good to see you! You're home at last! I hope you're not gonna leave again." Mary drew herself away looking into his eyes. She saw the dark shadows there. Shadows of youth faded, a stronger, wiser gentleness surfaced in the pale blue of his eyes.

"Jay's dead, Mary. I hung him like he did our paws. There's no satisfaction in it, girl. Where's the joy, the glory? I feel empty and wasted. I broke the Lord's commandment again an' killed another man. I'm glad Mary, glad he's dead, but I grieve that it was by my hands. I should have brought him back for the law to take care of. That's what I should have done. Then, I wouldn't have this on my conscience. I let my hate get the best of me. All I could see was how he'd done our families. But, it's done! It's over! I'm not sorry he's dead. I'm only sorry it was me what done it!" Tom confessed.

"Sorry! What's to be sorry for? Course you ain't sorry! The bastard got what he deserved! I only wish I could a been there to help!" Matt said with venom, disappointed at his brother's lack of excitement over Jay's death.

Mary smiled at Tom and kissed him full on the lips. "Thank you Tom! It don't bring mommy and poppy back, but somehow it's good to know that black hearted weasel won't hurt anyone else. We are free of him!"

Tears filled her eyes as she smiled at Tom. The snow was now coming in huge flakes that lay lightly on her moist face. She brushed it aside and took Tom's hand.

"Let's go home Tom. Kylee's been waitin' many days to see you!"

A ray of light broke through the flurry of snow and rested fleetingly on the slickness of the muddy road. Tom's glance followed the light to where it came to rest mockingly upon a dormant branch. The bare limb swayed slightly in the breeze and he envisioned for a second Jay's body dangling there in the gathering shadows.

Would his crime haunt him forever? Would Jay's body always be before his eyes? He was hopeful it would dim the horror of the atrocities at the Gap. But it wasn't so. The nightmare was still there. The grief for his father and the Stewart's still a raw wound. Killing Jay had not erased a single memory.

"Come on Tom, let's go see Kylee," Mary coaxed pulling on his arm as she watched him stare blankly into the trees across the road. "She'll have our hides if she knows we are keepin' you out here a jawin' when she's dyin' to see you!"

Kylee watched in wonder the large snowflakes coming in flurries under the sheltering porch roof. She gazed with awe as the white fragments landed on her damp hair. The delicate difference in each lacy flake was discernible on the surface of her dark locks.

With a large cotton towel she was drying her long tresses while standing under the protection of the low roof. A heavy sigh rose to surface as her thoughts dwelled on Tom out in such weather. The breath stilled in her throat and was replaced by the thumping of her heart as she recognized Tom coming with long strides into the yard.

Waving the towel wildly in the air she went on a high run to meet him. Without thought or a minute of shyness she jumped into his arms, locked her legs about him, fastened her arms around his neck, and kissed him soundly on the lips.

She withdrew her lips a fraction and whispered, "I love you Tom! Oh, how I love you! I'm so glad you're home. I don't care what happened, I ain't never gonna let you out of my sight again. Never!"

Her lips were only a whisper away from Tom. Her long damp hair fell in a cascade around them. Tom claimed her lips again then lifted her away and sat her feet on the ground. Kylee held her eyes closed, breathing slowly, savoring every facet of the kiss.

"Look at me Kylee," Tom demanded sternly.

She opened her eyes, green orbs sparkling with joy at the sight of him. She was puzzled.

"Look at me Kylee. Tell me what you see. Tell me if I've changed," he requested seriously.

There was nothing familiar about the man before her with the beard and long hair, no similarity to the old Tom with the clean-shaven face and neat appearance. Nothing was the same except the pale blue eyes and inevitable lock of hair falling across his forehead.

"I see you haven't shaved," she told him scrutinizing his face and looking deep into his eyes.

There behind the pale blue she could read the sadness and hurt. She could see the older look carved deep in the lines around his eyes. She could see the need for him to forget the things those eyes had seen.

"Now, Kylee, be serious!"

"I see you're tired an' need a bath," Kylee teased, wrinkling her nose at the fowl smell of unwashed clothing. "But most of all, I see that you love me just the same as I love you! That's all that matters in the whole world!"

Tom drew her back into his arms, bent his head, and kissed her.

"I have killed another man, Kylee. Can you still love me knowing I'm twice a murderer? Jay's dead. I hung him same as he did my paw an' Jan." His eyes staring into hers were filled with misery.

"Now we can forget all the hate," Kylee stated firmly. Her eyes expressed the joy she felt at the sight of him. With both arms fastened around him she hugged him tightly. "We can spend the rest of our lives loving each other," she promised looking up at him with wide green eyes.

"It ain't that easy Kylee. I should have brought him back to Virginia. I have to tell Snow. It's something I have to do. I don't know what they'll do to me."

"You'll not tell them! Then they can't do anything. Anyways they'd only say he got what he deserved." The statement and matter closed as far as she was concerned.

"Let's go in. You'll catch your death with that wet head. I couldn't stand that!" Tom chided her.

They walked to the house arm in arm. The snow whirls came faster now and seemed a refuge from the burden that filled Tom's heart.

"That roof sure needs some new staves. I better get that done before spring rains come," he added.

"Matt's room does leak some around the window," Kylee remarked.

"The barn needs some repairs too," Tom sighed walking a little slower. "I guess it's been too long since anyone cared enough to do anything seriously around here."

Tom felt a sudden urge to see to it all. He was home and his love for the place was strong inside him. The memory of his father and Billy became a warm cloak around him. He would never leave again. He was home to stay. He was encouraged with the news about Tanner and Ferrell Hall.

Kylee, Mary, and Matt were elated at Tom's return. They felt things would be almost perfect, except for the memory of their loved ones and Hail's absence. Now that Tom returned Kylee's worry over him was replaced by a nagging urgency for their friend's return home.

Over the months while Hail had been with them Kylee had grown very fond of her. She had filled the hole left in Kylee's life by the absence of her mother. Then the letters implied that Hail and her father had been sweethearts. The knowledge caused her to feel even closer to the woman. Finding out that Val and Nan weren't her real parents caused a deeper bond toward Hail. Kylee was anxious for her return so they could discuss the letters.

Kylee's desire to learn who her parents really were grew more and more each day. She wouldn't discuss the contents of the letters with anyone, not even her dear friend Mary. She would keep them a secret until Hail could unravel the puzzle.

"I'm goin' to Gladeville an' report to Snow. Matt, you comin' with me? Mary and Kylee will be all right while we are gone. There's no Mitchell's around to hurt them. If Hail ain't back by the time we get home, we'll go find her," Tom announced to Matt as they worked replacing the seal around the window of Matt's bedroom.

"I got a better idea; let's take the women with us. I want to buy Mary a ring. It seems to me it would be a good time for you to buy one for Kylee too, seein's how I see you snugglin' up close to her every time you get a chance. You are serious about her, ain't you Tom?" Matt questioned, stopping his pounding long enough to look squarely at his brother.

"I'm serious, Bub!" Tom answered emphatically.

"Let's go then. Let's go right now, Tom! If Hail ain't back by the time we-uns are, we'll sure go lookin' for her. I feel the same as you; she's been gone too long. I want to know what's happened to her too. There ain't any snow on the road. Looks like the weather will be good for a while, what you say Tom? Come on!" Matt declared, throwing his hammer down. He crawled down the porch roof to the ladder and climbed to the ground.

"Okay! Okay, Tom! I'm believin' you! I told you not to take the law into your own hands. Now you have really put your head into the noose. I'll go with you to bring the body back. I guess you know if Jay's where you say he is, an' the varmints ain't got him, we are in trouble. That's Kentucky. You might have to face a jury over there. No one will blame you Tom for what you done, but they might not understand your reasons over there. Maybe we should forget the whole thing. Without the body they wouldn't hold a trial, an inquest perhaps. Your confession without the corpus delect-i, well, let it go Tom. Let it go! Forget it! I'm busier than all get out. They've set Hensely's trial up after Thanksgivin'. That's gonna drag things out even more," Snow told Tom.

"You gonna be here, Tom?"

"Yes, I'll be here," but Tom could not feel any excitement at the thought of watching Hensely hang. "Right now I want to bring Jay home, then it'll be over an' finished Lorenzo."

Snow promised to be at the mill in two days. He told Tom to be ready for a trip into Kentucky.

Tom and Matt's shopping spree with Mary and Kylee was a great success. The two women agreed whole-heartedly to the idea. Both returned to the mountain with sparkling engagement rings on their fingers and wedding bands tucked safely in the men's pockets. They both firmly refused to wed until they knew of Hail's whereabouts. Their worries would soon come to an end.

CHAPTER SIX

Kylee and Mary were feeling the bitter chill of the day as they returned to the mill. They huddled tightly together under the warmth of a down quilt in the back of the wagon. Matt and Tom shared a fur robe around their legs on the wagon seat. The young women were glad to be home and hurried into the warmth of the cabin.

A song came loudly to Kylee and Mary as they climbed the porch, a little off key and out of tune, but a joyous sound to their ears. Kylee knew there was only one person who sang that badly.

"She won't come an' I won't fetch her,
Ho-hum come a tiddle-dum day."

"It's Hail, Mary. It has to be Hail, she's home. Hail's home!" Kylee said as she hurried faster into the house.

Sparks flew in swirls up the chimney as Hail stirred the fire under the big coffee pot.

"Well, there you-uns are. I was beginning to worry about you all. Here I am comin' home from a long journey an' no one to greet me," she chided.

The young women fell on her with hugs and chatter, both talking at the same time. They demanded to know where she had been and in the same breath telling her what happened while she was gone.

"Why didn't you tell us you were leavin'? You just up an' disappeared. We was so worried about you! You have been gone so long," Kylee said.

"I had things that needed tendin' to. Now, they's done an' I'm back. I see Tom has returned. I saw Jole' in the barn. We-uns are together again, that's all that's important! Do not question me about where I've been. It will do you no good. You needn't know!" Hail was firm and final about her explanation.

"Oh, we don't care anyways, Hail. We are just glad you're back. Now we can have our weddin's an' we'll all live happy ever after like it says in the stories Matt reads to me. I'm so glad this mess is done, I only want to forget it all an' start all over." The huskiness was close to the surface in Mary's voice. Kylee put her arms around her, quick to offer comfort before Mary broke into a storm of tears.

Tom and Matt came in bringing with them a blast of cool air. They greeted Hail with hugs, reminding her that she was family. Tom insisted that she must reveal to them where she had disappeared.

"Never you mind. I'm home now an' we-uns are gonna get ready for a double weddin'. That's the next thing we-uns are gonna do!"

Tom repeated to Hail a detailed description of his encounter with Jay. He gave her a full account of Lorenzo Snow's reaction of his report.

She gave him a smile that twisted the side of her mouth and clouded her eyes. Tom wondered what brought the strange look to her face. It disappeared as quickly as it appeared and she assured him nothing would come of going after Jay.

"Mark my words Tom, if it's as far back in the mountains as you say, you'll never, never find that place twice. You should forget lookin' for Jay's body. Sides, what's gonna become of Rueb? What did Snow have to say about Simeon an' Trace's killings? You said you left Rueben with a bullet shot through his leg. You suppose he might be dead?"

"Could be Hail. I didn't have the heart to go back an' finish the job. Snow promised they'd bring Rueben in sooner or later for his part in our folks killin's. You know Hail I have a new outlook on things. I'm lookin' more to the forgivin' side. I think even if it's somewhat late, it's time for forgettin' an' forgivin' an' gettin' on with things at hand!" Tom looked at Kylee with a deep love showing in his eyes and went on talking with Hail.

"It is funny no one has found hide nor hair of Polly. She has fell totally out of sight. If the law does find Rueben Mitchell perhaps he can shed some light on the mystery," Tom was thoughtful.

The hill people buried Trace and Simeon Niger in the village cemetery on a hill behind Donkey complete with markers and floral bouquets. The disappearance of Polly Trace would become an unsolved mystery; part of a bad memory people wanted to forget.

Evening was always a favorite time for Kylee. She always loved the firelight; the dimness of the cabin, and the closeness of her loved ones. The pain of death was healing and even Mary was beginning to cope with the loss of her family.

Sitting in a half circle around the fire they felt the darkness closing in. Mary rose, lit a lamp, and set it in the center of the long table. She was beginning to feel weary from the trip into Gladeville. Sleeping the night at Jennings had not been the joyous occasion it had always been when she was younger. Her body had felt every ripple in the plank floor. She was about to make her goodnights when Kylee turned to Hail with eager questioning that made Mary decide to stay in front of the fire.

"Now that supper is done an' we-uns are relaxin', there is somethin' I must ask you Hail. It is important that you tell me true. I must know more about my father. You are the only one left who can tell me. Uncle Ira would never talk of it. I quess it was because he didn't want to dig up old memories. But now Hail, you must clear up the puzzle," Kylee pleaded.

"What are you talkin' of child? Make sense! You know more of your father than I do. It has been many years since I have seen him. He is gone now, an' so is Ira. I have to agree, let the past lie," Hail said wanting to avoid the conversation.

"Wait Hail. Wait a minute!" She rose and left the room.

Placing another log on the fire Matt stood watching the sparks whirl in a frenzied dance up the chimney. His eyes were as puzzled as Hail's.

Tom sat in the shadows in a high back chair absently stroking Boy's ear. The big dog, always his companion, lay beside him on the floor with his head resting on Tom's knee.

Kylee returned with Hail's Bible and her father's letters. She sat both in the older woman's lap and turned the pages of the Bible open to where Hail's letters were. She had tucked her father's letter to her Uncle Ira carefully in her apron pocket.

"Tell me of these things, Hail. Tell me so I can understand their meaning. It took you so long to come home I almost gave up ever knowin'. Now, you must tell me what the letters mean."

Kylee was filled with excitement. Her eyes were large pools of expectations and eagerness now that Hail was here to tell her everything.

"I can never marry Tom until the mystery of who I am is cleared up."

"Mystery? Cleared up? You never said anything about a mystery to me girl. What's this gotta do with your gettin' married? Can't see's how it would have anythin' to do with that! I was a mind that everythin' was settled," Tom stated defensively.

"Well, it is Tom. But hush about that for a minute. This is somethin' I must know first. Hail can tell me. I know she can. Tell me Hail!" Kylee demanded.

Hail had been turning the letters in her hand and reading through them. A hint of tears misted her eyes.

"Who gave you permission to be snooping into my Bible?" Hail inquired wondering about Kylee's interference into her private possessions.

"I'm sorry Hail. I was movin' your things into Ira's room. Quite by accident I happened onto them. Don't be angry at me, please. I was glad to learn from the letters that you was sweethearts with my paw. What happened Hail? How come you turned him away like the letters say? How come?" Kylee continued firing questions and demanding answers.

"Cause of somethin' that happened long ago. Let's not talk of that Kylee, it's over! I never want to think of it again. Can we let it go at that? Can we just feel closer to each other knowin' that we both loved your father?" Hail pleaded wanting that information to be enough.

"No! We can't let it go at that, cause of this letter! Tell me now, Hail! Tell me of its meaning," Kylee demanded again reaching in her pocket and taking out Val's letter to Ira and handed it to Hail.

"What's this?" Hail questioned seeing Ira's name on the letter.

"It's from my father to Uncle Ira. You are the only one that can tell me of its meaning. This letter tells me that my papa an' mama weren't my real folks. It says you know who my real parents are. Tell me Hail! I had parents until I read this letter, then I found I had no one at all. I am an orphan with no father or mother. Tell me. Tell me where I come from!"

Hail read the letter, listening at the same time to Kylee. She raised her eyes and stared into the shadows in the room. She thought the blackness in her life had dispersed, but she had been wrong. One can't hide the darkness with more darkness, hate with more hate. Her eyes wandered to Tom's face revealing plainly the torment he was going through. The slight smile on Mary's lips, told Hail she was returning to a world of reality. Matt stood straight and tall before the fire, which was visible proof of his recovery. They were all victims of a black hate she thought was finished and done. Then there was Kylee, dear sweet lovely Kylee, whom she had grown to love. Hail could feel the dark despair creeping in and getting ready to devour them.

Hail fumbled with the letters in her lap. She gazed at the fire casting long shadows in the dim room. A bitter smile toyed at the corners of her mouth. The terrible scarred skin on her cheekbones stretched tight as a drumhead. Her green eyes so dark with shadows, they appeared black.

Hail knew now why Ira had never revealed to her the secret he kept buried from her. Her heart beat wildly, at last she knew. The letter in her lap ended the search for the truth Ira held hidden from her for so many years. She thought of her happiness when she learned of Tom and Kylee's wedding plans. Watching them sitting around waiting, she sighed. She realized if they were to understand they would have to know it all from the beginning. She must tell them everything.

"Please God, help me to make them understand," she prayed under her breath. Out loud she began slowly. It was hard for her to start. In a voice so low, the listeners had to lean closer to hear; she began a story she thought had been buried forever.

"Never in my life had I seen a place lovelier than Tandy's Mountain. As far as I was concerned, it held everythin' I could ever desire, trees, water, flowers, birds, herbs, lots of herbs for medicines an cooking. My father loved it here too, but my mother grieved for her home near the sea an' died longing to return."

"Please be patient with me. I must tell you everythin' so you will understand what I am goin' to tell you. After my mother died I became my father's helper, I went with him often to doctor the ill, it became my whole life. I stood next to Mattie when she married Ira. I fell in love with your father, Kylee." She took Kylee's chin in her hand and looked deep into her eyes.

"I loved him very much dear. So much I never thought anythin' could separate us. We planned to wed. Then it was decided he would go to the mines to make money for the mill. We were both anxious for the mill to be finished because it would be our future. Ira's health was growin' steadily worse. My father an' I worked what time we could helpin' him an' Mattie on the mill. We became fast friends," she continued on with her story.

"I helped most of the youngin's in these hills be birthed. Mary, an' her sisters, an' Billy. At the time Val left, Jay's wife Sarah was heavy with child an' very ill. There was danger from the beginnin' that she would never survive the birthin'. My papa said it would be God's will whatever happened. Sarah died but the child, Bob, lived. Jay was filled with bitterness. He blamed my father for Sarah's death. He declared my father was on the Phelps's side an' was tryin' to destroy his family too. Bess Stewart had just lost her first child, a boy, an' was grievin' somethin' fierce. My father arranged for her to take little Bob to wet-nurse him. The infant helped Bess think of somethin' else besides the death of her little son. Bess an' Jan had hearts as big as all get out for youngin's. They took in Rueben an' Blaine too, but there was no pacifyin' Jay. Oh, he was satisfied that his boys were bein' takin' care of, but he had revenge in his heart toward my papa," Hails voice failed. She lifted her cup for Matt to refill her coffee. Taking a sip of the hot liquid, she sat the cup on a corner of the table and continued.

"The weeks passed. We thought Jay had forgotten us. Then one day he appeared at our cabin," she paused, "he wanted me!"

"I want to wed Hail!" Jay demanded. "You owe me, White!"

"I'm sorry Jay. Hail is already promised to Val Bentley. The promise will stand that way. They will be married when he returns," my father told him. "I am truly sorry about Sarah. The fault was not mine." But Jay was not appeased.

"Next to gettin' folks healed, my papa loved to go huntin'. One day while he was gone Jay returned to our cabin." Hail continued.

"You're comin' with me girl!" he ordered me. "You won't need anythin'! I'll see you have everythin' you need! You ain't gonna be a bride, so you won't need much!"

"I was frantic. Of course I refused to go with him so he bound my hands an' feet an' tied a gag over my mouth. He tied me to the side of the wagon bed. There was no escape. I had no idea what he had in mind for me, but I was soon to find out."

"I knew Jay was filled with a burnin' hate for Phelps's, but he had treated my father an' I fairly an' with kindness. I thought he only aimed to scare my father into consenting to our marriage. I was so wrong. His intentions were only to take me with him down into the same black hell that tormented him. I thought after Jay's death it would all be over. Oh, my God, will it ever end? Am I to suffer more for my ill deeds?"

"Hail, what are you talkin' of? You could have never done anythin' as bad as Jay Mitchell has!" Kylee comforted her. "He is never gonna hurt any of us any more. You forget him an' get on with tellin' me who my real parents are. You do know, don't you Hail?" Kylee sat on a stool at Hail's knees waiting anxiously for what Hail would tell her.

"In time, Kylee. I will tell you. I only want to make you understand. I need to make you understand, an' forgive me."

"I can forgive you anythin' Hail. You are most like a mother to me. I'll forgive you anythin'," Kylee promised, "Tell me!"

Hail smiled faintly, a haunting terror misted her eyes.

"I wonder, Kylee. I wonder. You shall know soon. First I must tell you how it was. Jay took me to his house. You know Kylee how it is in the Mitchell's house? He chained me to the legs of the bunk beds. There was no escape for me. It was not a mother for his boys he wanted, but a woman to satisfy his lustful pleasure."

"He would unchain me long enough to take me to his bed. He raped me repeatedly. If I resisted he would beat me unmercifully. Bread an' water was all he allowed me to eat. I became weak an' sick. I grew wise to the fact that Jay's pleasure in attacking my body was in the brutality. He wanted my resistance so he could beat me. When I resisted him no longer, he grew tired of the game. He left me chained to the bed post days at a time."

"Time became endless. My arms ached from bein' in one position. I could lie on the bed an' watch the rats play around the slop jar of my own waste. It was at the side of the bed an' was never emptied. The odor filled the darkness of the night an' the dismal light of day."

"I prayed that my father would rescue me. But he never came. My prayers ended. I gave in to the knowledge I would die chained to that bed. I would die before I could kill Jay Mitchell." Hail had withdrawn into a world of her own, a world that until now, had been shared with no one other than Mattie and Ira.

"Jay's home had become my prison. I only moved when it became necessary. My bones ached. My head became an uncombed mess of gray substance, a snowy roost for vermin. I lay upon the bed, a shrinking clump of growing madness."

"Then, when I thought Jay had forgotten about me, he returned. He came into the room an' undone my chains. I cowered to the back of the bed. He pulled me forward an' stood me on the floor. This time he didn't drag me to the bedroom, but to the door. He pushed me out to the porch where a beautiful girl stood with a bundle in her arms."

"Get out'a here, you bitch! I ain't wantin' the likes of you anymore! I'll let you stay on Tandy's Mountain. I promise you that much, cause the people here need you, not that it matters none to me! But I'll let you stay 'cause legally you own part of my mountain. Don't let me look on your face again! You hear me? Now get!"

"I stumbled down the stairs past the woman, Mae, who would become Taynee's mother. I looked back at Jay and warned him, "I'll kill you, Jay Mitchell! You hear me? I'm gonna kill you! When you're dead, I'll burn your body in the hottest fire hell has to offer an' scatter your ashes in a hog-waller!" I screeched at him.

"Get out'a my sight before I decide to get you out'a your misery, an' kill you first!" Jay called after me.

Kylee's eyes stared at Hail, her body becoming tense. Her lips set in a ridged line, hands clenched tightly in her lap bracing herself for the things she thought would surely come.

"I swore I would kill him, but killin' a man in cold blood was not as easy as I thought even when the man was Jay Mitchell. I left that evil place. I tried to hold my head proudly. I was weak an' sick, at the point of madness. I thought of my father. I needed him."

"He had always told me that time heals all wounds, but it does not. He wasn't around to remind me. He had been found on the road near Stewarts shot in the head. I knew then why he had never come lookin' for me. He hadn't forsaken me. There was no proof, but I was certain it was Jay who had killed him. Jay always got away with his heinous crimes," Hail faltered and stopped to take a swallow of coffee and looked at Kylee's rigid body.

"In a few months I had regained my health an' was certain beyond doubt that I was pregnant with Jay's child. I thought of gettin' rid of the baby inside my body. Oh yes, there are ways! But I was afraid of destroyin' myself. I wanted to live to see Jay die! Of course I had to write Val an' tell him I could never marry him, an' never wanted to see him again. He made the decision to never return to the hills. I think he found happiness with your mother Kylee. I think he forgave me," Hail stated and stopped. For a long moment she sat staring at the letters in her lap.

Mary was crying quietly. Kylee, unstirring, knew the truth at last.

"Go on Hail," Tom encouraged.

Hail could see Kylee had guessed the truth and she had to make her understand. "I hated the child that was growing in my body because of the man who had fathered it. When it became impossible to hide the evidence of my condition any longer I took Mattie and

651

Ira into my confidence. Ira was fired up to take revenge on Jay, but I begged him not to. He had his little ones an' Mattie to think of. Who would finish the mill if he'd get killed because of me?"

"Ira suggested if I still felt the same about the baby after it was born I should consider givin' it away. When the child was born I was ready, but Mattie insisted that I nurse the little one for at least six months. My breasts were heavy with milk. She was afraid I would get milk fever, so I agreed. I could not stand to look upon the child. All I could see was the face of the black-hearted devil that had sired her. I was glad when Ira found a place for the child an' had made all the arrangements. Ira kept his secret well." There was a long silence upon the room even the crackling of the fire had ceased.

"Oh, my God! My God! How could I have been so heartless?" Hail sobbed. She fell to her knees in front of the young woman attempting to embrace her. Kylee pushed her roughly away.

"It was me! I was the baby you hated!" Kylee stated bitterly. Her face drained of all its color and all expression, a pale mask in the dim room.

"Since I read the letters I thought many things about what kind of parents would be mine. Never once had I thought I would have been born to a mother who hated me so fiercely she couldn't even look upon my face," Kylee hissed between tight lips.

"Kylee! Please forgive me! I hated the man that had fathered you with such a passion that I let it blind me to any love I might have had for you. If there had been any way to find you I would have. Ira would not tell me. He was afear'd if I brought you here Jay would find out who you were an' harm you."

"I would have been better off dead!"

"Oh, Kylee, don't say that! Can't I make you understand? It's been so long ago. Can't I have a chance to make it up to you? I have known many days an' nights of loneliness. I have suffered for what I done. I could feel you in my arms; feel you there nuzzlin' at my breast nursin'. When I'd look, my arms would be empty. I have longed so, to hold the little daughter that was mine. My hate for Jay was the only thing that kept me goin'." Hail tried again to put her arms around Kylee.

Kylee pushed her away again and stood up. "Now, my hate for you will keep me goin'," Kylee said looking at Hail then lowered her eyes to the floor. "You will be punished for denyin' me!"

"You think I have not been punished?" Hail asked rising from the floor to stand in front of her daughter. "Do you think I could have helped birth babies into the world an' not know the torment of hell for not keepin' my own? God has punished me many times for my selfish deed. Look at me Kylee!" Hail screamed. "Look at me an' say I have not been punished enough!"

But Kylee kept her eyes downcast. She would not look at Hail's scarred face.

"Soon as Ira had taken you away I knew I had made a mistake, but it was too late. I have lived with that all this time. I have loved you, Kylee. These many years without knowin' you, I have loved you since you came to the mill as a dear friend. Now there is only hate in your face for me. Please say you'll forgive me an' let me love you! You said you'd forgive me anythin'! I don't ask that you love me. But I need to know you forgive me! Please, please let me make this up to you. Give me a chance, Kylee!" she pleaded as Kylee turned away from her keeping her back to Hail.

"You will never look upon my face again, never!" Kylee stated bitterly. Without a word to any of the others in the room she walked into her bedroom. She closed the door and dropped the latch.

There were no tears for the woman that was her mother. There was more hate for her than for the wicked man that had been her father. At least, he had never known about her. Kylee understood many things now, but the knowledge did not soften her heart.

She knew why Ira was reluctant to talk of her parents, he had known all the time. She could acknowledge the look on Hail's face the night Nell's baby was born, the reason for Hail's undeniable hate for Jay. She certainly had cause. There had been a reason for the magnetism between her and Taynee. They had the same father.

Outside her window a chilly darkness embraced the world. Her ears were deaf to the song the pines created as they swayed in the cold breeze, a soft whisper in the gathering darkness of the night.

CHAPTER SEVEN

The fire in the potbellied stove inside the mill warmed Tom's body but his heart held a chill the heat couldn't touch. Kylee's coldness toward the entire household puzzled him. Her insistence to remain locked up baffled them all. She would not open her bedroom door to anyone, even turned away Mary's offer of food. She stubbornly refused to leave her room until Hail left the house.

Tom was totally confused and mixed up. He couldn't bury his emotions for Kylee yet her attitude about Hail completely angered him. The need to hold her in his arms and tell her how much he loved her pressed in on him. He was certain, if she would only share her trouble with him, he could help.

He understood how hate could consume you, tear your life apart, and leave you wasted and drained. With his new found love for the Lord he knew there was another way. It was all about forgiveness and he wanted to share his discovery with Kylee.

It was hard for Tom to believe how quickly she could forget their promises to each other. She promised to never let him out of her sight for an instant. Now, she refused to see him, closed the door between them as solidly as she had between Hail and herself, shutting him out completely. How could you talk to anyone with a four-inch plank door between you?

Tom picked up his mother's Bible, put it under his arm and stepped outside.

Matt was driving the small wagon and team of dapple-grays up to the steps of the house where Hail and Mary waited. He'd better hurry and go say good-bye.

Mary made the decision for both Hail and herself. "It's time I went home Hail. Matt an' I have decided it's where we will live after we are wed. I have to go sometime. I am sure it will need a heap of cleanin' knowin' Uncle Alvin an' his lazy house keepin'." Mary stated with a small laugh.

"It's not goin' to be easy for me. With you there Hail, it will be a heap better! After Kylee has time to think what a wonderful mother you would be, she will change her mind. Until she does, I'm gonna adopt you. I need a mother somethin' fierce! Hail, we can go home to my place as soon as you're ready."

Now, waiting for Matt to come with the wagon, they were both dreading saying good-bye. Tom helped them into the wagon giving them each a squeeze and a kiss on the cheek. He gave Matt strict orders to drive carefully.

Hail had been withdrawn since her confession. As she took her place beside Mary on the wagon seat she announced her decision to Tom.

"After Matt an' Mary are married, I'm goin' back to Norton to the hospital. It's somethin' I have thought a lot about. There are many things I can learn. If I have any years left, I aim to put some purpose to my life. My life has been wasted in hate an' selfishness. It is too late to make up to Kylee for what I done."

"You needn't do that, Hail," Tom protested, but Hail stopped him with a gloved hand over his lips.

"No! You can't talk me out'a this. If I leave, Kylee can forget an' live for herself an' your life together." Hail smiled faintly fighting to hold back her tears. "Thank you for all your kindness to me. I love you as if you were my own son. I'll never forget that I owed my life to you the night of the fire."

"Nonsense Hail! It was really Kylee who saved your life. I am certain if you give her time, she'll take a different look at things."

"It's too late, Tom. I only hope she can forget who her real father an' mother are, an' remember the ones what raised her. I should have told her nothin'. It would have been better to let her believe she was an orphan. It is very satisfying to know, even if she never forgives me, that I have such a sweet lovely daughter. She is much more than any mother could have hoped for, Val done well raisin' her. She is more than I had ever dreamed of. Don't blame her for the way she feels, it is fittin'." Hail patted Tom's cheek.

"Tomorrow is the day Snow will be by to go up the mountain. Will you be back to go with us, Matt?" Tom asked his brother.

"I'll not go with you Tom, but I'll be here to look after Kylee until you get back. I'll take care of things."

"I was hopin' as much, Matt. I was hatin' to leave Kylee alone. I was thinkin' on puttin' it off until she feels better about things. It'll take us a few days."

"You don't have to go at all. You could forget about the whole crazy thing. Forget about Jay! We'd all like to put him behind us Tom."

"I can't, Bub. I need to know that one of these nights when I think it's all over, I won't wake up with the law chasin' after me for murderin' Jay. I want it settled an' over. I don't want it comin' up later to haunt me." Tom's decision was final.

Tom watched the wagon cross the bridge. Hail's scarf was a bright splash on the cold November day. He watched until they disappeared among the trees then turned to go into the house.

For Kylee everything had ended, her life with Tom and her life at the mill. She must leave this place she loved so much. A place that had been part of her papa Val and although he hadn't known it, a heritage he left for her. How could she stand to stay in a place that would remind her every day who her father really was? A man so black hearted and tainted with evil that he had even murdered his own kin. He had killed all the people who were so dear to her. How could she stand to live with the memory of such a man as her real father? And Hail, the fact that she had denied her as an infant, even refusing to look upon her face. How could she ever forgive her, how? There was no forgiveness in her heart, only bitterness and hate. A hollow ache inside that would in no way allow the tender feelings she once had for the woman who was her real mother.

Kylee spent the days and nights sitting cross-legged in the middle of her bed. She denied herself any sleep and refused all offers of food. She would talk to no one, turned deaf ears to Tom's pleas to let him in so they could talk. She was afraid that if she stood face to face with Tom her decision to leave would crumble.

The rumble of the wagon caught her ears and she rose to her knees to look out the window. She watched Tom help the women onto the seat. She could see Hail talking to Tom and patting his cheek. "Hateful, hateful woman!" Kylee hated her with a fierceness that burned in her throat. She couldn't swallow. She clenched her hands into fists and fell back onto the bed.

So, Hail was going! Why did she have to take Mary? The sadness welled up inside her at the thought of her dear friend leaving. The young woman had become very much a part of her life. She allowed herself a moment of grief at the thought of her parting. But it was quickly gone and she was again encased in her hate and bitterness for Hail. At first she ignored Tom's knock. Then when he kicked the door roughly with his boot, she reconsidered and opened it.

"Well, you should be satisfied with your self my dear. They're gone!" Tom showed little warmth toward Kylee's stubborn behavior.

"I didn't want Mary to leave, believe me Tom. I didn't want Mary to go." She must be careful; the tears were close to the surface. If she allowed them, her staunch bull-headedness would crumble.

Tom looked at her pale face, the large emerald eyes pools of misery. Why had he never noticed before how much they were like Hail's? Her long auburn hair was breaking away from the long pins that restrained it and hung in long tendrils down her shoulders. Kylee made no attempt to control it. Tom's anger at her was gone. He needed to hold her in his arms, to comfort her. He reached for her, but she refused him.

"No Tom. No, this cannot be! Forget about me. I am leavin', I cannot stay another day here."

"What are you sayin'? Of course you can stay. You own part of this place. Hail is gone. She'll not be back. She's goin' to Norton to study at the hospital. Sides, you want to see Mary an' Matt wed don't you?"

"No! I don't care! I'm leavin'. The sooner, the better!" Kylee's voice was cold and without feeling, but definite and final.

"All right Kylee, if that's your decision. I can't talk you out'a it?" Tom backed towards the doorway.

"I want to leave tomorrow," Kylee said, shaking her head no as she came from the bedroom.

"I can't take you tomorrow. I'm goin' back to the mountain to find Jay an' bring his body home. I'll be gone for a week, or more. I'll take you when I get back if you're still wantin' to go."

"Can't Matt take me?"

"Sure, but promise me one thing Kylee, at least you owe me this. I want to take you. Promise me you'll wait until I get back. Promise me!" Tom hoped that a little time would give Kylee a chance to see things differently. He took hold of her shoulders firmly and forced her to look at him, shaking her slightly.

"Promise me, promise me!"

Kylee could hear the pleading in his voice. The love for her was still in his eyes. She could allow him that much. Besides, she had to get her things together. It would take a little time. She nodded her head.

Tom could see the consent in her eyes. He wanted to see more and searched for the love he had seen there the day he'd returned home. But it was hidden, blacked out, covered with her stubborn misery. He could see no hint of the love he thought she felt for him. It was over, he told himself. With no further comment he turned and left the house.

Marshal Snow arrived early in the morning before dawn. Frost lay heavy on the gray leafless trees and gleamed white on the road. Tom rode out along side of him with heavy heart. Kylee had been awake to send him away with a warm breakfast but there was no happy smile or cheery good-bye to follow him down the road. Even Boy preferred the warmth of the fire and had refused to go along. Tom's heart was heavy for his long trip and the chill he felt only added to the darkness he could see gathering.

Tom was afraid he had forgotten the place where he left Jay and Rueben. But once on the crest of the mountain the terrain became familiar. He recognized the place where he had rolled down the mountainside. He had no time to reminisce over his experience at the bottom of the ravine.

The spot on the mountain was empty and eerie. Silence hung about the place. The noise of birds and squirrels were absent. The rope no longer hung from the limb. The only resemblance to the place was a heap of ashes from a long ago dead fire.

Tom stirred the ashes with a limb. As he turned the rubble he uncovered the remains of a badly burnt boot sole and a charred heel, nothing more. They searched the place. There was no evidence anyone had been at the spot.

"I don't understand it Lorenzo. Rueben was lying right here."

"Well, Tom. It's been a few weeks an' any blood spots would be gone long ago. I'm believin' what you told me was true. But let's face the facts Tom; there ain't a thing to tie you in with a murder here. Now, let's go home an' forget this whole ridiculous dream," Lorenzo said mounting his horse and fastening his collar up tighter from the brisk wind that was stirring. "This wind is goin' to bring up a storm. I want to be down off this mountain when it does."

"Dream?" Tom screamed at the marshal and reached up to take hold of Snow's coat front. "It ain't no ridiculous dream! I promise you, I left Jay hangin' on that big limb. Rueben was a layin' there bleedin' badly from a bullet in his leg. It wasn't no dream!" Tom added in a quieter tone and freed the marshal's coat.

"Come on son, let's go home. Let's go home an' get drunk an' forget this whole mess. Forget it Tom, it's over!" Snow advised as he rode out of the clearing and down the trail.

"He's right!" Tom said out loud to himself. "The mind plays funny tricks on one. But I know, it weren't no dream. I know it weren't."

Tom was left with a deep bewilderment at what could have happened to Jay. Perhaps Rueben had not been injured as badly as he had thought. It was the only answer. Either he had buried him or else he had taken him down the mountain.

As he rode closely behind Marshal Snow he was silent, but his mind was in turmoil. Would the secret of Jay's disappearing body remain forever a secret, deep in the shadows of the pines?

Kylee kept herself busy while Tom was away. She cleaned the house from top to bottom. There was plenty of clean linen to last the men for a time. No one could say she had left a dirty house. Tom should be home soon now. She kept her promise and waited for his return. She smoothed her hair, coiled it in a long rope and wrapped it around her head, then straightened her skirt. Absently she picked up the wool cards setting on the window seat. She sat down in her rocker and began working on the wool she had washed, dried, and stuffed in a feed sack.

She glanced out the window and saw Tom and Matt talking at the gate. Matt shook Tom's hand and was gone on a high run to the barn. Kylee supposed he was going to Mary's. It had been six whole days since he had seen her.

Kylee kept her head bowed as if preoccupied with her work. She paid little attention as Tom came in. She was silent and sullen. So intent on her own misery that she would not offer him even a casual welcome.

He hung his coat and hat, greeted Boy and patted his head at the dog's insistence. Laying a new log on the fire he turned to Kylee.

"I'm home Kylee, in case you hadn't noticed. I'm tired, an' I'm cold, an' I'm hungry. Now, I know when I rest, I won't be tired any more. When I stand by the fire, I'll not be cold any more. When I have some corn bread an' buttermilk, I'll not be hungry anymore. Now, I can solve all them things. But, I have another problem that only you can solve. I'm dyin' from lovin' you an' wantin' you. I thought of you every minute while I was gone. I see you have your things ready for leavin'. I need to talk you out'a that. I want to convince you to change your mind about leavin'. You're the only one that can save me from dyin' of love."

Kylee remained silent carding the wool into handfuls of white fluff. She stuffed the clouds into a basket at her feet.

"Kylee, I want to marry you. I want you to stay here an' be my wife an' have my children. The mill is half yours an' it's your duty to keep it runnin' same as it's Matt's an' mine. Now say you'll forget this leavin' nonsense an' stay here an' marry me." Tom was beginning to sound desperate. He even flashed a warm smile in Kylee's direction.

"Kylee! I love you. I'm dyin' from wantin' to marry you. If you'll get up an' come here, an' give me a kiss, I will love you forever!"

"I can not marry you Tom, ever!" Kylee finally said without raising her head.

"What kind of nonsense is that?"

"I'll not stay in these hills another day! I am leavin' tomorrow." Her tone was decided, but Tom detected a slight softening. He was hopeful.

"Never, Kylee? I have no intentions of lettin' you go anywhere. We're goin' to be married!" Tom crossed the room and took the cards and wool from her hands and laid them in the basket. Lifting her from the rocker he put his arms firmly around her. How good she felt. He had wanted to do this for days. He bent to kiss her, but she turned her head. The kiss landed on her ear.

"I can't Tom! I can't! How can I ever forget I was Jay's daughter? The man you hated so badly was my father." Kylee tried to hold back the tears. Tom's arms around her had softened her. She was beginning to crumble.

Tom could feel her yielding. He pushed her away slightly but still held her. "You mean you couldn't forget that I killed your paw. Go ahead, say it!"

Her eyes opened wide and she looked at Tom directly.

"No, Tom, No! I meant we'll never be able to forget it was my father that did all them dreadful things to those beautiful folks we loved!" She cried openly almost to the point of wailing.

"Whenever you think of Billy or Uncle Ira, how could you forget I was his daughter? Do you think Mary could ever forget? Every time you looked at me, would you always wonder when the cussedness that is surely in my blood would surface?" Kylee asked him through her tears. "If we were to have children, wouldn't you be afear'd they'd be like him?" She pushed herself free of Tom's arms and turned to run.

Tom was quick, lifting her in his arms he sat down in the rocker cradling her like a baby. He smoothed her silken hair and kissed her tears away.

"Have you forgotten Kylee, you have other blood too? There is no better person than Hail. Her father, your grandpa was a great gentle man. And about Mary forgettin' who your father was, she knew he was Taynee's father, she loved her. It will make no difference to her." He soothed her with his words.

"Taynee, she was really my sister. I wondered why I loved her."

"See, Kylee. That's what it's all about. Lovin' an' forgivin'. We are gonna forget all these things, sweetheart. Jay's dead an' the evil with him. Our children will be fine because we will teach them in the way of the Lord. We will start our lives together with love an' forgiveness. Everythin' will work out fine as long as we have each other." Tom lifted her apron to dry her eyes and wipe her nose.

"Look at me, Kylee. Do you love me enough to start as if these last few months have never been? Do you love me enough to do this an' marry me right away as we planned?"

"I love you more than anythin'!"

"No more talk of leavin', no more tears. No more nonsense about Jay, understand?"

"Yes," Kylee promised and smiled at him trying hard to stop her tears. She wrapped her arms around Tom's neck and kissed him soundly. He was quick to respond. He held her tightly as he returned her kiss.

"Oh, I do love you Tom. I love you!" Kylee sighed against his lips.

He could feel the beating of her heart; hear the huskiness in her voice. The warmth of her hips lay directly under the palm of his hand; the pulse at his temples began to throb. He kissed her again, easy at first waiting for her parted lips, and then kissed her again with steady pressure. He felt her relax in his arms.

He could feel her submission. Here was the moment he had longed for. But in his eagerness he recalled the morning under the mulberry tree. There had been a change; he was not the same man, eager for another Polly. He had become a man with new faith, a man who could control his desires and curb his passion. He was a man with discipline. He knew when the time was right Kylee would be the fulfillment of his dreams. He loosened his hold on her, broke away from her lips, and smiled softly at her.

"One more thing, sweetheart. Are you goin' to forgive Hail? You could help her to forget some too." Kylee stiffened in his arms.

"Kylee," he spoke firmly.

"I don't know, Tom if I can forgive what she done to me, givin' me away an' all."

Tom rose from the rocker and stood Kylee on the floor. His eyes were still charged with desire, but filled with love and tender understanding.

"Well, do you think it's gonna be easy for her to forget what she suffered at Jay's hands? Lookin' at you each day, but she wants to try."

Kylee looked at him with cold eyes. There was no spark of compassion or hint of forgiveness. "I can never forget what a beast that terrible man was. You'd like to think you could have loved your father."

"You don't even want to love your mother!" Tom's exasperation was clear.

Kylee was stubborn to the point of denying herself any joy she might feel in forgiving Hail. She would stay on at the mill, marry Tom, and be a devoted wife, but there was nothing in the marriage vows that said she had to accept Hail. For her, the matter was closed.

"Did you find out what you went to the mountain for?" She questioned Tom, wanting to put the subject of Hail aside.

"No, Kylee, there was nothin' there."

"You mean he could still be alive?"

"Not possible! I left him dead, that's for sure! But Rueben was alive an' I'm thinkin' he's buried Jay some place or brought him back to Tandy's Mountain. I'm goin' over an' talk to Bob in the mornin'. Perhaps he can shed some light on Rueben's whereabouts. I reckon he's the only chance we got of ever knowin' what's happened to Jay's body, or Polly Trace," Tom explained watching Kylee closely as she set out corn meal and salt to prepare supper.

"Its most time for Thanksgivin', Kylee. I'll go down to that bottom cornfield behind the barn an' get us a young fat rooster turkey. I saw several of them back there one day when Matt an' I was huntin' squirrels. Wouldn't it be great Kylee, we could have Mary, an Alvin, an' Hail. We'd be one big family like Thanksgivin' used to be," Tom suggested with a big smile taking over his whiskered face.

"Hail? Never! Never!" Kylee screamed at Tom. She slammed the bowl she was holding onto the tabletop and ran into her bedroom and pushed the door closed with force.

Tom was as good as his promise and the next morning he rode out on Jole' for Tandy's Mountain. He found Bob and Nell finishing up the tedious job of butchering a hog. Nell was cleaning up the mess and Bob was getting ready to hang the pig in the springhouse to cool out.

"Hey man, let me give you a hand with that," Tom yelled at Bob when he saw the young man struggling to carry the armful of pork down the stairs.

"Yeah, you bet! Would sure appreciate it Tom. What in tarnation brought you this way in this cold?" Bob inquired as the two juggled the meat to a comfortable position to carry.

"I had to come tell you Bob, I found Jay. I hung him. Whoops, watch it man. Nell wouldn't take it lightly if we drop this bacon in the dirt."

Bob's surprise and shock was soon over. He gathered his composure and asked Tom to the house for coffee. He didn't know how he was going to break the news to Nell.

"I went back to bring the body home an' someone had already been there for it. Rueben was the last person in that spot alive. You haven't seen anything of him or Jay's body, have you Bob?" Tom asked the young Mitchell, watching him closely as they walked to the house.

"I ain't seed hide-nor-hair of either one of them. The law keeps comin' around hopin' Rueb'll show up an' know somethin' about Polly Trace. But he ain't been home since I left the two of them over in Kentuck."

Tom listened as Bob told Nell of Jay's death. He watched as the young man held her in his arms comforting her.

"I ain't sorry he's dead! I'm sorry for his wasted life. I'm glad the youngin's won't remember him, as we knew him. By the time they are older, perhaps, people will forget what he done," Nell told Tom. She stooped to pick up the baby at her feet. Little J.B. was walking now and his dark curly head was a duplicate of his fathers.

Bob noticed Tom looking close at the baby in Nell's arms. He was quick to assure him.

"He ain't gonna turn out like Paw, or Blaine, I promise you that. I'll see to it. I'm gonna make somethin' out'a this place. I got plans. Nell an' the boys are part of them. We'll be fine Tom, fine."

Tom drank down his coffee, black and hot. The strong liquid reminded him of Hail. Somehow he had to fix things between Kylee and Hail. There had to be a way. He put on his hat ready to leave, shook Bob's hand, and left them with an invitation.

"Come down to the mill for Thanksgivin' Bob an' bring Nell an' the boys. It's time to forget all the things that are past. We are goin' to learn to live in these mountains in peace. We'll raise our families together so they will have good memories instead of hatin' an' killin'. What do you say?" Tom suggested.

"I'm for that! We'll bring a leg of pork, what do you say to that?" Bob laughed and gave Tom's hand another shake.

Tom rode out hunching his shoulders to the cold thinking over his visit with the Mitchell's. He wondered how Kylee was going to take to his plan to bring her family together. But it was going to happen, whether she liked it or not!

On Thanksgiving Day Matt left early with the wagon and team of grays. He spent most of his time at Mary's now that Tom was home. Their wedding day was drawing close.

Kylee thought it odd that Matt had left so early and hadn't said anything about being back for dinner. She wondered why Tom had insisted on such a big dinner. He brought in the turkey the day before, pumpkin pies were cooked and cooling on the marble counter, corn bread dressing stuffed into the turkey, and lots of sweet potatoes and gravy.

Kylee watched Tom crossing the yard from the mill. She stood on the porch shaking the flour from her apron and waving at her sweetheart. Tom had been wonderful the last week and had even stopped nagging her about Hail. It was amazing just being together. She noticed the skiff of ice along the edge of the millpond and thought of the night Matt and Tom had fought because of Polly. She felt sadness over the disappearance of Polly and was afraid her fate had been as horrible as the Stewarts and Ira. She had unconditionally forgiven Tom for his association with Polly.

Tom took Kylee in his arms and stood holding her leaning against the porch post. Her arms were clasped tightly around his waist, her head rested on his chest. He turned her around and positioned his arms around her waist enjoying the sweet smell of her hair. Tom had resumed his well-groomed appearance, hair cut above his shoulders and beard trimmed very short.

The sun was bright this Thanksgiving day and a soft smoky haze lay lightly over the mill creek and Pound Mountain. The two stood silently gazing out at the tall barren trees. They watched, as the shadows of the pines grew shorter in the noonday sun.

Kylee noticed the dark spot on the bottom step marking the place Blaine had fallen that day so long ago. The spot had lessened from the rain and winter snow.

They stood as one, even their breathing was timed. Tom held Kylee closer, loving the feel of her in his arms. Her hair was scented with rosemary and he breathed in deeply of the heavy aroma.

In the distance they heard the sound of rolling wheels coming down Tandy's Mountain. Perhaps it was the Mitchell's. At the same time a wagon emerged from the mist along the creek and crossed the bridge. Tom was not ready to share this sweet moment with anyone.

"It's Matt, Mary, an' Alvin," Kylee remarked as Tom hugged her closer.

"Someone's with them," she added, pushing her back in closer to Tom's chest.

Tom could tell from the bright splash of color that the other visitor was Hail. Kylee had also noticed. He felt her stiffen in his arms.

"Kylee, you're gonna forget this nonsense, you hear? She's the only parent you have left. Let's not shut her out because of your stubbornness. I want my children to have a grandmother!" Kylee struggled to free herself but Tom held her firmly.

The wagon rolled in closer and turned in at the lower gate. Matt and Mary waved them a greeting. Tom released Kylee slowly. She looked up at him and took a deep breath and smiled. The smile was filled with love and forgiveness. A bright sunshine filled her eyes and a few shining tears. Laughingly, hand in hand, with arms open wide, they ran down the steps to meet their family.

The talk followed the red headed stranger as he traveled across the hills. He stayed to himself and lived in caves. Some thought he was tetched; others gave him the benefit of the doubt.

"He only likes to tell wild stories, Bernus, he don't harm no one. He comes in to the store every month or so an' trades these carvin's here for some supplies. Anyone what can whittle like that can't be too bad."

Bernus looked with leering eyes at the carvings behind his brother. Horses, dogs, wagons, and small toys with moving parts lined the shelf.

"An' look at this one brother. I never seed an animal like this one with a horn comin' out'a his forehead. Look here at this girl with all the curls at the back of her head all perfectly carved, even a bow in her hair. Her eyes, they look as if you could see right into them."

"They certainly are beautiful, Wally. I'll grant you that! But you gotta admit that story he tells must be just that, a wild story. How could you believe such a tale about a wild man hangin' his paw? Then shootin' him in the leg an' leavin' him for dead, I almost could believe that. But what about a witch lettin' his paw down onto a blazin' fire with limbs crossed back an' forth? Then sittin' down on her haunches an' watchin' his paw burn to ashes," Bernus took a deep breath and continued. "Did you see that wild look in his eyes when he told about her scatterin' the ashes out over the mountains an' lettin' the wind blow 'em across the Blue Ridge, settlin' among the hills an' nestlin' into the hollers? How her head was all tied up in a red scarf? Witches don't wear red scarves! Then she rode away on an ol' red mule into the night wavin' her arms an' screechin'? Cursin' anyone what rode alone in the woods at night?" Bernus shivered as he finished the tale. "Anyways, it makes my blood curdle. Look a there, there he goes, ridin' that big black mule. I swear that's the biggest mule I ever see'd!"

The red headed stranger spurred the mule trying to encourage her into a run up the mountain. He looked frantically around him as if seeking a place to hide deep in the forest, dense enough even a witch could not find him, if she so desired. Sputtering and muttering to himself:

"You shouldn't have refused me, Polly. You shouldn't have. It would have been best if you hadn't refused me! I didn't want to kill you Polly, I didn't!" He confessed to the trees, unable to forget the beautiful young woman he had left buried in a lonesome grave deep in the shadow of the pines.

THE END

EPILOGUE

The Pound Mountain Massacre actually occurred on May 14, 1892. At the time M.B. Taylor (Deputy Marshal Tanner Hensely) was guarding Talt Hall, a well known outlaw who was on trial for murdering a Virginia man. M.B. Taylor strutted up and down the court room aisles pompous with authority. While guarding the murderer he disappeared to become one himself.

At this time Taylor was a sworn enemy to an invalid man, Ira Mullins (Ira Phelps). He along with another collaborator (Jay Bird Mitchell) planned his death. They ambushed Ira and members of his family and friends at a place called Picket Rock on Pound Mountain.

A member of Ira's family, Deputy Marshal Booker Mullins (Tom Phelps) tracked down and executed his own vengeance on Jay Mitchell.

M.B. Taylor was also referred to by other novelists as the "Red Fox". He died on the scaffold at Wise, Virginia on October 27, 1893 for the murders on Pound.

I have used these events to create a story of fiction.

Printed in the United States
41880LVS00003B/7-42

9 781420 863758